# ALSO BY JAMES D MCCALLISTER

**NOVELS**
*King's Highway*
*Fellow Traveler*
*Let the Glory Pass Away*
*Dogs of Parsons Hollow*
*Dixiana*
*Down in Dixiana*
*Dixiana Darling*
*Reconstruction of the Fables*
*(2022)*

**STORIES**
*The Year They Canceled Christmas*
*Fables of the Reconstruction*
*(2022)*
*The Night I Prayed to Elvis:*
*The Edgewater County Stories*
*(2023)*

# MANSION OF HIGH GHOSTS

MANS[I]
OF

A NOVEL

# GHOSTS

JAMES D
MCCALLISTER

Mind Harvest Press
Columbia SC

Mind Harvest
Press
Columbia SC

*For Allyson and Andria,*
*Jason and Jack,*
*Alvy and Max, too*

I would not want to make you unhappy by detailing pain, but there is
a crucial sort of difference between pain and the narration of pain. I
am telling you what happened. If there is vicarious pain in knowing,
there is actual peril in not knowing. In aversion lies a colossal risk.

PHILIP K. DICK

# PART ONE

# A MAN IN THE GRIP OF A THEORY

## SPRING 2004

# ONE

## —

## DEVIN

The crash of the vehicles in the intersection, an everyday light-running near tragedy, came to the drunk's attention through his gauzy, fermented scrim of consciousness only as a muffled *thud*. Had a chunk of headlight not glinted across his field of vision after glancing off a municipal wastebasket, Devin Rucker, be-bopping along the cracked sidewalk with a decent AM buzz, mightn't have noticed the accident at all.

Once he did notice—a hard knock between vehicles, smoke, a woman crying, nobody even out of the cars yet—he perambulated into the intersection without missing a beat or increasing his pace, waving lazy cig-stained fingers in the four cardinal directions to discourage approaching vehicles.

At the cracked side window of the car with the crying woman Devin grunted, spat and asked if she could get her door open.

"Smoke'll kill you faster than fire, usually," Devin's wisdom, delivered through a cloud of his own. "Better get on out, now."

"It's stuck." The woman, flustered, held her hands a-flutter. "I can't find my purse."

"Make sure it's unlocked."

Once she diddled the knob Devin heard a faint *clunk* inside the door. He pulled. The door hung. A frame issue. They'd total it for a bent frame. Devin's Uncle Hill, a car dealer, was among numerous voices from back home offering advice on a daily basis. The ones he couldn't drink quiet, anyway.

Devin pushed his yellowed fingertips along the top of the door frame until finding gap. He might have been close to dying, and with nary an ounce of fat nor much muscle, but this drunk knew when he needed to get a woman out of a busted-up car. And how to do it.

He panted his left leg and found the most leverage he'd experienced in ages, yanked. The door all but peeled back like aluminum foil. He hollered, primal, and finished ripping it off the hinges. Tossed the door aside like the Hulk.

By now others had gathered to gawk. "Damn, bro," a stout Latino man in dusty work clothes said as he went to help the woman get out of the car. The sound of a first responder's siren came from a point increasingly less distant. "How you did that?"

"The Lord helps those who help themselves. S'all I can tell you."

The workingman crossed himself, praised God.

His part played, Devin went on loping his wobbly, untroubled yet disconsolate gait; not yet noon, he had already been ejected from his favorite daytime watering hole. It happened.

Before long, however, messages left by his sister slapped a bigger fish down on the sizzling grill than another soul's minor traffic accident, or, for that matter, where to get another drink.

Getting booted so early in the day from the joint over in Silver City—cut off, and before the sun had gone down—represented a stinging rebuke. Amateur hour. Now he'd be drinking alone. Driving back to Commerce City on the other side of Denver, with the vehicular mishap written off as a hallucination brought on by encroaching sobriety, Devin pouted about getting the boot from one of his go-to joints. The sports bar a few towns over, where his shenanigans were not quite so notorious, would now be crossed off the list.

Yeah—a barroom badass, only two ways his best stories ended: jail, or the hospital. Felt like that kind of scene coming on later tonight, in fact. But the outer intention of the world in which he operated often frowned upon such misadventures.

One or the other—injury, or imprisonment. Sounded like a goal, though in lucid moments one he suspected already achieved. Neither outcome bound to conjure much emotional reaction, though. Not unless he failed to drink enough to quell what ailed him.

Out of liquor at home in this shitty apartment, he cracked a microbrew. He'd need forty such libations to get right.

Wisdom, here gleaned from inside a clever bottle cap coexisting with itself also as a fortune cookie:

**Moments only pass
to make room
for more Moments!**

Devin, trembling, sat on his balcony and balanced the bottle cap between his thumb and forefinger. He had found it in the apartment complex parking lot. He tried snapping it between his fingers to make the smart-ass bottle cap, literal garbage, fly away into the air like a little frisbee, the way he and his friends in college once did in the dorm rooms with numerous bottle caps, or at one of the many bars they frequented in the Old Market entertainment district alongside campus.

He dropped the moment-cap three times. Cussed. Gave up.

Devin Rucker's moment: His apartment, once fresh and clean but now a pigsty, lacked any semblance of stewardship. Long abandoned to forces of decay, an entropy had taken hold which featured garbage piled in the corners, food rotting in the refrigerator, and a general décor designed with the eye of a distillery rep.

The sheer volume of empty liquor vessels, Devin often thought in admiration, lent a pleasing aesthetic quality to the surroundings, a preponderance of *objets d'art* representing the scope and entirety of one man's life's-work project. Of many men's lives; they who'd done the distilling and the bottling, the labeling and QC-ing and shipping and delivering and displaying and selling, and bless their hearts and pointed little heads for all they did to make the world a better place.

For Devin.

For everyone.

*A-men.*

To Devin, a drunk's drunk, a pro—they called him Ruck, or his friends did, anyway—the bottles weren't trash, rather trophies suitable for display in any All-American high school lobby: records of achievement, though for outstanding effort in his own peculiar, dyspeptic field of athleticism. This, no mere trash pile. Grad students would one day sift this find for clues to the essential nature of his philosophy.

A line of black ants, swarming, a bountiful day for the mound: a sack of dry cat food lay wounded and bleeding stale kibble onto the yellowed vinyl of the cheap and dirty kitchen flooring. A sack Devin had thrown against the wall and left lying there, split open. The pet food had been there fur-ever, it seemed.

For a year, now.

Longer.

From somewhere in the apartment complex came the thumping of a hip-hop tune that copped the hook from 'Love is Alive,' an old 70s pop number Devin remembered from listening to rock radio with his sister Creedence back home in South Cack-a-lack.

The beat, boring into his pickled brain.

Stoking his rage.

Pounding his palm against the wall, he gave a hoarse shout: *"Turn that mess down, you goddurn college fucks."* A nearby state university satellite campus meant students lived in the complex, and often tunes could be heard thumping day and night. Devin, never nostalgic enough to join in with their parties.

The bass-beat, undeterred, thudded on.

Pacing.

Trapped.

Needing a drink.

But not alone.

And not here.

Making for the outside world. Relieved, as always, to push his way out.

But his apartment door, it wouldn't close right. Like it no longer hung quite square. Swollen, like from the kind of tropical air Devin grew up breathing in the South.

No mystery. His door had acquired a big crack down the middle. One night he had needed to kick his way out. Or rather, in. Kick his way in. To get some shuteye. A golden threshold of inebriation existed which had to be met, during which sleep would come dreamless. A big project, becoming dreamless, but the long journey was always taken as a series of individual steps until arrival. Someday.

At last, the bolt clicked into place. Nothing worth taking inside anyway —locking up, a habit from the days of his cat Prudy. To keep her close and safe.

A brilliant light, flashing behind the aviators hiding Devin's amber slits from the glare of the beer signs in the windows of Chubby's Ale House: Not so much like a flashbulb, rather a glinting reflection of high midday sunlight off a surface of polished chrome. The image, coming accompanied as always by a disharmonious roar, a black-throated screech, an enormous out-of-tune instrument blown from on high: thus, the signal of his descent into abject, non-intoxicated despair. This condition loomed with nigh inevitability, but this a precursor, in his grand plan, to the blessed unconsciousness which awaited; else veering across the center line into wretched sobriety, as polarizing an intention as could be reckoned to a man like him.

Short version: He needed a drink. Before the shakes took hold.

Jim, his bartender at nearby Chubby's, greeted him with a measured and cautious air. A softheaded idiot, Jim, but one who cared; who knew how to pour.

A small freestanding tavern on the other side of I-70 next to the pyramid-like Marriott hotel—on the weekends bikers congregated here, and recognizing his condition steeped in past trauma, treated Devin with dignity and patience—the bar lay only three safe minutes of flat highway cut from the prairie-dog scrubland near the big soccer stadium. That made Chubby's homebase.

On the satellite radio—Jim liked oldschool authentic country, which they featured on one of the four or five channels devoted to the genre, the kind they'd have listened to back home at The Dixiana in Edgewater County—Devin enjoyed good-old Loretta Lynn warbling about 'Somebody Somewhere,' a plaintive number full of longing and loss and syrupy soothing steel guitar. This is music his father would have listened to, all of which reminded Devin of being back home. Which, as it happened, also made him annoyed enough to bite a nickel in half.

Grumbling, wincing, clutching his right side and settling onto the stool at the corner—his spot, near the cigarette machine—Devin sparked a smoke with his typical aplomb and hollered over to a couple of the neighborhood guys shooting a money game. Other Saturday drunks, sitting hunched over and nursing lonely libations, ignored him or otherwise glared. A familiar and comforting scene.

Jim, noting that Devin clutched his side, asked if he'd been injured.

"These barbecue ribs? Yeah. A bit tender." Devin, probing and pressing under his armpit, sucked in his breath and cussed. "You could say so. Training for the '04 Olympics chugging squad."

*Nyuck-nyuck.* "What happened this time?"

Leaning over, shaggy hair hanging down, beak shot through with spider veins, nail-bitten fingers; aviators perched, hiding the eyes. Confidential: "This lot lizard, see, she took a notion to go and take a kick at me."

*"Kicked you?"*

Dismissive, waving a hand. "Pretty standard stuff. I had passed out, and this party girl, she figures to roll me."

"Not again."

"But damn if I didn't wake up to catch red hands rifling my jacket. Foiled, I says."

"You kick that bitch's ass?"

"She had a weight advantage. Clocked me in the kisser and knocked me onto my ass. And then kicked me square in the side, all punitive and shit. Had on one of them—what ya call them spikes they wear?"

Jim, blinking and rapt. "High heels?"

"The colloquial term for them slides they wear."

Jim, confounded by this digression. *"That who wears?"*

A comment came from Darla, another regular sitting a few stools away, drinking and playing trivia. Dry: "Alex, I'll take 'Come Fuck Me's' for two hundred."

"Right right right," Jim said. "Like—high heels."

"There we go," Devin said.

"Was she a decent lay?"

Insulted. "Christ, Jimbo. Why you want to ask me a question like that?"

"*Like what?*"

"How the fuck would I remember? If she was a decent lay?"

Jim, ever more confused. "Me, I'd have those ribs checked out."

Devin, regarding 'his' bartender, as much as any bartender could be possessed, with renewed trust and pleasure, pronounced an alternative cure: "Ain't nothing wrong a double J-D rocks, and a pack of Reds, won't fix."

"Pour it on top?"

"On top of what?"

"The round you already ordered."

Devin, discovering a half-consumed cocktail sitting in front of him, broke into a grin. "Make it so."

Jim gurgled the liquor, filling the drink to the rim. Colorful bar-light glimmered on the surface of the whiskey. Devin felt a shudder like reverence.

About that time the Man in Black came on—'Can't Go That Way.' Devin, thinking, *nah*; he could and would go that way. In his own time; and biding his time. Waiting for the moment.

Through a hot, acid belch: "Bless your heart, Jimbo. A real drink at last."

The ballgame on the muted high-mounted TV set ended, and the late news began with a headline story about an alleged drunk driver having plowed into a van-load of innocents on their way to church. With an angelic six-year-old girl cold on a slab and additional victims in near-critical states of bodily distress, outraged community members howled on-camera for the perp's literal blood.

"This scofflaw has three prior DWIs," a middle-aged activist, someone's grandmother, shouted in the hospital driveway where others clutched signs demanding justice. "*Something's got to be done.*"

"See, that's why Chubby's keeps our list of cab companies taped over here." Pointing to a laminated card taped next to the wall-mounted pay phone, an old one they'd kept at Chubby's as decoration rather than as functional technology, Jim nodded with grave responsibility: "Have your fun, drink your fill. But arrive alive. That's what I say."

Devin, noting with disgust how his bottle-boy spun it all so positive, felt desirous of having himself a good solid raging volcanic puke all over the bar. As well as another drink. It was a Zen-like place of consciousness to dwell, familiar and frequent. Soon as he got drunk enough, he'd drive back home and get some decent shuteye.

His stomach burning and sloshing, Devin stayed swilling and bullshitting with Jim and the other drunks all the way up to witching hour. He felt better, but not quite there. As such, he sat bitching and moaning at last call, trying not to sound as desperate as he felt.

"I know you're gonna be in here counting down and sweeping and shit. Lemme stay."

Jim always turned frosty in the run-up to last call, and more so afterwards. "That's why it's called 'closed.'"

"Let me drink a couple more, ya stingy goat. I ain't broke."

Steadfast. Jim, a meaty limb pointing to the door. "Closed. Out."

"Make me, fratboy."

In under a minute Jim, larger than the recalcitrant drunk by fifty pounds and six inches, manhandled the situation all the way into the parking lot. In Devin's condition the action seemed magical, an act of teleportation. They were at the bar; they were by the car—*snap*.

Devin's intuition tingled. This was the Moment. He would goad this dumb fuck into killing him. Finally—a plan.

He took a boxer's stance. "All right, you simple-minded fuck. Let's go. Dirt, prepare to meet dick."

"Dude. Not this again." Jim stood watching with sad eyes. "I'm-a call a cab."

The first actual threat came. Devin, with a few under his belt, planted fast his feet and held up a fist. "Don't you pity me. And don't let that bullshit on TV earlier make your nuts draw up, boy. I'm right as anyone."

"I'm calling Checker. Don't move."

"Da-fuck you are."

"Got to."

"Wait, wait, wait—look here." Devin, patient, calm and now impossibly, lucidly sober, kept his words measured instead of rushed to avoid the inevitable sibilance coming with alcoholic anesthesia: "I don't live but a half a goddurn mile on the other side of the slab," gesturing in the general direction of his apartment complex across the freeway, a rough, dusty slog on foot: Commerce City, a place of industry and warehouses, burgeoning vinyl villages, and to the east behind them, nothing but motels and the expanse of DIA, and beyond that, the fecund infinitude of the American prairie. "I'll go. But it don't make sense to take no cab."

"Ruck—you sure?"

Devin, a supplicant, palms out: "Steady as rocks."

"I dunno."

"Relax, pal. It's me. It's Ruck."

Sighing. "You got yourself one hollow leg. All I know."

"It's one for the books. I'll see ya tomorrow or next-day. Like normal."

The bar door slammed. The lock clicked. The light in the sign high up went dark.

In his car, a battered, nearly twenty years young VW Jetta, Devin found himself shaking, sick and scared. Knowing that the pussy Jimbo would give him grief about driving, he had held off. Hadn't had his fill.

And, now? Not only late, but also Sunday, with no liquor stores open, and none to be for a ghastly and unimaginable thirty or more hours. Colorado, as it turned out, hadn't been much more progressive than South Carolina on liquor laws.

Terror-struck at having no further drinks at hand, at not knowing why he was still here, or why he'd come in the first place, years ago—it'd been 'away,' he supposed, with him and Prudy on the lam—but mostly the no-drink part, he considered options.

Prudy. But now it was only him.

Better this way. No responsibility. Devin had finally left it all back East, where it belonged.

To the West? The mountains. Through which he found he could not pass; could bring himself to traverse. Even after so many years, the Pacific remained unseen. This brown desert, as far as he'd made it from his Carolina home. Got to Denver one afternoon, took a hard glance at those white peaks, thought about Libby and something she had said this one time, got shitfaced, and woke up here in this moment. Whenever it was. Two thousand zero-zero-something.

Why here?

Devin, if he were a narrator, saying, Well-sir. I'll tell you all. The roads in this part of the country—so flat and straight. A motherscratcher could see his ass for miles in every direction. Could see for himself what was coming. That all ended once you got past the mile-high city, though.

Devin, thinking that those bad-boy peaks, and the bigger ones farther west, made the tiny Carolina hump-hills back home seem puny indeed. As small as he felt. If only he could feel less than that—if he could feel nothing —then Devin Rucker might receive the one true revelation he craved most.

Back at the apartment complex—safe as a kitten, no accidents, no DUIs despite seeing multiple center lines down the highway—he admired its cracked stucco, with a ghastly ochre paint job now faded to a xanthous, dull cast, the units boxy and crude and functional and cheap, especially when compared to the newer nicer condos farther up the hillside, which were the absolute jewel of Commerce City. Devin, climbing two flights of exterior wrought-iron stairs with a pair of reluctant stumblebum legs that threatened to give out by the first landing, trudged upward with the kind of grim determination born from the bleak dregs of having no other choice at hand.

Inside, he squinted out a grimy window at his most decent view of the night-lit Denver skyline, and he remembered, yea, oh, did he remember how he'd found his way here: A good spot, this, a prime vantage point from which to debate the conundrums and vagaries of existence; the skyscrapers, Devin thinking, like his own accusatory fingers pointed ever upwards into the violet void.

Devin, flipping on the light in the wrecked and disastrous kitchen, liquor bottles and beer cans stacked and gathered in slick black yard-trash bags, diverted slitted eyes from the plastic mat upon which his dearest Prudy had eaten her food; her water dish sat in its spot outside the kitchen, never moved since the time of her passing.

Time.

Time passing, yes.

But wounds yet to heal; the sight of the dish, avoided. If possible.

Please.

But the disposal of said cat's food dish not possible, the thought of doing so causing Devin's thin breath to vanish with a wheeze, and a wellspring of revulsion to gurgle up from his wasted gullet like landfill methane. Screaming through his teeth. Not crying anymore, no matter what. These days he'd been getting so drunk he'd pass out before getting to the crying phase. These days had turned into years, when he allowed himself to admit this horrid truth.

Years. Only a couple since Prudy died. Near as he could reckon.

Prudy led to Libby. And there wasn't no going there. *Nuh-uh, beau.*

Devin, desperate, snatched up bottles from the glass forest standing upon the counters. He foraged backwash out of several, dribbling each remnant into a tumbler until managing a finger or so of diluted alcohol flavored with fermenting saliva. A decent hint of a smidgen of whiskey, a wee taste to splash into his parched throat.

Drinking, slurping. Bemoaning the now empty glass.

Trembling.

The dusty food dish.

Prudy.

A long night ahead, now, lying on his rank mattress, wishing he'd gotten to That Place: drunk enough to get the spins, and finally unconsciousness. But instead, nowhere close to passing out, what he lived for.

Devin, preparing to sweat it out. Maybe he'd go ahead and detox. Had to happen one day.

Didn't it?

Maybe he'd sprout fairy wings, flutter around like a big, drunken redneck butterfly, too.

Devin, knowing that none of his choices sat well, lay twitching and nauseated in his sour bed for who knew how long. He begged for an answer, feared the detox to begin anytime now.

Up from hell the answer blew.

Invigorated and optimistic, he sprang out of bed on his skinny chicken legs, pulled clothe onto his wasted, bony frame and hurled himself downstair and out driving in search of a bar, any bar, that might still be open.

But carefully—driving real, real steady and good. No way would he be responsible for anyone getting killed. Not unless it was himself. Which wouldn't be an accident at all. Now would it.

Fade in.

Words on a glowing LCD screen typed by big boy Billy Steeple, y'all, sitting here in whitey-tighties, dude-bro repping a tight, bronze, sculpted body like that of a magazine model.

Like a god, a golden god. But on the inside? Not so godlike.

Billy, suffering, anxious and enervated at the notion of starting yet another screenplay, yet finding the work on scripts as the only activity which felt wholesome, productive.

And so, what else a practitioner of ass banditry to do?

Get high and watch the tube?

Commit another in a series of murders?

Wait—scratch that. Accidents. Not murders. Revision: *Let another one of those pesky accidents happen?*

That's better. No good writing, they say; only good re-writing.

Billy made no apologies for spending endless hours a day farting around on his alleged writing career. Failures aside, the effort took him back to a happier time, and in that sense, had become an end in itself. Satisfying.

Most of the time.

Well—often.

Often enough.

Mostly.

His head swimming with THC, Billy became distracted listening to a jamband cover version of 'Will It Go Round in Circles' broadcast on Southeastern University's WSEU only a few blocks away. "Will it fly high like a bird up in the sky." The uptempo tune, a tenacious bastard of an earbug, would stay stuck in his head for hours.

Billy, bathed in the cool light of his laptop screen, stared straight ahead.

The scribe, with two strawberry glazed donut holes for eyes, tried to empty his mind.

Willing the muse to submit.

Saying AUM like Melanie, with her ridiculous white-girl meditation routine.

Nothing.

Chanting: "Sky. High. Bird."

Crickets.

The floor creaked in the room next door—current bedmate Melanie Pinckney had begun to stir from her half-hour trance session, the Indian incense she burned but a bare whiff subsumed within the sharp, smoky pall in the office. Billy sighed—now she'd want him to screw again.

And with the act of coitus, always a risk. Of an accidental accident occurring.

And then? The rest of the night, and possibly the next day, mired in removal, recovery and cover story concoction. Steam-cleaning the Mercedes after dealing with the remains. Planting clues and evidence to support alibis. Searching through the blank spot in his memory for the trigger.

It had been a few years now since the last accident, but like riding a bike. A problem, a wrinkle, an occasional twist for a man who so loved women; who theorized how he completed them by his presence alone. Add in the pendulous meat hammer, and—well.

But, those eyes of hers, Melanie's—imploring. Sincere.

He could see the train coming. Three months with this one. The talk was coming. It will start with hints about giving up the lease on her own apartment.

No surprise, this growing affection. Not only had he taken Melanie to the highest highs right out of the gate, the first night, total control over all functions including accidental ones, but expected considering the awesome Billyness of both technique and physical stature brought to the table.

He'd succumb, of course. Give her what she was after. But grudgingly, and rougher than she liked it, which for a six-and-a-half footer like him offered a sound method of scaring off distaff adherents like Mel, but, damn if their feints toward S&M weren't skating along the keen edge of stoking an accidental accident.

You talk about blade running—Billy's has to be, like, times-infinity ice-cold frozen razor sharp tippy-toe traverse over the icy stream, yo, to keep from slipping and falling into accident country. It's the method most guys use to keep from coming as soon as they shove it in there—Billy distracted himself.

Thought about great scenes from classic movies.

Ones his old pal Libby had loved.

Movies they had watched together, back in the day, the 80s; all the greats.

Yeah.

Except Mel, she liked their tumbles rough and ready. Almost as though his dream girl had come along. One who beamed love to him in every movement and motive, each angelic glance and delicate gesture the beautiful young woman seemed capable of offering.

The thought made Billy feel kicked in the stomach.

She had to go.

Before he accidentally accidented her and her sweet self.

Yeah. No. Seriously.

Billy opened the vertical blinds to better enjoy his view of the diminutive, twinkling skyline of ten- and twenty-story structures glowing orange from thousands of streetlights casting heavenward: Columbia, South Carolina, a capital city to be sure, but by any standard a modest one. His condo, the galactic center of the metropolitan area, a corner unit in one of the quote-unquote skyscrapers. He lived about as high as one could get around here.

By day, Columbia, like a slice of Southern heaven: the light of morning would find the neighborhoods and thoroughfares redolent and verdant and color-splashed, shot through with clusters of honeysuckle and dusted yellow by pollen; Bradford pears blooming white, dogwoods blazing pink, Confederate jasmine like a spray of baby's breath in an April wedding bouquet. Springtime, the first season in which he'd seen the city and the Southeastern campus, with its ungodly endless bevy of beautiful young women like no collection he'd experienced. Not growing up in the Northeast, in boarding schools full of born-to-the-manor bluebloods thinking they were the center of the universe. Especially the birds all a-feather with their birdiness.

Did they not know who was in their midst?

Arisen, a pole star.

Billy.

His true feelings about women—a pained, grudging acceptance of their disgusting, suppurating wet holes, which he attributed to myopia—mellowed as he hit his bubbler, *gurgle-gurgle*. Got a little mind-tickle as he held in the rich, vaporous smoke.

The notion occurred to look up 'myopic.' Nah. He was using it right. Words. Helluva problem for a would-be writer, keeping them all straight.

But spring offered a chance, always and eternal, to begin again; a season filling Billy—a man of sentiment, though loathe to admit so in mixed company—with peace and an arguable sense of nearly permanent satisfaction, a feeling impugned upon only by the ineffable, occasional twinge of what was missing, which was everything: Libby.

Ignoring Melanie's calls to rejoin her in bed, Billy instead concentrated on the screen. He cursed the cursor, drummed his fingers and wondered if he needed a better idea. Home from the archive for hours, he ought to be farther along on this new script than Fade In. With his job as media librarian keeping him stuck down in an annex south of campus, he could work on screenplays all day, if he chose.

Not that he got them finished. The pages and scenes were ghosts of the past, tugging at him.

Wondering about Devin—what had become of him, where he was. Googling his name, and not for the first time, but like always, never finding a single hit. As though his old buddy didn't exist.

Cool.

Reminding himself: Libby's not here, Libby's not coming. Devin could walk in any day, maybe; Libby, not so much. No amount of screenplay writing would resurrect her.

Decades of stewing over this crap.

His goal of late had been to achieve a type of psychic comity with his pernicious past troubles by the age of forty, which loomed in a few more transits around the sun. Between that and grandfather being sick—finally—Billy'd be hitting his prime years in time to receive his full inheritance—millions. He'd head west like he'd planned so long ago. Write scripts, direct, perhaps act in a few, like Fritz Lang and Sam Fuller working for Godard. Take over the movie biz.

He had to try. For Libby. To achieve her dream. He'd been telling himself this since the last century.

But didn't achieving a dead girl's dream entail being chained to the past?

So what. Life, meaningless. Nothing is true; everything is permitted.

No—nihilism will queer the deal, and turn accidents into willful acts of malice. Billy had no such bone in his body. He needed to seek polarity, a cosmic balance, in accepting the fact he'd never get to fuck Libby Meade. But after almost twenty years of trying, he still failed daily to get over this incontrovertible fact.

And so to stave off the terrors of acceptance, the work of his waning youth, endless in its calling: all Billy needed was a new, fresh screenplay idea, marketable, sellable. A rom-com, let's say, modest in scale; ninety, a hundred pages tops, with an HEA. Commercial. A winner. An audience pleaser.

Or—what about a horror movie?

Nah. Too personal.

Billy looked askance at the stacks—reams, actually—of draft-this or version-that of his previous magnum opus, a tower to the heavens representing the same project forever teetering upon completion. Over the years spent tinkering with the script—he'd begun it in college, when he and Libby shared one precious scriptwriting class—he'd retained every scrap ever written, stacking the pages up scene after scene, sequence after sequence, act after act, all pages printed on twenty-four pound bond; Billy, feeling even his first drafts emerged so shimmering and polished, like the Florsheims and Weejuns in his shoe closet, that such pages deserved inscription only upon the finest of manuscript leaves. Billy, speculating how, one day, he feared the project would at last force its way up through the smooth, nine-foot ceiling onto the roof, reaching for the stars.

He wondered if he'd ever be able to say he had finished.

He wondered what *finished* meant.

What time was.

Why writing a movie mattered—a script wasn't even a complete piece of art, not like a novel or an epic poem. It was a diagram for an actual artist, the director, to follow.

But Billy's script would be different. It would be complete in itself. It would be so good it would never need filming.

The dream project, the masterwork, lengthy, yes, but chock full of excitement: a high-concept sci-fi action epic featuring such awe-inspiring set pieces as a pre-credits, 007-style teaser depicting a thrilling jailbreak from a lunar prison run by the insidious forces behind a totalitarian, solar systemwide government; an extra-thrilling opening title sequence set in the Mars colony as our heroic, desperate protagonist seeks to save a hermetically sealed-off city from a disastrous dome breach; scene after scene of political intrigue peppering the talky-by-necessity sequences of complicated exposition; a bit of the old in-out here and there between the leads to break up the rhythm; three lengthy monologues (from two different characters) fully explicating the theme(s) of the piece; extremely desperate, enormous battles between mammoth, combat-hardened armies on the dystopian home world of Earth that included a breathless hovercraft chase through the overgrown, flooded canyons of an abandoned New York, an homage to Friedkin's THE FRENCH CONNECTION, Miller's MAD MAX 2: THE ROAD WARRIOR, Spielberg's and Kubrick's AI, Carpenter's ESCAPE FROM NEW YORK and THEY LIVE!, and most obviously the Death Star canyon run from Lucas's STAR WARS EPISODE 4: A NEW HOPE: SPECIAL EDITION, but also the asteroid chase from STAR WARS EPISODE 5: THE EMPIRE STRIKES BACK: SPECIAL EDITION, and of course the pod race sequence from STAR WARS EPISODE 1: THE PHANTOM MENACE.

Finally, a *gotcha* post-resolution action beat all his own—a heart-stopping, indescribably desperate climb to the top of a giant laser cannon set on overload, a hidden, forgotten weapon which must be disabled before the readouts all go red and the digital timer counts down to zero hour and everybody still lucky enough to be alive after the huge, deadly, now *penultimate* action sequence ends up getting smoked, too.

Which can't happen, not in a movie. Not a successful one. At least one of the heroes must live to experience a moment of redemption. The hero's journey.

In the denouement following the shatteringly heartbreaking climax, WE SEE that, on a personal level, the victory is but pyrrhic—the hero watches as the heroine makes it in time to disable the cannon, but staggering back out WE SEE that her body has been ravaged by radiation. The protagonist, crying out in pain Kirk-to-Spock through the transparent aluminum of the engine room; the heroine, sacrificing herself to save them all.

During every rewrite, Billy, suffering a lump in the throat. *I will wait for you on the other side* was the current choice for the heroine's dying line.

*I will wait for you.*

Deep breath.

Still waiting.

As a result of all the time and tweaking, the current draft of Untitled Science Fiction Epic, as Billy thought of his script—he'd yet to come up with a just-right title shimmering with a frisson of epicness—had now grown to a monstrous three hundred and twenty-six pages, far too long for any one feature film production to contain. A freaking doorstop.

No—an epic. A masterpiece.

All for her.

For Libby.

To make her proud. To lend meaning to her short tragic life.

*For Libby...* a dedication. It had accompanied all drafts, all the way back to the first scenes in the stupid screenwriting class with her, though that dedication had been imprinted only in his heart, and never on the page.

Except perhaps upon the letters he'd written following her rejection on the night of the Dead concert. All of which had also been rejected.

Next, a blurring flash-frame, and she'd been dead in the car accident. Later that spring—1990, to be exact. Fourteen years—it only felt like twenty. He heard the words in the voice of DeNiro as the redneck rapist in CAPE FEAR, bemoaning his 'unfair' prison sentence.

Was Billy crazy, or did he feel sympathy for that bad guy? How does a writer do that? The day Billy could answer that question, perhaps he'd become a real writer.

Twitching, he gasped at a sharp pain in his chest. No—a dull, burning pain. Bothersome. Dull, burning, bothersome heart pain often led to accidents sticky and sanguineous in nature.

And, people? All oblivious to his pain. No earthly idea. They thought he had a sweet life: brilliant mind, movie-star looks, thick luxurious hair, a fat trust fund, hung like a stallion, a master of the modern age. But no one knew the real him, as though Billy a tenth-rate Andy Kaufman, one lacking both the courage to adopt false faces as well as the innate talent to pull off the a hat-trick of manipulating the perception of reality. No one, living or dead, knew the real him. Either a curse, or else by design.

If Billy were actually smart—and he intuited this while not knowing it, or so that's what he pretended to tell himself—he'd take the family pecuniary largesse almost kinda-sorta at his fingertips, forget about his ridiculous 'career' at the middling academic backwater that was Southeastern University, and upon the occasion of the next peach-colored Carolina sunrise? Hit the road for the left coast with the latest version of the script under his arm. What, pray tell, could stop him?

Who would have the stones to try?

Only himself—and a ghost or two.

A dam burst inside his head, suppressed images, a vision of an angel: Libby Meade, strolling these streets. Libby, falling in love with Billy, willing her to love him. Making it so. Before, that is, their love had been forestalled first by Devin, and then months later, by the tragedy that took her from all of them. The cool hand of death. Irrevocable. Inexorable. Both of those smart words at the same time. Maybe they meant the same. Couldn't remember.

So, Billy, staying here. Walking the same sidewalks year after year, seeing Libby waving to him from the pedestrian bridge or in front of the coffee shop in which they used to sit in quiet conversation, knees bumping under the table, a memory of which nagged as representative of the most intimate and legitimate contact he'd enjoyed with her. Billy, desperate to hold on; seeing Libby in the young women tanning themselves beneath the benevolent Southern sun on the Elliptical, the park-like center of the two-hundred year-old institution, a blaze of fecund youthful bodies lying supine among the towering live oaks and the buildings exuding historicity: unlike the rest of the city, the old campus at Southeastern's core, the horseshoe of green crisscrossed by a webbing of uneven cobblestone paths, had been a fortunate survivor of Sherman's storied and terrible march through the Confederacy. Upon its tended grasses sprawl the children of the middle class, studying, learning. Dreaming of the long life ahead. That she never got to have.

Billy, sensing a piece of Libby in all them, returned life to her by seducing them. Making love, furious and sustained like he'd never had the chance with her. Climaxing, but never getting to the place he knew they'd have gotten. Together. And sometimes so frustrated, as he had been by a problem of bothersomeness long predating the drama of Libby and Devin that, well... accidents happened.

Such frustration threatened on this night. But it could not manifest. Could. Not. Billy, a badass Gen X master of all he surveyed, Judd Nelson pumping fist in freeze-frame against a sunset sky, would maintain control.

Melanie, calling again from the bedroom. "Honey?"

"Busy."

"Doing what?"

Keeping his voice even and calm. His tongue felt thick, like a sick anaconda slithering along a slimy rainforest floor of peat and fungus looking for a damp hole in which to finally die in peace. "I'm working on the new project. Like I said was planning to do. Understood?" But he said that last bit so low she wouldn't hear.

Dainty, shuffling footfalls approached the office door. The knob, twisting.

Locked.

"Billy—you locked me out?"

"It's for your own safety."

"Ha-ha. Maybe I don't want to be safe."

He couldn't work with that. Sat in silence. Pretended to clatter keys on the iMac.

"Honey—let me in. And then I'll let you in."

"I'm in the middle of a freaking sentence. And then I want to get caught up on the news out of—Iraq."

"Since when do you watch the news?"

A standoff.

"Are you gonna open this door? Or not?"

"I'll give you what you want. But later."

"Promise?"

"You can depend on me, ma'am."

"Gonna hold you to it."

"Seriously—a few more minutes, and I'll be all caught up."

She demurred, finally, and he heard the bedroom door close.

Hitting the bubbler again, the herb simmering, a tiny cauldron. A mood enhancer—maybe not the right drug, but all he dared sample.

Billy, a man with appetites.

A man who needed to stay in control. To manage indulgences. Doing so to avoid one of his troublesome accidents, which, when they occurred, were enormous pains in the ass to deal with and clean up without complications and rigmarole like nobody would believe.

Melanie, no; no accidents in her future. They'd been together too long, now. They'd been seen, all over the campus and surrounding community. A couple. He might as well marry her as get out of this the good-old accidental way.

Which sometimes happened.

Whether Billy wanted, or not.

And had almost happened with Libby, back in the day. The night his so-called Devin snatched her back.

Devin Rucker—now here lay a tired, worthless, useless eater of a drunk, one from whom the world would benefit, let's say, if a little accident or two happened to him. If not an outright act-of-malice style, premeditated murder.

Wait—*murder?* Billy, incapable. Crimes of passion, now, these were different. The courts often said so. And in Devin's case, a mercy killing.

Or—an accident.

An accident.

*Yeah. That's all it was.*

This explanation for when the bothersomeness happened worked best. It had to. To believe otherwise constituted madness, and Billy Steeple, y'all, ain't crazy. Not with all his charisma and money. In the house, yo. A golden god, who only needed a queen, one he could never have, to at last complete him. A conundrum; more than a plot point.

Further, this was no damnable movie. This was real life. And big dick, money or not, life sucked. Not as much as when Devin's sister called to ask a favor, mind you. Favors opened cans of worms, especially between people with history like he had with the Ruckers.

He'd put off calling Creedence back; he'd put off properly grieving for Libby, and, to be truthful, for Devin as well, for nearly twenty years.

No rush on regaining his sanity, or anything. Nah.

The disappearance of the last accident, a pickup in a bar, had been investigated and reported in the media, but Billy, an angel, hadn't been interviewed as a suspect; had skated consequences yet again.

Better still, the murder allowed him to blow off steam, but the risk had made it a close one. His grandfather, clinging to life as it was, would disown him if the truth about Billy's thus-far occulted series of sex murders ever came out in the press.

One day he'd settle down with the right girl and be cured of his unbridled and murderous libido. Maybe that woman was Melanie. Nah. Not enough like Libby. None of them would ever be.

# THREE

## —

## DEVIN

Devin, leaning over his balcony, squinted hard into the morning sun illuminating the Denver skyline and mountains beyond. He tasted bile like battery acid lapping at a raw uvula, tide-driven waves hurling against a craggy shoreline in sprays of what felt like napalm-soaked razorblades.

The urge to hurl. It came in a sick gray-green wave. Again. After the violence of the earlier purging, the stomach, a tender sack under the best of circumstances, now felt as though he'd swallowed shards of pulverized glass.

Feeling covered in glass.

Glass returned to base elements, reduced, again, to beach sand. And, as after a day trip to the beach, the glass in his ears; in the creases around his eyes; in his navel; between his toes. A dream of sand.

No—glass.

Glass.

Sunlight.

Blood.

The phone, buzzing in his pocket. His sister, calling from back home. Creedence—*what a revoltin' development.*

Leaning his weight against the balcony railing, Devin choked down a slug of a long, cold, early tallboy. Ragged and all but unintelligible: "Dingleberry and Ass-ociates, LLC. What can I do ya for?"

"Do what, now?"

"Just funning with ya, girl."

"That's how you start the first conversation you've had with your sister in almost a year?"

"Don't be like that."

Their version of awkward, near hostile pleasantries. "How's tricks back yonder in South Cack—*oh, shit.*"

A cracking sound as the wooden railing, already splintered from a good kicking one hazy night, gave way against his weight. The flat horizon and upside-down buildings appeared upside down in his vision, the morning air kissing his face as Devin tumbled from two stories up, crashing to rest in a sitting position on the hood of a Toyota Corolla with the tallboy and phone still clutched in his bony talons.

His sister's voice, tinny, rang out from the phone. "Devin, what the hell's all that racket?"

"Fell off the balcony just now."

"P'shaw. It sounded like you was going to the bathroom like last time. You better not have been."

"Promise I wasn't," with a wince. Damn them slow-smoked ribs of his. Now his back would join them in a dance of pain.

Stiff as hell, he slid down off the dented hood of the car. Maybe he was injured for real. That'd be dealt with, forthwith, in his own way. Fuck allopathic healing. He tipped back his beer, miraculous, nary a drop lost. God, watching out for him.

This kind of crap happened to him with a fair amount of regularity. He'd been through so many close calls, the old boy had begun to believe he couldn't die at all. The windshield of the Toyota, however, had been irrevocably starred from the dent his bony drunk ass had made. Tough break.

Now from Devin's sibling came an uncharacteristically forthright speech. Creedence, normally prancing around themes and narratives the way Southern families do rather than talking about them head-on, yet here, precise and explicit:

"Now that I finally got a hold of your skinny ass, here's the news. Mama —your *mother*," as though necessary for Creedence to remind him what 'Mama' meant, "needs you back here."

"Bullcrud. Ain't none of you needed me."

"That ain't true."

If it weren't true, Creedence said, I wouldn't waste time on calling. "What you been doing with yourself, anyway?"

Devin, cussing and smoking, thought his red-haired younger sister a nosy-assed little turd. "Ontological studies."

She asked for clarification. Growing up, Devin had been the bookworm who knew words and such.

"Nothing," he said. "So what's this nonsense really about, girl?"

"I don't, and Mama doesn't"—*duddent*—"deserve the way you traipse around half-lit, treating us all like dirt. We're your dad-blamed family."

Grunting. "That you are. But that don't present a new crisis."

"It could be a crisis."

"I'm the last thing any of y'all need hanging around."

A spell of silence. "How long's this gonna go on?"

Devin mumbled, "What do you think I been asking?"

"Do what? I can't hear you."

He recoiled from the telephone as though burned. Glancing up to the ceiling with exasperation. Shuffled to the fridge for a fresh dose of breakfast. "I'm touched to know I'm missed in this fine manner. Deep inside, like." He balanced the phone on his shoulder long enough to crack the beer. His ribs hurt. His hands shook. He got it open, took a blessed slurp. "Ain't coming home."

"If it's left up to me, you can just as soon stay gone."

"A wish likely to come true. You must feel right blessed."

"But Mama, now. She says she can't"—*cain't*—"stand it no more."

"Stand what?"

"You not coming home for birthdays and Thanksgiving and Easter. And everything in between."

"Yawn. Try a different reason."

Her tone changed. Small and grim. "There's more: she's sick inside. One day soon she's going to be gone."

"Sick?" Devin, grinning. "You better not be shitting me."

"Hush your mouth."

"Sounds like a tragedy. But I ain't coming."

"She's dying, Devin."

A sharp pain in the center of his forehead. A phantom roar. A flash of light. "Who ain't."

Creedence, clearing her throat and changing the subject. Devin thought she did so with casual non-urgency, at least for having delivered such heavy news. "You know I finally took and went through her check book."

"So?"

"So is that I seen how much money she keeps sending you."

Devin sat in silence. The shame he felt over cashing those checks caused a real and visceral need in him to drink. "Uh-huh."

"She's been sending you money all this time? All these years?"

"Never asked for a penny of it."

"I'm sorry, but I think it's the same as stealing. From her. And from me."

"Neither stole nor asked. End of subject."

"You ain't no better than them gypsies who come through and scam old people."

"I'll have you know I donate half that money to a charity of my choosing."

"Bull."

"I don't always cash them things anyway."

"Bull-shit. I seen the statements."

"You ain't all wrong."

"I know I ain't."

"That money ain't hers to give."

"It's out of her account."

"Her account? Shit. She didn't do nothing for it. That's daddy's money."

"I wish you'd shut your smart mouth."

Scratching week-old chin stubble with one ragged nail, Devin faked being drunker than he was by offering Creedence a string of slobbery gobbledygook.

"Lord have mercy. Listen to you."

Fighting to control laughter, he pinched his nose; tears ran down ruddy cheeks. More sibilant shit, his throat deliberately froggy and phlegmy, like a man drowning in his own juices. Whimpering, pleading, apologizing. Saying how broke up inside he was. Insisting how he still couldn't get over it all. All while trying not to bust a gut, either in laughter, else from acidic bile the color of rust inside his gut, a stormy gastrointestinal squall line which a few morning beers could never temper.

A hushed whisper: *"Edward Devin Rucker, I ain't never heard you this bad."*

Devin's merriment threatened to turn to genuine tears, like an unattended pot of mama's grits boiling over onto the hot orange spiral of the stove burner. Taking off his shades and putting them on the plastic patio table covered in cigarette burns, he took a deep breath. "None of you know what 'bad' looks like, woman. Don't forget that. But I know."

As he drank, belching, Devin listened to nothing. After a moment he realized he could hear his sister sniffling.

"Forget Mama, which considering how sick she is—I think it's cancer, by the way, but I ain't sure. But, she might not last long enough for you to make it home. So, come home and do it to me."

"Do *what* to you?"

"For me, I said. Do it *for* me."

"You said 'to'."

"P'shaw. Are you drunk already?"

"No. And don't remind me of this sorry fucking state. The bars ain't open out here yet."

Speaking of his physical condition, in the last year or so the weight had really come off. It probably had something to do with the fact of Devin rarely eating solid food. Every third day or so, he'd switch to screwdrivers or Sea Breezes to get vitamin C. Otherwise, he got by nibbling on dry toast, or, on a real good stomach day? Maybe a fast food hamburger, plain, no cheese, no condiments, don't drag it through the garden, because that's vegetables, and that's good for a body.

These Rucker women and their dramas. If some croaker had told him he was the one dying, finally, Devin would have danced a jubilant jig.

He barked, "'Do it for me?' You self-centered little Edgewater County prick-tease. Mama's a goner, but it's all about you? Damn if you ain't just like her."

"I can't sit here on the phone all day going back and forth with you."

He cussed her bloody. Called her a dried up old biddy. Said he might have to come home just to spite everyone. She hung up.

At the breaking of the line a flash of affection flitted in and out of his heart, a pale remembrance of love once held for Creedence, a sensation like actual emotion trying to claw its way out of the recesses of his abyssal insides. Devin, a besotted island unto himself, a vast, brackish sea of alone, but undeniable of his sister's existance as the one and true life connection with meaning. The only one he'd allow.

Furthermore: Devin, thinking that showing up back home for real could indeed serve as the ultimate fuck-you to them all. A lark. A hoot. Home again might possibly end up being the funniest, most entertaining stunt since the last time he'd been back in the Carolina midlands, when everyone got their drawers all bunched up at the old man's funeral over the Rucker ruckus he'd perpetuated.

As it often happened in his life, a sudden sea-change, a thunderclap, the turning of a page. A plan; a destination. For once.

He called back. She answered. "Yes, yes," his diction now clear and precise. "I believe that I will come home, dearheart. Yes indeed-y. As you wish."

Officious. "Fine. How, and when?"

Devin, ready to get moving, but not about to give anything remotely close to resembling a firm ETA. "Don't fret about the whys and wherefores, girlie. You'd get lost in the details." Purring and oozing charm, his words now a mellifluous, *basso profundo* Barry White incantation. "I'm-a be there before you know it. Ya big brother—he's coming home."

"Thank god. If you mean it."

"Say what I mean and do what I say. Count on it. Et cetera."

But Devin, his stomach stabbing with cold: Back home meant Libby. Even if she were dead.

*Wait—that's a metaphor. She's with Dobbs.*

Libby, her name holding an implication of wickedness and abandonment not unlike that of his own wretched mother, and all of her ruinous and pernicious foolishness. Still having a score to settle with both of them, but especially Libby—maybe once there in Edgewater County he'd track her down. Finally have matters out with his ex.

For keeps.

"You taking the bus, I hope?"

Absolutely, he lied. "No way I'm getting behind the wheel."

"Fine. Dusty'll pick you up from the station in Columbia, if he needs to."

Devin, cringing at the thought of her husband Dusty. He'd warned his sister to move away, far away, before something like Dusty happened, but Creedence, unheedful of his valuable and studied advice. And now? Stuck married to that sad-sack chubby Wallis turd, the only boyfriend she'd ever had; his sister, trapped running over the same old sandy, pine needle-strewn ground, so bored out of her mind she couldn't think of a blessed goddurn thing to do but call and monkeywrench his perfectly cozy, comfy trajectory of unrepentant alcohol consumption.

"And you listen to me," she continued. "You better not worry us by not coming after all—we don't deserve to be treated that way. There's too much at stake this time."

"Reckon you probably don't."

"'Probably'?"

"Put it this way: The situation's taken under advisement."

Creedence, telling him to hush with his mess.

The siblings paused, neither hanging up. At last she continued. "Wait—I got some other news, too."

"Mercy." Cracking open a fresh beer, quiet as possible. "Go easy."

"We're *pregnant,* finally."

Ouch. Horrible news. "Well, I be dog. A joyful occasion. Good job. And so on."

"Dusty's so happy. We both are." Sucking in a shaky breath. "And so I want to say how I'd like to believe my baby'll have an uncle to play with one day, and to love, and to look out for her. One who loves her back."

"Sounds like a fairy tale."

"Just think about things like that. There's a future for this family now, Devin. *Please,*" voice breaking. "Don't turn into a story I have to tell my child about one day."

Back out on the balcony, Devin peeked over carefully to see a college dude in a Colorado Rockies jersey, hair corkscrewed and face puffy from last night's party, walked out stunned by the mysteriously cracked windshield of his Toyota. The kid whipped his head around everywhere but up at Devin. He stalked away, stabbing at his phone and threatening the endless expanse of prairie-dog pockmarked American scrubland how *You fratboy bastards went too far this time.*

"Whoa, that's a noble aim. Proud of ya. Didn't suspect for a minute old Dust-ball had it in him."

"I only wish," her voice breaking, "you could bring back little Prudy with you. She's still okay—isn't she?"

A bucket of cold pig blood, dumped onto his head like that of Stephen King's oppressed literary Carrie. Rage threatened to pass his lips. Devin, instead managing syllables sounding like DUH followed by GAH.

"Devin: tell me. *How is Prudy?*"

His inner vision flaring with coruscating fire-white light, Devin cussed with vituperative invective into his flip-phone, shut it with a vicious snap of finality, threw it across the room.

Now, dang it—Prudy being dead wasn't Creed's fault. But, but, *fuck* that girl for invoking the cat's name, unbidden and out of the blue like that. Was she trying to kill him?

His heart pounded and the snakes under his skin, they began wriggling with aplomb. Truth: He'd sooner die than go home to South Carolina. Instead: Devin, needing to go and get extra superduper intoximacated.

But wait, wait, wait—to get their goats but-good? And make it stick this time?

*Go home for real.*

He chuckled through the shakes and the churning stomach-sickness. Show his ass to them all like he done at Daddy's funeral, but up the ante. Toss down a handful of Devin-change, that's change in which they could believe, onto the gaming table felt. Double down on it all. That would show their disloyal cracker asses.

What specific act of betrayal this campaign of revenge centered around, he could not currently recall. But he had a long drive ahead, and time to mull the reasons for wanting to put his fist through someone's ignorant face as soon as he saw them again.

But which someone?

Dobbs.

Billy.

Libby herself, the disloyal little so-and-so.

His mother.

*Ooooh.*

Getting warm.

Giving this familiar puzzle a toss precipitated a wave of the nightmare detox shakes, but Devin nonetheless managed a wry, dry laugh fraught with rueful intent—a road trip lay ahead. But this time, it would be the last one.

First? A drink, but only a bracer or twelve; however much to ease the wrinkles out of his slacks, get the hands steady enough to not only plan out a safe route back home across the country—safe for whom?—but to actually get behind the wheel, say grace to the God who looks after innocent drunks and little children, and hit the slab for home. What could possibly go wrong?

# FOUR

## —

## CREEDENCE

Brushing a salty tear from the corner of her eye with a flick of a pale, freckled finger, Chelsea Colette (Rucker) Wallace stifled a scream, holding back the ire against its will. She touched deep, weary creases in her brow above heavy auburn eyebrows. Her phone, still spinning on the slick countertop where she'd tossed it after Devin had hung up on her.

Reflux crawled up her gullet. She belched, spat into the sink. Overwhelmed for no good reason—when hadn't he acted like this?

Sounded strange hearing Devin call her Creedence, though. Chelsea, rarely thinking of herself as that anymore, not since losing her Daddy. Chelsea, this sounded like a woman's name. Creedence? A skinny ugly dumb redneck girl stuck in Edgewater County, South Carolina. Stuck stuck stuck. Maybe Chelsea, on the other hand, would one day get herself free. They'd called her Colette as a child; her middle name. It had always felt inauthentic. What was wrong with using her first name? Lord, but her mother was a mess.

Eileen, in failing health for real, though. That much true about what she said to Devin. The weight loss. The fatigue. Her pallor. The trips to the bathroom, frequent. And yet, the woman wouldn't admit to her own daughter that all those mysterious treks down to Columbia were to see doctors.

It was more than speculation. One of the guys in the body shop at the dealership, or rather his wife Felicia whom Chelsea had been in school with since the first grade, had told her that yes, Eileen had been in a number of times to see Dr. LaFreniere, but also that privacy laws were such that to say more could cost her a career. But that she was sorry—so so sorry, those extra so's like knife wounds in Chelsea's gut—and to let their family know if anything they could do.

Friends. She could count on Felicia more than her own people. Sad and pitiful.

Chelsea, almost shitting a brick—nobody in the healthcare industry would say 'sorry' that way if whatever was wrong with Eileen Rucker wasn't serious, damned serious. If it wasn't cancer from all those horrid cigarettes, she'd be surprised, mighty durn surprised, ladies and gentleman watching at home, if it wasn't terminal.

For once, the sister could understand her brother's need for a stiff drink.

Other voices in her head besides that of her mother: the babbling televisions and radios at the car dealership running constantly like a harsh, constant wail of white noise, the words spoken by the newsreaders and actors only half-noticed as she sat behind the switchboard in the Hampton Motors showroom, a glassed-in cubicle on a small stage, elevated. Her work: sending people and phone calls this way and that way, all day, every day, a task so all-mighty highfalutin' that on most days she ended up wanting to curl in a corner of the break room and croak from the boredom.

Not amusing. Not with Mama croaking.

Forget it. That couldn't be true. It was fine.

When not staring at the showroom television screens tuned to Fox News and ESPN, pointing, or punching line 1 or 2 or 3—Sales, Service, Parts—Chelsea now had her own computer and could sit quasi-discreetly surfing around to internet celebrity gossip sites and other online destinations. After going down the rabbit hole of links, she'd gotten caught up in UFOs, 9/11 conspiracies (what a crock), One World Government paranoia, faked moon landings. After a couple of hours of such surfing she'd feel dizzy from worrying about the Elites and their nefarious plans for humanity, so much she had to finally make herself stop reading and thinking about the idea of a cabal of humans controlling everything and everyone, earthly power wielded with godlike consequences, the shadowy puppet masters laughing at all whom they called the Great Unwashed. Chelsea, intrigued but unable to accept that the government would do things to hurt their own people. Insisting that the nature of reality was indeed how it appeared as depicted on TV. Her mother, agreeing.

Then, a new tangent, one ongoing, reminded by the cloth tube hanging on the wall into which she shoved all the plastic grocery sacks: after stumbling across a story about a giant island of plastic crap floating around in the Pacific Ocean, Chelsea had begun to read and learn about environmental problems. How plastic wasn't going away, but instead broke down into pellets tiny shrimp out in the ocean mistook for food, mutating from eating the plastic or dying off. How, since those tiny shrimp were a minuscule but crucial base of the entire food chain, a potential catastrophe of future worldwide nutritional privation loomed...

What was anyone to do?

Nobody was going to stop using plastic, driving cars, and running AC units, particularly in Edgewater County, so hot in the summer that people called the Carolina midlands the armpit of the South.

But impossible to ignore, these fears of food running out or the world getting too hot or too cold: Chelsea now had her own legacy to consider in the form of a daughter.

Or maybe a boy.

Certain to be a little girl, though.

One like her.

*Another me. Another person.*

*To replace Mama.*

*Once she's gone.*

Eileen's beloved and only daughter groaned.

The phone rang, scaring a scream and a poot out of her.

Mama. "Did you talk to him?"

"Yes."

"You got him on the phone?"

"Did I stutter?"

Chelsea's mother, a burst of weeping. Mama Eileen had gales of grief at times. They came and went, almost like she could turn it on and off like a play-actor. "Is he—? Did you—?"

"Yes, Mama. I lied to him and told him you were sick. That he better get home soon, if he was gonna see you again. It made me want to puke. But I lied for you."

Her tears, evaporating. "Good. That little shit. He doesn't deserve anyone to tell him the truth."

"I also told him about the baby. Thought that would help."

"What'd he say?"

Remembering his nastiness. His disdain. "He sure sounded happy. Hoping it'd be a little nephew for him to play with."

"Nephew? P'shaw. If it ain't a little girl, it'll be the first time I was ever wrong about anything, Colette. Won't it."

"Sure, Mama. Whatever you say."

Digging around in the fridge and suffering innocuous small talk and enduring waves of her Mama's dry, choking cough, Chelsea begged to be let go and was, but only with great reluctance. They talked three times a day, usually saw each other once or twice. Mercy.

Stooped over in lounging pants and oversized Jeff Gordon T-shirt, one of Dusty's, Chelsea's house-clothes hung loose, threadbare and stained, fuzzy bedroom slippers worn, stinky. She grabbed a head of iceberg lettuce out of the crisper, the bag of carrots, half a tomato left over from the sandwich Dusty had taken to the hardware store for lunch that day. Trying to eat better, all these salads. Half the time it was still pizza and burgers. Not much of a cook. Her mother had never had the patience to teach her.

Thinking: Maybe this will bring meaning. Us having made a baby.

Us.

She barked a laugh. Caught herself. Suffered a bout of revulsion at that one awful remark of Devin's.

About the daddy.

Of the baby.

Just morning sickness, her twinge of nausea, only a few hours late today.

The baby, the baby, the baby; the baby represented another chance, a new beginning for Chelsea, her husband, her demented-acting mother. For all of them, in fact, and this included poor shattered Devin.

Devin. Driving everyone up the wall with his morose behavior, now, then, always. One particular summer, changing from his sweet former self into a troubled angry little shit, and never looking back. Getting caught drinking, constantly, from that fifteenth year, drinking drinking drinking— Devin, not like your typical kid, getting beerdrunk and 'partying.' Hell no. Guzzling straight liquor. She saw him do it, time and again, when it was only the two of them at home. He went from being a happy boy who played games with her and did funny voices and dances and laughed all the time straight to a mean redneck drunk like you see hanging around that nasty honkytonk The Dixiana in downtown Tillman Falls. Like adolescence in his case meant skipping the healthy and productive adult years to go straight to alcoholic, sad and confused curmudgeon.

Later, Libby's death at the hands of a drunk driver would seal his emotional deal, but ironically enough, it had not been Devin himself. That mess represented the final nail in an actual coffin into which Chelsea thought her brother should have crawled along with his dead girlfriend, for all the years he'd lost to grieving and drinking, anyway.

She didn't have the words or ideas for what ailed Devin. Considering the circumstances of what happened to Libby, one would have thought he'd never take another drink, not so much as a drop.

In his case? The opposite. She wondered if he considered that the universe had sent him a message to chill out and clean himself up. Only drinking more, though, after that day. No one could blame him.

And then there was sweet Dobbs, Devin's best friend who'd been riding with them, thrown from the car and paralyzed, living just up the road with his mother. He seemed to have let the tragedy finish him too, only in a different way. Everybody gave up.

Even her, in a way.

Dang.

Chelsea, so lost in rumination that she'd shredded an entire mound of carrots.

She finished making the salad and envisioned her brother's imminent arrival in Chilton, not even a goddurn actual place, only an unincorporated collection of subdivisions with the only real town center being Hill Hampton's car dealership, and quite unlike pretty, preserved Tillman Falls, the county seat, with its town green and statues and sense of history. How she wished she could at least live in one of those nice old southern houses on Whaley Way, with their massive magnolias and oaks and crepe myrtles so ancient they towered high as trees. Old South money back in yonder.

What she wanted couldn't be bought: Chelsea, and the rest of the family, at last managing to heal Devin—ushering him, processional, down the path of wholeness and sanity, at the same time making her saintly mother's passage from this life to the next comfy as possible. An act of generosity, a kind of filial duty, one fraught with inherent meaning; her current life felt bereft of said meaning; a no-brainer.

Fix Devin.

And as for Mama, maybe not as sick as she imagined. Her pal Felicia, always such a gossip, going back far as Chelsea could remember.

Myriad other worries besides Devin bobbed to the surface like Big Ma-Maw's homemade dumplings in broth bubbling with greasy fat.

But she'd been gone twenty years now, her granny, the first dead body Creedence and Devin had ever seen, and nobody'd had them good dumplings since. Now, with Dusty acting distracted and frightened over the impending birth of their child—yes, she had lied to her brother about Dusty's enthusiasm—more immediate concerns sat poised to take precedence over old tragedies such as lost-soul brothers, dead grannies, and lost old friends like Libby and Dobbs.

*Old friends.*

*Old friends who could maybe help her brother.*

*Get him back home.*
*Get Devin back to himself, whatever's left.*

Covering her salad bowl with Glad wrap and putting it in the fridge, she chewed her lip and glanced sidelong at the phone. Chelsea should have been turning on the oven to preheat for the taters, thick cut steak fries that she refused to put in the Fry Daddy anymore because of Dusty's growing gut. Instead, she plopped down on a kitchen stool and began doodling on the message pad sitting next to the cordless phone base.

Kitty-cat faces.

Dusty caricatures.

A hollow-eyed skeleton wearing aviator shades.

Devin.

Looking around her home, gripping her stomach, panic at the idea of having been born and living in a South Carolina pine barren with a man she didn't love.

With his child inside her.

*Billy.*

That's who she'd call. The logic, irrefutable. Chelsea—Creedence, as he'd remember her—would call Billy Steeple down in Columbia. He'd know what to do about Devin. Chelsea, in need of a hand; one of handsome Billy's hands, doing nicely. The idea of talking to him after so long came as a rare thrill; the fantasy of doing more than talking, as they had almost managed so long ago, left her weak in the knees.

Thinking long and hard before deciding to look up his office number in the Southeastern University online directory, at last she jotted it down with a hand that shook the way Devin's always did.

Naughty, bad girl thoughts flooded into her belly all around the baby. She stayed so mad at Dusty all the time. And him so mamby-pamby, dull and unsexy. And her horny and feeling lonesome while he played his dumb games.

But, what had happened the last time she left herself think naughty thoughts?

Deep in her heart, of course, she would always think of the child as Dusty's. Uh-huh. Wasn't no doubt. After all, she'd only done it with Buddy Lawler, one of the car salesmen at Hampton Motors, twice last month. So far. Now he would not stop pestering her for another go-round.

But, it hadn't been no better than Dusty. Seemed impossible that sex so lame could produce a little baby—but one of the two doofuses had managed the feat. Thank god they both had pudgy bodies and brown hair. This was a pathetic lifeline, one to which she would cling as she prepared for a lifetime of pretending which lay ahead.

A revelation, cold, wicked, but also appealing—*but now, if I went and finally done it with Billy... we could pretend my baby was his.*

*I could pretend, rather. Not we.*

Secrets must be kept close. This idea formed the core of Mama's wisdom.

Chelsea drew in her breath—Billy, not only a person of means but a gentleman. He would consent to marry as soon as her divorce was final—and divorce it would be, the second Dusty saw with whom his dumb redneck ass would have to compete.

A way out of Edgewater County. But she would have to hurry.

The pencil point broke on the pad. She tossed it aside. *Argh.*

Outside on the porch of her manufactured home she drank in the springtime Carolina air, but sneezed from all the pollen coming off the trees in yellow waves. Cussed at the layer of orange longleaf pine straw Dusty wouldn't rake to save his sorry life. Cringed at the sound of a logging truck *choo-chooing* on the hill down toward the highway. Heard dogs howling at a far-off siren.

Billy. They had all-but screwed that one time. It could finally happen. Still wasn't clear what had gone wrong.

A way out.

Her mind raced. Devin, Billy, Dusty, the baby. Mama. What people would think, if they only knew how she was scheming.

But above all: The baby.

Chelsea, perhaps at last finding her one true thing. No one could get mad her for a little messing with people's hearts and minds, if it meant the best for her baby. She got up the nerve, made the call, and at last he answered, the sound of his voice like music in her ears. Billy.

And, at her tears and breaking voice over poor Devin, why, you should have heard how Billy sounded—like Superman ready to race to the rescue. By the time she pressed her body into his in gratitude for helping her brother, his heart would be hers.

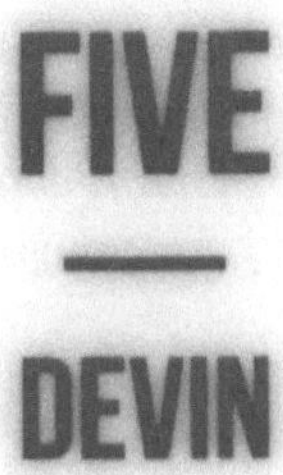



With cold liquor gurgling down his ruined and painful gullet, only one problem loomed with any true immediacy—another motherfreaking phone call.

But, this time? Epic.

Steeple.

No shit.

His best boy. All chummy sounding on the message, checking in. But like, to call back. Super important, actually. Not just checking in. *Please*, his oldschool college friend's final entreaty.

Settling into a dim nook far away from the scattered barflies and yammering televisions at Chubby's, Devin punched up Billy's number and waited, humming the melody of that Gary Wright tune 'Love is Alive.' Hadn't the foggiest how that'd gotten into his noggin. Hadn't heard that one in twenty years. Longer.

"Ruck?" Billy, sounding out of breath, answered on the third ring. "How fantastic to hear back from you so quickly."

"You acted like it was an emergency. Going all *please* on me like that."

Billy paused and grunted. "Yeah, no, well: Hard to believe it's been so long."

"Time keeps on slipping-slipping. Don't it, though?"

Billy, asking how Devin had been. What he'd been up to. And so on. Devin heard a strident female voice, muffled, in the background.

Billy, faraway, saying, "Go back to bed. *Now*."

Tickled. "Don't tell me I interrupted you in the middle of getting some."

Back to Devin, a softer tone. "Nonsense. We were doing yoga. So, I hear you're coming home soon? Is this right? That would be *fantastic*."

Devin, a pull on his triple house bourbon, hot right out of the bottle into his glass and down it goes. So Creed, behind the call from Steeple after all, the conniving little red-haired busybody.

"Bill, I can't stand the place. You know it just as sure as I'm a stone drunk. Creedence might've got some silly idea-r in her punkin head I was coming back, but damned if I do anything because she wants it. Or cause anybody else fucken wants me to. That much we know."

"God knows it must be hard for you back here. I know it is for me, sometimes."

"Hard. Yeah."

The spots, silvery simmering and boiling, blotted out the view across the stained and picked velvet surface of the pool tables—B-girl Darla, a frequent drinking buddy, sat hunched over a gin and tonic in need of refreshment.

She noticed Devin noticing her; she winked, blew him a kiss, and hit the response on the bar-top trivia machine without looking; the CORRECT ANSWER fanfare blared.

"So you'll come? For me?"

A tremulous recitation of hoarse, coiled animosity masquerading as enthusiasm:

"Bill, I can't wait to get home and try all this out. We'll schlep on over to the new Sizzler they got in Chilton. Yeah, we will. Creedence says, she says, she says they got a *huh-huh*-hot bar where a mo-fo can slop macaroni and taters and slaw and mustard greens on the side of them ribeye and T-bones like it's Sunday dog-gone dinner at the preacher's house."

"Hardy-har. You're making my stomach growl."

He gulped hot liquor. Fought back a stupid wave of panic and tears no set of aviators able to conceal. Faking laughter, wet and thick, Devin going, it's a beautiful plan, bro. "I'm halfway out the door."

"I'm relieved to hear it," Billy said.

Belching into the receiver. "There's some words what's gotta be said."

"By all means."

"Serious shit."

"Go ahead."

"All right. Here goes..."

"*Yes?*"

"Can't remember what we was talking about."

Cheery, now sounding like a game show host introducing today's contestants, Billy said, "We're talking about you coming back here to South-Cack to visit with us for a spell! To get yourself fixed up! That's all we were discussing. That's the whole deal, Rucker-man!"

Nobody was getting 'fixed up' or detoxed. The last time, too rough. No way. Hell, he'd only done it because of Millie anyway, but what had it got him but more headaches and heartaches and empty bottles.

"Sounds *dee*-lightful."

"Can you get yourself to the airport?"

"Fly home on your nickel?"

"Quicker, easier, over in a few hours."

Curious to hear Billy's version: "What's so gall-danged important back home, any-hoo?"

"Well. Creedence reports you haven't been home since your Dad passed away."

"Objection. Hearsay."

"That's no good, brotherman." His tone turned gentle, as though speaking to a child. "Your mom. Sounds like they—she—could use a visit. Before too much longer."

"You wanted to give me a goddamn reason to come back home to that shitty ass place? Partner, you done it right there."

"I did?"

"I tell you what. I'm-a gonna kill their lying asses. All of 'em."

"That's so not-even funny, bro."

"Every comic drops a clunker. But I'm here all week, folks." Turning reflective. "You done a lot for me, son. You picked me up when I was down, once, in the summer of '90. Near as I can recall."

Billy made a strangled sound. "I didn't need to be told the date."

"You okay?"

Strained. "Three words: Just come home. I know if you give me the chance, I can help again. Like before."

"This is a shit assignment you're volunteering for."

"There's nothing I want more. And nothing Creedence wants more, either."

"Help me the way you helped Libby?"

Billy paused so long Devin thought the call had dropped.

He ignored the reference to Libby. "Come back to the world, dude. What do you have to lose? And what are we talking about for a plane ticket? The money—it's nothing to me."

"Okay, Scrooge McDuck. I get it."

Pleading: "Let me do this, big chief."

Devin, chastened and contrite. "I don't deserve it."

"From the Enough-Already files comes a sad tale of martyrdom."

Devin, finding a true voice inside, for once. "I'm drunker than shit right now. Which is the only time I feel okay. That's the god's truth. If I come, I come. But lemme figure out how on my own."

"Two thousand miles? Too much freaking driving."

"I'm careful. Wouldn't want any accidents."

"Accidents—they're pernicious buggers, they are."

The rest of the bourbon disappeared. Devin, his throat raw. "That they are."

"But look. It's like a noted philosopher once said: the more you drive, the less you think."

"Maybe that's why I like it so much."

Billy mentioned again how with his USAirways Platinum status he could book Devin in a skinny instant; had done so recently for a conference to which he'd be flying to in San Antonio in a mere two days. Expressing hope that by the time of his return on Sunday, Devin, by whatever means, would be waiting there in Edgewater County.

Devin, a sea-change of mood. "You'll be in Texas? That ain't but two states away."

Billy's voice became small. "It's for work."

"I'll drive on down and meet you there. Hang out."

"You'll do *what*?"

"Ain't never been to old San An-tone. I hear they got themselves some nasty tight little brown Mexican pussy down that way."

"You can't be—you're not serious."

"If we don't leave with Spanish-speaking crabs, m'boy," slapping his thigh, "we ain't done our jobs right. Fuck-all if we ain't."

"This sounds crazy."

"Beau, you wanted a plan. There it be. *Boo-yow*."

Devin, downright stoked: this, no mere peregrination like all his other travels; here, one with a tangible destination: San Antonio, Texas, an American city, meaning bars and liquor stores like every other crappy two-bit berg in the whole lousy country. Might take a bit longer to get himself back east than heading straight that-a-way, but Devin, in no real hurry.

Not to get home.

Billy, strained, mumbled his hotel info. Sounded like he wanted to take a dirt nap over the whole Devin-popping-by idea.

*Perfect*.

Devin, bursting with vigor at the notion of getting moving. And so: A light-heeled shuffle over to the bar, waving his empty glass around and calling for Jimbo.

The bartender, a pothead, emerged bleary-eyed from the back room. "Need a fresher-upper, Ruck?"

Devin, holding out his hands. "Almost steady. One more round should do it."

"Coming up, old buddy."

In a moment he found himself sipping a fresh double and chased it with the first of the beers Jim would line up.

Devin, regaling Darla and a few others, announced he was headed back home to visit family; he spun stories about his sister, about Libby and Billy and fuckers like Dobbs, too. All had betrayed him.

"But here come the judge," to a variety of hoots and boot-stomping. The regulars cheered but had heard it all before, but still they listened and nodded and drank and smoked with Devin. Like family.

After a while he got drunk; after a longer while, he forgot about the folks back home, as well as his impending trip to San Antonio. Forgot it as much as he forgot anything which had happened in the past. Which wasn't a god-damned bit. But it didn't hurt to pretend, every now and then.

Billy, anxiety ridden, not nearly high enough, slumped at his desk in the Media Archive, a musty crumbling converted warehouse shoved way out on an outer spiral arm of the sprawling Southeastern campus.

Staring at his cellphone, chewing his lips.

Jumping at every small sound.

All tremendously bothersome.

Ever since the conversations with the Rucker siblings Billy had suffered a deep and abiding fear that at any second, the phone might again sound bearing the voices of mad, babbling ghosts.

To recap: Devin, on his way back home, is now to 'swing by' and meet him this week in San Antonio. To hang out and party and reminisce.

*Mark it down—my shizzle is now fazizzled.*

Billy, recovering his wits enough to call Creedence Rucker and inform her of his horrifically hard-won success regarding the engagement he'd achieved with her brother, said, "Maybe I got through to him. And who knows, it could be good that we hook back up on neutral territory out there."

"Bless you."

Insincere and gut-knotted furious at the imposition of troubled old dicknut Devin back into his life, Billy could barely get the words past his teeth: "It's my deepest joy and honor to assist."

Heartfelt, broken-voiced gratitude in response. "You're the best. I hope I can do something one day in thanks."

"Are you kidding?" He owed her one. Said so.

"You always were the sweetest." She sighed. "Among other qualities."

What a guy. A real mensch. Creedence had been cute as a teenager. He had almost had it off with her, too, before coming to his senses.

But now, it felt refreshing to hear her flirt. So much it gave him a bothersome, half-mast trouser snake in need of wrangling.

They rang off pledging to see one another soon as Billy could get Devin back home. He noted how she expressed a husky and determined desire to 'get together soon.' She repeated the phrase no fewer than three chuckling, nervous times.

The call, troublesome; for some bizarre reason, now Billy started obsessing about nailing the living shit out of Creedence Rucker. Profane and naughty, thrilling by default, bucket list material.

Yes: He would do it at first opportunity. She'd wanted it a long time; she wanted it now.

Christ, how he'd have to be careful. In his size, excitement and strength, he had often injured sexual partners.

On purpose.

No—by accident.

Or: sometimes both.

He'd only killed a few along the way, though. A couple-three. Four or five. In the ballpark of a half-dozen. Ya know. Those he allowed himself to recall.

He could barely remember what the victims looked like. He hadn't meant any of it—the killing part, anyway—and so, and so, you had to give him a freaking pass, yo. Unintended consequences. Acts of God type-deal.

His memories of dumping various bodies, both in South Carolina and the ones back at various prep schools—a couple of girls, also a dude who'd made the mistake of talking Billy into an interesting mutual masturbation experiment gone terribly wrong—all lay hazy, inaccessible. Like shitty movies remembered from watching late at night all by oneself, stoned, lonely, confused, murderously depressed and angry from missing Libby Meade so goddamned much.

Movies, more memorable than the victims.

Accident victims, he meant. Semantics were key, here. If 'semantics' was the right word for what he meant.

Eyes slitted, Billy peeked through the window of his office at neat rows of steel industrial shelving which held the 16mm, VHS, and DVD elements making up the Southeastern academic film library. His forgotten kingdom.

A nerdy, introverted girl holding a clipboard pushed a gray cart of film cans by the open door of Billy's office. His new intern from the Mass Comm college had circles under her eyes, a labret piercing, orange threadbare Che Guevara babydoll T-shirt, strawberry blonde dreadlocks pulled back by a tattered puke-green paisley bandanna that revealed jug ears rattling and jangling with piercings. Morning breath. This grungy hipster trollop was far from Billy's type, which of course seemed for the best—fucking the interns to death, probably not considered ethically sound leadership of a department like the Media Archive.

Oh, but so lonely and secluded down here. You could fuck until bloody and screaming, coming and coming until emerging from the trance to find carnage; a crime scene, yeah, but really an accident. The mess; the sadness and terror in their cold dead eyes.

It was why he didn't drink. His issues—the accidents—required a high degree of self discipline to manage. A double-edged sword: concentrate, don't come; concentrate, don't fuck them to death.

Which wouldn't have happened with Libby. What that nasty little drunk Devin stopped that dreary night after the Dead show was the two of them, Billy and Libby, on the cusp of falling in love, but forever forestalled.

Oh, but now Ruck's the one talking about killing people? *Fucking amateur, dude.*

Billy's life, unfolding quite different now but for that redneck's meddling. So what if Libby had been Devin's girl. So what.

Look—there's a chick right now: Damn if Marleigh didn't present as appealing and bright. Best of all, possessing a wealth of cinematic knowledge. Beyond sexy, into the realm of threatening. Stinky, but smarter than him.

Awesome.

Billy, swearing to himself to be careful on the approach here, feel her out, and if or when it happened, exhibiting precise and sedulous caution to not break her as had happened before with other rosebuds of such small stature.

Accidents. Nothing that feels as good as coming could be associated with any true malfeasance. Accidents, he insists.

Libby, she'd been smart as well. A cinephile, and a writer. The smartest and coolest girl he'd ever known. But Libby, gone gone gone.

Billy leaned way over, stared out the door at Marleigh standing on her tippy-toes. Scrutinizing a stack of film cans on a high shelf, she scribbled a notation on her clipboard.

"Remember to tell me if you smell vinegar. Those are the cans we're going to want to deal with first, if we 'can' at all, ha-ha."

"Can-do," she said.

"Sounds good, punkie."

The intern shot him a curt, terrified glance—her normal response to any communication—followed by a dispassionate, professional nod of understanding. Here in a university environment, Billy suspected he ought to lose the cutesy terms of endearment. But only putting her at ease. Making her feel attractive.

Marleigh. What kind of lay would she be? All hippie and hairy and grungy? Earthy? A wildcat, he surmised.

Women, sensing his power, seeking his essence. Billy, like, hey: giving the people what they want.

Khaki fabric stretched and strained, zipper teeth threatening sensitive nerve endings. *SPROING!*

Billy Steeple, needing to chill the eff out, brothers and sisters and all the ships at sea and grandmama listening back home on the NBC radio network: Chill out, lose the incipient chubby, be cool and stop this; don't let this happen. Marleigh's a good girl. She's an employee. She's becoming a friend.

Like Libby.

Except that Billy didn't love Marleigh, so there. Another reason to ignore the bothersomeness that made him want to fuck this decent kid to death.

Ah. He felt better. Relaxed. He'd nail Mel to the headboard later. She got into being held down; threatened. She came—hard, screaming and thrashing —while Billy pretend-choked her.

Melanie Pinckney: the most dangerous and perfect girlfriend he'd ever had. She had to go.

Marleigh's knowledge of cinema, he understood, probably offered the majority of the reason for Billy's incipient lust. Discovering to his delight the young student could keep up in a discussion of Bergman or Kurosawa made her a rare breed indeed among her peers. This lady had seen movies, knew the work of the masters. Could talk the talk of both critic and filmmaker.

Melanie, for all her welcome carnal vigor, was quite the opposite. Hating all that *auteurist* stuff. Finding his favorite art films dull, turgid. Preferred rom-coms, revisiting Disney or other jams from her youth like CLUELESS.

Billy, in many cases agreeing with her taste, albeit in secret: Most of the art-film selections in his collection were to lend street cred with other media academics. Yeah. He had close to five hundred Criterion spine numbers on display. Add in the screenplay stacked to the ceiling, and here, a film scholar beyond reproach.

In truth?

Billy dug mainstream, popular titles the most, classics he'd loved as a youth: starships and heroes and time-tripping luxury cars and heavy makeup effects and happy endings. Whether they smacked of *deus ex machina*, whether contrivances made sense, it didn't matter so long as the conclusion reached left him feeling as though satisfying resolution had been achieved.

Further, he followed the weekly box office results less like a baseball fanatic following stats than a solemnly penitent monk memorizing lines of scripture. He often commented under a variety of nom-de-gueres—*BO Sock Puppet, Emilio Lizardo, AlexDeLarge420,* a few others—posting arch and smarmy flamebait on various industry blogs, engaging in vicious and cutting comment threads sometimes amassing into the hundreds of responses. While trenchant and apt, his prognostications made alongside knowledgable and bonafide industry insiders nowadays left him empty as most of the plots of the megafilms sitting atop the top of the charts.

The art movies, however, sat displayed upon bookshelves to protect his rep as a cineaste, and while he purported to have watched them all, the truth was that in the last couple of months alone, he'd passed out during (or otherwise bailed on): Bergman's WINTER LIGHT, Ozu's LATE SPRING, a Mexican Buñuel, a postwar Kurosawa, the early Herzog about the dwarfs, Satyajit Ray's APU trilogy (after only twelve minutes, a record), Cimino's HEAVEN'S GATE (the four-hour version, so he had an excuse for passing out), Bertolucci's 1900 (the five hour version, stopped after only ten minutes, new record), two Altmans (NASHVILLE, THREE WOMEN), two painterly Malicks (DAYS OF HEAVEN, the three-hour extended director's cut of THE NEW WORLD, which with all the whispering, awestruck narration made for a mean soporific), an award-winning, universally praised Errol Morris documentary, a bare-bones Dogma 95 effort from Lars Von Trier, a brutal Michael Haneke, a chilly Atom Egoyen, and the Bresson featuring a donkey as protagonist.

All dull, pretentious claptrap; all of it like homework.

No one knew of Billy's completion problem but him, thank god. Thanks to the arrival of capsule internet reviews, his ability to fake his way through a conversation about either an artist's oeuvre or a particular picture remained impressive, even fooling the film studies faculty into believing him an expert.

Billy, a magician. They saw the reality he wished them to experience. Godlike, I tells ya.

Movies. Before Libby, he'd barely given a shit about them. He'd been into music, his punk band Choking Hazard, was headed toward rock stardom. Libby's interest in cinema, though, had changed all that. Until she went and died on him. Till Devin killed her by letting a drunk hit them head-on.

Devin, a drunk himself.

But not drunk that time.

Which at least would have given him a decent excuse. He heard the character from SEINFELD asking, "What's irony?"

Billy, crying out, shoved back from his messy desk as though stabbed. He gripped his side, the ribs on the right, which tingled and quivered with incipient panic. He felt grateful Marleigh had moved out of sight.

Ruck.

With all of Billy's problems, to babysit a volatile drunk like his old friend, especially at this academic conference about which he'd been so eager and anticipatory, offered an additional layer of BS. Spoil-sport Ruck.

The conference, a little vacation, had nothing to do with his work as a media librarian; a fun trip to hang out with other erudite pop-culture geeks like himself, presenting papers and talking late into the night about movies or great albums or whatever, fucking some chicks, but not hard enough to kill them. Not ones he knew, anyway.

Calm blue ocean, he thought.

He had bigger issues.

Melanie.

Eh. He'd bang her silly tonight. Fill her head with bullshit, go to Texas, come back, kick her ass out and, and, hell, who knows? Put her head on a pike. A warning to others who dared transgress.

Or?

Start.

Fucking.

Creedence.

Rucker.

A capital idea.

Despite exhaustive experience with such matters, though, dumping Melanie had so far presented a wee small amount of difficulty. Like, her totally not picking up on all his signals and subtext.

He'd taken matters to the next level by ignoring her all day, with resulting frenzied and frantic jabbering messages left on the voicemail, a lengthy email screed hysterical with capital letters and exclamatory punctuation, over three dozen text messages. Billy feared she'd come strolling into the Media Annex at any moment to create an uncomfortable scene, if not worse— maybe his was the head awaiting prejudicial removal. A wild-woman, Mel.

With said possibility in mind, he pushed back from the desk and folded up his tent. Almost four. Enough for one day. No one to make any hay out of closing up shop early.

Media—who cared? All his beloved film reels and videotapes, now supplanted by the exchange of pure information through every dorm room's hot T-3 connection to computer services. The DVDs, yes, were available to students. Still, few ever came his way but maintenance folk, custodians, the occasional film geek wanting to screen an actual print for a class.

No one to care, no one to bother him.

Not stuck way down here like this.

Tomb of the unknown Billy.

Slipping on his tweed sport coat, he strolled down the long metal racks of film reels to tell Marleigh of his departure.

"Let's wrap it up for today."

"Already?"

"Tragic, I know. I've an important meeting up the hill with the Dean and the Vice Provost."

She dropped the clipboard onto the metal cart with a clatter. "Hate to quit in the middle of a shelf and all."

"Pish-posh," flopping a hinged wrist. "The stuff has already lain here long enough awaiting its savior to come along. A few more hours, days, weeks— they won't matter."

"Time is an illusion."

"How's that?"

Some mumbled horseshit about it 'all being right now'.

Bright, this one. Or pretending, anyway. Billy, down with all that. "And 'right now,' I have an appointment. So let's skedaddle."

"Okay, Dr. Steeple." Marleigh cast her gaze at the tips of his loafers, a titillating display of obeisant respect.

Billy, glowing inside; he yet to correct her about his academic pedigree. He hadn't gotten near a piled-higher-and-deeper.

"See you tomorrow, young lady."

Outside, Billy, thinking about what lay ahead with Ruck, watched Marleigh peddle on her mountain bike up the steep hill toward campus proper. Maybe in San Antonio he'd be able to understand Devin's fucked-up mental state. No choice but to ride out this mad episode and find out what awaited.

The nailing-Creedence angle. That was the spice in all this Rucker activity. If he could manage to keep from having some unforeseen accidental accident go down—a pernicious problem, no doubt—he'd be golden.

# SEVEN
—
## CREEDENCE

The checkout lines at the Piggly Wiggly snaked lengthy, daunting, and inescapable. Chelsea, on her standard midweek grocery trip, had found every other chucklehead in this misbegotten corner of Edgewater County of similar mindset. Still not as bad as the cattle-call at the Wal-mart on a Saturday, though. So she had that going for her.

Sighing and rolling her eyes, Chelsea surveyed the contents of her cart—preservative-laden, processed crap piled on top of a small cluster of fresh fruits and vegetables, her customary list all but memorized, garbage Dusty relished like manna.

But, didn't everyone?

As her mother often proclaimed, though, 'they' wouldn't sell food which wasn't no good for people. Worrying about such matters made Chelsea feel like an alien from Planet X.

A voice from behind, despite its softness and affection, caused her to jump out of her skin. "Colette?"

Chelsea turned to see Miriam Vandegrift pushing her son Dobbs, in his wheelchair, along in front of her. So many people still called her by that stupid childhood name. Between her father's nickname and her proper first name, she'd fixed that. Mostly. "Mercy. You scared the mess of out me."

Dobbs, blinking at her with a grimace, speaking with a slight, moist lisp. "Daydreaming again?"

"It's what I do."

"Fancy seeing you at the Chilton Piggly Wiggly."

"Ha—we oughta both have our durn mail delivered here."

Winking at her; a joke. Often did they run into one another at the store. Small town blues.

Squeezing her eyes at her brother's old childhood friend; for the first time in a long while, she felt fresh sorrow at his broken, irreparable body. Her brother's other passenger. What a day that was. One of the worst.

She got a flash—of Billy in the hospital, looking so grownup and handsome, so calm.

Except when they told him Libby was dead.

And he peed in his pants. In front of everyone.

The small-talkers exchanged weather-chat and Chilton gossip, capped off by Chelsea's announcement she'd become heavy with the seed of life.

Miriam, awestruck and joyous, hugged her neck. "That's grand, Colette. I can feel the Lord's hand in this."

"Me too, me too." Dobbs, nodding up to his mother. "I bet Mama Eileen's fit to be tied."

"Yeah. She's over the moon about it."

Dobbs, wise and knowing, squinted at her: "What about Dusty?"

The fake smile she produced actually hurt. "He's excited, and all. Everybody's real—glad."

"It reckon it's time, Creedence."

"Reckon so."

The line, moving forward. An enormous woman in a floral-print dress like a bed-sheet swiped her EBT card and billowed out the automatic door, her cart weighted down by unhealthy food, a smorgasbord of frozen containers over which Dusty would drool.

Chelsea unloaded her cart onto the belt and handed two canvas sacks to the bag boy, who looked at her like she'd lost her mind—the reusable bag craze, yet to gain a foothold in a place like Chilton.

"Now, you get everything into those bags. I don't want none of them durn plastic ones."

To the Vandegrifts she offered one more shred of news, one fraught with portent, but making it sound nonchalant: "Oh—Devin's coming home, by the way."

"He is? When?"

"Real soon, we hope."

She stole a glance and saw Dobbs's smile now troubled, as was his mother's face. "Good," he said. "We can't wait to see him again."

"He said to tell y'all 'hey.'"

What a liar. Her brother had never been able to face his friend, perhaps the coldest part of the post-accident Devin storm of grief and hateful behavior. The world had been cruel to him, she supposed, so he started giving back—but with much emotional collateral damage. *A car wreck wasn't no excuse for how he'd treated Dobbs.*

"I need to witness to him. He's got to let me, finally—please help me do that."

"Praise the Lord." Miriam whispered. "Fifteen years."

"Well." Imagining Devin not taking such a conversation too well. "I'll do what I can."

"Once I do? Everything's gonna be made right again. With him—and with me, too."

She couldn't possibly imagine what he meant—would Devin's reappearance heal the lame? Doubtful.

"I'll make sure you're first on his list."

"That's right. We're gonna get him fixed up. Sure as I'm sitting here."

Chelsea put the last box of frozen, processed meat products onto the conveyor belt. "Devin's right hardheaded, as I'm sure y'all remember. But I'm hoping this time'll be different."

"This time will be with God's help."

"Yeah."

Fat chance. God hadn't helped her do anything yet. The job, too vast, too complicated. Near as she could figure.

God? He seemed weak and cruel, or perhaps worse, indifferent.

A cold chill rippled through her. Bad thoughts again. Thoughts of Devin's return gave her a cramp, hard and sharp, down in her pelvis. She was sure these pains were a normal part of pregnancy. On the way out of the automatic doors, she waved to the Vandegrifts while trying not to double over from the pain.

All this stress over Devin. And the baby. That's all these aches amounted to—worries. She'd quit worrying. Soon.

Maybe Billy would take away her worries. Who knew what he future held? A girl could daydream.

# EIGHT
—
## DEVIN

The drunk's mind, racing to picture the scene awaiting him in San Antonio. Billy had always been such a kind soul. Even now, with his old friend knowing what a hopeless waste of drunken flesh old Ruck had become, still being 'that' guy. Selfless. Supportive. Caring. Such efforts made Devin feel only further grief.

For a brief moment, he tried imagining a move back home to live again. Hanging out together like best friends, scoping out the chicks, tossing back a few beers on Friday nights, growing old and fat and wealthy like two proper American gentlemen. Laughing with wistfulness, warmth; remembering the good times.

The fantasy, turning dark: Sunday dinners with his mother and Creed and Dusty and their little monster of a child, or children, should his sister and her husband make the stupid mistake of reproducing themselves over and over again; his guts, twisting as he allowed himself to think about running into Libby and Dobbs: together, married, a house and jobs and their own children; a sweaty Dobbs lying on top of Libby, thrusting, obscene, moaning.

Graven images.

Devin, blotting out these visions by chugging the juice hot of the bottle, right in the middle of the room naked, stupid-crying and drunk-sick. Check.

Such melodrama. How bad could going home be?

Devin, rewinding the hazy playback to consider the possibilities: The last time seeing Creedence, the morning after his father's funeral. Two years ago —or three? Ballpark was the best Devin could do on the passage of time.

Closing his eyes, seeing his sister sitting on the huge deck at the back of their parents' house: Creedence, sorting through a plastic grocery sack of old family photographs never properly scrapbooked: Polaroids and Kodachromes of trips to Myrtle Beach or Disney, or the time the family drove all the way to Abilene, Texas to visit Dad's dying great-grandmother, a hundred years young.

The thought of being forced to exist so long, waiting and hoping for the blessed end to come and wondering each day *when when when,* made the teenage Devin uneasy and aghast.

Was he pushing forty, now?

What would that make Libby?

*Same age, dipshit. You were the same age.*

Creedence, calm and quiet that damp October morning; unreality settled over the scene. Methodical, she sat going through the photos and placing them into organized stacks on the round patio table wiped dry of the dew. She wore an old gown and robe, new, fluffy-red bedroom shoes on her feet, long legs crossed, one slipper dangling and exposing a narrow pink heel.

Devin, thinking how she'd always hated her slender feet, how when barefoot she'd scrunch her long toes into little fists, try to hide her deformities. Creedence, thinking the rest of herself ugly too, but the reality simply not jibing; Devin, always trying to reinforce the concept of her frecklefaced pulchritude, but failing. Rucker women tended toward the stubborn, and his reassurances had never taken, not that he knew. Maybe she finally thought she was pretty, now. He'd ask.

The bag of photos, the morning dew, her white, freckled legs covered in goose flesh from the breeze that swept in through the long back yard dotted with hardwoods and pines amidst other gardening and landscaping projects, a sloping, manicured expanse resplendent with greenery, clusters of azaleas arranged around dogwoods and Japanese maples and older oak trees, bright red mulch from the Home Depot, a smattering of forest pansy redbuds scattered along the tree line where the woods behind the house began to get thick, bushes which in April bloomed brilliant with rich purple, the flora bursting with vibrant color like a scene out of a SOUTHERN LIVING magazine cover.

Devin, head pounding with each beat of his diseased heart, a hangover for the ages, watched from inside the sliding glass doors: *my sister, how cold she looks.* Planning, then, to get her a sweater for Christmas, or her next birthday. Should he live that long.

Sliding open the heavy door, shivering, hacking up thick, bitter spit, he shuffled out and stood behind her.

Without turning to face him: "Everybody in these damn pictures— they're either dead, or else someone I loved a long time ago, but now can't stand no more." She cut her eyes back at him, finally.

Devin, swaying back and forth in stained white t-shirt and faded Felix the Cat boxers, underwear his mother'd sent for Christmas some holiday long in the past, the cartoon animal on his thigh sporting an insouciant, knowing wink and a word bubble—*Life is Just a Bag of Tricks!*

"Don't know who half these people are. If I ever did before."

"I'm sure they feel the same way about you. After yesterday."

Drunk as a coot before his father's funeral had begun, of course, he had caused a scene. Devin, his back hurting, recalled being pulled off his mother at the gravesite by strong arms. Maybe Uncle Hill Hampton. Hot breath hollering in his ear to quit showing his ass. A funeral fight scene like out of a movie.

"So you can't stand me no more?" Devin asked. "That what I'm hearing?"

"I'd say that's about right." Strained, an aggrieved stage whisper. "*What the hell's wrong with you?*"

Sincere: "Which part?"

"You tried to strangle our Mama, damn you."

Trying to light a smoke and dropping his lighter, he explained best he could: "Guess it all caught up to me, I reckon. What you want a motherfucker to say?"

"Like our mother had anything to do with the things that've happened to you. That you've pulled. You haven't changed in twenty years. Getting drunk and hollering at her—y'all at each other. You think I didn't see all that go on?"

Fury, rising but forestalled; throat clenching shut at his sister's truth. His mother, for all her sins, not having much of anything to do with what'd happened to Devin. Not the substantive tragedies, anyway, like losing Libby to Dobbs.

Ah, but Creedence, uninitiated, not realizing how Mama's sins were concealed like esoteric truths kept from the profane masses by secret society gatekeepers. More than Eileen's daughter would ever find out, at least if Devin had any say in the matter. And he did. Keeper of the key to the vault. A sad duty.

"You even care about any of us anymore? Or yourself, for that matter?"

"You, I do. Not so much myself."

"I get that," clenching her teeth and shoving stacks of photos back into the plastic sack. "You act like you're the only one who's ever had to suffer."

"I've seen some shit you ain't."

"That don't make you special. People get hurt and killed every day."

A flash of light, a booming echo—phantoms, but real. "Nobody knows what I been through. Nobody but Prudy."

"Why do you hate her?"

"I don't hate my cat."

"Our mother."

He couldn't tell her the truth. "You talk to Daddy before he kicked?"

"Talked to him every day, you son of a bitch."

"You think she gave him what he needed?"

"Daddy?"

"Who else?"

"They wouldn't've stayed together so long otherwise."

"And if I hold a different view, for the sake of propriety," a word he could barely pronounce through the tremors he felt all the way into his tongue, "I'd as soon keep it to myself. For everyone's sake."

"I think under the circumstances, that'd be best."

"Another time."

Leaving his sister and mother that night with their grief, he not seen them since, neither to say 'boo' at Halloween nor 'Hallelujah!' at Christmastime.

But now? Now, Creedence pregnant; their mother sick, or some such bullshit; and so, Devin, having to go home. A clusterfuck, this.

It would be fine. He could drive two thousand miles on beer and the occasional nip on a flask. He would get through fine; get himself settled in South-Cack in time to have a good long binge.

Sounded like heaven; like worthy aspiration.

Leaving, now, for good. But he couldn't depart Denver yet.

Driving around, thinking about Millie. She had been good to him, back when he needed a friend. Needing to say a proper forever-goodbye.

Intending to let her know he'd never come back this way, no sir. Not now; not ever.

*She'll be relieved to hear it.*

A call made, surprising agreement, and a half hour later, Devin, sitting across from Millicent Haverford at the diner they'd once frequented for lunch, back in the days when they worked at the Community Thrift store where they met. A bizarre interlude, this era, both the romance and the steady job. He had been drinking way way *way* too little, what with holding down a regular gig.

The diner: red vinyl stools, polished chrome, a checkerboard floor, milkshakes so thick a spoon would stand on its own, a jukebox stocked with cheesy 70s pop hits. 'Already Gone', as The Eagles now reminded him. Yep-yep.

And yet, retaining a shred of errant decency buried somewhere in his mania, enough to bid him to tell Millie goodbye in person. Well, the real deal, honest-to-god, *goodbye*-goodbye, anyway. The first iteration had been thoroughly covered when they broke up, and in unpleasant detail.

Devin, sliding into the booth, hoped his breath t'weren't too fiery and sour; he'd needed multiple bracers.

"It lives." She always could be a smart-ass. "It moves and breathes."

"Babygirl," an old term of endearment. "Let's sit a spell and get caught up."

Millie: healthy, radiant, thin, had stayed sober. That much clear. "First: don't call me that."

A gravelly, wasted croak. "Looks like you might've lost some weight."

Millie regarded him with cool suspicion, but a measured softness dwelling in her eyes. A tall, midwestern farm girl with strong shoulders like those of a competitive swimmer, she'd slimmed down by twenty pounds since their time together. But of course, Millie, sober for several years, now.

"Taking all that excess sugar out of the diet's bound to change anyone's body into a beanpole."

"See, that's never been a problem for me. I don't need to change to lose weight. Dang if that ain't the truth."

"Anyone with a sincere wish to change, changes. I've seen it happen with you."

Ignoring the remark. "Dry wasn't sober."

"It was a start."

"I reckon I can't smoke in here, huh?"

Sarcastic. "No one has smoked in restaurants for twenty years. Thank god."

Devin's rage, unbridled and sudden, burbled up like blackest pitch: "*Bastards*. Laws and rules, and more laws on top, and I'll be damned if a goddurn man can't take a shit no more without some pencil-neck peeking over his shoulder."

Millie ain't got time for this mess. "So to what do I owe this alleged pleasure?"

Devin, holding her gaze for the first time since he'd sat down, dropped the rage-monkey bit. Felt the muscles in his face relax. His hands, shaking hard, though. He hid them.

"Want to get right down to it, do ya?"

"Well?"

"No big whoop. I just might not be back this way for a while—for good, like—and I figured, the way we finished up wasn't the most graceful scene."

Her screwed-down frown broke. Millie, snorting and laughing. "Understatement king enters conversation."

"But I thought about a do-over on the fare-thee-well, if you'd have it."

"What, like a spite-fuck? You got a better chance of hitting the Powerball, mister."

"Furthest thing from my mind."

Her eyes, gray and flaring, changed color depending on the light and time of day. "So—you remember those awful things you said?"

Devin's turn to scoff; Ruck's time to lie. "'Remember' is a strong word for a sot like me. But I can imagine well enough."

"No, you can't—it was worse."

Devin, knowing this truth. Guilt and shame imploded inside his drunk-sick gut; twin towers of steel and concrete collapsing into their own footprints at the speed of gravity, billowing clouds of disgust flooded the steep canyons of his quivering sick heart.

"I was just trying to get rid of you. For you own good." Millie didn't deserve being saddled with a short-timer like Devin, he explained, for whom recovery was impossible outside of a sort of nebulous retribution awaiting back home; a vague idea in his mind of receiving long withheld recompense, justice. The details would gel once on the road, and he got a few beers in him. He kept that part to himself.

Devin, telling her to forget the past; nor to invite a future that included any further such scenes or sentiments as those he'd employed to scare her off. "I'd take what a drunk like me has to say with a grain of salt the size of a cantaloupe. You're a sweet soul who done better by me than I deserved."

"That's nice to hear." She looked down. "But I'll never trust you again. How could I?"

"I don't blame you."

"I can't do this." Her anger took a turn for the melancholy. "I've never been more wrong about anything. Gave you my whole heart. Told you my secrets."

"A Wisconsin girl and a Dixie chicken like me? Man, that wa'n't gonna work no matter how hard we tried."

Millie's turn for a mini-meltdown. Hot-blooded and aggrieved. Her eyes shone like steel. "You know what's so pathetic about all this? Back when we were dry together, I'd have bet my life on the fact you were better. That I had helped you to pull out of whatever hell it was you were trapped inside. I *wanted* to bet my life on it. But Ruck, damn it—you repaid me by tearing my heart out and shitting all over it."

"Please don't remind me."

"Forgiveness is a thing; I get it. But, boy," her voice finally breaking, "you are a project. That's all I can say." She sat back and put a hand over her eyes, massaged her temples with thumb and forefinger. "A project."

"Suckers get born every minute, or so's I heard."

"Tell me one thing to let me off the hook. So I'll stop wondering."

"Off the hook? Now, that's a deal. Shoot."

"What happened in South Carolina? When you went home that time? And came back a wreck all over again?"

Black ice inside; dark boiling spots, blotting out her face. "I told you—my Daddy had died."

"And, what else?"

Now Devin needed a drink; he wasn't gonna put up with any more of her psych-out foolishness. "If I didn't let you in on it when we were fucking, I certainly ain't gonna tell you now."

That seemed to hurt. Millie, flustered, dropped money on the table for the coffee she hadn't drunk. "We're done, now," a hot, hissy exhalation of sad syllables. "Done for reals."

The sky leaden outside, a spring snow shower in the making; as she got into her Accord to leave, Devin's worm turned and found his alkie-ass rushing over to grab Millie, hold onto her like a drowning man grabbing at a bobbing, Styrofoam cooler of rock-salt cold tallboys, a crumbling life preserver at which he clutched amidst a raging sea of horrible lucidity.

But, too late. Cursing himself. Millie—sweet to him. And, loving her back; more than anyone since Libby.

Until he made himself stop.

Again: inevitable his impending death would end up hurting her. You couldn't make them see it, though. You had to show them by manifesting the coming shitstorm in the moment, in the now. Make them want to run.

Coughing and trying not to puke, Devin's facade crumbled. Hot tears dripped from behind the aviators.

She glanced over and saw him weeping; put the car back into park before lowering the window.

"And now," she said, weary, "the tears."

"I'm weak, angel. Ain't nothing you, nor anyone else, could've done to help me."

"You forget—I know the real you. When you were sober, I saw the real Devin Rucker. And, this little act? It isn't him."

"So you claim." He held out his arms. Snowflakes landed on his arms like butterflies. "But this is this. And it's all I know. It's all I got left."

Deep breath. "Ok, last-chance-charlie: if you want to get help, I'll forget all our nonsense and be a friend to you again. An advocate. But nothing more."

"Aw—I'll ease off the throttle again, like we done it before." A soothing voice, lying like a dog. "Hell, I'll call you soon as I get settled in back home. I'm'a get in treatment this time. Get right again one of these here days. You'll see."

Melancholy Millie returned. She didn't believe him. "Take care."

"So I'll call. We'll maybe write letters sometime, like they done in the old days—"

But way too late for such talk. Devin, watching her peel out into the traffic on the foothills highway like she had somewhere to get to; somewhere to be.

West. Toward the mountains. She lived in Boulder, now. Probably fucking college kids and professors like Billy Steeple.

What a load of hooey; what a load of melodrama. Who cared who she was fucking? Off the hook, now—remember?

"Yeah, I remember." But no one to hear the affirmation.

Trying to light a smoke, the wind too stiff even for his Zippo, Devin, searching his mind for the next step. Right then a floral delivery truck with a spray of yellow roses pictured on its side trundled along the highway.

Billy Steeple.

A road trip.

Devin, slapping his thigh. "Deep in the heart of Texas—shit-yeah, boy. Enough of this piddly-ass pooting around."

For once, his gut churned with something beyond aching nausea; instead, a twinkle of anticipation. But no need to get moving, not yet; why not enjoy a last round at Chubby's? Sure. Get a few under his belt before hitting the road, jack. It's the American way.

# NINE

## —

## CREEDENCE

Sitting in the crapper paging through last month's SOUTHERN LIVING, Chelsea thought she would hurl. As though the iconic periodical hadn't covered Charleston a million times before.

She announced to her empty bathroom: "Charleston? I wouldn't live in that stinky old marsh if you paid me."

The magazine had been a blurry faraway object in her hands anyway—Billy's smooth and flirty voice on the phone earlier still rang in her ears like a church bell.

Billy, agreeing to help with Devin.

Her shining knight, Billy.

What might have been.

How stupid, letting herself get knocked up. The timing.

Despair.

Chelsea, flinging the slick publication into the basket beside the toilet, finished up, or at least hoped she'd finished. Ever since she'd peed on the stick and seen the two lines, she'd suffered a stomach best described as rotten. Nerves, maybe. Or part of the process, like the morning sickness and cramps. A puking and peeing and squirting vessel of life, her.

Charleston. So close, so far. She lied to herself—of course she'd love to live there. In fact, doing so remained her dream.

Chelsea, on her infrequent visits to the Holy City, adored strolling one of the few preserved pieces of colonial America left besides the theme park version in Williamsburg. Sure, Tillman Falls down the road had beautiful old houses and the courthouse and the Revolutionary War battle monument and the gurgling, wide Sugeree River and the lake country below the nuclear plant, but nothing to her came as romantic as the idea of strolling the Battery on a cool morning, gazing up to the night herons asleep in the branches of the enormous live oaks, tasting the salty breeze blowing in from beyond Fort Sumter. Feeling a tingling, untethered sense of freedom staring out at the enormous freighters chugging, lugubrious, through the shimmering green harbor to disappear, finally, in the haze along the watery horizon.

*Lugubrious?* Listen to her. Must be some dumb word she'd picked up reading one of those bullshit, purple-prose Pat Conroy doorstops. Had had to look up the word, made herself try to remember it. She much preferred Dotty Frank or Mary Alice Monroe or Jo Humphries anyway, all giants in the pantheon of South Carolina low-country family melodramas, characters standing ankle-deep in the pluff-muddy inlets of their gauche narratives of suicide and adultery, sea turtles and grass baskets and class struggles. Such novels and stories often revolved around nearby, good-old Charleston and its sea-island environs.

Reading about the city, however, made it seem like a thousand miles away. That's how little interest Dusty showed in her desires, including going to Charleston, "Where everything's so high-priced nobody can't have no fun."

Chelsea held a vivid memory of her teenage self standing on the battery one evening with her father during on a beach house week on nearby Isle of Palms. Devin and Libby had stayed behind, and she knew why—Creedence, naughty, had spied on them making love one night in Devin's car parked outside, late, their parents long asleep; moonlight fell across Libby's back as she rode with rhythm on top of a shadowy, unseen Devin. Creedence knew what they were doing, but still did not 'know' what it was, exactly. She kept waiting for her mother to have the talk, but at thirteen, it had yet to come.

Watching a massive ship vanish into the distant violet nothing, squinting, the experience frightening as the vessel disappeared, its running lights twinkling like receding stars, she smiled with comfort as her dad draped an arm around her.

"Life is long and beautiful, my dear girl. Make the most of it."

"I will. I want to be an artist, someday. And live in one of those houses—like that one," pointing behind her across the battery.

"No," he said. "Not an artist—let's call it being a designer. Designers get jobs. Artists don't make no money, sugar."

"I don't understand the difference."

"You will. They way you love to draw, you ought to think about getting into making Hallmark cards."

"That's dumb," she had heard herself saying. "I'll be rich and famous for my paintings and what-not."

He had laughed with gentle affection. "You'll find out, sugar. Don't nobody live as an 'artist' unless they already got somebody paying them to do it—maybe Daddy will get rich, though, and he'll pay for it."

Otherwise, nobody had encouraged her. Wouldn't let her go off to SCAD down in Savannah. Mama always told her she was silly about wanting to draw. That she needed a man, and later a job or career as well, if she wanted. But a real one. Nobody was wasting money on a college degree to draw horsies. Her mother had all but said it that way.

"You find a man to take care of you," Mama had instructed. "That you can trust."

"What you mean, trust?"

"Like your daddy." Scoffing. "He wouldn't do nothing out of turn if it killed him."

At last one day, Creedence had realized something—this had been her mother's version of 'the talk.'

She was in prison. Her, and now, her baby.

She had finished in the bathroom but stayed sitting on the closed toilet lid. Yeah—fighting off another wave of cramps.

No more recounting of old grievances against Mama, though. Doing so all the time made Chelsea sick. Maybe her sour-patch attitude was the origin of all these cramps, she thought, and not her pregnancy. She needed attitude adjustment. She needed Billy to spirit her away. She needed his baby in her belly. Not Dusty's.

Speak-of-the-Dusty rolled in from the hardware store about six-thirty, in time for the start of the second of two episodes of SEINFELD. The show sometimes seemed over her head with its silly, sarcastic humor. She didn't have the word for it—how unrealistic it was, like, letting the audience know how the show and its characters kind-of knew it was all dumb? Like the one with Elaine on the subway telling the lady that something was ironic, and the lady going, like, what's ironic, like, no, *what does it mean*? That type-deal? She had a hard time explaining herself when it came to the 'why' of things like SEINFELD.

For instance: One night while watching the Kenny Rogers Roasters episode, she'd tried to verbalize her complicated thoughts to Dusty about irony, celebrity and fried chicken. He'd looked at her like she had six heads.

Forget TV. She needed to get it on—pregnant horniness was a real thing, evidently. Would it be like this the whole freakin' pregnancy? She'd starve.

But she also needed a decent conversation. Dusty couldn't talk about nothing worth a durn except NASCAR, video games, horror movies and hamburger meat. That's about it.

After he hung a greasy ball cap in need of laundering onto the coat hooks by the front door, her hubby smacked a perfunctory kiss on the cheek; the cracking of a can of Bud Light.

Creedence—Chelsea—looked at him and him at her.

"Busy today?"

"Busier than I care for. How about y'all?"

"I didn't go in. I was sick."

"What'd you do instead? Lay around?"

"I went shopping."

"You didn't spend much, I hope."

"No more than last week."

"Better not." Shooting her his mean look. "Can't work no harder. Not for no better'n I'm getting paid."

Her head got so hot she started sweating. But she couldn't start anything. Not feeling as peaked as she did.

Instead, Chelsea saw an opportunity to broach a familiar subject. "I worry about Mr. Vincent going under."

Dusty jerked and jiggled as though goosed with electric current. "That hardware store's been in business sixty years. It ain't going nowhere."

"The way you hate working, I'm surprised you care."

"Kiss my ass."

"It could happen, though. And then what?"

"Lord, don't say that. I'd have to start over. Ain't nobody else gonna pay me ten dollars an hour like Mr. Vincent."

"It's because you been there since high school. He ain't got no other choice."

"It's because I'm his top employee."

Time to put in the knife. "Employee—not manager with salary and benefits."

"That's coming."

"So I keep hearing."

"He ain't lying."

"Dusty—the manager is his daughter. She ain't going nowhere."

He shrugged. Poked out his lip. "It's what he says."

"Maybe you should get on at Lowe's once it opens."

He all but shouted, *"Down in Columbia?"*

"No, dummy. When it opens here next year on that parcel they cleared across from the dealership. Mr. Hampton told me about it."

"So it's true."

"There'll be a Lowe's, and a new grocery store, three or four chain restaurants. Personally, I can't wait."

Bitter. "He could probably build it himself, with all that car money of his."

Uncle Hill lived in the biggest, oldest house over on Whaley Way in Tillman Falls, but he wasn't that rich. "We ain't selling that many cars lately."

"Shit. He's got money gone to bed. Ought to pay you more." Dusty gurgled soda and belched. "Damn, I hate money."

Hill Hampton, a close family friend for as long as Chelsea had memories; rich, a second generation car dealer, a Hampton, South Carolina royalty in his blood. He had the run of the county, and damn if oftentimes her Daddy hadn't been at his side. Men like them had a special club which met all the time—sometimes at The Dixiana, sometimes out at a lodge in the woods near Big Rock and Jensen's Pond on the other side of Tillman Falls near the country club, where rich people had houses back in the woods. Had no clue what that club was all about. Like the Masons, she guessed, or those dudes with the little fezs who drive the mini-cars in the Christmas and Fourth of July parades. Daddy wouldn't never talk about it.

She felt safe working for Uncle Hill. Stable. Like family. Plus, weak sales figures or not for the quarter, wasn't no way in hell people around these parts were going to stop buying F-150s. Not completely. Best truck on the road.

But Mr. Vincent's little two-bit hardware store? *Sayonara, señor*. Like every other oldschool business in Tillman Falls. The only original ones left were The Dixiana, and Lucinda's diner, and the Congress Street Grille. Antiques and closed-up storefronts filled out the rest of what was once a thriving township with furniture stores, jewelry, appliances, the original downtown Ford dealership, offices and a bank or two.

Mama, an officer of the Edgewater Ladies Munificence Society, said they were raising money to restore the old Palmetto Grande movie theater, transform it into an arts center for theater, music, dance as well as film society screenings. Such a move would 'revitalize' sleepy old Edgewater County, she and the others said in their campaign to county council.

*Mercy*—what did those highfalutin bluebloods think they were up to, turning Tillman freaking podunk Falls into downtown Charleston, or Savannah? Please. So full of themselves, all because their husbands left them money. Damn old baby boomer biddies. They needed to die off. It was bound to happen eventually, she supposed, like all the old businesses.

Like Mr. Vincent's, soon. It had to be.

But Dusty pish-poshed. "It's like Mr. Vincent says: if that durn Wal-mart down in the lake country didn't finish us off—"

"—nothing will. Honey, you can't sit on your hands and wait for him to close up." She poked him with a freckled finger. Felt a twinge in her side, way down low. "You got to make a move. Maybe get a tech degree. Something."

"You want me to quit? Who would he get to work my shifts? That's worth a durn? In this town?"

As though Dusty Wallace were a retail hardware genius. He didn't even know what half the tools did.

He sat down and pulled off his work boots. "You can go back to school all you want. Get Eileen to pay for it, or Uncle Hill. Or, go start selling your Mama's Valium and Xanax over at the high school, for all I care. But I ain't gonna go sit at a little desk at that tech school with that bunch of shit-turds I see running up and down the road every afternoon. What you trying to turn me into?"

She broke. All the sarcasm and flinty antagonism washed away in a barking, hollow gale of sudden water from her eyes. "A father."

"Don't start with your mess."

Something he'd said struck her: "Really? I should go to school?"

"What, with a baby on your hip?"

"You ain't never heard of daycare?"

High and whining: "How you planning to pay for all this?"

"By you getting a better job, dummy."

He walked into that one. Turned red as a beet. "Told you I don't give a flying fudge whether you go to school or bake a cake. Besides, Mr. Vincent says that if I play my cards right, he'll make me the GM in a few years. I'll get bonuses and all kinds of incentives, then. That 'better' enough for you?"

"He's been telling you that tale for ages, now."

"Ain't lied to me yet."

"That shriveled up old money-grubbing peanut? He talks out of one side of his face and then the—"

"*Shut your mouth about Mr. Vincent, before I shut it for you,*" Dusty roared from the couch, his face a mask like the Devin's own. The devil's own, she meant.

Chastened and furious. Simmering. Ever since getting pregnant, her emotions, a rollercoaster. Hot-cold hatred for Dusty. Seething. Making her cramp as she smushed down the bun of his chicken patty sandwich.

"You better quit hollering at me."

"Just hush up about Mr. Vincent."

Sick of his mess. Pushing in a hot, secret knife: "Buddy Lawler says electricians make good money. Welders even more."

"Who cares what that fat little queer-bait thinks?"

"You could get your certificate in a trade like that. Have your own business, like Daddy did with his insurance. Plumbing. Good money there, too."

"If Buddy Lawler's so smart, why's he selling cars for Mr. Hampton instead of pulling wires through walls, hanging up breaker boxes and getting the shit zapped outta him? Or unplugging toilets?" *Toe-lets.* "Say."

"Buddy makes good money already. Believe you-me."

He eyed her sidelong. "How would you know all that?"

"Because I watched him close on six deals, all new-truck buyers, this week. That's almost one a day."

"Thought y'all wa'n't selling nothing?"

"Buddy's selling. Getting fat paychecks and commissions."

"Goody for him."

"Yep—it was good for him, all right."

"I'm sure. He still driving that Mustang?"

She really had no clue. "I think it's blue."

Her husband, disgusted, shook his head. "Y'all women don't pay attention to nothing important."

Dusty's earlier outburst unnerved her. She should tread with care. He had been angry. A lot, lately. Grabbed her by the arm a couple of times. Finger-bruises. He had been drinking too much beer. That was all.

In a way, she had wanted Devin home for a secret reason of her own: To protect her from Dusty, who had pushed her around a few other times through the years. And now acted like he was finally going to hit her. Hadn't yet. Not with the baby and all.

Wouldn't that be something. Waiting until she got pregnant to pop her a good one, at last. She wouldn't put it past him.

Diffusing the tension. Her tone became gentle, loving. "But if I went to school, honey, don't you see I'd have a better job afterwards, too? For all of us."

"A bigger paycheck—now that would be sweet." His eyes flitted over to the game console, the TV screen. It wasn't mounted on the wall like he wanted. Dusty gnawed at his thumbnail. "Both of us getting more money would be cool."

"More would be nice. More things."

"We could get the better movie package," a cable TV add-on he had lusted after for months. "I been wanting Showtime."

Whatever worked. "Sure we could, baby. More movies."

"And games."

Every time he had extra money it went to a new game for the console. She wanted a computer for the house, finally. He hated them, computers. The game controller, those he could handle. Little raised callouses on his thumbs from shooting all the lasers or whatever it was. If only he used those fingers on her occasionally, she might have felt more relaxed and less pushy. "Sure."

But her smile, forced, hurt. Felt hard around the edges. Felt fake.

Sliding around sock-footed, she brought in Dusty's dinner of breaded chicken-patty sandwiches and mac'n cheese for him to eat in front of the television. At the sight of Elaine Benes doing her silly, awkward, white-girl dance, Dusty snorted with mirth.

At times, Creedence danced around all crazy like that. But in her case it made her look like a lunatic, he said. Wasn't funny.

"Shit. I feel like we seen this one four times in the last month."

"That might not be a bad idea, me going to school. One of us has got to start thinking bigger."

"Enough about school for tonight. It'll all work out."

Dusty pulled the Ace Hardware polo shirt over his head, threw it on the couch like Chelsea had begged begged *begged* him not to do. Yanked down the white V-neck T-shirt underneath to cover, best it could, his hairy muffin top. Turned up the TV too loud, in case she started talking again, she reckoned. He squirted condiments and crunched into his sandwich. Thursday night. Yay.

After he finished eating, his attitude softened.

"I know you's worried with the little one coming and all. It's fine. But, we worked hard all day."

"It was busy?"

"We was *real busy* with all them contractors building houses over in that subdivision off River Ridge Road, over by Pike's Bait & Pawn? Them gonna be some choice houses they got going. Maybe we'll get ourselves one, after I'm manager."

"That would be something. Now wouldn't it."

Back to mean as a snake. "But for now? I wanna relax and play my game."

"Sure. Far be it from me. To give a durn."

"There we go."

Dusty, an X-Box aficionado, sat in fond embrace of the car-racing games, currently fixated on one involving sordid activity: driving around committing crimes, beating up prostitutes, shooting people, all manner of distasteful acts. Chelsea, getting the creeps whenever she watched him play, face red and eyes glassy; afterwards, for some strange reason, Dusty often wanted to mess around—*yuck*. The only thing nastier was walking in and catching him biting his own toenails, most often on Sunday afternoons while absorbed by NASCAR.

Shaking her head, poking at her salad greasy with oil and sharp vinegar, she spied one of her own hairs wrapped around the tines of the fork. Feeling her gorge rise. She dumped the salad, uneaten, into the trash.

Chelsea cleaned the kitchen and put Dusty out of her mind. The house would now be quiet but for his small grunts and sighs as he jerked his controller around—she'd made him buy a pair of headphones to wear when 'jacked-in,' as he called his game-time. Those sound effects. That music. It had driven her to distraction. Out of her skull. Her numbskull, like he called her sometimes. Ironic.

Done tidying up, Chelsea yawned and reached down to pet her big boy kitty Mr. Bubbie, an orange barrel-stomached tomcat who ate and ate and ate. A pitiful stray she'd found in the parking lot of the Piggly Wiggly, so skinny the vet said he was only a day or two away from death, he had what they called starving cat syndrome. Mr. Bubbie, her special rescued angel, rubbing up and down, back and forth on her lower legs, a graceful, feline dance of gratitude.

But getting so old. Hadn't a clue how long he'd been on the street before coming to her for rescue and salvation. He had stopped washing himself, his fur greasy. He could be fifteen, for all she knew. Older.

The other cats made their way into the kitchen, mewling and stretching and yawning from the deep slumber of their early evening naps: Pickles, a midnight jet-black female Chelsea'd also found as a stray; a spry, undersized, affectionate calico girl named Bootsy she'd had since kitten-hood, bought from a flea market for two dollars; and a newcomer male, a gray-striped, nervous fellow christened Arthur because something about his face reminded her of the large-eyed cartoon rodent of the same name.

Dusty hated Arthur—he had prohibited his wife from adopting yet another cat. Scoffing and unmindful of his concerns she'd taken in this latest newcomer anyway, who didn't seem undernourished or in any particular distress. After petting him and falling in love with his funny face, she'd removed the collar he been wearing, including a tag with a phone number and a name she didn't like—**TYGER**—and had thrown it in the trash. Taken him for herself. Once coming inside to live he'd been a tad stressed and had indeed marked a few spots, but had now settled in nicely and was using his boxes. Happy as a kitty-clam. He stuck his kitty-butt up and peed against the wall instead of down in the litter, so she had started taping up newspapers all around the boxes full of gray dusty sand. Who cared? He was so cute. He had needed her. She had needed him. The extra trouble and odor was all worth it.

Chelsea bent down to stroke each of the cats in turn and when possible in tandem, so none of them would feel diminished or left out. Her cats looked up to her; she was their god, the fount of their existence. On most days taking care of her pets was the one skill that Chelsea thought she'd mastered, one thing she could do well—modest, perhaps, but at least something. And everybody needed something. Didn't they?

Cooing, a gentle lullaby. "Arthur didn't break us. Nor will one more in the house. Tell me. Tell me the truth. Yes yes yes. Mama's precious babies. One more to come. My baby girl this time. Mine this time. Not a kitty-cat baby. One just like me. A little angel."

Lord, she thought in sudden detachment sliding into revulsion, but, sometimes? She simply could not stand herself. Truth be told, the last thing she probably needed was another little smart-mouthed 'her' running around. Too late now, though. Wasn't it?

Deciding on the walk home to make a pit stop down in the Old Market neighborhood to look up a mutual chum of Ruck's from Edgewater County, good-old Roy Earl Pettus, for a consultation, Billy strode with purpose up the hill from his office. His boy Roy, a homey to all the principals in this sordid tale, understood the history. He'd know what to do about Ruck.

Now a successful small business man, Billy, admiring the dude like hell for Roy's normalcy and kindness. Sounded like he never got laid, though.

Hell. Maybe that's the answer. Get beyond sex, once and for all. Be done with it. Less trouble in his life, that much for certain.

High-stepping his way up the steep hill of South Main Street and drinking in the springtime air, angling out of his to avoid the spot were he'd first asked Libby to have coffee, where their romantic relationship began. Billy, saluting the oak tree upon which she'd leaned and smiled at him. Quelling the urge to head-butt the stately tree.

The campus, alive with flip-flopping girls that, thanks to springtime, had been peeled and stripped down to shorts and T-shirts—a cornucopia, overwhelming, awing, tempting him; Billy, in the spirit of the mating season, all but getting the heebie-jeebies and embarking upon a killcrazy rampage of bloodily unbridled, rapine carnage. God, but the women around here were glorious, fecund flowers into whose pink squishy pistils he so wished to insert his one and true special purpose and thing. Yo. Like repeatedly.

Trying not to follow one of them back to their home. Off-campus best, but Billy's ID, getting him into all sorts of campus buildings.

Billy: being silly. No accidents, not for a long long time now.

Alcohol, when he drank, which he did for a few years after Libby's death, a serious factor in perpetuating accidents. The weed, however, keeping bothersomeness at bay. Better for everybody. Weed weed weed. He went through an ounce a week. He attributed his runny eyes and dazed countenance to 'allergies.' In a place like South Carolina, covered in springtime pollen, no one doubted his alibi.

Billy exited campus and tromped past the magnificent Victorians on University Hill near his condo building until finding himself on the streets of the college ghetto, the commercial district next door to the enormous state university, a neighborhood of bars and funky little shops for which generations of South Carolina college students and folks from all over held great affection. A cosmopolitan few blocks in an otherwise sleepy Southern city, albeit one with a big swinging dick of a school attracting students from across the region and the country and the world, the Old Market had attracted Billy back when he matriculated to college from prep school. Thank god Columbia could support at least one hipster neighborhood.

Angling down toward the main drag he eagle-eyed his destination: the South Beach-pastel cube of The Spotted Banana, a smoothie stand owned by Roy. A good man, maybe the nicest human being Billy had ever come across. He admired the man's decent, dutiful soul.

Roy Earl had characterized his stewardship of the Banana, as well as an iconic, college-hipster coffee shop around the corner called the Carolina Beanery Café, as a kind of manifest destiny: back home in Tillman Falls his grandfather had run a notorious tavern and music hall called The Dixiana, so in the Pettus family the hospitality trade, as such, had been in the genes. He'd been halfway toying with the idea of franchising out the coffee brand, if not the smoothie joint, too. Already had other locations—in one of the suburban malls, another up in Charlotte, too. Billy bet Roy had a million bucks stuffed into a pillowcase under the bed.

And hating him for it.

Harsh. But Billy, unable to get at his family money. Not yet.

A trust fund, sure, but only a couple grand a month. Coupled with his proletarian Southeastern University salary, he had sufficient funds to keep himself in Criterion DVDs, weed and pussy. And, he could get more, occasionally. His father, a Washington power-attorney and prick who danced up and down K Street in various guises, still whipped out the checkbook whenever Billy—pushing forty, as he tried to forget—whined hard and long enough.

The Spotted Banana, a small, self-contained building of a thousand square feet on the corner of a busy intersection with a few small tables scattered around inside and on the sidewalk; inside, golden afternoon sunlight streamed into the serving area, the countertops and floors impeccable—spotless stainless steel, waxed and shiny checkerboard tile flooring, bright colored menu boards and walls, the smell of strawberries and other fruit coming high, cold and sweet like in an ice cream shop.

Billy smiled at the iconic mural of anthropomorphic bananas with oversized cartoon eyes and toothy grins, giving thumb's ups and flashing peace signs with one hand while clutching disproportionately-sized smoothie cups in the other, nattily-gloved cartoon hands like those of Mr. Peanut. Roy Earl said he drew the icons himself.

*Talented little redneck*, Billy thought. It didn't seem fair.

A roar came from one of the industrial blenders operated by a smiling, natural beauty of a college girlie wearing a pink Spotted Banana T-shirt one size too small. He noted a pooching belly—the freshman fifteen—that featured a fake-gem encrusted fairy dangling from a pierced navel, but still a beauty.

Billy zoomed in, racked focus. Convinced himself he could see the light tuft of fine blonde hair lying against the tender skin behind the jewelry. Yearning to trace his fingertip under that dangling fairy, tearing the jewelry out with his teeth, ripping those white shorts off, seeing that ass pop out like a ripe peach, shoving his tongue into the back of her throat, filling her up and make her hole whole.

Billy, the bearer of answers to what ails ya, ladies. The answer man.

But: what would be the answer to the answer, man?

Like a head-rush—a flash of blood splatter on the checkered floor, white and black, a pattern for the world like on the floor in the Masonic temple to which his father and grandfather belonged, the big one in DC. The main one. Billy, having none of their fraternal foolishness. Decrying their sad attempts to initiate him.

Blinking his eyes. Losing the urge to rip the girl's head off. Seeing the young woman for what she was: Nineteen, smiling, innocent in attending to her part-time college job. He wasn't a monster. C'mon. He could be satisfied with holding her down until she only *almost* suffocated. Not all the way dead.

The blender stopped and the counter girl dumped a viscous, oozing tendril of purple smoothie into a Styrofoam cup the size of a small bucket. She handed it to an ethnic type, as Billy thought of the bespectacled Indian gentleman waiting with graceful and studied patience.

The studious-looking young man gurgled his beverage and thanked the girl in precise, elegantly accented English. "Remarkably delicious," he noted to Billy in passing.

"Hey now, sweetheart," Billy purred as he bellied-up. "What's shakin'?"

Fake smile. "I'll be right with you, sir."

She took the blender to the cleaning area and immersed it in a foamy tub. The rhythmic motion of her elbow, enchanting, allayed his annoyance at being made to wait like some regular Joe.

"Wondering if the boss-man's around."

Hollering over her shoulder: "Mr. Roy—there's a man for you."

Roy Earl Pettus, beaming like the sun, popped his rounded, shorn noggin from behind a door. "My boy Billy—now it's on, y'all."

He charged around the counter in what Billy'd termed the Standard Roy Earl uniform, sported by him since college: a fresh, black pocket T-shirt stretching taut across a substantial belly, a pair of ragged, aged cargo shorts scarred by rips and frayed edges and stains of all origin and hue, wide feet shod by rubber sport sandals that Billy suspected could only have provided modest support. Self-described on a dating service posting he'd shared with Billy as *Possessing a genuine curiosity about other people's lives, a better listener than a conversationalist, loves sports and music and sunsets and beauty and life,* whenever he spoke about matters over which his passion stirred, spots of color rose in Roy's cheeks: Southeastern Redtails football, the price of fair-trade Nicaraguan coffee beans, the perfect ripe banana for the perfect smoothie. Meeting the girl of his dreams. He dated—hell, he had money, so you know plenty sniffed around. Said they were too serious too fast for him. Waiting for the right one.

Roy Earl. A doofus compared to god-Billy. And yet seeming to trump Billy's own sorry life in every respect. So what if he didn't get much pussy.

Jesus—if he'd never gotten a whiff, wouldn't Billy's life have been simpler? Less bothersome, no doubt. Yeah. Made him roll his eyes with all the subtlety of Jim Carrey.

Requesting an audience. "Got some back-home news for ya."

"Back home?"

"Well—*your* home. Edgewater County."

A shadow fell across Roy's eyes. He already knew. "Devin?"

Billy, nodding. "Ruck."

"How bad?"

"Bad. But not like you're thinking."

Roy Earl hustled Billy out on the sidewalk, directed him to plop down onto one of the wire-mesh outdoor chairs, the aluminum tabletops reflecting afternoon light back into their faces. Billy, rueful, wondering what the hell he had in mind by burdening innocent, happy Roy Earl with news of Devin's incipient return, but here he was spreading the joy.

"What happened to him this time?"

"Nothing—yet. But, later in the week I'm to spend some time with our old Ruck," as Billy explained the call from Creedence, the nonsense leading to the ridiculous San Antonio meet-up.

The soft Pettus countenance fell troubled, cautious. He asked about

Ruck's condition. "On the sauce, I assume."

Grim: "The endless, epic bender. Epochal. Whatever."

"Did he call?"

"Are you kidding? His sister rang me up to complain. Ask if I'd reach out."

Roy Earl, coloring at the mention of Chelsea Colette Rucker, clutched his ample stomach. He grimaced. "How's that lovely Creedence doing?"

"What's the matter down there?"

"Think I got ahold of some bad barbecue tailgating at the spring scrimmage last night."

Billy, going all Leonard Zelig: "Say, how's the team looking, bro?"

"Hale and hearty." Roy described the physical characteristics and statistical achievements of the standout returning players. "Wouldn't be surprised if they do real good this year."

"The Roy I remember didn't care much about sports."

"Well," sounding shamefaced, "in this neighborhood, you almost got to love Redtails football." A belch behind a pink fist. "So anyway, Creedence—? Maybe I should call and check on her."

Billy could see Roy's attraction for Ruck's sister. He had no memory of them being an item, however. Not to mention how it was he who had gotten close to busting a nut with Creedence, more than Roy could dream.

Time for misdirection. "The point is that she wants to make some last-ditch effort to bring Ruck back down to earth. No easy road, but I can't blame her for wanting to try."

"I always wondered what it would be like to have a brother or sister. I guess it would be hard to give up on them."

"Hell of a thing, watching someone you love do the slow, drunk fade out." Suddenly hot all over, Billy wrenched loose his color-drenched J. Garcia tie. "You should have heard him. Makes sense for a while, then doesn't."

Headshaking pity. "I grew up around a bar, and not any old bar. The Dixiana's a place that—well. Sat there with my granddaddy my whole childhood, both of us watching drunks of various pedigree come and go, until one day they didn't come no more. Because they were were dead," he added to make sure Billy got it. "Started serving them myself, after I turned fifteen. But it's different when it's someone you care about."

"Ruck's mental condition—it's quite something."

"What else is he on? Pills? Powders?"

"What are you, the heat?" Blowing out his lips. "Haven't a clue, Sgt. Friday."

Shifting the focus. "You ever talk to Dobbs?"

Guilt flooded into Billy's gut, a dull spike. "Not as such. You?"

"Not like I should."

"May we end this interrogation?"

Roy Earl cast doleful eyes onto the sidewalk. Billy followed his gaze—cigarette butts, a crushed Spotted Banana cup, scraps of newsprint.

"I'd like to catch one of these little dorks out here littering."

"Be worth it if you did."

"I'll get Nicole to sweep up—I mean, *Heather*. These gals start to run together after a while."

Chortling. "Welcome to my world, dude."

"Lucky prick."

Billy, lowering his voice and shrugging. "What you want a motherfucking N-word to do?"

Roy Earl, blushing anew. Frowning. "Like I said."

Billy set aside the issue of his self-evident sexual prowess to fill in the rest of the lousy details: Devin's intention to intrude upon the conference in Texas. "Not to sound like I don't want to help him, because I do—it's the least I can do for an old friend—for Ruck—but, still."

"Heard that."

"But if the girl I'd loved—? If I'd watched her die right in front of me, on the side of the road?" The words caught. "Who knows what would've become of me."

Roy Earl reached across the table to pat his friend's forearm in a series of exuberant, meaty smacks. "I'll never forget that day. Me and you going to the hospital."

"No. Burned into the synapses."

"Not that I want to remember it, but I was sure glad to have you there."

"It's what families do."

"I hadn't seen you all spring. I had missed hanging out."

Swooning; her smell came to him. "Libby. An ethereal angel, then as now."

"So I listened to the Dead show just the other day."

Billy's throat, like a vise. "Collegiate Coliseum?"

"Man, it really holds up."

"Yes, it does. It surely do." Folksy, hiding the shock and horror twisting inside him. "A barn-burner."

"Hell of a night."

And yet, Billy noticed, his old pal looked more chagrined than nostalgic.

Wait: Had Roy found out what went down with Libby that night?

*Had he?*

Christ—Billy hoped not.

He tried to speak again but choked off; a single sharp, weapons-grade sob escaped. This time Roy Earl's hand stayed on Billy's sleeve. Billy, placing his own huge paw on top, squeezing.

His crying jags could be monumental. Gargantuan. If it happened in public, they'd put him away. He'd barely been able to hide these episodes from Melanie, as well the ritual masturbation and snuff films and other weird secrets Billy occulted from everyone.

Some secrets he kept even from himself. Yeah. Mind=blown at the notion. All rather circularly self-reflective.

Composing himself. "I don't mind helping. But damn him, it's the timing. I'm presenting a major paper on archival film preservation."

"I'm amazed at what you do. It's so much more important than—all this."

"It ain't show business. That much for certain."

"It's academic, dude. It's history. Me? They piss out what I sell within the hour."

"The work's significant, sure; one only hopes to make a contribution to the general knowledge base."

"To me, what you do is heroic." Now Roy's turn to get choked up. Billy remembered big talk from him, an English major, of becoming a poet, not a smoothie salesman. "Look: once you and Devin get back, I'm here for him."

"I know you are."

"I'll do whatever I can. Have a cookout. We'll listen to the Dead tape." Roy betrayed a flash of consternation at how lame such suggestions must have sounded in the face of Ruck's travails. "If everybody wants to get together."

"Yes: We will get Ruck back onto the narrow way. Straight and narrow, rather."

A buzzing sound; Roy Earl, cursing a vibrating Blackberry produced out of a cargo pocket. He squinted at a text message. Wrinkled his nose as though sniffing a funky sock. Slapping his hands together, a busy man, time wrap it up. "Gotta split. I'm treasurer of the neighborhood association. Time to go write checks."

"Civic leader as well as merchant class. Most impressive."

"Small business—man, I tells ya. Every time you turn around, there's a hand reaching into your pocket."

"So long as you get a decent hand-job out of it."

"Right." Bitter, sarcastic. "A hand-job nobody in their right mind wants."

On their feet: back-pounding, one-armed man hugs. Roy said into his ear: "I'm not gonna let you and sweet Creedence go through this alone."

Billy, so touched water again sprang to his eyes. Pernicious, these peskily genuine emotions. More bothersome in their own peculiar simmering way than the urges causing the dreaded, unavoidable accidents.

To quell his nettlesome humanness, Billy fantasized again about the blonde counter girl Roy sent outside with a broom and a dustpan, swish swish, purposeful and glowing with youth and sufficient feminine vitality befitting a potential goddess. On his way down the sidewalk, Billy, snatched the broom handle from her and smashed her over the head, dragged her by the hair back to the condo where he would stick his entire head into her sopping, pliable innerness. Claw all the way inside, curl up, rest until suffocating from the gooey viscous pleasure, amber waves of film-grain fading into vinegar syndrome color shift, later crumbling into powder and blown wind-borne into endless nothingness; no more bothersome anything.

Peace.

Maybe that's what Devin got out of drinking himself into incoherence.

Consumed with the need to do forty massive bong hits before dinner and get his headspace together before the inevitable Melanie Eruption, possibly occurring within minutes, Billy, willing to bet his inheritance that she awaited him outside his building. Panicked, furious, a shadowplay of hyper-uncool emotion crawling across her strained, shining face. The girl had it bad for him.

But, who could blame her? A tiger—Billy, not her.

And later, the make-up sex, sure to be a pleasurable enough distraction. Melanie, helping him forget. Like every girl had since the day Libby had been taken away from him, on a wind black, bleak and unforgiving.

To fuck. To forget. This was key.

But not too hard, now. Don't take your shit out on the rest of them. One or two, here and there, maybe?

It'd been too long. Or not long enough. On the old accidents.

Head spinning, like back when they got so beer drunk in the dorms and passed out. Spins.

Now, Melanie, though, could appreciate—and take—a good solid sex-beating. Who came hard as Billy did. Who pinched his nipples and squeezed his balls—hard!—slapped at his erection—harder!—and dominated him, all of which somehow helped keep the accidents from happening. Walked on the dirty floor and then made him lick her feet clean.

He had thrived under the whole role-playing rubric. This was how he got away with all the rough stuff. Safety words. Heh. Billy's was 'Hothouse Cucumber.'

Wait—Melanie didn't sound so bad.

Yes; but. If being unfaithful to Libby didn't sting so much—she was still The One, no matter who came along—he might consider keeping her. With the looming Ruck drama to come, however, ditching his rider, in the Delta blues sense, could wait until next week.

# ELEVEN
—
## DEVIN

Devin, sick but purposeful, regained wretched consciousness early in the morning, got his bloody vomiting over with and started putting his gear together for high-speed travel.

For once he knew, unprompted, what lay ahead.

The end.

Impressive or sad; he couldn't decide which. Only a conclusion.

The road. Had to get this part over with. Had to get somewhere and settled, soon as possible. Or he'd start detoxing. Remembering he needed to get on the road today was a sign he hadn't gotten nearly drunk enough last night.

*Fuck. Way too lucid, yo.*

He cracked a beer, drank it. Felt steady.

Steady enough, anyhow.

He puked it up, drank another. That one settled in real nice. As did the next.

The preparations already made, all left now the proverbial hitting of the bricks: gas tank topped off, oil changed, last Eileen check cashed. Ran around the corner to the convenience store, a cooler slap-full of ice cold beer stashed in the trunk, along with two liquors—one clear, one brown. With providence on his side the distilled elixirs wouldn't be touched until stopping sometime later in the night, otherwise this road trip potentially brief.

This time Devin, like, actually wanted to arrive alive.

To catch up with Billy.

Bidding adieu to the apartment; what meager belongings he owned to be left behind. Flushing the door key down the toilet. Intending to leave the dump wide open for whomever wished to try their luck with the evil spirits dwelling inside.

*Or, do you carry your troubled spirits with you?*

An old saw. Something his mother or grandmother probably used to say.

Devin, starting out the door, but going back to pick up Prudy's dish. Rinsing dust from the ceramic bowl and wrapping it in a red bandanna, reverent, he wedged the artifact into a safe corner of the trunk. Saying to himself, got to remember where it is. Can't forget. Can't let myself forget, ever again.

A rush of sick memories: waking up the day after discovering the cat's death, her body lying curled and cold, under the bed where she'd gone to die. Drinking it all away. Until awakening again.

And reliving the horror.

Devin, bundling the stiffening corpse into his backpack, a faded, threadbare Army knapsack he'd carried since adolescence. Shaking and sick, driving until he on the other side of Denver from dusty flat Commerce City, where the foothills of the Rocky Mountains began in earnest, and behind them, the big peaks.

Getting as far as Golden, at the edge of the mountains. Never ever taking the canyon road, the Golden Gate parkway, up into the hills. Too dangerous even for a shaky old hand at driving plastered like Devin 'Ruck' Rucker.

Sometimes he liked heading on up to Boulder, taking 93 on past the big brewery looming over the tourist-trap town and up through the flatlands to the college town, and thinking about Millie being there and what she was doing but never looking her up; drinking, watching the carefree kids going about their business, then toodledo-ing his way back down the parkway and onto I-70 and out to Commerce City, where the real glug-glugging could begin: at Chubby's, in the apartment, anywhere he didn't have to travel too far for a decent place to puke and pass out for a few hours. But always taking the straightforward and safe path to Boulder, the flat highway. Never attempting the scenic route up and round through Nederland, a beautiful but challenging drive. He'd driven up the canyon road in the past, following South Boulder Creek. Sure—but with Millie. Back in the day. But not since.

Not in this condition.

What about today? A big day. The cat dead, and all.

Not drunk. Not hardly at all. Not yet, anyway. That would change.

Why not?

A voice saying, *Go for it, tough guy*.

Keeping one eye on the backpack with Prudy's body, he passed through Golden until taking the highway turnoff to the west. After a micro-hesitation he hit his signal to take the canyon road, which began to twist and turn and rise in its snaking track up into the hills.

He'd thought about it a thousand-thousand times: getting hammered as shit and attempting this drive. But never doing it. Tempting fate, that. Too easy a way out.

Shaking and nearly incapacitated by the rampaging need for a bracer, Devin drove, gripping the wheel of the Jetta which seemed to protest on the inclines, the engine whining and knocking; Devin, fearing he'd leave more than Prudy up here in the hills. Wondering if the transmission would finally drop out of the undercarriage. But it didn't.

Devin, chewing the insides of his cheeks and thinking about the rum in his pocket and the dead cat in the back seat under the blanket. Negotiating the turns with confidence and a modicum of unlikely grace; the mountain air came tinged with the scent of fire. A controlled burn, probably.

He pulled into turnouts a few times to let tailgating nitwits be on their hurried way. He wouldn't be rushed.

This, too important.

This, to be done right.

Not to have an accident, no; taking the Golden Gate road a test and a testament and statement of purpose and intent and invulnerability, which Devin, perhaps alone among all the peoples and humans of the world, seemed to possess. Why else was he still around?

Preternatural, his ability to survive car crashes and falls and alcohol poisoning.

*God, that old rascal, he musta got himself a plan going.*

But for Devin? The plan was to bury the cat. Anything else, like his own death, could wait.

Finding what seemed the right turnout, finally. Parking the car and gathering the rucksack and other accoutrements including a pint of Bacardi 151, Devin followed the track of a stream back under the highway, into the wooded hills stretching above. He and Millie, hiking the trail many times. They'd even made love in the woods, once, next to the flowing mountain brook.

Memorable; sober days, then.

Millie begging him to say, *I love you.*

Devin, unable. Unwilling.

Climbing, the land becoming steep. Carrying his pet, cooing reassurances. His body, aching with the effort. Stopping at several points to rest sore, spindly legs.

The stream: Colorado mountain water scrubbed pure and clean by the stones over which it ran cascading foamy and white down tumbles of falls, the sound clean and purifying. Once making it to a level run of the stream—

here the water placid, the surface like glass—Devin, hacking into the stony ground near the bank with a small gardening spade. Stabbing at the wet, sucking mud, grunting. Sweat rolling down his brow, stinging his eyes, the physical labor feeling good, meaningful. Digging a hole, harder than he'd anticipated.

Into the damp hole she had gone.

Covering up Prudy's body with the thick mud.

Clasping his lips shut to stifle curses that threatened to claw through his cheeks.

Devin, his back and knees on fire, threw the spade end over end into the forest behind him, staggered into the river up to his knees and struck the water's surface openhanded, shouting and raging until his clothing soaked through and cold. Hurling curses at the sky, an inexhaustible torrent of vituperative invective.

Spent, wet, he dragged himself to the bank. Lay immobile atop the grave. Wished for death. Doing so had never worked.

Pulling himself together, he produced the pint of rum out of his jacket, a special treat he'd brought to follow up the burial. Cracking the tax stamp seal—a marvelously wondrous sound—and chucking away the cap, he choked as the powerful liquor exploded on his palette. Devin, managing to drain the bottle in four enormous gulps.

His stomach, ravaged, convulsed in protest. It all came back up into the river.

Devin had wept at his failure to get drunk with a modicum of competence. This idea, almost worse than the notion of Prudy being dead. What, indeed, could he offer the world but this one and true talent?

He'd driven on to Nederland to have a pitcher or two of beer, enough to steady himself for the trip back out of the mountains to his lonely flatlander's apartment where he could drink and drive with impunity. It had been going on unabated for however long, now.

Not that much longer. Devin would be dead soon, too. Because without the cat, what was left? And yet, years later, he waited still.

Devin, in the parking lot of the apartment complex, and for the last time, smoked and considered the sandy earth blowing across faded asphalt by wind mournful and easterly. He cracked two PBR tallboys, not giving a shit who saw. Chugging them both in about five minutes, one after the other. Throwing the cans on the ground, but picking them up and putting them into a blue recycle bin. He wasn't a litter monster, belching loud and long there on the asphalt. Only thirsty.

Feeling centered.

For once.

The Jetta, getting to be a beater, but cranking right up. A sign—a positive one.

Devin, another cold beer poured into a silver coffee mug, now ready. Screwing the lid on and stashing the vessel down in the cup holder with a hand as palsied as a Parkinson's victim, he pointed the nose of the Jetta hard east on I-25 and drove into the true flatlands. Later, he turned south, toward Texas, and the promised apotheosis of reconnection, and retribution, with the ones who had done him so wrong. Soon as he remembered not only which ones, but what they had done to him.

# TWELVE
—
## CREEDENCE

"Well, I'm not sure *what* I would do, darling."

"Wouldn't you? This is a quite a change."

"Hush your mouth. Before I hush it for you."

Mumbling. "I'd like to see you try."

"Shit. You young'uns don't know your butts from holes in the ground."

Their lines, all but rehearsed. They talked to one another so much there was nothing for it but to recite routines like the folks on the TV babbling its soap operas, commercial breaks and terror alerts about the war, or whatever theatrical plays were showing that week on the news channels.

Eileen Rucker spoke between puffs of a slender feminine cigarette, its smoke blue and rich with menthol and toxins. She coughed after every toke yet kept puff puff puffing away. "Sometimes men get funny when there's a little one on the way."

"Funny how?"

"Like they ain't got a lick of sense all of a sudden."

"Dusty never had none to begin with."

"Hush your mouth. That's all this is."

The daughter, skeptical, lay stretched out in Daddy's recliner, her loose clothing a familiar uniform: ratty bright green sweats and one of Dusty's stained **Dale Earnhardt RIP** T-shirts, now far too small to accommodate his paunch. Whatever Chelsea's complaint, Eileen could be counted upon to take Dusty's side. Inexplicably. "Think so?"

"No—I *know* that's what this is. Once you've been through things, you know. You don't *think*."

"You always was the smartest one in any room."

Ignoring the dig. "You'll understand one day. I hope."

Eileen Rucker peered over her glasses, a pair of ugly, cat-eye frames she'd had since about 1970, appropriate considering how Chelsea's mother's hairstyle had not changed, either. Then again such a style, American Bouffant, continued in favor by a veritable multitude of aging Eileen Ruckers across the American South. Sometimes their daughters as well.

Not this girl. Long and straight, like the girls wore their hair back in the 1970s. Took a long-ass time with the hot iron, though. Pain in the butt.

All she knew was that her mother needed to start eating more. Eileen must have lost twenty pounds in the last couple of months, and with doing essentially nothing different. Must be a part of getting older, Chelsea thought.

It wasn't illness, because Eileen stayed too busy: Right now her mother sat hunched over piles of folders and check stubs and documents spread all over the Rucker dining room table. This year it was Eileen's duty to serve as treasurer of the ELMS. Folks in downtown Tillman Falls called the group the power behind the throne. They had secret meetings, like the Masons, with initiations, liturgy, dogma. Chelsea sure as shit hadn't been asked to join. The club existed to support women of means and breeding, her mother had told her, not bring them up to speed.

Get a load of that. Her own Mama thinking about her daughter in this way.

Mercy.

Today Eileen's chitchat felt different. Lecturing. Of greater importance that the normal small talk in which the mother and daughter engaged.

"Dusty's never acted like this before. Since I got the news, he don't want to—you know."

Eileen chuckled through a plume of smoke, coughed. Dismissive, she patted the stiff crust of her beauty-shop hairdo with nails impeccable as always, rings in place, wedding band still worn in deference to her beloved late husband. "Darling, darling angel of mine. Once she gets closer to born, he'll be excited and happy."

"Be better if I could at least get some along the way."

Her eyes, lidded; Eileen, tsk-tsking. "Big Ma-maw taught me that you ain't supposed to do nothing when you're pregnant. Your grandmama always said to read a ro-mance book. Take hot baths. Hot as you can stand."

"You mean cold showers." She gulped iced tea, so sweet and cold it gave her a forehead spike. Thought about the times with Buddy Lawler. And the idea of parenthood. She needed a shower, all right—her skin was crawling.

But for all the guilt and trouble, Buddy Lawler, as it turned out, hadn't made for a better lover than Dusty.

Coming fast the first time by necessity, back in the parts department and in a dusty closet as they were, so yes yes, of course it had to be quick; damn stupid decision had been made on a whim, the morning Dusty had called to say he had forgotten to pick up the cat food and litter she had told him to get on his way to work. Selfish little piss-ant. She'd show him.

Sliding into her and feeling good. Telling Buddy so. But his thrusting was awkward, spastic and propulsive, an event primal and brief. Buddy, who'd flirted and cajoled and flat-out told her how effing hot she was and how he dreamed, dreamed, of giving her the high hard one, as he put it with such tact; giving her the high hard one, a state of grace that'd lasted for all of thirty seconds.

How she'd wept, later. Like after the first time with her husband, too, for that matter. They'd been sixteen.

Considering the circumstances she decided to give Buddy another chance, but damn if it wasn't with the same result despite being conducted under reasonably private conditions and with a six pack of Bud Light, there in her car under the Sugeree River bridge where the teenagers, at the time all still in school, would go to make out. That time she'd climbed on top, planned to control the flow and rhythm. Get what she needed, one way or another.

But Buddy, bless his heart, he'd been extra excited, it seemed, by her being on top. Once she'd peeled her panties off—the smell of her sex had filled the car—and climbed onto him, drawing in her breath, he was hard as a railroad spike, a little thicker than Dusty.

Easing him in.

Moving her hips. A few times. Maybe three or four.

"Oh, wait now, hold on girl...*ahhhhh.*"

"You *finished* already—?"

Grunting again in assent, moaning, saying how sorry he was; how sexy she looked and felt; how tight her pussy. "Keep on going. Get you some."

Grinding, trying, but he popped out of her. "Dude."

"That's that."

Words escaped her. Flustered, she pushed off him.

"We need to get in a bed, honey." Craning his neck around. "I'm too nervous out like this."

"Yeah. Okay."

"Give me one of those beers," like changing the subject, yanking up his pants. "On the way back we need to stop and get some gum."

Disgust—with herself, with him, all of it. Feeling only this at first rather than the guilt she'd expected. That came later. And for nothing. The idea that Buddy could have made a baby that fast—or Dusty, for that matter— seemed ludicrous.

"How did Daddy act when you was carrying me and Devin?"

"He acted like your Daddy—a man. A father."

"'Funny' like Dusty's been?"

She went *nuh-uh*. "Your daddy had the opposite problem."

"Which was?"

Demure. "Honey, I couldn't keep him off me."

"Lucky you."

"P'shaw." Eileen gave Chelsea her full attention. "Dwight, always working so hard, even before my sweet little angels came along, didn't have time to feel funny about nothing. Work work work. His own daddy had worked hard, and so he did, too."

"He was gone a lot. That's for sure."

"That's what he always said, that working hard was the least he could do, to honor his daddy and all that he had done for him. And that *y'all*," meaning Chelsea and Devin, "were never to want for nothing. *Nothing*," stabbing that crooked old index finger of hers, the one she'd caught in the blades of a whirring beater many years before, a break that'd healed badly. She'd refused to go to the doctor. Had wrapped it up in an ace bandage and popsicle sticks. It had hurt her for a year before it fully healed, Eileen always said. After enough time had passed, she had started exaggerating the time it took to heal to two years. Milking the pathos.

Eileen cut two slitted hateful dashes for eyes over at her daughter. "Let me tell you something, little girl."

She waited.

"You'd best not be mean to Dusty. Not after what he's done been through in his life."

Chelsea slammed down the footrest of the lounger. "Mama, Dusty's a grown man now. His drunk daddy and dead mama don't excuse everything."

Eileen drifted into a nostalgic trance: "Poor, poor Dusty. Always so sweet with those big brown eyes. And not having no one to care for him. Not like we did. His two-bit daddy laying up drunk in that trailer, this one time with *a black girl*," gasping in horror.

Chelsea's Gen X snark erupted unbidden. "Oh, lord help me—not a black girl. Heaven forbid."

"I can't even think about it. But in spite of all that mess, and then later his grandmama getting sick, poor Dusty come up just fine. Thanks to us. And to you. Now he starts his own family. Sweet, poor Dusty."

Chelsea started to make a pointed remark about the unrewarding labors of such service, but didn't.

"But despite it all, Dusty was always darling and goodnatured about everything. And so grateful to have us all."

"Mercy, but you lay it on thick. It's like Dusty has something on you."

Her eyes twinkled. "I swore I'd never tell you this," tittering, "but not too long after y'all started dating-dating—after a few months at least?—Dusty come to me and says, he says, 'Mama Rucker, I don't understand. It's like once a month Colette acts like she don't love me no more,' and I laughed and laughed and I says, I says, oh my goodness gracious, poor little Dusty." Beaming and delighted at the memory of his naiveté. "Bless his heart."

"I guess you set him straight on our little mood type-deals."

Analytical. "It's difficult to explain the way things work—things that are complicated, grown-up."

"It's just basic biology. How hard does it have to be?"

"Because you mustn't let children grow up too fast. Once you've lived for a good long while, everything's right easy to understand, but until then—? No. *No no no no no no no.*"

"You'd just as soon nobody grew up at all."

Eileen, a rueful smile. "That's right. I wish you all could've stayed little forever."

Thinking her mother nuts. The opposite of the way it ought to work. Saying so.

"To retain the purity and innocence of childhood?" Eileen glared at Chelsea, got up from the couch. Stooped and grimaced, she reached back and put a hand on her ribcage. "Such would be a miracle in this wicked world."

Mama had gone back over to the dining room table and her stack of ELMS paperwork. She sat down, licked her thumb and turned over a sheet. She began punching numbers into a calculator, peering down her nose through the glasses.

Chelsea, exhausted, shuffled into the sparkling white kitchen and put her sweet tea glass down on the magnificent granite countertop. Dwight had installed these gray marbled beauties the summer before he died. Feeling more than seeing her mother's disapproving head shake, she correctly anticipated the familiar 'appearances' speech:

"Chelsea Colette Rucker. Heavens to betsy."

"What now?"

"Why on earth don't you go and get you some nice things to wear?" Mortification. "People will think we don't got no money."

"I was sick this morning. What should I have put on? A prom dress? My durn wedding gown?"

"Sick don't mean you can't dress yourself like a normal grown woman."

Screaming from the kitchen. "*I was puking my guts out!*"

It was true, but the nausea and dizziness had passed by eight o'clock that morning, but she'd called into work anyway. Doing so made her feel naughty, as when she'd faked tummy or girl trouble to get out of school.

"You better watch raising that voice at me."

Chelsea snatched her keys from the countertop. "I'm going to go home now and get supper on for Dusty. Maybe he'll be more like himself tonight."

Eileen, wringing her hands, looked surprised. "Well, darling. Do you have to go already?"

"I think I should."

"I feel like—we should talk more."

Chelsea got a cold feeling inside. "About what?"

Coming over and fussing around with her daughter's hair, stroking her arms, and putting a hand on the pooch where the baby would live until born, Eileen appeared to shake off whatever had been on her mind: "I wish you'd never moved down the road."

"That's silly. It ain't but five minutes away."

"Yes, but there's room here for you, and for Dusty, and your kitties, and this little angel, too." The budding grandmother stooped down with a grunt. Nuzzled Chelsea's midsection, baby-talking the unseen fetus. "Isn't that right my little angel? Oh—I can't wait to get my hands on you."

"We'll have time to talk later in the week. On Sunday, when you come over for dinner? Dusty's grilling steaks."

"Sounds like a lot of trouble for only the three of us."

Leaving through the front door, Chelsea's eye caught the Thomas Kinkade painting hanging in the foyer, one called *Christmas Moonlight*. It an arched bridge leading over a stream to a snow-covered, inviting family home, golden windows glowing with warmth. The house in which she stood remained her home but lacked that sense of connection. Rather than caroling in joy, the argumentative voices of the mother and daughter often rang out, strident and spectral, in the spacious rooms and high ceilings.

She paused. "Maybe there'll be more than three. Maybe we'll have a guest."

"P'shaw."

"I'll get extra meat."

"I don't know what for."

She could just tell her mother Devin was coming. But that would make her too happy.

Nevertheless, her brother offered a solution: Devin, filling up this house.

Devin, dealing with whatever was wrong with Mama.

Devin.

And as for Chelsea? Or little Colette, as her mother would call her until her dying day?

Billy.

Buddy.

Somebody.

She wished, and wished hard, for a better way to excuse all those thoughts. Maybe an answer would come along. A way she hadn't considered to feel free and fully alive. Other people obviously had it, even Devin in his own sick and perverted way. She kept guessing in her head; her heart always seemed far too clenched to make any contribution. Hard-hearted—it was a hell of a way for a new mother to feel. It wasn't right.

Nor was Dusty's behavior.

*It's because of the baby. He'll settle down.*

But the tail end of a mysterious phone call last night. That Dusty took. When he didn't realize Chelsea was listening. A new wrinkle. The real reason.

But she had to have proof. If only she had had the courage to tell her mother the truth. Having affairs was one subject about which Eileen Rucker might have held insight.

# THIRTEEN

## ——

## DEVIN

Road rolling on beneath Devin's worn tires; drinking, steady, but not getting drunk, a kind of empty plateau with steep drop-offs on every side, frustrating but necessary to Arrive Alive—not usually the goal, but damn if seeing Billy didn't make sense. Talk about some heavy shit, oldschool stuff. Hanging.

When not dialing through the sparse selection of radio stations, Devin, playing the same cassette over and over, the bootleg Grateful Dead concert tape Billy'd given him the semester before the sad summer, the forgotten time, 1990; the cassette, the only media Devin still owned in any form, battered and worn, the mechanism making a faint squeal.

The recording of the show the rock legends had played at McNabb Arena.

An awful night. Nothing good came of it.

Or everything good, actually.

This represented a pernicious state of confusion. Good, bad, all of it mixed up in his mind. Certain he'd eventually get drunk enough to reason it out, though.

Devin, recalling how after the band appeared in Columbia 'hippie' seemed to become a fad, with tons of people besides Billy getting into that noodling Deadhead crap: everywhere you looked roamed girls in flowing skirts and Birkenstocks, and guys, Billy included, growing their hair long and rocking Guatemalan shorts, tie-dyes. The aromatic odor of exotic tobaccos wafted from dorm room windows. That part he understood was not so fresh a development on a college campus. Not in their dorm room, anyway.

*Shit's always made me squirrel-nerved. Gimme a few brews, yo, to feel less present, not more.*

The best song the band did at the show came warbling out of the tinny Jetta speakers—'Wharf Rat,' a mournful ditty about a drunk knocking around the San Francisco docks grieving for a lost love, to this day Devin's favorite bit of music he'd ever heard the Dead or any other rock group play. Recalling how at the concert he'd held his paper cup of overpriced soda pop up in the air in salute as Jerry Garcia, singing about doing time for other fucker's crimes and stumbling around drunk on bur-*gun*-dy wine, had held rapt the houseful of fans eighteen thousand strong, all standing silent and reverent and worshipful in the massive basketball temple. The lyrics, giving Devin chicken-skin, that song, every time.

The work, resonating.

*But a big fight later that night. You and Billy.*

*Over Libby.*

It'd all worked out, though. Until it hadn't. After which Billy a hero, rather a villain. A vague savior to Devin in some amorphously mysterious manner forever escaping clear recollection.

Next? Dobbs messing around with her. Dobbs, of all people. Had known each other since first grade. Best pals.

*Not to mention that Dobbs is gay.*

It didn't add up.

*Stop thinking and let the mind lie fallow, boy. Like you done got so good at*, as a soft inner cadence called to him. Now here came a voice of reason.

The miles, the clicks, piling up. Boring his way on toward Texas, the awful spots boiling, infinite, all consuming.

But Devin, making it through the first day's drive fine. No cops, no accidents. A Super 8 in Boise City appeared on the side of the road, some shitburg nowheresville in the panhandle of Oklahoma. No man's land, which suited Devin's unique brand of emptiness fine, fine as wine. Ice in a plastic bucket that stank, and then knocking back the fifth of vodka he'd brought until crashing.

Shocked in the morning to discover not how much he'd drank, but how little. Upon arising not long after the sunrise, Devin, starting his day on a high note by retching—hard and sustained—into the stained and mysterious motel toilet, but over pretty quick by his standards. Seeing a gratifying pink accent of blood. Check.

Devin, in the parking lot, cursed the sunlight striking his optic nerves like white-hot daggers. The air, rank with diesel exhaust from big rigs rumbling across the overpass a hundred yards away. The acrid char-smell from What-a-Burger next door smelled like death, but tasty death. Devin, swooning with fresh nausea, felt a sensation mistaken, briefly, as hunger.

Not yet nine, but almost. Time, and the road, waited for no Devin.

Somewhere close by, a man inside a room screaming and jabbering in angry, broken, drunken Spanish; a woman's voice, equally as passionate, seemed to counter his every vituperative threat.

"You want a date?"

Devin, cussing and nearly coming out of his skin. A sad little lot lizard had sidled him in the doorway of his room.

They had words. He cursed the petite, tattooed Latina girl. He was extra mean. Told her to 'quit sucking dicks.' "The world prefers you to get a real job."

"Yeah, but all me and my kid need is something to eat."

"Fair enough—take this." He gave her some of his mother's money, a twenty. Money wouldn't spend where he was going. Not this time.

She shoved it back at him. "You don't got to pay me yet."

"It's so's you can get your kid a McMuffin for breakfast. Take a break this morning."

"For real? You don't want me to do nothing?"

Devin looked over the shades. His stomach convulsed. The shakes were all over him. "Go on, now. My junk don't work no more."

Relieved, she scurried not over to the fast food joints, but probably to the next john. It wasn't his problem.

After getting fixed up with a quick bracer from the heretofore unopened Henry McKenna—hair of the D and knock that hangover right out; McKenna, despite the name, a brown-eyed woman if there'd ever been one —Devin chased the blessed nip of whistle-wetting Kentucky firewater with a semi-cold tallboy lying in melted cooler ice-water, brewski slipping down smooth and dry of finish. Seeing as how he'd regurgitated it soon after, shocking and propulsive through his mouth and nose and necessitating a change of shirt, the second beer of the day tasted even more especially crisp; refreshing and clean as the mountain air he'd left behind, or so he convinced himself.

Devin, now time to remember where he was and what he was doing. A parking lot in the midwest somewhere. Hungover. Calculating how much to drink and still be a functioning motorist. Like a broken record.

Then, okay, the novelty of it all; the whole Billy deal, yeah yeah yeah.

"Maybe another quick bracer."

*No, don't do that, not with hundreds of miles to go.*

"It'll be fine."

*Don't drink no more McKenna, beau.*

"Just a taste. I'll spit it back out."
*Order toast from the diner over across the way.*
"Kiss my ass."
*All right. Drive. Smoke. Sip brewskis.*

Nodding and listening as his voice of reason found a decent perch, Devin shuffled back into the room to brush his teeth, forgot what he was doing along the way and lay his wearied body back down.

An hour later he repeated the whole routine, to include the bracer and tortured inner debate about hitting the bourbon a second and third and fourth time, but not doing so.

Having ginned up the gut to get going for real, he fortified by nibbling rabbit-like on a packet of Nekot cookie-crackers, sixty pesetas out of the vending machine and sweeter than hell after the beer. But he kept them cookies down. The sugar, giving him a charge and a spring to his step.

Squaring the trunk away, cooler packed with free motel ice and beer, and checking on Prudy's dish. Safe. Holding it made him want to drink, though.

No. Drive. For once, he was on a schedule. Which he kept all day, picking a time and looking at his map and saying, *I will be there then.*

And, as if in a dream, a few hours later here he was, skyscrapers and a fancy hotel and down the block the freaking Alamo, yeah; and a bar. Billy? Immaterial whether he showed or not. Far from the point. A bar was all Devin needed to stoke his sense of arrival. Like always having a home away from home—until they kicked you out.

# FOURTEEN

## — CREEDENCE

Chelsea, a knot in her stomach, raced over to Mr. Vincent's hardware store in her little blue Ford Focus. Her eyesight: blurry. All but sleepless from vivid, anxiety-ridden dreams all through the night.

Her day running the switchboard at the dealership, interminable. Clicking around online to some of her old favorite celebrity gossip or conspiracy and secret society websites—baldheaded Britney and baby-maker Angelina, or the video 'proving' no planes hit the towers—the ocean of information at her fingertips served only to make her more nervous, a torrent of helplessness threatening to sweep her away.

Dusty's behavior after she asked who he'd been talking to tucked away in the whispering shadows? Obvious and busted. Face gone red, apple cheeks making him look like a tryout for the center-court mall Santa.

She'd overhead how his voice had come out so soft, like back at fourteen when he'd been trying to talk his way into her drawers for the first time, tickling and poking and probing around with his stubby index finger while begging her to let him 'take it out.'

Hearing him say, quiet, to whomever he spoke: "I can't wait, either."

Chelsea, having heard him express such sentiments before.

On the phone.

To her.

Startled by her presence outside the laundry room he'd lashed out: "I swear to goodness but I wish you'd quit creeping around this house on me."

Arms folded. "Who was that?"

"Mr. Vincent. He was—today, see, I give him an idea-r on a sale. On having a sale. An idea-r I had. And I was only calling him to thank him for taking me, taking me up on it. The sale, it's gonna start soon. That's manager stuff right there, boy."

'Idea-r.' It drove her up the frickin' wall. Hillbillies from Parson's Hollow or Red Mound said 'idea-r.' Not folks like the Ruckers, from the eastern half of the county, on the other side of the ridge from all them rednecks.

She speculated on the praise Mr. Vincent had offered to deserve Dusty's buttery hand-job voice, one full of gratitude but also ripe anticipation of future events. She knew it well; she knew what she'd heard. "And you can't wait for it to start."

"Do what?"

"The sale."

"Hell yeah I can't wait. I'm—he said—I'll get a bonus. If it goes good."

Pushing by her, he went through the dark kitchen and living room. He grabbed the remote and shut off the movie at which she'd been staring, oblivious to its content. Creedence, daydreaming about Billy Steeple, and Charleston, and cat stuff.

"That exciting, is it? This hardware sale?"

"I'm right stoked." And on into the bedroom.

She followed. "When's it start? How much are the discounts?"

Sitting on the bed he peeled off his work socks, which looked stiff. Being a good boy, attentive and mindful of her rules, he tooted the can of Glade a couple times. "I don't remember."

Against the doorjamb, hands on her swelling belly, fake smile: "But, what was your 'idea-r'?"

His mouth worked up and down. Had him there. Fake-yawning to buy time.

"Well?"

"Fasteners and tools under fifty dollars," he finally blurted. "For those little household fixer-upper dealies. That's what the radio ad's going to say."

Not bad.

New tactic. "Heck of a thing, this sale. Can't say I ever seen you call Mr. Vincent after hours."

"I'm just trying to do what you wanted." Stomping into the bathroom he called out, high-voiced, "I'm trying to impress him, girl."

"Maybe I'm the one you need to impress."

"Ain't that what I just said?"

"Not exactly."

"You're talking in circles. *I don't know what you want.*"

That chubby little cashier.

It all came to her.

Clicked in.

What was that look the little shit had gotten when she walked in that one day last week? Chelsea had brought Dusty the lunch he forgot. The way the girl had crossed her arms and smiled all crooked, almost sarcastic—and Dusty himself, tense and annoyed at the appearance of his beloved spouse. His beloved, pregnant spouse. Said he would run to Mickey D's. But that he appreciated her bringing his brown bag.

Buddy Lawler, now, that had been foolishness and nonsense and weakness ascribable to hormones and boredom and whatnot. Dusty messing around with a young girl? That was a whole-nother ham sandwich.

Pulling into the parking lot of Mr. Vincent's hardware store she saw no sign of Dusty's beat-up Toyota Tundra, with its variety of NASCAR iconography, **Power of Pride** flag sticker and two different **Never Forget** decals—one for Dale, one for 9/11.

At her appearance inside, spindly old dried up Mr. Vincent brightened. She asked where on earth her husband might be in the middle of the workday like this.

Dentures whistling, the proprietor reassured her with a lingering hug, rubbing the small of her back and leering through thick old-man's eyeglasses taking up half his puckered face. "Said he was going to run errands for you, honey. I let him clock out for the day."

"He's off work?"

"Quiet as a tomb around here. But we'll pick up again."

With a shrug he glanced sidelong at the only customer in the large store, another crusty old fart in suspenders and dusty work pants and ball cap holding the tines of a cheap rake up to the light and squinting, Chelsea thought, like one of those Jewish diamond merchants in New York City.

"I shouldn't have come without calling first."

"Dusty says you been a fretting and worrying too-*too* much, now."

"Hard not to."

"I been worried, too. What with these Mexicans piling in on top of everybody. And Wal-mart, of course."

She drew breath to say *And Lowe's, too* but stopped herself. Salt in the small business owner's wounds.

Mr. Vincent saw Chelsea's troubled face. "Dusty's job ain't going nowhere, sweetheart. Not until I do."

None too reassuring. Mr. Vincent had to be in his mid-70s. "I appreciate hearing you say that."

"All these earthly travails—Redtails football squads and expensive coaches that ain't worth a toot, terrorists, Wal-mart, eye-rack, hardware, chicken feed, nails, washers, tools, cash registers, money, et cetera et cetera," gesturing with both arms at his place of business. "Once the Lord comes back? And takes us home with him?"

"Yeah?"

"All will be moot and forgiven and forgot and immaterial."

"The world is a troubled place. It needs fixing."

"Not for very much longer, my dear."

She hotfooted it back to the car and pulled out onto the main road right in front of a school bus, the short one. A horn blew. She waved, 'sorry.'

*Dusty didn't have no good god-durn errands to run.* Where were they?

Passing the old Pecan Market, a mom and pop gas station and diner frequented by school kids from James F. Byrnes High, at first she didn't notice Dusty's truck parked outside. Or Dusty himself, for that matter. Leaning with his arm against the hood of the vehicle—like they had once done.

Scores of times.

Hundreds.

Since childhood.

Together.

The Pecan Market, an Edgewater County teenaged right of passage. They still went there twice a month for hot dogs. Didn't stand around, however. *We bring them home to eat. Like grownups.*

Tires squealing, she cut a U-turn in the middle of the road and cruised back by the market. This time, unmistakable: Dusty, his back to the highway, gestured and flapped his gums while standing next to the little strumpet Ashleigh—that was her name. A pimply, chubby checkout girl, ripe and red-haired.

Little Ashleigh, standing right next to her husband. Another redhead. Worse, a fat girl, the way so many modern teens had become. Myrtle Muffintop was more attractive than her?

And, standing right up *against* Chelsea's husband. A not-pretty redheaded fat girl. There in front of God, and everyone else, too.

Chelsea, shitting a golden brick, did all she could not to cut another U-turn to confront him there in the sandy, unpaved Pecan Market parking lot. Instead, she hit the gas before Dusty noticed her and could see that she'd caught his little red-handed ass in action. Surprise would be key, now.

Driving home, a pulse beat in her temples. Her abdomen, tight with anger and shock. Sweating. Cramping down there. Only when in the house by herself with the kitties did she finally begin to cry.

# FIFTEEN

## DEVIN

"Excuse me, sir?"

Devin, realizing 'sir' meant him, pushed the empty glass he'd killed in one sweet blessed cold swallow over to the bartender, a young woman in her hotel uniform with a gold nameplate who'd watched with concern as he gulped the first round. The barkeep's expression, he thought, betrayed grim experience with such customers of great thirst showing up so early in the happy hour shift.

Fiddling with his mustache, crusty in places, he rattled the ice at her. Cheery and bright: "Got any more li-bations back yonder? Or did I clean you out already."

"Sir?"

"Fill me up, buttercup."

"No—behind you." She gestured. "Someone's calling for you."

*"Do what?"*

A looming, shadowy presence fell across the bar. Billy.

Pale as a ghost, sweating, but the old boy, looking all hale and hearty. Wellsir, good on him.

"Ain't seen you in a coon's age, son."

"It's been a few. You're looking—good."

Doing what I can. Devin repeated it a few times. Tried not to boohoo. Felt all crumbly.

"Your drink, sir." A fresh one; a napkin. All was right with the world.

Hugs. Smalltalk. Ordering another round. Billy, saying the magic words, "It's all on me."

This was gonna be fine. Devin could easily run out of cash before getting his fill. Billy. Good old Billy.

Hours later, Devin's prophecy, true.

Helping Billy along, they were trying to get back to the hotel. They'd been drinking, Devin-style, until last call at no fewer than three different joints.

But unsatisfying—all small talk, all the time. Big laughs. War stories. Pussy and drinking.

Good times.

But nothing about Libby.

Billy, a pit stop; emerging out of the bushes and onto the San Antonio Riverwalk pathway with the contents of his stomach in his hair, on his shirttail, and splattered on top of one polished Weejun. Billy, incoherent, incapacitated. Kept saying, ain't used to drinking, pardner. Devin, going, yeah-well. We'll see about that. Showing him how the pros from Dover could do it.

Even in the orange light of the streetlights Devin could see that his friend's color was *no bueno*, and that one of his eyes looked bloodshot as though he'd gotten the stink-eye from puking and heaving with such gusto; in Devin's judgement a 10-level expulsion of fluids.

Far as he could remember, many adventures had occurred—kicked out of the Marriott lobby bar; ejected from a cantina for vociferously alleging false advertising after the server had displayed unwillingness to serve Devin a beer the size of the prop promotional bottle they had standing out front; trying a second Mexican joint, and Devin behaving long enough to sneakily order Billy a giant party-sized margarita meant for four to six drinkers and then insisting that he chug it 'like a man.' Devin, talking smack to the hostess trying to calm him down, in the process knocking over said giant frozen drink. Being escorted out, and rushing over to accost a boatload of tourists passing by in the dark still waters of the canal and singling out an obese woman, he later 'splained, for having the temerity to snap a photo of the T. G. I. Friday's coming up around the bend nearest the Alamo, like the chain restaurant was the local tourist attraction of note. Offensive to those who had died in service of American freedom, et cetera.

Hustling away from the scene in the dark recesses of the walkway back to the hotel, they'd found a tucked-away cigar bar. No arrests, and no fights, at least. But Billy, now drunker than a skunk.

Devin, too. Smoking and grinning. Pleased beyond measure.

But for a time, concerned: after the giant margarita, Billy, entering a fugue state. Starting to speak with glassy-eyed distance about being interested in two things and two things only—pussy; and getting some—and how history would judge them poorly if they didn't get themselves fucked and fucked but-good by some of the local snatch. How he wanted to eat the motherfucking juice out of some quality pussy. Went on and on about it.

Yawn. Devin, saying, hell no, bro. "Just keep drinking."

But it didn't matter anyway, because Billy soon became so ridiculously potted that he forgot about pussy and instead turned weepy. Slobbering and crooning remember-when, holding onto Devin and calling him Ruck, Ruck, beloved Ruck. Hugging him hard, big old body heaving and sobbing and mewling sentimental nonsense until damn near breaking Devin's brittle spine.

A few more drinks at one last late night joint. Only some beers, no big whoop, but these had brought stomach upset and incoherence to Billy, a case of severe acute projectile dyspepsia, all of it Devin's bread and butter, maybe, but for an apparent lightweight like Steeple, devastating and final. Far as Devin was concerned, the only pussy in the house was Billy himself; the downfall, the end of the party.

For tonight.

"Almost back to the Ponderosa." Devin, steadying Billy on his size fourteen loafers in a darkened tunnel, wanted to take a piss, but too close to the entrance. "We is two drunk, sitting ducks out here for the po-po."

Billy, holding his stomach, belched and moaned. A towering oak of a sot standing ready to tumbled earthward at the first whack of Paul Bunyan's mighty axe, he said, "*Mumble-grumble*."

"I know; I get it. But we need to git ourselves moving now, Big Bill."

The two of them staggered down the walkway, now only a block or so from the hotel; passing under a bridge, above them Bowie Street. Devin, saying 'howdy' to a couple strolling arm in arm, and who cringed away from the stumblebums.

After a few lurching yards, Billy, stopped and pled: "Water—I've got to have cold water."

"We're all but there. Just get your card key out in case we get hassled."

Devin, kind and fatherly, voice lucid and sober, but no surprise: this was his balance time, his soul and spirit attuned in perfect harmony with the right frequency of the vibration of life, which for Devin meant being drunk enough to forget he existed as human.

"The key's not here." Billy, digging in a pocket of his stained khakis, wept over its loss.

"Hey." Devin, tender. "I'll talk our way in, if I got to."

"No. I let you down." He sobbed, echoing off the walkway and the water. "*I let everybody down*."

Oh, lord. Not this kind of drunk. Devin had finished with the crying phase of his disease years ago. Well. Hours ago, anyway.

"Look here, spud." Devin did a pat-down. He found the key card nestled behind Billy's overstuffed wallet full of twenties and fifties. Rich bonehead. Always was.

Regarding the sartorial mess that was his oldest and best-est bud, Devin, musing: "Here, tuck in that goddurn shirt. Wait. On second thought, keep it pulled out." Pitching his Marlboro butt into the canal; it perished with a tiny hiss. "Looks like you done pissed your drawers."

Filled with self-loathing, his sorrow turned bitter. "Would it surprise anyone at this point?"

Devin's memory lousy, no question, but he truly never recalled a Billy quite this wretched. Or—did he? "Settle down."

"I want to kill myself. You don't understand."

"Why the fuck you want to say something like that?" Rage. "You ain't got nothing wrong in your life."

"Leave me alone. Please."

"Hell of a thing to say." Devin, grumbling. "To your old pal."

Several mini-dramas followed in getting the card key to work, first in the reader to access the lobby of the hotel and then in the elevator—Billy, staying on concierge level, required the card as an extra step before being allowed to engage the button—and last in the room's door lock. The entire front of Billy's shirt was now stained with endless tears that dripped. He was a sight. Devin, thanking god it was late.

The blind-drunk leading the shitfaced, both at last tumbled into the chilled, manufactured air of Billy's double suite, immaculate as when the housekeeper had left it:

Billy, busy from the moment of his arrival.

Once in the room, Devin, tripping over the suitcase and dancing, nimble-footed, in a mad search for the mini-bar, which he found in the cabinet below the flatscreen TV. Out of the corner of his eye he saw Billy dive into the bathroom, tearing off his puke-stained shirt like Superman in the phone booth. Buttons, scattering with a crisp clatter on the tile floor.

Devin, cracking open a mini Chivas Regal and gurgling its contents, sky-hooked the empty across the room into the plastic waste can by the writing desk, nothing but net. Pulling out a Marker's Mark, a tiny version of the distinctive normal bottle with the red wax seal. Gulping down that sharp mercy. Another successful free throw.

Going whoop, whoop at the top of his lungs, a kind of dry wheeze; meanwhile Steeple, retching all epic-like into the toilet. Peeking in the bathroom Devin could see that Billy had the dry-heaves again. Ouch. After the bushes you'd've thought nothing left inside but the thin and bitter bile of his stomach lining, ravaging his throat.

Billy, collapsed beside the white commode, the cool of the tiles against his flushed, red skin likely a blessed event, long golden-boy hair spread out on the floor in a fan around his face: a corona. Devin, leaving him to sleep there.

Stretching out in the easy chair, sipping on a chilled mini of Jack Daniels and trying to get some shuteye before he'd need to start drinking again, Devin, remembering passing out in the college dorm to some movie, Billy sawing logs on the floor or on the couch, and him drunk but still unable to go to sleep; always the last one up, lonely in the night, haunted by old ghosts in his head.

Billy.

Devin.

Like old times. Fade out.

Chelsea, sitting on the edge of the unmade queen-size bed, holding her sides, rocking back and forth but not rockabye baby, and not from the ever-present cramps, instead from finding a purple elastic hair-tie, clenched in one angry fist—an unfamiliar hair-tie. Dusty, his buzz-cut not requiring any pulling back; Chelsea, using the black ones and the black ones only. So, whose, this purple stretchy unfamiliar rubber hair band?

With a frizzy, god-durned red hair tangled all around it?

Frizzier than hers had ever been, and by a damn sight?

The question moot, now. The answer, hers. This, constituting evidence.

As though her eyeballs hadn't already done the job.

They'd come here first, before they went to get their hammy burgers and Frenchie-fries and choco-shakes. They'd fucked. On the bed. She could smell it, still, in the air. And gone for a snack afterwards.

Dusty and his routines. Lord have mercy.

This? Much worse than the martial perfidy she'd committed with Buddy.

This? Their own bedroom.

Dusty and his little girlfriend, not even a grownup woman yet, *messing around* on this bed. The one upon which Chelsea herself lay night by night. On which she'd lain on her back for Dusty to impregnate her, bidding him repeatedly to try harder. After she'd missed her period a month after letting Buddy come inside her, bareback, she had to make sure it was Dusty's baby for sure. So, she'd made sure. Was sure.

Or rather, certain.

Not sure, but certain.

That sounded more final and formal.

Buddy Lawler didn't mean squat. Impulsive and stupid, her behavior, but not designed to rub Dusty's face in things. Not like this. Not like standing around at the goddurn Pecan Market for all to see. Whichever one had the made the baby in her, well, that was nobody's beeswax. Insider trading. Inside baseball. Whatever they called it.

A secret to be kept.

Forever.

That's what it was.

Chelsea stopped crying and got mad. Who was this Ashleigh?

She already knew: Another little slut, like all the others back in school.

*Kookie Colette*, the popular girls and boys had called her. A bony beanpole with freckles and big feet, gawky and awkward and semi-friendless, never dating anyone but Dusty; the cheerleaders and jock girls and even the bookworm girls, all so lovely and with boyfriends like them, smart and beautiful and talented. But, her? A dorky goofball, bony and long-legged, freckles. Her mother, calling her a mess and a wreck.

Chelsea, also remembering calling herself that. "I'm a mess," she would say to people. And so she was.

Cramping like mad for a day or two as it was, now with this fresh stress... Sick.

Bolting headlong into the bathroom. Heaving, but nothing coming up.

Realizing the hair tie still clutched in a fist. Screaming and throwing it into the toilet. Flushing, twice before it would go down.

Coming out of the bathroom, sipping a Dixie Cup of tap water that smelled of chlorine: needing to be sure. Mussed sheets meant nothing. She'd not made the bed up that morning, and rarely did so. Unlike Mama, who made sure all beds made up before the day got started. Even on Christmas morning.

Searching, sliding her hands around, she stumbled upon forensic evidence, jerking back from the find: a damp spot on the comforter, wadded down on the floor. Like it'd been kicked off, the way it did from Dusty's wiggling fishy-white legs during his and Creedence's three minutes of glorious marital congress that occurred every now and again.

Yuck. *Blech*.

She knew, knew it all. Could see them in her mind's eye as clearly as a movie up on the big screen: the wet-spot.

Incontrovertible.

Chelsea, revolted, smelled her fingers, the stench acrid, almost like piss— not his gunk, this, but hers!

*He gave her a girly-squirt.*

Dusty, making sure that Ashleigh got hers.

Never caring a bit about Chelsea getting hers.

Or Colette.

Or Creedence, either.

But Dusty, conscientious enough about this girl to give her an orgasm.

At the grim revelation Chelsea was not hurt beyond words, but beyond reason itself: Hollering through her raw throat and kicking up a mad dance of frenzied frustration, like she had in her room so often as a teenage girl bored out of her mind; cats and long freckled legs, all going every which way. Until she collapsed on the couch, hurting her back on one of his damn controllers lodged between the cushions.

It had been a long tough morning at work, but at least she had a caring boss.

"Colette, sugar—what on earth's the matter?"

She still couldn't get Uncle Hill Hampton to call her by her grown-up name. They wouldn't learn, the old people. Wouldn't change. "I'm fine."

"You look peaked." He leaned over the switchboard desk, had broken out the seersucker already, a lime green one that looked new out of the tailor's bag, like all his suits. That had been Daddy's thing, too. They had gone suit-shopping over in Columbia and Charlotte and Atlanta together more times than she could remember. Mama always scoffed and said, suit shopping? Golf? *Don't you believe it for a minute.*

Her boss and substitute-father seemed troubled by her puffy eyes, her obvious unconcealed distress, sniffling into a tissue as she did for about the four-hundredth time today. She'd yet to confront Dusty. Had spent all night locked in the bedroom feigning—or perhaps actually suffering—physical illness. Had sneaked out and overheard him again in the laundry, talking on his phone.

The hand-job voice. Again.

They must really like each other. All that phone talking.

Down-mouthed. "Nothing's wrong. Something in the air, maybe. A spring cold."

"That don't look like no cold to me. C'mon back into my office, now."

Hampton, a barrel-chested, prehistoric cave-bear of a towheaded Southern behemoth, boomed out the orders across the expanse of the showroom filled with gleaming automobiles awaiting inspection and subsequent purchase by starry-eyed motorists. "*LAWLER*—get your butt over here and look after the switchboard while I consult with Mrs. Wallis for a minute."

"I'm the top sales associate this month. This here's a misuse of my abilities."

"Well, do it for me as a favor, then." When Uncle Hill sounded so friendly, it was usually him at his most threatening. A weird kinda talent. "As a friend, Buddy-bo."

Buddy knew this deceptively collegial tone, a precursor to getting one's ass handed to them. "Anything you need, chief."

Chelsea, sticking her tongue out at him, a raspberry.

Buddy looked all disappointed. Mouthed, 'come on, now, girl.' Sad-eyed.

Oh, lord. Don't let Buddy get pitiful on her, too.

Too late. Having already told him not only to stop picking on her and calling her Susie Freckleface over the intercom, but now also how she didn't want to do it with him anymore and how it'd all been some weird bizarro-world anomaly destined for consignment to the memory hole of shameful acts never spoken of again, both ideas exacerbating deep-seated insecurities. Since, he'd been either needy or else a little petulant shit; Buddy and Dusty, she thought, ought to take their act over to open mic night at The Dixiana. Start a comedy duo. A franchise. The Wee Weenie Brothers.

In the office, Hampton motioned her over to one of the chairs. Chelsea knew she must look disheveled in her slacks, a pink V-neck blouse and modest heels, clothes wrinkled as though pulled from a hamper. Her makeup smeared, she sat ramrod straight, tearing her damp tissue into smaller and smaller pieces.

"Are you worried about that little baby a your'n in there? I bet that's all this is."

Chelsea leaned forward onto the edge of the desk. Hot tears dripped, but she pretended not to notice. "I reckon you're right."

Hampton's kind smile evaporated into a distressed grimace. He lurched around the desk and patted her on the back, gentle.

"Here, honey—you want a cold drink? Let me get us some cold drinks." His bellowing, elephantine voice likely carried all the way back into the clangorous body shop: "Cheryl-Ann—go to the lounge and get me two Co-colas. *Chop-chop, you hear me?*"

Chelsea, now in better control of herself. "Truth be told, I ain't sure Dusty loves me no more."

He scoffed like Mama. "Dusty not loving you? I can't imagine it. No sir—oh, heck. I'm just gonna say this, and I'm hoping you ain't gonna take it the wrong way."

"What?"

"I remember your Mama, now, when she was carrying you? Lord help me, but that woman, she was a handful. I don't know how your Daddy put up with it like he did."

"Is that right?" Creedence, lightening the tension. A little towel-snapping humor. That's how they rolled at the dealership. "Mama says the same about y'all, back in the day."

"We wa'n't nothing too bad, girl."

"Do tell." She missed her Daddy so much. Hearing Uncle Hill talk about him made Dwight Rucker real again.

"Playing cards upstairs at The Dixiana, or in the back room at Pike's Bait & Pawn. Taking Burnie Sykes's money, losing my own there and on the Redtails. Drank some beer. That's the worst we done." Casting his eyes down to the tips of his gleaming hand-tooled cowboy boots, his voice now came chastened. "But don't tell your Mama I told you all that. If she knew we used to gamble and get all drunk-up, she'd have a hissy fit."

"I don't think it matters too much now."

"She's your mama, ain't she?"

"True that." Chelsea, sucking her teeth. "She'd cut your behind, wouldn't she. Like she did Daddy's."

Hushed and serious as all get-out: "I don't doubt that she would."

Cheryl-Ann, a sort-of friend from way back, came in carrying two cans of cold soda pop, already opened and with bendy straws inserted. Her eyes, probing: "You all right?"

"Ain't no thang."

"You let me know if you need anything else," soft and maternal. Cheryl-Ann, not too close, but a longtime friend. "Buddy keeps asking what's going on in here, too."

"Tell Buddy to kiss my foot, please? Would you?"

"With extreme prejudice." Cheryl-Ann winked and exited.

"Now look here," Uncle Hill said, slapping his thighs, "anytime you want to talk to me—and I don't know why I got to keep telling you this—you get up from that durn desk and march right in. You hear me?"

She said she would.

"Tremendous." He pounded the desktop; Uncle Hill, a man accustomed to cutting the deal and moving on. "Feel better?"

"I might need to go home a little early again today. If that's okay."

"Are you kidding? Go on right now, matter of fact."

"But the switchboard—"

"Shut your mouth. We'll get old Buddy to sit and answer them phones. Hell," Hill Hampton shouted, a man in the grip of a theory. "I'll work the goddurn floor myself. You'll see us move some of these cars then, boy. Like in the old days."

She grinned. "I'll bet you could, Uncle Hill."

"Damn straight."

Hampton came back around the desk and helped her to her feet, chivalrous and deferential. How handsome he'd always seemed. Daddy's best friend. Her dead Daddy's rich old best friend. Her benefactor, her protector.

Putting her arms around him, head against shoulder. A single, silent heave, but no fresh tears. She held onto him.

He squeezed and patted and went *mm-hm*. "You're gonna be fine, my angel."

So powerful and strong.

A thought, racing through her whole body like electricity. Terrible but wonderful and naughty and exciting: Uncle Hill—in no way shape or form her real uncle—could probably fuck like a racehorse. As big as one too, she surmised.

She looked up into his eyes, not letting go. His arms, dropping. Chelsea, standing up on her tippy toes. Putting her lips onto his. A kiss.

A real one.

Her heart, pounding; her tongue, starting to probe—

His lips, frozen, but not breaking the kiss.

Until he *freaked the freak out*. Uncle Hill, pushing her away and staggering back, had turned the color of a brick.

"Colette, lord have *mercy*. What's wrong with you?"

"I didn't mean it like that. Just a kiss."

Breathless and flustered. "Get on home now. Pull yourself together. Lord have mercy on our souls, girl."

Outside the office, she felt faint. *Whoa*—that had happened. Big dummy. Impulsive. Why didn't she fuck everybody who worked at the dealership? Cheryl-Ann and Alejandro included, who was always looking at her feet, the little pervert?

Skittering out and across the showroom floor, she averted her eyes from the toad Buddy Lawler, sitting at her personal and private workstation.

"In a hurry?"

"Yes. Move so I can get my stuff."

"What happened in yonder?"

Chelsea, ignoring Buddy, gathered up her purse and the sweater she put on when the AC got too cold. But noting the car salesman—her erstwhile lover—clicking around on her computer with impunity, she pushed him back away from the monitor.

"Quit snooping at my history, you butthole."

"You been reading some weird ass stuff, girlfriend."

She whispered, *"Don't you dare call me that."*

"You telling me you think they wasn't no plane that hit the Pentagon?"

"Well, I don't know. And neither do you."

"Bullcrud. I think the government ought to keep an eye on your ass."

"It ain't like dirty pictures. Now, turn it off."

Lawler closed the browser. "You quit? Or get fired?"

"I don't feel good, if it's any of your business."

"See you tomorrow, Susie Q. Freckleface." He dropped his voice. "Unless you want to see me sooner. I got something so's I can keep going. You know." He showed her a pair of blue Viagra in his sweating palm.

Buddy, a lout, unchanged since school days. What had been she thinking? "They're melting."

"I got more." He threw them into her trash can, wiped his hand with one of her crying tissues. "I still want to talk to you some more, sweet girl."

"Not happening."

"Since last time, I ain't quit thinking about you for a minute."

She felt a flash of anger—at him, at herself. Hissing. "What I got from you I can get at home, and just as shitty. You little-dicked redneck nincompoop."

Chelsea, striding away and leaving him gape-mouthed. Mean as shit, and for no good reason than to hurt his feelings.

Confused about what'd happened with Buddy, with Uncle Hill, and at wit's end regarding Dusty, she thought, *if Dusty admits the truth and shows repentance, what then?*

*Do I even want him, now?*

Had she ever?

More complicated than she'd let herself believe. And perhaps not entirely a bad thing—except for the baby.

The baby.

The baby.

She drove home a cold statue, ready to see what her husband had to say for himself. Her life was going to change tonight. She didn't know how, yet. But it would. Her heart spoke the truth even when her head didn't. This time she would listen.

Composing herself by drinking a Zima, she hit 1 on the speed-dial and waited for Mama to pick up.

Eileen answered, weak-voiced. Her daughter found herself sobbing and sucking in breath, words half-formed and thoughts unclear. When finally managing to make sense—Dusty, a lying little cheat; her, having the proof—Eileen's response was only to scold for scaring her poor mother half to death.

"Don't do that to Mama, now. I thought someone had died."

"It feels that way."

"Nonsense. You come right over and we'll figure out what's going on."

"I can't. I got to wait for him to get home."

"To do what, exactly? Pray tell?"

She didn't know. Dusty, still keeping that old .22 rifle, loaded, in the closet. He might be greeted by her, shot dead in his unfaithful head and laid to rest on a bed of pine needles out front. Crying again. "I'm-a kill his ass, Mama."

"You need to cool your jets."

"He should—he should have his thing cut off. He should die."

"Colette," admonishing and shocked and disapproving. "Don't be so damn hateful. You act like he's done hurt somebody."

"I'm serious."

Last straw. Furious. "Have mercy. I swear."

Wait. Mama was right. Did Chelsea wish to go to prison over Dusty? After being in prison all this time already?

*A jailhouse of your own making, dearheart.*

Devin's voice, coming out of nowhere. A subtle whispery nagging hint of his nasty, mocking, drunken laugh.

A cosmic answer, now revealed, for her zeal at getting Devin home: Chelsea, persuading her brother to kill Dusty.

Yes—Devin, acting like he didn't want to live anyway. So what difference would going to jail make, or getting the gas chamber?

What difference between yes and no for him? Nothing to lose.

She got all tingly inside. Chicken-skin.

Once Devin got home, Creedence, his sweet little sister, telling him *this* was the real reason she needed him back. Getting him all drunk and mad, at last taking out all his pain and grief over Libby by ripping Dusty apart and dumping the leftovers into the Sugeree; Dusty, his bloated pieces-parts bobbing up in Lake Hollings downriver where the catfish would eat his fat, cheating ass.

Oh! Chelsea thought. It's like a plan in a movie.

And as for Devin, wait wait, she had that figured out: he didn't have to be a sacrifice; he'd get off scot free. They'd call it a fishing accident. Dusty, only an occasional fisherman, with evidence in the form of a tackle box and a jon boat sitting out back filled with last autumn's leaves and straw.

Oh, but Dusty, on the water, always frightened, always a clumsy oaf. How sad, poor Dusty. Drownded whilst fishing for his supper. Dusty, who could not swim.

*I tried to save him,* as she would coach Devin on what to say. *But he panicked and went under. Sorry.*

Ugly thoughts.

Too much TV.

"You must give Dusty a chance to explain."

"Mama—you don't know what this feels like."

Eileen, quiet for a heartbeat or three. A small cough: "No, I don't."

Chelsea slammed down the phone. A pang, a cramp. Resentment flooding in like nausea.

But the child, undeserving of such animas for having been put inside her by a stupid boy she'd allowed herself, ruinous, to believe her one and true great love, mainly because he'd been the only one standing there. Believed it enough to get tied down to, and talked down to, for eternity, by Dusty—or whichever doofus to whom the damn stupid baby belonged. Mercy on her soul.

"I got a bone to pick with you." Dusty at the kitchen table, waiting for Chelsea to serve him his supper, leaned back and looked smug. "Let's have us a talk."

Shaking inside, she hoped to betray no hint of her tension. It wasn't easy. "Gladly."

Chelsea, eyes red-rimmed and puffy and in blue and yellow Blockbuster Video T-shirt color-splattered with food stains, plaid pajama bottoms hanging low, her grungy awful oldest slippers, back hurting, head hurting, waddled into the kitchen holding kitty Arthur, who after a complete and total scouring and frustrating search of their entire eighteen hundred square-foot manufactured home she'd found cowering under the living room sofa.

"Why's my Arthur so scared? Why's he acting like this?"

"I've about had it with that durn cat of your'n."

"Too bad."

"All these cats."

"This I got to hear." Arthur jumped down and leaned against her freckled legs, purring—his little motor, the loudest and sweetest!—and beaming undying kitty love up to her. "What exactly about my precious little one seems to be troubling you?"

"I can't keep on with this mess."

"I keep this house neat enough."

"Work all day and come home to this mess every night. He keeps peeing outside the litter box."

"I keep that clean."

"Cats cats cats, that's all I hear out of your mouth lately. That, and the baby the baby the *baby*."

Here was the opening. "You've been working hard all day every day, have you?"

"Yes."

"At Mr. Vincent's?"

"Where else?" Eyes darting, lips pursed. "Why?"

"Three times, eh? Is that how many?"

"Three times what?"

"Days this week you've worked."

"Yeah," Dusty mumbled, frowning. "At least. Wait—it's Thursday. So, four."

"How many, again?"

His voice tight, strained, cheeks burning. "Four, like I said."

"Which one was the best one? The first time? Or maybe the one today? Does it keep getting better?"

"What the hell you talking about?" Panicking. Dusty couldn't act worth a durn. "Do what, now?"

She explained that she meant not his working days, rather the cat-messes. Arthur's accidents. What had happened; how many times. "The details."

"Exactly. That's what I'm talking about. The one today was the worst yet. It had splattered on the wallpaper and baseboard. He ain't pee-peeing, girl; he's spraying."

"I got him fixed. He is not 'spraying'."

"Told you a durn tomcat was gonna spray. That it would stink up the whole house."

"And so what do you suggest I do about Arthur and his dreadful peeing?"

Folding his fat arms. "I reckon he's got to go to the pound, is all."

Enough. This was getting ridiculous. "Shut up about my cat. I seen you. At the Pecan Market."

"When? I told you I would bring you hot dogs, but you didn't call back."

Sad. "I saw you with her."

"At the where, now? Who? What you talking, talking about. You better not—*you better not have found another cat*. At the Pecan Market."

"Wasn't no cat I found."

"Better not be."

She could barely breathe. Felt all floaty and weird, like that time she smoked dope with Billy Steeple and he almost screwed her, but didn't.

Chelsea, Colette, Creedence; rage, volcanic, that threatened to cook her guts like a forgotten crock-pot left on high for hours too long—a crust, forming around the rim of her heart. Hard inedible black char. What the devil served up on Thanksgiving. "We ain't talking about that kind of pussy no more. Boy."

Now Dusty looked scared. His eyes bulged. But his voice remained steady. She had to give him that. "That's exactly what we ain't talking about."

Chelsea's anger, now reborn as mad laughter. "Tell me you've just gone *crazy*. Anything to explain why you'd do this to me."

"It ain't nothing but a stupid cat. Ain't nothing stopping us from getting rid of it."

"Well, it's too late," shrieking. "What are you saying, motherfucker?"

"*The cat.* You better watch your mouth."

"You ain't heard nothing yet." Clutching her stomach. "I got this in here to think about now."

"That's what all this mess is. You having this baby." His words, frustrated and caught and on the verge of piteous tears. "I didn't know pregnant women got like you, which is half-crazy."

"'Me' having this baby? Who you think done it with me? The Easter bunny?"

"You let yourself get pregnant on purpose."

Incredulous. "What?"

"I seen you spitting out your pill one night. You didn't know that, did you?"

"*No I didn't.*" Chelsea howled and wept, high and dramatic the way she had learned from her mother when caught in the act. Leaning over the sink, hair hanging down into a pot with mac and cheese residue around the rim, wishing for her statement to be so but knowing otherwise, wishing and dreaming, now, she'd made any decision but the one that'd allowed Dusty Wallis, or Buddy Lawler, to impregnate her. The baby her mother'd pushed her to have. Pushed pushed pushed. In the last year, more than ever.

"You're just making stuff up, now," she sobbed. "To hurt me more."

Arthur, purring and dancing against her leg, reaching with his cute paw up to check on his crying kitty-mom.

"Sweet angel," she said.

The cat, sashaying back across the kitchen, bumped his gray striped head against Dusty's shin.

"*Get off me.*" Dusty kicked at Arthur with one dirty work shoe, the steel-toed ones Mr. Vincent said they had to wear as though they were out on a job site. The cat, flinching and sliding crazily across the slippery floor, paws desperate for purchase, his kitty face, terrified. No howl or sound. That was only in the movies. Real cats suffered their pain in silence. He bolted out of the room

Creedence, a war cry; she lunged across the kitchen at her husband, hurling invective and slapping and clawing at Dusty's fat, jiggling face. She beat him with her closed fists; a knuckle, landing hard and true and in collision with cheekbone. Putting her knee up into his groin. "Don't you ever do that again to my baby."

Dusty hollered, pinwheeled his arms, fell backwards across the table. He upended the lazy susan and the dinner plates, a rain of yellow spice tins that scattered and burst open.

Creedence grabbed at the warm tea kettle and flung it across the table at his face; he batted the ancient, heavy iron object away—it had been Big Ma-maw's—with a forearm then clutched in pain.

Not done: She grabbed at the big skillet hanging behind the stove, yanking at it so hard she pulled the whole bar off the wall, the other pots and pans tumbling onto the stovetop and the floor in a shower of sheetrock and paint chips, the big heavy wok landing on her left big toe and causing her to collapse and miss Dusty's roundhouse swing at her head that now went high. Creedence, collapsing and holding her foot, wailing in agony, calling him an SOB and every name in the book.

Down on one knee by the table, she looked up to see a caul of anger coloring Dusty's normally soft round features. The brown doe-eyes Eileen so loved were now hooded and red and glazed. Teeth bared, snot hanging out of his nose. He loomed over her, yanking the belt from his pants. Doubling the leather strap.

"Oh, please," scoffing and struggling up onto her knees. "You ain't got the balls."

Dusty, lightning fast, struck his wife across the face with the worn leather, stinging and hard.

Creedence, gasping and falling to the laminate kitchen floor, heart trip-hammering, hollered out for her mother. Thinking, *this can't be real, this can't be happening to me.*

As she cowered Dusty raged and cussed, beating her again, and again. He kicked at her. She rolled away. He whipped her across the back, three times, four times, one last brutal lash across her buttocks.

"Don't you never call me no son of a bitch again," he wept in anger, breathless, a demon. "*Don't you never do that.* You hear me?"

Creedence, on her back, cowering and whimpering and holding up her hands. "I won't. Please. I won't."

He broke down, sobbing. He dropped the belt and slithered out the back door, slamming it so hard it bounced back open.

"You shut that door," wheezing into her breath. "Before my kitties get out..."

Her stomach aching where he'd kicked her, she crawled over and pulled herself up by the doorknob, yanking the storm door shut and locking him out. Her back stinging, she got to her feet and went to find her scared babies to reassure them that they, and kitty-mom, were now safe.

A line had been crossed.

She wondered if she were lucky to be alive.

*Shit*—Dusty, not having the guts. What'd happened, an anomaly. Not forgivable, but not the Dusty she'd known. Chelsea had become another domestic violence statistic. Her mother would be horrified.

But for all the pain and disbelief, the upside? Now she had license to say and do as she pleased. Could get out of this thing with Dusty, which she already knew she wanted anyway. People thought she was a dummy, but it wasn't so.

Still scared and stinging from the belt—a more visceral sensation than she'd ever gotten from screwing the little squirt—already the pain seemed to empower her. She'd get photos of the wounds. Rock solid evidence. It couldn't have worked out better.

And then? Billy.

Billy, whom she wanted most.

Needed.

Old business, unfinished; the longest foreplay in history.

Still, she could wait a little longer. In due time. Dusty'd beaten her into the arms of a rich boy, as she'd show him.

She'd show Billy, too. Show him how sexy she could be—years of anticipation would erupt like a dam bursting.

Into the bedroom, fixing herself up best she could and putting essentials into a suitcase; next she assembled the cat-carriers in a neat row in the living room, an action causing the vet-phobic pets a new round of demonstrable, vocal distress. She called her mother, said she'd be home in ten minutes; how she had her proof of Dusty's infidelity, and that she'd be checking into the Rucker Inn for an indefinite stay.

Eileen, sounding breathless and thrilled and tantalized, bade her daughter to come with all good but safe speed; to be careful; that home was waiting. That her mother stood at the ready, dutiful and eager, to care for her only daughter. That she could not wait to hear what had happened this time.

# SEVENTEEN

—

## BILLY

Awakening face down on the scratchy hotel bedspread, Billy found himself dressed only in boxer-briefs and sporting his customary morning redwood, jutting and painful. Throat sore. Vision blurry. Sour, sticky tongue.

Sticky. Checking his hands, fingernails, torso—no blood, but crusts of yellow between a couple of fingers and around his mouth.

He gagged—if some accident had happened with Devin, Billy must have cleaned it up.

Jesus—booze. What a moron. No control at all. Who knew what had happened. All he could remember was puking.

Devin, helping him with the puking. Being kind and jovial all night.

Okay. Other than a nostalgic raging bar crawl, no perfidy.

Rolling over, he saw through a blurry eye his boy Devin in the lounger, the television screen glowing with shimmery LCD unreality. Devin, at first appearing to be asleep, but as Billy's own hungover, sleepyhead vision cleared he realized his old friend's eyes were slitted open. A finger on the remote, moving, changing the channel from Headline News to ESPN, skipping over in favor of QVC, then AMC, then BET, a rap video with bootylicious women gyrating behind a gold-toothed wordsmith flashing bling and hip-hop *bons mots* at the camera.

All had gone well last night. Libby's name hadn't come up once.

As far as he remembered.

His rigid porkhammer ebbed and withdrew against his thigh.

"You been up all this time?" Billy asked as a hoarse good-morning. "No way."

"Couldn't nod off." Pitiful, small and shaky. "Drunk everything but that shit Amaretto."

At the sight of all the empty mini bottles, his tender stomach pulsed with a sharp and unpleasant sense-memory. "You can't be serious."

Devin winced, sudden, and put the heel of a hand to his forehead. "S'cuse me." He went hobbling toward the bathroom—his leg, seeming to be asleep.

An epiphany felt through Billy's hangover: no more conference. No more paper. He didn't know what he was going to get up there and say, particularly in this wretched physical and mental shape.

And so: Ruck, flying back with him. Today.

After seeing his friend's pathological condition—from the sheer volume, end-stage alcoholic seemed about right—Billy, the triumphant, returning soldier, a would-be Captain Willard, but this time returning with the mad recalcitrant Colonel Kurtz, captured alive and ready for court-martial and debriefing and mental health counseling and a return to patriotism and sanity and fit for duty to command troops in the field. Once again morally fit to do so.

And to Creedence, Billy, a hero. She would be grateful beyond measure. Willing to do anything in return.

He hadn't stopped thinking about her and believed it would come to pass, but also feared the eventual moment of coitus; that he'd need more control than he'd ever mustered so as not to have an accident.

All of it, stoking his desire. Billy; hangover hornies. Soon as Ruck got out of the shitter, he'd need to pop in there and rub one out, a hard ugly dry mean jerk that'd leave him sore enough until he got some proper tail.

With the man's own sister, if it all worked out.

Fuck yeah. A plan.

As for Ruck, the more Billy recalled, his buddy had been fine last night. Profane, disgusting, an inebriate—brothers in arms, Billy thought with a modicum of chagrin—but not a threat. They hadn't discussed much of substance, only the raising of the wrist, Ruck's Olympian prowess in this regard, the missing years. Impressive, but sad.

Billy's hangover, intensifying.

While Devin made all manner of interesting sounds in the bathroom, Billy dialed up room service and tried to figure a way of sneaking out without running into anyone he knew. Fuck this conference and fuck the paper, which had been some lame-ass shit about reading THE BIG LEBOWSKI as political metaphor. He'd only wanted to get away from Melanie, obliterate some fresh pussy, maybe have an accident or two far away from home where it'd be easier to blow off steam, get evened out. Accidents, easier to deal with, theoretically, with a stranger. The ones he'd known, eh—those had always been the ickiest and stickiest. Besides, who knew how many bodies the opaque waters of the canal already concealed.

Billy, ravenous and determined to beat the hangover with food, ordered eggs, potatoes, a rasher of bacon, fruit assortment, breads and pastries, coffee, two kinds of juice, a pitcher of ice water with lemon. A lumberjack breakfast, a shower, a wank, and the two of them, BOOM, to the airport and home in three hours.

The situation: Ruck claimed to drink like this all the time. Not good. He needed to be in the hospital, if they could find one willing to detox a case like this far gone.

Hell—Billy, detoxing Devin himself if needed. Getting him smoking some grass and chilling out and living the high life instead of all this soul-sick, ruinous tippling. Billy: a savior machine. Forget killing Devin's ass. Forget Libby. Forget accidents. He had to help his buddy. The past was still the past, but it wasn't worth the trouble. Not with a problem like this on his hands. Right on. Time for Billy Steeple to do some good. The change-of-heart moment on the hero's journey. About time.

# EIGHTEEN

## —
## DEVIN

Squinting against the Texas morning sun, Devin eructed with such violence his sunglasses slipped down his nose. The whole-wheat toast he'd managed to choke down, not sitting too well. No sir. But he done it for Bill. He poked the aviators back into place with a finger he had trouble making work right. He looked forward to his impending beer-breakfast, and the beginning of the long march to steady hands.

Billy, trying all through breakfast to talk him into flying back, but Devin, not abandoning the Jetta, not after all this time. He'd get home when he got home. What bullcrud, he'd said. "Like I can't drive a day or two."

Billy, though appearing stricken by the idea, finally saying fuck it—they'd drive back together! Through Texas and onto the bayous of Louisiana, and Alabama and Georgia and finally home to Columbia, the jewel of the Carolinas, the Paris of the southland. A road movie. Devin and Billy, in a car for a couple of days. Somehow it fit; somehow it all made sense.

Devin, finally giving in and saying, WTF, hells yeah, beau. They could stop in New Orleans. Halfway home. A place to get a couple of drinks if there ever had been one.

"You ready, Freddie?" Billy, impatient, his bags piled at his feet, head on a swivel. "Where the heck is that valet?"

"Probably rifling the ashtray for roaches. Little greaser looked like a damn refugee from a Cheech & Chong skit."

The engine knock-knocking, a pall of diesel exhaust in its wake, the dented silver Jetta appeared from behind a huge round concrete column. The valet, getting out, held a troubled look.

In English halting and broken he cautioned, "Had a hard time to getting it to start, sir."

"What are you talking about."

"Better to have it checked. The ignition."

Billy waved it away. "As long as it's running right now, we'll be fine. I have comprehensive roadside assistance, platinum elite status. The kind of coverage where you get your dick sucked while they change the tire."

The valet laughed. "Very nice, sir."

"Well, hot damn. But there ain't a goddurn thing wrong with that car anyway." Devin, chucking his backpack in the back seat, threatened the bellman. "And be careful putting them bags in the trunk, ace. I got important shit stashed back in yonder."

Billy eyeballed the horizon. "Which way's east? Or rather, the freeway out of town, toward Houston?"

The valet shrugged and pointed in the direction of the rising sun hidden by skyscrapers. "The bell captain, he can forgive you directions."

"Forgive? What the hell you talking bout, Willis."

"Directions—the bell captain. He can give them."

"Ah."

"We'll figure it out, dude. Relax."

Devin, stretching and popping his neck and picking his nose, struggled to flick the bloody, stringy booger onto the sidewalk. Three, four good shakes to lose it.

Billy, groaning and gasping at the leg room, squeezed his bulky frame into the compact vehicle. "Jesus, I hope this seat goes farther back."

Devin, hopping into the back, said, "I'm right tired, Bill. Sure you don't mind driving?"

"I live for it, Ruck. Going to need tunes, though. What you got in here?"

Devin, not listening, digging around for a smoke.

Billy, squinting into the rearview. "Tunes?" asking with insistence. "Cassette and CD capability, I see. So we have that going for us."

Seventy-five degrees outside, yet Devin's body shook as though the temperature below freezing. He mumbled about a tape in the deck, the cassette all that he had, as well as filling up the cooler.

Billy, popping the eject tab, held the Maxell XL-IIs up to scrutiny, a heavy, hearty shell and quality of tape offering top drawer high-bias recording capability.

When he saw the label, Billy gasped, but tried to play it cool. "Maybe we'll save this one for later." He stashed the tape in the glovebox. "We have much time to fill."

Devin, not giving a shit and saying so. "Wind-whistling's enough entertainment for me, but we got to get some ice. I got beers in the trunk." Adding in a tremulous, weak voice. "And listen to that tape. Eventually."

"You sure?" Billy asking more about the latter request than the former.

Devin, managing a wry smile. "Sure as I am about anything."

He cracked the window and smoked and stuck his snout out like a dog.

Sitting back, drumming his fingers on the dirty knees of his jeans, holding Billy's reflection in the review, he started with more small talk. Before they got to the big talk, which was how they were going to handle the Libby and Dobbs situation back home—whether he knew it or not, Billy would be helping him straighten out those two cheating motherfuckers once and for all. "Nice day for it."

"Yes—here we are on the road."

"That's where we are, all right."

"Speaking of roads, you know which ones to take?"

"Roads." Billy, gunning the engine, merging into traffic, slipstreaming a big rig, a mocking laugh like a super-villain. "Oh, dear Ruck—don't you realize?"

"Do tell."

Sticking his arm out the window, waving at the trucker, getting the big bleating horn-blast in response, Billy yelled: "Where we're going, we won't *need* roads."

# PART TWO

# FACING COLLEGE STREET

## AUTUMN 1989

# NINETEEN

## —

## BILLY

O pening scene slug-line, screenplay format, which Billy struggled to master:

EXT. CAMPUS SPORTS ARENA — DAY

A Handsome Lad — BILLY STEEPLE - shorn of hair but long of wallet-chain, waits in A LONG line to buy concert tickets for his friends. He's handsome and tall and with big feet, and you know what that means.

The sun is bright. He's outside a columned cube, a basketball shrine: the revered, sacred Southeastern Redtails basketball venue of that championship season of '78. Blah blah blah.

But if what the screenwriting teacher Max de Lisle taught held true, here Billy would need a title card. No way to convey all that information from a master shot, however elaborate, of a punk kid waiting in line with a bunch of hippies.

That's right—today, the hallowed basketball ground defiled by the spirit of rock'n roll: these specimens queuing up were not the hoops faithful, instead a motley and unusual collection of music lovers—hippie kids standing alongside professors in suits, houndstooth mixed with tie dye, all awaiting the moment to buy Grateful Dead tickets, a ritual in itself ...

But one figure in particular knew that he, by design, cut a most unique and incongruous presence. Billy Steeple—skinny, shorn of hair, and with a pair of gold hoop earrings in each ear—rocked back and forth with hands jammed in the pockets of his greasy, ripped blue jeans. Scratching at his chest through a threadbare Dead Milkmen T-shirt, he waited to buy tickets to see the hippie band.

The punks, having discovered acid.

He didn't belong.

Consumed now more with movies than popular music, Billy, skipping from one Doc Marten to the other and imagining a smash-cut in from a high angle, a swirling Chapman crane shot zooming down upon him Him HIM, "I Am (Superman)" blasting out of his small headphones, a fuzzy-guitar powerpop soundtrack to a scene of a punk bass player buying tickets to seeing the most lumbering dinosaur act of them all. Weird and incongruous. A thing. But to what end? He knew not. Only that his intuition said, do it do it do it.

Not cool seeing the Dead, right-right, but so long as Billy maintained his chosen image—he hadn't listened to too much hardcore, but had a shelf of LPs and CDs to prove his bona fides—it didn't matter, and he didn't give a flying fuck, what people thought. He liked what he liked, consumed and absorbed it at his discretion and pleasure, and put out whatever image was necessary at the moment to be noticed, yet invisible. Paradox Man, his alter ego. If he ever ran into himself, the universe, collapsing and sucked down a swirling blue cosmic drain, like in Disney's 1980 critical and financial disaster THE BLACK HOLE.

Billy, boning up on movie trivia like the other cool kids in Mass Communications seemed to have at their fingertips. A filmmaker. Directing, and scriptwriting, of course, was Libby Meade's concentration. And having her had become the ultimate goal. This week, anyway. That's what he was to be, now—a filmmaker.

*It's been decided.*

Billy, pleading with his Meat Mallet bandmates to work up a punk version of the new favorite self-reflective alt rock anthem, but to a member they accused Billy of being out of phase with the edicts and ethos. Suggesting a stupid pop ditty by old men like REM, establishment richie-riches nearly ten years into their lame-ass mainstream superstar career? Bullshit ROLLING STONE cover boys with money sticking out of every hole? "Fuck those assholes. And their little ditties."

"We'd be subverting convention by adding covers like 'I Am (Superman).'" Billy had taken off his bass, made to leave yet another unsatisfying Choking Hazard practice. "So far all we've achieved is utter ossification. How far is scream-rock supposed to take us?"

Frontman Mucky Turnbull had replied, "What the fuck is ossification, brainiac?"

"We're turning to stone."

Mucky, calling bullshit. "If you ain't serious about the scene, then here's my advice: quit."

"Don't tempt me."

"You got stage presence, man. Give you that. We ain't gotta be best pals. Or see the same way. Don't quit."

Mucky, a local scream rock demigod and legend, made for a true frontman who had brought fans. With his prior band Horselick, he'd opened for names like GG Allin. Drew some water in the town. It got them bookings, but he lorded his exalted status over Billy. Worst of all, here had a point. "Appreciate the compliment."

"But, don't forget we can get any number of nimrods to thump their way through this slop. So like, shelve the REM dream, bro. Stuff it back in that ear of yours, the one that first heard it."

"You dumbshits. I was only fucking with you cats."

"That's more like it. Now get that axe back on and let's play."

"Aye, captain."

Mucky grabbed his microphone. His voice, raw and ragged, echoed in the rented storage unit where the band rehearsed, a row of them taken over by hardcore musicians and in constant conflict with the surrounding neighborhood regarding noise, garbage, excrement, called out the countdown right as Billy had plugged his bass back into the amp. *"Save the paradigm subverting for our breakout art-rock album one of these days, Steeple. For now, just scream."*

This whole ticket deal, a generous outlay of cash and time, but Billy, eager to please. What real friends had he had in his life? Few. None he could point to as people who could be fully trusted. Who knew the real Billy.

Not that the Carolina crowd knew the real-real him.

Billy, hoping the accidents at prep school in New Jersey lay behind in more ways than temporally. Also the ones in New Hampshire. And outside DC. The variety of schools through which he passed. The bothersome nature of his adolescence, an issue. But dealing, finally.

Best of all? Never caught.

Still.

Wouldn't be here, otherwise.

As for the kids he'd started hanging with, locals, Billy, feeling a particular kinship with Rucker. Ruck, the only other person he'd ever met who, like Billy, carried himself as unafraid of anything or anybody.

Rucker, morbid and mordant, a deep well. Always seemed to be looking around corners. Acting as though he knew some arcane secret. How his eyes seemed to mock his human brethren loping about in blithe ignorance; his, a bad-assed attitude. Billy's brand of no-bullshit, thoughtful spunk. A guy to have on your side in an argument.

Or help in dumping a body in the wee hours on some future night. Should such an awful and quite accidental task ever again need doing.

Billy had gone so far as to make Ruck the star of a documentary for his first video production class.

Billy asked his few subjects only the heaviest of questions; showing his fellow students how intellectual and sophisticated he would be one day as a professional filmmaker mattered to the budding artist. Ruck's answers, by far the most probing and serious:

Billy, off camera, as though one of the 60 MINUTES interlocutors, asked, "What is truth?"

Ruck, puffing a smoke. "That which is verifiable."

"And how do you verify truth?"

"Through what they call the empirical method."

"What does empiricism mean?"

Laughter, mocking: "Beau. You ain't got me here to define empiricism for you. What is it you're scratching around at?"

"What happens to our consciousness when we die?"

Ruck, blinking and thoughtful. Shifting in his chair, face going halfway out of frame. "I think we wink out of existence, and that all you knew and all you were is just gone. Poof."

"So you don't think there's such a thing as a spirit world? Or a soul."

"I think that's equally as likely."

But which one do you *believe*, Billy had pushed.

"If I had any real insight, I wouldn't be here to tell you about it."

Billy, screening the piece for the class with a hard cut to black following Devin's last response. Perfect.

The professor, a lesbian named Hedda Gamble who hadn't cottoned to Billy's charmer of an alpha male vibe, had proffered measured praise. "The smash-cut to black has become a familiar trope, but Mr. Steeple, that one gave me goose-pimples. Very nice work."

In that moment Ruck had made Billy a star, if only an ersatz *wunderkind* who'd yet to produce anything else of merit since then, now almost a year in the past. Billy owed his friend, big-time.

And yet, planning to snatch Rucker's girl from him.

Hell, it wasn't like he was planning to have an accident with her. This one Billy actually liked. As a person, and all. Libby.

After scoring decent side-stage tickets Billy loped back up the hill from the arena box office with a twinkling of anticipation. Grateful Dead—the name, always holding a portent of immense, dark mystery, one he couldn't yet define. No question, however, about the possibility of admittance—with the stack he'd secured, he, and all his friends, were inside.

Fuck the tickets—his lust, personified and magnified to exponential critical mass in a sudden, horrifying wave of bothersomeness by the appearance of one Libby Meade hurrying ahead of him. Distracted, face a mask of annoyance, she seemed a million miles away, hadn't noticed him.

Billy, heart leaping into his throat, butterflies in the gut, knew the moment had come: Clear kismet, running into her like this.

Undeniable.

Fate.

But: Ruck's girl.

His buddy.

Trying to remind himself.

Not trying too hard.

C'mon—fruit was there to be picked. Guys traded them back and forth sometimes. Billy, from money, from up north, way too evolved to suffer such base emotions as jealousy. Nor would Ruck, sophisticated beyond his years.

On another level, Billy needed to talk to Libby about schoolwork: to get the tickets he'd had to blow off the scriptwriting class they shared. But the assignment, far from his mind.

*She doesn't really love that guy she makes it with. Now does she.*

"I am Superman," Billy declared to a passing ROTC shavetail with a bulging book bag. "*And I know what's happening.*"

"Congratulations," the budding soldier said.

Billy walked on, contemplating the compliment, but said, hey: save it for the real victory. Hurrying, he strove to catch up to Libby. Soon, she'd never be far from him again.

# TWENTY

## DEVIN

Dobbs, knocking, insistent, calling from outside Devin's locked bedroom door:

"I've come to draw master's drapes and change out the chamber pots!"

Devin, groaning and sweating upon fetid, yellowed bedsheets; a hangover for the ages. A death rattle. Epic night down in the Old Market. Far as he could remember. Wednesday morning hangovers the worst, somehow.

No—Thursday. It had been Hump Day Happy Hour all night.

Terrible sleep, even with all the booze. Nightmares of the dead body in the country club pool, the one he'd found five years ago at his dumb summer job. Nothing new. Dreams, ever since.

His narrow, iron-framed bed offered little more than a glorified prisoner's cot; it creaked in tandem with his moans. "Leave me to finish cooking in here," he pleaded with his best pal from home in Edgewater County. "The sunlight is roasting me."

"Open up and I'll fan you, princess."

"Takes one to know one."

But Ruck wasn't in prison, only in college, pursuing the life of the higher mind; his dorm room, sterile and austere, a grungy room in need of painting and curiously denuded of the posters and personalizing totems typical of college men like him, as though Devin a transient prisoner awaiting sentencing to a more permanent holding cell.

A corner room, he had lucked into windows affording two views—of the huge oak tree with boards nailed onto it for roof access, a prime sunbathing spot, and also the grassy yard two stories below where in the evenings the roommates, four in all, would grill hamburgers and hot dogs, or barbecue chicken and marinated steaks on Sundays, as though they were all still living in Edgewater County and going to Roy Earl's granddaddy's cookouts, or at Devin's own grandparents, when they were still alive.

University Terrace, near-decrepit student housing, was part of a block-long complex of 1940s era, two-story buildings comprising sets of over-and-under flats in the middle, multi-level suites on each end, with a mirror structure across a concrete fire lane. All of it sloped down a steep hill toward Blossom Street. Cruddy or not, unlike normal dorm rooms the abodes more small apartments, with full kitchens and bathrooms, than dorm rooms; it made for an on-campus luxury only a hundred yards from the student union and five minutes to any class. Devin and Dobbs, lucky to get in together from year one: Hill Hampton and Dwight Rucker, both football donors, pulled strings.

Best friends, familiarity making the transition to college life an easy one; another Edgewater County native Roy E. Pettus, good old boy, sensitive English major, and fellow pothead to complement Dobbs; another roommate named Mike Cassidy, from Ohio, an outsider—okay guy, but when drunk a thug, a lout who got off on vandalizing property on their drunken walks back from the Old Market after last call. Mike, barely there most of the time.

Inspired, Roy had written a short story for one of his English classes called 'Eye of the Vandal' but: "Too close to real life," had been Devin's review.

"I tried to make the Cass Mickle character seem like it wasn't him."

"Not enough. Make him have blonde hair instead of brown. That way Mike won't realize."

Libby, an observer and good judge of people, had called Cassidy a minor character in the ongoing story of the dorm-suite, Fall 1989 semester. "I predict his role will be small."

"Like an extra in the background?"

"No—some minor detail in a subplot. Mike will have one decent scene where he says something that matters, but on which the overall story doesn't turn in any huge way. Again, a subplot," she'd explained, half serious.

"You and those movie classes."

"It'll pay off."

Devin, knowing he needed to spend more time with her. Happier getting drunk enough to pass out and forget all the weird crap that wouldn't leave him be. Dead black dudes in the pool. His mother and her rank disloyalty to the family. Buncha dumb shit. You had to drink to not think about it all.

"Are you going to let me in? Or not?"

"It's, what do you call it—under advisement."

Dobbs, refusing to relent, continued rattling the tarnished, ancient brass doorknob until it fell off onto the hardwood floor. The door creaked open to reveal him standing with judgmentally folded arms.

"And I advise you to pull yourself together."

"I already got a mother back home, chief."

Slight and stooped, a shock of unruly blonde curls like a small helmet atop his head, Dobbs; the one time he and Devin let their hair grow all summer, before senior year at James F. Byrnes, he ended up looking like Harpo Marx; the high school back home, known colloquially as Byrnes Hell, actually a top high school in the state, serving central Edgewater County to include Tillman Falls, Chilton, Red Mound, Parson's Hollow. Strong school for such a rural county.

Dobbs, his voice, soft, slight and high-pitched, a manner gentle but sarcastic. His eyes, drooping—by now, he and Roy Earl had had pre-class AM bong hits.

"Enough with the repartee. I bring news."

"So dish, Cronkite."

"You may not have realized it, but in your convalescence, the outside world has continued to endure."

"Do tell."

"It's almost lunchtime."

So it was. "Explains the light and the heat."

"More to the point: that's three classes missed."

Devin stretched. The spare tire around his midsection rumbled, his hangover turning to hungries. "Don't sweat it."

Dobbs, giggling. "Look, y'all—it jiggles like a great big bowlful of jelly."

"Fuck your mother."

Clapping his hands together. "What'd you bring me this year, Santa? A twelve-pack? A beer-bong?"

"Why don't you eat the fucking dingleberries out of my ass?"

"With sugar and cream? Yay, Santa, *yay*!"

Devin's cheeks, flaming; and, yes, feeling self-conscious about burgeoning weight, but the point of being in shape was, what? His end was nigh.

Yeah, no; the dead guy in the pool had told him. Not with words. You couldn't explain it.

But, still, Devin certain: Aches and pains. Award-winning benders, shots of straight liquor chased by cases of cheap beer, PJ parties, drinking games, a universe of possibility when matters turning to those of incipient mortality. Taking chances. Hopping the slow moving freight cutting through the southern end of campus, riding until crossing the Old Market trestle. Jumping off, drunk, stumbling and rolling down the steep incline of the trestle hill. Only last year, a kid got killed pulling that stunt. Legs cut off.

Bled out there waiting for help. REMEMBER JEREMY, screaming caution-yellow billboards read. DON'T HOP THE TRAINS.

"Are you planning to go to classes again anytime soon?"

"Will you get out of here?"

"But seriously, son—you have got to do better. With Libby, too."

Libby had been distant lately. Asking what she had to do with anything.

"If you care about her, you'll ask her yourself."

Devin pulled on a gray Redtails gym shirt that stunk of armpit and beer. "What'd she say?"

Dobbs, an air of supercilious disdain. "You're as dense as an ever-loving block of cement. Did the doctor squeeze the forceps too tight when you was birthed from your Mama's belly?" He flopped down on the bed, skinny legs in the air as though in the stirrups. "Push, Mrs. Rucker."

"I may puke."

He made a fart-sound. "There he is. Oh, my—this may be the fattest baby we've ever seen here at Edgewater County General Hospital."

"I get it; I get it. I'll take care of Libby. I'll hit the gym. And the books."

"Be serious, if you're serious."

"What's the rumpus?"

"I hate to see her treated like an afterthought."

"Who is doing that to her?"

Dobbs, punching Devin in the arm. "She deserves better."

"Leave Libby to me."

"Do you still care about her?"

Somehow neither surprised nor caught off guard. Knowing now that Dobbs a true surrogate. Asking Libby's question for her. Fraught with portent, but not unexpected.

Devin, the same answer he'd probably offer his girl: "C'mon. What do you think?"

"Never answer a question with another question, Ruck—you might as well be saying 'no'."

"When'd you get so wise?"

"Since you decided to get your ears flushed."

"You wish."

Dobbs, leaving with a sharp glance, slammed the door shut behind him.

Serious shit. Devin, on notice.

But a part of him already found acceptance. Devin's clock, ticking fast. A concept already having taken hold, now reinforced. *That's what Libby deserves. Someone with a future. Someone alive.*

Libby: coming alive at Southeastern and out from under the yoke of home life—taking to her scriptwriting, fluorescing into young adulthood as a mature and self confident survivor of a sometimes unsettled home life, a drinker for a father, a mousy, nervous mother, cowed, fearful, and kids suffering unpredictable verbal and mental abuse. But Libby, strong, seemingly unscarred by grim experiences of her youth, more implied to Devin than depicted in detail. Libby, healthy and smart, telling Devin, "it's all material, my family's foolishness. That's all it is. Fodder for fiction."

"Fodder." Devin, with a nod. Understanding. *Been there.*

"Yes. Nothing more."

Libby, already working on the final assignment in her screenwriting class, one not due for two months, a twenty-five to thirty page five-scene epic. Devin, sitting in her room one night, watched her with a small stack of three by five note cards: a project to be later expanded, she hoped, into a first feature length script, a special section taught by Max de Lisle for upper level Mass Comm students. FACING COLLEGE STREET, the title of the piece; plot, the trials and tribulations of a young woman from a dysfunctional home who, after going off together with her longtime boyfriend to a fictionalized 'Mid Carolina State,' enjoys a crisis of faith—but only after her lover begins to take their relationship for granted.

Where she got this stuff, he had no idea.

Devin, that afternoon, telling her how much he liked her story idea, took Libby off-campus for dinner and a movie. Holding her hand. His girl, back to beaming and happy.

Weeks ago, now. Back to feeling isolated, though by his own volition. For whatever reason. Entire days would go by with only a phone call.

Devin and Libby.

An acknowledgement: drifting apart. It was fine. She would be better off without him.

Devin, soaping his body in the shower, the steaming water blasting against his forehead; trying to beat back the headache now getting a foothold. These lasted until first of the day—beer, not class.

A vague recollection of gripping the sheets as the spins overtook him, as though bed and room and building all twirling counter to one another—and perhaps to the earth itself—in a nauseating maelstrom of severe intoxication. Hot water, pores opening, cleansing.

After getting out he felt better, almost like a normal human being. Fleeting—an unusual sensation.

Remembering the floating man. That crazy morning. Devin's first dead body.

Pedaling his ten-speed through the woods cut-through, a sandy path meandering through rows of skinny loblolly pines, a shortcut from the highway to the eighteenth green, the country club beyond; the Ruckers, longtime members, his father a businessperson of respect and relative good fortune, a man of means. Chilton, while still unincorporated, had become the most outlying of the bedroom communities serving Columbia down past the lake country. That's how Devin's daddy described where they lived. Devin told people Tillman Falls instead, when they asked. Nobody had heard of Chilton, but Tillman Falls had famous steeplechase events and history going back to the revolutionary war. Chilton, whatever it was, had an Piggly Wiggly, two gas stations, a McDonald's and a flashing light.

Devin's daddy, a Nationwide man, was lifelong best friends with the guy who'd become the millionaire car dealer in the county, or rather, whose daddy had back in the fifties and sixties. They ran in town with others like them, men and women who lolled around the country club and together in other fraternal organizations. This particular club counted upon its rolls member of both the bourgeois Old South town of Tillman Falls as well as the exurban areas like unincorporated Chilton, where the Ruckers lived in the real nice Pine Haven subdivision right off the interstate, though certain characteristics like race and social standing played a part in determining membership eligibility.

A go-getter, an early riser like dad, an insurance man who owned his own firm and now had locations in three towns, nearby Union and Chester a little farther—*futha*, as Dwight Rucker would say—to the west; a work ethic, instilled. Believing his father's wisdom about idle hands and evil hearts, seeing with his own eyes that the man worked hard, lived to work, long hours.

Peddling with strength and purpose along the best part of the trail, Devin, sweating already despite the hour. He had skirted Jensen's Pond to pass through a copse of hardwoods and down an ancient creek bed dried hard and flat by years of South Carolina sun, wiping his forehead and wishing he had put on the terrycloth sweatband stuffed down into a new, neoprene waterproof book-bag slung and hung on his back. Inside, his lunch, a change of clothes, a paperback or two. Always.

Devin; the books. More than people.

He couldn't account for it. Didn't fit there in Edgewater County. Felt hatched instead of born'd.

He had approached the golf shack and the pool house, the club patio, outdoor bar, the upstairs dining deck; his domain as lifeguard (Boy Scout certified), cabana boy and sometimes busboy for the restaurant. His first job-

job. It paid well. Again—Old Money, and some new, among the swells in Edgewater County. Enough to demand a top-flight club, anyway.

Devin, frowning at an anomaly—he froze and felt a chill: the heavy wrought iron pool gate, gaping and open. Unusual, unless an earlier bird than he already at the club. "You don't never leave that gate open, or even unlocked, at the end the day," as he had been trained by Mr. Raymond. "It's an in-surance liability for the club."

"Oh, I understand, sir. My dad's Mr. Rucker."

"I know who he is, son. Why you think you got this job?" Mr. Raymond, burned brown and wrinkled from a lifetime of toil in the sun, looked seventy from smoking but was only in his 50s. He cut through the guff, as he put it. Told it like it was. Devin could get down with it, so long as it jibed with his worldview.

The sun, cresting the top of the tree line, a reflective bright twinkling streaking across his vision. A glass vessel—a liquor bottle—lay label-down in the grass by the hard concrete of the pathway leading to the narrow gate.

He turned it over with the toe of his sneaker stained amber by the clay around the pond. Henry McKenna, a bourbon. All but consumed. A trickle in the bottle. Devin had found out what liquor was like while away at Scout camp last summer. He had thrown up, but also liked the way it made him feel.

A lot.

Better than this:

Devin, heart flopping in his chest, glancing around, pushed the heavy iron gate all the way open. Creeping toward the pool, head on a swivel, he saw a man in the water.

"Hello?" all too soft. "Hey, who is that?"

Not a swimmer. Devin, seeing a dark shadow floating down in the shimmering deep end—a body.

A real body, arms outstretched.

A man.

Floating.

A pink cloud.

Blood.

Hurrying over, stiff-legged and uncertain, Devin's Scout training kicked in. He leapt into the water, thrashing over to the man. Devin, gasping a lungful of air and diving under.

Devin, grabbing at the rough sleeve of a black man with dark skin, work clothes, a billion tiny bubbles clinging to his body. Hanging upside down, turning now in the turbulence caused by Devin's presence.

Devin, panicking, ridiculous, his lungs exploding, screamed under the water: *Are you all right?*

The man, eyes lidded but open, turned to look. His wrinkly, swollen fingers brushed against Devin's stomach. A flash of morning sunlight from a silver necklace floating out from around his neck. His other calloused, dead fingers tickling against Devin's leg. All in an instant.

A gurgling sound, air escaping from the dead lungs.

A voice from beyond: *HUH*.

Devin kicked back and away, catapulting himself up out of the pool onto the night-cooled concrete of the decking. Hacking and gasping and spitting out chlorinated pool water, his chest tight, throat ragged, he cried out HELP HELP HELP but it was choked, aggrieved. He puked—pool water, milk, soggy breakfast cereal.

"Devin Rucker—is this yours?" Mr. Raymond, standing in the gate with the McKenna, looked horrorstruck. "Boy, what ails you?"

He couldn't get the words out, like a recurring dream of smothering under a great amorphous dark weight—of trying to yell for help, but having no wind. Devin, croaking: "*In the pool.*"

"I'll be shit." The old man, noticing the body. "Son, is he drownded? I'll be damned—is he drownded?"

"I think so."

"Oh, lord."

Mr. Raymond grabbed the pool net and made to fish the corpse over toward the shallow end.

Devin, stammering and sobbing all sudden, like a kid. "I tried to help him."

Raymond, a startled look—a realization. Withdrawing the long pole back away from the body, left there to float. The oldtimer, squinting and sweeping his gaze around the pool area. "Son, don't touch another thing out here. Come on, we got to call the sheriff's department."

Devin couldn't stop staring at the body. "I think he was still alive when I jumped in."

"Don't look at that no more." They hustled over to the golf shack, neither of them looking back.

A whirlwind of events had followed—the police, the ambulance, his father, a rubbery black shiny bag with a heavy shape inside, the reporter from the EDGEWATER ADVOCATE, begging and pleading but who was not allowed to talk to Devin; the worst was having to explain that the puke had been his. "Are you certain," the coroner had asked twice in a row. "Are you certain that's your vomit?"

He had felt three years old. "I ate Frosted Flakes."

Devin, closing his eyes in the shower, why was he thinking about it all again. Seeing the flash of the light from the necklace and the empty eyes, dead like that of a shark, piercing him. Seeing through Devin. The dead man's voice, a last gasp: trying to tell him a secret. The sorriest part for Devin was that it seemed to have worked.

Considering this moment as *before*. For both the floating man, as well as himself.

The questions. Relentless.

Endings—what they meant.

How they would feel.

Worst? *When* they would come.

When.

Devin before; Devin, ever after. Did everyone feel this way? The rest of them seemed untroubled. As was Devin Rucker, who figured, among all his hard partying friends, that the way to deal with a wicked hangover on a class day was to have a cold beer with breakfast. Nothing crazy. A Natural Light. After all, Devin wasn't a drunk. He liked to party. Sue him.

# TWENTY-ONE

## — CREEDENCE

Chelsea Colette Rucker: rebellious, fifteen, a recent burning desire to be called by her first given name rather than middle, yet still Colette to every dumbbell who didn't already think of her as Creedence.

Colette, a dumb little girl's name. Creedence, that one's special, her Daddy's name for her. *Chelsea*, however, needing a name to call her own.

They all thought it silly. If that's what they thought of her, well: silly's what she would be.

Her mother, of course, number one on the top forty of having no truck with her name-changing. Calling it foolishness. Telling her she would slap her smart mouth if she didn't shut up about it. Her Mama, at the stove stirring a pot of greens that'd stunk up the whole house, working her lips, soundless, furious, a coiled jungled cat of maternal rage.

Composing herself. A flinty, precise statement. "The name that I chose is your name. That's the end of it."

"What about what I want?"

"That's not the way the world works, young lady."

Tonight's kitchen contretemps, with pots bubbling and biscuits baking, was not truly about names, rather a big brother's offer of a wild time at an upcoming concert by a famous rock band with a scary name.

"But Devin said I could go if I wanted. He would look out for me."

"No."

"He'd get me a ticket and the whole dang bit."

"I said to forget it."

"But Mama—it's the Grateful Dead."

"You think I'm going to let you run around Columbia? At your age? With the likes of Coy Wando out there?" Eileen, during and since the time of the Wando murders, more protective than ever.

How stupid old people could be, though. How fearful. Granted that Wando had killed three Edgewater County girls and taken credit for about a hundred more, all up and down the eastern seaboard, so he was definitely a monster. But still: "P'shaw. They caught him and locked him up last year."

Ignoring her facts. "And I remember those San Francisco hooligans from before you were born. Not from their terrible music, mind you, but *from the news stories about their various drug arrests.*"

"But, Devin said—oh, fudge."

Vicious and low, like a mob boss Chelsea'd seen in a movie on TV referring to an untrustworthy henchman: "When it comes to my little girl, I don't give a good-god-durn what your brother says. Or what he thinks." Brandishing a slotted spoon, collard juice dripping on the tiled kitchen floor. "Is this understood?"

Chelsea, the Dead show, how unbelievably cool and strange and different the night was sure to be. Burning for the chance. Begging. "But Mama— everybody's going."

"What about Dusty? You haven't said a word about what he thinks. He's not invited?"

Not giving a thought toward Dusty also going. Not wanting him there. "No. I want to do this with my brother."

"But, poor Dusty."

"Mama, he likes *country* music. Don't you understand nothing?"

Sounding hurt. "Well. I guess I don't, then."

Chelsea, beyond curious about her brother and his friends, about the person she'd once known as a happy-go-lucky sibling, and what he'd become. Devin, changing so much through the years, starting back when she'd been twelve. It was after he found that black man in the pool. She had figured it out, one day. She didn't know why. It all sounded like her Boy Scout brother had tried to save the man, at least according to the story in the EDGEWATER ADVOCATE about it.

Devin was sneaking liquor after that. He never did it before. A little sister notices these things.

Remembering ugly scenes: Once, she and her parents coming home from the steak house to find him in his room drunk as a skunk. He was playing his old Atari game console from years earlier, a bottle of Henry McKenna procured from god knows sitting at his elbow half-empty—"Brazen, just brazen," her Mama kept saying. "Henry McKenna, Henry McKenna," she wailed, as though the distiller, a long-dead brand rather than a living human, had personally shamed the family.

Rather than being contrite or ashamed, however, Devin had staggered around, waving his arms and slurring his words; *so* sarcastic and hateful, pointing his finger and cursing at his own mother. He tried to explain himself, but it all came out like gobbledegook. Creedence, remembering the *smack* of Eileen striking Devin openhanded across the face, and her poor father Dwight, standing by, horrified, helpless.

But what happened next had been so much worse: Devin, pimp-slapping Eileen right back. Clean across the face, boo-yow. How it'd all slowed down like in a movie—Mama falling backward, staggering down the hall boohooing her way into the master suite at the other end of the house. How Chelsea's heart dropped into her stomach like on the rolly-coaster at the State Fair.

He had meanness in him. It was scary. Where'd it come from? Devin, always sweet to her, though. Protective. Like a big brother should be.

As for hanging out with Devin on campus, precedent had been set:

"You let me go that one other time."

"That wasn't for no damn rock and roll concert. That was for a cookout during the goddurn afternoon."

Enough whining the previous semester had resulted in her riding over with Libby to the building where the boys all lived, when Devin and Dobbs and their friend Roy Earl held a cookout in the tiny yard next to the building, a gathering like folks held every Sunday back home in Edgewater County, but with college students: Steaks and baked potatoes and iced tea, cold cans of beer, the girls drinking wine coolers.

Libby had let her have a couple of Seagram's white wine coolers, sour-sweet. Her stomach had been cold, then warm. It had been so wild. Drunk at college. Couldn't wait to do more of it.

And then, Billy Steeple. Like nobody she ever saw. No punk rock kids in Edgewater County, not at her school. She hadn't known what to make of him, except that she could see how handsome. How sophisticated he spoke —he wasn't from no podunk Edgewater County. Roy Earl Pettus, who followed her around the whole time, was a sweet but round-faced doofus too much like Dusty Wallis.

Too much like back home.

Chelsea pushed her chair back from the kitchen breakfast table with a scrape. Letting loose, she jabbered in describing her need for adventure and experience; in hysterical detail how bored she was out here in the country; in shrieking injustice how Devin being away made her feel as though she were constantly missing out.

Her Mama, fed up, slapped her. Creedence quieted. But she didn't cry. She had been slapped a hundred times in her life.

"I'm getting tired of you acting like you can't stand to be here where your little smart-butt mouth belongs." Grumbling about Devin running wild, how it'd not happen again, not with her babygirl. "No more trips to Columbia. And that damn university. It's already took one from me."

"I can't wait to get out of this house for good."

Back to the mob boss voice. "Hush your damn mouth. Before I hush it for you."

Now came childish tears of disappointment, a sudden downpour, feeling stupid and diminished here in the grand two-story all brick with a huge island and the high ceiling of the great room, a dream house her Daddy had had built for Mama and them two years before here on the best cul-de-sac in Pine Haven, the nicest subdivision this side of the Sugeree River Plant and the Tillman Falls/Chilton exit off the interstate. The county had a good many new subdivisions going, and so being called best said something, as her mother liked to point out.

Nobody at school treated her like a girl who had money, though. Too goofy, she guessed, or like Devin, way smarter than them. And they knew it.

She wished. She didn't feel smart. No faking those report card Cs.

"I can't wait get out of here and away from you," in her own most dreadful cadence. "I hate this place."

"Stop trying to sound like Joan Crawford. Go fold that laundry I told you to do an hour ago."

"No."

Mama ran out of steam. Muttering, unable to form a cogent verbalized response, she wiped her hands on a kitchen rag hanging on a butcher-block island stained by legions of steaks tenderized upon it. "Please, honey. Mama's getting one of her headaches from all this."

Chelsea, feeling half the time anymore as though she could *scream*, and if everyone wasn't careful, someday she might. Everyone including Dusty, hell-bent these days on putting it all the way in. Chelsea, thinking herself all-but ready to do so.

But, on the other hand? Not yet. A tingling at the back of her neck. Lessons taught about the putting inside of peterpiper being an activity only for the betrothed. And in love.

*Don't let it be Dusty. He's like your cousin, somehow.* This voice was the one always right. But she didn't listen. Not enough.

Chelsea's resolve, hardening like the spike in Dusty's shorts whenever they made out. What Eileen and Dwight Rucker would and wouldn't allow, soon a moot point. Go to the Dead concert or be damned, yessir. Sneaking out, if she had to.

A close-up on Chelsea's scheming eyes; cue the dramatic music before the commercial break! Lord, but Mama loved them stories all day long. That TV never went off for a blessed minute.

Chelsea, smiling a big Cheshire grin. Saccharine, hugging her mother tight: "Mama, I'm sorry. I'll forget about that silly concert just like you want me to do."

Eileen's puckered grimace melted into a smile, not so much in affection, but in triumph. "That's better, sweetheart. Now, let me get this damn supper on before your Daddy gets home. Not another word about this at the table. Is that understand? He'll be too tired at supper for one of your little to-do's."

"'Our' little to-do's? Ain't that what you mean?"

"Hush."

Singsong, the fluttering of eyelashes. "I'll be a good girl."

"You'd better be. That's all I know."

The next day, Dusty Wallis, in theory not allowed home alone with Chelsea in the afternoons, lay back and sighed. Leaving almost as soon as he'd quite literally come with his patented, wide-eyed yelp of pleasure, *splurt splurt* all over her bedspread, his entire body convulsing as though jabbed with an electric cattle-prod; this time, he touching her down there for about twenty seconds. Not interested in a blamed thing except his own squirty-squirt. That turd.

Powerful, in a way. What she could do with a little tickling and tugging. And yet he'd rubbed and poked her till she was all-but sore, with no equivalent result.

In any case, the horse out of the barn for Dusty, now.

For both of them.

Maybe, thinking, she should let him put himself inside her. Maybe owing him that honor. Poor Dusty.

Not without a rubber, though. He kept hinting riding his bike all the way out to the Food Chief by the interstate. They had condoms in the bathroom there, he reported.

Chelsea, aghast at the thought of something from a nasty filling station bathroom on Dusty's winkydink and then up inside her. "They have them there for you to just take? In a basket?"

Dusty, grinning and rubbing his hands all up and down, rough and clumsy. "They're in a machine for a quarter," *cort-der*. "Like the ones at the Piggly Wiggly."

"At the Piggly Wiggly? *Where?*"

"Not rubbers. The gum and bouncy-ball machines."

Oh, she said, I get it. But panicking. "Daddy'll have a fit if he catches us here alone."

"Please," he had pled showing her the pup tent in his pants, the damp spot at the peak. When they made out, he sometimes would end up with a huge wet patch.

A few minutes later, the front door was hitting Dusty on the ass with a thump as he bolted out before Dwight's arrival home from the Union office. Chelsea, left to get a damp washcloth to wipe up the glob of Dusty's semen on her arm and bedspread. He hadn't even wanted to kiss anymore once she started her tickling.

Her princess phone ring-a-linged, vibrating an old glass ashtray of Mamas where Chelsea kept her rings and other jewelry. Delighted to hear her dearest Devin, calling back already.

Her mood brightened further at his report: that he'd done as she asked and talked an initially reticent Roy Earl into coming for her. "For some dumb reason, he's agreed to spirit your little frecklefaced butt over to the Dead show."

"But—I'd rather you came and got me."

"You're breaking my heart. It'll be fine."

"That's easy for you to say."

"He likes you. He'll take care of you."

"Wouldn't you take care of me?"

"Not as good as somebody who actually liked you."

"Kiss my foot."

"Serious question."

That usually meant Devin was funning with her, and she warned him he better not be. "Go ahead."

"Anything else I can arrange about your life for you?"

She said no, thanked her brother with deep and abiding sincerity. Chelsea, elated, slammed down the phone and spun about her room, long legs and feet and frizzy hair going every which way. She shrieked, long, raw, her throated shredded. Mama's cats went running every which way.

Suddenly self conscious, she froze. Collected herself. A grown woman going over to party with college boys in Columbia didn't hurl herself around her bedroom like that demon girl in THE EXORCIST.

Still, she twirled one last time and danced her way downstairs in time to see Mama arriving home and closing the back door and calling for help putting away all the groceries. Pork chop night. They had a routine. "You'll understand men and their routines later, sweetheart," her mother always said.

Supper: Mama had not liked the looks of the chops, so it turned into fried chicken with mashed potatoes and greasy, yeasty dinner rolls from the deli at the big new Publix fixing to run the Piggly Wiggly out of business, or so her Daddy kept saying. Their take-out deli was excellent, however, and besides: Mama had had too much to do with the ELMS, the civic organization in town, and this and that and the other duties she also had on her plate, to do justice to pork chop night. Not this week.

If this pace of seeing to everyone's needs here and downtown at the Edgewater Ladies Munificence Society lodge kept on, Eileen threatened, she was going to have to hire help to cook and clean—a Mexican, she specified, or a young woman from another 'latin' country as she put it, not one of those light-fingered colored girls prone to pocketing spoons and heirlooms out of spite if nothing more, or so the family legend went about a previous hire of housekeeping help; or else they'd all be eating takeout and TV dinners to the end of days. Back like when they'd started out, she would say in at this point in the speech, "when Dwight hadn't yet been worth a plug-nickel, and we thought open-faced sandwiches smeared with beef, gravy and potatoes out of a Dinty Moore can made for a king's feast."

Next, Lord, how the children had come; and no struggle that'd come before come compare, nothing had been the same. Not for her. Not for any of them. "Mama's little angels," she'd say, but her tone sounded more like some work obligation than her dearest life connection.

The Mama monologue. Chelsea felt like she had heard it all, through countless versions and iterations. A work in progress, ever more baroque in its recitation of sufferings, as her gay English teacher would say it. For queers to be so awful, he was the nicest teacher they had at that school.

Surely grownup life wasn't supposed to be all opposites and lies. With all the complaints. It felt like Mama had so much resistance inside her that it would one day snap like when that plane crashed at Edgewater County Airfield and broke the power lines.

Chelsea and her father, now home and at his table-place with iced tea in hand, ignored Eileen's prattle from inside the kitchen. They talked between themselves and paid attention only when Eileen came in through the swinging door, yap yap yapping the way she did, about how the food, such as it was, would be coming out as soon as she microwaved the chicken. If not going on and on about what interested her, instead gossiping through the meal on the phone with Chelsea's aunt or one of the ELMS women, or in years past, Chelsea's grandmother, Big Ma-Maw, rest her sweet soul. Called her twice a day, Mama did, till the day the woman had died. Hadn't picked up the second time, that day; how everyone found out.

And, expected the same one day out of the daughter, Eileen had warned. The way of the Bevinses was closeness, and now Rucker women as well. "Your grand-mammy's watching from on high. We can't let her down. You got to call me just like that. Every day. When it's your turn."

"My turn for what?"

"To be the god-durn daughter. Calling on the phone."

A million years in the future. Ha. She *might* call, occasionally. From wherever she landed. Besides far away from here.

Chelsea, happy and excited about her plan of subterfuge regarding the concert, and while it caused a sting of hot guilt, far from worried about poor dead Big Ma-Maw, who had suffered in the end and was now at peace, as Daddy had explained when it was just him and the two children talking after the funeral.

As Mama took a hushed phone call in the kitchen—another ELMS crisis —Chelsea made small talk with her dad at her own breakneck teenage girl speed. She banged her knee up and down against the underside of the table, jazzed on the Cheerwine she and Dusty drank before messing around in her room; teenage girl-gossip, school dramas, the spoiled privileged cheerleaders and dumb redneck girls alike who picked on her, thoughts and observations tumbling out unbidden.

Finally her father managed to break in. "Sweetie, can you quit with your knee?"

"What with my knee?"

He informed her of the bouncing and bumping. "Poppa's had himself a long day."

"Oh—sorry." She pretended not to have known she was doing it. Stopped. "That better?"

"Much."

"Well, la-ti-da," in mimicry of Diane Keaton from a movie she'd watched with Devin and Libby, one with the little squirrelly New York Jew, as her Mama said of the man, talking right into the camera. She'd never seen an actor do that. She threw up her hand like the actress and laughed, ha-ha-ha, I-don't-care. "La-ti-da."

"Quit being smart now, sugar. Pretty please? One day, you'll have headaches."

"How was work?"

"Spent all day up in Union," Dwight said, pleased at being asked. Beginning his own more languorously paced small talk, he catalogued the minutia of his endeavor running "over yonder" to talk to a man about partnering up and expanding further into the upstate—the people of mountainous upper South Carolina could use more insurance. No question about that part.

The Rucker patriarch, as Chelsea thought of him when he was crabby and cross and trying to rein in Eileen's foolishness, made good money. Had been a success—more, he said, than he'd ever dreamed of having when he'd started out. He came from millworkers, back when mills existed in which folks could work, as he often said and she had seen when Gray-Peele had closed the last one here in Edgewater County.

Dwight had grown up near Spartanburg, he said, barefoot and fishing in the Pacolet River, and with not a brain in his head. Proud, then, of all he made of himself—entrepreneurship. Civic leadership. A home and family well beyond the means from which he'd come. She had heard his little speech so many times. He told her this was his way of showing gratitude to the God who had made all this possible. Had given him a chance, the gumption to make a man of himself.

The magic formula? "You got to love what you do. And be happy doing it. Folks will respond in kind by loving what you do and being happy." Among the family record albums were two or three to which she remembered Daddy listening years ago. No music, only these old men speaking in their deep voices—Acres of Diamonds, one was called. Think and Grow Rich was another. "Success is always right there waiting for you. You just have to learn to look for it with the right eyes."

Always so full of good advice and stories and parables. It wasn't nothing but old man horse-doody, of course. But she always listened and nodded and went uh-huh.

"I wish you didn't have to be gone so much."

"Well—that's the card I done drew, sweetheart. That's my path. I hate the driving. You can't get a blessed thing done except, well, drive. Can't stand wasting time having to drive places."

Drive places.

A tingling. The moment. She'd had an announcement simmering for weeks, now, since before wanting to go to the Dead show. Much more important. With Mama out of the room, maybe now the time.

"Daddy—I need to tell you something."

Dwight, who'd turned one eye toward the Jeopardy Tournament of Champions fanfare blaring from the living room set, put down his fork. "What, angel?"

"I want to go to SCAD, for college."

"What's 'SCAD'? Sounds like an off-brand bug spray."

"It's in Savannah. Savannah College of Art and Des—"

"Do *what*?" Eileen had burst back in.

"Me and Daddy were talking."

Eileen stared down the daughter, took her time in getting seated. The presence of her impending disapproval preceded any words she might say, and knowing this, she took her time: stubbing out her cigarette, messing with her napkin, finally starting to daintily eat without making eye contact with her daughter. "Don't start no mess tonight, Colette. I told you Mama feels like she's run a durn race all afternoon."

"That's the god's truth," Daddy said. "Mercy."

"We decided, the Queen Mother and me, that I ain't going to go through with a 'little to-do' tonight about going to no rock concert. But we didn't say nothing about college."

A stand-off. Eileen, daggers for squinting eyes hovering over her readers.

Dwight cleared his throat. He looked at her like *go ahead*. "Tell us about college."

"The Savannah College of Art & Design. That's—that's where I want to go. That's what I want to be."

"You want to be a *what*?"

How dumb were they? "An artist."

Her daddy beamed but with a little frown, caution knotting up his eyebrows they way they did when he was looking at bills or having to sit listening to Mama pestering and instructing on this'n that. "I think that's wonderful, honey. Now, can you make a living being an artist?"

"If I go to college and learn how."

"Can't you do that at Tri-County Tech?"

"I don't want to be no plumber or electrician. If I go to SCAD, art is, like, what the whole school's for."

"The whole durn school's for art." Mama said it like it was filth in her mouth.

"For—drawing. Stuff like drawing." Chelsea's words were barely there. Her mother's diatribes when she wasn't getting her way came enormous, vicious. This felt like one brewing. She cowered.

Dwight spoke up. "Here's where I come down on all this: If you can make a living at what you study, I'll pay for you to study it. And, long as Mama thinks you going to Savannah for four years is all right, then it's fine by me."

Chelsea watched as her Mama quelled and controlled anger that nonetheless bled from her eyes like tears. "*Drawing pictures ain't what people go to college for*," she insisted. "Least not someone who can already draw as pretty as you can. I ain't never even heard of SCAD. You could at least pick a school with a reputation, not some fly-by-night foolishness coming from the back of a comic book." Scoffing in her savage hateful way, as though her daughter had uttered one of the stupidest remarks ever imagined. "All the way in Georgia? For god's sake."

"*It's not but three hours away*."

"Not only is college still *years* away, you're not going out of state. Furthermore: people like us do not become 'artists.' Trust me, in planning and executing the Spring Fling Festival each year," an annual Tillman Falls to-do with vendors and crafters and artists and music, "being an artist seems to do something terrible to the normal functioning brain. Lord help me at such wanton, childish foolishness. Bless your heart—so young. You'll find out."

"But Mama—it's what I want."

"Since when does the child get to decide? I'll tell you—when she has her own babies. Until then? *No way, José.*"

Nothing rankled like when Mama would say 'No way, José.' Chelsea's face and eyes burned like somebody was cutting up onions. "I hate you."

"Now Creedence and Eileen, let's not start—"

"And I swear, if you don't quit encouraging her, Dwight, I will put arsenic in that tea you drink like well water. You both make me so durn mad I could bite a tire iron in half."

"Devin says you made him go to Southeastern too, 'just so you could keep tabs on my ass'." Chelsea, mimicking his deep voice.

"Don't bring your brother into this. He ain't got nothing to do with none of this. And watch that mouth."

"Mama?"

"What."

It was time to make it clear. "I *hate* you."

Her daddy cussed and popped her on the forearm with his butter knife, hard enough to hurt. "Don't you talk like that to your mama."

Mama sat mortified with shock. "Dwight Rucker—don't you dare hit that angel with a knife. What's wrong with you?"

More breath than voice. "I hate you both. I hate myself."

Here came the tears.

Not Chelsea—Mama. Eileen began to wail and boohoo, melodramatic, reminiscent of the day two summers ago when Devin announced he no longer believed in God, if he ever had in the first place. "I can't go through this again, Colette," sobbing. "I can't lose you, not like Devin. I can't let you go, I can't, I *can't.* You're all I *have.*"

"All we have," her Daddy added. "Don't do us like Devin. Please, girl."

Chelsea, ripping apart inside. Cussing and pointing at her mother, vicious, the way she'd heard the woman herself curse any number of people —her husband and son and daughter, people like Uncle Hill (which seemed inexplicable, and only when no one else was around), repairmen, salesmen, waitresses, her so-called friends in the ELMS, random passersby. Even Big Ma-Maw here and there, when she was alive. Cussing a blue streak over the old woman after she got sick with the stomach cancer and laid there dying for two years. Chelsea's Mama had really turned pissy back then, boy. Yowzers.

"I hate all this mess," she shrieked, throwing her own silverware across the room against the wall. "I'm dying upstairs in that room, and at this table with y'all still treating me like a baby!"

With adrenaline squirting, Chelsea ignored their pleas and admonitions to bolt upstairs, fake-wailing like her mother. Feeling thrilled by her profanity, and at disobeying her father's orders to come back and sit down and apologize and yadda-yadda, she slammed her door and screamed for the second time today—primal—and flung herself across the bed, bouncing to a place of quiet and stillness where she could only hear the thudding of her heart. Leaping up, doing a crazy Creedence dance, herky-jerky, in a circle around and around. Collapsing again.

Crying for real. Hard.

Chelsea, at last feeling cried out, came to a fuller understanding of her brother's animus toward their mother. Dried her eyes. Sat up. Glad no one could see her spazzing out.

How the little sister had been in denial, a fool. How she'd have to be strong to get her way.

Or else, if necessary, to run away. Maybe on the night of the concert, when she would sneak out and have a head start—the lie was she'd be staying at Shelby Fordham's house to study and watch movies. Leaving and not coming back.

How much money did she have stuck away in the piggy bank? Fifty? Sixty? Maybe she would call in the morning to the Greyhound station and see what a bus ticket to Charleston or Savannah would cost.

*Ain't much, girl. What then?*

"I don't know, Devin. Shut up."

Chelsea, contemplating what she could stuff into her overnight bag. What she would need, where she could go. Her mind, racing, kept her up half the night.

When she did sleep, she suffered vivid, lucid dreams—of running with Devin and his friends in Columbia on campus, but the city changed into the woods, where they were then galloping like a pack of deer or those cute little pygmy goats they have on the Glasscock farm over yonder off River Ridge Road, little animals running free and crazed and directionless; like the wind, unbridled. Directing how and where she ran in the dream, in control and thinking that what lay ahead was marvelous. Calling back to the others, come this way this way this way, this is the way I just know it, a big meadow full of freedom always right there out of sight. And Devin, laughing and running crazily, encouraging her to run faster, to keep going, to find that place, whatever and wherever it was. A dream that had been more real than the life to which she again ascribed the nature of reality in the morning light. Another day. The same. Creedence.

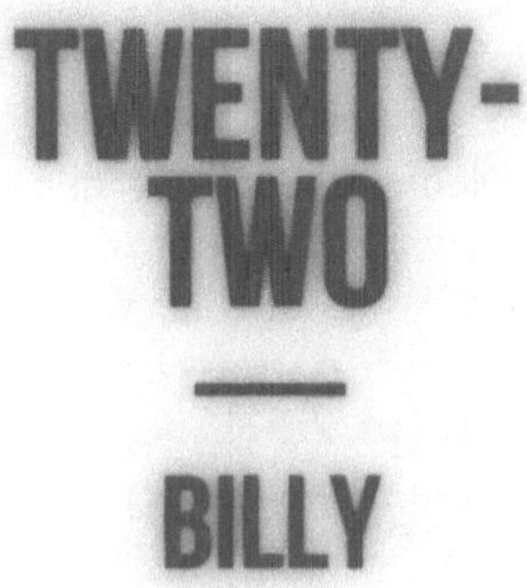



*ibby Libby Libby Libby LIBBY.*

Billy, at his high-rise condo on the southern side of campus. Two bedroom, nice, a corner unit, no roommate needed or wanted, the building overlooking the slender city park running parallel to Blossom. A quick shower and a soapy wank—*LIBBY*—with an explosive release that left him weak-kneed. Three slices of cold pizza, book bag repack, ready to jet off to afternoon classes. Billy.

On the walk back home from dinner in the student union dining hall, he thought through the play-out—the approach, the score, the follow-through —and in the process, a tortuous but naughtily thrilling idea came to him: Billy, calling for a sit-down summit with Ruck. Not to lay things on the line, no, but ostensibly to help him and Libby, thus demonstrating his own level of caring sensitivity. How wonderful a man he was in every way. How considerate.

Later, once the switcheroo occurred, they'd meet again over drinks like gentlemen, with Ruck seeing that her instincts were best—she wanted Billy, and *who could blame her*. The perfect and right-thinking idea, unfolding in its own immaculate moment.

Furthermore, how Billy, unique, privileged and ravenous, deserved to have her. Repeatedly, vigorously. At will. A birthright—when one wielded a knobby, pendulous elephant trunk such as his, you put it where you would, and the few who couldn't see the boon in receiving its energies were too shortsighted to live. The results of this attitude often manifested in shocking and sudden occurrences of emotional release. It was what it was; he was learning to deal with it.

No Choking Hazard groupies had ended up in the swamp. Not yet, anyway.

As for his friend's reaction to losing his gal? How Ruck would understand what Billy saw in her; a given. How Ruck was moving on with his morosely chubby and nihilistic self. Win-win. He's smart, granted, but a drunk suffering a simmering, low boil fixation on mortality? At their epic age of princely abandon? The bars they frequented seethed and roiled with drunken girls. He'd find himself a partner in crime soon enough.

Ruck. A mook, a bringdown. Interested in nothing but his own morbid navel. But Billy still loved him, as far as that went.

Yes. Billy Steeple, snatching that pussy right out from under his boy's oblivious nose. The logic, irrefutable—if he thought necessary, he'd hit up the Boolean sages over in the philosophy department for confirmation. But Ruck, making this reality himself; Billy, an innocent. Train, leaving station.

Christ, though. He had to be careful. If had an accident with Libby, he'd never forgive himself.

Out on the balcony he inhaled the scent of the city, warm and greasy with afternoon automobile exhaust, and gazed toward campus proper and all future glory awaiting him thereupon.

A light breeze; he convinced himself he detected a hint of crisp fall, always welcome in muggy South Carolina. The first graceful kiss of cooler air reminded him of childhood at prep school in New England during his various semesters at schools like Marvelwood, Androscoggin Academy and Portsmouth Abbey, his three alma maters spread over eight years of fitting-in attempts. These never worked out, not in the face of his pubescent penchant for petty vandalism, poor grades and disruptive classroom behavior, the notorious Androscoggin Pornography Ring scandal, and so on. The two accidents, salacious, tawdry and surprising affairs, had upped the stakes.

He had been caught at plenty of wrongdoing, but not the deaths of students, one of which he disguised as a suicide by hanging, no great scandal at a prep school full of rich neurotics. As for him, always an explanation of his whereabouts. Always the right alibi. Billy, watched over by angels. It had continued. The latest, a groupie—a transient girl with terrible teeth and skin, filthy clothes and safety pins through her ears—hadn't been missed. She had been a pressure-valve, that grungy trollop.

Gazing at the buildings where Devin and the others lived, including the twelve-story women's dorm within which dwelled the damsel, the exquisite Libby Meade, Billy sighed with vague worry, a pernicious sense of impending accidental doom. He shook it off. No more accidents. Only with background players like the nameless groupie. To do so at this early point with one of the principals, as the main characters in a screenplay were known 'in the industry,' would spin the story perhaps too far in a shocking direction. "Only Hitchcock could get away with PSYCHO's conceit," as the screenwriting guru had taught them, "of killing off the ostensible lead after only the first act. The true artist may break rules, but only after he becomes master of them."

The rolling, hilly campus lay beneath a steel-gray cloud deck: contemporary block-like buildings sprouted among verdant patches of greenery like hideous, angular Eastern Island heads, concrete monuments to mediocrity jutting up in obscene relief from the natural topography that, in this part of town, tested bike riders with steep inclines more reminiscent of the San Franciscan peninsula rather than the midlands of South Carolina. The land, cut through over the eons by the confluence of three rivers a mile or so to the west, must have seemed idyllic to early colonists, indeed worthy of a future state capitol.

Billy, pondering the unnatural incongruities, the buildings housing the student body. One far day ahead they'd be excavated, studied. He pictured a group of intrepid archaeologists, serious and driven, wearing hazmat suits while sifting through layers of beer cans, used rubbers, Madonna CDs and textbooks, those mostly left pristine, untouched. Wrinkling their noses and snorting with condescending disgust, if not outright bewilderment, at the degeneracy of the ancients on display; a vision of empire's end.

Billy, in the throes of one of his fixations, cared little for what the future might think of him. Not with Libby in one of those buildings. The thought of her, along with the breeze flowing across the balcony, threaten to provoke another dizzying, persistent erection; Libby Meade, star of COMPULSION, A Film By Roman Polanski.

Soon, he would have to act. A successfully nonlethal seduction of her, and eventual real human relationship between them, would put to bed once and for all any hint of the bothersome, murderous rage often sweeping through him during the physical act of love. A healing angel, Libby. He just knew it.

But not always compulsive about screwing another human being to death. Sometimes Billy went ballistic over the collecting of objects—high-end audio equipment, albums, VHS tapes. So far, the desire for Libby like how the ravenous need for a spike of heroin must feel to a junkie.

How he'd watched Mucky Turnbull shoot up one night, he said, in honor of GG Allin, who'd died not shitting on stage but with a needle in his arm. And how Billy'd told Mucky he was a real douchebag poseur, and drugs weren't that cool and how straight edge was what their band should emulate;

this attitude needled the lead singer, with his drooping eyes and drooling mouth, of what they'd decided that night to call Choking Hazard.

Billy, believing Mucky to have now gotten hooked, keeping it from everyone else in the band. Wasn't hard to conceal. They barely practiced, much less gigged. Needed to get motivated—the band was Billy's only serious side-artistic outlet, next to his burgeoning scriptwriting career, of course, with music fame and fortune now only the backup, but still important.

They needed to try harder. Not party so much.

Needling.

Need.

Needing to acquire.

Now.

In Billy's case, love being the drug. Forget the band, Mucky, music, movies.

Libby.

The spark, ignited, whether she knew it or not.

The best part?

Billy wasn't a complete and total snake—a foundation had been laid: Libby, confessing to him a week earlier over an impromptu coffee chat outside the Humanities building that, as much as she might still love Devin? Wondering how much he cared for her anymore? If theirs was a high school romance now running out the clock?

"These things happen."

"Yes," Libby said. "You'd tell me if he was seeing someone else?"

"How would I know?"

"Because he hangs out with you more than me lately."

"Can you blame him? I'm a super-friend." And sharing a warm chuckle. "He'd be a fool to let you go."

"I'm more trouble than I'm probably worth. I'm as moody as he is."

With most women, they made their intent known within ten seconds, like the au pair who'd deflowered him at eleven. She'd seen what he had. Wanted a taste.

But Libby, not as clear-cut in her desires. Cutting her eyes under wavy short hair, a perm. Tasteful makeup. Demure. An arts goddess. "Thanks for the coffee. I think I'll go and check on Devin."

"Ruck's a rock. But, I'll go with you." They didn't find him.

The au pair—the first accident.

Renee, how she'd walked in on him beating off. A French girl.

Had laughed, at first, at the hung horsemeat he wielded even at that age. Her giggle, it made him freak. Laid a kernel of anger that he still rolled around in his head to this day.

He stood frozen. It glistened in the half-light of his room, a rainy morning. She came over. Started tickling it.

Playing.

He'd erupted within seconds, ropy and thick, with a roar—and from her, another gale of laughter.

He had picked her off the floor by the throat. How the girl kicked and fought him off, fell to the ground choking, skittered out and bolted.

She quit later that day, tending her resignation to his father's secretary. Offered no reason other than *unhappy*.

Her loss.

Women were all the same. Except for Libby. She had her own music. He had to have her.

Afternoons.

Throughout October Billy made sure he met Libby at least twice a week; for coffee at one of the downtown lunch-counter places on the other side of the Capitol Complex, or to study together. This allowed ample and expansive time for her to kvetch about Devin, or the scriptwriting class, or her dreams, which included standing on the AMPAS award stage one day, clutching the gold man near the base and trying to remember everyone deserving of thanks.

He finally broached: "Does Ruck know about our coffee talks?"

She colored. "He doesn't mind."

"C'mon. That's why it's always all the way over on this side of campus—so we won't run into him."

"Yes," clear in her discomfort at his blunt incursion into the truth. "I don't want to hurt his feelings."

"Talking is not doing anything wrong."

"Here's the thing." She snapped into focus, taking charge, chopping at the air as she spoke with a trio of petite fingers like a Boy Scout salute, digits Billy wanted to lick and suckle like teats. "Devin's in a funk. It's a bring-down."

"I've noticed this tendency."

"I keep wishing it were time for him to think about growing out of old routines. What the future holds. What he really wants to do with his life, which he still doesn't know. My poor baby."

"What you need to do—as I see it—is date other dudes. People, I mean."

"Billy." Understanding what he meant. Shaking her head, *no*. "We can't. We're all friends."

Billy calculated, resisting the urge to force his impatient hand: Pooh-poohing, saying *of course of course of course, no no no that's not what I meant.* "What kind of cad do you think I am? There's a code among gentlemen. The thought of betraying a brother officer of the lodge shakes me to the core."

"Oh, please."

Asking her, finally, if she would be his date for the concert, yes; but only in the sense of accompanying one another in platonic friendship and collegiality: as fellow writers.

"I want my mind blown alongside you. It's the Dead."

She nodded. "Legends of psychedelic rock."

"Chance of a lifetime."

"Sure, sure. I get it." Libby, reminding him she was more of a movie gal.

"We're kindred spirits."

Giving him a forearm slap. "It's a deal."

"If I get out of hand—"

"—like breaking some code?—"

"—yeah; I'm sure your Ruck will set me straight."

The slap, her energy, lingering along his skin like a trail of ants. Her smile. The eyes, holding his; darting away in recognition of the undeniable heat.

Billy had her. Almost too easy.

They parted with a chaste, quick hug that caused tingling deep inside. He brainstormed the rest of the day about an appropriate gift for her, something cool, not ordinary; no flowers, not stupid, not clichéd. Layered with meaning and metaphor. He'd work on it.

After jerking off a couple of times back home the idea of a CD came to him as apropos, counterintuitive considering what she'd said earlier about preferring movies over music, but whatever. It was his idea, it was his and no one alive could stop him from executing this plan.

Billy rinsed off his horsedick and bolted up the hill, three stairs at a time, to the record store in the student union mini-mall.

He scanned the racks—no punk for her; no bombastic classic rock crud; no bubblegum pop; no fucking Beatles. Not even the Grateful Dead, about whom Billy knew less than nothing. His next conquest deserved tunes with class and style, an album of music befitting a luminous and sophisticated specimen like Libby Meade.

Browsing, his fingers dancing across the rows of CDs. Coming upon a

Dire Straits called MAKING MOVIES, a semi-recent critical and artistic smash. From the title alone he knew he'd found the right present for his newest and best girl:

Making movies.

One day, he and Libby would be making them together.

*Steeple-Meade Productions Presents.*

Making movies and fucking with joyful abandon. No more accidents once kismet and love joined hands. Heavenly.

No more bothersomeness.

And as for Libby Meade, soon reveling in the eventuality of their union. Whether she wanted to, or not.

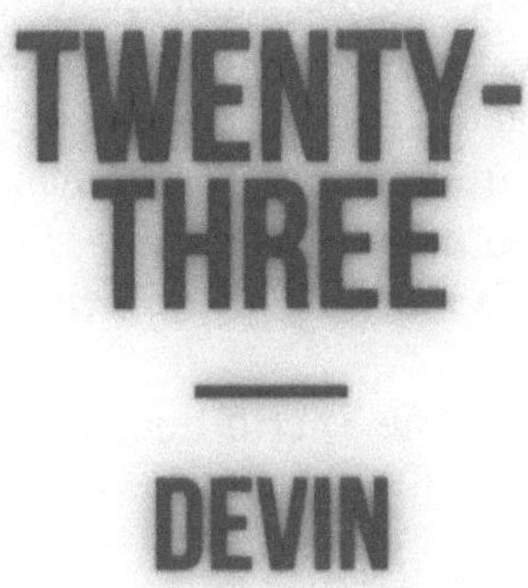


Every night in which he failed to drink himself into unconscious oblivion, Devin, re-encountering the dead fucker floating along, peaceful, easy and asleep. Forever. Could rarely drink enough, it seemed, to avoid these stupid dreams.

The flash of sunlit glass off the liquor bottle left by the gate.

The man turning toward him with those dark, dead eyes.

The blood in the water.

What a day it'd been already, but after Devin and Mr. Raymond found the dead dude, all heck broke loose at the country club.

The police and ambulance arrived. Bill Wimmel, editor-in-chief of the Edgewater Advocate, drove over to personally report the story. Men in suits and uniforms alike, huddling, pointing, nodding. Yellow incident tape across the pool area gate.

Devin, made to describe what he had seen, where and how, what he had done.

At last Devin's dad showed up, sliding the Oldsmobile into the country club parking lot in a spray of grit and small stones like one of those 70s car chase movies the family enjoyed. Running over to the pool area, wild-eyed, desperate to find his son.

Once he did Dwight hugged Devin close, a gesture more intimate than most the teen and his father shared.

"My boy—are you okay?"

"Of course." Devin, lying. Inside, he couldn't stop trembling. "It just— surprised me."

"Shook you up, I'll bet."

"Nah."

The Sheriff, a fat Southern redneck named Whardell Truluck, his gut as big and hard as a bowling ball, greeted Dwight Rucker with one of their grown-man special handshakes.

"Sorry you had to go through that, young man. This here boy didn't do nothing his whole sorry life but cause trouble. Drowning in that pool and scaring y'all half to death this morning ain't nothing but one last time."

"What kind of trouble?"

"Hush, son. You don't ask the Sheriff questions—he asks you." The men winked at one another.

"Young Mr. Rucker?"

Devin said 'yessir?' to the Sheriff, whose breath stunk of onions and nicotine.

"You ever seen a body before?"

"When they showed us the traffic safety movie at school."

"That don't count. That's in a movie."

"Then I reckon it was."

"Best advice I can give you is to forget it." To Dwight: "Y'all get on out of here. Your son can't tell us nothing we don't already know about what happened here."

"Who is the man?" Devin, a squeeze from his father's arm suggesting impertinence.

Sheriff Truluck, a blank face and a snort that seemed to say *what difference do it make?* "Albert Nixon. Worked on Bledsoe's landscaping crew. That's when he seen the pool— when they's working around here. Reckon he come back wanting to take himself a dip. Hot night last night."

"Nixon? He related to that Reverend Nixon across the river?"

"Them SOBs all related, one way or another. Autopsy'll tell if he was on drugs. Either way, this SOB wasn't right in the head. A drunk and a layabout, dead in the decent folks's pool. If that don't make you shake your head, I don't know what would."

Devin, going to the Olds and getting inside. Dwight Rucker pulled the driver's side door shut with force.

"You don't dwell on none of this, son."

Devin watched the ambulance carrying Albert's body go down the long tree-lined drive of the country club, a median of flowers and shrubbery Albert had tended many times. "Daddy?"

Dwight, waiting.

"When I was in the water with him, I imagined what it felt like."

"What what felt like?"

"To be dead."

"Nothing more natural than feeling scared when you see another person like that."

"I reckon."

Dwight groped at first for words. Nodded until he had his thread of discourse figured out. Devin knew this look. Dwight could sell insurance all the livelong day but not always express himself on an emotional level with his family. Here, an exception:

"I'll never forget when your great-grandmama passed on. I crept into that funeral home like I was being asked to go into a haunted house. I wasn't but a year older than you are now, back before you wasn't so much as a twinkle in me and your mama's eyes."

"Were you scared?"

"For a while I couldn't stop thinking about her being gone, but later, the preacher took me aside. He told me how she was okay." He'd leaned in, a teachable moment: "How she'd be waiting for me, son, once I got there. Smiling, and waiting. Like she's still waiting for all of us. And then? I felt better."

"You think all that's true?"

Dwight, whom Devin knew considered himself saved despite the fact they never went to church, beamed an expression of self-satisfaction at having done the job required of him: imparting the selfsame assurance offered by the pastors of the world. "Never more sure of anything."

Devin, processing. "Mr. Raymond said they had to drain the pool, now, so I could go for the day."

"Well, let's go, then."

"I'd rather ride my bike back home."

"Get on your way, then. Enjoy your summer. You'll be fifteen soon. Time to get your learner's permit and get old Uncle Hill to start looking for you a car. How's that sound?"

It sounded great. He said, hell yeah, Daddy. And they slapped secret skin. Eileen would never approve of Devin having a learner's permit, not with all the accidents people were having these days.

But Devin had not gone straight home. Instead, he lingered in the quiet woods by the place kids called Big Rock, a huge boulder jutting up from the ground with one jagged corner carved and chipped and spray-painted to look like an owl's head staring out toward the placid, dark water of the forest pond. A few rich people had houses near the opposite end of the pond, an oxbow lake that had once been part of the Sugeree River, but on the whole

Big Rock lay tucked away, private, where people came to party untroubled by cops or parents.

A carpeting of cigarette butts, condoms, beer cans attesting to its status as a place of leisure and revelry among Edgewater County youth covered the ground around the rock. Devin found this place lovely and peaceful, hated that it was defiled by all the detritus. Wishing he had a trash bag to clean it all up. Maybe one morning he would come early and do so, before it became too muggy, and try to redeem clean the Edgewater County cretins who'd defiled this otherwise lovely forest glen.

Devin. Consumed by the concept of the end, what being dead felt like. How one second a person could be filled with emotion and knowledge but in the next transform into an inert, floating hunk of meat. Doubts about salvation and eternity, of streets of gold and a place alongside the savior, or God himself, or whatever it was supposed to be. Doubts. Fears. The impossibility of the him inside him being gone.

God seemed over-there somewhere. Inaccessible.

Doubts doubts doubts.

But Devin, feeling safe in the woods, away from everything and everyone that defined him as a person. Remembering a line from a science fiction book he'd read:

*Fear is the mind killer.*

Alone, Devin felt that he could not die, not here among the trees and the lichen-covered rock, birds singing and cicadas buzzing, warm, humid air hanging heavy and alive, worms beneath his feet and catfish in the pond. Wondering if death might sneak up on him the way It had the man in the pool. Cruelly and sudden.

A paradox, intellectual, spiritual: Knowledge of death, tomorrow or perhaps in another sixty or seventy years. Knowing, but not-knowing.

When.

How.

What awaited.

Now well past the lunch hour, at last his stomach growled. Heading home, he pressed 'play' on a cassette in his Walkman, turned up the dramatic music—The Who—and started forgetting about the man in the pool, except for the problem of seeing his dead face every time Devin closed his eyes.

His Mama, wild-eyed, greeted him at the front door in one of her states of agitation. Clearly she'd been informed by Dwight of the morning's tumultuous and thrilling events, now beside herself with worry.

"You get your skinny ass in this house. *Where have you been?*"

"Just riding around, Mama. Out in the woods."

Grabbing him by the upper arms, hard enough to leave oval fingertip bruises. "You can't go off somewhere and not let someone know. *Your Daddy called to say you were on your way home over an hour ago. He's driving the roads looking for you right now.*"

"I wouldn't have been here till later anyway. So what difference—"

Releasing his arms, she slapped him across the mouth. "You better quit with this back-talking. I don't care how many dead black boys you found in a swimming pool today."

Holding the back of her hand to her forehead, Eileen snatched up a copy of WOMAN'S WORLD and began fanning herself. Sudden, eyes flying open, dropping the magazine to the floor and grabbing Devin again, now crushing him to her bosom, she wept, "That could have been my poor sweet little baby in that pool. You are not going back to that damn country club *ever again.*"

Devin, unnerved, pushed her away. "Let me go, now. I know where the deep end is. I know how to swim. And that's my durn job—I got to go back."

"You'll never understand, not until you have your own children."

Going upstairs, lying on his bed, he flipped through a collection of Poe stories he'd been reading. Now that his soul had been scrutinized by the glassy red eyes of a dead man, the dark nature of the material seemed less entertaining than horrific.

*It could have been me.*

Wondering about the nature of time and space, matters cosmological, spiritual. Unable to shake the big questions, pondering the notion of how long he might have until ending up floating in some pool. Thinking about the man's body turning toward him, as though wanting to look at the boy who'd jumped into the water with him.

Devin, giving in. He felt afraid. He still did.

The next day, a screaming match with his mother about going to work. She'd tried to physically restrain him from leaving. And for his part, Devin felt unnerved and anxious about being where a man had died. The pool, drained and cleaned and now being refilled.

Not wanting to look into the water, to see the sun glimmering upon its surface.

With the pool cleaning underway Devin had no formal deck duties, and Mr. Raymond again dismissed him early in the day.

When he tried to discuss the events of the prior morning, his boss had shown no interest. "That ain't worth none of your worry. Not now. Put it out of your mind."

"I keep seeing that man in the pool."

He patted Devin on the shoulder. "I was in Korea when I was a young man. Did you know that?"

"No, sir. Like on *M*A*S*H*?"

"Lucky I didn't end up in one of them units. But I seen men suffer, men I knew, bleeding out into the snow all the way on the other side of the world, so far from my Mama I damn near cried myself to sleep every night. I couldn't help the fellas no more'n you could help Albert Nixon. Only thing you can do is put it out of your mind."

"I'll try."

"Go on and play. Enjoy your summer."

Again through the woods, not especially wanting to go home but having no other place to go but Dobbs's, in a neighborhood too far to ride to in the Carolina heat. Hoping instead for a deserted Rucker house: not only Dad gone, but Colette at the Fordhams for a picnic with little Shelby and her brother. With luck, his mother, off shopping instead of sitting in front of the television, or at one of her ELMS meetings.

Devin. Craving *alone*.

And yet not.

Pedaling out of the woods and onto highway 79, a quarter mile later along the shoulder and through the brick-gated entrance to his subdivision. He felt an odd stillness and sense of loneliness in the air.

A couple of turns to his cul-de-sac; upon arrival, Devin, noting a Lincoln Towncar parked in the driveway. Hill Hampton's car. Uncle Hill, friend to Dwight and to all the Ruckers. Family.

Devin, not giving it two thoughts. Nothing too unusual about seeing Uncle Hill at the house. Except, perhaps, time of day.

Coming into the house and slamming the door.

Out of Devin's line of sight came a cacophony of noise, banging around in the formal living room.

His mother, screaming out in surprise. "Who's there? Devin?"

"It's me, Mama."

"Don't you move."

Devin, barreling on through the foyer to discover Eileen wearing only her robe, the same one she'd had on first thing. Her face, white as a ghost. Standing beside her was Hill Hampton, his shirttail out and checked sport coat off. Boots of finest leather, hand-tooled, lying willy-nilly on the floor like he'd kicked them off his wide pink feet in a hurry. The throw pillows from the couch, scattered around.

The two of them.

Together.

Devin, not comprehending. Not at first. Not letting himself.

Then, oh shit, a different fear: "What are y'all—"

"Well, looky here." Hill Hampton, barefoot and stuffing his shirttail into his trousers. "What you know good, Devin? Your Daddy told me y'all was talking about riding over to look at cars for you, soon."

Devin, backing out of the room. "What. Are y'all doing. In here." Narrowing his eyes at Uncle Hill. His inner voice, verbalizing itself unbidden: "This—I can't figure this out."

"Uncle Hill brought papers for Daddy to look over. On the new Cadillac we're looking at—thinking about—maybe buying. And—" This lie seemed to pain her. "And about a car for you, next year."

"That's right." Hill tried to seem casual about sitting down to yank the boots onto his wedges of feet. "I sure appreciate you rubbing my feet, Eileen. She's been doing that for me since we was all in high school together. But Devin, the 86 model-years will be rolling off them trucks in a week or two, and if I was you? I'd tell old Dwight to let you test drive one yourself. In fact, I'll tell him that myself. *I'll insist*. We don't need to wait for no learner's permit to get you behind the wheel. Not in Edgewater County."

"There now." Eileen, swishing past Devin in her robe and making for the stairs. "Thank you for bringing those papers over for Dwight, Hill. We'll— we'll see you on Sunday for the cookout," his attendance a regular occurrence: the Ruckers, the Hamptons, going back many years. Devin despised Uncle Hill's two meathead sons—McNabb, after the famous championship Redtails basketball coach, and McIntire, maiden name of one of the grandmothers. They had thankfully gone off to college at Clemson, where both played football. Were going to the pros, to hear Uncle Hill tell it. These days usually only Hill came over, though—his wife Lenore had died several years before.

Uncle.

Hill.

Devin fell against the wall in the short hallway leading to the kitchen. The frame of his 6th grade portrait jabbed him in the shoulder. His heart, beating in his ears like a bass drum.

Hampton, his cheeks splotched the color of a beet, paused at the front door and called back. "Wait, Devin: You happy working at the club? If you ain't, we can put you on down at the lot. I know finding that boy in the pool like that must've been awful."

"*Bye, Hill.*" Eileen, hollering from the kitchen. "*Can't wait to see the new car.*"

It all sunk in. "Damn, y'all."

"Devin." Hill Hampton held out his arms encased in seersucker, shirttail still half untucked. "Please."

Two simmering gray blobs boiled in Devin's line of sight, obscuring Uncle Hill's fat, freckled face. "You just better go on."

"I will. I will, now." Hill Hampton, out the door. The engine of the Towncar roaring to life. All but peeling out of the cul-de-sac. Devin, ignoring a line of patter from his mother about helping her decide about supper, skulked up to his room.

On his bed, staring at the ceiling, a sickening sense of his mother he'd never felt before—thinking of her as a woman.

And Uncle Hill. As a man.

"Ye, gods." Devin, revolted. Unable to stop imagining it. He forgot about the dead man, at least while the sun was up.

The next day, a Saturday, he helped his father rake pine straw in the back yard and asked: "Daddy? Are we getting a new car?"

Dwight, laughing, said, "No, son. Not just now."

"We're not even planning to look?"

"Not unless your mother said something."

"Or test drive? Or nothing?"

"What's this all about?"

"Uncle Hill said the new Cadillacs were coming in next week." Dwight's was an '82.

"He's been on me to trade. When'd you see Hill?"

Devin shrugged. "Can't remember."

Dwight mussed his son's hair. "I know what this is about."

"*You do?*"

"Of course I do. And I think it's fine."

Devin, his mind a blank—they had to be talking about two different things. "Well, dang."

"Putting the cart before the horse, though," prideful rather than in annoyance, "thinking about that learner's permit next year. That's my fault. Guess I put it in your head the other day, though. Didn't I."

"Uncle Hill said he'd let me test drive a car sometime soon. That's all it was."

"That rascal. My boy's growing up so fast. All in good time, son. My sweet son."

At the Sunday cookout, Devin, watching Uncle Hill and his mother's every interaction with a keen discernment. Seeing in their darting, furtive eyes the nasty truth. At least Hill had had the sense to bring a beard, a woman he knew from Columbia. Devin's Mama made such a production about welcoming her to the fold it was like watching a Broadway play. Devin, seeing his mother's layers, her little fibs and exaggerations, with a new lens.

Secrets which he had held close for five years, now. They burned him up worse than finding a dead stranger in the pool. But he didn't have nightmares about his mother. That sordid mess he truly did do his best to push out of his mind.

But ever since, eaten alive with all this grim knowledge. From the dead man in the pool, Devin, unable to articulate any verifiable wisdom, other than an ability to describe the condition of post-life dead-eyed meat; with his father, wanting to tell him the sick and true-truth about what he knew, but unwilling. Believing this both an obligation but also a prohibition, the breaking of which an unimaginable impossibility—looking into his father's eyes and telling him.

How. Could. He. Do. It.

Easy—he couldn't.

Not making it over to the car lot to test drive cars anytime soon, but a different sort of venality and bribery began that week—his mother, plying him with unexpected money. Slipping twenties into the pockets of his shorts and under his pillow. No notes. No words between them. No exchanges between them regarding Uncle Hill, other than Devin's occasional piercing stares across the dining room table.

"What's this money for?" he finally asked her one day.

"Extra," she called it. Her eyes, hooded, opaque. Like always. "Just our little secret, extra little deal type-deal. You save that money. Spend it on something you want. Something special."

Devin, a year passing, another momentous season of change: sixteen, a birthday celebrated with new girlfriend Libby Meade. Prior, vivid tragedies fading in the face of sensual exploration with Libby.

A transplant from Delaware, her dad was an engineer at the Sugeree River Station. Libby herself, a doll, an absolute angel, smart and witty and sexy, dark-eyed, petite, matching Devin book-for-book, except maybe for the sci-fi. A slightly jaundiced eye about the world; cynical like him, but a sweet cynicism. He could not have prayed for a more compatible soul.

Libby. The coolest girl he'd ever met. So different from the belles and chubby rednecks and ignorant poor farmer's daughters of Edgewater County. After that terrible summer, the only time Devin really felt safe—and loved— had been with Libby.

One afternoon he played her Dylan's BLOOD ON THE TRACKS. Singing along to 'Buckets of Rain,' the lines about loving the 'cool way she looks at him'. She had blushed and smiled.

Later, he'd find out about her family problems. Darkness in the past. But together, life was all fresh and innocence and felt like rebirth from the summer before him. A respite. A way out—Libby.

Love.

And sure enough, upon that sixteenth birthday milestone, Devin, receiving his car—a midnight blue Mustang straight off the lot of Hampton Motors, sticker in the window, huge red ribbon, new car smell, tires shiny, a stick-shift, a fastback, one of the slickest new cars in the county, in Uncle Hill's words.

Indeed—Devin, standing with his hand on the fender, felt awe.

Getting away now seemed tangible.

Freedom beckoned.

Uncle Hill, his mother, father, Creedence, and Libby: the young girls stoked and wound up and excited beyond reason, his sister doing one of her crazy involuntary dances Devin called the herky-jerk. The lot of them, all looking to him for a reaction.

His voice, coming small and timid. "Thanks, y'all. It's amazing."

Dwight slung his arm around his best friend's neck. "Uncle Hill picked it out for you personally."

"That I did, Devin. Had it shipped down from Charlotte just yesterday."

Devin, meeting Hampton's eyes. "Thank you."

A warm smile. "Nothing but the best for my boys—all my boys."

Devin extended his slender hand, swallowed whole by Uncle Hill's lion's paw. Leaning in, letting Uncle Hill give him a big backslapping hug, followed by his father, who wanted to do the same.

"Take her around the block, son."

Cutting his eyes at Eileen, who had busied herself pulling off the oversized ribbon. Devin grabbed Libby's hand. "Let's go."

Creedence all but shouted, "Oh my god, please, *please can I go, too?*"

Devin, laughing at his crazed little beanpole of a sister. "Sorry. First ride's for me and my girl. Next time."

Backing out of the driveway, peeling out, he caught glimpses in the rearview: of Creedence standing with her arms extended in disappointment but also his father, who shouted in anger at the youthful display of automotive machismo. Devin, knowing a lecture awaited his return: about safe driving, about not showing off and being careful, especially with a passenger in the car.

Libby, in the passenger seat for the first time but not the last; this, a weird, vaguely fearful thought which came to him sudden and cold and that he could not figure out to save his sorry life.

Shivering in his cramped dorm-bedroom, smoking and cursing the names of a dead man and his mother and her not-so-secret lover, Devin, remembering all as though five minutes ago. Wakeful after his nightmare, he needed to stop running the past through his mind and get down to the books—if he didn't take Dobbs's advice, his grades this semester would be shit.

Devin, ready for a beer, not studying. In drinking one he ruminated about the upcoming Grateful Dead concert, and with it the acid Billy said he'd get if anyone wanted an authentic 1960s-esque Deadhead experience.

Unsure about exploring some weird hard drug scene, but Devin, maybe participating anyway, if only for the shear risk, more than the thrill. Death was real. He seen it. And Devin, fearing no consequences from taking a pussy-assed party drug. Or pulling heroic, bravado shit, like driving around drunk as piss but still arriving alive.

Maybe the night with the acid would be *the* night: One last big blowout, and then done. No more anxious fretting. None of this guessing game of wondering where Devin's pool awaited, and when he'd jump into the shallow end and break his neck.

Devin, nodding and serene; no one more ready than he to finally be grateful. Hell, he'd celebrate by going to class, for once. The ones he hadn't already ditched that day, of course. It had been a late night. With one or two under his belt, however, he had enough gut to put off the real partying until later.

Speaking of the concert, at Libby's news Devin became livid:

"You're 'going' with Billy?"

"He asked me to be his date."

"What in the freaking shit is that supposed to mean?"

They met for burgers, fries, and Libby's indulgence of a chocolate shake at a cacophonous lunchtime fast food joint. She claimed to suffer a budding addiction issue. "These shakes," she said, "are killing me."

"C'mon. What's this Billy nonsense?"

"He asked, I'm going."

"I heard you—but what does it mean?"

"He asked. I accepted. Are you deaf?"

"But we're all going together."

"Well, he asked me like a proper gentleman, and so I said yes. Why should I have said no?"

Devin, seething, hot blood rising in beer-swollen cheeks. "You're breaking up with me. *Over Billy?*"

"You're being melodramatic. It doesn't mean anything."

Anger. "Don't insult me like this."

"It's like Billy himself says. We're all friends. He's a big-hearted goof."

Devin, familiar with Billy Steeple and how he operated with women, felt as though a bucket of ice had been dumped into his gut. "He wants to goof your panties right off."

"You sound like my father. And you know how I feel about that."

"Sorry."

Libby's turn for rank annoyance. "But you're right—nothing's going to happen. We're to all party together, go to the concert, and that's that. You're overreacting." The half-smile, beaming at him. "Billy, whatever he is—well. He's not my type."

She took a moment to consider. A smoldering, sexy look that sent a thrill and chill down his spine. "You know who I'll be going home with."

"Sounds like we'll be up all night afterwards on the acid."

"We will." Libby had done acid at fourteen back in Delaware. "It'll be better than drinking."

"Nothing's better than that."

"You'll see."

Devin, feeling possessive. "I want us to live together. Or, I guess. I'm asking. Would you like to?"

Eyelids aflutter. "That's so sweet. When?"

"Next year."

Libby clutched herself. "Um. Wow."

"Well? We love each other—don't we?"

At that statement, she snapped to attention. "All I've wanted is for you to show it more often. Like you used to."

"When you said that about a date, it was like a corkscrew to my heart."

"People don't go on one date and then fall in love, like in the movies."

"We did."

Considering the veracity of his statement; knowing he meant a misty February day walking in the woods near Big Rock when they'd kissed, the moment they considered their anniversary. "So we're the exception."

Parting on the bricks that night, both agreed to talk on the phone later. Libby, off to finish up classwork.

Devin, on the pedestrian bridge connecting the old campus to the newer buildings closer to the Old Market, pressed for additional details about the next day's activities. "Is he, what—picking you up on this magnificent date of yours in his Mercedes?"

"He offered, but I said 'I'll see you at Devin's.' Good enough?"

"That's better."

"Relax. Billy's as chivalrous a gentleman as I've met."

Devin, trying not to choke, spun on his heel and headed toward the dining hall—Billy Steeple, a poon-hound of a most egregious order. Snowing them the way he'd snowed Libby.

Devin would keep tabs on the situation. Cock-block the fucker, but good. It would be easy enough. Libby was his girl. All was right. And yeah. Maybe he would give up the juice for her. Dial it back. Have a couple of light beers with dinner instead of hitting the hard stuff. Drink it over. It was a plan.

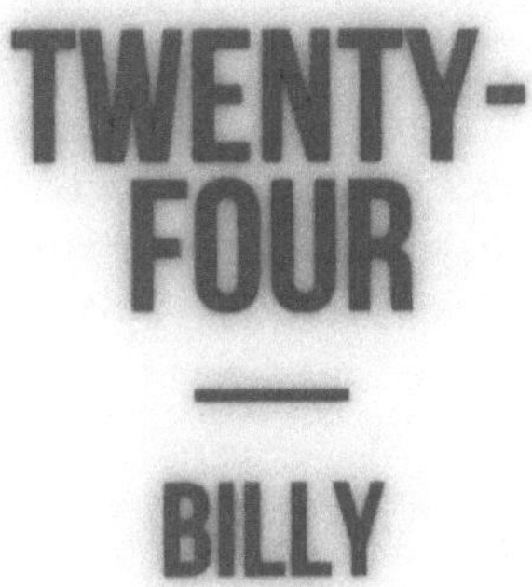


After a hot shower Billy shaved for the first time in a week; rubbed one out; paced around the condo almost literally bouncing off the walls with anticipation.

*Tonight, tonight.*

*But damn, son. An accident this time would be spectacular. I mean, terrible.*

"Get out of my head," he said to the walls of his room, papered in rock and movie posters. "I'm in control, now. Understood?"

*Sure*, the voice answered. *You got it. Anytime. Et cetera.*

He sought the cleanest T-shirt he could find, a plain black pocket T by Hanes. Meat Mallet wore them onstage, their signature, a three-pack available in any store rack in any town in the country. A band shirt that said it all, showed how punk they were. Black—endless, black, nothing. Billy, showing loyalty to his mates and not this hippie crap by sporting a tie-dye.

All of it was incidental to nailing Libby Meade. The exclamation point that would appear over her head the second she got a look at it.

Billy, for reasons obvious now considered ditching the punk persona altogether, a reinvention not unlike when he'd switched from shaggy-haired outdoorsy dude into paddling and rock-climbing to a straight-edge, thrash music and hardcore anarchic punk rock bad-ass slapping a bass as hard as he jacked his red, crooked vein-fed meat bollard, pulsing and hot-cold, all glowing and humming with purple neon like this one bass he'd asked his grandparents to buy for him back in prep school, on the afternoon he'd decided to become a rock god.

Besides—the punk band was going nowhere, the music scene in Columbia was TOTAL MOTHERFUCKING BULLSHIT, and he flat-out did not have his heart in thrash anymore like, at all—if he'd ever. His dad, not seeming to give two shits anyhow what Billy looked like, so the shock value the punk-guise once held now diluted and thus useless.

But if Libby and her circle of friends were going hippie after tonight, Billy, ready to jam. He'd already snooped around at The Happy Accident, the last head shop from the 60s still in business, now mostly clothing instead of bongs. He'd fingered the bright Dead T-shirts on a rack, a woven beret called a tam designed to corral dreadlocks, the basket of hacky-sacks on the counter by the register, the jars of incense, the spinning rack of leather 'Jesus' sandals 'Road-tested on the streets of Damascus' as a dangle-tag promised. As long as they carried his size—big boats down there, don't you know—he'd be in business.

And if Libby didn't work out—not an option in his world of occasional sex murders—accidents, rather—Billy'd noticed a slew of cute hippy chicks dotting the campus and the Old Market; a veritable fashion trend. Who knew how hot granola slit might be? Hairy and earthy, he surmised, such as the unshaven European girls he'd diddled on vacations with his father, with only one accident of record barely noticed there in a high-crime area of Rome? Yeah, boy.

Long as they were tough. Had stamina. Weren't fucking virgins. Could take a serious Steep'ling.

Crucial—no V-cards. Or, never again. Too easily frightened. Too fragile. Too much blood.

As additionally promised to the revelers for whom he'd purchased the tickets, Billy also procured through one of his Meat Mallet bandmates a quarter ounce of what appeared to his untrained eye as decent, smelly buds of marijuana, a package of Joker brand rolling papers, and most importantly, a ten-strip of allegedly heady blotter acid. Friend of a friend selling the doses got them from a West Coast brother at the Hampton Dead shows a couple weeks before, he said, back at the start of tour that'd hit various cities along the Eastern seaboard.

"You will walk upon beams of light," Mucky Turnbull said his friend had promised. "Participants in the ritual will *become* the light."

Billy understood from chatting up obvious Deadheads on campus that many fans would attend the two Atlanta dates right before the tour finale in Columbia, and he wondered if the real attraction had to be the drugs or hedonism rather than the music. Why else would people pay to see the same act night after night?

But Mucky, troubled by Billy's plan: "You'r losing a metric ton of cred for even thinking about getting near any of that hippy shit, Steeple."

"It's the pussy," Billy reassured him. "That's all. I swear."

"Good. I'll dance a jig the day Jerry Garcia finally croaks."

"Dude."

"Well—I will. It's stoner bullshit, dude. The whole hippie movement came out of MK-Ultra—the fucking CIA, dude."

Billy, calling balderdash, had grabbed Mucky in a headlock. A coffee table had been broken in the ensuing melee, and lucky no instruments damaged. The rehearsal after their spasm of violence had been their most vital music ever, raw and primal. Peak punk. No one would ever hear it but them.

Libby told Billy she'd done acid once or twice, back during freshman year at McKean High when she still lived in Delaware. She'd been running around for a while with this senior guy named Todd, a small time dealer, but that relationship didn't last because, she said, what he really wanted from her, she wasn't ready to give. She recalled those doses more as an amped-up drug experience than a psychedelic, transformative one.

"I might smoke some pot, but that's all." Libby, setting parameters, never a welcome development with one of these skirts. "I have class in the morning. And so do the rest of you."

"How can you say you want to be a filmmaker—a visual artist—and not trip out?" Billy had challenged.

"I told you I'd done it. My body, my choice."

"Killjoy."

"I'm quite serious. Cool it with the peer pressure."

"As you wish, m'lady."

Libby, so together and confident. Deserving of a more exciting partner than dumpy doofus Devin. And after the Dead show, she'd have one.

Jacked on Jolt Cola and anxious beyond measure, Billy got real and called the UT dorm. The soft-voiced redneck boy Roy Earl answered on the second bounce.

"Y'all about ready, Freddie?"

Roy Earl, a party hound, sounded stoked. "Just back from the last class. I got to run home in a little while to pick up Devin's sister, but the Edgewater County turnaround won't take but an hour."

"Plenty of time. A high school girl, eh?"

"Well—?"

"No judgement here, bro. I say initiate her. She'll thank you later. Trust me."

Roy Earl sounded embarrassed, mumbled a sort of faux-macho assent.

"But if you've cracked the first of the day, I'm getting my shit together and heading on over."

"Sweet. But Bill, look here now: grab another case of Bud on the way. I'll pay you back. For my ticket, too."

"Money is meaningless tonight. We'll settle accounts another time. One day when we're old, and we've forgotten the details."

"Righteous."

The night of nights, Billy realized, now upon him.

Libby.

In this bed.

It would fix what ailed him.

But a last-minute issue: his bedsheets, stiff with dried semen from sexual encounters as well as incessant, tortuous self-abuse often leaving him so raw the last sensation he wished to experience was the touch of another's skin upon his. He threw the bedclothes into the small apartment-style washer and dryer in a hallway alcove, put a fresh set on the bed. At last he hauled ass, ran his errands. Big man on campus, coming through.

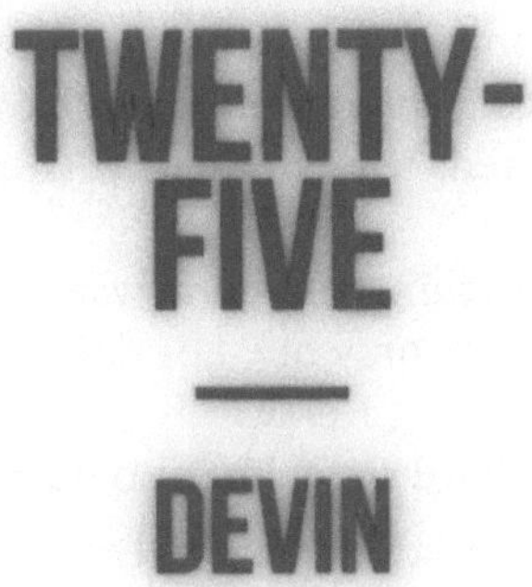


Six o'clock in the dorm suite, the air thick with smoke and laughter. A half dozen people drinking beer, passing joints, bubbling the two-foot purple, plastic U. S. Waterpipe-brand bong, laughing, screaming, having a blast. Music, thumping on the stereo—not the Dead, instead the Led Zep, side three of Physical Graffiti, Devin's choice.

Devin and Libby, sharing glances fraught with gravity and portent. Psyching each other up for the trip ahead. After finished a big class project that day, she'd decided to party-hearty with the rest.

To this end, Billy, busying himself in the kitchen with a razor blade. He cut apart the hits of blotter acid, same blade they used to cut up lines of Bolivian marching powder he'd scored last week, which Devin had declined.

A couple of weirdo Mike's friends, all three high and watching Danger Mouse with the audio turned off, their eyes giving off a sheen like the glaze on an Easter ham back in Edgewater County. Roy Earl, a jabbering idiot, seemed spun in advance of his upcoming drive—too spun; Billy had persuaded him to eat his dose at about five o'clock. That it wouldn't come on for a good long time.

Billy, articulate and emphatic about the necessity of experimenting with the substance in the presence of the Dead, while having less than no experience with the substance in question. "Worry not. You can drive like a champ on acid."

"But—I need to go all the way home and back—"

"Need. That's a strong word. You want to go. Big diff."

Roy, tabbing the dose on his tongue. Cracking a beer. "I've driven it a thousand times. I'll be fine. Plenty of time."

"There we go."

Devin, thinking, *Don't go now, pardner. You'll get in an accident.*

Roy made eye contact, sipped his beer, wandered upstairs to his room.

Devin, hoping he'd gone to call Creedence and tell her it was off. The fallout would be brutal. He should never have gotten her hopes up—neither one of them. Awesome.

Dobbs, the missing element at the party, who at the last moment had begged off. Devin, speculating the reason might have been the acid-talk.

Indeed, Dobbs had fretted, "I'm afraid of what might come out of me on that mess."

"You don't have to do anything you don't want to."

"But, I don't want to be the only one not doing it."

"Nobody's keeping score, bro. Relax."

Devin, not giving him a hard time, but also decrying his journalism-major friend's lack of curiosity. But, whether to party down or not, a personal decision: America, a free country, its proud citizens the possessors of will, drive and individualistic God-given thinking brains. Look at him—here, choosing to smoke dope with them all. Passing a joint heavy with resin. Tasted like sucking on a lavender sachet. Made him want to drink a beer.

Billy, offering half-doses to Libby and Devin. Noting Billy's leering, fevered, glassy-eyed stare. Faraway. Weird. They nodded to each other and took them.

After Billy distributed the rest of the doses like a shaman, Devin and Libby went out onto the concrete steps leading down to the fire lane between the buildings. They gazed down the hill as concert traffic backed up along Blossom Street. With daylight savings time ending the weekend before, the light of day faded quickly into the gray of a low cloud deck building in the sky all afternoon.

"Look at all those cars," Libby said. She sat close to Devin. He leaned into her.

Devin, head buzzing, felt the weed creeping on cat's paws into his consciousness. He stayed girded to notice effects from the acid in his system. "Answering the call of the dead?"

"Isn't that what we're all doing?"

"How so?"

"Life—it leads to death."

"Yes." Devin, knowing this better than most.

The world, seeming real; Devin, feeling the opposite of intoxicated. Grounded.

"Pot puts you in the *now*-now," Roy Earl had explained one night. "Like this guy used to hang around my granddaddy's honkytonk said: you're either remembering and processing the moment that just ended, or you're anticipating the one that's to come. Trying to get ready. When you smoke, see, it lets you be in the *now*. The moment you're in right now. No past. No future. The moment is all, he told me. And that the moment was forever."

"Whoa. What is time, anyway?" Billy had asked, blowing already stoned minds engaged in a late-night dormroom bull session. "Past and future are but constructs, but right now, is right now. See, there it is again. Now. Now. *Now.*" Devin, *now* feeling the sensation of which his friend had spoken.

He put his arm around Libby. She scrunched over next to him. Warm. Head on his shoulder. The two of them, watching a squirrel foraging in the grass underneath the oak at the end of the building, a big, ancient tree like the one in the front yard of Devin's house back home. Libby, eyes droopy and relaxed from the weed, a slight smile playing about lips covered by a thin sheen of gloss. Precious and beautiful, a rare creature. Devin, eyes tearing at her beauty, so natural, so innocent.

Devin, leaning over to kiss her, pausing. Anxiety swept through him. Imagining a world—his world—without her.

Silly. From whence this foolish feeling?

Libby, looking at him with a familiar expression of affection.

"What is it?"

"Someone walked over my grave. Let's be careful tonight."

Laughing, eyes sparkling, she stuck out her tongue. The small piece of paper, melting. "Too late."

Roy Earl came bounding out onto the landing wearing cargo shorts and filthy Adidas sneakers, a Blue Öyster Cult T-shirt pulled taut across a not insubstantial belly. He bellowed at the top of his lungs. "Whoop-whoop-*whoop*! I'm a whooping crane."

"Are you, now."

Flapping his arms, laughing until tears streamed from the corners of his eyes with pupils swimming dark and huge. Sweating. Breathless, gazing around with wonder. His dose had kicked in.

"What did my sister say when you called to bail?"

Roy Earl, a shadow falling across his face. His mellow, harshed. "I didn't."

"Dude. What time were you supposed to get her?"

"Oh, y'all." Libby pushed away from Devin. "She's going to be crushed. Devin, you've got to at least call her."

"Not me."

"Then you have to do it, Roy."

"Nuh-uh."

Libby, her disapproval total. "You boys are awful."

"All right, dag-nabbit." Devin, grumbling his way inside. "Buzzkill, this is."

Dwight Rucker, verbally pleased to hear from his son, picked up on the second ring. Curious about a request to speak with little Creedence, whom the father reported not now at home.

"What you need with your l'il baby sister?"

Devin, calling from the upstairs house phone, dragged it into his bedroom to muffle the peals of ribaldry from downstairs. "She wanted to hear all about this crazy concert scene over here. That's all."

"Son, I'll be honest—I wish none of y'all was going. Now, I've always been frank about the drinking and drugs and all, but I'll say it again: You a grown boy, and can do what you want. But should the day come when you're standing in front of a judge over drugs—a judge who can just as well ruin your life as sneeze at you—I might not be able to fix things as easy as I could here in Edgewater County. You understand?"

Devin, his scalp pulsing and the walls starting to breathe, tried to keep his voice steady. "So, Creed isn't there?"

"She went to the Fordhams. They gonna work on some project together till late. Your mother had a fit, since it's a school night," dropping his voice, "but when don't she."

"How many rounds?"

"Colette put up such a fuss that Mama, well, she gave in. As for your music concert, you'll have to tell your sister all about it tomorrow. If there's anything worth telling."

Devin, ringing off, burned with irritation at being dragged back into a situation he had already managed; out of his hands once Roy grabbed the baton. Colette—Chelsea, damn it—would have to understand.

*When Roy Earl doesn't show, she'll get the message. And for once, it won't be my fault. This case is closed.*

# TWENTY-SIX

## —

## CREEDENCE

Chelsea, sequestered behind the elaborate landscaped gateway to Pine Haven where she'd instructed Devin to tell Roy Earl to pick her up, squatted under a huge magnolia tree that loomed above her head like a sentry keeping watch.

The damp wind chilled her; the slate sky looked as though about to weep. Time passed fast-slow. Checking her watch; after about forty-five seconds, checking again. Roy E. Pettus, now only five minutes late, but still.

After yet another stupid argument with her mother—about spending the night over at a friend's house one neighborhood away, for heaven's sake—Chelsea got so angry that on the way out, she swiped one of Daddy's Budweiser tallboys out of 'his' fridge in the garage. Now drinking it, ice cold and yucky, yet good and bold. Of a piece with the whole enterprise.

She burped, and some of the beer came back up into her throat. She threw up the rest.

Chelsea, wiping her eyes, regarded her overnight bag stuffed with more, much more than she'd need for a sleepover. Enough to get by for a few days, until she got stuff figured out.

*Good-bye, Mama. For all I care, you can suck a poot straight out of my butt.*

But: a cold rock in her stomach. Her mother's dewy-eyed doting face, weeping for her lost daughter.

The minutes, slipping by, and the sky turning darker. A bobwhite, sounding off in the distance. Well out of sight, she yanked down her tight jeans and urinated in what seemed like an endless torrent. Feeling silly and exposed. Wiping off her privates with a magnolia leaf.

Every car driving past made her jump with anticipation. Now fifteen minutes late.

Where was he?

What time was this damn concert supposed to start, anyway?

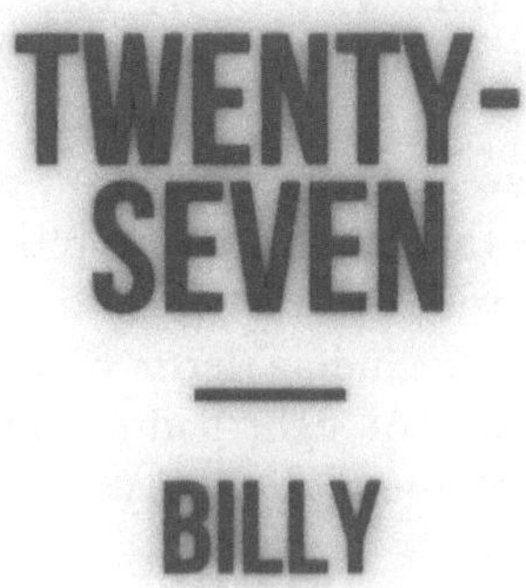


Cacophonous voices in the humid, crowded arena lobby, smells coming in waves: patchouli, cannabis, B-O like you wouldn't believe. Skin crawling, hesitant to touch anyone. Billy, tripping hard.

And fretting.

Feeling bothersome.

Fuck.

Inside the cavernous basketball hall, an empty seat between Devin and Libby. Billy plopped down between them, clunking Devin on the skull with a rude elbow.

His friend, eyes like saucers, almost exited his body. *"For fuck's sake, man."*

Billy, sweating and bopping to the house music, nudged Libby. "Hope the lights go down soon."

"Settle down, stretch."

"I'm scared," Libby said.

Billy, concerned. "What's wrong, angel?"

But she didn't look scared—she was writing a screenplay. "What if they're coming to kill us all."

Ruck, intrigued. *"Who?"*

"The Dead," Billy said, nodding. "They have at last risen from their cold, uncomfortable graves."

"Exactly." Libby scribbled a few lines in a small notebook she'd started carrying on the advice of her writing teacher. "Somewhere George Romero is smiling."

That was his movie girl. He didn't know about this Romero cat, but if Libby was into it, it was cool.

Libby, collapsing in laughter, slapping skin with fellow movie buff Billy. He nudged Devin, gave him a shit-eating grin.

Time and space slipstreaming all around him, light bending, Billy felt himself transcending into LSD warp drive. The band hadn't yet played a note. And poor Ruck, green around the gills.

*Excellent.*

Without warning, the arena lights winked off to a stupendous, chicken-skin inducing exultant roar that swelled up from the multitudes and crashed like a wave against the colorful bandstand now holding a unit of exceedingly ordinary-looking rock stars including Jerry himself, fat as the Goodyear blimp. Everyone in Billy's line of sight had already leapt to their feet and started grooving even though the music had yet to start—everyone with the noticeable exception of Ruck.

Creedence, almost soaked through from the mist hanging in the air, still crouched concealed behind the Pine Haven sign. Sobbing and heaving until nothing left.

No one.

Not her brother.

Nor that bastard Roy Earl.

No one was coming.

Well, 'no one' not entirely accurate: at one point Dusty had gone past the entrance to the subdivision in his grandmother's dark blue Ninety-Eight. He wasn't supposed to be driving after dark, not on a learner's permit. Dusty ought to have had his license by now, but he kept failing the test. Like Mama always said, with a dead drunk for a daddy, poor Dusty didn't have no one to show him how to do nothing.

Chelsea, needing to pull herself together. She could go on to the Fordham's after all, she supposed. She'd had to bribe Shelby with five dollars out of the precious stash-money for cover in case her mother called. Which with ever-protective Eileen Bevins Rucker on the case, a distinct possibility.

Shivering and soaked, at last she trudged a half-mile to the Amoco Gas Chief to call Dusty and tell him to come get her. No intention of explaining what'd happened, no—she'd say that Mama and her had had a fight, et cetera et cetera, all quite believable; Chelsea, later telling her mother than she and Shelby had had the fight, and that she'd gone to Dusty's to get him to go and beat her up, or some such dramatic prattle.

The Gas Chief. The bathroom inside. The rubbers.

Letting Dusty finally put his peterpiper inside her.

The grandmother would be asleep on her couch.

They would be good as alone.

Sure. That would show them all.

On the walk, she considered instead snagging a ride with somebody—anybody—else. Hitching into Columbia, only thirty-odd miles; a truck driver, kind, would buy her coffee and chat about life on the road.

In Columbia, finding them all. Beating Devin and Roy Earl until bloody. Ripping them to shreds with her woman-teeth.

A stranger passed in a Chevy van. Watching as he rolled on by her, fog lights cutting through the mist.

But how to know a stranger's intentions? So many serial killer stories, including Coy Wando right there in Edgewater Country. People saying, oh, it's not like it used to be—it's not safe.

*No. No hitchhiking.*

*Something safe.*

The Gas Chief payphone.

She made the call.

Chelsea, sitting against the wall under the pay-phone, her makeup wrecked, watched as Dusty squealed tires into the parking lot. She told her fibs, including plenty of detail to sound realistic; he believed her.

"Don't you need to use the bathroom while we're here?"

Dusty, frowning and wrinkling his nose at her bedraggled, wet-rat appearance. "You got mascara running all over."

"The bathroom," she repeated. "Shouldn't you go in there?"

"But I peed before I—" Her wriggling eyebrows sparked awareness. "Oh —*you really want me to?*"

She shrugged, coy, but kept one eyebrow arched. "One way to find out."

Hands shaking, Dusty fumbled change out of the cup holder of his grandmother's sedan and hurried inside. He stumbled over the mat in front of the automatic door. On the brief drive her back to his grandmother's house, he rubbed her leg above the knee, over and over.

Chelsea, hating the Wallis house so much. It stunk like his grandmother, of camphor, Lysol, and fake-sweet flowers all mixed together. When they got inside she went to clean herself up, ate leftovers while Mama Wallis blathered on badmouthing one of her rivals at the church. They sat together watching television until the old woman went to bed.

Alone.

Dusty's face, shiny in the TV light.

He rubbed and squeezed and smooched.

Okay, Creedence thought. Okay okay. Why not. One way or another, the night would be memorable. Big time. Once Dusty's grandmother had begun snoring from the other side of the thin walls, Chelsea Colette Rucker wiggled out of her jeans and set to losing her virginity.

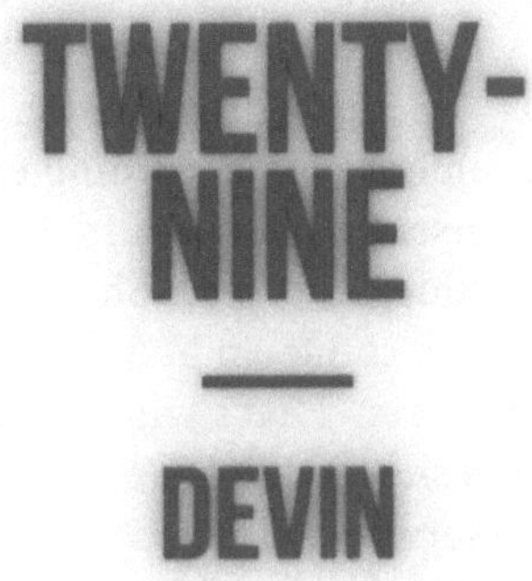


Devin, on the roof of his apartment building. The concert, still going, for all he knew. Enough already. That's what he'd said.

The experience had gone bad for him early on, but for Libby's sake he'd hung in as long as he could. The band's first set of mostly straight-ahead rock tunes, a country-flavored pair of songs sung by the younger, skinny guitarist, a long, droning Bob Dylan cover, 'Desolation Row,' seemed fun and exciting—to all twenty-thousand in the arena but him.

After the set break the band came out and played music much more strange, flowing and mysterious. Devin, not understanding where one song ended and the next began; the stage lights went dim and the band eased into an insane, dark improv jam he'd sworn capable of conjuring up demons.

Devin, gripped by terror, the urge to bolt overcoming him, yelled in Libby's ear, "I'm sorry."

Libby, rapt, cringed away from his shriek and continued to sway, uncomprehending of the danger he sensed. Pounding drums, driving him from his seat, up the steps, through the horrendous lobby full of twirling hippies and bemused authority figures.

Seeing Dobbs. At the show after all. With a guy. A big dude that Libby knew, from another of her media classes, wearing overalls, a tie-dye, almost as tall as Billy but heavier. Dobbs and big bear dude, standing tucked away behind a throng of spinners in an alcove with a door leading to offices, conferring; Dobbs nestled right up next to him.

"Devin!" His eyes like saucers, Dobbs jerked away from his new friend. "Where are you going?"

Why his old friend tried to hide being gay, he'd never understand. Nothing had ever happened between them, other than the time when they and Roy Earl all jerked off to porno mags on a camping trip. They had known each other too long for pretense. He might not be ready to tell his mother, or the rest of the world, but Devin, a best friend. C'mon. "I'm too fucked up. Enough, already."

"Ah. Your loss." Dobbs seemed to dismiss him. "See you back home."

Devin had fought his way out through the dancers and twirlers, a maelstrom of color and movement. Time, turning elastic. Mirrors of mirrors reflecting inside his mind. Noise. Pungent odors. Blissful faces, glassy eyes.

Libby. He'd meet her outside, he'd said. She nodded like she had heard, turned back to the music, which to Devin had been incomprehensible.

Fresh air, and a couple of beers. That's what he needed. Billy had laughed like a maniac when Devin had shouted in his ear that he had to split.

It all seemed like many hours ago, now.

His stomach clenching, Devin gazed in the direction of the distant football stadium, now dark following the conclusion of the Thursday night pep rally. Having to remind himself that what he'd felt and seen at the concert wasn't a threat. Meant nothing.

And yet: The Dead were all hippie and love, but some immense power had vibrated in that room alongside them all. The white-maned man at the center of it all, hunched and burdened by the weight of his guitar, as well the immensity of the nightly experience. Devin, sensing this, wondered if these people fully understood the energies they too the risk of calling forth. Either way, the conclusion came to him as a monstrous, idolatrous, biblical-scale immanentizing of the eschaton-style epiphanic reveal. That kind of type-deal situation. He wanted no part of the ritual, that much for sure.

Salvation remained possible. Escape was at hand for the traveling man. The phrase had lodged in his mind, until at last he acted.

Inside, the close ceiling in the apartment had been too confining. Up on the roof, a fine mist somewhere between light rain and fog floated in the air, reminding him of the thick haze of smoke rising into the rafters of the coliseum.

Libby.

He left her behind.

With Steeple.

Also Roy Earl, Mike, Carmen, the sexy neighbor who ran hard with the party-boys. All of them together, tripping balls and raging the concert. All fine. They'd be back here to collect him before all headed out to the Old Market, which after a concert like this would pop with revelry all night.

In the time since—an hour? more? less?—Devin leaned back against an air-conditioning unit, pounded six beers and became fully in the *now*-now, placid and whole in the peace of the nighttime roof. Also pissing like a racehorse, belching, drinking, damp, tripping, listening to the swoosh and swishing of the passing traffic on the wet pavement. Catching hallucinations on the periphery of his vision. The acid, tidal, waned but returned resurgent, a cycle.

"Well, this is another fine mist you've gotten yourself into, beau." And laughing. Devin could usually have a pretty good time by himself.

Devin, breathing, staring with wonder, open and alive. Thoughts traveling at lightning speeds inside his cerebral cortex, synapses opening and closing in patterns unfamiliar. Orange streetlights, already glowing due to the mist, streaking across his field of vision. The beer cans in his hand, huge; but then small, way too small.

A parade of marching anthropomorphic emergency vehicles, klaxons wailing and looking to Devin like animated cartoon versions out of WHO FRAMED ROGER RABBIT, approached with ghostly anticipation until blazing along Blossom Street, a swelling of orgiastic light and sound, the cacophony eclipsed in dramatic impact by the shocking and vibrant color-splash of first-responder reds and yellows playing across the buildings, the trees, the hillside park, the cars parked down South Bull Street. Across his own body fell the colored light, as it had from the concert follow-spots in the arena; thinking, then as now, he could feel warmth from the light.

In the wake of the firetrucks Blossom Street again fell into silence, the atmosphere on the roof still as glass; getting late. A dog barking in the distance sounded like the sound effect from Pink Floyd's ANIMALS; Devin wondered if next he'd hear the bleating of sheep. Instead he heard laughter, and the approach of feet on wet sidewalks. Libby—with Billy.

As their spectral voices bounced between the buildings, Devin, creeping over across the roof and crouching down, watched from the shadows holding his breath like a sniper:

Billy and Libby, skipping down the concrete path from the student union on top of the steep hill at the geographic center of campus, were holding hands.

Gut-punched.

Billy, stopping to gaze down at Libby. He now held both her hands in his. Devin could barely hear Billy's voice, out of breath, husky. But he heard enough.

"Everything's gonna be different now. I can feel it."

Libby, laughing low and strange. "How?"

"I'm on Dead tour after this. You heard what I heard. And you're going with me, doll-face."

"Be my guest. But I have class in a few hours." Libby, giggling, pushed Billy's hands away. "Come on. Let's find 'Ruck' as you keep calling him."

"Let's not, but say that we did our best."

Libby, uproarious. Slapping Billy on the arm. "You're awful."

"Everything's gonna be different," he repeated. "You'll see."

They ran over to the building, laughing and skipping like little kids. Disappearing under the balcony, Devin could hear the jangling of keys—Libby, having her own to the apartment, one Devin swiped off Roy Earl's ring back at the beginning of the semester. Poor Roy, gaslit to the point of near madness over how a key could, of its own volition, migrate off a ring like his had apparently done.

The voices, muffled and echoing from inside. He heard her faint call—"*Dev?*"—followed by the hollow thumping of footsteps up the stairs.

Devin crunched on the roof grit over to the corner of the building, his room below. One of the windows, cracked open to let out his cig smoke, gave him a reflected view of the room, albeit upside down and distorted. He wanted to observe, see if Steeple was making moves on her for real. An intuition. The acid had opened up meridians and neural pathways. Maybe he'd switch to this stuff from the booze.

His light came on. Billy's black T-shirt and bald head appeared in the reflection, Libby beside him in her tie-dye babydoll-style shirt.

Billy, sounding impatient. "See, Ruck's not here."

"Well—dang."

"His ass is already warming a stool down in the Market."

"*Or*, he's back there in the hippie village hunting for us."

"Let's go back, then."

"I'd rather wait. They say you should wait for someone who's lost in a crowd, not start searching. That's what the lost person is doing. You just have to wait for them to find you."

Devin, not believing his eyes. Billy, putting his hands on Libby's shoulders. Spinning her around. Crushing her to his body.

Kissing her.

Libby shoved him away. "Stop."

"I hear what you're saying. The time is perfect. So—so is the place."

Devin's blood, pounding in his ears. Waiting to hear Libby's answer. Incredulous, laughing, high, too high. "*No*, Billy. I—I'm not making out with you."

Confident and insistent and shoving his face into hers, he said, "You told me you thought it might be over with him."

"I didn't say it that way. I said, I hoped he still loved me."

"A woman should trust her intuition." Billy, pushing Libby back down onto the bed. Looming over her.

Devin's bed.

And now Libby kissing him right back, albeit with moderate reluctance. Head drawn back, one hand pushing away rather than embracing him.

Finally pulling her mouth away from his with a wet smack.

Devin, frozen. Watching her kiss someone else.

But putting a stop to it. "Okay, mister. Cool your jets."

"It's too late for that."

"This is not happening. This is Devin's *room*." Libby, sounding as angry as he'd ever heard her. "Are you out of your mind?"

"He's not even here. Who cares?"

"I can't do this—I don't *want* to."

"Yes yes yes you do. "

Libby, a quiet, tender, conclusive effort: "Billy—*no*."

"It'll make it better, being in here. Exciting."

Billy Steeple—dead man walking. Devin, seething, got up to go put this asshole in his place.

Libby, screaming.

Devin, finding his voice, his vision distorted by anger and LSD, shouted and lunged down toward the window.

Off the roof.

And fall-fall-falling, one tripping frame at a time, to the wet ground below.

# THIRTY
—
## BILLY

Billy's concupiscence now beyond the point of no return, a throbbing, explosive need pulsing throughout his circulatory system straight to ground zero, zooming, rushing, the peak of his trip going on and on, the concert all but forgotten, now here Libby, ready to receive his infamous gifts, the top of his skull feeling about to come off, edges of his vision rippling in a grand, revolving vortex, at its center his cock about to enter Libby's pussy. This, his destiny, and hers too, whether yet realizing such. About to climb on board Billy Express, promised-land bound.

He didn't care what she was bleating on and on about. He unzipped his greasy jeans. Showed that pounder to her. Ready to go. Leaking a clear stream of lube. And Libby, screaming like they all did—with delight. One problem: someone else screaming, too. From outside. What in the actual fuck?

The concert experience and been profound, Billy lapsing into a state of complete and open perception, the world on fire, stage lights a pulsing blob of color, the music, whether improvised or otherwise, loud and incomprehensible. Staggering epiphanies with each passing moment, sensations like what he mused a STAR TREK transporter experience felt like, every molecule broken apart, accounted for, analyzed, scanned, assessed, put back together. A quivering mass of manmeat, aware, alive, sentient, whole frickin' bit. Aware of Libby, of Devin, but beyond his two friends only a writhing colorful glob of humanity manipulated by the two maleficent drummers, their flailing limbs attached to gossamer strings extending out into the crowd like spiderwebs, puppet masters to the gathered throng, their movements tied to the anarchic loose-limbed dancing of the hippies.

The hippies; the tribe, as Billy'd begun to think of them. His people. Yes.

And they, too, he realized, were thinking of him, Billy Steeple, standing at the center of the great circle; no, astride the arena like the Colossus of Columbia, all of it occurring not only at his discretion and pleasure, but by and for said satisfaction.

Next, however, the band, played a lilting, mournful encore, disappeared with a wretched suddenness and reality again descended. Billy sat stunned after the lights came up and the world begin to again play out on a more prosaic level.

Now? No Ruck, only Libby. Now, saying to himself, time to act.

Slipstreaming back to the block of flats, the idea to take her in Ruck's room had gelled. He prayed the old boy was off somewhere drinking away his hallucinations.

Prayers, answered. Each unfolded moment had been so perfect, like one of the screenplays they'd write together—starting tomorrow. As soon as she'd gotten her fill. The acid gave him perfect clarity of purpose—no accidents possible. *You was cured, all right,* Billy heard an exaggerated voice like a black vaudevillian whisper in his ear.

But Libby, pissed and flopping around on Ruck's bed. Kicking at him.

Awesome.

The way he liked it.

It was all working out!

His tongue, thick, eyes crossing, getting the spins, pulling at the button of her jeans, his dick hurting, hurting with incipient pleasure. Smothering her with his Billyness.

Falling forward into the pools of her angry eyes. Pleading, his voice cracking. "Hush. It'll be different with me. I'm special. Look—"

Tugging at the bulging button-fly of his 501s, his Attribute flopped out accompanied by a sound effect he hoped would diffuse the tension. "*SPROING,*" he shouted.

"Oh," Libby said. "Jesus."

But then?

Laughing at him.

Not.

Sexy.

Fury, instead. Accident-level fury. *Put that cunt in her place,* a stentorian voice like the late actor John Houseman. *Make her pay for her offensive laughter.*

"BILLY, LET HER *GO.*" Ruck's voice, raw and huge, came booming from outside in the fire lane.

Libby shrieked anew—Devin fell past the open window.

Billy, untethered and busted; the one thing that could not happen:

getting caught. Because then his life would be over. Except, the accident hadn't happened.

Thank god.

Frantic, shoving his dick into his jeans, begging and pleading *I'm sorry I'm sorry* but Libby, slapping at him and cursing, bolting out the doorway.

Ruck had swooped in to save Libby.

God-damn, man. Like a superhero. Like 007. Like a freaking movie.

Shoving his dick dow into his jeans, best he could, Billy rushed to chase after Libby and Devin, to straighten out this fortunately forgivable—surely, certainly forgivable—misunderstanding among friends.

Yes—Billy could explain himself. This LSD, it gave him pathways to new space. They would all stay friends. This incident wouldn't queer the deal. It couldn't—Billy would be lost without these folks. He'd be left alone with himself again.

# PART THREE

# A BAR CALLED HEAVEN

## SUMMER 2004

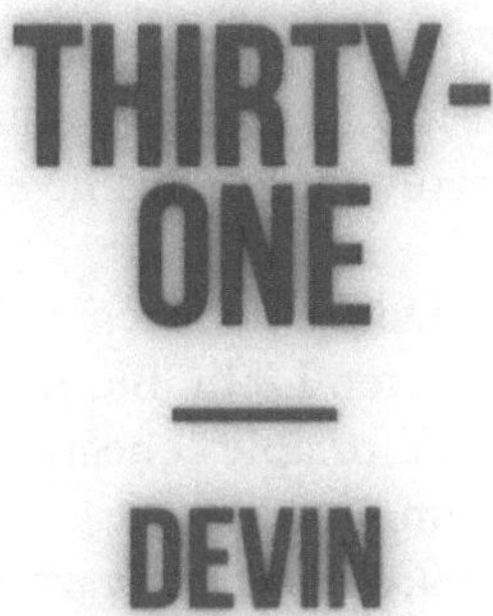


Devin, staring into the hotel bathroom mirror, regarded his pasty haggard killah ghostface. Scowling, disgusted, sick. Vague unpleasant memories of the past few days. Lots of drinking.

Which meant: All was right in his world.

Mostly.

At the moment, his feelings, hurt:

Late Friday night on the other side of their two-day haul across the southern tier of American states, that jackleg Steeple had deposited Devin at a downtown hotel in Columbia, checked his ass in like baggage and said, well-sir old Ruck old fella, gimme a shout sometime tomorrow. Had a blast driving from Texas, pal. A dry handshake, and gone.

Fucker.

Devin, struggling all through the day Saturday, paralyzed, depressed, freaked at being back in South Carolina, especially downtown Columbia. Emptying the hotel mini-fridge as he had back in San Antonio.

Not enough to do the trick.

He'd considered ordering a bottle of liquor from room service, but with costs starting at fifty bucks, saying, forget it, you thieves. Once Devin had refused to be driven to Edgewater County, the whole stupid reason for this ungodly clusterfuck, as Billy kept saying through a forced smile and bulging cartoon eyes, he had been dumped like an unwanted pet. And so, despite Billy's pledges, he might or might not show back up to settle the bill. No room service liquor, then.

Devin, sitting in morose repose. Turning on the television, flicking it off again. Sipping away at the minis and feeling unnerved—hotel rooms were like cages.

To pass the time, trying, for once, to sort through the clutter of his mind. To see back into the past with clarity, with veracity. No mean feat.

Cracking open the last mini-bottle, Beefeater gin. Gin sucked. But all he had left.

Sharp pains, exploding in his gut. A fluttery feeling as the tissues struggled to remain living in the face of constant onslaught from the toxic elixirs constituting Devin's waters of life, his flowing, forgetful waters of the blessed Lethe.

Devin, knowing he'd see Dobbs soon enough now that he was home. Well, he'd be seeing everyone, even Libby, but most definitely Dobbs. Ready to have matters out with that priapic, cheating, lying little bastard who seduced her out from under him.

Next, to deal with Libby: *You broke my heart, you disloyal Delaware yankee bitch. We were lovers in mind, spirit, body. But you left me behind.*

Panic, an adrenal eruption, full body tremors, images rushing through his mind.

Blood.

Glass.

Sunlight.

Now we were getting somewhere.

Sunlight bleeding in through the slatted blinds of the corner room to which Billy had insisted on upgrading, Devin made haste for the outside world. He exited the hotel in a daze, stopping only long enough to ask the bellman the precise whereabouts of the nearest liquor store, and thanking God in his Heaven that the day was not Sunday—in South Carolina, as in Colorado, the Lord's day remained a dry day, except in bars and restaurants.

The bellhop, probably a college student, recoiled from Devin's crisply astringent breath. "Around the corner," gesturing, shooing, offering a forced smile to a pair of well-tended guests exiting past the odiferous drunk fumbling around with a crushed soft-pack of Reds from the jean jacket pocket stained brown from the many packs of smokes that had gotten wet therein. The jacket, far from necessary on this nice spring afternoon, but a character like Devin needed a costume so the studio audience would recognize him as he walked onstage in his side-character comic relief role, a Latka Gravas or Steve Urkel for the modern age.

"Right on." Devin, extending a wrinkled, thin dollar. "For your trouble, ace."

The bellman, eyes narrowed and hard, really didn't like Devin or his breath. "Keep it, sir."

Shakes coming on now. It always made Devin emotional: "You little cunting bastard. Too good for my motherfucking tip, are we?"

"Sir—the bill was wet."

"I'm-a tell you what, son, as goddurn guest of this here fine hotel-iery, I demand to tip ye this dollar." Devin produced his card-key, held it up like ID at a checkpoint. In the other, he held the dollar by one limp corner. "I'll not have such impertinence. Now take it. And spend it wisely."

Now the slits widened. "If you insist."

"That's more like it."

Devin, crumpling the bill up and tossing it onto the hotel driveway, skipped away in one of his little drunk-dances. He called over his shoulder, "You best watch that disrespectful shit, buddy-row. I'll fuck you up six ways to next Wednesday."

Now, where'd that twink say the liquor store was? Guess he shouldn't go back to ask again. Bridge, burned.

Maybe he should call Creedence to come get him. Instead of buying liquor.

Nah. He'd show when he showed. That had been the agreement. Far as he could remember.

Wandering west until crossing Main Street, after another block turning onto the wide, six-lane thoroughfare of Assembly Street, he froze in midstep. Shock flooded in.

In front of the glass and chrome of the modernist public library glimmering in the midday sun, rows of mature Bradford pear trees stood in full bloom. White blossoms shimmering brilliant in the Carolina springtime light dropped in clusters and clouds in the morning breeze. Beautiful, if diseased trees; Devin recalled that the local paper called their planting a poor longterm planning decision on the part of prior city leaders.

The wind picked up—the blossoms, falling like snow.

Devin, hotfooting his way back toward the hotel. Away from those damn trees and their white blossoms.

He stumbled on the liquor store, tucked away on a side street. A fivespot from Billy's wallet later and Devin had procured a pint—only a pint, worrywarts—of crisp, clean Skol vodka, affordable sweet relief and peace of mind. They had said you couldn't buy it. Bullshit, he thought.

Ducking into an alley and cracking the seal, he gulped the hot liquor. Guts in spasm, gurgling with pleasure and yet not, he retched, coughing, but somehow forced his gullet to receive the vodka with the goodwill in which he'd offered the sacrament. Drinking another couple of good solid toots.

The nausea abated.

Ah.

Heavenly trumpets sounded; no, only the siren of a passing ambulance.

A sense memory, vague and unsettling.

Ambulances, fire trucks; their sound set him off.

Walking east away from downtown, shaking off the hellish image of the pear trees, he knew the campus of Southeastern University lay only blocks away. Not going there. No way.

And wherever he looked, yea, unto him: more white blooms, pink dogwoods, other vibrant displays of color sprouting from the rich and loamy Carolina soil. Devin, unnerved by the indicators of the earth's annual renewal; drinking, walking, trying to blank out his mind. Swatting at a display of wisteria flowers dangling like a bunch of lavender grapes, this at a law office in one of the few historic old houses Columbia still had, the lot of them full of lawyers and dentists and real estate companies; he crossed through a whole oaktree-canopied district of such structures, what passed for historicity in a city whose antebellum form had been otherwise rendered to ash by Sherman and his gang of retributive avenging yankee angels.

Feeling a modicum of steadiness, Devin now headed across the downtown plateau toward the hilly Southeastern campus and the flood-prone basin of the Old Market beyond. Danger lurked—these stomping grounds lay lousy with ghosts which might be impossible to drink away, to ignore. Devin, pretending to be a wandering drunk instead of one heading straight down into the hellish heart of the emotional maelstrom that'd gotten him into this condition.

Devin struggled down the long incline of Gervais—too steep, sidewalk root-bound and uneven, he kept almost face-planting his way to the low point underneath the train trestle.

Deciding to ankle the hillside, he braved a skulk through the nice Victorians and Craftsmans of University Hill. More huffing and shuffling took him by a tall, white condo building. He felt steadier on a level street, now. He noticed the pyramid-shaped shrubbery art out front; he saluted Old Glory hanging limp from a flagpole, all the while nipping the vodka. Hot belches, stomach sloshing. But in a good way. Mostly.

Crossing the railroad tracks, the smell from the fast food joint a block away either nauseating or tantalizing, here, the Old Market lay spread out before him—bars, stores, restaurants, shoppers. They called the area that because it'd been anchored by a Winn Dixie grocery store, a newfangled supermarket serving Herndon Hill, Columbia's first actual suburb built back around the turn of the twentieth century, making this area the area's first commercial shopping hub of the modern age; now it offered much more character as a college ghetto than the corporate big box-anchored strips choking out every traditional merchant neighborhood the country over. Going farther back, it was said that slave trading had gone on at the far top of the hill, in a market building up that way, so maybe that, too, had informed the naming of the neighborhood.

Only one or two newer buildings loomed over the old one-story rows of family-owned businesses he remembered. A lovely, lovely Saturday afternoon. The soul of the Old Market remained uncorrupted by corporate tenants. It was a relief.

Devin, shuffling by a smoothie stand called The Spotted Banana, glared inside at the young girl behind the counter busy operating a whirring blender. Cute as a button. No booze to be had here.

A blatant jaywalking decision carried him nimble-footed across the busy highway to a lovely bricked fountain, one built in the interim since he'd last haunted these streets. A couple of crusty, red-eyed dudes, African-american men from the nearby poor neighborhood, panhandled him. He told them to open their eyes wider and check out who they were asking; that they should shine it on. That there was hope right around the next corner, but not in his threadbare pockets. It was half-true.

Making his way down the block toward a coffee shop, mostly college kids sat at the tables outside sipping and smoking and reading.

Devin, staring through the open door. A figure inside, catching his eye— an avuncular-acting, heavyset man, a pleasant smile, laughing and talking to a customer. The voice came familiar and unforgettable, a voice beside which Devin had slept on camping trips and sleepovers, a best friend from back when friendship was more than a word:

"This Sumatran is so good it'll make you want to slap your mama. That's the one I take home with me at the end of the day."

*Well, I'll be a monkey's uncle—Roy Earl. My old buddy. Can't be. I must be dreaming.*

*But, I'm home now.*

*So I guess this is real.*

Devin, seizing the moment: marching in through the open doors, mumbling a string of nonsense syllables, waving his skinny drunk's arms around in a gesture of pleasant surprise.

Rather than embracing him, his old pal hustled around the counter like a shot. His cheeks had reddened: "I done told you fellas to keep out. Now get on before I call my boys in blue. Again."

Devin, freezing in mid-chortle. Backing out of the doorway. "I wasn't bothering no one."

"Sure you weren't. Skedaddle." Roy Earl, tough and mean. "And I don't mean five seconds from now. I mean now. Sir."

Acquiescing; unlike Devin's peers shucking and jiving up at the fountain, Roy's peepers were working right.

What an a-hole.

Some friend.

Slipping into the cool dim comfort and succor of the first bar to cross his path, Devin, down to it money-wise, would cocoon inside for as long as he could get away with it; to forget, divine.

They all wanted to forget about him, it seemed. Why not forget about himself for once? Only one way to do that; a liquid lunch in order. A hearty one, as much as he could swallow.

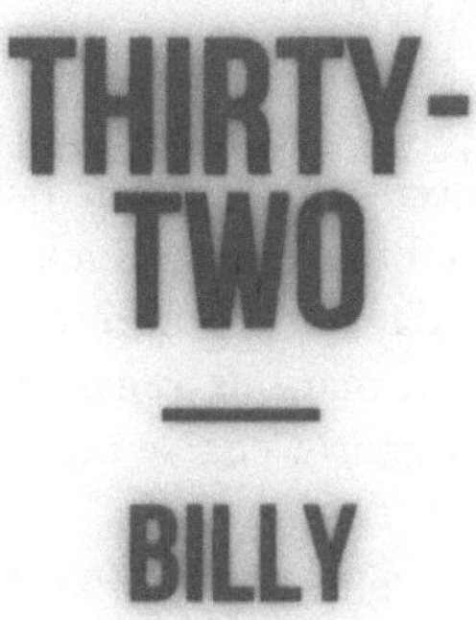


By the time Ruck's clunking, smoking Jetta finally crossed the Savannah River into South Carolina, Billy, descending into paranoid near-madness from exhaustion; swearing he could *smell* the radiation from the government's upriver nuclear-bomb factory. Seeing glowing shapes in the water flowing under the long interstate bridge. Malformed mutant cartoon animals leaping out from the side of the road. Startled into lucidity by the crack of another in an unending series of beers opened in the back seat. A running monologue of horseshit and lies and filth. Ruck, for two days, on a roll.

He didn't seem like the same guy Billy had known in school. For one, he looked about sixty, at least first thing in the morning. By the time of his first drink, Ruck seemed to lose about ten or fifteen years. Also: the more the fucker drank? Yep. He got downright lucid. One of those types.

All too lucid.

Gaslighting Billy. Pretending not to remember what happened.

They managed a decent night's sleep in New Orleans after the first leg. On day two Billy expected to be better rested, but wasn't.

Teeth on edge the whole time.

Waiting.

Waiting for Devin to stick a knife into the back of his head, or putting him in a headlock, jerking the wheel and running them into a concrete abutment or off the long bridge over Lake Pontchartrain leading from the west into New Orleans, or all through rural Alabama, or on the beltway skirting around the Atlanta megapolis.

But his old drunk, deranged compadre hadn't made any such moves, nor shown any antipathy or ill will. Had only sipped beer, told filthy stories and farted. Pissed into the liter-sized bottles of Aquafina Billy sucked down. Wept or cursed to himself, occasionally; went into twitchy fugue states, episodes Billy worried were leading to a full-blown seizure. Another beer or three usually took care of the problem.

When Ruck enjoyed his moments of coherency—Billy'd discovered that during the daily cycle one could expect a number of such periods, alternating with gurgling mad silly nonsensical drunken babble—he enjoyed chatting with his old buddy, much as Billy dared; Ruck, cynical, cannily observant, ironic and subtle, at times flat-out uproarious. Only when the discourse veered in the direction of intimations regarding subjects Billy wished to avoid did his voice take on a gnarly, coarse edge, Gen X sarcasm marinated in soul-sick brine for fifteen years.

But forget all that. In Ruck's presence, the grief over her, voracious. Billy, maybe finally getting it. Why the boy-o drank so much—Ruck hadn't even mentioned Libby the whole time. Didn't obsess over her. The motherfucker was free.

After the long slog across Texas, measured not so much by time as the consumption on Ruck's part of a half-case of tallboys, they'd arrived at the hotel at which they were to stay in New Orleans, a Renaissance-branded Marriott property located right across Canal from the Quarter and pre-arranged via cellphone. Billy, he explained, enjoyed gold elite status, comp upgrades, concierge level, all please and thank-you and sucking his royal and prodigious dick. Literally those words.

Ruck had remarked at that point: "Nothing changes with you."

Billy had feigned innocence. No, really. He was like, *what?*

Once checked in, Ruck, acting as though he'd died and entered the gates of the promised land, had dragged Billy down to Bourbon Street. Five minutes later they strolled by Larry Flynt's Barely Legal Club drinking Hurricanes and subsumed within a parade of like-minded hedonists clothed in various stages of dress, undress, inebriation. Sloppy, wild-ass, whooping it up—and this on a non-Mardi Gras weeknight. From the youthful demographic on display, Billy suspected college spring break accounted for many of them.

Ruck, declaring with remorse how, in all his years of sodden foolishness, he'd somehow never made his way to New Orleans; ruing how shortsighted this omission. "Get a load of this place."

"It's extraordinary." Billy had shuddered, a weird vibe to it all. "You can feel the ghosts lurking up on those balconies. Watching us."

"Ghosts? Fuck that noise—it's the drunk's Disneyland. That's what this play is. And we ain't going there. We *are* there."

"So we are."

Ruck had moved over, a sudden close-talker. "You got us this far. But this is my world, now. And you'll defer to me. Understood, old buddy?"

Playing along. Billy could snap Ruck's neck and dump him in the Mississippi. "Commodore, the bridge is yours."

Contemplative. Three grunts' worth. "You want to go and fuck some nasty Cajun slit? Bet it tastes like seafood gumbo, extra spicy and shit."

Billy, mumbling how, if given the choice, he'd pay for pedigreed poon before slumming it. If it were all the same to Ruck. "If we're that hard-up, I belong to a network of reputable escort services available in all major American cities."

"Nah. Pussy can always be had for nothing."

"True; semicolon. But thank you, no." Billy, unsettled by Ruck's veer into sex talk. "I have a girlfriend back home."

"Do you, now." Ruck, amused. "Serious?"

"Afraid so. Unless—I do something about it."

"That's more like it. You get tied down, it's over. Right, Bill?"

He could but nod. When Ruck was right, he was right. That part hadn't changed.

Acknowledging this stung Billy. An end-stage alcoholic had more sense than he did. No wonder he was still being trolled along by his father with that pitiful trust payout every month.

*It's because they all think you a retard. And you are.*

Leading Billy along, Ruck orchestrated a wild scene indeed: The Quarter, and with it, unbridled abandon. Billy, however, sipping and nursing this time. But Ruck, oh, mercy, without a care. Not like the previous night in San Antonio, when he'd been a drink-pusher. And had pushed Billy over his limits. New Orleans or not, it wouldn't happen a second time.

After getting a decent buzz going they stood by the open front of the Maison Bourbon, listening to a Dixieland combo inside tearing it up. Ruck, ordering and chugging a Maker's Mark, triple, rocks.

The band finished. The small crowd—in addition to buskers on every corner, seemingly dozens of joints had bands playing—applauded and called for more. Ruck whoop-whooped and tried to clap but dropped and broke his glass. He made a fuss about 'sweeping it up himself,' which had not gone over with the staff. The drinkers moved on.

Hereafter they strolled and stopped in for quick drinks whenever Ruck raised his hand; he settled into a reflective and confessional state—a place of honesty—in which he told Billy a strange, personal story:

Speaking at length of catching his mother doing the nasty with a family friend, like a scene out of some redneck soap opera. From the sound of it, nothing more than a case of typical, old-fashioned adultery among small-town intimates, naughty but banal and commonplace. Shocking, sure, at that moment—he was only a kid. But these things happened. Any atavistic humps still hung up on sex or pussy or nontraditional relationships here in the modern age might as well hang it up.

The next bit of Rucker lore, however, piqued Billy's interest much more than his mom *schtupping* an uncle, or whatever the relationship was: "And around that time, I went to work one day at that piss-ant country club back home. And damn if I didn't find this here dead mo-fo floating in the goddurn pool."

"You found a dead body?"

"Deader than dogshit."

Billy felt icy inside. He'd seen much worse than a drowning victim. "Ghastly."

"Finding that old feller floating there, it just fucked me up beyond all reason, beau. On a fundamental level type-deal." Ruck snorted and shook his head in frustration. "Nothing was the same after that. Like his ghost is following me around and stirring up shit. Like I pushed him into that shallow end head-first."

Billy felt nothing. Less than nothing. "Death be not proud. Sounds like the fellow had some tough luck."

"Along those lines." Ruck, shrugging and smoking, enshrouded vaporous and blue in the glowing light from a bar's brilliantly beckoning neon signage. "He done it to himself."

"You wouldn't call it an accident?"

"There ain't no accidents."

"Nonsense. It's all accidents."

"Now there's a debate for your black robes back on campus."

"Those philistines at Southeastern? Philosophers they are not. They don't even know art movies."

Ruck, uninterested in movies. "But this pool-fucker, he told me shit no little boy's supposed to know."

"He 'told' you? I thought he was dead."

Ruck, shrugging, eased into a joint to get his liquor topped off. "Three of us in the pool. Me, his body, and his ghost."

So melodramatic! Billy scoffed. Finding a body at fourteen? By that age he had killed his first classmate and concealed the corpse in a storm culvert; it wasn't found for months. The locals in the town near the boarding school blamed it on a pedophile who had been apprehended on a morals charge; his apartment yielded a cache of death- and child-porn. Case closed.

Dead guy in a pool? That Ruck had not killed himself? No big whoop-

whoop. Billy, again, t'was a pity. He could ill understand Ruck's longstanding guilt over the death of a stranger in which he had no hand.

His boy had come back slurping bourbon and belching with wincing, strangulated aplomb.

"Let's banish all talk of death and pools," Billy suggesting with good cheer and an arm around Ruck's shoulders.

Ruck, who tensed up at first, relaxed and agreed. "Let us banish ourselves. If we can."

"Yes," Billy said. Chicken-skin. *If only.*

The moment, broken: a stumble-bumming group of preppy college fratboy types brushed through. One elbowed Billy, who sloshed tepid draught beer onto expensive shoe leather.

Ruck, hard-eyed and serious, knocked back his drink and flung the glass against the wall with a burst and a tinkle. Gurgling with menace: "You little son of a whore. Get back here and lick this boy's penny loafers clean."

The college guys, laughing and hooting, flipped them off without breaking stride.

Billy, snorting high-voiced with frustration. "Look at the cuffs of these trousers—*at my Weejuns.*"

Ruck spat and cracked his knuckles. "When we see that boy again, he'll apologize, Bill. Finally. I can promise you that."

A chill fell in Billy's gut. "Who'll apologize?"

"You know who."

Sudden, Ruck ditched the darkness. Happy and gregarious, he hauled Billy through every bar left in the Quarter. For hours he spun filthy stories and leered at every shocked and chagrined woman whose misfortune it was to run into him, ultimately becoming so shit-faced that, at last, into the hotel bed he went to pass out.

Ruck, snoring like a drugged ogre, twitching and spastic but unconscious, a condition for which Billy, exhausted, felt duly thankful. Billy, cracking the seal on a brandy from the mini-bar, sipping it like a gentleman, shaking his head at his old friend.

Wanting to go find the fratboy. Make him sorry for his disrespect. Such fine clothing as Billy's, none of this comes cheap. Someone always must pay in stories of wrongdoing, injustice. Payment for sin offers the only path to redemption. If such themes weren't true, they wouldn't make movies about them.

Ruck, as though still coasting on the previous night's glorious, besotted pinnacle of intoxication, greeted the morning lucid and upbeat, receiving the startling room service knock with a stretch and a smile and nary a cross word. He ate dry toast with relish and aplomb, going so far as to enjoy a smear of orange marmalade, the sweet taste of which appeared to have a profound effect on him. Instead of guzzling vodka first thing as he insisted ought to be the plan for day two of driving home, Ruck, instead only a pitcher of mimosas, chasing the champagne with ice water and going "*Now this is real class, here, boys.*"

Good, Billy thought. A baby step.

"Hell of a town." Ruck, crunching through a mouthful of sourdough and draining a slender glass of orange juice and champagne. "Might ought to just stay here. You and me. What you think about that?"

A bemused Billy, with an acid stomach, demurred on the notion.

Hours later, a proper piss and lunch break at a Georgia rest stop. Ruck, munching crackers and petting an elderly couple's small dog; the couple, but not the animal, regarded him skittish and wary. Sidelong glances from faces pale and pasty and liver-spotted. Billy thought them prudent.

Billy, slumming, procured a vending machine sandwich, his mostly vegetarian diet already perverted and debased by the charred pigflesh he'd apparently eaten while drunk in San Antonio, or so Devin had reported. This explained the gurgling and rancid bowels, which since leaving Texas had continued in mild distress.

Back on the road. Billy, the whole trip making his way through a stack of discs he'd stopped and bought at a suburban big box retailer outside San Antonio. One after another the silver discs, a format rendered obsolete by hard-disk storage on small devices capable of holding a hundred albums, a thousand, slipped in and out of Ruck's VW factory combo stereo with clunky 20<sup>th</sup> century energy, digital but still antiquated: live Dead releases, Lou Reed's apocalyptic NEW YORK, Neutral Milk Hotel, the Minutemen, the Pixies, Dead Kennedys, Television's seminal MARQUEE MOON, but most poignant, Billy, every fourth disc or so spinning up MAKING MOVIES. Dying inside, track by track. Note by note. Guys like Garcia and Knopfler, pouring out his soul merely with the touch of flesh to a vibrating metal string. Billy, trapped in his own skin, forever struggling to get across via music, screenplays, human interaction.

Ruck, into a fresh beer, upbeat. "So when you want to listen to that tape, bub?"

Swallowing hard. "Tape?"

"The show. Our big Dead show."

"I've heard it so many times. Not just now."

"Don't it mean nothing to you?"

"You know it does—I gave it to you."

"Not the tape." Ruck, eyes moistening behind the aviators. "Us being together again."

"I wouldn't be here if it didn't."

"Cool. Forget it. The tape."

Billy, with immense relief. "Maybe another time."

For the next couple of hours, Ruck, regaling Billy of further misadventures both depraved and humorous, self-inflicted depredations of the spirit, horrendous and painful sexual encounters, beatings, muggings, fights, but above it all, drunk, drunk, and more drunk: Ruck's, a soul-sick existence, blackout nightmares of degradation too sordid to recount in decent company. Waking up having performed oral sex on a fellow drunk, discovering that she had received her monthly visitor, and finding in his teeth and in his mustache a surfeit of sanguineous, clotted evidence.

Billy, mopping at his brow with a monogrammed silk handkerchief produced out of a pocket with a flourish. A metallic taste at the back of his teeth. Apart from being vehicles for his own orgasm, women's bodies disgusted him. "God help me. I'd—I'd have killed her."

"Wasn't like she done it on purpose. The sheets, they was embarrassing enough. Worst part came when I tried to pay her."

"Were you light?"

"Nah, she started boohooing."

"Did she consider having her period a lapse of professionalism?"

"This was some chick I picked up all legit—she wasn't a Jane. But, I didn't remember."

"Ouch."

"Literally. Kicked me in the ribs, took off. Called me a worthless drunk. If you can believe the—" Ruck blinked and zoned out. Shook his head. "The temerity. I'm starting to lose all them words I learned as a kid. All them books."

Billy, taking a risk: "Any actual girlfriends along the way?"

"For fifteen minutes at a time."

"A real girlfriend," choking on the words.

Ruck waved it away. "N-word like me gets tied down, he might as well be dead."

Billy, saying, right with you except on the racial epithet.

The Dire Straits CD ended again. An interval of time, heavy with portent, passed in silence but for the *chunka-chunka* of Ruck's weary VW engine, the maddening, whistling whine from a back window that wouldn't roll up all the way. Tire rubber on varying grades of interstate highway.

Finally Ruck continued, as though the conversation had been ongoing. "There was this one old girl, back yonder in Colorado. Millie." He cracked a beer, gulped, belch. "Yep. She was right sweet on me."

"What happened?"

"I let her be my girl for a while. Yeah I did. Lanky, lucky old redheaded thing." Ruck, relating the story of meeting Millie while she was working the checkout at this goodwill thrift store, smoked and nodded, an archness to his voice making him sound like a fabulist. Him getting a job there, normal friendship, taking her to lunch, all leading to courtship; movies; hand-holding; hooking up, moving in together, an actual couple.

"And getting dry," he finally admitted.

"No kidding."

Holding up his hands like *Can you believe that shit?*, Ruck said, "It didn't last long enough to be memorable."

Now, the way Ruck had said her name, Billy, he knew this a lie. "She was a juicer, too?"

Ruck, sparking up a smoke and shrugging, slit-eyes peeping over aviators. "We kicked. Got detoxed. Until I said, eff that noise." Ruck, his voice coming now clearer and less affected. "We did it together, me and her. What a pip. What a lark it was. But ephemeral, alas."

"So it didn't work out."

"You're watching me drinking a god-durn beer, ain't you?"

Billy, with sad resignation. "I guess I just meant with Millie in general."

"No steady chicks. Not even her—it was all pretend. Call us 'the pretenders'. That's what we were."

His gut tightened—did Ruck remember how much Libby had loved Chrissy Hynde? Was that a reference to her?

Unprompted, Ruck added in a pinched whisper, "There wasn't no one but Libby for me, beau. She was the one."

"I know, Ruck. If anyone does..."

"It's you. It's you, Bill." Ruck, holding up his beer at Billy, a salutation. "It was always you. Wasn't it?"

In response, his hackles stood end-wise. "That's right, Ruck. Whom did you believe the protagonist of this sordid tale?"

"Not me. That much I know."

"That's right."

Ruck, grinning, had yet to look this serene and gentle on their road trip. When he had taken off his glasses, Billy had seen in the rearview not the drunk, but the boy Devin Rucker had once been. "I get it. We're all on pins and needles waiting to see what you're gonna pull next, Big Bill. You bet we are."

The closer to home, the more a grim torpor of fatigue and tension settled inside the Jetta, already reeking of flatus, stale beer and cigarettes even before this trying and odiferous journey.

Pulling into Columbia, a furious row ensued about taking the passenger up to Edgewater County, only another half-hour, but no; an adamant Ruck instead squared away at the hotel with another stocked mini-bar and few parting words. Billy, gratefully and at long last, stashed the Jetta in the hotel garage and left a note for Devin with his address, taking a cab home across downtown to his building.

Sure, first thing real soon, he'd be back to scoop him up. They'd go see Creedence together. Sure, sure.

Billy, finding a perfumed note from Melanie taped to his condo door. It read in part about how much she missed him, but also describing plans within plans, the salacious details of which made him tense with involuntary anticipation, and this despite the modest regard held for the so-called girlfriend he hadn't missed and still wanted to dump into a blackwater swamp, the hallmark move of South Carolina's homegrown serial murderer Pee-Wee Gaskins.

Billy, thinking about a bumper sticker seen during the drive:

**NO MATTER HOW HOT SHE LOOKS,
SOMEBODY SOMEWHERE IS SICK OF HER SHIT!**

Billy, wanting to get T-shirts and ball caps made, coffee mugs, fridge magnets, Beanie Babies, children's picture, chapter and middle-grade books in which to indoctrinate and initiate the next generation in this wisdom. Billy, pledging to buy billboards around town. He wasn't sure there was a single one of these women worth the trouble they put a man like him through. The stresses and accidents their pheromones and pulchritude caused, false markers of attractiveness masking a black widow's nest. Except for Libby Meade, whose rejection of him had been merely shortsighted and not foolish enough to warrant killing her over it.

Once inside his condo, he tossed his crap down in the foyer and headed straight for the bong; thankfully, neither Melanie nor anyone else expected him home until the next day. Four massive hits of the put-back 'secret' stash of Mendocino County's finest left Billy with heart palpitations, panic. He fought off wave after wave of terror, at last subjecting himself to a brutal, dry wank with a rough cleaning cloth, harsh friction lasting until getting a decent pop. Then, only then, did he doze off into a dreamless, fitful, comfortable sleep.

Bliss, this unconsciousness. Like the other night in San Antonio. When he had been drunk.

Other than awakening the next morning without his customary flagpole of rigid morning wood—unusual by any standard—he felt rested and even-keeled. Thinking, whether with Ruck or Melanie or Libby, a silly voice insisted on adding, if it all doesn't simply work itself out, he'd be surprised and perhaps a touch disappointed.

Billy, working his magic, in control. Accidents, from now on, happening only if absolutely necessary; only by choice. Starting with Creedence Rucker, he'd never lose control again.

# THIRTY-THREE

—

## CREEDENCE

When not fending off desperate phone calls from Dusty, to whom, adamant, she refused to speak, Chelsea's head had been set spinning by her mother with a series of rationalizations and explanations for his behavior. Eileen, in one of her shiny wind suits and matching lime-green Espadrilles, tried to make Chelsea think all the beating and whipping had been imagined.

Reclining in the La-Z-Boy and feeling the pain from the rising welts on her back, she considered the reality beyond dispute, beyond spin. And yet Mama, emaciated and coughing and fussing about in the kitchen, spun and took up for him.

Amazing. But, she'd been pretending so long about her illness that she could pretend about Dusty, too.

About anything.

Changing the subject, Chelsea brought up the subject of Devin's imminent. Eileen reacted with surprise and anger at this sudden news; Chelsea play-acted at forgetting, said she was sure she'd mentioned it. That when his bus got here, Devin would set matters straight with Dusty, if it came to down to it.

Eileen laser-beamed a daughter who swore she could feel her mother's ire like a shaft of warm sunlight. "I would've paid for him to fly home. I would've paid any amount of money. I swear, but y'all don't have the sense that God give a damn turnip. You put him on a bus?"

"You don't want him driving, do you?"

Eileen's anger turned on a dime to grief-stricken, brokenhearted despair. "Please watch over my poor baby and get him back to me soon, Lord."

Creedence, disgusted. Her mother had never been a churchgoer. In any case, thinking how a bus trip sounded like a romantic, mad adventure;

further, that all of them might soon regret wishing Devin back. Who knew how he'd show his ass this time.

Wishing, with horrible stone-cold guilt, she didn't have the baby in her stomach. How she could take whatever money they had in the savings account—not that much, of course—and hit the road. Like Devin had done all those years ago.

Fuck everything and run.

Was it too late to *not* have the baby?

Women did it every day.

Flushed unwanted children from their bodies.

The law of the land.

Getting a cramp, sudden and sharp.

"Do the two of you overgrown children realize what kind of people ride those buses? He's probably the only white face on it."

Chelsea, thinking her mother sounded like some hood-wearing Klansman like they had in Edgewater County back before integration and civil rights got settled. But furthermore, Eileen probably hadn't been on a bus since the yellow one she rode to school nearly fifty years ago.

The cordless sitting on the glass of the coffee table rang with jarring suddenness. A look shot between the women. Again.

"Mama, I ain't talking to his ass."

"You're just heartless to poor Dusty."

Eileen, scurrying into the kitchen, picked up the cordless. Chelsea heard the sliding doors outside the backyard shut as Mama went *uh-huh, uh-huh.*

Five minutes later Eileen came busting back in from the deck humming and smiling.

"First of all: I'm relieved."

"Oh, lord." Creedence, a mocking singsong, chin aquiver. "Let's hear his story."

Eileen's demeanor now fell reserved and careful, like conducting the treasurer's meeting around the heavy oak table in the red-draped ELMS inner chamber downtown. Enumerating bullet points: "He says the girl is nothing to him. That she's been the one calling and pestering him for it." She cussed the girl, lit a cigarette, said, *I swear to goodness.* "That she started the whole mess with him down at that durn hardware store."

"Mama—how can you excuse him?"

"He's sorry, darling. That's why."

Stupefied with confusion. "Did you ever have to forgive Daddy? Is that what this is?

She p'shaw'd at that. "Dwight didn't have the guts to screw around on me. Not that it's any of your business how your Daddy and me conducted our lives." Another Virginia Slims, lit off the butt of the last. "Now. It takes two to tango…"

"That's more like it."

"…and Dusty explained how you were confused and worried about the baby you've been. How *cold* you've been." Eileen pursed her lips at the salaciousness.

"Confused'? About how many times they done it? Or which way they done it? On my bed? In my house? Or Mama, how many times he whipped me?"

"Colette—hush your filthy mouth."

"I'll be damned if I will."

Now her fury burbled over like hot oil. A viciousness like no mother should ever show a child. Or a daughter, rather. "*He told me you hit him first. That you damn near bashed in his head with a skillet full of hot grease.*"

"Yeah—so what. I'm just sorry I missed."

Eileen had begun coughing into a pink hanky. It had once been white. "We can't have y'all carrying on like this. Not with you pregnant."

Hating herself for sitting and listening to this nonsense. "You're letting him sweet-talk you. 'Poor Dusty, poor Dusty.' It ain't normal. The way you're defending him."

Aghast with indignation. "Who are you to tell me what normal is? You haven't half-lived yet, girl."

"I'm gonna be thirty-two this summer."

"Age is a number. Experience is the gold standard. All this you're going through?" She chortled. "This is only the beginning."

Chelsea muted the television set, a ridiculous program about how many assistants Donald Trump goes through—bottom of the barrel, all these reality shows. She missed the old detective shows and comedies from when she was little. It was like they just didn't want to pay nobody to make up stories anymore. Cameras following folks around doing shit. Devin should have a show like it for drunks. Dusty, for fucking high school girls. "What are you talking about?"

"The beginning of doing what you have to do. To be happy. Do you understand?"

"No."

"To get by."

She barked at her mother to just say what she meant.

"Dusty understands. And you better, too. If you know what's good for you—for all of you."

Chelsea hadn't a clue what the old woman, addled from disease and nicotine and old Southern lady foolishness, meant by her opaque statements.

Enough. She stood and pulled the T-shirt over her head, revealing the welts across her back. "So this is what Dusty has to do to get by?"

Eileen cried in alarm, made her pull the shirt down.

"No, damn you—he don't get away with that part. Don't you think I already explained that much to him outside?"

"Did you, now."

"There are lines, Colette." Eileen, face puckering and a shadow across her eyes. You did not want to see this face coming. Not from Mama. "I spelled out consequences."

"Such as what."

Offhand. "That he'd never put that pee-pee of his in another little strumpet ever again. Nor my daughter. Because he wouldn't have it anymore."

"Don't give me no ideas." Draping the shirt back over herself, Chelsea winced at the touch of the fabric against her back. Another cramp down below, a depth charge. "Lord help me, I got to go lay down. My stomach hurts."

"I don't like the sound of that."

"If he calls again, tell him he's lucky I didn't put the Sheriff onto him." They didn't have no old redneck like Truluck anymore. Sheriff Oakley was not only a younger black man, whose election had given the ELMS set the flutters, but an ex-Marine and straight-arrow. He had exposed dog fighting and cleaned up a few of the worst honkytonks and juke joints, had instituted a DUI campaign, and best of all, had spoken out about the high rate of domestic violence in Edgewater County. He'd lock up a punk like Dusty Wallace. "Tell him, one phone call to Garen Oakley, and he'll be sleeping on a hard cot tonight."

Eileen said she'd hate to think her savior a smooth-talking black like Oakley. "He's gotten too big for his britches, too fast."

"Save that talk for your girls downtown."

Upstairs Chelsea caught Arthur, terrified at being in a new house, urinating against the door to her room. Not unlike her own decision about what to do about Dusty, and Devin, and with any luck, Billy Steeple as well, she put off the detailed attention such a mess would require. But she couldn't put it off long.

She wouldn't. Dusty's whipping had beaten sense into her—the Billy plan. His attention and resources would release her from this bondage. A warm glow inside—she recalled how excited he'd been with her all those years ago, before acting freaked out and pulling back, telling her no. At last she'd show him what he missed; that it wasn't too late to make up for lost time. And her baby would then be theirs.

Devin, heartbroken by Roy Earl having sent him packing, as though his old pal only another drunken reprobate panhandling asshole, saying fuck you, Roy E. Pettus. This kind of shit? The reason he hadn't wanted to ever set foot in this pissant burg again. Disrespectful, ungrateful asswipes, the lot of them. Where was General Sherman when you needed him.

Needing a cocktail, a proper libation served in a decent watering hole, where a gentleman could go and get some thinking and drinking done—wiping the mind clean—Devin had not far to go. Bar-shopping and killing the last of his vodka unmindful of passersby with shopping bags who glared, he slipped the empty into his jacket pocket and belched fire.

The elegant, half-lit room he chose—The Parlor, a classy joint unfamiliar to him—found Devin the lone Saturday happy-hour patron. Dark, peaceful, soothing, but for the incongruity of the modern rock playing at a reduced volume through the sound system. A comfortable, pliant, amber womb from which only a fool would wish birth into the harsh lucidity of sobriety.

Devin, considering a celebration with all due pomp and circumstance of this glorious return to the land of his youth; demonstrating the appropriate reverence and acknowledgement of this momentous occasion's arrival. A fat cigar; getting shitfaced shit-ass drunk as a coot; killing Dobbs Vandegrift.

And now Roy Earl, too. The disloyal fuck.

How after catching them together? He'd beaten Roy Earl. Yeah, he did.

*No—it was Dobbs, you nitwit.*

Dobbs.

*Billy.*

Bullshit.

Everyone was fucked up that night: Roy on acid, Devin and Libby and Billy too, none of them knowing what they were doing.

But Dobbs, he had been the one.

Dobbs, his thick dick jutting out like a purple veiny viper. Dobbs, waving the damn thing around right in front of Libby's face.

Her yelling at him *NO,* unheeded.

Dobbs, determined and depraved, pushing her down on to the bed—Devin's bed. Devin, faraway, unable to stop them, yet unable to look away.

Cold vodka sluicing down Devin's throat, sharp elixir; ice clinking against teeth white-hot with cold pain. Ordering another.

Wasn't Dobbs gay?

And he and Libby best friends?

And the last time Devin saw him, wasn't Dobbs in a wheelchair?

At the funeral?

Which funeral? What funeral? Whose funeral?

*Well, it wasn't Libby's, that's for sure. Because...she's not dead. She's with him.*

His father's funeral. A couple of years ago; lost years since.

Devin, downing his fresh drink and ordering yet another, calling out as though the bar crowded and noisy. The bartender, a kid not looking old enough to drink much less serve, his face a pale and impassive oval in the dim light, a glow from the far glass of the door, the only window into The Parlor, sighed and ambled over.

"That firewater's going down mighty quick, chief."

Devin leveled a grungy index finger but stopped himself, pulling back the rage. "Listen. Give a dude a break, kid. One more, and I'll be on my way."

Skeptical. "One more's okay."

"This's oldschool, me being in this neighborhood. Good to be back. I'm celebrating." Devin, relaxing, leaned back on his stool. "Place get busy later? All these kids from the college up yonder?"

"Dude, you can't get in here after ten o'clock, especially on jazz night. Line down the block."

Adjusting his colorful tie, tucking it into a vest out of which hung a pocket watch chain, the young man set down another vodka tonic, smooth, no clunk, a pro barkeep. They had their servers here dress all nice and shit. Devin noted a glimmering tie-tack that he thought looked like the compass-and-square Masonic symbol.

"Notice you ain't got no jazz playing now." The satellite radio seemed set on an early 80s station, Talking Heads right now.

"When it's this early, the officer on deck takes liberties."

"Understood. You from around here?"

"Went to school up the hill. Never seemed to leave."

"Same as it ever was, same as it ever was," Devin sang-spoke with a wink. Talking Heads had been one of those CDs they listened to on the ride back home.

Billy and his music.

All those CDs he bought on the trip. Throwing money around. That had been so crazy, him stoping and buying CDs to play.

After Devin said that all he had in the car was the Dead tape.

The Dead tape.

The Dead tape.

The Dead tape of the show they'd gone to.

Libby.

Dead since that night.

Wait. Or, not.

Was Libby dead?

*C'mon, boy. The car wreck—who the fuck do you keep trying to blame?*

'Wharf Rat.' There you go. Devin had wanted Billy to hear 'Wharf Rat,' the song about the drunk. But Devin, he'd missed it—it'd come late in the show, after horrified and claustrophobic he'd bolted from the arena, away from the gesticulating crowd of hippie acolytes reveling in their orgiastic frenzy of twirling and dancing. Hearing the recording of the second set a thousand times since, yeah, but missing the actual moment of performance of that song. Ruing.

Regretting.

A detail about Libby: that next day, her telling him how cool 'Dark Star' had been, how happy the fans had all seemed when the band played the psychedelic tune. But Devin, missing the moment. No 'Dark Star' for Devin; no 'Whart Rat,' either. By then back home. On the roof.

Remembering the fine mist, the low cloud cover. The wailing of the fire truck. The color-splashes of the lights.

Falling to the ground.

The pain in his shoulder.

Libby, screaming out his name.

Twice. That night—and once again. Months later. Not at night. Not on the roof.

In the hot sunshine.

Dobbs and Libby. In the car. With Devin.

Libby's face.

Libby's face, kissing Billy. (*Dobbs, you idiot, Dobbs!*)

Billy on top of Libby, holding her down.

*Billy!*

Libby's face, drained of color but for her lips, turning blue.

*Billy, stop!*

Dobbs's slight body, bloodied and broken on the side of the road.

*Billy, let her go!*

A flash of light, and an awful roar.

Blood.

Glass.

Sunlight.

Prudy, howling in pain—his cat, too. In the car.

Libby. There beside him.

In the wrecked Mustang.

Devin, his skeletal frame wracked by tremors, saw silvery spots boiling. Images poked their way through the screen and scrim of his oblivion.

Libby and Billy.

Libby and Billy on the night of the Dead show.

Billy, trying to rape her. On Devin's bed. But yelling for him to stop.

Libby's savior.

But that next spring, Libby calling his name again, Libby's face, dead in the car, the steaming, hissing engine block sitting in her lap. Twin peaks of horror. The rape, the accident. Months apart, yet connected. The flash of the sunlight in his eyes shining down where moments before there'd been the roof of the car, the brilliant light reflecting off a thousand-thousand tiny shards of glass, off twisted metal and viscous leaking fluids. Devin's seat—the driver's seat—the only part of the car not obliterated; that he and his cat and Dobbs survived, a miracle. Or so they said.

The light. The flash of light. Like in the pool that day, too. The light; the death rattle from the man, and from Libby, *huh*, into his screaming face. Cold water. Blazing hot sunlight. Fire into ice.

Devin, a horrific yelp of recognition. Rearing back on the stool, snatching up his fresh drink, gulping and gasping like a dying man in a desert more arid than the devil's own. Howling up to the ceiling, pressed tin panels that may or may not have been authentic. "Oh, fuck all your mothers, you motherfucking ghosts—!"

"What the fuck, dude."

He flung his empty glass at the bartender, who ducked as it went tumbling and clunking down the bar onto the tile floor behind. Devin's spine, cracking with the effort of the throw, diseased warmth sweeping into his extremities, a fever, his thin blood raging, pumping.

Alive and awake.

Strangling out a tortured series of words. "I thought I killed you all. But you keep coming back. You keep coming back..."

The young bartender, brandishing his slicing knife, shouted, "I should have listened to my gut about you. *Now get out*," in a voice more tremulous than steadfast.

"Boy, I will knock your ass three blocks over onto queer street." Devin, sliding down the aviators onto the craggy beak. He felt a drop of snot fall out of his nose. "Now pour me a fresh goddamn drink before I feed your nuts to the squirrels in them trees out front."

Dropping the weapon onto the cutting board, the barkeep now pleaded rather than threatened. "Pay up and get out."

Devin, trying to smile, the muscles in his cheeks jumping with spasms, drew out money with a trembling claw—the last of his cash—and placed the folded bills on the bar. Wheezing, barely able to get out the words: "I'm sorry. I'm sorry. I'm sorry about the glass."

The bartender, snatching up the cash. "You drunks suck."

"You little dick-weed. 'Drunk'—you say it like it's a bad thing. If it weren't for drunks like me, you wouldn't have no damn purpose in the world."

"This is a part-time gig, asshole."

"Am I a drunk? Is this a bar? Is this real? Is this really real?"

"I'm calling the cops." The kid, snatching at the cordless with his own shaking hand, dropped it onto the floor with a clatter.

"*Well call them, then.*" Devin, pounding the bar and hurling invective, primal and piercing and ravaging his ruined throat, cocktail napkins and swizzle sticks leaping into the air; pushing back, kicking over a few of the heavy stools, clattering onto the carpeted floor, he began screaming epithets, hurling invective-laden threats at the floor, the walls, the ceiling, and the doorway leading outside into the light.

In the light.

You will.

Always.

Know.

Devin, the mad vestiges of his bitter and occluded memories torn asunder, knew his purpose here. Now his primary mission in life redefined, the quest now consisting of finding and killing Billy Steeple, lay beyond that door. Steeple the liar, lying all week, as he'd done so many years ago. Devin, sensing a wearing out of the welcome at The Parlor anyhoo.

"Catch ya on the flip side," he shouted, high-stepping his way outside, ready to go and get himself killed, finally. "Bigger fish, and all."

Those three drinks had settled nicely on top of the breakfast vodka. And getting enraged about all the shit from his past, why, he almost felt human again. Now all left was to make some trouble about it all. He'd start, as always, with himself, and another drink somewhere. Then he'd know what to do.

The phone buzzing interrupted the first normal crap Billy had taken in a week, caused him to jerk and pull a stitch in his lower back. He grunted out what more he could. His diet, a wreck for days, now. Too enervated to cook a proper meal. Too much cheese, bread, processed foods.

The hits kept coming. Roy Earl, aggrieved, called to explain that a bum he'd ejected from the Beanery earlier looked a lot like Ruck; he wondered if they could be back in South Carolina already? How he'd run after the guy, but the skeletal figure wearing aviator shades had disappeared, wraithlike, into the afternoon shoppers and weekenders strolling about on the sunlit sidewalks of the commercial village.

"Did I fuck this up?"

"We got back last night. So—yeah. Could be him."

"When I said to vamoose, he got this look on his face. Like he was hurt. I finally seen his eyes, then. That part don't change about a person, even when the rest does."

"A hug probably would've been better. Yeah."

"I thought he was—just a drunk."

"We both know Ruck's more than that."

"I'm as dumb as a bag of ball-peen hammers."

"No, Roy. It's on me. I shouldn't've left him alone like this."

Billy, suggesting they pool forces to track Ruck down in the Old Market. Finish getting him delivered to Edgewater County. "You bear no responsibility."

"I'll fix it. Fix it all."

"You will?"

His worm had turned. Confidence, now; his words came flat and cold like black ice. "I'm the bossman," Roy Earl said. "Bossman solves problems. Our boy's as good as found."

"Word."

Billy'd been ignoring the Devin Problem all day now, instead getting stoned, calling Melanie over and fucking the shit out of her a few times and trying to watch DVDs, but getting bored with every movie he chose. He had a number of messages on his phone he'd also ignored—his area chair from the conference in San Antonio, a fellow film archivist and colleague from San Jose State, sputtering with concern because Billy had bailed on the BIG LEBOWSKI panel without a word.

*Yours was the showcase paper, Steeple. Our big gun. Jesus, man. Well—I hope you're all right.*

Embarrassing, but unimportant. Deleting the message unreturned. What was he doing wasting time with these movies, these fictions? Libby awaited.

He meant Creedence.

Billy, Melanie, and Roy Earl Pettus all stood in foot-shuffling stasis in the open doorway of the Beanery. All clutched comped coffees courtesy the bossman.

He had circled the block, Roy reported, but hadn't seen Ruck.

Billy, sniffing the air. "He's close. He's real close."

"What's the plan?"

"We think like a drunk and start crawling—he's in Lupo's. Or, Little O's. McHaffie's. The Back Porch—"

"—or Eddie's Saloon, The Patio, or The Parlor; Lucy's, The Red Tub, or Yesterday's."

"Right. The task in this neighborhood is somewhat herculean."

"We should wait here," Melanie chimed in. "Maybe he'll come back by."

Billy, staring down the LEBOWSKI-esque bowling lane of forty, questioned his sanity—what was he doing with this ignorant child? He restrained himself, barely, from snatching Melanie out of the chair and turning her into a broken Pez dispenser.

Savage and abrupt: "Why don't you keep quiet and let the grownups sort this out?"

Her angst, tumbling out in a rush. "But Billy I haven't seen you all week, and then you show up with this awful drunk? And, like, I want to be alone with you but now we have to find him and do what, then *do what with him*—?"

Roy Earl, bug-eyed. "If y'all got something else on the sked, I'll look for him. Drive him home to see Creedence. I don't mind," nodding with bright-eyed vigor.

"You need help. Trust me."

"If I can't settle him down, y'all sure as hell ain't gonna. Me and Devin, we used to be tight." Explaining with wistful pleasure to Melanie, "We were kids together."

But Billy, thinking Roy Earl suffered a condition of overstatement in conveying the depth of his friendship with Devin. Billy and Ruck, they had been real running buddies. For a while, anyway. Deep conversations. Couple months, anyway, before it fell apart.

Meaningful as hell.

The sharing of Libby.

But when that drunk took her away from them all, yeah. That's when he and Devin became the closest. Until the day Ruck split for keeps. Sad times all the way around.

Melanie, plopping down at one of the tables, rocked a fuzzy Ugg boot while sipping her giant iced mocha. "You can't help someone who doesn't want it. Unless, of course…"

"Now this I have to hear."

"You think he might hurt himself. Or someone else."

Billy, seething. "Ruck would not hurt a goddamn fly. I could be persuaded to hurt somebody, however. If pushed any further."

"Please quit fussing at me about every little thing. I didn't do any of this."

"We all have our parts to play."

"True—we are co-creating this scene together, you and I. And you too, Mr. Pettus. And my part is all about love and light, whereas yours, hon? Stress and strife. You need to chill and allow rather than trying to control this chaos."

Billy, trying to breathe, wished for Superman's heat vision to roast this recalcitrant disrespectful slit right where she sat. The gall of her insulting New Age platitudes and self-help crap. Soaring, operatic heights of indignity at the thought of expending breath trying to explain Ruck; Ruck and Libby; Ruck, Libby and Billy, and the past and everything else to this, this youthful trollop would take more honesty than Billy could dredge. He had that much self-awareness.

Billy, risking a deep-dive into her moist, pleading eyes, felt a glimmer of human contact. She held out her hand, which he took.

"I'm sorry, angel."

She squeezed. "I know; I know."

Blowing out his lips, he continued in a tone kinder and gentler. "Ruck's like my own brother. You can't fathom the mental duress he suffers. It's more than the booze—the mania I've witnessed goes beyond that."

"It started young," Roy said. He fretted and paced. "When I was getting a buzz off two beers, Devin was already pounding hot liquor."

"We'll get him into alcohol treatment. That's the easy part."

"But will it take? There's the rub."

Melanie, a quiet grace note. "It's all about connecting with the higher power."

Billy, at fault for so much that'd occurred, or so he'd now begun to understand, ignored her sentimental hoodoo about a benevolent God waiting nearby to heal hearts. Billy was the one who made up stories. Not her.

"If it takes more than one facility; if he needs more than one chance, the one thing we won't do is give up. No, sir." His voice cracked like Jimmy Stewart finishing up a stem-winding populist soliloquy from classic cinema about which Billy professed deep and abiding insight as well as trivial knowledge, yet hadn't actually watched with any keen or specific interest, if at all.

He held up a finger, kept his eyes on Melanie. "Here's the deal: I wasn't there for Ruck, when it counted the most. I let him down. I let him get away, all those years ago. And I won't to do it a second time. We won't debase our history and friendship and debt to Devin Rucker by turning our backs on him again. I won't have it. The thought sickens me."

Roy Earl, fired up, clapped Billy so hard on the back that a pen leapt out of his shirt pocket: "Who said anything about giving up?"

"*That's the spirit,*" Billy wheezed as his breath left his body.

A police cruiser rolled down the street; its siren blipped in staccato salutation. Inside, a bulky cop lifted a veritable tree-limb of an arm at Roy Earl.

Roy waved back. "McWhorter's been on the Market beat for twenty-five years now. Better hope we find Ruck before he does."

"I remember the good officer ran my lead singer Mucky Turnbull downtown on a D&D one night during load out. We had to bond him out later with cash from the gig. Hard to believe the same cop's still around busting balls."

Roy, staring down the street, gape-mouthed. "Holy shit, there's Devin reeling down this way—but looks like McWhorter's made him."

Melanie, raising her hand. "Remember what I said about staying put?"

Billy, whipping around. The prowler, pulling over a few car-lengths down the block, disgorged an enormous, African-American cop whose shape and gait Billy remembered well.

And sure enough, there on the sidewalk, Ruck, still in his same denim jacket and greasy dungarees from the long drive home. Waving his arms and shouting at the huge cop, whose body language stiffened and froze... except for his hand, which drifted to the butt of his service revolver.

This could get out of hand.

"You people stay here," Billy ordered with a slashing gesture.

He trotted down the sidewalk toward Ruck and the cop, barking orders at Devin Rucker to halt in his tracks. But no, Ruck, drunker than shit it seemed, kept coming down the sidewalk hollering invective, calling the cop a fascist pic, hurling epithets at Billy, until finally they ran into one another.

It was an explosion of energy, like Hulk and Abomination crashing into each other. A flash of red light, a huge crushing release of energy. Sky-rockets in flight, afternoon delight: Ruck, the skinny drunken bastard, had clocked him a good one.

The force of the blow had sent them both to the sidewalk. Billy, crumpling in a heap of khaki and loafers, heard the cop's shouting voice calling for backup all filtered and faraway, like in a dream sequence.

A scream from Melanie snapped him out of a painful, foggy reverie. Billy, realizing that his face lay upon the gritty concrete, a smushed cig butt only an inch or so from his eyeball, had only been hit one other time in his life. And that had been Devin as well, come to think of it.

McWhorter leapt over Billy's sprawled body and straddled Ruck, who'd rolled onto his stomach. The cop, twisting one of Devin's small forearms back while grabbing the other wrist, cuffed his detainee in a flash of practiced movement.

"That's the last punch you throwing today, my man."

Now a flopping, subdued sidewalk seal, Devin said, "Let me up, motherfucker."

McWhorter, breathless, lamented the sorry scene. "Saturday night underway already, but the sun ain't down yet." To Billy, in a more officious tone: "Sir, are you all right?"

Billy climbed to his feet as Roy Earl and Melanie blustered onto the scene. "Yes, I'm fine."

"Knocked you on your booty, he did."

Billy squirted the cop with smarm. Fingering his jaw he said, "Oh, is that how we're writing this up?"

McWhorter seemed unaccustomed to processing Gen X sass. "We would probably call it 'assault'."

Billy shook his head with vigor, *no no no*. "Officer, this man is ill; he's under my care. So if you don't mind, I'll have to insist you allow me to handle him from here." Billy, folding his arms and expecting only acquiescence from this servant, whom he considered one notch above the Mexicans who kept up the landscaping around campus, stared and wiped grit from his cheek. Cops—pains in the ass; to be avoided at all costs. Especially at three in the morning with a warm body in the trunk of the Mercedes, heading over toward the Green Hole.

McWhorter answered a voice on his shoulder-mic with a staccato bit of police code. "Your patient here just clocked you one, doc. We got multiple eyewitnesses."

"So you keep pointing out."

Considering a bald-faced lie but after a millisecond's deliberation thinking better of doing so, Billy gestured toward the campus. "All right, dammit. I'm not a doctor. I'm a librarian. Up the *hill*." His inflection meant to indicate superiority as part of the august tenured class of learned employees of mighty and venerable Southeastern University, a long way from the police academy. "A media archivist, to be precise."

"A do-what, now?"

"But what I do for a living's beside the point. The point is that—that—"

"Here's my perspective, sir. This man's not only D&D, but looking at assault. He matches the description of someone who threatened a bartender not ten minutes ago," cocking an elbow back up the block, "at The Parlor over yonder."

Billy, irritated beyond measure. "So a national emergency, in other words."

Another cruiser, pulling up. McWhorter waved and went to drag Ruck to his feet. "Sir, *can you stand up?*" he shouted. "Help me help you, all right?"

Ruck's sad expression, a contortion of possessed agony. "Just shoot me right here, you fucking pig." Pleading and pitiful. "Do it do it do it *do it*."

"Oh, my goodness," Melanie said.

Roy Earl, his eyes swollen and face the color of a brick, stepped in. "Alvin, don't listen to him—our friend's sick. But we can help him."

Skeptical. "Mr. Roy—you can?"

"Billy's right. Let us help him. Let's not put him in the pokey."

The cop, pissed. "Now Mr. Roy, when you was president of the neighborhood association, I sat across the boardroom table and you looked me in the eye and says, 'Alvin, I want you to lock up all these drunks, and I don't want to hear no excuses from the CPD, all going on till y'all merchants was bluer in the face than this uniform.'

"C'mon. It wasn't that bad."

"So let's clarify: Do you want me to lock up the drunks? Or not?"

"I might not still be president, but I can assure you I speak for this neighborhood." Roy Earl gave the cop a do-my-bidding glare. "And in this case, no arrest is happening here. That's the end of it."

Damn. Billy had never seen this side of his old buddy.

McWhorter greeted the backup cop, Boykin, a hard-eyed whiteboy dwarfed in size by his fellow officer. Drawling, a good old boy from someplace like Edgewater County, he wrinkled his nose at Ruck. "Smells like somebody done messed their drawers."

"Kiss my ass," Devin growled. He hurled the N-word and told them both to suck his dick dry.

McWhorter, yanking Ruck to his feet, slammed him onto the trunk of the cruiser. "Sorry, folks," he said as though telling Clark Griswalk that Wallyworld was closed today. "But I feel certain we taking him on downtown."

Billy, snorting with dissatisfaction. "Bullshit, this is."

"Hold on, there." Boykin, frowning at Billy's profanity. "Watch that potty mouth, or we gonna put two guests in the back seat."

Billy snorted and scoffed. "Uh-huh."

A standoff. While Devin drooled on the police car, the cops stood now watching Billy with suspicion.

Fools. They had no idea the snakes in his gut and head that threatened to uncoil at a second's notice. Billy's greatest fear through the years? A public hulk-out one day like he'd always managed to avoid. Thank god he had gotten completely baked on sixteen hits of a hybrid strain of Sour Diesel before they left.

"Up the hill," Billy reminded them of his higher social status, "we don't take verbal breaches of decorum lightly. But, an arrest for what?" Steady and stentorian. "Even here in 2004, somebody verbalizing such a racial epithet can hardly be held actionable in any legal environment of which I'm aware."

"He's got a point," Boykin said, snickering. He probably used the word himself with frequency, Billy suspected.

Roy Earl, enough of this. "He's drunk. Needs a shower and coffee, not a jail cell. Let him go, fellas."

Billy, maintaining enough control to seem as unhinged as he'd begun to feel: "Gentleman? All perfectly goddamned delightful, to be sure, out here before God and country. But as you can plainly see, my friend's in a high degree of distress, and so I must insist that you allow us to take care of him. He—it—" Putting half his fist into his mouth, he composed himself. "He's suffered an absolutely terrific loss. Needs the kind of help. That a night in the lockup can't possibly afford him."

"Oh," McWhorter said. "We can sober him up."

"You have counselors on staff? Who handle such cases?" Clutching his torso with arms that strained and vibrated with the desire to beat them all to death, Billy managed at last to smile. "Or, we could go ahead and get actual attorneys involved. Wouldn't that be fun."

"God help us," Roy chimed in. "Ain't that the truth."

"Sir, this man is a danger." McWhorter, sad and tired. "To himself. To all of you."

Billy brandished his phone like a weapon. "Dude: my lawyers squat in one of those tall shiny buildings downtown. Think about it."

"Mine as well," Roy added, his eyes cold, all hint of conviviality with the cop now vanished. "This has gone on too long already."

McWhorter, sighing and weary. "Ain't no arrest, ain't no need for no downtown attorneys. Sure enough."

Billy, murderously relieved. "Expect to see a letter to the editor soon in the *Columbia Record* praising the CPD for sound judgement of its fine, working-class beat cops."

McWhorter, unlocking Devin's wrists, offered only pointed and sarcastic cynicism. "Don't do us no favors."

As the cops drove away, Ruck, unsteady, wiped snot onto the sleeve of his jean jacket and regarded the three people watching him like a hawk.

"Well, I be dog—Roy Earl. I seen you earlier, but you didn't act like you knowed me."

Roy, shamefaced as could be. "You all right?"

"I ain't doing too good these days." But he sounded cheerful about it. "Not at all."

"Ruck, let's get you cleaned up. Get some decent food in us. I've got seven-grain bread—we'll make all the toast you want." Ruck, ambulatory but buckle-kneed, his face slack, held tight to Billy for support as he led him down the sidewalk.

Glancing back to see Melanie lagging behind, the dragging of pedicured feet; Roy Earl, tagging along off to the side of the cool kids, trying to keep up. Probably the story of his life.

Next steps, other than getting off the street?

"Do me a solid," Billy called back to Roy Earl. "Call Creedence for me. Let her know Ruck's coming home."

His pained face split into a grin. The phone was already in his hand. "Now that I can do."

Appearing at the back deck stairs, the intruder startled her out of a reverie, times playing frisbee in the backyard with Devin. Having sneaked around through the woods, her erstwhile life-partner had crept into the backyard like a dad-blamed burglar.

Dusty.

Who done it with a high school girl.

Had kicked at her cats.

Who'd beaten her.

Chelsea had been sitting outside trying to clear her head by reading an article in *Entertainment Weekly* about how lovely and smart and talented and rich some teenage girl already was, and there, Dusty. Trying to act all jokey and smiling and saying hey, now, Creedence.

This, all she needed right now—more of Dusty's whining bullshit. Him and Britney Spears both needing to take a chill pill. To get over themselves.

"Get out of this yard, boy. My daddy's dead, but his shotgun is still loaded."

Dusty's cheeks were inflamed as though he had rouge smeared upon his face. "I ain't done nothing and this is silly and you coming home with me. We—we got this durn baby to think of, now."

"Will you stop? Those ain't nothing but words Mama's put in your mouth."

"It's my baby. I got say in this."

"I don't need you and my baby don't need you neither. I ain't never been so sure of nothing in my life."

Cramp.

"You need to go to the doctor. Get some of them antidepressants or whatevers. Mama Eileen says they give them out to pregnant women like candy-corn now-days."

Cramp, cramp.

"I'm not the one who's acting crazy and needs pills. Screwing some teenager. Beating on me like you done."

Dusty, an edge creeping into his voice. "You can't prove nothing."

"I can't 'prove' nothing? You just admitted it all, you big dummy."

"No, I didn't. Quit trying to confuse me." Coming up the steps and grabbing her fleshy upper arm, he warned, "We married, and that means you do what I tell you."

"That what Mama says, too?"

He grabbed her face and mushed it in. "It's what I say."

Chelsea, now scared, yanked away from him.

Circling each other on the deck like wrestlers, she feinted toward the sliding glass doors; Dusty, blocking her way, grabbed at her and knocked over one of the heavy iron chairs around the patio table.

Moving back toward the steep steps down to the sloping back yard, she felt dizzy, losing her breath. Cramp cramp cramp. "You just admitted it. You told me everything."

"You ain't scaring me. Ain't admitted nothing."

"Your little—teenage—honeypot." Getting the spins, grabbing for the railing. Reduced to monosyllables. "Done. Go. Now."

Lunging for her again. "I didn't do nothing and you can't prove it no way."

Chelsea, hissing and striking back, but before she was able to right herself, her head swam anew and she tumbled backward—that feeling, the chair tipping over.

Down the hard wooden steps, a tangle of legs and arms and onto her hip and elbow; her head, bonking the patio concrete *hard*, a flash of red—and Chelsea, all grayed out.

He had killed her. Dusty had killed her. She couldn't believe it.

Her senses returned. Their voices came to her as though she were inside an enormous, empty auditorium. Dusty and Eileen seemed at odds with one another.

Vision doubling, Chelsea found herself lying halfway on the rough patio pavers and the dry, scratchy grass of a yard that needed the tending it no longer received since Daddy had died.

Eileen's voice came hard and urgent, a kind of vitreous scorn notable even for her: *"If you don't get back, I'm going to tell them what all you done, god-durn-it."*

"But she tripped over her own big feet, Mama. I swear."

"Dusty, go take your redneck Wallis ass around front and wait like I told you. Do it. Do it do it do it." Eileen, offering a further string of epithets. "You asking us to forgive so much, son. So much. Lord have mercy on my soul."

Dusty, blubbering, went with his gut jiggling around the corner of the house. "But I swear I didn't do nothing—*she just fell over.*"

Chelsea, the cramps; flaring like electric eels buzzing in her lower body. She held herself.

Moaning: "Mama, my stomach—it hurts so bad."

"Oh, sugar. He didn't mean it. We gonna get you fixed up. Hush, now."

Her baby, dying. She didn't need a doctor. Her heart knew it.

Eileen, standing back up, held her side and groaned with pain. She went over and sat down heavy, but only after righting the chair Dusty had overturned. She lit a cigarette and put her forehead in her hand. "Now every neighbor's gonna be on the phone to each other, yap yapping—I hope you young'uns are happy. Finally embarrassing me to death like this."

She heard the ambulance siren on the highway, turning into the subdivision, approaching. "I'm glad Daddy ain't here to see it."

"You hush your smart mouth," Mama said.

# THIRTY-SEVEN

—

## BILLY

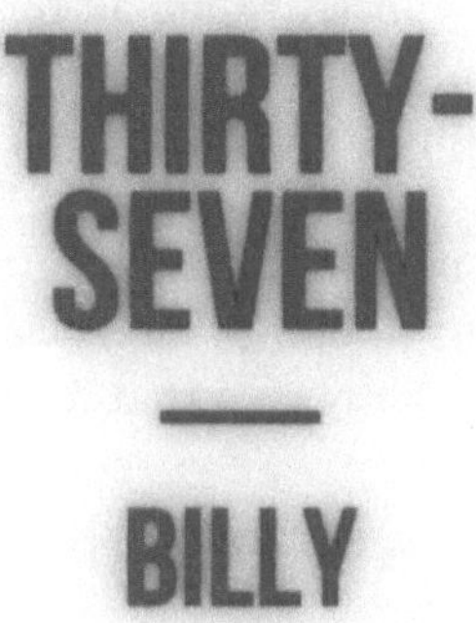

Billy, in the kitchen with the other participants in the ongoing drama, came up with a take-out meal plan. He wished for death rather than spend another second with any of these wretched nitwits. But here it was.

One issue: he couldn't drop off Devin at his family home, not in this condition, not tonight. Tomorrow. Sober, cleaned up. Billy, not going to Edgewater County looking half-assed, not in front of Creedence.

Besides, he hadn't been able to raise anyone in the Rucker clan.

Tomorrow.

Yes: they'd get a couple of those morning beers into Ruck, even himself out enough so Billy able to present him in a reasonable state before punting and hightailing it with the wind at his back. Despite his fantasies and lust for Creedence—or because of them, rather—he held no desire to spend any undue amount of time with her. More he thought about it, too dangerous. Too much pent up desire. Hard enough not to break Melanie in half these days.

Ruck, sneakers off and ensconced in the media hub—his feet smelled like the effluvium from the chicken processing plant across the Congaree River; like death itself—had quieted down since Billy presented a dusty, half-full liter of Crown Royal kept on hand for his father's infrequent visits, a libation otherwise untouched by the younger Steeple.

Billy, figuring: in Ruck's condition, what could another few drinks hurt? He'd chug that brown liquor, pass out—God willing—awake to puke his guts out, and next into the Mercedes for a quick jaunt past the lake country up to Chilton.

Seeing Creedence; maybe making time for Dobbs Vandegrift, too, another sad case. Visiting the lot of them, all reunited. Fly the missing man formation out to the memorial garden of grave sites. No reunion of this crowd complete without Libby.

Wait—*what?* No way.

He hadn't been to the memorial garden in almost ten years, not since Jerry Garcia died back in 1995. Oh, how Billy had wept for Garcia, grief that dredged up a fresh round for Libby. Not that it ever truly went away.

Drunk for the first time in ages on the night of Garcia's death, Billy had howled and wept alongside a dozen fellow Deadheads gathered for a candlelight vigil in Mojeska Simpkins Park, on the other side of the Old Market from campus. Chugging vodka. Cursing and crying until deep in the night, not realizing everyone had left except him and the crackhead denizens of the park who were shuffling around the small circle of melted candles, wilting flowers and other sentimental totems left to the entertainer's memory.

"Yo, bro," one dude in a grimy Army jacket said. "Gimme a slug of that white lightning."

"White lightning?" Billy, shitfaced, had been incensed. "Why is it always racial with you people?"

The memories hazy, all Billy recalled was that a scuffle had broken out, a knife pulled. Hollering and bolting across the dewy damp grass of the inner-city park, deep in the humid August night, Billy had run awkward and heavy-footed, the crazy whiteboy freak crying over the dead fatman, Billy's unbuttoned Oxford shirt flapped behind him like the limp wrinkled cape of a half-assed superhero, one about to shit himself from fear.

The assailant caught up, grabbed for the bottle. Another brief struggle. Billy, huge, drunk, and terrified, struck the thin black man with the heavy vessel hard as he could, a considerable amount of foot-pounds per square inch of force.

As such, the man's head had cracked open in a spray of brains squirting out of his mouth and nose, viscous splatter later found lodged in the crevices and tassels of a pair of loafers. He had thrown them into a campus incinerator often used in vanquishing accident remains.

Leaving the body crumpled in an overgrown vacant lot and wiping clean the bottle of prints before carrying it to a back-bar dumpster full of the same, Billy had staggered home in a daze. When the body had been discovered the next morning by a resident, the death was blamed on neighborhood gang violence—the man had had drugs on his person, meth and crack and pills. Black on black crime. Nobody had given a shit. For some reason, this killing had haunted Billy. The dude had wanted a drink. That was all. He hadn't deserved it.

In any case, deliriously hungover and freaked by the shocking incident of the brains in the nighttime—no accident, this; extreme ultra-violence, random and weird—Billy had called in sick. He drove up to the cemetery in Edgewater County, one to which he often traveled to pay respects and talk matters out with Libby, usually on Sunday mornings, his little church service.

Listening to the tape of the second set from the Dead show. Weeping like a little bitch over Garcia. And Libby. And yeah, even Ruck too, who by then had long vanished.

Trembling and nauseous, Billy had placed an elaborate spray of two-dozen red roses on Libby Meade's grave, and lay there alongside the blooms for hours excoriating a God in whom he didn't actually believe for having shown him the grail, but snatched it away again. Screaming useless and ridiculous threats until hoarse. Finally convulsing on the ground, dry heaving with multiple layers and iterations of blackest grief and alcohol sickness from his profligacy of the previous evening.

Seeing the brains splatter.

Remembering Libby's sweet innocent face.

Seeing it contorted in terror as he had loomed over her in Devin's room.

Begging forgiveness. But only the wind and the birds singing.

An Edgewater County sheriff's deputy, called by a concerned groundskeeper, rolled into the cemetery on the small road nearest Libby's grave. Billy, by now, had gotten back on his feet and pulled together his disheveled self.

The cop, strolling over, hands on belt, asked respectfully if all was well.

"It's the anniversary of my wife's death." A lie, and yet not. Gesturing down to the grave. "Another few minutes is all I need."

The cop's demeanor changed in a flash. A young black dude, he took off his hat and seemed genuine in his concern. "So sorry, sir."

"Car accident." Billy, explaining unprompted. "A drunk took her from me."

Anger flitted across the cop's otherwise impassive face. His words, expressed with grim thin-lipped frustration: "We do what we can about that. But it's never enough."

"Bless you," Billy said.

"You're not drinking out here today, are you, sir?"

"No. But I admit to tying one on last night."

Accepting this the cop split, after which Billy tried to weep some more, but inside now felt only dry and cold. Wanting to take it all out on someone. Anyone.

Devin Rucker. But no Ruck. Not then.

The next day Billy'd sent a sizable donation to the Fraternal Order of Edgewater County Law Enforcement Officers, not that it would stop any rednecks from getting plastered and killing young women in horrific day-lit, head-on collisions. But, we do what we can.

Roy Earl and Melanie, dispatched to get takeout from Golden Chopstix over in West Columbia, thirty minutes round trip, gave Billy a chance to peek in on his friend.

Despite the plethora of content at his disposal, the wall of DVDs and CDs and a few old VHS tapes kept around for sentimental reasons, Ruck reposed in the dim gloom of the hub in silence. Billy, noting with curiosity how Devin sat sipping, not gulping, the whiskey, the open bottle sitting balanced on his knee, a tumbler clutched in his other claw.

"Going down smooth."

"Told you I'd take care of you."

Avoiding Billy's eyes, cradling glass against chest. "You always were a class act."

"Ruck?" He squatted down, held out an open hand. "Do you remember what happened now? Is that what this is? With Libby?" No harder words ever said. "All of it?"

Ruck's flinty eyes shifted in Billy's direction. He set the heavy liquor bottle down on the coffee table strewn with scriptwriting and movie magazines, issues of VARIETY and THE HOLLYWOOD REPORTER from the last few months. "You son of a biscuit eater."

Billy, touching his own swollen cheek, hung his head. "We never did talk about that night again, did we? Not after—the accident."

"Why are you making me think about this shit?"

Amending. "Because I want to help stop this madness. What would Libby say about all this? If she were here?"

"No telling."

"She'd be so mad at you for acting this way. At both of us, probably," a quiet addendum.

Ruck, immobile, an air of calm. His posture, relaxing. "You said her name."

"Libby. Libby Meade. There, I said it again."

"I've been waiting days to hear you say her name. Years, even."

Morose. "Have you, now."

Totally chill, Ruck fished out a smoke. "You ready to talk about some shit?"

"If we must. No smoking in here."

"You was sucking on that bong earlier like it's going out of style."

"That's different. Melanie, she's the Nazi about it. She'd kick our asses, dude."

Ruck, nodding, accepted this line of reasoning. Putting down his drink and taking Billy by the arm, he said, "On the balcony, then."

Outside, the city and the campus lay splayed before them, streetlights and windows in buildings glowing like stars fallen to earth.

Ruck, leaning way over the sturdy metal railing, drawing in the smoke, cut to the chase. "What were you thinking?"

"I wasn't. I was young, foolish and—full of myself." *And if you hadn't intervened, she'd have fallen in love with me. She'd have been the one to fix me of the whole accidents problem.* But, Christ; he couldn't say any of that.

Bold. "I loved her." Some true gospel he felt willing to risk expressing to his old chum. "There, I confess. Happy? Feel better?"

"And so 'love' manifests in the form of you raping her, right there on my own bed," in a voice steady and dispassionate, "like it wasn't nothing. Like she'd be into it." Ruck, gesturing across campus in the direction where University Terrace, torn down in the late 90s, had stood, flicked ashes. "Damn, son."

"We were all fucked up."

"An excuse, but partial." Ruck, again counting off the charges, phrase by phrase: "In my room; on my bed; under my nose; against her will."

"That'll do."

"Fucked up or not—that's your idea of friendship?"

"Enough."

"Or of 'love'?"

"Stop it."

"Are you nuts, beau?"

"*No.*"

Ruck, smoking and nodding in the dim evening light. "All right."

Billy, desperate for his friend to understand, clutched at his denim sleeve. Ruck's body odor stung his eyes. "Almost nuts, sure. But that whole night with Libby, it was a total miscalculation—an accident—but most important of all, no, I *didn't* rape her. You stopped us."

"'Us'?"

"You stopped *me.*"

"An accident, eh?"

Well—now Ruck was talking his language.

"Yes. But you swooped in there like the caped crusader. Like James freaking Bond, saving the entire world. A hero."

"Sounds more like rose-tinted glasses talking."

"Of course, it was only that you fell off the roof, but the effect was all that mattered—like breaking a wicked spell. Hell of a thing, I tell ya. At the most anomalous moment in my whole life, my low point, you swing in to save her. From me," Billy concluded as tears leapt over his eyelids. He made no move to wipe them away. "Which was the best thing. For all of us."

Ruck sat down heavy in a canvas deck chair. "I saved her, did I?"

"You did. You saved me, too. Thank god."

"Do me this one favor. If you loved her so much, then tell me about her."

"Excuse me?"

"Tell me about Frances Elizabeth Meade."

Billy, not knowing where to begin. Wheels turning. Gears grinding. Now, the gulf of years seemed vast indeed. Groping for ideas, for words. Panicking.

"Tell me who she was, Bill. Or, can't you?"

"Stop it."

Ruck's disgust now palpable. "You didn't even know the girl. How could you love her, dipwad?"

Billy, eyes dancing faraway across the nighttime cityscape. He felt bothersome inside. If Ruck didn't watch it, they'd find him in the hedges fifteen stories below. "All too easily, Mr. Bond—you of all people ought to know that."

"Granted. But go on, now. Tell me one blessed thing about her. Just one little detail about who she was—who she really was, in here," placing an open palm on his chest, "and then I'll believe your innocent and wholesome tale of love."

"I remember her eyes the most—oh, those beautiful eyes. And she was smart, and so confidant... and we seemed to have similar taste in movies."

Ruck, nodding with deep satisfaction. "You through?"

Billy, shrugging, imploring: *What more do you want?* "Her smile. That little crooked smile of hers. And the bumpy nose."

"You could get that from a picture."

"Her sardonic, fatalistic Gen X worldview."

"That's all of us, dude."

True enough. Billy sat in shame.

Ruck, lucid yet trancelike: "Now listen up, William, and let me tell you about Libby Meade. She loved animals. Loved Prudy, couldn't wait to get another cat for her to have as a companion. She loved photos—taking them, looking at them. Scrapbooking, that kind of sentimental shit a man like me's got no blessed use for."

Ruck drank deeply of the Crown Royal before continuing. "Despite her family being kind of screwed up—Daddy a weirdo drunk like me, some Freudian thing, maybe, that she liked me? who knows?—she loved looking at pictures of everyone. Loved taking pictures. Her and her brothers, back when they were little."

A snatch of The Cure's 'Pictures of You' flitted through Billy's consciousness. Eighties tunes reduced him to rubble. "She had a Canon AE-1 when we took Still Photography together."

"Taking pictures—that's what got her interested in movies. A teacher asked her, do you have an interest in the visual arts? Before that, she told me, she hadn't even thought about 'visual arts' as a thing somebody could do for a living. One moment changed her life."

"Oh—this is solid gold, Ruck. Bless you."

"Least I could do for my old boy."

"I always dreamed of having a brother," putting his hand on Ruck's forearm. "You were the closest thing."

Ruck, shaking off Billy's paw and sparking up a fresh smoke, leaned with his back against the railing. "Lemme see what else is in our storehouse of intimate knowledge... she loved butterflies. She loved giving butterfly kisses. Know what those are?"

Billy, rueful, ached at the idea of being close enough to Libby to receive any kiss at all. Slack-jawed, he absorbed with detached wonder these fresh details like springtime blossoms.

Like an incantation: "Photographs. Scrapbooking. Butterfly kisses."

"She had secrets, too."

Billy, breathless: "What were they? Tell me," in grave desperation. "I beg you."

Ruck, shaking his head. "I can't."

"Oh, fuck you, you can't say something like that and then—*and then not—*"

"I only knew her about five years. Not nearly long enough to learn them all." Gripping the rail. "I killed her before she got the chance to finish showing me, or any of us, who she really was. Or was to become, anyway."

Billy stood facing away from Devin, now, at the rail. "The book says, 'you might be through the past, but the past ain't through with you.' I never understood that before. I do, now."

"What book would that be?"

Billy, snot running out of his nose, wiped his mouth. He leaned his weight on the rail, prepared himself for what he had to do next. Cold fire exploded in his gut, but he kept his fear of what awaited below to himself. "Only another stupid movie line."

"That was my death in the car. Mine."

His antennae twitching, he relaxed his hands. "What do you mean?"

"I knew death was coming—by then, I had known it for years. Had had this knowledge *foretold to me from almighty God*," shouting and gesturing like a black preacher. "By a man in a pool."

The idea settled around them, fogging their shared air like mist. Billy, thinking Ruck on a tangent.

"But death kept missing me. That day, it missed me and took her. And that, my boy, has been a tough row to hoe."

"I understand, now, brotherman. Enough."

"You say I saved her. Maybe that night on the roof. Yeah. Saved her from you—"

Interjecting, "Yes! And by extension—"

"—or else condemned her to me," like a prison sentence.

"Dude. Poetic, but nonsense."

"What if she'd fallen in love with you?"

Billy, aghast. "What are you saying?"

"Maybe she'd still be here now. Wouldn't she?"

Gorge rising again. "That wouldn't have happened. I was out of control."

"That's not what I'm saying, dicknut."

Billy, flummoxed in mind, but the truth already settled in his heart like lead. "Go on."

"What if you took her ass to dinner or to a goddamn movie instead of shoving her down and, and—? Don't you see?"

Billy, his jaw clenched, shook with fury, an odd one, a bizarre admixture of anger and admiration. Ruck, the alleged end-stage mad alcoholic, had been reading his fucking mind the whole time. Moving him around like a chess piece.

*God help me—I'm in the presence not of a drunk, but a master.*

Devin's perspicacity only sharpened: "Maybe you'd have dated and broken us up, and all would've been well. That night, you were out of your head. I accept the excuse—you'd never have done that to her otherwise. Why do you think I was willing to forgive and forget? I knew how easy it was to love Libby. And I knew how fucked up you were. And—after all, it had worked out. The worst had not happened. But enough to ruin it forever. From her perspective. Which I get. Boy—looking at you again, do I get it, you fucking ape."

Crushed into nothingness. Devin was making this decision easy. His throat clenched. The wind tousled his hair. He pushed forward against the railing. "If only we had the DeLorean, then we could go back and fix all this."

"But we don't."

"We'd only create paradoxes."

Ruck snorted. "I'd say we're full up on those."

"My brother, don't ever take back that forgiveness you showed me back in the day. And that you obviously hold for me now. It's too important. To lose it would finish me."

"People like you don't got a clue what 'finished' feels like. About being broke and alone and on your last damn leg. About needing to fuck strangers to put food on the table. But, yeah. I forgive you. Like I said—it all worked out. Mostly."

Ruck stood, draping his arm around Billy. He leaned against his friend. Soothing and crisp, the air held a cool hint of the season that'd passed rather than the hot Carolina summer to come.

Billy, one foot poised on the bottom bar of the railing, pondered, "I never asked, but: What happened to your cat?"

Ruck, casual, plumed smoke from his nostrils. "Died."

Billy, a fresh wave of grief, a finality he'd never before felt: Libby, gone; Libby's pet, another of the survivors, now also consigned to memory. Dust upon the pages of a forgotten book. "I guess she was old. For a cat."

Devin sounded nonchalant. "Well, yeah, but not exactly. See, I got so durn drunk after my Daddy died that, well, I took off for a spell, and..."

"And what?"

"Aw, you know. I let my beloved pet starve to death."

"Fuck you—no way. You didn't. You couldn't. Not Prudy." Billy's desire to kill himself turned to disgusted rage. "You stupid redneck."

"Yes, I did. Went away for a couple weeks, and forget to tell my old girlfriend to feed her." Shrugging, he picked a flake of brown tobacco off the tip of a darting, reptilian tongue. A blackness surrounded Devin Rucker which belied his chill countenance. "You know how it goes."

Billy, dumbstruck, felt aghast for his friend. For himself.

"But, look here—do you remember Libby, Billy? Tell me the truth."

"Why do you keep asking me that?" He no longer cared how it sounded: "On some days, she's all I think about, still."

"Lucky you. Because I barely can." Ruck, crumbling, dropped the act. Sniffling, he extracted a small photo creased and dogeared from years of handling: Libby's high school senior portrait.

Holding the wallet-size picture out to Billy.

Trembling, he reached for it.

The image leapt out from the paper: Pulchritude and youth, dark eyes staring straight ahead. Not truly smiling, a look of dignity, of determination: a young woman ready not only for the lifetime ahead, but also the tragedies and trials accompanying the joy, adventure and success; a face exuding strength, capability, and tenacity.

Brilliant; beautiful; breathtaking. Billy's epiphany came quiet and without warning, stabbing him in the gut like a silent assassin:

*Libby was the strongest, most centered person I've ever known. Everything I am not. No wonder. No wonder I loved her.*

*Love her.*

Crying out, sudden, he shoved the picture away. "Don't make me look at it," he shouted.

Kurosawa's wind machines kicked into action at this moment of highest drama and emotion. Ruck, spastic, fumbled with the photo. Picked up by the wind, it disappeared over the balcony, fluttering into the darkness.

Billy, screaming in grief, lunged for the rail: "Oh my god—!"

At the last second before Billy's weight sent him over, Ruck hollered and grabbed his old pal away from the railing. The force, however, sent them both tumbling backward and through the glass of the patio door, which shattered in a huge explosion.

About the time Roy Earl and Melanie came through the door with the takeout food, Ruck and Billy, arms around one another like lovers, came to rest on the carpet in a shower of tinkling glass.

Melanie screamed; Roy dropped the bulging plastic sack of Styrofoam containers and yelled out "*What in the freaking fudge factory is going on here?*"

Devin, laughing, picked glass out of his mustache. "Well—that happened."

"It's not what it looks like," Billy called out, rolling over and facing them with his face covered in small cuts. "We're not fighting. We're okay, now. We're fine."

## THIRTY-EIGHT

—

## CREEDENCE

Chelsea, alone in the emergency room examination bay with white, gauzy curtains pulled all around for privacy. Everything seemed so clean, neat and orderly.

Thankful for the quiet after a whirlwind: the ambulance ride, getting checked over. The cramping. The dizziness. Dusty and Eileen's stricken faces, his in particular. Looking like he was about to shit his britches.

And now, Chelsea, truly alone: Estranged from her husband, yes, but following this miscarriage, her body was no longer the vessel for another life besides her own.

Her brother. Why she thought of him, she didn't know. How she ached for Devin. How she longed for the innocence of their childhood together, their absent friendship. Before he started drinking. Before the car accident. Maybe he'd come back and they could finally work all that out. Stranger things had happened.

Crying to herself—hiding the tears from whom?—and guilty for not wanting the child, she worried that despite Dusty's culpability, it had been her own will which caused the spontaneous abortion.

Thinking: Maybe it was Buddy Lawler's anyway, and feeling a rush of revulsion and despair like a gust of hot wind.

Guilt, but also relief.

Complicated, these emotions. Nothing as easy as they led on when you were little. Get a husband, get a baby, get yourself fulfilled. All else would work itself out.

Bullcrud.

Feeling queasy, like the hangover she had after that party with Billy and Devin, right before her brother left South Carolina like he was never coming back. Teenage girl hangovers had left her system with haste; wondering, now, if the aftermath of this experience would fade in quite so efficient a manner.

The doctor, explaining that the miscarriage might have happened whether she'd fallen on the stairs or not: An extremely unfortunate but common event, miscarriages. The tumble after she tripped carrying the bag of groceries—that's right, she only stumbled and fell; that's what both Dusty and her mother had said to the paramedics, nodding to one another—may have simply accelerated a process already in motion.

"These things happen, Mrs. Wallis. We don't always know why. I wouldn't worry about trying again in a few months. But be a little patient. It'll be a while before your body's back to normal."

Not far enough along to need a D&C, as a nurse explained, Chelsea's body would rid itself of the remaining tissue over a period of a week to a month. The worst news? That she could expect to continue experiencing a kind of phantom pregnancy, likely manifesting as ongoing morning sickness and cramps. Joy.

"You'll have all sorts of odd little troublesome feelings." The nurse, a huge African-American woman, spoke with a caring, patient tone. "You being clumsy didn't have the first thing to do with this."

"No?"

"We try to sort out what happens to us in life. Figure out ways to blame ourselves for things we don't have in our control. But, sugar, the way it all plays out? It's all only in God's control, not ours. That's the notion we got to give ourselves over to. That's what makes it all add up."

Enough of this hooey. "I heard what the doctor said. When can I go?"

"Let's keep you a while. Check that bump on your head. See how you feel later."

After the nurse left, Chelsea lay listening to the buzzing of the fluorescents. She asked God that He get busy making all this add up.

While waiting for an answer—it didn't come; surprise!—the quiet was now disturbed by a murmuring of voices down the corridor. She heard Eileen's raspy timbre, echoing, shrill and piercing:

"*You goddurn quacks better let me see my damn daughter,*" coughing and sputtering and croaking. "And I mean right god-durn now."

Seconds later, Eileen, bustling and flailing through the curtain followed by a perturbed RN insisting, "Ma'am, you can't be back here."

"Oh, kiss my foot, woman." Eileen, collapsing across Chelsea's legs, wailed and grabbing at handfuls of the thin hospital sheet. "Lord have mercy. My sweet angel."

"Mama, quit it. I'm fine."

Eileen's eyes, bulging and feral. "But the baby—?"

"I lost it." Now the salty tears came, her chest and throat tight with a rush of realization. "My baby's *gone.*"

Holding one another, the women wept and sobbed until Eileen suffered one of her abrupt mood-switches. She shut off the torrent of grief and sat up dabbing at her eyes with a tissue, one she didn't deign to offer to her daughter.

"Poor Dusty—his heart will break." A theatrical gasp. "Now: We got to get him back here so y'all can be together. Talk through it all. Start getting right again."

It seemed so much like playacting Chelsea didn't have much of a reaction, not now that some fresh tears had cleansed her, disabused her of sentimental notions. Getting out of this baby thing was good.

Except for the part about tricking Billy into loving her. She'd regroup on that.

"I don't think I was supposed to have this baby anyway, Mama. Not after what Dusty done."

"Hush your hateful mouth. Besides, don't forget," her Mama said with one of those trademarked, pitying, sad smiles of hers. "Y'all can always try again."

"But, Mama—I don't love him no more. That ain't no way to make a baby."

Eileen scoffed. "Folks do it every day."

On that note Eileen pirouetted out with a flourish of the curtain worthy of a diva having taken the last of several bows. Coughing into her handkerchief, she called out for Dusty to come and begin making the family whole again.

Billy, sprawled nude and greasy beside Melanie, sweated out the booze of the last few days. Feeling all sorts of lousy, he nonetheless insisted on getting a BJ. Melanie had been reluctant, what with Ruck in the other room, but Billy, ya know ya know, had his way of insisting.

After slapping her in the face with it a few times she went to work, tracing a languid finger up and down, licking and tickling her way from navel to the start of his pubic hair.

Right as she started getting into it, he changed his mind. After seeing Libby's face earlier, this brazen sexuality felt profane.

"Mood pocket. Raincheck."

Melanie, like, *what*? "Well mister, here's a suggestion. I'm into it, now. You get yourself in the mood."

"Hell of a night. One for the books."

"All the more reason—you're so tense. Besides, your friend? You're right —he's dead to the world."

True-that: Ruck, once the Crown gone, had been further placated by a twelve-pack of Bud tallboys procured by Roy Earl from a gas station around the corner. Ruck, consuming every can but one, belching and pissing and going through mood swings of lucidity and profane, mad soliloquies until finally passing out on the media hub couch.

As he snored, the other three sat in the kitchen and discussed past events, filling Melanie in on the days of old—a sanitized version, anyway. Roy Earl, never having heard about Devin on the roof, about Libby and Billy making out in the dorm room, which is how Billy termed the incident, now looked at him with different eyes. Making to go home not long after. Asking what else he could do; telling Billy for the fourth time to 'let Creedence know' of his willingness to help.

Again, though, all too much. Begging off from her ministrations. "Sleep. I'm whipped."

"Besides," breathy and insistent. "I can be quiet—you know I can," while brushing her fingertips along the shaft of the now half-mast meatwhistle.

His Billyness, with its one good all-seeing eye: *Shall we come, you and I, while we can?*

Billy, trying to relax. Quelling the thoughts of bothersomeness that made him want to kill Melanie outright. For it not to be a sex accident like all the others through the years, nor the self-defense incident with the black dude that night.

Yeah—out-and-out kill somebody. The next person who didn't do what the fuck he wanted. *You talk about relieving tension, boy, I tell ya,* hearing Rodney Dangerfield and seeing the bulging eyes of the late pothead comedian. *That'll get you some respect.*

Forgetting all that: Melanie, going to work with deft tongue and teasing fingers, gentle at first, a true blow job, using her warm breath as much as her flesh to stimulate him; a fingertip, pressed with gentle intention against his tender taint. A dance of delicate flesh and nerve endings.

All in one exhilarating rush, at last she took him fully into her mouth, no small task.

Billy's reddening watchtower, now grew harder than the roadway upon which he and Ruck had traveled all those miles home, harder than the steel in the hull of a great starship blasting off from a barren moon. Took so much blood to fill it all the way up he often grew lightheaded during intercourse, suffered dissociative reveries leading to the accidents.

In the dim light, Billy, glancing down and meeting her eyes, which announced:

*I love you I love you I love you—oh, how I love you, Billy Steeple.*

Terrifying.

But why not go with this? A decent pop to wind down a stressful, whirlwind week of events; a woman, willing, to serve all these needs, and more.

Aw—did he halfway love Melanie?

Did he feel like, maybe he'd found the one? Since Libby, he meant?

Did he love this woman?

Billy, an emotional highway accident. His mind, a mess.

His control, tenuous.

Ready to explode, he realized.

Because, of course, Billy, incapable of *not* imagining Libby down there instead of Melanie. Melanie, a woman everything that Libby was not—as available and perfect and willowy and blonde and crazy and *alive* as much as anyone could reasonably hope for, and not really all that crazy, either. Not in the grand scheme. Even digging the fake-rape bits, the cherry on top, so long as nobody let it get all accidental. A little clingy, perhaps—but who could blame her? Billy Steeple, in the house, y'all. Who wouldn't cling.

Melanie, loving him, yes; but Libby's eyes flashed in front of him, her face the way it had looked in the small fading picture Ruck had stupidly lost over the railing.

Billy, a pressure building, warmth and energy ready to flood out of him. *Libby—oh, Libby*.

A sudden, spasmodic eruption. Melanie, gagging and choking out Billy's thick semen through her nostrils like lunchroom milk. Falling back, overcome.

"Surprise surprise." Breathless, his face hot. No incidents like this ever, not even the first time. Control, his watchword, an ethos by necessity. Mel, not a swallower.

Looking at his spasming organ. *What gives, bud?*

Realizing, then. How close he'd come. To an accident. A premature pop, why, it had saved everyone a whole lot of trouble.

Think about it—if he'd had an accident, he'd have needed Ruck to help deal with mess. That would have taken too much explanation.

Billy, feeling that his friend would help, though. They already enjoyed a bond going way, way beyond helping your boy dump a muh-fucken body somewhere, yo. Billy wouldn't even *need* to explain. Shit happened. Devin Rucker knew this. He'd be a little judge-y, sure. But, he'd still help conceal the corpse. No question. It's what friends did. Adolescent loyalty like theirs, Gen-X and solid as granite, was difficult to impugn. Particularly in the face of explanations, like, well, the death of this woman was only an accident.

"Sorry, girl—the excitement, it got away from me."

"That was epic, and not in a good way," thick and wet and disgusted. "Uncool."

Billy's nuts re-tightened as gravel rumbled from the doorway. "Oh, you cheating bastards."

Ruck.

"Dude—*shut the fucking door*."

But no, Ruck, trancelike, a silhouette in the doorway, dropped the last of the beers onto the hardwood floor with a hissing *clunk*. Slobber ran from his mouth in a string like the spew hanging out of Melanie's hair and off her chin. "I'm-a kick some ass now, son."

Melanie, screaming, grabbed a blanket to cover herself. Billy, flopping like a harpooned tuna, got twisted up in the silk sheets. "Ruck, not *now*—"

But Ruck lunged forward with an aggrieved yelp: "Libby, don't let him do this to you—to us."

Billy, not the only lunatic in the condo, threw his forearm against

Melanie to send her tumbling headfirst off the bed. Her bare feet flew in the air before she hit the unyielding floor, *thud.*

Billy, grabbing at Ruck, the two old friends now grappling like costumed wrestlers on television: Bigdick Bill versus The Shitkicker, one fall, winner take all. But no fake wrestling kayfabe playing to the rubes in the cheap seats: Ruck, flailing away and moaning as if in a waking nightmare.

Billy, shrieking high and nasally, bundled the skinny drunk into a naked bear hug. "Give up, Ruck—*quit.*"

But no; Ruck, struggling and refusing to quit.

Billy, slamming him onto the damp sheets and holding him down, the two of them sucking wind and bouncing to rest.

Billy, thinking that maybe the time had come to call for help—duh—but neither he nor Roy Earl had been able to raise anyone at the Rucker household earlier. Out for a big Saturday night in Edgewater County, perhaps?

Billy, now speculating he should have let the cops take Ruck after all. Let them shuttle him off to the drunk tank or the psych ward, or maybe a lonely field or bog somewhere. Put the dog out of his misery.

After all this Billy, feeling like a failure, but only for the second or maybe third time in his life. But wishing poor deluded Ruck dead? From whence these awful thoughts?

Ruck, rolling off. Staggering out of the room. A thud, vibrating the walls: The heavy front door, slamming.

"Oh, fiddlesticks." Billy, face in hand. "Now I've got to go and stop him."

"Let that crazy asshole go."

"Can't—I'm the protagonist. I have to fix all this."

"Billy: *let him go.*"

"You really want to help?"

"Of course."

"Go and rinse that disgusting glob of spooge out of your hair, you trollop."

Billy limped with heroism across the bedroom and grabbed a silk kimono —for their one-month anniversary present Melanie had bought them matching robes, and dutiful, he often sported his with pleasure and comfort.

Bolting, best he could, down the hallway toward the front door, he heard Melanie calling out. *"He was going to kill us both."*

Billy shouted NO, disagreeing in one sense because he didn't want the little shit to think she could tell him what to do, but with all the weed on hand, no cops.

The distinctive cell phone ring-tone from back in the bedroom, a piece of music familiar to Deadheads as the principal melody of 'Dark Star,' stopped him in mid-swish.

Melanie came out holding up the phone, the backlit screen reading ROY E PET.

"Roy, thank god—we've had a fresh eruption over here. How'd you know?"

The bossman's voice came thin and shaking: "It's Creedence. She's had a bad fall—Mrs. Rucker said they had to take her to the hospital."

At this news Billy felt nutted anew, beleaguered and suffering death by a thousand unrelenting crises. "Is she all right?"

"Think so, more or less. But still... Mrs. Rucker started crying about how she'd never get to see her grandbaby, now."

"*Da-fuck* that mean?"

"I reckon Creedence had a miscarriage."

Unable to process: it all sounded like a soap opera subplot complication in which he had no emotional investment.

"Well, this is like the seventh circle of Hades with these people." Billy, charging out into the shared condo hallway, whispering so as not to disturb sleeping residents. "That's all bad, yes; but Ruck's had an episode. He's out on the loose again."

"Fudge."

"Let me get back to you on this Creedence sitch, all right?" He rang off.

Billy stabbed a finger at the down button, which opened the doors. Once inside he realized with a start that, if the elevator were sitting on his high floor waiting for a passenger, no way possible Ruck had taken it downstairs. In a mad rush he leapt back out of the closing doors just in time and raced for the fire stairs. He burst through the door head-first and started down, his big feet slapping on the cold concrete steps; Billy, calling out Ruck's name.

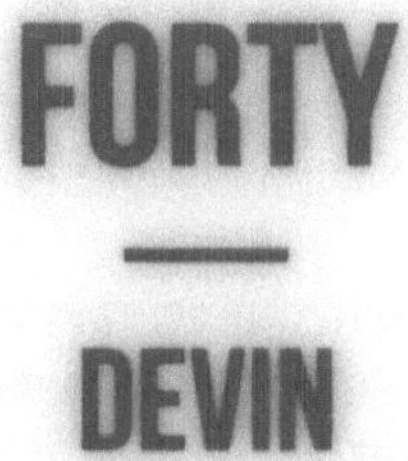


Devin tried to eat the hot food they'd brought to him, but the spices and vegetables had been too much. Only the bland little cubes of tofu had gone down without making him gag.

Feeling downright sober.

No head games.

No confabulation.

Way way way too lucid, y'all.

Devin, drinking the beers and making Edgewater County smalltalk, reminiscing type-shit with Roy Earl. The times they camped by the river on the back-land. Partying and drinking in Roy's grandfather's pickup truck. Spray-painting the Blue Öyster Cult hooked-cross symbol everywhere that one summer. And at last, Devin, pretending to fall asleep so they'd all give him some peace.

To sleep the dreamless drunk's sleep.

To rest.

And 'twas thus that Devin, whilst he did sleep, it would not be for long. His dreams, incessant and troubled as ever, but soon interrupted by noises from the other room.

From a place outside his consciousness.

Reality versus dreamworld.

Or was it?

Awake yet not, Devin, floating toward the door and into the hallway and through another door; on the other side seeing, to his chagrin, Libby.

Libby, at last, real and alive.

But making love to Billy.

A miasma of images and activity and struggle, a minute inner voice questioning after such a long separation what business Libby's love-life was of his. Devin, late to the party: she'd fallen in love with Billy after all.

Devastating.

Lashing out, a blur, a moment of lucidity, and of shame: The now-now, unobscured, unmitigated consciousness. Sobriety, of a kind, at seeing Billy's girlfriend.

Not Libby.

A tall woman who looked nothing like Libby.

*Oh, shit.*

Rushing through the condo in shame, the crashing sounds and the flashes of light pursuing like a pack of dogs, the clangorous howling roar that'd been the sound of the two cars plowing into one another opening up all around him on the road that day roaring in his ears. Snatching up his jacket and shades like Indiana Jones's hat, stumbling and racing and fumbling with the door-lock, wrenching it open, into the corridor.

Frantic. Head whipping, searching for the stairs. Finally seeing the dim red of the EXIT sign at the end of the hall. Kicking the fire door open; thankful for no emergency alarm.

The top floor. A long way to the bottom. The reverse of Jimmy Stewart's pursuit of Kim Novak—VERTIGO had been Libby's favorite Hitchcock. It had been rereleased on the big screen, they had gone to see it on a date back in high school. He wondered if Steeple had known that juicy little fact, her favorite Hitch. He hoped not.

Several landings of stairwell lights seemed out. A code violation. He started down.

Staggering and groping along in the dimness, the echoes of his own footfalls reverberating, plangent—the sound of an army chasing behind, an organized militia of Death's minions ready to do the work at which they'd thus far failed, ignominious and incompetent. Down, down, down, ankles turning and claws grasping along the cold metal rail.

Remembering this feeling at the Dead show all those years ago. The minions of death, chasing him out of the arena.

Wait—why was he running? It was time to let them take him.

Devin turned on his heel and spread his arms wide to greet his tormentors, his pursuers, to welcome the dark riders with open arms... but seeing no one behind him, in his disappointment he could but only lose his balance.

His grasp, slipping from the railing. And tumbling down the stairwell, legs and arms flopping like a rag doll, his head striking with a sick crack against the concrete of the landing.

For a brief instant, the stairwell shone bright as though lit by a flashbulb. Light that redshifted, then grayed out.

All quiet and dark, the Now becoming Then; Devin, suffused with peace and satisfaction. Endless, black nothingness—just like heaven.

# PART FOUR

# ARCADIA

## SPRING 1990

April in South Carolina: the white-petaled Bradford pears in full blossom, granulated pine-tree pollen sweeping through in sandstorm gales of yellow, cool mornings and warm afternoons, dappled light, the smell of petrichor accompanying a morning rain shower, the breeze tickling Devin's cheeks like butterfly kisses. Oftentimes spring didn't last long before it got thick and humid. Devin, hoping that wasn't the case this year. They would be living together near a small park with a gurgling creek. It would be nice to spend time out there. Maybe get a leash for the kitten.

The spring semester not yet over, not quite, but Devin and Libby had already signed a lease on a funky duplex over in the Arcadia Mill Village, a neighborhood about a mile from campus across the railroad yard. The first of May signaled a new life together, young love in full bloom not unlike the trees whipped up by the steady breath of the springtime, blossoms swirling and dancing like fluffy wet snowflakes.

Devin, Libby, a mixture of petals in their hair as they carried down cardboard boxes of record albums, books and other random possessions. Stowing the boxes in the Mustang parked in the concrete fire lane, trunk and doors open like a midnight blue, metal mockingbird flexing its wings and tail.

"Maybe we'll have enough money for me to replace my VCR, too," Libby said. Her access to movies, mission critical.

"I'll do without food if I have to, angel."

The Arcadia neighborhood they'd chosen was filled with old houses where the mill workers had once lived, at least until that culture faded away and the city became more urbanized, not to mention all the textile jobs going overseas. At the peak four such enormous mills operated in Columbia, with one of them, located at the confluence of the three rivers, enjoying historic status as the first all-electric textile mill in the country; it had been wired and built by a small startup called General Electric, their first industrial installation. Devin, knowing this only because of a field trip back in high school to the museum now housed therein.

Another of the big mills, now student housing for the university that, being adjacent to campus but not under the school's administration, a zoo, a party destination, one having key appeal like the Old Market—walking distance.

Only the Arcadia village had survived unchanged: the workers, now living elsewhere, but in 1990 the mill still operated. Owned by an upstate conglomerate, the last chugging old lady of a dying breed, not long for this world. The one in Edgewater County had shut down when Devin, Roy Earl and Dobbs had still been freshmen in high school. Their future lay elsewhere.

Libby, happy and productive all semester, taking her Mass Comm courses and trying to figure out the third act of FACING COLLEGE STREET, her epic feature-length screenplay. Her writing guru Max De Lisle, seeing her work as strong and commercial, wanted her coming out of his class with a full-length script to serve as a calling card, a writing sample, or perhaps if the stars aligned for Libby, a contest finalist or winner; signing with an agent; an actual sale. Nothing impossible, as he tried to teach his students. If he had come from South Carolina to make it in Hollywood, anyone could. That de Lisle had had an uncle working in production for RKO in the 1930s and 40s to open the door for him didn't seem to factor into his calculations of possible success.

Libby, thankful Billy dropped the advanced writing class after the first meeting earlier in the semester; seeing him around campus bad enough. Billy, not coming around anymore to the dorm-suite. The Dead show had changed the dynamic among them forever. Her fondest wish, she said, for him to bail on the class.

Devin, explaining to the roommates and friends that they'd suffered a falling out, him and Billy, over who had paid for what on the night of the Dead—the tickets, the beer, the drugs; a disputed accounting. That Billy, holding a grudge over it despite already being a rich fuck. Libby, helping Devin concoct the story. Wanting the details as embarrassing for Steeple as could be.

Roy Earl, oblivious to the other dramas of the concert night, reported how he had had his mind blown, couldn't believe to save his life they would let a dispute over money tarnish the memory of what, for him, had been a transformational experience. So much so that Roy ordered tickets to go see the Dead on the next tour coming through the region, as well as talking about getting LSD and trying it again—this time, though, not going to a concert, but maybe another intense but comfortable and familiar set and setting—like, say, a Redtails football game. Devin, thinking, yeah, I'll take a big Pasadena on that action.

The dreams of the man in the pool, leaving him alone for now. Devin, considering the apparition's prognostications about early demises and cruel unavoidable fates nothing more than childish, hyper-imaginative poppycock. Devin, now fallen from a roof and nothing much coming of the event; his fixation on mortality, mitigated. So what if, one fine summer's morn five years ago—ages; an epoch—he'd found a dead motherscratcher in a pool? So what if he'd been fascinated with rock stars who died young? Didn't mean squat.

So: Devin, more serious about his coursework. Considering journalism like Dobbs; considering a future: with Libby.

Alive.

Not-dead. Not anytime soon, anyway.

A voice said, *This may be what growing up feels like.* The lovers kept packing the Mustang.

Dobbs, watching them load the Mustang from his bedroom window on the second floor, held his nose to keep from breathing in the pollen.

"You can't leave me here with these rednecks, Ruck."

"Maybe you could move in with us." Devin nudged Libby. "We only need one bedroom."

Libby, brighter-eyed, fresher and prettier than Devin had heretofore understood beauty to look, had her dark, wiry hair pulled back from her face by a wide white band, rubbed a long finger under her prominent nose. Like Dobbs, she suffered allergies. Through a nasal voice: "I'd be in heaven having both my favorite men there with me."

"Forget it. I've had enough of this bonehead."

"You don't speak for Miss Libby, Ruck."

Devin, flipping a casual middle finger; Dobbs's rejoinder, a nasty wet raspberry.

"But seriously: let's think about that for fall semester," Devin said. "No need for any of us to come back to this dump."

"*Yay.*" Libby, an airborne split like a cheerleader. "Sure would save us money."

Dobbs, nodding with vigor. "I'll do it."

Devin and Libby, together doing a ridiculous, high-kicking jig; she finished with a handstand as Devin's feet got tangled up and he fell, laughing, to the grass of the small yard outside the two-story building of flats and suites, colorful tapestries and flags of other countries in view—many international students lived in the complex, giving it a cosmopolitan flavor. But time to go.

The blossoms floating down.

The bright sun shining in Libby's hair.

From somewhere nearby, a kitten meowed.

"Hey," she called out. "Is that my baby I hear?"

Dobbs bent down and reappeared with a gray tabby six week-old cat. "She's hungry again, mommy."

"I'm on it."

Devin, untroubled for the first time in his life, or so it felt. His mother's affair, dead dudes in pools, Billy Steeple's mad attempt to rape Libby. It receded into fiction, almost, in the face of Libby reaching down to help him up from the grass, then bounding into the apartment on strong legs gamine and coltish, still, like the young girl she was, to feed the kitten she'd found and that they had agreed to adopt.

Only what lay ahead matter. And what was at hand.

His hand.

Closing the trunk.

"I ain't gonna miss this dump," he yelled up to Dobbs, who stood cooing and kissing the top of the kitten's head.

"Me, neither. And neither is little punk-punk, here. Too noisy."

Libby asked Devin: "Shall we go? You and I? While we can?"

"It's a plan."

Over the months following the Dead show, Billy, on a number of chance occasions, had run into one or both of them. Each time, Steeple had made a mad fool of himself making heartfelt pleas to have an audience, and about talk therapy and a way forward to understand what'd happened; furthermore, the undeniable fact remaining that they'd all been in a drugged stupor, that Billy, in 'real life' as he kept terming it, wouldn't have hurt Libby in a thousand millennia. That he'd never touch LSD again, not on his life. Never again drink so much as a beer in anyone's presence. If only. If only. He could be given. A chance.

Oh, but in the heat of the moment after the incident, Devin, not so magnanimous. Witnessing his lover's assault by someone he thought a friend more than enraged him.

The heroic, injured, half-drunk, tripping Devin, his mind blown and ears ringing from the concert and the hard but cushioned fall onto the grass, had lurched limp-footed into the apartment, exploding through the front door they'd left open in time to see Libby, bounding down the stairs screaming his name.

Billy, following close behind and tucking in the black T-shirt he'd worn to the show, his eyes blown out and simmering dark with unnatural dilation; the drug had rendered him a dancing, jabbering idiot all night.

"Ruck, you all right?" he called out way too loud. Devin could see his dick, a monster, still bulging against taut denim. "What happened, bro?"

Libby threw her arms around Devin's neck, a death grip, making them both off-balance, almost tumbling over onto the coffee table filled with beer cans, overflowing ashtrays and a filthy bong stinking of weed resin. Wincing in pain the next day, Devin didn't know later if it'd been the fall from the roof or Libby's embrace leaving him more sore.

"Get him away from me!"

"Steeple, you are a dead man." The shoulder, throbbing. Tripping—but sobered up, too. Grounded, literally. "I ought to call the campus heat."

Libby shrieked. "You—you *rapist*."

"*Libby*, no, I—" Billy, ashen and gaping, blinking stupidly like a suffocating, caught fish. "Confused. I misunderstood. *It was an accident.*"

"Misunderstood." Hiding her face against Devin's shoulder. "That's rich."

"Please—this is all fucked up."

Libby, having had enough. Pushing away from Devin. The acid, going bad —her face, an evolving mask of fear and anger. Devin, trying to hold her back, calm her down. She grabbed at half-full beer cans and pitched them at Billy's head. The coffee table tipped over after all, a huge crash and mess.

"You motherfucker. Get out."

Billy, collapsing onto his knees, let loose a torrent of wet grief on the scale like Devin's mother would pull, howling and crying uncontrollably, mewling apologies, rolling in the trash on the living room carpet. Eyes rolling back in his head, Adam's apple bobbing as he spoke in silent tongues, his lips moving but nothing coming out. His erection, gone.

Mostly.

"You need help, beau. Look at ya."

"Just get out, get *out*." Libby, cursing and kicking at him.

Billy got onto his knees and put his head down on the filthy carpet like a Muslim facing Mecca. Sudden and spastic, he sprang to his feet and grabbed for her. For them both, to be fair. Begging.

Devin, tossing Libby aside onto the couch with a yelp, launched himself at Steeple. A furious struggle, punches thrown—weak—and awkward grappling; Devin, outweighed by fifty pounds.

But Devin, more in control than Billy. Pulling a knee up into the Steeple hip-bone, beating him with his fists as hard as he could, feinting and faking. Ducking a Billy right-hook and landing his own hard and memorable blow into Billy's tight stomach. Beer cans crunching underfoot. Libby, screaming.

Doubling over from the gut-punch, Devin now swung a left, swift and true, smack into Steeple's drooling mouth.

Shoving Devin back, Billy knocked him onto the couch. His lip, busted and bleeding, began swelling.

Libby, now charging in and smacking Billy's red face with a roundhouse slap and a kick to the nuts that sent him reeling backward. He clutched himself, crashing over the chair in which he'd once sat watching movies and drinking brews with the boys.

Down for the count. "Enough," he wept. "Please. I'll go."

Devin, on his feet. Unsteady, but a fighter's stance. "You better, pardner. I know what death looks like."

Billy, wild-eyed and nursing his lip, hurried outside, the screen door banging shut in his wake.

A curious buzzing silence. Humid and misty inside the apartment as without, the damp night leaching into the building. Devin and Libby, looking at one another. Tripping.

"Babygirl—what just happened?"

Libby, holding her arms out, helpless and childlike, hands all twitchy and spastic and fumbling around on her body like she itched all over. "I want this acid to stop. I want it to quit. I loved it before. Not now."

Devin and Libby, up to his room. Libby, staring at the mussed bed in disbelief, barking another of her strange acid-laughs.

"Well, okay. *That* happened."

"Should we go?"

"No. I'm taking back this place from him."

"I guess we don't really know the guy, after all."

"No—whose friend was he, originally? Mike's?"

"Hell, I don't know. Billy just started hanging out."

"Not anymore."

"Train has left station."

Taking their shoes and damp clothes off and crawling into his single bed together, spoons, both trying to calm down, hours seemed to pass. Talking, soft; ignoring the sounds of the party coming back to the apartment, finally, and the shrieks of dismay at the condition of the living room.

By now it was after four in the morning. But they both still lay awake.

"I don't think I'll ever sleep again. This is stupid. I thought the concert was wild, but this is going on too long."

Devin, stroking the swell of her hip, trembling, feeling as though an epic arc of events now winding down: "This doesn't feel like me. Or you."

"Yeah; no. I get it."

"Let's just be us from now on. Be ourselves again."

Libby, quiet.

"Does that make sense?"

Shrugging, demure, hiding her face. "I suppose it has to."

Kissing, gentle. Libby, tentative at first, but melting into his affection, grabbing at him, hands all over. Wiggling out of underwear and into position. Making love, slow, careful. Libby at last rolling Devin over, grinding him, yanking his shaggy hair.

Devin, staring into her dilated eyes. Unable to ejaculate, it went on for what seemed like an hour until they both gave out, gave up.

Finally slipping out, holding her. "It's good. I'm good."

"Now what," Libby asked.

"Maybe we should drink a few beers."

"That's a good idea."

"Oh, shit—listen."

"What?"

"The birds are singing. The sun's about to come up."

"Shit."

They pulled on sweats and crept downstairs, finding Roy Earl sitting up by himself clutching a smoldering bong and watching *Five Easy Pieces,* his favorite movie for some strange reason, but with the sound turned off. Devin scared the shit out of him at first, but then Roy seemed glad to see them—as he put it, relieved.

Until sunrise came they sat sipping cold beers and tripping and talking about the Dead show, how it looked as though sleep wasn't going to be possible, and how all would have to shine it on through classes.

Roy, saying they needed to get a tape of the show from one of the people making recordings down in the crowd. "Hey—what happened to Billy? And where's Dobbs?"

Libby, irritated. "Oh my god—I have class in one hour. I knew this is what would happen."

"Only one thing to do," Devin said. "Have another beer."

After Devin and Roy successfully talked Libby out of class, the still-sleepless lovers went back upstairs to shower together and fool around some more, then up the hill for breakfast at the North Tower cafeteria; both exhausted, both still tweaked, but now famished and a little drunk, food became all.

Taking their Southeastern-burgundy plastic trays outside to the patio and setting up camp on a damp wooden picnic table, they unwrapped breakfast burritos and ate in silence.

Devin's comment, finally: "So, you and Roy Earl had an amazing show, it sounded like."

"Unbelievable, so so strange. You left right as it started getting good."

"Story of my life."

"They played this song 'Dark Star,' and everyone erupted like it was the second coming."

Libby, explaining that a Deadhead told them on the way out of the arena that 'Dark Star' was special because it had been away for a long time and had recently come back.

"You just gave me chicken skin."

"It really was as though a presence had descended."

"Freaky."

Libby, tired as all get-out, purple smudges under her eyes, hair style courtesy Devin's pillow—anyone seeing them would know these two had spent the night together. Devin, looking at his extra-crispy, disheveled girlfriend and thinking himself a lucky young man indeed.

The rest of the fall semester: Devin, a new clarity to this thinking. Drinking less, going to class. Trying to finish out the term with dignity and enthusiasm. His own acid trip seemed to have flushed dark clutter from his mind.

Libby, a new hobby: trying to avoid Billy's gaze as they passed on the street.

Devin, finally running into Billy one day not far from the arena, with its classroom level containing the Mass Comm college. Billy insisted on grabbing a beer together. To give him a chance.

Something in his eyes like sincerity. Devin, agreeing.

A dump down near the State House called the Rainbow. Devin, Billy, a pitcher of draught, in a booth, tucked away; MTV on the projection screen in the corner, a video for one of Robert Plant's solo tunes.

Billy offered rambling, sorrowful analysis bordering on confession. "Feelings, along with the foolishness. That's my point."

Devin, sipping his plastic foamy cup, touched by the display, nodding. "Feelings."

"Look, I can't describe it any other way. I was confused. Libby, she—"

"Libby what?"

"I misunderstood."

"You're fucking delusional, is what."

"I was screwed up, man."

"What if I hadn't been there?"

Shame, cheeks rubicund and shiny, running his hand over the stubble growing out on his scalp, Billy looked sick. "Hell—I would've stopped before anything happened, Ruck."

"Yeah."

An announcement: requiring Libby's forgiveness as well. Seeking facilitation. Billy had never looked more imploring, which was at this point was saying something.

Devin, unable to offer hope. "I can't help you with Libby. This is guy stuff we're working through."

"'Guy stuff'?"

Nodding. "Women, they have their crap, dude. We have ours." Devin took a long draw on his beer. Belched. "Be glad it's not the kind of crap where I kick your ass again."

Billy, killing his cup of beer, turned chilly. "So it's settled between us."

Devin, saying sure. "But Libby, you should leave her alone, bro. All's I'm saying."

"As you wish."

Devin, seeing the worst fake smile in history on the boy. He would keep an eye out for this crazy fuck. His dad had guns at home. He'd drive up to Edgewater County and get one, if necessary.

Over the course of the next month, Devin, doing his boy a solid by seeking out avenues of recompense and reconciliation. Seeing in Billy a contrition that burned with an insistence perceived as genuine, culminating in a lengthy letter found under his windshield wiper on a late winter's morning, a missive that included a sub-letter to Libby he asked Devin to deliver.

Billy, pleading in the cover letter he'd submitted how Devin should feel free to peruse the letter-letter, the one to her, for his sanction and approval and rubber-stamp, after which passing the document to the other victim, as he termed them both—victims of his headstrong, ruinous stupidity. All of which he explained would sort of at last kinda codify the matter as legitimately resolved and the akashic records expunged, whatever that meant, as well as to consign memories of the events into what might be termed a friendship foolishness archive, dusty and forgotten and sealed forever.

Too many words saying not enough. Devin's takeaway.

Sitting in the Mustang reading the cover letter, three pages handwritten in Billy's distinctive, blocky print, Devin smoked and sipped on a lite beer from a six-pack he'd grabbed after class. The Libby letter? A dozen typewritten pages, single-spaced. Jesus. So much print Devin didn't give a shit what it said, so long as he didn't have to read it all.

One passage in the cover letter, however, stuck out:

---

Ruck, as I leave for the Dead show in Greensboro next week, I have to say that you, Libby, Roy Earl, everyone, 'y'all'—see, I am one of you!—feel like the only real friends I've ever had in my life. You are like real people compared to the robots whose tutelage I grew up under, ostensibly smart and urbane types, whatever, but in reality nothing more than soulless moneysuckers, the lot of them! My father, my mother, the stepmothers—like a sitcom!—everyone in my life have been leeches and whores. My life, before last semester, that is. And meeting all you cool cats.

Seriously. You don't know how often I prayed for a brother, someone like you, someone with that same jaundiced eye like mine, asking the big questions and taking no guff from that bunch of bipedal nincompoops running around this old redneck college campus here in the heart of the Confederacy. You feel like that brother to me, you did before I fucked up, and you still do now.

I know that's hard to believe but I swear it's true, and I'm not sure if what happened wasn't me only trying to be closer to all of you, not just Libby. God help me but I swear I believe that, so much so that I don't know anymore whether it sounds crazy.

Okay okay, it probably does. It probably sounds fucked and sick, but what can I tell you, I thought I owned the universe that night. I thought I was a hundred feet tall. But instead, I was only an amoral, delusional intellectual dwarf. Ruck: you have to know that it was all an accident. And again, a delusion. Like you said.

---

Devin, noting a strategic round splatter, a faded blue asterisk courtesy of the author's own tear duct. Folding up the sheaf of pages, putting them into the envelope to deliver to Libby, his spider-sense told him some aspect of all these words represented bullshit.

Libby's response? She mashed Billy letter, unread, into a festering wastebasket muck of old takeout Chinese food, sweet and sour sauce soaking into his unheeded literary plea for understanding.

How it had all worked out, man. Like, big-time.

Not.

Bursting apelike from the apartment, Billy, his legs rubbery, face and stomach hurting from Devin and Libby's punches, heaved his body up the hill from University Terrace. The streets wet and shiny, his breath pluming in the cooling misty air, he ducked into alcoves and alleys and shadows to avoid being caught, to avoid capture. He ran for miles. At last he collapsed against a slick green trash dumpster a resident had forgotten to take back in from the sidewalk. Puking into it. Hard.

Recovering from the spew, he pondered what had happened: They'd called out the big guns on him. In his mind a squad of ten trained, fearless cadres had descended and beaten the living bejesus out of him. A pride of lions, ripping him to shreds. A looneytune of Tasmanian Devils. And now, flaps of skin hanging down, contusions, blood, viscera, even his dick shredded like hamburger meat flopping wet and useless with gore.

Except, no; jeans and a black T-shirt. No blood. A little puke.

Finding himself standing on the corner of Blossom and Barnwell, reality locked back in. Surrounded by students coming and going from the concert down to party in the neighborhood, he'd barely run three blocks. No gang of militarized toughs.

*Only the girl you love and her boyfriend, whipping your ass.*

Wanting to go back, to explain, to apologize.

Or to kill them both.

Surprised it hadn't happened.

Yeah. Earlier, he'd had to run—his control, slipping.

She'd laughed at it. Women didn't love his dick—they thought it ridiculous.

How hard. It had been.

Not the steeplemeat. Not hard—difficult. To prevent an accident.
With Libby.
That would have ranked right up there with his greatest fuck-ups.
Relief.
But pent-up with bothersome energy. What to do?
To have an accident on purpose? Finally? Just to blow off the steam?
No. Hadn't he made enough mistakes tonight? Accidents were what they were and needed to stay that way. If that made any damn sense.

Billy, back home to his condo by himself to watch movies until the acid wore off, trudging through the dense pilgrimage of thirsty college students heading to the bars; being recognized from Meat Mallet by one dude, which was cool.

One after another for hours, jamming VHS tapes into the deck, pulling them out, winding, rewinding—scenes, bits and pieces. Finally realizing the sun had come up. A class day. Light bending around the edges of everything. Tinnitus from the ungodly loud, albeit crystal clear, Grateful Dead PA. Most impressive concert sound he'd ever heard. They had a following of worshipful millions. Maybe the punks had been wrong about the hippies. Every punk Billy knew, except for him and Mucky, whose dad had plenty of bread, were poor as shit. Like an ethos. Fuck punk.

Seeing Libby in de Lisle's scriptwriting class that next Monday, the one for which he still owed scenes from last week, much less the current assignment, made for a tense morning. Her face, a mask of icy revulsion. After Max's lecture, about a concept the teacher called 'separate sentience', that is, imbuing the characters with the sense they lead a life outside the story and the page, she had all but run from the classroom.

He trembled all over as the tall, wiry old writer, who had actual credits on Hollywood features and TV shows back in the 1950s and 60s—WRITTEN BY MAX DE LISLE in forty-foot typesetting on a movie screen—peered almost eye to eye.

"Where's the promise we saw in the early scenes, sir?" Max called everyone sir. Well, the dudes. The girls he called 'ma'am' like any good Southern boy does, or so Billy had discovered after spending time in South Carolina thanks to his grandfather's enormous plastic bag plant in the upstate. Consumers all over the world purchased their goods in Stemplewicz blister-packs they then toted home in a variety of Stemplewicz plastic containers. Dustin Hoffman should have listened to his Dad's friend.

"Prof, I don't know what to tell you. The muse has left me."

"I know you're in a rock band that 'gigs' late in the evening, as Paul Simon sang. Is that the problem?"

"Why don't I bring in the late work tomorrow. I'll bring the rest in on Wednesday."

"It's a deal. 'No excuses' goes a long way with me, and in the industry. Just do the work and step back. The path to serenity."

That next week, however, Billy decided to drop de Lisle's scriptwriting class and take an F for the semester—oooh, how scary. Like that hadn't happened plenty of times. He'd drop off a note saying that he had lied; that he had a drug problem and would be back in the spring after rehab.

He was a rock star. Max de Lisle was in show business. He wouldn't only get it, Billy's proactive behavior would only bolster the man's respect for him. Blowing off the last month of classes to avoid the reproving stares? Win-win.

Billy spent the holidays first with his father in his DC townhouse, and later taking the train to Manhattan two days before Christmas to visit his harridan mother and fiancé, a smooth-talking, African-american razor-jawed looker a dozen years her junior named Trenholm Whitaker, a hot-shit I-banker worth seven figures. It was nothing like Billy's family fortune, of course, but her beau nonetheless acted the part with aplomb—in other words, a tiresome Princeton nimrod whose impossibly white teeth looked too big for his erudite mouth.

Money. The Steeples already had plenty, pal. Get over yourself.

Besides—money alone didn't get you into the club.

Hell, Billy's grandfather was a member of both Skull & Bones and Bohemian Grove, as well another fraternal organization or two. You didn't talk about any of those, though. Nobody's heard of them anyway. Another world from the simple folks down in Edgewater County and at Southeastern University, far off the Ivy League track that delivers masters of commerce and the world like his granddad.

It was a world in which you didn't know who to trust. And people who talked out of turn got disappeared. The folks down in South Carolina seemed to be merely going on about their ordinary lives. Billy felt relief from bothersomeness among them. Unlike his own family.

New York, alive with holiday cheer—snow flurries, traffic, human beings bundled in animal skins and burdened by clusters of shopping bags.

But Billy, deader than dog shit inside. Wandering in the slush, glimpsing Libby out of the corner of his eye in every smiling, happy female face; seeing his failures in every worthless rag-wearing malcontent, in every stumblebum drunk. For all the money and family pedigree, no more powerful than they at exhibiting control over his circumstances.

Billy, walking for blocks in cold sleet, considered heading to the tip of the island and to the top of one of the massive twin obelisks there; hurling himself off, plummeting to the sidewalk below. Or else out wind-borne over the frigid waters of the harbor, his London Fog coat flapping like a cape and providing lift. No guts, no glory; but if followed through upon, no chance for Libby.

Yes—as long as Libby Meade lived, he clutched at the possibility of redemption. Had again come to believe such was possible; like a manic depressive, the peaks and troughs of his Libby obsession a wild and undulating high-frequency waveform, forced by occasional lucidity into acknowledging the unlikelihood of ever winning her heart.

Conjuring scenarios in which Rucker stepped aside—either willingly, or through misadventure.

Flashes of Libby, falling grief-stricken into Billy's arms at the news of Ruck's death. Remembering in her time of crisis the nascent connection they'd enjoyed—savored, even—prior to the almost-accident on the night of the concert. Both devastated at the sudden, tragic loss, the gravitational attraction provided pulling them inexorably toward one another, two cosmic bodies destined for collision and personal apotheosis. Ruck's sacrifice, an alchemical dissolution necessary to get to the gold.

Anything possible. Anything he wished—arranging for Ruck's death. Delegating so as to avoid the obvious emotional entanglement of killing his best friend. Paying one of those crackheads over in Simpkins Park.

Now he knew—Ruck.

Ruck would be the first non-accidental killing.

He felt a pulsating warmth inside like intuition; it seemed to say Not-Ruck.

Soul-sick and confused, he ducked into the first dive he came across, a Blarney Stone. The smell of cheap draught reminded him of Lupo's, in the Old Market where Meat Mallet gigged. Or the Rainbow, where he and Devin had shared their pitcher of forgiveness.

After two hours of drinking and watching television with the daytime drunks in the pub, Billy, half-lit and near tears, alone as he'd ever felt yet eager to get away from the filthy snow and the smog and being in the same city as his preening, self-centered mother, went about a charade of buying halfhearted gifts.

In the epic biographical film of his life they'd someday make, the mother character would not merit so much as a walk-on, much less a supporting or featured role: the all-but unseen villain, Elisabeth Gallard Steeple Barrett or whatever her next surname to be, estranged from her old Brahmin bloodline of the Boston Gallards and now holding sway and power over nothing, not even her own progeny, would be portrayed with brutal honesty.

No disloyal *fille de joie* like her held any power. Or could. Only the sexual ministrations making men vulnerable gave them any hope of dominance.

Now his mother, there was a potential accident which would do the world some good. But Billy, gagging in revulsion at the Oedipal implications of such a bothersome notion.

Billy sobered up enough to put on a sport coat and slacks to meet his mother for dinner. He told them both at Twenty-One how he'd completed no fewer than three feature length screenplays, two of which had already started making the rounds at agencies out on the coast.

"My god, son." Elisabeth, slurring already from holiday cheer, shone with approval. Her face, which he tended to remember from the brief time they had lived together in his early childhood, as narrow and youthful where now it had grown puffy. "You never fail to astound me."

"I understand the coverage on them has been uniformly positive." Billy, sipping a velvety, oaky Malbec, swished like an oenophile and swallowed in slow motion. "So a quick sale is likely, if not a bidding war. Or so I understand."

"A *sale?*" Whitaker, who had been eyeing Billy with cool detachment through his wire-framed gold glasses, leaned forward and squinted. "I thought you were shopping agents."

"That's what I meant—an agent, to manage such matters. As a quick sale." Billy shrugged. "I'm just telling you what my professor says. He knows the business."

"Fantastic," they'd cooed, *oohing* and *aahing*.

"You're going to make so much damn money," Whitaker said.

"And he's the man to tell you where to invest it, son."

"Sure, guys. Sure thing."

All smiles. But wanting to puke. He was making all this money to show Granddad. Well—one day, he would manifest these current lies.

Enough of this shrewd maneuvering. Contemptuous but quiet, when his mother went to the powder room Billy smirked and said to Whitaker, "As though my grandfather's people aren't available to help me manage my money."

"Listen—I'm not trying to stick my beak in the middle of family business."

"So we have that going for us. Know your place, son."

By the time they finished the rest of a dinner whose temperature had turned cool and he made excuses to leave, Billy'd gotten the distinct impression that his mother's boyfriend would refrain from making any more ridiculous entreaties. Next time it happened, Billy would make his point with prejudice.

Billy, getting to the meat of his real reason for visiting, took the train out to the Connecticut countryside where his grandfather still respected the old ways, celebrating the high holidays with an eye toward tradition; not so the younger Steeples, who eschewed their Jewish heritage, held no religious beliefs that Billy'd ever witnessed. But of course, like all good Americans, they had celebrated Christmas like the unrepentant Philistines they were.

Or so Grandad often declared. "I warned Bill Senior not to marry outside the tribe," he'd confided to Billy. "Now look at the family."

Llech Stemplewicz toasted his grandson's arrival. "Billy—my boy. You look so much better now that you've got some hair on your head."

"I feel like I'm starting to get my 'head' together, Poppy. Feeling grown up, finding myself."

Telling his forebear about plans to make films and become a living Hollywood god—the author of his films, and his own destiny—Billy knew it wouldn't be enough.

"Movies? You wouldn't rather make something of yourself in the real world?"

"It's an industry."

"It's make-believe."

"A billion-dollar pretense."

"Men like us are destined for greater things than mere play-acting. The stories we tell become other people's hard reality."

The old man, rapping his knuckles on the arm of the sofa; a fire, crackling in a fireplace almost as tall as Billy in the mansion's enormous family room the size of a meeting hall. Troubled and uncertain about his grandson trying a life spent in the arts, a look crossing his face like *one day my grandson will be grounded, will see his way through to the life he should be living*.

But for now satisfied, satisfied his progeny had at least come to visit. "So long as there's money in it—real money. Remember—that's the only path to true satisfaction in this life. The money is what matters. Without the money, you don't have the power."

Billy, concluding the holiday visit by discussing his new girlfriend Libby, how by the next time he came, he hoped to bring her along. "From a good family back home. They own half the county."

"Old money?"

Billy winked and nodded.

*That's the stuff,* his grandfather's twinkling eyes said.

This final lie, needling Billy by slipping out unbidden as it had. He'd tried to stop thinking about her.

Tried. But with each day, it only got worse. The sense of loss. Of separation. At times it could feel downright bothersome.

Without announcing his departure to anyone, the next morning Billy called a car service and headed for La Guardia, his destination not South Carolina but west, to the golden coast for the Grateful Dead's annual four-show New Year's run out in Oakland. Just the ticket. Also a hotbed of punk as well out in the East Bay area to be explored.

The concerts long sold out, at the last minute he'd procured the tickets from a 'broker,' a service that'd set him back nearly a grand for tickets with a twenty-five dollar face value. Ouch.

The week before Christmas he'd called Uncle Leap, in name only, an L.A. entertainment lawyer and pal of Billy's dad—his lawyer, one day, when ready to sign with an agency. Cal Leaphart made his own call and found Billy only the best of seats, a pair for each night. Uncle Leap, beside himself with pleasure. One of those old 60s hippies turned moneygrubbing yups, they 'rapped' for twenty minutes about the Dead. Had all kinds of stories. Endless dope, endless pussy.

"But they say if you can remember the 60s, you weren't really there. That's what I've heard, Uncle Leap."

*Bah*, he said. "Old wive's tale. The dope back then wasn't like booze. High was wide-awake, son. Not asleep."

Billy, his true intention with all these ducats? To call and surprise Libby! Make up, finally! Talk her into letting him fly her out to meet him in Northern California, on a romantic Deadhead getaway fantasy, all expenses paid, with no skin off anyone's nose—but he couldn't speak for other sensitive body parts, no sir, only that this time—this time—he'd take it at her pace.

Even if sex didn't end up happening at all.

He could wait.

Let her decide.

This, Billy thought. This here's growth, y'all, in Ruck's yokel voice he trotted out from time to time to make everyone laugh.

At the time of formulating the Oakland Gambit, Billy had been tipsy on mimosas at Mucky Turnbull's father's lake house where Meat Mallet had a weekend-long songwriting session going, and the logic of his plan had made sense amidst the boredom he felt working in a musical genre that now left him cold. And foolhardy, a cockamamie scheme, one thankfully not pursued. Other than blowing money on the tix, which he might as well use.

As though Libby would ever trust him again.

Get real.

He quelled these nettlesome worries. It would all work out. Except for the problem of her absence.

Arriving in California after lunch West Coast time, Billy took a cab from SFO to Union Station, got hustled by a drooling nitwit trying to carry his bags down onto the cavernous BART platform for a tip; Billy, rebuffing the con artist with a reasoned threat of sudden, violent evisceration.

After a different sort of hustle—waiting for the train and dealing with jostling holiday crowds, grifters, drunks, and San Francisco weirdos—he got himself checked into the Days Inn across from the Oakland Auditorium Arena, busted out a tie-dye and a fresh pair of Birkenstocks purchased at Bergdorf's back in New York, and hit the Dead scene.

Billy, raging and partying with the Deadheads who'd already set up camp in the neighborhood, made friends fast. Getting stoned, but taking it easy on headier materials. This, an academic experiment, not a bacchanal. That formula had proved all but ruinous.

In any case, these shows, as Billy had learned, represented the peak Dead event of every year: the culmination of another turning of the calendar's page, a symbol of steadfast longevity by both musicians as well as followers, the gathering of the tribe, the summation of another spin around the sun. The New Year's run. A finish line. Hottest ticket of the them all, and for a band whose shows were always SRO.

Billy, admiring their success. Bunch of lucky-ass, filthy hippies. Talk about shoving it to the man—fifty-million a year bought a whole heap of fuck-you.

The parking lot of the motel remained a roiling, raucous circus throughout the run, with hippie busses and other vehicles parked on every available square inch waiting for the official arena parking across the street to open. His room on the ground floor, right outside the window a guy had started running a nitrous operation out of his VW pop-top. All Billy had to do was wave money and the vendor handed him ice-cold punchballs through the open window; nitrous, a good thing, a calming, headtrippy, albeit ephemeral experience. Weed and hash and pot brownies and goo balls and shrooms and shroom tea, oh my. Liquid LSD in little vials. Sheets of blotter. Even white powders, but that was way on the Q-T. Billy, less a participant in all that than being in observer mode. Looking for the right partner for his little experiment in control.

Inhaling the gas until getting aural hallucinations—sirens in the distance going *wah wah wah*—Billy began passing out. He fell forward, conking his head against the screen of the soft babbling television set on which he'd been watching a cable rerun of THE BIG CHILL. The nitrous had made him feel as though he were in the movie with the characters, sitting on the couch with the actor William Hurt when he says, "I think the man in the hat did something terrible."

Imagine if Libby were watching it right now back home in South Carolina. And saw Billy in one of her favorite movies. Imagine it.

Hearing Libby's voice calling out to him from the other side of the television glass.

Seeing her reflection in the glass of the open window.

Reaching out.

But not Libby—a real girl standing in the open window.

The nitrous buzz wore off. "Word, sister."

"Hey now, brother."

"Join me?"

"You bet."

Voluptuous, dark-eyed hippie girl, voice deep, sexy, alluring; Sophie Sunflower, she said her name was, a ridiculous, made-up identity which made her no less attractive. Not unlike Libby in some ways, but in others not like her at all. Libby, no hippie. Down to earth, maybe. This chick, Jesus, she had dreads and armpit hair.

"You been on tour for a while?" he asked as though he'd been following them since the sixties.

"Ever since Jerry's coma," whenever that had been. He didn't ask. His ignorance as a newbie would have outed him. "But like, West Coast only?" she clarified.

"Right on. It's like kismet."

"How's that?"

"These are my first West Coast shows." He held up his hand for a high-five that she returned with gusto, laughing and sucking on her own punchball of gas. "Meant to be."

Billy, improving backstory, said he'd been hard on board since Dylan and the Dead back in '87; had done shows from New York to Timbuktu but never here to motherland, somehow.

To which she said, right on, right on. "Never too late."

Glad to hear that of her status as one of the vagabond followers—if the experiment went south, maybe nobody would miss her.

No back home, maybe. A romantic notion.

"Where are ya from?"

"South Carolina," Billy lied. "You?"

"You don't sound like a southerner."

He shrugged. "My parents were from the city. New York, I mean."

"Mine, too."

"How about now? From where do you hail, maiden?"

"Right here and right now," she said, nodding, her voice lowered almost a full octave by the effects of the nitrous oxide. She'd lost the thread of the conversation. She tooted her balloon. Laughed.

After a micro-hesitation, Billy, accepting a hit of X she offered. More nitrous. Puffing the amazing weed.

Sophie, like, literally BLOWN AWAY to discover Billy's set of tickets sitting on the small desk attached to the wall.

"Holy crap—*you have an extra for all four nights?*"

"There they are."

"I'm still searching for the thirtieth," she enumerated by holding up a finger and scrunching up the side of her face as though in deep calculation. At last she said, "And New Year's, too. Of course." She finished in a whisper, her pupils dilated, already spun.

Billy purred, "If you're unencumbered, they could be yours. Or, ours—if you know what I mean."

She asked what he meant. He explained.

"Right on. Right on..." A sparkle of connection. "What do you want for them?"

"I just want somebody sweet to party with, babe."

Now she got squirrelly. "You don't look like a Deadhead. You're not like, a cop. Are ya?"

"I've got the Deadheady credentials right here," said Billy, hand over tie-dye covered heart. "I am not *de* po-lice."

Smiling at him, beatific, sloe-eyed, alluring. Jackpot. "The lots are open now. Let's go get happy."

"Yeah—let's do that."

Focusing on Sophie Sunflower throughout the concert, hands all over one another, X-ing like crazy, Billy half-hard and ready for a decent, accident-free pop or three; he barely looked at the stage.

Jealous, though: his new free-spirit ticket wench seemed to have more close friends than Billy could imagine in his own life. Embraces, long lingering hippie hugs with both sexes, twirling and swirling with other guys, gals, the ushers in their sky-blue BILL GRAHAM PRESENTS windbreakers.

*She's like the mayor of Deadville. Half the audience would be looking for her if she up and vanished.*

*No accidents.*

The Dead, rocking the arena, Garcia grinning and shredding his Doug Irwin; a double encore, rare, all anyone could talk about while streaming back into the parking lots for the massive post-show party already underway outside, percolating as though it had never stopped during the concert.

But Sophie and Billy not tarrying, heading straight back for the hotel across the highway; both horny as hell, literally running.

Tender sex, turning wild and wooly. Sophie, a game companion for Billy's intensity. She met every thrust, howling and clawing at him.

Shoving her arms back. Holding her down.

Fighting back with him, scratching at him.

In later repose, Sophie, stroking his sore cock, said she'd never seen a more beautiful specimen. "What an angel man."

"Man of your dreams?"

*Mm-hm*, she cooed.

But as it often happened in the afterglow, her face—shiny, swollen and sweaty, nasty hair all dreaded like snakes, hairy as an ape—turned ugly. He wanted to shove her hippie head through the TV. Wanted to fuck holes she didn't yet have.

Calm.

Blue.

Ocean.

A technique he'd picked up.

The next morning, with approving lust in her eyes, she went to grab her stuff from a friend's van. Moving in with him for the duration. More practice awaited.

Billy, awake on New Year's morning, still tripping from the rip-snorting three-set Dead show, sat across the room staring at the inert, seemingly lifeless body on the bed.

His mind, a blank—he'd killed her after all.

But then the body farted, low and long.

Sophie Sunflower, who'd chosen alcohol as her New Year's blowout drug of choice, lay flabby and stinky and hairy, only passed out and snoring, not dead. Dirty, calloused feet blacker than printer's ink stuck out of the twisted, stained sheets. Bruises and scabs all up and down her shins. Drool down the pillow, leaves in her hair where she had fallen down outside in the a patch of landscaping on the stumble back from the show.

But still alive.

He'd fucked like a madman for four nights with no accidents.

*The test is over.*

Sneaky, quiet as a church mouse, Billy gathered his various accoutrements and pieces-parts, much of which he'd packed before the show last night. He slipped on his travel wear of an oxford shirt and khakis, rinsed out his mouth and combed through his short but growing hair. Left a note with a phony name and address in New York, 'William St. Hubbins,' a condo on Park Avenue where he and his father had lived before Bill the elder got into politics and moved to DC, a secure building that wouldn't let a skunky trollop like Sophie into the lobby if her life depended on it.

He signed it, *See-ya, wouldn't-wanna-be-ya.* Tears of laughter, streaming down his face. Snorting and trying not to guffaw. Desperate not to wake her.

At the last second Billy filched money from her purse, a hemp bucket-bag covered in ribbons and bows. He took what little cash she seemed to have—maybe seventy dollars in wrinkled, assorted bills. Took out her ID and debit card, slid them both in between the mattress and box springs. A prankster.

Downstairs he handed the hotel clerk the wad of her money to "keep his trap shut when the crazy bitch in room 111" calls asking for information on the former room registrant who'd decamped for fresher climes.

Confidential: "I made a terrible mistake hooking up with her, one of those whacked-out hippie losers. Now I need your help disposing of her."

"Goodness me."

"I beg you—let her sleep it off until late checkout time."

The young clerk, gay, dapper and dimpled, flattened his lips into a hard line of disapproval. "I wouldn't dream of giving out your information to anyone not registered alongside you. It's prohibited by law."

"So we're 'down by law'?" Billy, a little sparkle, teasing him with an art movie reference, the kind Libby would get. "You and me?"

"We're down, all right."

"Bless your heart," he said. "See ya next year."

The first week of January, a fresh start, a new dickhead—he meant 'decade'—found him back in his Carolina condo. He looked around, excited about the spring semester.

Vowing: *I don't need Libby, or any of them.*

But if he could have her, now he was sure he could exhibit control.

Could be normal.

Normal as she required.

Months later, however, upon hearing that she and Devin were planning to move into an apartment together—like the committed lovers they already were when he first met them—Billy, gut-punched anew.

Despondent.

Leaning over the railing of his balcony, inches away from hurling himself over the edge, but lacking the stones to do so.

Billy, since the awful night, lying to himself every second. Truth? He hadn't stopped thinking about her for one blessed moment, nor the possibility of reconciliation.

He sat down in the cool Carolina winter air to write a letter—two letters, one for each of the friends he'd wronged. One more attempt with her. Before he tried more desperate measures, most of which he wasn't yet willing to define.

# FORTY-THREE

## — CREEDENCE

After missing the concert, Creedence fell into a deeply persistent depression. Despite having let Dusty do it inside her—a mistake, she now believed—she proceeded to break up with her confused and heartbroken first-time loverboy. He had cried in the car next to her for an hour. Pitiful.

This act precipitated no shortage of fresh turmoil and animosity between Creedence and her mother. A drama. Tsunami-like, in fact.

"How could you do this to him. *To us.*" Eileen, weeping and wailing, clutched a damp tissue and smoked like a demon. "You'll never find a boy sweeter than our Dusty. It always worried me you wouldn't grow into good sense."

Creedence, her powers of speech devolving into wet slobbering incoherence, knew her mother correct on one point: the daughter suffered from retardation. Learning disabilities. Who knew.

Dusty might be the only one to love her.

*This is Mama talking. There ain't nobody who don't do what she says.*

Bullcrud. She'd show them all.

But by the holiday season, Dusty's own whining and pleading persuaded her to grant him a repreive. Welcoming him back by letting him put his peterpiper inside her again, this time without the rubber he had forgotten to procure, and since he promised to pull out before 'it' happened.

Said eventuality occurred, however, sudden and abrupt, on a downward stroke—the fourth or fifth—when he groaned and his eyes rolled back, a familiar visage of pleasure.

"Don't!"

"Cant help it—*oh.*"

Pushing him away. His rock-hard, short mushroom of a penis popped out still spurt-spurting. Some got inside anyway, the rest all over her thighs. She didn't know how such a stubby thing could produce so much.

For three weeks Creedence, terrified of pregnancy, praying and wishing to never be pregnant for any reason; and then voilà, her visitor arrived. Afterwards, she made Dusty buy a whole thirty-six count box of Trojans. He kept them stashed in the spare tire in his grandmother's car, like a kilo of dope he was smuggling.

After another dozen instances of him not lasting long enough, a question, nagging—when would Dusty be able to make her feel good too, to achieve a kind of release like he enjoyed, volcanic, cathartic? She knew from the times in the bathtub what it was supposed to feel like. Creedence started keeping in an ill-used girlhood diary, a growing log of hash marks for each time they had intercourse, planning to put a red asterisk, or maybe a gold star, by the instance in which she at last found an equivalent satisfaction. Dusty needed an instruction manual.

At Thanksgiving she spoke to Devin for the first time since the Incident of October the 27th, as the concert outrage had been called in her diary, a ledger of accumulating milestones, transgressions and hash-marks awaiting an asterisk.

She lay on the bed in Devin's old room, still used by him on school breaks and in the summer, as such preserved in a state of relative stasis: Movie and rock posters, an Atari video game console still hooked up to the orange black and white television set, an old toy box in the corner with junk piled on top. The toy box, a keeping place into which she suspected Devin had not peered for a long, long time.

Sitting in his desk chair, leaning back against the wall by the window looking out on the driveway and cul-de-sac, Devin seemed wearied by her continued anger: "I've explained in every way I know how that it simply could not be helped. Now put a sock in it."

"I don't believe you."

"I even said I was sorry, too," in a voice that sounded like Yogi Bear. "*Ah* sure did. Boo-Boo did, too."

"Boo-Boo? Is that what y'all call Roy Earl?"

Devin, shrugging. "Nah."

"But that's who you mean."

He held out his hands. "The Dead will be back next year."

"I can't believe you left me here."

"I didn't do nothing—Boo-Boo was supposed to pick you up."

"So why didn't he?"

"I'm not at liberty to say."

"*Why the freak can't you say?*"

A circular conversation. "Because we were all drunk as piss-ants already, you little turd. You didn't miss anything but bullshit." He jumped out of the chair and grabbed her by the arm, hard. "Now let it go before I pop you one like Mama."

It would take more than a threat like that to scare her. Not in this house. "Let me go. Y'all were too drunk *before* the concert?"

He went back to his chair. "Pre-game got out of hand."

Trying one of Mama's tactics, rage followed by tears. Boo-hooing: "Don't never again promise me something you ain't gonna do."

"Quit acting like it's the end of the world."

"That's easy for you to say. You got to *go*."

"You'll be able to do what you want in a couple of years. There'll be plenty of concerts."

"Think so?"

"Course there will. There's always concerts."

"No—that Mama's gonna sit by and let me do what I want."

"Stand up to her—she'll cave. Always does."

"With you, maybe."

"Bullcorn."

Her guts twisted. "How do I stand up to Mama?"

Devin's eyes turned cold. "Sneak yourself one of Daddy's tallboys. Instant courage."

"I tried that."

Little placated by apologies or further discussion concerning the matter, now she wanted to call Roy Earl and bless him out, too. But, whomever the driver was to have been, Devin bore the ultimate responsibility.

She stayed pissy with him the whole, long weekend. He didn't care, not with him and Libby wrapped up in each other. They didn't need anyone else.

And Creedence had Dusty. For whatever that was worth. Letting him come back over again made Mama so happy she left a hundred-dollar bill in between the pages of the diary Creedence thought she had so carefully hidden under her mattress.

*Now, don't y'all do it again without him wearing a thing on this thing*, Mama had scribbled on a note clipped to the bill. *There will be time for that later.*

The Christmas holidays brought winter weather which seemed harsh by South Carolina standards, with tension between brother and sister, son and mother, all colder than the frigid winds sweeping down from the north.

On Christmas Eve, Creedence overheard Dwight and Devin add to the mix with an argument that'd begun over matters unknown:

"Son of mine, I do not know what's happened with you. You act like your mother and me's the enemy."

"Not you, Dad. Not you."

Dark, angry, more so than she could ever remember seeing her Daddy behave. "Me and her done lived our lives for you and nothing but you, and your little sister—don't you understand?"

Creedence noted how Devin's voice shook. "There's a lot I can't explain. It's—hard to—I don't—it's weird."

"Quit trying to make up some story."

"Oh—the stories I could make up, Daddy."

"I figured you had more respect for me than that."

Devin, ending the conversation with a teenage-boy grunt.

Later, when Creedence passed by his room she noticed him staring red-eyed and blank, like Jack Nicholson in THE SHINING, drooling, insane and on the verge of an axe-murder spree. Devin, however, only looked as though he'd been crying—unusual for him. Most of the time he was like a stone. Except maybe with Libby, when his face looked more relaxed. His Libby-face.

Why didn't she change around Dusty?

Why didn't Mama change around Daddy?

Creedence, journaling that maybe she didn't much want to figure out all these marriages and relationships and mess, hiding the diary in her new spot way up in a nook above the closet door in her room. And yet driven inside to connect, but not feeling it with Dusty the way she thought she ought to. But going along. For now. Going along to get along; if for no other reason than to keep Mama off her back.

It was okay. Devin was right. High school would be over soon. She would do what she wanted, one day. Mama's hundred bucks would become the first of a secret stash Creedence—Chelsea—would use to leave all their stupid asses in the dust. Soon.

Christmas break, bleak around the Meade house as well as home at the Ruckers. Devin, sneaking liquor every chance he got, which he hid by covering it with a beer or two. Libby didn't mind a few beers.

Source of the bleak: A revelation in which her father faced a mortal challenge, a family crisis into which Devin found himself swept: cancer had been diagnosed just after Thanksgiving. That drunken sot, her father, had come up with Stage IV lung and liver, the disease progressing unabated, but the family, her mother Eunice and brothers Kevin and Harold, older and established adults with their own families—Libby called herself an 'accident' baby, born ten years after the next youngest child—still managed to put on a shiny, happy, holiday façade anyway.

The father, as Devin judged, was a complete asshole—as though he hadn't hurt his family enough, now putting on this cancer drama. Libby, informing Devin her dad had suffered alcohol-induced anger management issues, hadn't painted a kind picture.

No wonder she was always encouraging him to lose the Ruck persona. The hard-drinking cynic. World-weary at nineteen. Libby had had enough of this persona already.

Devin, lucky she had stuck with him. A reason to not drink as much. He needed one—a reason. Not a drink.

He took a drink instead.

Libby, her older brothers and the Meade parents along with Devin, all gathered around a tinseled tree under decoration on Christmas morning after the gifts had been opened at Devin's house, which his mother had insisted upon. First among mothers. The only reason Devin agreed is he knew one of the Meade brothers wouldn't arrive until lunchtime. She'd won nothing, had gotten nothing over on him.

Frank, shaky but participating by hanging ornaments with his wraithlike fingers, suffered a sheen on his face of perpetual surprise, as well as an occasional shadow: Realizing, maybe, this would be the last holiday.

"You don't recover from what I have," he'd told Devin outside as part of a speech about being sorry for keeping Libby's boyfriend at arm's length. "It's in my bones, too."

"I'm sorry, Mr. Meade."

"You want to know what fucked feels like? Do you? Well buddy, this is it."

Maybe he couldn't say any of that to the people inside the house—Devin, a near stranger. Frank's intimacy made him feel like a member of the family, in a way, for the first time.

In any case, quite a change in temperature. Frank hadn't always been so kind.

One night after dropping Libby off, he'd popped out of the hedges to accost Devin by the Mustang parked along the street in the newer subdivision where the Meades lived, closer to the nuclear station where he worked. Frank might have been a drunk, but he held multiple degrees and made six-figures, which in Edgewater County was real money.

Barely intelligible, bleary-eyed and red-nosed, exhaling a bitter cloud like he'd been gargling pure ethanol, in this guise Frank got in Devin's face to warn that Libby was special. That it wouldn't be just any little smart-ass Edgewater County redneck good enough for *his* little girl. That South Carolina was not a place to which he'd wanted to come in the first place, but money—he kept calling it 'mammon'—had ruled the day. Doing so for the good of his family. Devin, if he were smart, would watch his good-old-boy, cracker ass around the Meades.

"I have stories that end with the hospital. I have stories that end with *jail*," he boasted, poking two fingers into Devin's chest. "You don't fuck with me."

Devin, who had been yelled at by his Mama with such vituperative invective that it took a lot to scare him, didn't flinch. "If I get out of line," trying to sound like some bad-ass movie character, "I'm sure she'll give me the boot herself."

Frank laughed. "She'll choose correctly. She possesses the wisdom of the ages, that girl. No question. Like the woman of the wilderness. A fecund, white goddess."

Whatever that all meant.

"But you, son? You're nothing but *vaginal feces*. All of you are. You realize that?"

"I'd like to think that I do."

"Fuck you know about anything?"

"Well," Devin had said, running short of subtle back-talk. "There's the rub. I really should be getting on home."

"Get off this property. And if you come back, I won't be calling the law, son. We'll be handling it right here ourselves. Understood?"

Devin, for once liking the cut of the man's jib—Frank's boozy bluster dovetailed nicely with his own ripening, cynically burgeoning worldview. He decamped with haste, hoping Libby had locked her bedroom door.

The next day he'd of course seen Frank again, who held no memory of the prior conversation. Shuffling around the Meade household in a bathrobe, hungover, eyes and nose scarlet aircraft beacons, complaints of a wicked cold that'd come upon him, he greeted Devin with relative bonhomie and good cheer.

"Young Mr. Rucker," he'd said, bidding Libby to go fix them both cups of coffee. "I've been wondering where you'd gotten off to."

But now Frank was dying, which made him more interesting to Devin than anyone else but his daughter. He'd watch closely how Frank handled Death when it arrived. Devin was keeping a registry, he'd decided. That way when it was his time, he'd be ready for anything.

Outside at the curb as Frank smoked and coughed and watched as Devin dragged the last bulging black bag full of cast-off wrapping paper.

Pulling a pint of cheap scotch out of his bathrobe, Frank took himself a good nip. Furtive, a small gag and cough. But another before starting to put it away.

He paused. "Oh—you want a snort, son? It being Christmas and all?"

"Might be a touch early for me."

He was starting chemo next week, he'd said earlier. What did he have to lose now by continuing to drink? "Suit yourself."

Devin, marveling yet sorrowful at Mr. Meade, who, with cancer in his guts and bones, could still stomach hot scotch. "Changed my mind."

Handing him the bottle. "That's the ticket, son."

The liquor, hot and harsh, exploded in Devin's stomach. Good.

"Gonna tell you something, young Mr. Devin. Something none of them know."

The idea of secrets sickened Devin. "Sure."

"I knew I was beat before I ever got the diagnosis. Knew it sure as I'm standing here. Almost from the first time I drank—it was when I was your age, so don't make a habit of it, now. But as for being *sick*-sick...? Like this. I knew for real months ago. But I didn't tell anyone. Not until I had no choice. Want to know why?"

Devin, irritated at such news being kept from loved ones, couldn't say that he did.

Frank glanced up to the shining Christmas day sun. "You think I lack self-awareness?"

"How do you mean?"

"I know what's it been like to live with me. When I let myself know, that is."

Devin again took the scotch from Libby's father's hand, the skin mottled and dry. Unscrewing the cap, he took another pull. Wincing at the burn. "That does kinda hit the spot."

"Like I said—don't make it a habit. Not this early. Always try to wait until noon, at least."

"You can depend on me, sir."

"Take care of her, you hear me?"

"Libby."

Nodding. "If you would. My little Frances Elizabeth." The liquor in his gut has steadied him, given him a happy glow. "You know she was a surprise to us, don't you?"

"I've heard the family legend." Devin handed him the bottle. "She's everything that makes sense to me about this world."

Clapping him on the shoulder, nodding and seeming relieved, Frank gestured for them to go back inside for Christmas dinner. "So you'll handle things, then?"

"Things?"

"Whatever she needs. The boys, now, they have their own families, and their mom, I suspect, will go and live near one of them. They'll have each other. But my daughter, she'll need someone."

"I told you—she's my life."

Inside, Devin lacked conviction—he didn't feel in control of himself, much less of the world. But he gave no hint. Learning to show scant emotion around his mother had given him a carapace of stolid stoicism sufficient to mask the persistent anxiety and paranoia only alcohol quelled.

At the kitchen door, comrades in booze, they shook hands.

"Thank you, son."

"I won't let anything happen to her—I promise. I'll die myself, first."

Frank Meade's funeral, much sooner than anyone anticipated, only six weeks into the spring semester.

Back in Edgewater County at the newer Memorial Gardens near Chilton rather than the old cemetery downtown. February, gray, threatening rain. A funeral day like out of a movie.

Later than night, Libby, asking Devin to drive her back to the cemetery.

Tramping through the darkness up the gentle slope and finding Frank's grave, fresh—the smell of rich, tilled earth, of the impending springtime, of planting season. The ground, his resting place for all eternity. A plot next to him, secured for his wife.

Frank Meade, Devin thought, left body intact; whereabouts of soul, unknown.

Libby, silent, clinging. "It's over."

"What did that asshole do to you?"

Shaking. "Nothing that's worth saying out loud."

"Then you made it, babygirl. You made it through."

Libby, striding with head held high, already halfway into the next row of graves. Calling back after Devin, who lingered.

Libby, echoing across the hillside of grave sites. "Shall we go?"

"Yeah. Getting the creeps."

"The next scene is the one where I move on," she said.

Frank had been wrong about one thing—Libby didn't need Devin. One look in her resolute eyes the day her own father got put into the ground told Devin all he needed to know about the love of his life. Tough dame. That much he understood.

At last, Billy's best opportunity to petition Libby in person came in a chance encounter on the street, late, after another raucous Meat Mallet gig outside dingy rock club Slim Lupo's, punk pogo, sprays of beer, hardcore thrashing for an hour or so. All of it had left him empty. Going through the motions. Quitting.

Lurching out of the stage door and down a short alley, hunched over, rolling his heavy bass amp, shiny and black, the nicest piece of equipment of any member of Meat Mallet, or for that matter of the precursor band called Choking Hazard, Billy had yelped with surprise:

Devin and Libby, arm in arm, appeared wraithlike from around the corner. Her beautiful eyes, popping open. She drew close to her man.

Awkward.

Billy, emitting a series of squawking sounds outside Mucky's beat-to-shit step van, realized he had club-ears, shouting at the top of his lungs from the near-deafness he'd suffer for most of the next day. The band had inherited the van from the Turnbull family business, a successful and longtime plumbing concern down in Charleston. Wealth or not, how anyone had come to such a proletarian and scatological career Billy hadn't a clue, but proof may be found in the pudding, and the Turnbulls lived in a mansion South of Broad, the old money part of Chucktown. The plumbing, maybe a front for Southern-fried organized crime. Who knew.

Who cared.

Libby.

Smiling and going for nonchalant, but his breaking, high voice, Billy knew, blew his cover. "Just had a fantastic gig inside."

"Cool, dude."

"What about y'all?"

"We caught Miller's Crossing at the Bijou."

Billy had seen it earlier that week, but halfway through had fallen asleep. "Those Coen Brothers—geniuses. Damn their eyes."

"Time will tell," Libby spoke up. "It wasn't as satisfying as BLOOD SIMPLE."

"Brilliant movie, there."

"I couldn't half figure out what was going on," Devin said.

"You dozed off, is why."

Devin, Billy; secret, sleepy comrades in arms.

Libby, fake-yawning. "Well. I'm tired. C'mon."

Billy, watching an opportunity slip away, blurted, "Libby, please—there are things which simply must be said."

"Tell them to my boyfriend."

"Just let him say his piece," Devin said, weary. "So we can get on our way."

His heart thudded. "Is it all right with you, Ruck? Five minutes?"

Devin, belching: "Told y'all what I think."

Libby, steadfast. "And the answer's still no."

Billy knew his desperation pitiful, but his inhibitions, tempered by alcohol. "It feels wretched to beg."

Libby, glaring with simmering animosity. "If it means I'll be allowed to go home, fine. I have a headache."

Devin, bowing, went across the street to wait. And, as Billy knew, to keep an eye on them both.

Passing in and out of the orange ovals cast by the streetlights, Billy and Libby strolled up the block. She stayed about four feet away from him.

"If you touch me, I'll scream. I swear I will."

"I wouldn't dream of it."

Libby stopped and hurled herself around. Her eyes, flaring. "So what do you want?"

"Don't be that way, please."

"You made this situation."

Billy, frustrated almost to tears—all he'd wanted out of the evening had been to tell his band mates to go screw themselves once and for all eternity, walk out of the bar in a moment of triumphant so-what, fuck-all closure on a chapter of his life no longer seeming to have any meaning. His quitting scene, it had been planned as a big post-show surprise to Mucky and the rest of those dickhead poseurs, now interrupted by the chance to see Libby. How when she'd appeared, he'd been rehearsing the way he'd tell them—the accusations, the epithets, the declarations. But now had to put that off to deal with this other stressful emotional crap.

Billy, irritated. He wanted to kill her as much as kiss her. Bothersome; that he felt unprepared for this confrontation; a new apotheosis of understatement. So much pent up shame and desire ready to pour out of him, his body feeling as taut as an overfilled water balloon about to burst at the slightest change in air pressure—the river of draught beer he'd consumed over the course of the evening didn't help. Nor had his recent cessation of pleasurable self-abuse for a routine of painful flagellation at his morning erections with a stiff hairbrush.

A lapse tonight, this drinking. Another reason to bail on Meat Mallet—Mucky, denying it, but still shooting heroin. A bad scene. Hooked. What a schmuck. Way off course—smack? What, was it the 70s again?

Besides—look where the drinking and drugging had led with Libby.

They stopped at the corner by a bus stop bench. Palms clammy, dying to touch her, if only in the smallest of ways, Billy, all but tumbling forward into those eyes of hers.

Allowing a kernel of hope to overwhelm his caution: "Oh, god—how can I earn your forgiveness?"

"You can't."

"Don't you realize how I've suffered? What you mean to me?"

Flabbergasted, scoffing, backing away. "Hasn't anyone ever told you 'no' before? You have no idea what it feels like as a woman."

"Not really, but that's beside the point."

She laughed, a small, mirthless snort. "You don't understand—I wasn't only frightened. I was also disappointed."

"Oh, but I do understand—I've been in agony."

"This happening wasn't all bad."

Shocked by her perfidious notion. "Maybe for you."

"No, really—since you haven't been hanging around, Devin doesn't drink as much. He makes more time for me. And me for him. If you know what I mean."

Billy, his chest tight, felt his breath rush out. Wheezing: "Awesome."

"So here's my advice. Stop thinking about me."

Trying to ignore the devastating and grievous insult of hearing how close they felt to one another, Billy, seizing on a new tack, offered in a hot rush:

"Ruck, now, that's who we need to talk about—he seems to have forgiven me. Truly."

"Devin grew up in Edgewater County. He's a tough Carolina boy. You're lucky, Billy. Maybe luckier than you know. That's all I can tell you."

Devin loved Billy. Her intimations of violence skittered off him. "He *knows* I know right from wrong. How we were all fucked up, and the show was so intense and you looked so beautiful, see? You get it? Luminous, amazing. And I misunderstood the signals."

"Billy—what signals?"

"That's right. I misunderstood where we were. Who we were. Who I was. *It was an accident.*"

She took her time digesting that. Billy, his knees weak, sat down on the bench. Noise from up the block, his bandmates continuing the load-out.

Libby finally spoke. "This is tragic all around. Want to know how?""

His eyes bulged with anticipation. His sat on the edge of the bench, stolid, motionless, his spine straight. "Please."

"Besides you ruining your friendship with Devin? And screwing up the scriptwriting class?"

Billy, flummoxed and groping. "I beseech thee."

"Don't you realize you were stealing my heart? Against my will?"

This, no admission of affection. He couldn't speak. His throat, closed like all the bars at 2am.

Libby, marching away down the sidewalk: "There hasn't been one fair thing about our relationship. Now—leave us alone. I'm not asking."

Billy, swooning, rose to follow, took two lurching steps like Karloff in heavy Frankenstein makeup. Watching her jaywalk to meet Devin down the block, he staggered back like a blind man to again sit down, heavy, onto the bench. He watched in sorrowful resignation as they vanished into the deepening night, the slap-slap sound of Libby's flip-flops echoing with finality.

The crying started. He fell to his side on the bench. He nearly convulsed with grief. If anyone saw him, they'd think him mad.

*Maybe she'll come around. Maybe I'll get another chance. So long as we all still draw breath, it could happen.*

Billy, pulling himself together, got fired up to finish the I'm-quitting scene. It would be so epic they would never forget it.

*Fuck 'em—I'll split without a word. I just won't show at the next practice, won't show at the next gig. Won't return phone calls. And stupid as they may be, they'll get the message. Bunch of lousy punks.*

As devastated as he felt after this debacle with Libby—it would turn from despair to anger, soon, if his moods followed the typical pattern—he needed to get away from his bandmates before one accidentally ended up dead, if not all of them.

He had to walk a narrow path. Stay out of trouble. No accidents. Not while Libby only a few blocks away. She might still forgive him, if he explained it a different way, next time.

Devin, sitting on a low wall across from the music club with an asphalt parking lot at his back, smoked and watched as Libby and Billy strolled in and out of the pools of rust from the high-pressure sodium streetlights.

Besides the coarse grunts and clicks of Billy's bandmates continuing to roll out their gear, he heard other voices—a group of loud drunks came ROLLING out of the Back Porch a block away. As they got closer, he saw that one of the group was his roommate, Mike Cassidy, the enigmatic fourth bonehead taking up space in the University Terrace apartment. Devin had made no real connection with Ohio Mike, as they called him behind his back, other than shooting the shit and drinking beer and ditching classes together, here and there.

"*Ruck*." Mike, thick-tongued, plowed under, grabbing his hand in a bro-shake. "Where's the rest of the crew?"

Devin, dry, a cool greeting. "Waiting on my gal."

Mike squinted across the street at Billy and Libby standing down at the opposite corner. "Not Steeple. I wouldn't trust that player with my girl, dude."

"He won't lay a hand on her."

"You sure? I saw them a dozen times last semester, walking around together near the State House. Going into the Coffee Shack this one time."

"Holding hands?" Devin asked, impassive. He blew smoke in Mike's face and licked his lips. "Were they skipping along arm in arm?"

"You better keep that tail on a short leash. Or else him on a longer one."

"Taken under advisement. It's under control."

Scoffing. "Ain't nothing under anybody's control."

Mike caught up to his friends, pausing long enough to turn over a newspaper box with a grinding, loud crash. The group of young men, howling like wild dogs loosed upon the night, ran in their pack up the hill toward campus. Their carefree attitude made Devin sick.

Libby, appearing at Devin's elbow, surprised him with a big hug. She said, now that's that with Billy Steeple once and for all.

Startled and intrigued by a telephone call from one Roy Earl Pettus, Creedence got a flurry of stomach-butterflies from irritation as well as intrigue. At last, she thought.

A typical afternoon in Pine Haven: Dusty, watching THE BRADY BUNCH on TBS, pouted; Creedence, not feeling like messing around, either the main way or any other, for that matter. For all his disappointment and whining, you'd have thought Dale Earnhardt had gotten killed in a racetrack crash.

"At least tickle him under his chin."

"Nuh-uh. I got a headache."

She took the call from Roy in the kitchen where Dusty, engrossed and drooling over Marcia, couldn't hear.

Whispering: "I sat for hours waiting for you. *Hours.*"

His voice, soft and gentle. Sweet. "I really screwed up. I know that."

"I can't believe you didn't show."

"I told your stupid brother he should've gone."

"Why didn't you?"

"Can't say on the phone why, but I couldn't drive. He could've, if he'd wanted to. But me, I couldn't have drove to save my life, Creed—or, Colette. Or is it Chelsea? Devin said you were going by Chelsea, now...?"

Charmed by the apology, and the way his voice shook—months late, true, but the chivalrous nature of the effort, assuming the Roy Earl hadn't been coerced, prompted a touch of forgiveness. "Call me Creedence, if you want."

"That's cool. I like that nickname."

"My dad gave it to me."

"What does it mean?"

"Because of my initials—CCR."

"Oh, I get it. That's awesome."

"So now, *why* couldn't y'all drive?"

"Too much, too fast."

"Do you even remember the concert?"

"Not really. Aw, it wasn't so great, anyway."

"Really?"

"Your brother even left early. Didn't he tell you that?"

"No—well, dang."

"See?"

Creedence gagged as she watched Dusty picking his nose and flicking the booger off in the direction of the TV screen.

"So, I reckon that's all. And I—"

"Yes?"

"If you ever wanted to go out again, or something?"

"*Yes*—?"

"I could make it up to you."

Lowering her voice. "I have a boyfriend."

"Oh, shit."

"But that's not—it's not that serious."

"Dang it. Just my luck."

"Roy Earl?"

Waiting; silent.

All courage leaving her. "Nothing. Thanks for saying you're sorry."

Dejected, he rang off by saying he reckoned he'd see her around. When he came to see Devin. Sometime.

Creedence, slumping against the kitchen wall, hung up the handset. She scratched at a zit on her forehead, which she swore had appeared over the course of the conversation—a stress-bump.

Dusty, shouting over a Captain Crunch commercial: "Creedence? Fix me a glass of Pepsi and bring it on over here."

Chelsea, pouring the soda, stared into the glass and watched tiny bubbles burst on the surface, vanishing as soon as they appeared. Creedence, wishing herself to disappear, to vanish into the air like her mother's cigarette smoke.

Libby and Devin, after a hectic month of gradual transition, now all moved in to the new pad; exam week, over and done, with a housewarming party planned for the second Saturday of May, the tenth.

Libby, trying out the new kitchen by baking cookies, sang along to the radio playing classic rock. Devin, in the living room setting up folding lawn chairs—they only had one couch, bought for twenty dollars at a thrift store. Time enough later for further furnishings.

All the time in the world.

The still nameless kitten, fuzzy, white paws, darted in and out of Devin's feet. The kitty-cat, priming herself, sprang onto a scuffed coffee table rescued from the Meade family garage.

"*Meeee*," the kitten called, yet to grow into her full meow. "Me."

"Watch it, little one," Devin admonished the gray cat. "Don't wanna squish you."

"Here, angel. Don't get under Daddy's feet, now."

Libby, squatting down, beckoned. The cat leapt across the coffee table and dashed over to her on little white cotton-ball paws.

"What are we going to name it?"

"Her. Not it." Libby, squinted at the squirming feline. "Her *purr*-fect name will come to me."

Devin, taking the cat. "So, I wanted to talk to you."

Libby bent over to pull a tray of overcooked peanut butter cookies out of the oven, rows of dark little hockey pucks. "I can't get used to this damn thing. These are fucked."

"So, now that you and Billy have finally talked?"

Dumping the cookies in the trash Libby turned, a slow-burn. "What about him?"

"Didn't y'all get it all worked out that night outside Lupo's?"

"I let him apologize. I didn't say I accepted it."

"I thought about inviting him over."

Stricken. "*Tonight?*"

"Tonight."

"Are you shitting me?"

Devin put down the kitten, where it chased crazily across the laminate kitchen floor after a darting housefly.

Libby slipped off her oven mitts and threw them onto the counter. "Let me ask you something—what if you hadn't been there to stop him that night?"

Devin, silent, held no wish to contemplate said hypothesis, which indeed took the air out of notions of welcoming Billy back into the fold. "But it did happen."

Repeating. "But what if it hadn't?"

Wishing to change the focus. "All I really did was fall off the roof."

"That was enough," touching his face. "Forget it, angel man."

And so ending the discussion regarding Billy's presence. Later, Devin made a furtive call, gave his buddy the bad news. He took it well, best as he could hide the sadness in his voice. Billy Steeple was a nut. Better he stayed away.

Dobbs, arriving first, poured himself a glass of white wine out of a box of Franzia. He pulled out the so-called 'white' Beatles album and put side two onto the turntable. Singing to the kitten in a pure and steady voice: "*Dear Prudence... won't you come out to play-hey-hey...*"

Libby, a fit of finger-snapping, ah-ha excitement, ran into the living room. "That's our baby's name."

"Prudence?"

"Prudy," Libby saying in clarification. "Prudy-kitty."

"Me likey. Cute."

And so it would be.

Roy Earl arrived, as did a new friend of Dobbs's named Aaron, quiet until getting a touch lubricated, after which he became gregarious and funny; from his flamboyance, he seemed a good match for the emerging, but still self-conscious and tentative Dobbs.

Devin, waiting for Dobbs to simply say the words to him. What his boyhood pal was, or wasn't, didn't matter—friendship, and trust, trumped all. But still that layer of secrecy, in a sense. An open secret. All very strange. It must be tough to be gay, is all Devin could think.

Of course it was. Look at the way most guys talked among themselves.

Some dorm friends of Libby's showed up, a couple of cute girls; later, other folks from the neighborhood rolled down the block and joined in, Deadheads who brought weed and got excited to hear the Southeastern Dead show, tapes of which Billy had left in Devin's campus mailbox and which were discovered sitting on the stereo console shelf.

Much conversation bubbling around, and beers consumed; Libby, on a Bergman kick, tried to discuss THE SEVENTH SEAL with a room full of cinema philistines who hadn't seen the classic, one she and Devin screened at the Bijou the week before during their Art House Classics festival.

She described her favorite scene: stalked by Death, a medieval knight and a troupe of vagabond actors gather on a sunlit hillside to rest and eat:

"The doomed travelers, eating strawberries and milk, enjoy a last instance of peace and grace before the dark-cloaked one again looms into the frame, inexorable. It gave me the chills." Almost in tears, she recounted Max von Sydow's fated knight, smiling and speaking of how he'd always remember the lovely afternoon on the hillside—the food, the light, the people with whom he'd shared the bread of life, a last respite before the end. It's about appreciating those simple moments for what they are," nodding and explaining. "Being in the moment."

Devin, grunting. "Be here now. I get it."

Roy Earl, after catching a decent buzz on some skunk weed he'd brought, said to Devin outside, "We should have run that sister of yours over here for this."

"Well—you shoulda asked her, Romeo."

"I tried, but she said she had a boyfriend." He raised his eyebrows asking for verification. "Right?"

"This little dicknut back home named Dusty. Would love to see you break them up."

"Not my style."

Devin, laughing, grabbed Roy Earl around his chubby neck. "I'll tell Creedence you were thinking about her. We're going home tomorrow to get some more of my gear out of the house. Maybe I'll see her."

"I was planing to ride back home, too, but my folks are coming over here to go out to eat—tomorrow's Mother's Day."

"Oh, shit. Guess I should get a card."

"If I know your Mama, she'll have your ass if you don't."

Everyone drifted away, leaving Dobbs and Aaron downstairs. Getting ready for bed, Libby carried Prudy on her shoulder like an infant; Dobbs, planning to sleep over and ride home with them the next day, crashed on the thrift store couch, bidding a private goodnight to what Devin thought of as his friend's first real boyfriend.

"Hey, y'all still awake?" Dobbs, whispering, came midway up the creaking, aged mill house stairs.

Devin, grumbling, leaned out of the bathroom with a mouthful of toothpaste. "What is it?"

"I don't want to waste time in Edgewater County too long tomorrow."

"Who in their right mind would?"

"Aaron—he wants to take me out to a movie."

"I wouldn't dream of staying longer than a New York minute, oh my brother. You can depend on me, sir."

"What did y'all think about him?"

Libby, sleepy, padded barefoot into the hallway wearing one of Devin's T-shirts, The Who bullseye logo: "He's a cutie-patootie."

Dobbs smiled; at last he could be true to himself.

For this, Devin felt glad. Golf-clapping. "Dobbs finds love. I'll alert the media."

Libby, pranced through the hall in her threadbare cotton panties. Hugging Dobbs's neck. "Yay for you."

"This all isn't some wonderful dream, is it?"

"No." Libby, beaming back up at Devin. "This is real life."

In bed Libby nestled close against Devin, silvery moonlight pouring in through the slatted blinds across the young lovers; Prudy, purring herself to sleep, had curled up on Devin's pillow beside his head. The twinned limbs and spooned bodies of lovers, a family portrait; a night like forever.

# FORTY-NINE

## — BILLY

Roy Earl on the phone. Grim news. "Some kind of car wreck. Dobbs, and Devin—and Libby." He had caught Billy at home, beeping in on a dreadful Mother's Day call to the Harridan of Park Avenue, an interruption Billy grateful to suffer.

Not anymore.

"Which one's dead?" The question popped out. That drunk Rucker, who had no fear of driving pissed as a skunk, finally killed someone. "Tell me."

Roy, saying he didn't know that anyone was dead. But that it was bad.

Billy, feeling faint, collapsed against the wall of his condo. Bright sunshine streamed in through the vertical blinds leading to the balcony. A beautiful, almost too-warm Sunday afternoon in May. The sky was blue.

"All of them taken to the hospital?"

"Far as I can tell. Palmetto General," he said in clarification.

Only a mile from campus; Billy, shouting in recognition of his proximity to whichever of his intimates lay clinging to life. "*I'm out the door.*"

"Pick me up, dude. Please."

Billy, saying he'd be at UT in two minutes, blasted out of his door and shoved by a startled neighbor, a fetching cinnamon girl in tight terrycloth shorts and tube-top carrying a basket of laundry—Marcy somebody. He'd normally have groped and pinched her, but no time, sweetie.

"Billy, watch the fuck out, dude."

Racing for the stairwell, he called over his shoulder, contrite: "Apologies; but a friend's been in an accident."

"Oh—so sorry, sweetie."

Billy left black streaks after roaring into the fire lane at University Terrace, where Roy said he had been moving out the last of his belongings.

Billy, greeted by the sight of Devin's old bedroom window, felt like puking.

Feeling a flare of bothersomeness.

Beating his thighs with clenched fists.

A voice, telling him that what was to come would be bad.

Sounding the horn.

If Devin, or Dobbs, or more crucially, Libby Meade, were hurt?

He'd tear his teeth out.

He'd shit himself.

He didn't know what he would do—accidentally kill every motherfucker in the room?

Himself, too?

Take them all with him?

Libby. It couldn't be her.

But Devin, Dobbs, they were all important to him now; all crucial pieces of the Billy puzzle, illuminating and healing and making him whole in ways he'd never known. He could not lose any one of them, now, no; not even well-meaning doofus Roy Earl Pettus. He needed them like he needed the air—besides, he'd alienated every other person here in South Carolina he could've counted as friends.

Every.

Last.

One.

Roy Earl, bounding down the concrete steps, the chubby good-old-boy moving quick and agile as Billy'd ever seen.

"Okay," jumping in and slamming the door. "Go."

Under other circumstances Billy would have driven fast and fantasized about being in one of his silly Hollywood movies, a buddy cop action extravaganza shot through with witty rejoinders and sly asides and references and in-jokes, images of 'splosions and stunts and mayhem, action and movement and humor, beast brain stuff. Instead, he clutched his aching side, a stress reaction, with one hand as both of them sat in silence. Racing through the city in his fine Mercedes with the top down, the breeze whipping his lengthening brown hair, Billy felt no joy or fun in his heart; Roy Earl, holding onto to a beloved Redtails ball cap with one plump hand, held no color in his cheeks.

Hurrying into the hospital lobby, Billy, all-but lunging over the information desk at a startled old lady; directed to a waiting area.

A few Rucker relatives already, faces Billy didn't know.

"Head-on," he heard someone saying, a man sputtering and angry, a ruddy, frecklefaced ginger chap in cowboy boots. "I should go call Whardell Truluck and get to the bottom of all this mess."

Roy Earl, nudging Billy, whispered, "That's Devin's dad."

"Who? Cowboy Bob?"

"No—there. With Creedence. The redhead."

Dwight Rucker, a crumpled, broken, balding and dumpy man in his fifties, sat slumped in casual Sunday attire. Holding his gangly teen daughter in shorts and T-shirt, both were quietly weeping.

Devin, gone.

Defunct.

We'd lost him.

A flash through Billy's mind: fantasy, made real—Devin, out of the way.

*Yes, dummy. It worked out just that easily.*

Oh, shit. Not that voice. His gut turned solid as granite.

Manning up. Getting ready to be strong—for himself, for the survivors.

He approached Mr. Rucker and the girl, Devin's sister Creedence, he halfway remembered from that cookout they had way back when. Glancing up to him through puffy eyes, boohooing and hiding her face again, she didn't want to talk to a stranger.

"I'm Ruck's—Devin's—friend from school."

Dwight, choked. "We can't believe this. We just can't believe it."

It was true, then. Ruck. Gone.

The competition over Libby or not, Billy felt a gaping, yawning maw open up inside him. Imagined his guts twisting into one of those David Lynch sand worms, eating himself from the inside: grief. He felt grief.

*Oh, Ruck.*

*RUCK.*

"You can't see him yet." Creedence, a harsh whisper. "But they think he's okay."

"Dobbs—oh, thank god."

"Devin. They still have him in the emergency room downstairs. Stitching up a cut on his forehead."

"Dobbs? Libby?"

Creedence, breaking down, sobbing. Mr. Rucker, shushing his daughter. "Libby's gone, son."

Roy Earl, understanding and yet not. "Wait—hold on."

"I'm afraid so. Now, please—my daughter's upset."

Billy, nodding, announced in a voice loud and cheerful to the others gathered in the waiting room:

"Excuse me, everyone."

The hubbub quieted down.

"Anyone know where there's a nearby restroom?" he asked as hot piss ran down his legs. "It's kind-of an emergency."

Devin.

On the ER examining table.

Still alive.

His body covered by a rough hospital sheet, he noticed the dried blood all over his arms—from his own wounds.

That's right—but for a blot at the corner of her mouth, Libby had not bled. Had looked peaceful, hanging next to him in the wreckage of the Mustang. Her face, in an inarguable state of peace if not demonstrable grace, held a final expression which could only be described as serene.

Her face.

The blood draining out of it.

Floating there next to him.

Devin: Unsure whether alive or dead, whether all that had happened in the last two hours had been real.

Alone for the first time since being transported here alongside Dobbs, the emergency room staff now off attending to the day's various other grievously injured from their own tragedies and illnesses and mishaps, he found his vision unfocused, suffering afterimages and light flashes—the sun, harsh as it beat down in his eyes for so long as he'd awaited rescue.

Until his vision blurred in the vehicle.

Ah, here was death, at last.

But no, only blood, his own, running into his eyes, thick and warm. As the jaws of life had cut away at the metal to get him out—and afterwards, Libby's body, which of course he hadn't witnessed—he had leaned back into the seat and held onto the kitten, who hissed and clawed.

"You're a lucky man, son." One of the ER doctors, sucking his teeth and scrutinizing the X-rays. "Except for that head wound, you're in one piece."

"Why don't you go and fuck yourself." Devin, all but screaming.

"You've been drinking."

Devin couldn't deny it. They'd pounded a beer before leaving. A single beer. "I'm not drunk, dickhead."

The doctor, scowling in his hospital blues, ordered a sedative for the patient and swished out of the curtain.

Devin, twisting around on the gurney, felt a sharp stick of pain in his stomach. Reaching under the sheet, running a hand across his belly. Horrified, he discovered a tiny cluster of shattered windshield dust had collected in his navel.

A strident voice came echoing from another part of the ER, followed by a staccato conversation in more muted tones. At first, Devin, thinking more accident victims being brought in—what was going on out there today?—before realizing the voice that of his own mother:

"Now let me back there to see *my son,* you god-durn quacks, before I kick your recalcitrant butts over yonder onto sissy street! Now! Now! *Now!*"

A flurry of brisk footsteps and voices, and his Mama, looking older and frailer than he'd ever seen, burst through the curtain trailed by a blustery ER nurse.

"Ma'am—"

Eileen Rucker, hard as nails. "Woman, let me see my son before I knock your black ass all the way into next Wednesday."

The nurse, sighing, closed her eyes and counted to ten. Taking the rancor in stride, she withdrew.

Clearly horrified by his bloody appearance, drawing in sudden breath but trying to smile, Mama patted him on the arm, gentle.

"Oh, my poor sweet darling—there you are. There you are, now. All fine. All better. Mama's here."

All the animus and pain toward his mother, the confusion over Uncle Hill, melting away—Mama. The first face you see.

Trying to speak, but choking off before getting out a single intelligible word.

"Hush, now."

Breathing, controlling, suppressing the tears, his throat raw and scalded, but damned if unable to say what needed to be said. The truth of the matter? That in the seconds after the car had come to rest, Devin, seeing the light go out of Libby's eyes?

Hearing her last breath?

"She was still alive. For a few seconds. Oh, Mama—she was still alive. But then—but then."

"Hush, sweetheart."

They held one another. He smelled the scent of her cigarette smoke. For a second or two, everything felt okay again.

Later, upon further examination, Devin's head wound was stitched up by a plastic surgeon who blew in dressed as though coming straight from the golf course—which, of course, he had: it was Sunday afternoon.

Another doctor, young, wandered in amidst the procedure. He leaned in alongside the middle-aged surgeon. Devin could see a frosting of dandruff in the man's curly black hair.

The younger doc pointed with curiosity at the gash on Devin's head. "How're we gonna fix that little bit there?" Devin could smell the man's lunch on his breath, onions and meat and vinegar—a sub sandwich.

"You're gonna watch the fanciest stitching you ever did see," the plastic surgeon said, tugging and pulling above Devin's eye. "Like you ER residents ain't *never* seen."

"Not bad." The younger physician, who shot a wink at Devin, wandered away in a cloud of Subway.

After the procedure Devin found himself moved to a private room. A nurse, young, cheerful, came by in her colorful scrubs to finish cleaning him up.

Informing her: "Think there's glass in my belly button."

Laughing and canting her head.

"I was in a car wreck."

"Oh—okay. I'm sorry."

Devin, glaring as the nurse went about her business, quiet and officious, sponged him off with deliberation and care. Many small wounds, tender flesh where he'd struck the steering wheel. This nurse, whose name he did not know and whom he would not see again, gently washed his contused body. She would become the first woman besides Libby Meade to touch his genitals.

Over the next day, the facts, trickling in. The man, a poor Edgewater County fella wrapped up a weekend bender which had dragged on into Sunday morning, decided to pass another car on a hilltop; on a double yellow line.

But as it turned out, the asshole wasn't a local—a transient. Not even a resident of Chilton, nor South Carolina at all, the perp had been passing through while moving from Kentucky to Florida.

After interviewing family members he'd visited, it seemed Maurice Reginald King had gotten off the freeway, dropping in on a cousin; the cousins had themselves one big Saturday night together, an apparently bacchanalian reunion which began at The Dixiana in downtown Tillman

Falls before moving on to a number of other establishments. Drinking all night and on into the morning, when Mr. King took a notion to continue his journey to Florida. His cousin had tried to talk him out of doing so, he said, but failed.

Ruinously so—Mr. King, dead like Libby; decapitated in the collision.

Devin, thinking, nice work there, God: transgression and retribution wrapped neat and clean into one package, King's misdeed punished well and true and final, like. No need for a jury or judge; justice served.

Case closed.

But no sense of actual justice—no bringing her back. Getting used to the idea already. Or so he made himself believe.

Devin, overhearing a highway patrolman outside the cracked hospital room door quietly going through the details with Dwight and Eileen:

"Are you saying he was drunk?" Devin's father, aghast. "On a Sunday *morning?*"

"The circumstantial evidence, open containers in the vehicle, says yes. Toxicology'll tell us for certain. Now—your son had been drinking as well, it seems."

"I know," Dwight said. "I know."

Devin's own blood drawn as well, the extraction in the ER overseen by a stony-faced, plainclothes law enforcement officer who'd presented a release for him to sign, which he did with trembling, bloody fingers.

"Honestly?" The patrolmen went on in a more conversational tone. "I don't see how anyone survived. Apparently, when your boy seen the other vehicle coming over the rise he had a split-second to react, and it appears that he turned the steering wheel," Devin seeing the shadow of the cop's arm pantomiming the action, "which is what saved him."

Devin could hear his mother sniffling.

His father: "He came so close. He came so close. Oh, thank god."

Devin, hearing every word.

Understanding.

Turning the wheel.

Enough to save himself.

But not her.

He didn't remember; all he knew was Libby yelling his name, and a flash of the truck and the roar and the sunlight, beating down. And then her face, turning blue.

Screaming, Devin began thrashing and yanking out his IV. Another sedative. Sleep, blessed and dreamless.

Libby's funeral was held two days later, but Devin, not there, instead still in the hospital room, alone with his mother. The docs, keeping an eye on his heart, which they said might have suffered a contusion from the impact of the steering wheel on his breastbone. Tests to be run. And so on.

Devin, wondering if he oughtn't pull himself together and attend the service. Feeling so empty inside, he thought he'd do fine. Kind of wanted to see her again.

Nah. Nah.

However: "Mama, you ought to be there."

"No—I want to remember her like she was." She snapped her fingers. "You know what we're going to do, darling? Here's what we do. Let's remember her like she was. Not how she is."

Later, a small knock at the door—Billy.

Their eyes locked. Devin's friend stood trembling in a blue oxford shirt and a conservative tie, awfully formal attire for a punk rocker. Devin, thinking, *he attended in my stead.*

*For me.*

*Billy, there for me.*

Indeed—Billy, explaining that he, Roy Earl and others had been to Libby's service. Billy, smelling of whiskey. Smiling, trying to keep himself together.

Devin, scratching at the bandage on his forehead, spoke in his silly redneck brogue. "Ah ain't never seen you in a tie, beau."

"And you probably won't again soon."

"Means a lot that you went." Devin, blinking, struggling not to crumble. Hardening inside. Wanting the source of the whiskey breath. "That you're here now."

Billy, without words, hung his head and sat down heavy on the bed beside Devin.

Shooting a look at his mother—Eileen, understanding, got up to leave.

"I'll let y'all visit while I go get us all Co-colas." Taking her purse, checking her appearance in the bathroom mirror, she gave Billy a big, happy eye-squeezing fake smile. "And some breath mints for you, young man. If I may suggest."

Billy, his face pink, said yes-ma'am. "I prefer Certs to Tic-tacs, if they have them."

She shut the door and left them alone.

"Ruck, I don't know what to say."

Devin wrenched his face away. "I let him run into us. I seen the truck. But it didn't compute. I killed her."

Billy laid out the case—the other driver was drunk. Not Devin. "He hit you. Not the other way around."

"I did this. I did this." Devin's mantra.

"She's not gone," declaring with Steeple certitude on display like plumage, a pulsating, tie-dyed superpositive vibe of energetic can-do optimism: "Here's what's happened—she just went on up ahead a bit. She's doing some re-con work for us all, making sure it's safe to follow. That's all." Laughing, high and strange. "Sacrifice, this is. To light the path." Billy, his half-full spin on matters devolving into wind-sucking tears. "Our guiding light. Libby."

Devin, thinking his friend gone mad, believing Billy's eyes might start spinning around like a cartoon character's. But only saying, I hear you, beau. I hear you. *She's right here with us, still.*

But Devin, his arms breaking out in gooseflesh—Billy, giving him the idea, the impetus, the method: Devin, following Libby. Drinking himself to her.

Yep. Drinking, in some ways, was what he did best; what gave him reasonable peace. What banished the man in the pool from his dreams.

Whom Libby would now accompany.

The last mystery, perhaps, he'd ever need to solve: "Bill—at the funeral."

Billy's jaw tightened. "A lovely service. Well attended."

"Did she look like herself?"

Billy, cutting eyes over his shoulder. He pressed his lips together.

"In the casket," Devin added.

"I knew what you meant."

Sweat popping out on his face, Billy yanked at his colorful tie. Unable to get the knot undone, he cried out in frustration and began ripping at his shirt, popping buttons, pulling it off over his head—underneath, one of his black T-shirts.

"She looked like an angel, Ruck. An angel, an angel, an *angel*—"

Devin reached out to Billy, pulling him over.

Billy: collapsing, heaving, begging.

Whispering. "Bill: we weren't drunk. But we—all of us—pounded ourselves a brewski before leaving. Before we drove over. The three of us. We didn't want to go, not really. We wanted to stay in Arcadia. Dobbie, he said he didn't care if he ever went back—ah!"

Billy had a sea-change of mood. Purring like Prudy, whom Devin now knew was all right and waiting for him at home, he began stroking Devin's arm:

"So you drank a beer. What is one beer supposed to do to Devin fucking Rucker? Tell me. Tell me what a single beer would do."

"Not much."

"Not *much*," repeating and beating his fist against a khaki-clad thigh. "Not to a motherfucker with a hollow leg like yours."

"There you go." Devin, patting Billy on the back. "That's what I keep telling myself."

"You keep on doing that."

The patient lay back against the pillows. The leg would be filled, and for all time. His ass would show everyone what a single beer could do.

The door opened and the others filed in to gather around the hospital bed, all reeking of booze. Roy Earl looked as though suffering a grievous stomachache; Creedence, the last through the door, seemed a shellshocked mess in a black dress. She carried her chunky high heels, shuffling around the hospital in hose-feet, her face streaked with mascara.

Devin, motioning for them all to stand down, stand back. Clutching the disconsolate Billy he whispered quiet words of comfort, a sagacity of cynicism he'd already begun to embrace and embody even before all this horseshit came raining down.

In conclusion he took another track, another tidbit of grave importance. "Bill? A favor."

"Talk to me."

"You got to do me a solid."

"Anything on God's green earth."

Devin, gathering the courage. "In the car—when it happened? We were listening to the tape."

"What tape—?"

"The Dead tape. From the show. We were listening to 'Dark Star'."

A ripple of fresh unease and averted eyes. Billy, his teeth gritted. "The tape."

"You got to go and get it. It's still in the car."

"I will, I will." Billy, swearing this. A mission. "I'll retrieve it. It's already done."

Devin, holding out his arms, accepting the succor of the friendship at hand. Handed a flask, he nipped at a fiery taste of Crown Roy Earl offered. With each sip, Devin started feeling better.

More like himself.

Rock on.

Riding with Dwight to the junkyard to retrieve the cassette, Billy played get-to-know-you with the elder Rucker.

The genial, gentle-eyed insurance man seemed stunned to learn of the Steeple family heritage, the vibrant industry of plastics, grocery sacks, blister packs and polymer foam-formed packaging materials of which Billy would be heir; his father's role as family consigliere, ensconced on K Street in Washington to advance the interests of the family's various business concerns and investments, which with tech advances diversifying the uses of fossil-fuel based polymers inspired continued expansion and growth.

"It makes for a complex corporate structure."

"A business you'll be learning."

A cold rush of panic. If Mr. Rucker meant sucking at the teat, certainly; having responsibility for any of it, nah. Beneath Billy's station as a budding artist. "Certainly. One day, all mine."

Full of questions. "Why, Devin never said a word."

Billy laughed. "It's because he didn't know. I just said I came from 'upstate money.' It's true that one of the plants is near Greenville. I may have left out the part about the New York townhouse and the Connecticut mansion."

"Well now, I'm working below my pay-grade, today." But winking. Billy could tell Dwight was a king in his own little world.

"It's an empire, but grandpa's no Rockefeller." Billy went on to Mr. Rucker in self-effacing, quiet dismissal of his family's wealth and lineage, which, he joked, stretched back in royal splendor all the way to a pair of oppressed, hungry Poles bobbing across the pond on a leaky Holland-America line steamship. They had disembarked at Ellis Island and gotten their immigration inspection cards with instructions on the back in seven languages including their own; stamped and cleared that they were relatively disease-free, allowed to set foot on the shores and make their way into the new world; and a new name, one with fewer letters.

"Self-made money," Dwight said with a glowing admiration which filled the car like the scent of his Old Spice. "Not an old world family line."

"Best kind—right?"

"No question about it."

Billy, musing upon the possible past: "Granddad says, if his people, certainly working class and of the wrong religion, had stayed? They'd have ended up in Hitler's ovens. Or so goes the family lore."

"Dang. Well, son—I'm sure he's glad they didn't."

Billy, a distillation of these pioneers, smiled and nodded; a purity of essence, the American dream turned living walking godhead of a whiteboy, y'all. They couldn't have guessed. Not in a thousand steamship journeys across the brackish and forbidding storm-swept Atlantic. Nope.

Raw confession: He despised the Jewishness angle, however, the adherence to holidays and rituals, the seders and candle-lighting and worst of all, the enormous family rift over Billy's refusal to participate in his bar mitzvah, though this antipathy toward faith would have been the case for him no matter the specifics or dogmas. All fairytales, to him. You talk about old-world thinking.

Billy: he'd make those immigrants proud. Except that they were dead already, those great-grandparents.

Ah, well. Perhaps they observed from on high.

Along with Libby—maybe she watched, now, from high heaven. Who now could see and know, into the past, forward to the future, eternity like a rolodex file at her angelic fingertips.

Which meant she had now seen the accidents.

*Yikes.* Gooseflesh, and a tight scrotum. The wrong kind. The thought of Libby seeing one of his accidents go down chilled him far more than being discovered by terrestrial authorities.

Waiting for the chain-link gate to allow entrance he scanned piles upon piles of automobiles, a landscape apocalyptic and rusted out, a wee patch of countryside dystopia near the reeking county dump. The place reminded him of the junkyard set in SUPERMAN III, the interesting scene where he must battle another version of himself. The combat with a darker self had seemed resonant alongside the Richard Pryor co-starring comedy schtick. Billy couldn't articulate how, exactly.

"Have you seen the car, Mr. Rucker?"

"Not yet."

"Better prepare ourselves."

He stopped his luxury vehicle. It sat idling like a single shining white knight having survived among piles of crusade corpses.

A grungy redneck in grimy coveralls, a pistol in a holster hanging on his hip like a Western gunslinger, shuffled out of a shack of an office near the gate. "Y'all hunting parts today?"

Dwight, explaining their mission that of retrieving personal effects from a recent total that had come in, a blue Mustang.

Pinched and weathered, the junkyard attendant, Billy noted, looked like a character actor who had stepped out of a Peckinpah widescreen oater. "That mess is back yonder."

Billy, unable to quell his curiosity. "What's that heater for, sir? High-crime neighborhood?"

"Heater?"

Dwight, who had served in the peacetime service, as he had told Billy, clarified in soldier-speak. "He means your sidearm."

"Oh. We got rats come over through the woods from the dump."

"Four-legged, or two?"

The junkman spat and chuckled, wiped his nose on a grimy overall sleeve. "Hard to know the difference, sometimes. Ain't it?"

The attendant cracked a cynical laugh; a bark of assent escaped Billy's dry lips.

The Oldsmobile rolled through the mountains of wrecked, abandoned cars until stopped around the corner behind a cinderblock garage.

Billy gasped—there sat the remains of the blue Mustang, a smashed, crumpled figment of its former self:

Every window shattered.

The roof peeled back.

The doors pulled off.

The engine block, sitting where the passenger seat should have been.

Billy, his entire body trembling, swallowed again and again, compulsive.

Cracking his knuckles. "I can't do it."

"You want to forget about this durn tape, or whatever it is?"

*You're the biggest piece of shit who ever lived. As faithless a friend as your mother was to you and your father.* Billy wished for a penknife to jab into his thigh, over and over. "He asked. I have to."

"Then hurry on, now." Mr. Rucker sat immobile, eyes straight ahead. He had yet to fully look upon the pile of metal which had been his son's automobile. "I'll wait."

Billy, dizzy, stood peering into the twisted wreckage, a shredded metal nightmare still stinking of antifreeze and gasoline, along with other acrid odors of which he dared not imagine their source.

The dashboard, shattered beyond recognition... but there, dangling by a pair of wires, the tape deck.

Gathering himself—Libby had died somewhere in this hell of jagged metal and shattered glass—he reached down with care not to cut himself. With a weak, shaking index finger, he managed to push the eject tab. The cassette, a heavy-shelled Maxell XL-IIS, popped right out into his hand, *ka-chunk*. He caught it before losing it down into the wreckage.

Billy, walking back, witnessed the scrawl of the label he'd stuck on before gifting the cassette to Devin, which in reality he'd been giving to Libby:

### GRATEFUL DEAD COLLEGIATE COLISEUM 10-27-89 SET II

Billy. A bothersomeness like never before, sweeping through him, a flash-fire. All he could do not to destroy the tape. It felt like Exhibit A in some capital crime for which he would be served justice.

He staggered forward and fell down onto his knees, blowing the chicken salad Mrs. Rucker had served him earlier all over the penny loafers and slacks he'd worn on this latest, now sacred visit to Edgewater County.

It was fine. He had the tape. Ruck had asked. And for what his friend had gone through, the boy would get what he wanted. What he needed, Billy would make happen.

Climbing into the car, he showed Rucker the tape and signaled for him to haul ass. Billy reasoned Libby would want it this way—that he and Devin reunite, now, in grief. They would again become the best friends they were becoming before the sad foolishness over Libby. That's what this tape represented.

Billy and Ruck and most of all Libby, three of a perfect pair. So long as the survivors stayed together, they'd never have to be apart from her.

"That sucked. But I'm glad we did it."

"I don't understand what's so important about it."

"It's symbolic."

"Some of your college-boy stuff."

Billy, rueful, remembered the scriptwriting class with Libby in which Max had discussed symbolism, metaphor, other literary conceits. "Here's the way I see it. Showing your son that this cassette survived intact, like his precious cat, will represent the first step in his salvation from all this horror," Billy announced as they pulled back onto the highway.

"But if nothing else, his mama and me's been praying that if one good thing comes out of this mess, it'll be Devin putting down the bottle once and for all."

"Our boy can drink us all under the table. No question."

"Any help you can give us on that, Bill, well—we sure would appreciate it."

Billy grinned like Alexander deLarge. "He'll be cured, all right. Sir, you can depend on me."

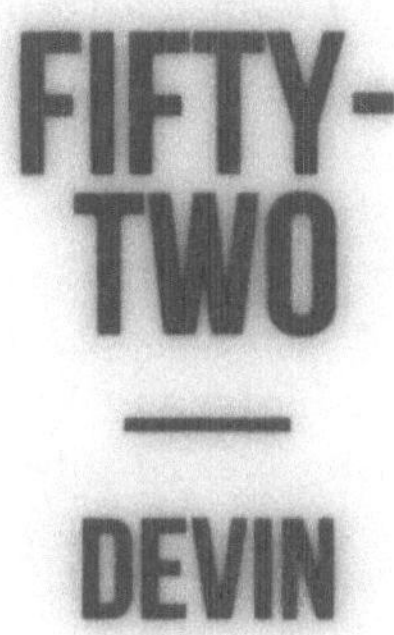


Devin, on the couch in the living room of his family's home, held Prudy, her back leg in a cast. He puffed on a Marlboro from a carton his mother had bought for him. This precious creature, like Devin, having made it through the tragedy relatively unscathed, all things considered, represented another of the small miracles associated with his own unlikely survival. Or so Mama kept insisting.

He had clutched the mewling, struggling kitten as he slumped bleeding in the wreckage waiting for assistance. In the few moments before the first responders arrived, faces of gawkers and rubberneckers had peered into the wreckage to glimpse the carnage.

"Help us," Devin had begged, but the car, a smashed disaster. No one able to extract victims until the trained paramedics and rescue equipment arrived.

But for one: "Give me your cat, son," a stout, lumbering black man with familiar nightmare eyes said to Devin, speaking in incongruously loving and gentle tones, reaching in through the space where only moments before had been the driver's-side window. "I'll make sure she's all right. I'll take care of her for you. I promise—I would not lie to you."

Devin, horrified. The floating man, come to collect his due.

It had to be him.

The eyes.

Wait—it meant Devin was dead, too. Libby, Prudy, all of them. Here, the Floating Man waiting to bear him heavenward.

It was fine. So long as he would be with Libby again.

Lifting Prudy up, handing her over, Devin offered a weak soliloquy of protestation. "Please don't take her. You bastard. Why are you doing this? Why are you following me?" Those eyes. It was him. "Who are you?"

"Don't worry, son. I'm going to help her."

"Are you coming back for me, too?"

"They're here." The sound of sirens, growing louder. "They're coming to help you."

"*Who are you?*"

Taking the cat, moving away out of Devin's line of sight. That's when the blood had run fully into Devin's eyes, and his vision had blurred.

Devin, shouting up out of the steaming wreck: "Don't you go and leave me here! Don't you go and take Libby and Prudy and leave me here! *You son of a bitch*! You goddurn shiteating son of a bitch! I knew you were coming back for me! I knew it in the pool that day! Knew sure as I sitting here! *What else do I have to do?*"

Onlookers in their Sunday clothes rushed over, shushing and quieting.

At last, the EMTs.

A frecklefaced boy Devin's age, looking in the window. His eyes bugging out. He put two fingers on Libby's neck.

"I'm sorry, pardner."

The sound of the saw, cutting away at the blue metal.

Devin didn't feel dead, suddenly. He felt all too alive.

The man who'd taken Prudy, Devin later understood, had not been the floating dude at all. Nah.

Being told that Prudy's savior was in fact a relative of that floating man, hence resembling him, however, still blew Devin's fractured mind all the further: the Reverend Roosevelt Nixon, of Calvary Full Gospel Church of the Holy Redeemer, a few miles across the Sugeree River from Tillman Falls, was indeed Albert Nixon's cousin.

Not a spirit; not Albert. Just a man.

Well, knock me over, Devin thought.

The Reverend Nixon had left his name and number with the police, who passed on the information to Devin's parents. Prudy, taken to Dr. Foy over in Tillman Falls, her leg set, and later retrieved by Eileen; on the mend.

Devin, thinking he'd have to apologize for all the shouting, which couldn't have made sense anyway. Another aspect of the accident he'd like to forget.

Hell—he smelled like beer from the one they'd chugged back at the Arcadia duplex. Everyone probably thought he was as drunk as the other guy. Untrue.

However: *Might as well have been. For all the good I did Libby and Dobbs.*

"I should go and thank that pastor."

"We already sent Reverend Nixon a lovely bouquet of flowers, as well a donation to his church from both our family as well as the ELMS," Eileen said from across the room. "No need for my son to have to go slumming in some black church across the river."

Devin put his cat down on a pallet Eileen had prepared there in the Rucker family room, with its high ceiling and fireplace and photos on the wall, a projection big-screen TV in the corner, a set wider and thicker than a refrigerator; the first in the neighborhood to acquire one. Devin hadn't so much as considered turning it on, preferring instead to sit reading in the dim, air-conditioned quiet.

To be left alone.

To ponder.

Devin, watching as Prudy, frustrated, struggled with her cast. Turning around and around, trying to get settled into a comfortable enough position to cat-nap. Four weeks of this.

Devin: Consumed with the notion of getting himself and the cat back over to the duplex. Understanding the breadth of the work to be done. To get where he needed to be. Much work.

Devin, getting started once his mother left to run errands by getting down the bottle of Jack Daniels his father kept around for when Uncle Hill hung out, which was often. Cracking the tax seal. Throwing the cap away. A plan, underway.

Back in Columbia the weeks rolled on unabated, hot and terrible like a good Carolina summer oughta be, or so the Rucks of the world would put it.

Billy, in Best Friend mode, all but moving in with Devin and Prudy. Bringing his top-of-the-line stereo over and setting it up in the living room. Playing great albums: Making Movies. Lou Reed's accomplished and fascinating excoriation of Reagan's crumbling, diseased America, New York. REM, Life's Rich Pageant. Dead tapes he'd started acquiring. No punk.

Billy, wishing to go back—not to the day of the Dead show, all the way to the morning of buying the tickets. A time so innocent and full of promise, him and Libby by the tree, chatting. All of it squandered—even while she still lived.

Only one answer—he needed the flux capacitor in Doc Brown's DeLorean to start fluxing.

But also, and this was a big but-also, the air in the Arcadia mill house gave him a modicum of peace—'twas the last place Libby'd lived, if only for a brief interval. Sitting on the sofa, he convinced himself he'd catch a whiff of her divine scent, the Egyptian musk oil she wore, tickling his nose as though she'd walked past. Hiding these notions from Ruck, tortured enough already.

To the outside world, for all appearances Ruck seemed normal as could be. Drinking heavily all summer, in good spirits, telling ribald jokes, speaking with a more pronounced Southern twang than before, which Billy thought odd but acceptably eccentric behavior in this survivor of a near-death experience; folks came and went checking on Ruck and Billy, bringing by sixers and good tidings. A tall drink of water named Carmen, who'd lived down the block in UT, had shown a particularly motherly interest in Ruck's recovery. After Libby dumped Ruck for Billy, next step in his plan had been to arrange Carmen for rebound duty with Ruck. And now? *Here we are.*

Billy, suggesting they visit Dobbs over in the rehab facility in the hospital complex, but Devin, refusing.

"I can't look him in the face."

"But Ruck—I feel like we're leaving him there."

"I got his blood on my hands, too. I can't."

"He's asked for you, man."

*Bill*, Ruck said. *I can't.*

Devin Rucker wept, then, for only the second time that summer, at least that Billy had seen. He let him off the hook.

Billy, visiting in Devin's stead; Dobbs, a mess, but coherent. Asking after Devin. Billy, trying to explain. That Devin's pain was so great, he sought to keep it to himself. To not spread it round.

Billy, coming home one night after a movie at the Bijou—Sex Lies & Videotape, a resonant work on more levels than he felt capable of articulating—cried out in shock upon stumbling in the dark over an unconscious Ruck.

Sprawled across the front steps, he looked dead.

Billy, yelping with alarm, collapsed alongside his roommate. He cradled Ruck like a lover.

Still breathing. Shirt covered in puke. Not dead—just ungodly intoxicated.

*Thank un-god.*

Unmindful of the vomit and the stink, Billy wiped his mouth and cooed reassurance. "It's okay, buddy."

Devin, incoherent, drunk as two skunks, called out in a cloud of astringent breath: "Where's Libby at?"

"Quiet, now."

A garbled string of gobbledygook.

"Libby's fine."

"She is?"

"Yep. You fell down." He held him close. "That's all."

"Ah," he gurgled. "Thank god."

"C'mon, brotherman. Let's get you inside." After helping Ruck to his feet, Billy managed to wrestle him upstairs. Quiet, penitent and careful as though he were a monk crossing a frozen river stream, he cleaned up his friend, undressed him and rolled him into sheets.

Only once did he allow himself to break down in front of Ruck, during the weekend when he finished unpacking the last of the moving boxes to discover a couple of her school notebooks.

Not too shabby, this one breakdown. Considering the depth of rage and the jags of privacy which often overwhelmed him into total lassitude and ill-contained accidental murderous rage, barely able to concentrate on the summer school courses he'd taken to keep up with the classes in which he'd received an F or W. It's amazing Billy hadn't gone out and killed someone just to do it, finally. Just to see if doing so would mitigate the pernicious and pathological weeping.

Libby's mother and brothers, still shellshocked over her loss in such proximity to that of Frank, came to Arcadia one afternoon in July to gather her clothing and other possessions.

Her mother had requested these items. Ruck, more than willing to offer them up. She was her mother, after all, he'd said with a shrug. "You don't say no to a dead girl's mother."

*That Ruck*, Billy thought. *You want to see someone bounce back from abject horror and tragedy?* He seethed with envy at his friend's fortitude.

Billy, watching with interest from the living room as Ruck carried a pair of Libby's sneakers—a pair of gray Nikes she'd worn the night of the Dead show—and stashed them away on a shelf in the top of the broom closet underneath the stairs. He placed them there along with a manila envelope of papers: her now forever-unfinished screenplay.

It went without saying he quietly died inside more each day in his desire to read the pages. Ruck would say yes. It was that Billy, feeling profane and unworthy, found himself unable to ask for the rare privilege.

Looking at her cover sheet—the title, the words 'first draft', her name Frances E. Meade, the date, now a few months in the past—he'd never in his life experienced such a pusillanimously rancid sensation of discouragement and despair. A yawning, opaque emptiness. A sense of disappointment bordering on the outright bothersome.

But, he didn't want to kill anyone. Not again. Those had been accidents anyway.

No—this time, he wanted to kill himself. Would that he had the courage.

Perhaps he needn't act—the planet would be turning to ice in the early 21$^{st}$ century, anyway. Real estate below the Mason-Dixon line would become so expensive even the monied classes like Billy's wouldn't want to live anymore.

And yet Ruck, he was the one. He had seen the worst of it all. A stalwart, strong mo-fo. To be admired.

After bidding Libby's family adieu, Billy drifted around outside. He kicked at an old basketball, half-deflated and covered with mildew, found in a forgotten corner of the weed-strewn backyard. A rental property in a college town, several residents' worth of junk had piled up against an ancient chain link fence.

A great rumbling came—train tracks bisected the neighborhood only a block away. Lengths of freight cars trundled through day and night, shaking the old mill houses to their foundations and residents out of the beds.

Ruck, appearing on the back deck, plumed smoke out of his nose and saluted Billy with the first libation of the afternoon. Skipping the beer stage, he gulped half of a bourbon and water he'd mixed for himself in an oversized iced tea glass.

They stood looking at one another. Billy spoke up. "That went okay."

"Glad it's over and done with."

Hiding an errant tear from his friend, Billy kicked the ball one last time, so hard it disappeared into the thicket of the weeds.

"Damn, son."

"Yeah. That hurt." He had to ask. "Why the shoes?"

Ruck seemed to cogitate on how to answer. He came down into the back yard and looked at Billy.

"To remind me." Having to clear his throat. "That she once walked this earth alongside us all. Was real as you are now. Like we are. Stuck here on this prison-planet." A long, cool drink. "That she wasn't just a dream."

Profundity, every hair on his body standing endwise—and Billy had been the one trying to become a writer. His fraudulence stung like alcohol in a cut. The dreadful voice laughed at him the way the au pair had tittered at his meatstick. He wanted to strangle himself.

"It does feel that way. Doesn't it? A little dreamlike."

"Just a little."

That wry fuck-it grin of his. What did the bastard know?

Billy seethed and agonized anew at his failings. Ruck had always been the smartest one of them all—no wonder she'd chosen him instead. A big dick, money, none of it could compare.

The shoes. "Treading the ground. Instead of gracing the sky."

"Now you've got the poetry of it, beau. And once I'm gone, you'll be able to explain the fable of them gray shoes."

"What's 'gone' supposed to mean?"

"Nothing," he said, barking like a dog and chugging his drink. "Let's party, beau. Let's forget."

Later that night, gone indeed, but only down to the Old Market to embark upon a gold-standard, obligatory and obliterating drunk which absolutely raged.

Ruck, gregarious to a fault, had the time of his life—roaring with bonhomie and buying shots for people; Billy, hitting on every halfway decent-looking filly who'd stop long enough to listen, and doing well with most, the ones who weren't totally turned off by a now six-months shaggy-haired big-ass Adam's apple dude the size of a linebacker.

Billy, cocky. Getting bothersome inside. Not taking a liking to the looks of some dude at one of the tables outside McHaffie's Pub. Words. Flipping them off, but keeping on down the block.

Later, picking a fight in the alley outside Group Therapy with a group of frat cats, who, while all smaller than Billy—but far less besotted—still managed to knock both him and Ruck onto their staggering asses. Their assailants strolled away, chortling and calling them dick-sucking pussies.

Another failure. It was as though Billy the one sitting on the other side of the desk where his grandfather sat, also father and assorted headmasters, in abject, stupefied disappointment at his obvious intelligence, yet poor academic performance and behavior problems.

Ruck, helping his buddy to his feet, said, dang, beau—a cut on Billy's cheek from someone's college ring dripped hot blood onto the front of his tie-dye, the dark color intermingling with the bright. They took a cab a few blocks uptown to Baptist Hospital to get his cheek stitched up.

At Ruck's insistence they filed a police report regarding the assault. He reported the 'college toughs' has taken roughly sixty dollars from his wallet —about the amount he'd spent that night on his tab—after assaulting both he and his friend. Ruck, having fun with it. The drunker Ruck got now, the more Billy swore he seemed sober.

At another bar, on yet another night of heavy boozing the day Billy's stitches had come out, both young men stood frozen in their tracks as Chryssie Hynde's voice came over the speakers.

It couldn't have been a worse track. 'Back on the Chain Gang' caused lightning fast look of horrid, unavoidable recognition between the friends.

The Pretenders, one of Libby's faves. Loved a kick-ass rock band fronted by a strong and confidant chick, she had.

Splitting the scene.

"I'm going to be the Chryssie Hynde of Hollywood," she had promised. "The movies I'm going to write will be like nothing a woman ever wrote before."

Billy, remembering that moment. How Libby's courage and ambition had made the true perfidy of his fraudulence, in every aspect of life, well inside him like a stomach bloating with gases from a rotting convenience store burrito.

Ruck, out on the sidewalk, the pop tune echoing out of the bar, became not so much weepy as withdrawn. "Ah, shit," he kept saying. "What a waste."

"Let's not go there."

"'There?' Fuck, dude—we're already there."

"I feel you."

Ruck, demanding to be led to another bar with less offensive tunes playing; Billy, cursing the night sky and kicking at newspaper boxes and trash cans. Punching a brick wall hard enough to break skin, but not bone.

Collapsing, inconsolable, into his friend's arms.

Ruck, supporting his friend.

And not for the last time.

Another milestone, fraught with tension and personal tumult: Ruck, finally getting a new car courtesy Edgewater County's automotive legend Hill Hampton, who procured the Ruckers a brand new 1990 VW Jetta at wholesale, the model chosen after Billy and Ruck went to the library to scan through the latest CONSUMER REPORTS vehicle reports. Hampton Motor Company sold Fords, but his Uncle Hill could get any kind of car that Devin wanted from his business partner's import place over in Columbia, or from the auction up in Hartsville or down in Lexington County.

Ruck, explaining to Billy that any old car would have done, but that he had what he called 'a marker due' him from Hampton, and so he might as well get what he wanted.

"This model," Ruck told Billy, "gets good MPG. It's got a deep trunk, too. You could just about live out of that trunk."

The price had also been right—the insurance pay-out from the accident covered the cost of the VW in full, a condition upon which Ruck had insisted. "My folks had just made the last payment on the damn Mustang. They ain't paying for no more cars for me."

Billy could have arranged to buy Ruck a brand new car, and would have offered, but felt ostentatious. Ruck's dignified and adult bargain further sullied the worth of the modest Steeple trust fund upon which Billy drew. What was money in the face of true human dignity and grace in the face of tragedy?

One night in early August, a get-together gelled in the mill house, with Ruck insisting that young Creedence be included in the revelry.

"More I think about it, I got something to make up to that little lady."

Billy, remembering—the Dead show, how the sister had been forgotten, precipitating a pernicious family conflict over the slight.

Had there ever been a stupid rock concert portending more drama and strife? he pondered. Had there ever been more to forgive than that night? The wretchedness concealed inside had caused his face to break out in acne, which hadn't happened since before the first accident back at Androscoggin, after which his skin had cleared.

At the party, the usual suspects attended save for Roy Earl, who'd gone on vacation to Myrtle Beach with his grandparents. One afternoon when he and Billy went to see Dobbs, soon discharged and ready to begin life in the wheelchair, he confessed how the drunk driver having started at The Dixiana, his family's bar, caused him enormous grief.

"The dude's people said they drank all over the county. Nobody's closing up their barns."

Roy Earl shook his head. "One day I will shut down that damn 'barn.' That honkytonk's always been the biggest embarrassment of my sorry life."

"It's kinda legendary in the country music world."

"That was forever ago. Now, it's just a dump where drunks drink. But not for long."

The festivities were centered out on the back deck, a keg placed in a blue plastic tub of ice melting in the heat of summer. The humidity heavy and relentless, the entire world seemed covered in condensation; everyone chatted, laughed, smoked, played music. Newcomers stood in shocked amazement when one of the trains rumbled through and blasted its horn.

Eschewing food all day, Billy, in particular, got ripped while pumping full the red Solo cups. In a fit of alcohol-induced delirium coupled with sudden-onset-empty-stomach syndrome, he bolted inside to order ten large pizzas, about three times as much food as needed. Thirty minutes later he paid for the pies with a stack of twenties fluttering out of his pockets like the confetti which had fallen from the ceiling at midnight during the Dead's New Year's Eve show, an experience he barely remembered but for the experimental sex with the nameless, chubby cooze he'd met out there.

Again: he let go about as much as he dared, yet hadn't fucked her to death. A win.

After wolfing down pizza the partiers drifted back outside, leaving Billy in the living room with young Creedence. She'd been dropped off by her dad with an overnight bag. A big family deal, this sleepover.

Buzzed, she lay kicked-back, narrow bare feet on top of the couch. Creedence, cute as a button, Billy noted, in cutoffs and a yellow, formfitting Madonna T-shirt.

Looking, Billy admitted to himself, sexy as hell.

How long had it been since he'd gotten laid?

Since the Oakland accident prevention experiment.

A rocket in his pocket.

Another test, maybe?

He leaned over, grabbed her foot. Her eyes lit up. He kissed her toes, a quick peck, and placed it gently back down beside its pink twin.

Breathless. She couldn't speak. He winked and sat down in the chair opposite her.

Billy, beaming dick-eyes at her while he twisted a fat number using a filthy yellow Frisbee full of stems and seeds for a tray, made small talk.

"You like smoky-smoke, fair Miss Creedence?"

"*Hale* yes I do," her Southern accent becoming more pronounced with each sip of beer. "Light me up one."

"You don't get your own joint—we share one."

"Sounds fun."

"A communal experience. Sharing."

"I know. I smoke all the time back home."

He finished rolling a bomber thick as a finger. "This will do the trick."

Her eyelids already drooping, Ruck's little sister gave Billy her own come-hither smile. Sounding tipsy and breathy, "So I guess you'd better come sit over here, then. So we can share."

Steeplemeat, twitching in his shorts.

The sleeper has awakened.

Sparking the doob and passing it. Telling her to take it slow.

Creedence, puffing and coughing. Puffing again.

Getting quiet, eyes beginning to cross.

Billy, now seeing her as the hottest little southern flower he'd ever imagined. Deciding to take direct and timely action about said revelation; running a finger along her smooth bare calf, passing her knee, and tickling a pale thigh.

"Oh!" she said, blinking. Seeing the shudder go through her body. Her hand upon his, her eyes saying *Yes*. He took her, and the huge joint, upstairs to his room before Ruck had the chance to notice them together.

# FIFTY-FOUR

## — DEVIN

The next morning, Devin, hungover as a dog, stood in the filthy, destroyed kitchen, the whole place reeking of stale beer and smoke—the duplex, as well as the bodies of the two friends. Creedence, yet to emerge from upstairs, had disappeared on him last night. Lightweight.

Billy, swaying on his feet, looked green, weirded out. "Announcement: I'm finished."

"Regarding—?"

"I'm done, that's what." Billy, searching to explain. "I'm going legit."

"Legit? What's 'legit'?"

"I'm done with the wet stuff."

"Goody for you."

"Seriously."

Beyond dismissive. "Listen to him singing the hangover blues."

"Like—seriously, bro."

"You must still be fucked up."

"I'm on the edge. I gotta climb down."

"What happened last night?"

"Nothing, that I know."

"With my sister. Seen y'all sitting on the couch. Then you were gone."

"She was about to pass out. I put her to bed upstairs. That's all."

"Better be."

Billy's lips, pressed into a hard slash across his face: "Give me some credit."

"Well-sir, Mr. Credit, I gotta get her on her feet before Daddy shows to collect his baby girl."

"I'll help straighten up."

Sipping a cold Budweiser, Devin went into the living room to slide the weed-Frisbee under the couch, pick up empty Solo cups, dump the ashtrays. Billy lit a stick of floral incense and started sweeping the kitchen.

"You telling me the truth about Creedence?"

"To paraphrase Mr. Garcia: maybe she had too much, too fast."

"Is that so. And then what?"

"I told you—I tucked her in."

Devin stared into Billy's eyes. He averted his gaze.

"My own sister, now?"

Rueful, sincere: "No, no, no. Nothing like that—for once."

"Keep it that way. She's just a kid."

"Don't you think I know that?"

"I do. Credit, due."

But Devin, heading upstairs to get his sister ready, said to himself: "'Credit'? Now that's a good one."

Chelsea. Queasy and crashed on the stinky futon in the spare room. Billy's room.

But Billy, declining to share the space last night after all.

With her.

Bailing on what she thought was about to be her second time.

Or first real time, depending.

But Chelsea, after their brief, aborted rendezvous, not seeing him again. And there in the morning light she lay hoping that, once it came time for her to depart, she wouldn't find him downstairs.

Humiliation.

Right as things got heated he'd gotten a look like disgust, an expression seared into her brain is if done with a red-hot cattle brand.

Disgust—then fear.

Yeah. *Fear* had been this beautiful boy's reaction to her tugging at the bulge in his shorts, tickling her fingers under his tie-dye.

Billy, those eyes—crystal blue like hers.

That voice—his accent, from someplace else.

Somewhere different.

Somewhere special.

Those eyes bulged not with passion, but terror.

*What the hell, beau?*

Billy, though, let's face it—he'd done her a favor, confirming what she already knew. That Creedence—Chelsea Rucker, Kookie Colette, pick one— wasn't worth a damn.

Didn't look good.

Didn't kiss right.

Something.

His thing had been hard. But he still didn't want to do it with her. At least she didn't need to wonder anymore if her mother was right about Dusty being the one.

Hearing her brother and Billy downstairs, Creedence, tiptoeing into the upstairs bathroom with her toiletries and a change of clothes, held her breath to keep silent.

Best she could remember she and Billy'd smoked pot, flirted, and the next thing she knew they were in his room sprawled on the futon, kissing and touching one another, so excited that her panties had soaked through.

Again, Billy, excited as well. So much bigger than Dusty. Like a different species of peterpiper.

But his penis wasn't the point: Creedence, about to make-it with someone who seemed to want her. Someone not-Dusty. About to take her, fill her up.

She hadn't even wanted him to put on a rubber. Desired to let him know how special he was.

But then, Billy jerking back from her as though startled. His erection, fading away. Awkward, mumbling.

"Billy—what's wrong?"

"We shouldn't do this."

"*Why not?*"

"We just shouldn't. I don't want to. I can't. I won't."

Speechless.

He rose to leave. "I'm—I feel too excited. It's not safe. You sleep here. I'm—I'll go downstairs."

"But Billy—!"

Too late. The door had shut with a click. He'd run out as though the devin at his heels. The devil, she meant.

It's not safe? What the hell? Had he read her thoughts about not wearing a rubber?

The tears flowing, the shock of his rejection kept her awake for an hour, listening and crying until the party died down.

Afterwards, the duplex still but for the grunts and bumps of intimacy coming from Devin and his friend Carmen in the other bedroom, the squeaking of the mattress springs therein—Libby's old bed. She'd watched Carmen follow Devin around all night. Had babytalked him and doted on him. Carmen, Chelsea thought, seemed to really like Devin.

She could hear him across the hall, doing it to her. The way Chelsea used to sneak and listen and even watch, that one time they thought the house was empty, as her brother and Libby had made love. How it seemed to make her feel, her back arching as she rode Devin to release. What Creedence should have been doing with Billy.

But not to be. It beat all she'd ever heard of, him bailing on her. She must be a freak.

She got dressed and sat down on the toilet to lace up her Converse sneakers. A knock came, startling in its urgency. She prayed it wasn't Billy.

"You up, sissy?" Her brother's voice, hoarse like he suffered a sore throat. "Time to get moving."

Relief. "I'm almost done in here."

"Everything all right?"

Uh-huh, she said.

"You sure?"

"Just feel yucky."

"From what?"

"From last night."

"Join the club." Devin, coughing. "But a little grease'll knock that hangover right out. Plenty of pizza left. If you can stomach it…"

In a flash, as though she could taste the beer at the back of her teeth. She suffered a wave of hot nausea. "I'll be down in a minute."

Her stomach roiling at the filthy tiles on which she knelt, Creedence retched into the grungy toilet bowl and thought, *Mama would have a fit if she seen the state of this bathroom.*

Clomping downstairs with her backpack and purse she found her brother waiting and smoking a nasty cigarette. Creedence, stopping in the doorway with her limp greasy bed-hair hanging down, arms folded, noted how rough her brother looked.

"Where's your new girlfriend?"

"She already split, and it ain't like that." Devin stared her down. "I wanted you to know something, before anyone else."

"What," sounding bored like when Mama had a big pronouncement about to drop, usually amounting to a hill of beans. "About that pretty Carmen?"

A low tone of confidence, discretion. "No, sissy. That I'm leaving soon."

"Where're you going?"

Shrugging, Devin flopped his hand in the air like a gay hairdresser. "Away."

"Away?"

"Away."

"From Columbia?"

"Yeah. Away-away."

"From South Carolina?"

"Far as I can get."

"Carmen's going with you?"

"Fuck, no. I mean—she's got to finish school."

"Y'all were up late. Together."

"How would you know?"

Cheeks burning. "Because I heard you."

Devin, a hint of shame, not unlike what she saw on Billy's face—what was wrong with everyone? "Carmen's just being friendly. Trying to help, I guess."

"She looked at you like she loves you."

Gasping, Devin face drained of color. Sudden, he leapt to his feet and grabbed Creedence by her arms, squeezing hard. Desperate, his eyes swum with a panicky bewilderment. "Don't say that. Don't you dare."

Chelsea, unable to fathom his extreme reaction. "I just think she likes you."

Releasing his sister, Devin rubbed his hands on his jeans and apologized. "Like I said—I'm outta here before—before I—ah."

"Before what?"

Certainty: "I know I've told everyone I'm fine. That I'm gonna go back to school. But you can forget it, man. You can forget Carmen. You can forget Billy. You can forget Libby," saying her name like a curse. Devin, cutting himself off at the hurt she knew he could see on her face. "I can't get right until I forget, somehow. When I forget again, I'll be able to live. And I'll come back. And it'll be the way it was before, when we were kids—like at the beach. When we'd go to Myrtle Beach and play. Remember?"

Tearful. "But I don't want you to go away."

"I can't get away if I don't leave."

*"But then I'll be all by myself."*

Shuddering as though an ill wind had blown into the room. "You'll have your chance to leave one day."

"What about Prudy?"

"I'll have to take her with me. I shouldn't, but the cat's all I got left."

"Of Libby, you mean?"

Devin, impatient. "Yes, Creedence. For fuck's sake—yeah."

Her brother stood watching as she held back a gusher.

It didn't work: She grasped at him: "Please take me with you."

"Oh, god no. Not on this trip. You're better off here, dearheart—believe me."

"I guess you hate me, too."

Devin, crumbling. "My love for you, sister girl—? It's the only love I got left. You and Prudy, I reckon. But I can't let you love me any more. I can't let anybody."

"Why? *Why?*"

"Because I'm not gonna be around much longer. The car wreck—that was for me, not Libby. And now? My marker's overdue. If you love me, you will lose. So my advice is to quit while you're still ahead."

"Quit loving my own brother?"

He smoked and smiled. "Why not? I certainly have."

Devin stood in the yard with his father, each with arms folded and ill-at-ease, chatting about this'n that. Creedence, already ensconced in Dwight's sedan in the back seat, lay with one forearm slung across her face. It was still quiet along the block—others had held nearby parties as well. Sleeping it off.

"I might need to borrow some money."

"You're not in a fix of some kind, are you?"

"Nah. Nothing like that."

Dropping his voice, Dwight searched his son's eyes. "You're not doing anything you shouldn't be? I see that my baby daughter don't seem to feel too good today after y'alls little 'cookout' over here."

"She's fine. And, I'm not in trouble."

"How's the new car running?"

"The Jetta? She's a peach. Looking forward to the first oil change."

"I'll make sure you don't got nothing to worry about." Dwight, clasping his son to his body, breathed heavy. "My son. Just concentrate on your schoolwork this fall. Let's get you back to normal. And—stay away from the bottle."

Devin, pulling away. Hoping the shame he felt going unseen. "I will, Daddy. A few beers now and then. Nothing more."

"How much do you need?"

"A few hundred bucks?"

Dwight, well-off at least by Edgewater County standards, scoffed at such a pittance. "I'll have Mama send you a check first thing tomorrow."

Devin watched as Billy came to the screen door and exchanged a brief wave with Dwight. His friend faded back into the shadowy interior without coming outside.

Glancing toward his sister in the car: "Y'all be careful going home on that damn interstate."

"You and Billy be good, now."

The Oldsmobile pulled away. Devin offered a lethargic, heavy wave. He let his hand fall to his side.

Afterwards he sat squatting on the front steps; Prudy, rubbing back and forth across the inside of the screen door, cried for him to return inside.

After a few minutes Billy came and sat beside his friend, draping a huge arm across Devin's stooped and slight shoulders.

Tense at first, Devin leaned into Billy. Heaved a deep sigh. Nothing needed saying.

But Devin, thinking how to find the courage, the right words, to tell Billy goodbye. How to drive out of Arcadia and not look back. How to bid farewell to Libby, and all these spaces she'd occupied, all the good along with the bad. He couldn't seem to remember the good without evincing colossal risk and consequences—a hell of a condition.

A fix, maybe permanent: strong drink.

The sun, blazing through a hole in what had been a solid, wispy bank of gray clouds, blinded the hungover friends. They scowled and held up forearms to shield themselves from the light. The end was nigh. He'd break the news to Billy later, after they had gotten a good afternoon buzz going.

His announcement didn't go over well.

Devin, not kidding, had begun the next day shoving crap into the Jetta. He folded a thick bath towel and put it inside one of Eileen's cat carriers he'd cadged from the Rucker manse. Prudy protested but allowed him to put her inside, along with a small dish of dry cat food.

Billy, watching Devin button up the car, paced redfaced and hollering like a wild-eyed, jilted lover.

"Ruck—for heaven's sake, you can't leave."

"Not you, too. Like I said to Creedence: I'll be back. Just going on ahead to do a little recon work for you all—remember?"

*"For the love of god, don't do this."*

"Aw—I'll still be around." Devin, tapping his chest and getting into the car, no direction home, grinned at his pal Billy. "As long as you remember me," quoting some dumb movie, the kind of discourse that made sense to someone like Billy Steeple, "I'll never really be gone."

# THE PRETENDERS

**AUTUMN 2004**

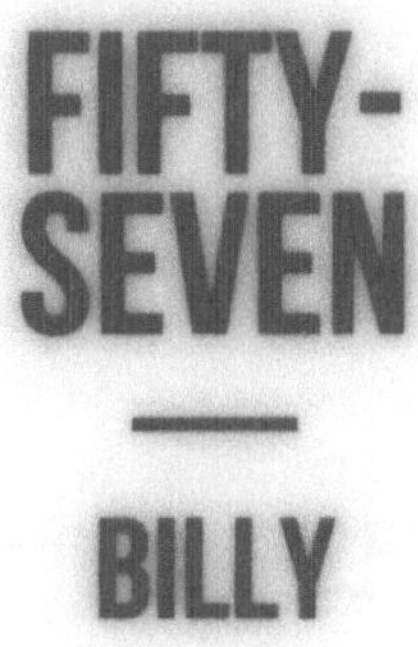



The dude elides.

Late summer, now. Lingering heat waves emanating from the sidewalks of the Old Market. Thick air. Yeah—everything held the sound of thick air.

Already drunk, Billy came ROLLING big-voiced into Slim Lupo's wearing a faded tie-dye over his khakis, grungy flip-flops slapping against the soles of huge feet. With a multi-day chin stubble, patchouli he'd smeared underneath his arms in lieu of deodorant, a growing potbelly hanging over his waistline and greasy hair pulled back by a purple bandana, he slapped skin with bouncers, greeted the sound guy as though he meant as much to Billy as Devin freaking Rucker.

Tweaked on six to eight TOTALLY MASSIVE bong hits and a snort or three of Crown, he'd chased the drink with a swish of Tom's of Maine all-natural, alcohol-free mouthwash. Trying to mask the smell of the bracer he'd needed to face this night. The guitar case, bouncing along against his tree-trunk of a thigh, a comforting weight.

Back to the music, now. He'd finally said, screenplays? Eh. Anyone could write one. Who gave a shit.

Music. The stage. Primary experience.

Immediate gratification.

Yeah—remembering his exhilaration, the zest of playing onstage with Meat Mallet during their heyday headlining *at the very club to which he now returned*, Bigger than life. Cue Billy's brassy and inspiring theme music, John Williams-esque and triumphal, as he plopped down the guitar case and bellied up to the mostly-empty music hall.

Billy.

*In the house, y'all.*

Nicole Braden, one of the bar's owners and a friend whom he'd known for a number of years, came over grinning. A petite honey, Nicole, with earthy, cinnamon girl curves, seasoned with hard lines around the mouth and eyes from working in the bar trade and who knew what else in her life. Billy, wanting to nail her in the worst way, but due to her status as a friend, he'd never made a move—after all, he wasn't a cad.

Affection tinged with curiosity: "Billy! You look—so good."

They hugged, brief and platonic. "Never better, toots. Never better."

The flickering TV set behind the bar, catching his eye, displayed war news and nonsense about the election. Billy never looked at the news, in print or on TV, not unless it was pop-culture related.

His father, of course, as a high-toned corporate DC operator never stopped hanging on every word coming out of the newsreader's mouths, in the polling, the punditry whispers on the wind. Having milked lobbying on the front end of the deal rather than after serving in office, the man was running for congress soon, and wouldn't the family business be looked after then, boy. Bill Senior, as he often told his son, succeeded because he took none of this world too seriously; that life is a game from which one should stay detached so as to avoid disappointment when the invariable shit hits the fan.

Knowing Nicole as a diehard lefty, Billy, pandering: "You think that silver spoon frat-boy will get himself reelected?"

She suffered a look like nausea. "Kerry will wipe the floor with Dumb-ya. I'll freaking leave the country if he doesn't."

"Word to that. What a clusterfuck. They didn't even find any WD40s over there in Iraq."

"No," she said, frowning a little. "They did not."

"It makes you embarrassed for the U. S. to be a player on the world stage. With all our technology, wealth, capital, manifest destiny, all that crud, you telling me we couldn't have at least faked some nerve gas canisters somewhere? For appearance's sake? Amateurs, dude."

"Right. Wait, I mean—*what?*"

"I tell ya, I just don't know about this country anymore."

"So, do I see a guitar in hand?"

"I'm afraid you do. It's time."

"Well, all right then. Lupo's is honored to welcome you back."

"It's been a hot minute."

"I remember."

Billy'd first met Nicole when she'd been a librarian at SEU like him, but after inheriting some money from a grandparent (*Oh!* Billy thinking with impatience, *How lovely that must feel!*), she'd followed her dreams by investing a fifty-percent stake in the floundering Lupo's, thereby keeping it going into the new century. A music lover, Nicole believed that Columbia, a troubled market for live music venues, could ill afford the loss of yet another hip room. An enormous sea-change of a career move, academia to merchant class plying the hospitality trade, but she'd succeeded.

Nicole, holding an extra special place in Billy's heart simply by giving validation to his youth: "I still recall a few Meat Mallet shows from back in the day," she never failed to remind him. "Wild times inside these old walls."

"You had a punk boyfriend back then, as I recall?"

Nodding. "Went to all those shows—the all-ages early ones, the late nights here and at house parties."

Billy remembered it all well. "Back in the day."

"We thought y'all were going to break out."

"We was bad; but we was not nationwide." A smile of gratitude, strained. "Alas, it didn't happen."

"But as I got older, less punk and more of a Swimming Pool Q's, REM, Let's Active kinda girl."

"I hear the ghostly sound of jangly guitars. Once I heard the Dead, I grew out of the whole punk scene, too." Enough small talk. "So here's the deal: I need to see who's doing what tonight. Get the lay of the land."

"How can I help?"

"Let's put me down in the middle of the bill. That cool?"

"Just sign in on the sheet after some others arrive."

"But I'm special."

"Yeah yeah." Winking. "That's what my mommy told me, too."

"Touché," in phony contrition. "All right. I'll wait for the signup. Like everyone else."

"That's the spirit. Don't try to control it. Let it flow."

"Let it grow."

"There we go. Now I gotta get back to work."

A beer delivery guy came bustling through the door, a stout fireplug of a driver manhandling a handtruck burdened by the considerable weight of two fresh Stella Artois kegs.

"You're late today, Freddie," Nicole said, gesturing to Billy. "We got thirsty customers in the house already."

"Traffic's a mess all the way the heck up Blossom. Dumbasses digging the new sewer over the other side of the Market hit a water main." He went to hand her yet another invoice. "They gotta get this road work finished."

"Paddy can sign for them," referring to her bar manager, a barrel-chested man who whistled while prepping the speedrails and fruit garnishes for the long night of drink-slinging ahead. Paddy, slicing citrus fruit with flair and panache the same way Billy had seen him serve customers, was a no-question, god-damn pro. Had worked in joints over the Market, and other places, too, for decades. A lifer, as Paddy put it over the last few months of Billy hanging out and getting pissed at this and other bars in the neighborhood.

Billy, a froggy Louis Armstrong voice. "Paddy, my man? You here is a righteous individual. Has I ever tolds you that? Has I? Has I?"

"It's all you, son," bumping fists. "Wet your whistle?"

"Hit me with a Crown, neat, and—"

"—a 'brown bomber' on the back," meaning a heavy English ale called Newcastle. "Right?"

"Guess that makes me a regular."

"Afraid so, my friend."

Billy, in the months since Devin's miraculous awakening and return to sentience and sobriety, haunted the numerous watering holes as his friend once did. Carrying the muddled and sputtering torch of forgetfulness, maybe, Devin had seemingly chosen to put down.

Paddy poured Billy a measure of the Crown. He tilted the bottle back and added a dollop on top. Not quite a double, but almost.

He placed the drink on the bar. "Where's that hot piece of chicken of yours?"

"Eh—laid up with woman shit." The truth was that he'd told Melanie he didn't want her ass there tonight. That it'd make him too nervous. "She's a dragon lady right now."

"On the upswing of that cycle, I bet that same dragon eats you alive. In a good way, I mean."

"I can't lie." Billy and Paddy clinked glasses, the barkeep having a diet soda instead of a cocktail. "She's a real tiger."

"We call that in life a trade-off."

Swooning with momentary vertigo, Billy stole a glance at the storied stage against the far brick wall, at the lights in the ceiling, the mixing board, the PA; picturing being on those boards warbling out his three open mic tunes, staring pie-eyed down into a viper's nest of drunks catcalling and hurling rotten vegetables, nabobs having no sense of history and respect for his legacy, of the youthful brio he'd demonstrated in the punk band, not to mention all the post-show tail he'd gotten without any accidents. Credit where credit due!

Shaking off the uncertainty, he strove to remember how fun it'd been thrashing around on that stage in a state of pure adrenaline, and yeah, afterwards, getting so much pussy he couldn't hope to remember them all: drunk girls, bar girls, punk girls, sorority girls like Melanie.

Every woman in town, it seemed, but the one who had mattered.

And the ones who didn't? Easy—they ended up in the Green Hole, or out at Congaree Heritage Trail in one of the deep, algae-choked ponds out there.

Accidentally.

If they weren't careful—if he weren't careful, that is. Billy, a sip of the draught beer followed by the Crown with nary a grimace. Chasing the liquor with another slug of brown ale. He was on his way to feeling relaxed. Ruck had not been wrong about the hard stuff. Wonder drug.

"Think we'll pack them in tonight?"

Paddy gave the for-now quiet club a squinted glance. "Hope open mic gets us a decent pop tonight. Open mic night, though, working stiff like me's gotta complete with the tip jar onstage."

*Oh, you poor thing. You should feel what hell it is with such a modest trust fund as mine.* "How's biz?"

"Been a weird semester around here—the students, they ain't drinking like normal, the little bastards. Not even turning out for touring bands."

"They don't have money like we did back in the 90s." Billy leaned in, whispering. "It's the Republicans. You know what happens when they get in power. Trickle-down my dimpled ass."

"Heard that. But, I'm pretty sure they're all crooks. Don't matter which letter's beside their name. Especially when it comes to the big guy."

"We got a real genius in there now, boy."

Paddy, disgusted. "And what'll it be like in ten years when my kid is ready to go to school up the hill? Ten-thousand a semester? Twenty? A hundred grand in the pot before you even get started in the world? Or what, go in the freaking Marines like I did, so they can send him off to another war off in the desert shooting at towelheads? Bill, we gotta do something. This country's a mess."

Billy, feeling for the bartender. Wondering why in God's name anybody bothered having children anymore. Why we had to talk about politics again when Billy wanted to think about songs and singing and banging beaver without it getting out of hand, he had no idea. The one-idea devil—the television—pumped the narrative into people's heads 24/7 now. No wonder it's all they talked about. "Whole shebang's collapsing under the weight of its own brief history."

"You can thank the president for all that, and the rest of his chums."

Billy, scoffing in disgust. "Strutting little popinjay."

"But Kerry, Bush—? Same shit, different piles."

"How so?"

"The both of them was in Skull & Bones at Yale together—that shit's fishy."

Billy, shrugging, decided on the fly to conceal his own family ties to such organizations. "Thought it was gonna be Howard Dean, anyway."

Paddy, brightening. "But then, Dubya's frat brother Kerry miraculously wins Iowa, and they started running that scream—the Dean scream. Again. And again. And again. Motherfuckers had it in for him—made him look nuts."

"But why?"

"They wanted Kerry. Or, somebody did, anyway."

"In any case, Bush won't win. It'll be nice to have a different bonehead reading off the TelePrompTers."

"Meet the new boss—?"

Billy, head throbbing, gulped down rest of the brown ale. "Say, leave my tab open, Paddy? Back in a bit—I'm doing the open mic tonight."

"Saw the guitar. Awesome, bro. Can't wait."

Quitting Lupo's Billy headed over to Roy Earl's smoothie stand and then the coffee shop, but his friend had already gone for the day from both businesses. Billy, alone, useless, bored and empty but for the cool buzz he'd managed to achieve, strolled the perimeter of the area, window shopping, sneaking discreet tokes from his one-hitter dugout.

Wanting to invite someone—anyone—who actually cared about him.

Billy, pushing away the incessant thoughts about Libby.

Succeeding; her face replaced by that of another girl.

A girl he hadn't seen in months.

A sudden, naughty idea.

Billy, placing a red alert, person-to-person, emergency call to Chilton, South Carolina, and not to Devin 'Ruck' Rucker, either, who of late had been mysteriously standoffish. Maybe it was because Ruck was sober and Billy was anything but. Nah. Must be over Libby. The jealous fuck. He should get over himself, Ruck. That's what Billy thought.

Creedence, on the other hand? Now she was something over which to get oneself, if one knew what Billy meant in euphemism, which would be nice, because he didn't.

All he knew? Something naughty with her, as naughty as it got. An urge. A compulsion. And thus a call.

Chelsea, as during adolescence, spent most of her time alone and sketching until her hand ached. Newly motivated, she had managed to coax muscle memory into a fruitful remembrance of a time when such endeavor had seemed worthwhile.

As for the part of this discipline she considered therapy, she'd begun working on a special piece—a practice run, yes, but one over which she nonetheless labored with focused intensity, adding shading and detail and layers, striving for accuracy rather than impressionism: Glancing squint-eyed into the mirror and back at the burgeoning self-portrait, the first she'd ever attempted.

Cautiously pleased at the result—a damned fine likeness of a not-unattractive face. If she could allow herself this small indulgence, please.

The process of rediscovery had begun over the summer while Devin lay about the house 'getting his sea-legs back,' as he kept calling it. Eileen, despite her obvious frailty, had catered to them both with her own brand of maternal, laser-like attention and effort.

Devin, all but unable to walk at first after his coma, now regaining his strength. Joking and laughing, gamboling with unselfconscious zeal around the house or yard with his cane, smoking, his spirits seemed light—but he had always been good at hiding himself, his darkness, behind a veneer of black humor.

Creedence had watched from the window one day as he'd tried to take a few running steps. Gasping as her brother nearly fell over. But Devin didn't seem frustrated. He merely nodded like, okay. Lit another cigarette.

But Devin, so much like his old self, cutting the fool and messing with everyone's heads. He'd freeze in the middle of a sentence and throw his eyes wide, shaking and pretending to have hair-raising flashes and visions. And busting out laughing whenever Creedence or Mama would rush over asking, what's wrong.

He'd say, I'm like that old fella in THE DEAD ZONE, bugging out his eyes and talking of having visions, like of assassinating the president and saving the world. But laughing: "Nah, nah—I'm just messing with y'all, now."

"Well, I wish you'd quit."

"Sheesh. At least it's an act, and not nothing worse."

Nobody needed such a reminder.

Devin, his hair growing out where they'd had to drill a hole in his head to let out the pool of dark blood that'd formed after his tumble down the stairwell at Billy's, still smoked like a fiend. But at least he didn't drink.

Devin. Lucky son of a gun. Living through it all, coming out of the coma stone sober and already detoxed. Hadn't been seen to touch a drop since.

A miracle, everyone said.

All of it. "It's like that car wreck, Colette," her Mama whispered after they finally got Devin home from the hospital. "The policeman told us he was surprised any of them lived through it. And now this fall, cracking open his head. Merciful god in heaven. My little angel—that's what Devin always was."

Right—his latest crisis had done so much for her mother. Now that he was home and better, she didn't seem half-sick anymore herself. Still thin as a twig, but with so much fresh responsibility Mama had picked up a late-life head of steam. She talked of running for ELMS treasurer again in the spring. Spoke of many future events and plans.

And, as her daughter had wished, Devin took up most of the mother's attention.

But all living together again. Under the same roof. And that was downright surreal at times. She sometimes expected to see Daddy sitting in his recliner looking at television.

In private moments, Chelsea—Creedence—poured over all of the old notebooks and sketchpads she'd pulled from a cardboard carton shoved up in the attic. Going through them page by page, lifting the paper up by the corners as though a meticulous archivist examining the original text of fragile, decomposing historical records. Some drawings made her smile, while others evinced winces. Many were not-bad, in her opinion. Or so she told herself.

Others tugged at heartstrings, drawings bringing back sweet memories of family pets, most of whom now lay in eternal repose beneath the lush Bermuda grass of the back yard, their lives memorialized in granite; the same as Big Ma-maw and Pa-paw and Daddy and Libby, all lying in their own eternal interment down the road.

Her Mama kept on her to make sure she'd see to the tending to the care

of all family related grave sites, and on more than Decoration Day, too—
year-round maintenance—once Eileen one day passed away. Chelsea didn't
hold no truck with any of it. She wanted to get on with her own life, not
think about dead people.

Such talk seemed to annoy Devin, who'd sit out near the pets' stones in
the back yard in a lawnchair, reading and smoking with fiendish and greedy
abandon—his only outlet, Chelsea guessed.

But, all in all? Her brother seemed like himself. Other than him looking
more like sixty than thirty-six, having his face sitting across from her at the
supper table almost passed for old times.

Eileen, Devin, in a race to see who could become skinnier.

With Eileen going on all sorts of 'errands' Chelsea suspected were her
own doctor's appointments, some of which seemed to leave Mama so tired
she couldn't move, that left it to her to deal with Devin's own visits.

His astounded doctors continued in a state of amazement at his recovery
—weak as a kitten at first and needing physical therapy to be able to walk,
with liver and kidney function in decline and who knows what else, in a
matter of weeks he had regained lucidity and a high degree of mobility.
Devin—his old self, albeit skeletal and wrinkled, cracking wise and seeming
unburdened by all that'd come before, told the medical professionals he
believed only a divine intervention—a Higher Power—could be assigned a
credible responsibility for this obvious miracle, and for all to kneel, as he
now did, in due gratitude.

At last, he said, enough doctors. She kept after him about doing further
tests, but his latest bloodwork showed improved numbers on the vitals.
Furthermore, once he could mostly walk again he seemed unconcerned, and
so neither she nor her mother pushed him.

And, of course, he got taken to meetings, put through the ringer of
substance abuse rehab. Chelsea noted, however, how he didn't attend as
many AA meetings anymore. Not as often in the first two months home.

But, not worrying. Her brother's good humor—and perhaps his soul—
seemed, by all accounts, restored. Despite the fall, whatever had occurred
between Billy and her brother on their trip together seemed to have healed
the grievous wound Devin suffered for all those years.

Billy.

She didn't know what he'd done, but wanted to thank him.

In a very special way.

She wasn't pregnant anymore. But that didn't mean it couldn't happen
again. She'd be divorced in another year, in any case.

Moments came and went, however, in which she thought she glimpsed glimmers of Devin's old pain, the melancholy near-madness flickering in the eyes hidden behind his shades, twitchy flashes of pique that bordered on seething rage. Or perhaps she'd only been primed to expect such out of him, and projected those expectations. She'd been thumbing through Oprah's line of self-help books, a subscription her mother had gotten for her and Devin, and her field of consciousness felt duly expanded.

The only real argument they'd suffered as a family was over their impudent smoking, in particular at the dinner table.

"I don't care if you both huff yourselves into the ground," she'd shouted, *"but I can't take this stink while I'm trying to eat supper."*

Devin's response? A rare flash of genuine hot rage, pounding the table and declaring how he'd smoke wherever he goddamn pleased and whenever it pleased him to do so, thank you very much, and for her to kiss his ass and piss up a rope all at once.

Eileen, on the other hand, had burst into tears, begging her children not to fight at their father's dinner table. Coughing into her pink napkin and not touching her food, she deigned, however, to snub out her own smoldering butt. So it went.

The separation from Dusty, ongoing; Chelsea, counting the months until said divorce would be final.

After the loss of the baby, Dusty had no longer pressed the issue of reconciliation. So far he'd agreed to Chelsea's demands, which by anyone's standards were modest and fair. Especially gracious, all things reconsidered.

After all, she could have been like chubby Shelby Fordham, who, on a stop-by last week to see Devin—and making goo-goo eyes at him the whole time, brazen and obvious to all but him, it seemed—told her that, after catching her husband making time with another 'bitch' as she termed it, she'd stayed married for another five years.

"Just to make the son of a gun miserable. To remind his ass who writes the checks inside this house. And I am not talking about the monthly bills, either."

Chelsea, horrified, said more power to her, but she's history.

But, also thinking of the enjoyment of doing Dusty that way—staying with him, but never getting near that peterpiper again.

Which would only make him stick it somewhere else.

Like they all didn't do it. It's what her mother always said. "You ought to just forget it and get on with your lives." Eileen still cussed her daughter occasionally for having 'made all this happen.'

Thinking about Buddy Lawler. Getting all shaky inside. Thinking of the few text messages he'd sent her lately. Wanting to get together.

*Forget it, good-time Charlie. I have my sights on bigger game.*

As with Devin and his Big Book recovery work, she'd taken inventory. Had done wrong, too—had hit Dusty first, she had to admit, on the night he'd beaten her down to the floor with a belt. Admitted this to herself that she had had a hand in creating this reality.

It didn't make his escalation any more right. But it did take two to tango, as the one Oprah book that covered addiction and adultery and abrogation of personal responsibilities had suggested. Also, that blame and guilt are childish games. She tried to forget and forgive. Sure. You betcha. But was moving on anyway. No apologies.

The house and lot had been put on the market to be sold, which had been a relief. Dusty, swinging by a few days earlier to deliver a box of kitchen items from the house, all-but wept as he told her how much he missed the cats— his way, she supposed, of saying that he missed her. Watching the way he'd put down the big carton of utensils and pots on the table, running his hand across the top, talking about the kitties he used to despise, she found his discourse literally incredible.

Chelsea, giving him a chaste hug and little pats on the back, could feel his legs shaking at her touch. He all but collapsed into her arms.

"I just still love you so much." Crumbling into tears. "I can't believe what all's happened. It don't seem real."

He almost got her. No—this was manipulation, like when she broke up with him as teenagers and he cried for a week. Emotional manipulation. Her mother yelled, or wept; Dusty, mostly weeping. Before the grownup him had started to try yelling.

And whipping with a belt.

They had both done it to her—Mama and Dusty. All this time. Beaten her into submission. She couldn't get rid of her own mother, though.

"Well, I'm sorry," she finally said. "But it is what it is."

Dusty, lingering rather than leaving, mentioned how after the house sold he had a plan to move into the new apartments over near the industrial park off the interstate. "They got a big-old pool area, with a hot tub. It's gonna rock on Saturday afternoons."

"They'll be real spiffy, I hear."

"I'm sure. Y'all come and swim all you want. I'll make sure you got a key."

"No, now. Nothing like that."

"It ain't far from the dealership."

"I know."

"In case you ever need something."

"Dusty—?"

"What?"

"Nothing. Awesome. Noted."

Now was the time. She announced she wouldn't be here much longer. "I'm going to college, finally. In Columbia."

"No you ain't. Really?"

"Yes, I am."

His eyes spun with wonder. "Naw—you ain't going to college. Are you?"

"I'll have you know I've applied to Southeastern. To start in the spring."

Bless his heart. He tried to sound happy. "That's awesome. I reckon."

"Mr. Hampton keeps saying he wants to pay for it all, too. But I was like, um, what? No way, José."

"I don't know why you wouldn't let him."

"Mama's got plenty of money."

Besides, she told him Hampton said he knew someone 'over yonder' who could help her figure out the financing. "Uncle Hill's always been a big Redtails booster. Hobnobs with all the big wheels over there, like him and Daddy always did. Anyway, I just need to get accepted."

"That's exciting. I reckon."

Creedence, not caring whether Dusty became disappointed, discombobulated, disenchanted, or disenfranchised like those black people said they were in the last county elections over in Tillman Falls, at least according to that Nixon preacher's claims in his Edgewater Advocate letters-to-the-editor he wrote every other week. Chelsea skipped over political junk, usually. Yawn.

Not long after Dusty left Eileen arrived home from the ELMS meeting, her group for which she seemed to live, determined to still keep the books for them as she'd done for years. Despite complaining of searing back pain from what she claimed to be arthritic old bones, she lugged a pair of heavy grocery sacks and a leather satchel bulging with ledgers back and forth every week like always.

Upon seeing the box on the floor, Mama dropped the satchel. "Dusty came?"

"You just missed the little shit."

Eileen grimaced in disappointment. "Oh, me."

"Wish I could say the same."

"I would love to've seen him."

"That makes one of us."

As she put away the spoils of her quick-stop by the Piggly Wiggly, Eileen, wistful, embarked upon anecdotes and memories of Dusty Wallis and his sad childhood—the drunken father, the familiar details recited like family scripture; how if it hadn't been for the Ruckers, he'd have had nothing. "Nothing at all. And us living high on the hog."

Chelsea knew every syllable, every inflection. At this point it sounded like an incantation of nonsense words.

"And now, here we've gone and abandoned him. Shame on us."

"Mama? It wa'n't only Dusty who done wrong."

Eileen, pausing in the act of putting away a jar of Ragù, cut her eyes across the kitchen. "Oh—did my little girl do something wrong, too? Do tell."

"Yes, ma'am. I did."

Her mother put down the spaghetti sauce. "Did he ever know?"

"No."

"Then don't tell him now."

"It would pour cold water on it, I bet."

"You little shit. It would only hurt him worse than you already done. Which in light of what you're telling me, seems like outright meanness. That's not how we raised you, Colette. Lord have mercy."

"I ain't gonna tell him nothing."

"You better not." This explicit threat, complete with devil-eyes and a crooked old finger thrust in Chelsea's direction, was as serious as it got with Mama. "I'm-a tell you what, little missy."

In any case, what was past remained past, and Creedence Wallis—soon to be Rucker again—was all about moving forward and doing whatever with whomever she pleased, now. One in particular.

But even with her freedom, Billy Steeple remained out of reach. How could she compete with Melanie Pinckney, whom she had met a few times during Devin's long hospital stay?

It would be wrong.

And for once, little Creedence needed to be right.

Still. The ache for Billy, it persisted. Like one last unresolved bit of her unrequited past still demanding attention. A final itch to be scratched. She had to know, if for no other reason than to ask him in their moments of intimacy to tell her, at last, why she had so turned him off. What she had done wrong that night. And what she could now do to make him love her, finally.

Devin, taking his daily hobble in the acre-large backyard among the tombstones and mosquitos and gnats, puffed away on the smokes in which Mama kept him stocked. A sacred routine.

He strove to recall the pets themselves. Having been gone so long, though, several he didn't remember at all. One of those, as explained to him, had been a kitten, Prissy, stricken by rare, juvenile feline cancer, with the animal living for only three months.

Devin, asking about it. He'd seen his mother weeping over this one.

"In that last summer right before Daddy died. Lord, son—don't make me talk about it."

Examining the fine-carved gravestone, Devin smoked and remembered his own losses.

### *My Sweet Miss Prissy*
### *May – July*
### *2002*

His heart, clenching at the brief life span. Grief welled for an animal he'd never known.

How long had Libby gotten to live, in cat years?

Sick in the head, still.

He could see dead people, like that little turd in the movie.

But this was no movie.

Devin, knowing damn well what he needed to do. Yeah. Pay a visit to the memorial garden down the road. To see Libby. These were the practice runs out here every day with the cats. The real tombstone still awaited.

Speaking of gravestones:

After his latest, spectacular plunge, or more to the point his amazing recovery, Devin, beginning to consider whether he could die at all. A vampiric bloodline, let's say, or a reincarnated knights-templar of the crusades, hacking through the modern world and invincible until justice and peace restored to the holy lands. Perhaps he existed as an All-American, righteous and upright exemplar of superhero: the invincible Dipsomaniac, able in a single bound to drink entire cities dry of liquor.

Devin, wondering if he should start taking insane risks in order to save people from themselves. See how many he could rescue from the cruel hand of fate. Build a watchtower over Edgewater County. Stay up there for months at a time, scanning the horizon for events.

Yeah: Picturing himself racing into a burning structure, an office tower or perhaps a private residence, escaping unscathed toting a pair of sooty, screaming toddlers and the family dog; his emergence from the rubble of a collapsed skyscraper like, say, the smoldering 9/11 towers, dusting the debris from his shoulders as though movie-rubble made of spray-painted balsa wood and Styrofoam. Lifting impossible weights over his head; undergoing intensive martial arts training, putting his invincibility to work on the mean streets of troubled American towns and cities, side-stepping bullets, bludgeons and blows with equivalent dexterity and ease. The flash of cameras blinding him, mobs of admirers and sinners in need of absolution, healing; microphones thrust into his face, television newsreaders weeping in open awestruck gratitude while describing his selfless and impossible feats. President Bush draping the Medal of Freedom around Devin's neck, both of them biting the inside of their cheeks to keep from corpsing with emotion at the fevered salvation that came part and parcel with such examples of triumphal American righteousness.

Devin, more than a hero—a savior machine.

Fantasizing about immortality: being buried alive, pounding on the coffin lid, decrying his entombment. But when he went down this road—thinking about death—it only made him want a drink.

If not forty drinks.

Or: how about a hundred.

In less fanciful moments, as instructed by a therapist he attempted mental healing by focusing on only good memories instead of tragic-leaning-to-horrorstruck. Forcing the issue, he found himself able to entertain hazy memories of the happy final months with Libby, the time between the Dead show and the mill house in Arcadia. Or pleasant, carefree times back in high school—giving Libby gifts, holding her hand, the first kiss, the warmth and sweet scent of her breath intermingling with his; making love on a scratchy plaid blanket in the sunlit woods behind Pine Haven, or in his or her bed when they had the chance; taking walks and talking about life and the future.

When Devin had felt like talking.

These wonderful moments, the only visions of her allowed.

Not her death.

Not her face, drained of color.

Not the sunlight and the blood.

Not, not, not. All that, over and done.

But the old dark spots, boiling in front of his eyes. The semicircle of granite markers at his feet, he could barely see them clean enough to read the names.

Searching again for the happy times: recalling a beach trip with the family when he and Libby had been seniors in high school. The Ruckers had taken a house on Isle of Palms for a whole week, but that chump Frank Meade prohibited Libby from going for the whole trip. Devin, however, would be allowed to return midweek to collect her, driving up to the midlands and all the way back to the low country, a plan over which his mother had caterwauled, her dissent mattering little to a pulsating set of gonads in the grip of seventeen year-young love.

Devin, his hand on Libby's thigh the whole drive down back to the beach house... remembering the feel of the hot wind on his face, and of his girl's bare, smooth skin. Her profile, her sloe eyes, defiant chin, happiness at an adventure with her boyfriend. Like grownups.

Free.

Down the shore, three days, the young lovers stealing moments to walk on the beach, read, play cards, and once the rest of the Ruckers retired for the night, to make love in the hot tub, all in a summer atmosphere far more pleasant than the stagnant air and buzzing nuisance insects of Edgewater County.

Heavenly, in fact.

Devin bought Libby a necklace at one of the gift shops, a simple silver chain from which dangled a small butterfly. Speculating about one day living in a place like this. Together. How fun it would be to live this way all the time.

On Friday night, the parents and Creedence went to dinner across the great erector set of a bridge to Charleston, to enjoy Southern authenticity in the form of low country legacy Jestine's on Meeting Street. But Devin and Libby, declining; saying they'd rather have hamburgers and hot dogs at the beachfront stand in the commercial district one last time.

Instead, of course, they'd climbed straight into Devin's bed. Later, drinking cheap wine and dancing around in their swimsuits on the rooftop deck.

After full dark descended, Libby had performed an immodest striptease to 'Brass in Pocket.' The song played on the boom box radio they'd carried up to the deck. Nobody else like me, she sang, a bit off-key. The next tune had been 'Back on the Chain Gang,' from a Pretenders greatest hits CD he'd given her on their six-month anniversary.

Devin, kissing Libby and holding her eyes as a full moon rose red and fat over the Atlantic, the sea shimmering, a billion diamonds floating upon the placid surface—he was back there now. He tried to hold on as the flashes of quicksilver lunar light reflected from the sheen of perspiration on her tanned skin, glinted off the butterfly necklace. Molding her to his body, and he to hers.

Hearing her voice in his ears:

"I love the beach." The hot oceanic wind blew back her curly, damp hair, dancing ringlets backlit orange by the halide streetlamp mounted on the side of the house. "But I always wanted to go see the mountains—any mountains."

"So why didn't you?"

"Too hard for my father to drive those roads. Not when someone drinks so much."

Devin examined the beer can in his hand. "It's a self-limiting thing. Isn't it?"

"If you want to drive your family to see the mountains on winding roads? Yeah, it is."

"If you want to drive them there safely."

"That's right," she had said. "But the mountains are for later. The beach, and this," taking his hand and placing it on the tie that held her bikini bottom on her hip, "is for now."

The beach and the night, now a thousand centuries ago. So present, Libby. Real enough in his mind to still touch her.

If only.

In the backyard? Only granite and crabgrass, skeeters and flies. He dropped the butt into the grass of the pet cemetery and ground the stub into the dry green blades.

Licking his lips, Devin went to get out the lawn mower, to change the oil and cut this shaggy yard. And to think about nothing while he done it, too, pardner. If he could manage it.

Cats, cats, cats—much fun had once the women sought to learn of Prudy's ultimate disposition. It had been the only time Devin had let himself have a good solid weep, all three of them together, over the story of Prudy's decline and the decision to say goodbye at the vet out in Colorado. Like all the other cats here in Chilton here under the grass. Like normal. That's right.

Before he could get going good on the yard work, Devin watched as his mother, waving for his attention, came hobbling onto the deck with two glasses of iced tea.

"Edward Devin Rucker—pick up that cigarette butt from the ground where my babies lay in repose. You little heathen."

Spitting and cursing, he nonetheless policed up the butt, stuck it into the deck ashtray, a rusted Charles Chips tin like they used to have delivered back in the 80s. Half full of sand, it stunk now of ash and nicotine rather than salty snack food. Sat by the wooden steps, which were slippery after a rain.

The steps Creedence said she fell down.

By accident.

Devin kept meaning to reopen the file on that case.

Mama set down the two tall sweating glasses of tea on the glass patio tabletop. Each beverage was graced with a slice of lemon and a sprig of fresh mint from her own herb garden.

"Devin, darling?"

He leaned forward on his cane at the top of the steps. "Yes, mother dear?"

"Why on earth do you wander in this yard every day?"

"Trying to keep off the roads."

"It's perfectly safe in this neighborhood."

"Yeah—but it's hotter out on the asphalt."

"Oh, p'shaw. Stubborn as ever. Come have a cold drink with me. It's so muggy today I'm liable to melt," she said, coughing. "Sit with me a spell."

Devin, pacing on the deck. "Fall weather'll com in when the State Fair starts. That's what Daddy always said."

"Your daddy would've known." She lit a menthol. "Son, I can't stand the way you don't hardly never sit down and relax. Standing there with your hands in your pockets. Hobbling back and forth on them bad legs of your'n."

"I spent a lotta time sitting before. I reckon."

"Like you're always late for something. Or waiting for somebody."

"I am waiting on something."

She asked what.

"For you to quit watching my every move and commenting on it."

"You hush that smart mouth and sit down."

Devin, relenting, opened the patio umbrella, a bright floral print of deep burgundy and brilliant green, cranking the handle, a sound effect. Sweat trickled down into an eye. He sat.

He and his mother sipped their tea, sweet as candy. They put down the heavy glasses in unison. *Clunk.*

"Sure is hot out here. Mercy-me."

"So you keep saying."

Eileen, humming to herself. Working up to it: "I know we ain't talked much all summer, since you woke up. I know how you haven't felt like it."

"No'm."

"But I thought—we could talk about some things."

"I've talked it out enough already with them pill-pushers and head-case quacks." Devin, a fresh butt scissored smoldering between fingers stained yellow, indelible, by nicotine; his mother, lighting her own menthol version. "Remember? You paid for it."

"But them doctors ain't your *mother*, son. I'm the only one who really loves you. Who knows you."

"We talk every durn day. Sometimes that's all we do."

"I noticed you ain't been going to your meetings like you did at first."

A slow burn. "You don't see me pounding cold ones, do you? Sitting in front of the TV every night with you and Creedence? Ain't like you can hide it."

"No."

Truth was that on many days, he still felt as thin and unreal as when he'd been drinking. Thinking about Libby, about Prudy. Wondering about the point of sobriety.

"Dry as a bone. Trust me. I—I ain't crazy no more."

Eileen, aghast. "Son, you wasn't never *crazy*. If you want to see that, go downtown and watch Howdy Shull," a notorious Edgewater County fixture, "marching back and forth with slobber hanging out of his mouth."

"Medical science would tell ya there's range on these things. But whatever."

"You just had a little alcohol problem. You didn't work on it too good for a long time. But now you have, and you're over things. It's all better, now."

Smiling at his mother, a sickly, insincere expression. "Ah, but Mama dearest, the first thing they tell you is you don't never really get over being an alkie. Part of the acceptance shit, or whatever. *Accepting that I'm weak, weak, weak*," mocking, fluttering his hands toward the sky. "That I got character flaws and shit. Yep yep. All packaged and inventoried and evaluated like a pallet of Spam fresh off the truck at the Wally-world."

"There's always a way to get over things."

"Mama: Let me ask you something."

"Yes, darling?"

"Did you love Daddy?"

"Well, *Devin*. I never in all my life." Her impugned Southern dignity, palpable. Eileen, fanning at cluster flies. Sticking out a defiant chin. "What possesses you to ask me such a thing?"

"Sometimes I wonder, is all."

"Maybe you do need to talk some more to a doctor. That's the most foolish thing I ever heard come out of that filthy mouth."

Devin, hating her, but losing his ire like a piffle of sour breath whooshing back out of a child's party balloon. He'd thought she was about to spill the beans about her obvious illness. "When we gonna talk about you?"

"Me? There's nothing to talk about. My children are the ones who need to talk through their various travails."

"Nothing to discuss?"

That Eileen fury reared its head. "I swear, but you children are driving me to distraction. There ain't nothing wrong with me. There's never been anything wrong with me. If there was? You'll be the first to know."

Hightailing his ass inside, Devin slammed the sliding glass door with finality; the conditioned air hit his damp skin, a cold shock to his system. Sure that she'd get up and follow him. Acting like nothing had happened, fussing around about dinner.

Cats, a brood, wandering in and out of his field of vision. Trying not to look at Prudy's food dish, which he'd placed without comment amidst the expansive collection of bowls found in strategic places throughout the house of now nine cats.

Phone ringing, Devin, startled, snatched up the handset from the granite breakfast-bar. "It's your nickel, start yapping."

"*Dude*."

His eyes rolled to the heavens—Billy. Not again. Devin, having a hard time of late talking to his old friend, who, for all the other issues, had become a bad influence to a man in recovery.

"What it be, beau?"

"Everything status quo up there?"

Noting a slight slurring of his friend's words. "Doing the best we can."

"Doing all right—with it all?"

Chuckling at all this concern from everyone. "Legs getting strong."

"I—didn't mean that."

"Right. I'm dry as Death Valley. No worries there."

"Thank goodness," a rueful tone. "Keep it that way."

"We try our best to maintain over here at old Teetotaler Plantation."

"Ruck, there is no try, there is only do; or do not."

"Okay, Mr. Miyagi."

"Yoda, bro. The fucking Jedi master. Keep it straight."

Devin, tiring. "So to what do we owe the extreme pleasure of this phone call, oh my brother?"

Billy, hesitant. "Say—could I yak at Creedence? For a hot minute?"

"Don't see why not."

Her face lit up at the mention of Billy's name. She almost fell off the chair. Prancing with the phone up the stairs to take the call.

Devin, of late peering into her crystal blue irises, thought for the first time since forever how those eyes looked so apart from anyone else's in the family. The big joke always made, not knowing from where on earth little Creedence had come.

The eyes.

The red hair.

The afternoon of his mother, and Uncle Hill.

A shock of recognition struck Devin in the kidneys like the time he gotten mugged and beaten by a Vietnamese street gang outside a bar somewhere out west. The revelation left him weaker in the knees than he already was. Devin collapsed back onto his narrow childhood bed, the mattress worn and thin, springs squeaking. "Well I'll be a son of a biscuit-eater."

Mama came into the room. "I didn't really want to talk about none of that mess earlier, darling. Mama knows you're not drinking anymore."

His words felt like objects in his mouth, like small spiders skittering off the tip of his tongue. His heart pounded. "What did you want to talk about?"

Tearful. "A problem I have."

He couldn't breathe. "Such as?"

"A problem I might need your help with."

At last—her illness. What he could do for her. Deep down, this is what he knew had brought him home. He could sorta-kinda remember a phone call from Creedence that started this whole cycle of events.

"What's the trouble? I'm sure it ain't nothing we can't fix."

"*Something I don't want your sister to know,*" she wailed, collapsing and telling him the truth. For the first time since she'd been sneaking away for treatments, she said, the tumor had grown. And how there was no more treatment.

Not pretending anymore felt like a relief. But the news, and her grief, made Devin count drinks in his mind like an insomniac picturing sheep.

Sure—he could stay sober and nurse his mother through her death. No problem.

"We don't got to tell little Creedence. It ain't even nothing worth talking about—is it, Mama?"

"No," she said, smiling through her tears. "It certainly isn't, my darling."

As such Devin hugged her, held his mother close; they both cried. Later, when they felt better, they went downstairs to fix dinner and smoke together.

# SIXTY

## —

## BILLY

About seven-eighths lit by the time his turn to perform at last came around, Billy had a hard time remembering which songs he had chosen. No punk, no jam-band Dead; instead, a populist pick-list of 90s radio hits he hoped would get the room on its feet.

Otherwise, no longer nervous about warbling out his little cover songs; instead, he fretted whether Creedence would show. When he'd called to invite her, she sounded cautious but excited. Unlike her brother. When Ruck had answered, he sounded only cautious.

Billy, fully primed and gargling another measure of Crown, no longer felt in need of the beer chaser. If only to find a convenient place to smoke a quick bowl, he'd be all set.

Eh. The weed, making him all too present these days. Better to have a quick snort or six. Take the edge off that way.

Wisdom, here. Ruck had just not known how to keep matters into perspective. Not getting too drunk was like screwing hard without having an accident. Billy, getting not-bad over the years at the latter. Working on the former.

The club, filling up, mostly with musicians about to play to one another, but a few regulars and drinkers hanging around at the bar or at the tables arrayed in front of the small raised stage against the far wall, a Slim Lupo's logo painted across the cinderblock wall, sound-baffling foam squares hanging down from the open rafters of the ceiling. The building was one of the oldest in the neighborhood, over a hundred years. They said in its original guise, it was used as a horse barn.

Nicole Braden's voice boomed over the PA. "Earth to Billy Steeple."

Paddy, waving a hand in front of a slack Steeple face. "Hey, ace."

"Howzat?"

"It's you."

"What is?"

Nodding in the direction of the stage. "The whole of it all, my man."

Nicole, at the mic, glared over at Billy with busy eyebrows.

"Oh," he said. "Shit."

The previous act, a pair of aging hippie chicks with frizzy hair and thick bodies clutching acoustic guitars, the duo heavy on the harmonies and calling themselves Nancy and the Cartwrights, had all-but shuffled their gear offstage. Dead air approached.

"Come on, old buddy," Nicole said into the mic. "I don't vamp."

Panicking, he downed a last-gasp of the good stuff and grabbed his guitar case, in the process almost falling over.

"And now, here's an old friend from down here in the Market. If you're as old as I am, you might remember him from hardcore acts like Choking Hazard and Meat Mallet. Billy Steeple."

On the depressed trudge up to the stage with his guitar—no one cared, no recognition, no cheers or hoots at the mention of his old bands—his frown next turned upside down. As he hit the riser, he saw, smiling and waving, Creedence! Making her way to a table in the middle. Creedence, appearing hotter than any redheaded Southern belle had the right.

*Yes!*

*SPROING.*

Billy, adjusting the mic stand to suit his impressive height, winked at her, broad and comic so she'd notice.

Creedence Rucker fairly glowed, her eyes like two diamond chips floating in the dim light beyond the stage.

"Hi everyone," Billy boomed, plangent and present in the vocal monitor at his feet. "A special shout-out goes to the lovely little redhead over 'yonder'."

Creedence, blushing, self-conscious, hid her face. "Hi."

"Hi, angel."

He got out his Alvarez acoustic guitar, strumming. Tweaking the tuning. Satisfied, clearing his throat.

But before beginning his first tune, Billy, shitting a golden brick—none other than Ruck St. Ruck himself came cruising in through the door, relaxed and insouciant like he'd been rolling down Bourbon Street.

Followed, to Billy's revulsion and shock, by a sneaky and thrilled Melanie.

Damn her. Not doing what told. Again.

Consequences.

Melanie squeezed her eyes and shrugged at him like a naughty little girl.

The two of them piling in on top of Creedence at the last available table on the packed floor caused a ridiculous bustle right as Billy about to serenade his way into that other woman's trousers.

*You selfish assholes. Way to ruin everything.*

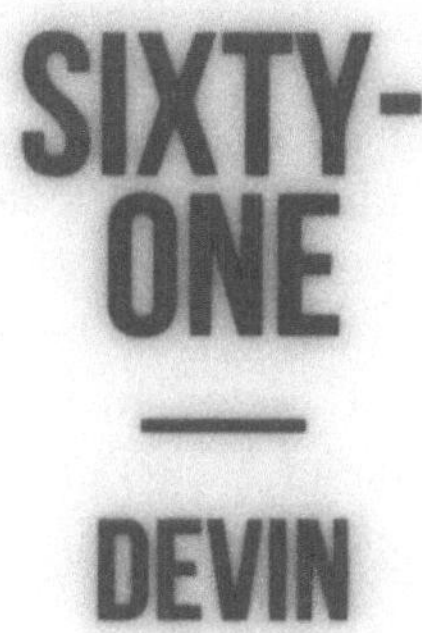


Devin, scrunched in the passenger seat of Chelsea's green Ford Focus, heading to Columbia.

To see Billy play at a fucking songwriter night.

Inside a bar.

*Yeah.*

But it sounded like Billy needed him there.

Fine.

His sister, skittish and spastic, motored south down the busy freeway toward Columbia like a scene out of a MAD MAX hyper-reality, road warriors on a last chance power drive of un-signaled lane switching, bird-dogging, wild speeding, and generalized near-mayhem. Since coming home from the hospital, Devin, much as he could, avoided cars.

A Suburban roared by followed by a convoy of big rigs four trucks strong, shaking the Focus frame, blowing their doors off.

"These people's nothing but maniacs."

"You the one going too slow, GF. At this rate, them wooly-boogers's liable to run us over."

"It sure is gonna be a pain."

"What?"

"Running back and forth to deal with Mama. After I move over here."

"You ain't gonna have to worry about it."

"But—I figured you wouldn't stay. That you and her—?"

"You know she's sicker than a dog, don't you?"

Creedence, gripping the wheel. "It ain't that bad. Look at how busy she stays."

"Horse-pucky." Devin, dying for a smoke. "Sicker than shit's what she is."

"Then it won't matter either way, eventually. Will it."

He didn't answer. Didn't have to.

The closest they'd come to discussing her mother's cancer had been after Chelsea found a pill bottle her mother had stashed away in the trash, had looked it up online and confronted Devin. It was for some kind of renal cancer. Mama's kidneys had gone bad.

Well, knock me over, he had thought. I would have figured the lungs, as he anticipated from his own predilections enjoying a bout of future liver cancer. He'd have to get he filter changed, if he wasn't careful. Hardy-har.

Devin, stealing glances at his sister. In profile she looked determined, almost defiant. She wasn't gonna let Mama's mess bring her down. Her eyes, sparkling with anticipation for the night out in the city. She was fine pretending for a while longer.

Since his earlier epiphany, he'd been unable to stop regarding her features, the small details, the color of her skin. Turning the apparent facts over in his mind. But not wanting to. Feeling nutted anew over the deception regarding his father's dignity and bloodline.

But hey—at least this fresh drama better than thinking of drunk driving accidents and dead girlfriends.

Creedence, the little mind reader: "Why do you keep cutting your eyes at me?"

"I was looking at a Ferrari going by on the other side."

"You were eyeing me back home, too."

Shrugging. "Thinking about shit. The past. That's all."

"You worried about drinking tonight?"

"Nah."

"Should you be doing this?"

"Nah. I mean—yeah, sure. Billy's my main man."

"What, then?"

Devin, grunting and shifting around in his seat, made a show of fiddling with the safety belt strap cutting into his collarbone. Dying to let his suspicions tumble out, the truth now clear:

Creedence, only his half-sister.

The enormity of his mother's duplicity now multiplied, exponential. Thoughts of it all made Devin quiver with thirst.

"Same old rigmarole." Casual, controlling his voice, acting up a storm. "Mama wants to sit and talk the way y'all always done. But, I ain't got it in me."

"She'd call me six times a day at work for updates on what I was doing. What Uncle Hill was up to."

If here was an open door, Devin, deciding not to go through it.

"Maybe I'm not much into family."

"Aw—we used to have such fun. You remember."

He did. "And Mama too, on all them beach trips."

"But you seemed to change. *Did* change."

Putting his hand on her forearm. "Only in certain ways. Never stopped loving my sister."

Creedence, reaching across and squeezing his knuckles.

But another shock of recognition, startling. Devin, jerking his arm away and yanking down the cosmetics mirror in the passenger side sunshade. Staring, now, into his own eyes.

*Now tell me, who are you? 'Cause I really want to know.*

"What on *earth*?"

"Something in my eye, s'all."

"Scared the mess out of me, boy. We need to arrive alive, now."

Wondering now how in God's name he could go and sit in a bar without succumbing, Devin tried to push the thirst out through his pores like sweat.

*The shit's got no power over me.*

*It is only I who've the power over my own actions.*

*For today, I will not drink.*

*One day at a time.*

Over the summer of recovery, Devin, suffering and soldiering through a few key tests of his sobriety, but so far coming through fine:

One bleak, boring afternoon he did at last hit up the cemetery to visit Libby, but instead of turning at the gates, driving around, aimless, for hours; haul-assing down every country road but the right one, giving the Jetta more of a workout than the battered car could possibly have wanted: up to Parsons Hollow and across to the national forest in the west half of the county, down through those endless pine barrens to Red Mound and what they called the sand hills, places where you could find seashells from zillions of eons ago when the coastline had been situated along what they called the fall line, where the rivers began to flow down to where the briny sea met the sand.

Ending up in Tillman Falls on the town green right outside of The Dixiana, Roy Earl's grandfather's beer joint. Sitting outside for an hour. Sweating, heart thudding. Watching a broken-down old redneck man hobble in to get his fill of whatever got him through the long afternoons. Itching to join him.

In the end, Devin had put the car in gear and driven home, proud of his resolve and yet shamed by his inability to view Libby's gravesite, to pay proper tribute to the ancients. In hiding, as them old Pearl Jam boys sang on the alternative rock station from down in Columbia. I'm in hiding, still.

No. Too much time had passed—Pearl Jam's now classic, not alternative, rock. The 90s, a blank spot in his history.

Creedence exited the freeway for the main thoroughfare into downtown Columbia. "I been meaning to ask you something."

"Lay it on me."

"When on earth are you gonna go and see your best friend?"

A distinct, different shame. "Aw, hell—Dobbs don't want to see me."

Creedence, stern: "If everything you've told me is true, about how you're all better?"

"Which I am."

"Then go and tell him, son. He's known all summer you're back."

"I don't know how I can look at him, girl. I never could, after the accident."

"Devin. He still believes it's all his fault."

This kind of talk caused ear-steam to leak out. "My boy wa'n't nowhere near the wheel. It was me."

"Devin?"

He grunted, waited.

"What were you doing all that time?"

"*When?*"

"When you was gone away. What'd you do with yourself?"

"Oh—then? I drank. And drove. And I drank some more."

"Not for the whole time. Nobody could."

Devin, even in sobriety continuing to elide the truth about his dry period with Millie, which had been a year or two. "And yet here I sit, having lived to tell the tale. A sturdy frame, I reckon. S'all I can tell you."

Devin, directing her on a series of turns that led them down into the Old Market; they wended their way through a gauntlet of orange traffic cones, backhoes, sidewalks with cavernous voids, all the old sidewalk trees ripped out—the neighborhood, a facelift.

Feeling it for the merchants. Devin had been told by Roy Earl how the construction had already caused no end of anxiety, but not yet halfway complete.

"Park in there." Devin, motioning toward the pay lot across from Lupo's, marveled at the lack of vehicles parked in the neighborhood. Thinking, back in the day? Even on a weeknight like this? The streets would have been crawling with students. Maybe the younger generation, a later crowd?

Who gave a rip. Devin, declining to join in their revelry.

There, the low wall on which he'd sat, watching Billy and Libby so long ago. Wondering what'd been said between them that night. He'd never asked her.

Getting out of the car, Devin, curious to see Melanie Pinckney, a nylon book-bag slung over her shoulder, sashaying down the sidewalk toward them.

Billy had done well. Hair ringlets like Libby, a lithe and tan goddess.

Creedence, a shadow crossing her features: "Tell me that isn't Billy's little college girly."

"Looks that way."

"Well, I'll be shit."

Devin asked what was wrong. She said, nothing.

Creedence, calling out and waving: "Hey, girl!"

Melanie canted her head over with a curious frown. Her smile, dissipating once she realized the identity of the people approaching her.

"Melanie, how are you? I keep meaning to get together with y'all."

Devin, fumbling with a cigarette. "What's shaking, gorgeous?"

A modicum of cheerful enthusiasm. "Are you guys here to see Billy play?"

"Yeah." The siblings, answering in unison. Devin, punching Creedence in the arm.

"Billy's so silly—he didn't want me here."

Creedence, mock-shock. "*Why on earth wouldn't he want you to come?*"

"Said he'd be too nervous. It's such a big deal, for some reason. But after hearing how hard he worked on his songs..."

Devin, chuckling. "Steeple used to be quite the rock star, back in the day."

"I can't imagine."

"A different Billy, back then."

The trio stood in awkward silence. The sounds of a female folk duo wafted from the open door of the club.

Creedence, peering inside. "I reckon we ought to go in."

Devin, smoking, cleared his froggy throat. "Say, Mel?"

"Yes?"

Stammering as though trying to ask her on a date. "Just a word or two. For a skinny minute or three?"

Melanie, crossing her arms as though cold. "Go ahead."

"Alone, I mean."

Creedence, getting it. "I'll go on in and pay for you. It's only five dollars."

Melanie, left with Devin in foot-shuffling discomfort, looked as though she'd scream if he said so much as 'boo' to her.

"I'm sorry as all get-out. Truly. For whatever happened that night I fell."

"Billy said you'd apologized to him. That's good enough for me."

"That's like, what, step four or six. Some shit like that."

"Excuse me?"

Devin, miming the quaffing of a beverage. "The AA routine."

"Are you feeling okay these days?"

"Dry as the Sahara."

"From your fall, I mean?"

"Oh—a bit stiff when it rains." He held his cane aloft, danced a delicate little side-step. "Otherwise? A hundred percent."

"That's amazing."

"One for the books, they tell me."

Chewing her lower lip, Melanie hesitated as though carefully choosing her next words. Her youth and beauty stood in high, ghostly relief next to Devin's crusty drunkard's countenance of pits and lines.

"I know how close you and Billy are, or were. But you must realize how much you scared us that night." Cutting herself off, her face reddening. "My goodness, but it was horrible."

"All Billy said was I had got all rowdy on y'all."

"In a word."

"Sorry."

"Should you even be coming in here tonight?"

Devin, smoking under the crepuscular lavender sky, that twilit moment of almost-dark. "Probably not."

"Then why are you?"

"He called Creedence, not me. But I came anyway."

"He called—who?"

"My sister. Chelsea. Creedence is what we call her."

Considering the revelation. "He called her? Not you?"

Devin, fibbing. "He called us both."

Melanie, a trace of angry recrimination. "Since you both came back from Texas, now he's the one drinking too much."

No *bueno*, Devin said, hand over heart. "Firsthand info."

"He barely touched a drop before."

Quavering and faint. "Now, look here—you ain't laying that on me. Ain't like I been out partying with him."

"He keeps talking about how he let you down. One night he even punched a hole in the wall." A harsh whisper. "And, crying."

"Crying?"

"He's been crying like nobody's ever seen."

"No shit."

"*Ruck?*" She parroted what Billy would call him, raising her eyebrows. "I've never seen him cry at all before. And so, I'm worried."

Trying to force his weak smile through a tight mask of degradation, Devin didn't know what to say. "He always was real emotional. With me, anyway."

"You know I'm a psychology major."

Devin busted a gut. "Hope you brung your notebook for this crew. Yee-haw."

A smattering of applause greeted the conclusion of the vocal duo's set. "Maybe we should go in."

Devin's energy settled. He sucked his teeth. "Yeah. Let's go in."

"What the hell happened between you that night on the balcony?"

Truthful as possible: "Far as I know, nothing. We just fell through that sliding glass door."

"You weren't fighting?"

"God no, girl. We was drunk. We'd just had too much, too fast. That's all. Now let's go hear him play."

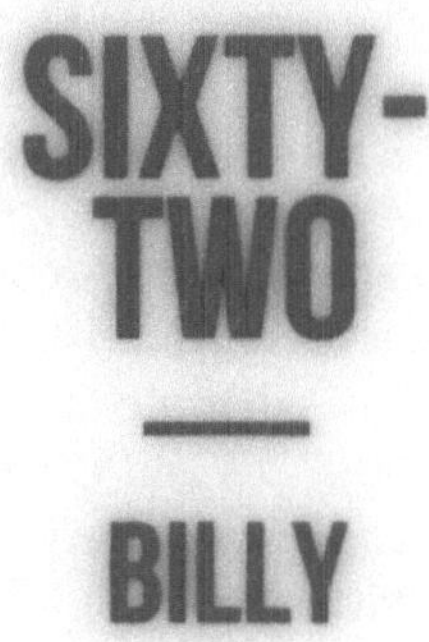


Warbling in his reedy tenor, Billy struggled through the first tune. In trouble.

It had been bad enough whittling down his lengthy pick-list. He'd been having early 90s nostalgia. He'd heard titters at the start after muttering "'Champagne Supernova,' by the Gallaghers," into the Shure S-57 microphone. As though anyone in this crowd of musicians and music lovers wouldn't recognize the overplayed 90s pop hit. He also had 'Californication' and 'Cumbersome' prepared, along with a few other grunge classics.

Having a difficult time maintaining the tempo, hands soaked with sweat, slipping on the strings, he couldn't remember in the least why he'd thought this song so fraught with meaning, nor had his attempt to goad the audience into a sing-and-clap-along of the chorus gone over.

Wrapping it up with a flourish. Silence. A few claps. The table of three who knew Billy whooped and goosed the applause best they could, Ruck telling him to 'tear it up, beau' in that ragged rasp of his and waving a cane in the air. Surreal.

Why had he played it? Libby hadn't even lived long enough to know the tune. What a colossal error.

Forget his fans—he fixated on finding the one wit out in the darkness who had the temerity, the rank discourtesy, to literally *boo*. Retribution awaited.

For others as well—peering at his old friend, waving, thumb's up, but inside? Rage monkey. What, did Ruck find out about her coming over here and have a shit-fit? Did he have some say over his sister's life?

The way he'd had over Libby's?

Billy, thinking about sending a message—an ugly one.

"Here's how I feel about being back here on the Lupo's stage after all these years." He plucked around, settled on a key which felt correct. "Here's one from the old days. From when dinosaurs roamed the earth. It's for my boy back there. He's home from the wars. He's a road warrior. This is for him."

"*Get on with it,*" the boo-er yelled to shushes from Creedence, Melanie and others.

Yep—Billy launched into a spare, hoarse rendition of 'Back on the Chain Gang,' the old lament for departed friends. The whole time he sang he stared out beyond the lights at what he hoped was Devin, a bitterness verging on outright sarcasm, the lyrics and cadence of a vocalist making fun of a song rather than doing it in tribute, the subtext of his message... well... that Melanie, sitting next to Devin, was no Libby. And that if Devin wanted Melanie, it could possibly save his life. As Creedence would save Billy's. He wasn't sure it came through.

After doing the first verse and chorus straight, he stopped strumming and began to sing-speak the rest of the lyrics like William Shatner. "I found a picture of you, yeah. Back on the chain gang. That's where we are. Yeah."

Devin, his hair and shoulders backlit, glowing and ethereal. Still as a stone.

"*What in the actual fuck?*" the lone voice of dissent called out.

Billy, holding up a hand, again strummed the chords and modulated his voice back into a straight, serious rendition. Getting choked up but holding himself together, he sang on through.

In fact ramping up the performance—Billy, flailing at the metal strings until slicing his unseasoned, callous-free fingertips. Belting out the bridge-verse. The words bearing down on his soul like lead.

Billy, hating Devin.

He who had had her.

Thoughts, out of control.

Now his voice shattered and broke. Trailing off and sobbing into the microphone, choking. Not giving a shit whether anyone saw him weep or not. His consciousness, awash in intoxication. A wellspring of fresh grief that hit him out of nowhere. He had been drinking nonstop since noon.

Wiping his blurry eyes, his vision cleared to see a roomful of hushed and shocked faces, bar owner Nicole's the most horrified of all.

She had already come onstage. "Billy-boy—you okay?"

Barking NO and waving her away, he asked for 'special dispensation' because of a family issue, a moment to recover and finish his set.

"No. Come on down," she whispered, gentle. "Please."

Covering up the microphone with his huge hand he caused the PA to screech with feedback. Flinching, releasing the mic, he shouted: "I've got one more. I picked it for you—'Just a Girl,' No Doubt. I know what you're thinking, but I assure you I can hit the high notes."

"That's enough, sweetie." Glancing around at a crowd held rapt by this drama, she begged: "Enough for tonight, now."

"*Jesus*." Billy, slurring. "I swear I'm okay."

A quick, cutting glance at the shadowy looks of confusion on Creedence and Melanie's faces. Devin's chair, now empty. No more catcalls—they all rubbernecked at a train wreck still unfolding.

"Thanks for *nothing*," Billy yelped into the microphone. He threw his guitar into the case so hard that the neck of the instrument cracked and broke; he didn't care if he ever played it again, nor if anyone else still alive did either. That bitch was Pete Townshend-bound for the splinter factory. Forget music. Back to the screenplays.

Ignoring the stares of the audience, he flip-flopped over to his people, asking, "You believe these Philistines? And where the fuck my boy Rucker at? Daddy's ready to party like it's 1989."

Chelsea, watching as Billy came down offstage, felt as though she had witnessed the man of her dreams not at his best; rather, losing his mind.

In front of God and everyone.

*Oh-kay, then.*

Revelation in a minor key; puzzle-pieces connecting. He hadn't wanted Melanie here. His tears, because they're in the process of breaking up.

*It's why he wanted me here. To show her.*

Devin, who'd gone outside to smoke, had not come back. Sudden, as though someone lit a fire under him, he'd bolted when Billy began the recitation. And her now left with a roomful of strangers.

Melanie, cooing to her man. "Honey—that was so good."

"I'm like so so *so* glad all you guys came. Anyone wanna get a drink?"

Tilting his head just so, his twinkling eyes, a little puffy and red, still bore right into her. "How's Miss Creedence tonight? Besides gorgeous?"

Felt herself flush. "Been forever since I went out."

"Have no fear, fair maidens; memorable times await. Drinks, dancing, debauchery. A night to remember."

Melanie, air out of a balloon. "Sounds more like one I'd rather forget. We should really get on home."

Billy scoffed and signaled Paddy for a round.

Paddy, who stood conferring with a troubled Nicole, gave him a little head-shake. Creedence could not blame them.

"Or—let's pay my tab and we'll find friendlier climes."

Or at least that's what she *thought* Billy had said—his words were coming in a sloppy rush.

He was piss-drunk.

*Well, dang.*

Melanie, however, put the kibosh on notions of further partying. Reminding Billy about obligations. Pulling him away from Creedence she said, firm: "We need to get ourselves home, now. We have ourselves a wedding to plan, don't we?"

Wait—*wedding*? But hadn't Melanie's cadence gone UP at the end? Seeming to Chelsea like phony enthusiasm?

Outside on the sidewalk, Billy froze. Devin, down the block, paced in a circle and smoked. Her brother looked in the streetlamp glow as though talking to himself.

Billy announced that he needed to rap with his brotherman for a spell. "Why don't y'all hang here and talk gal stuff for a bit?"

Melanie, harsh: "Just hurry up, now."

Billy, thrusting his guitar case at her, said thanks.

The women watched them stroll away down the sidewalk. The cherry-eye glow of Devin's cigarette faded in the darkness.

Melanie squinted at their retreating backs. She clutched Billy's guitar against her body. "Well, that's one thing I'm thankful for."

Feeling old and ugly next to Melanie, she tried to stand with one leg bent inward and hands on hips, nonchalant but sexy. Chelsea asked about the one-thing.

"That Billy doesn't smoke freaking cigarettes."

"Be glad. Mama and Devin's like living with two chimneys."

Melanie turned imploring, a crumbling facade. "But he smokes so much *marijuana.*"

"He does?" Shocking. Drugs—that explained tonight.

"He always smoked, more than I liked? But I didn't worry about it too much?"

"It ain't so bad. So's I've read."

"They say pot isn't as deleterious as alcohol, yes, and no one ever died from it. But, now he's drinking hard liquor *straight out of the bottle.* Sometimes early in the day."

"That's not too good."

Averting her dewy eyes, she said with disbelief: "He keeps blowing me off with the most ridiculous rationalization."

Chelsea asked what.

"'The people on TV all do it'. Can you believe that?"

This all seemed overwrought. *A little high-strung, Miss Priss? It so happens I used to smoke weed with him back in the day, so ha-ha to you.*

Knowing better than to make excuses for drinking too much, and yet: "He's partying a little too hard. That's all. You know men."

Melanie grabbed Chelsea by the arm. "Creedence—you knew him a long time ago."

"We hung out some. So to speak."

At that Melanie narrowed her eyes. "What was he like in those days? Him and Ruck?"

Chelsea, picturing Billy sitting on the edge of the bed that awful night, pulling his T-shirt on over a strong, beautiful back. How she had put her hand there, from which he'd recoiled.

"I didn't know him too good." She gestured down the block. "The boys are the ones who were close."

"I get that."

"Billy was real strong for him. After what happened."

"He says it was awful. A car accident, right?"

Chelsea held out her hands, a helpless gesture. "We got a lotta DUI in South Carolina. So sad."

"Billy... he's so different from all the other guys I've dated. So—what's the word?"

"Well-spoken?"

"Erudite? Yes. Billy's quite sophisticated. You should see his collection of art cinema. He went to present a major paper at a national conference only this spring." She sighed. "I went to private school, UGA and now almost have a masters from Southeastern, mind you, and I haven't even heard of half of the movies he likes."

"Don't surprise me none." Imagining Billy's fancy movies. Remembering Libby, and all her filmmaking dreams. "He's a character, all right."

"All of those Charleston boys back home, and the fraternity brothers here? Juvenile beyond measure. So weak and unmotivated. Did you know Billy has a producer in Hollywood interested in his screenplay?"

"Like—for a movie?"

"I'm certain his dreams are coming true. He's not always patient, but—" Laughing and demure, covering her face. "Goodness, but we fit together well. Like he was made for me." Now her tone turned chilly. "And me for him. If my meaning is clear. Little miss back-in-the-day."

Chelsea's envy, sparking into full blue flame like a burner on Mama's Jenn-Air range. "How wonderful for you both. And, I don't have a clue what you're suggesting."

"You're married, correct?"

"Yes," unwilling to admit the failure to have a successful marriage. "I am."

"Stick with hubby, Edgewater County. Understood?"

Chelsea Rucker Wallis, forcing a smile, hadn't felt this aghast since she realized Dusty was literally belt-whipping her.

With hand-flapping nonchalance: "It's wonderful when it's so right. I'm so happy for you both."

Shouting voices, in the distance; Melanie, frowning.

"Did you hear that?"

Chelsea got a cold-wash of anxiety in her gut. "It sounded like Billy and Devin."

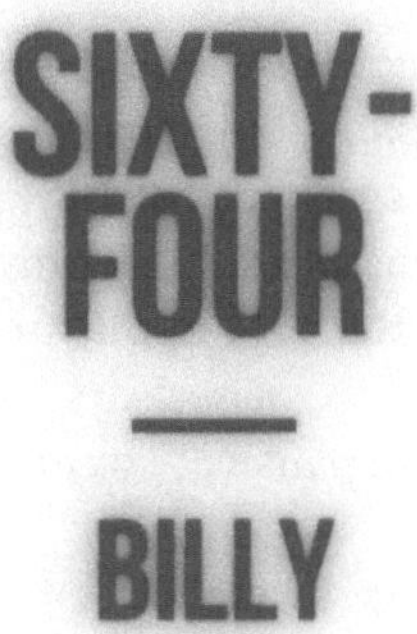


The two pals strolled around the corner from Lupo's. They shuffled along in the direction of Roy Earl's coffee beanery, which at this hour sat closed-up tight. Ruck, not only burdened with a cane but also pausing to cough and hack snort into the gutter, lagged behind Billy, with his big-legged strides.

He caught up. "I oughta chain-gang your ass."

"When I saw you, I called an audible with that one."

"Thanks."

"Not my best decision."

"What was that mess in there, dude?"

"It's just a song, after all."

"Much as songs mean to you, Bill?" Devin, low and rueful. "Hard for me to believe you on that one."

Billy turned haughty. "I wouldn't have done 'Chain Gang,' but it seemed like old times. But—I didn't invite you. Did I?"

"You called to invite my sister. Is what it sounded like. Which is why I decided to come."

Billy, short of breath, regarded his old pal with unmasked loathing. He worked his lips. Nothing came out but a liquor belch.

"Say what you gotta say, big man."

Billy, no thoughts in his head other than movie lines, song lyrics, other people's words. Thinking he might either vomit or cry; his lantern jaw working, soundless, until finding the right words, the right lyric.

"Maybe there isn't a vein of stars calling out our name."

"Do what, now?"

Collapsing against the wall of the neighborhood flower shop, Billy shuddered, wished for a drink.

"Bill—?"

"Cracks in the pavement," he explained in an exhausted wheeze.

"What about 'em?"

"You have to watch your feet for them."

A couple of sorority-girls passed by—passing as far away from the men as possible. They whispered and snickered at Billy leaning against the wall.

Examining his dirty Birkenstocks, big grimy toes sticking out, he cursed the young women and said to Ruck, "I'm not finding the right words."

"What's the issue?"

Billy's answer? A gesture, expansive; sweeping his arm in a vast arc as if to say:

The street, the cars; the sky, the stars.

Devin, smoking and exhaling, watched as his brotherman, mumbling nonsense, hung his head and choked off a sob.

"You is drunk as a coot, boy."

Billy raised his head. "Hypocrite."

"Not I, said he." Devin held out his hands—steady as rocks. "And for what it's worth? I didn't come back so you, or anybody, would swap out places with me and start drinking like there ain't no tomorrow."

"Don't get me wrong. This isn't about your issues."

"So what's it about? Creedence?"

"Not so much."

Devin smiled and shook his head, took a deep breath. "Before all that shit went down with us? I figured we could've been best friends, you and me."

"You mean over what happened this spring?"

"No, dicknut. Before the Dead show."

"Oh. Understood."

Devin took a step toward Billy, who drew back against the wall of the flower shop with what appeared to be earthly terror.

"But, Bill—I wouldn't mind another go around on the old friendship merry-go-round. If you're game."

"That's so sweet of you," cringing and biting the heel of his hand. "So generous."

"But, dude." Definitive. "I can't hang watching you slurp booze and blow fumes in my face."

"You shouldn't, maybe." Desperate. "But you could."

"Not worth it," without meeting Billy's eyes. "I have—my sobriety to lose."

Billy seemed gripped by a notion. "Ruck: a favor."

"Anything besides doing a shot with you."

"Gonna sound weird."

Devin, like: *try me, pal.*

"Let me suck your cock."

Devin, smoking and letting the offer settle. "Um—pardon?"

Billy, pulling his friend over to him. "Let me taste it."

"Dude, get off me." Ruck pushed away, stepped back. "Fuck off, bro."

"I beg you. You don't get it. I had this idea—I'll be able to taste her."

"You sick fuck."

"Oh, god—please let me get close to her. To you both."

"I'm-a whip your ass all over again." The men grappled across the street from the last spot they'd fought outside Roy Earl's. He tried clutching at Ruck, who swung with his cane, bonking Billy across the clavicle.

Hollering in pain, he let go.

"Now," Ruck said. "Dude. Let's get you some coffee."

Billy shoved Devin against the wall. His cane clattered to the concrete.

"Now let me fucking suck your motherfucking cock, you dumb redneck." He roared with insistence. "*I'm not asking.*"

The echo slapped back from the opposite row of businesses.

A stare-off. Both needed to catch their breath.

At last. "Bill? Love ya, but I decline this privilege."

Billy released Ruck. With an air of supercilious scorn: "Suit yourself. The point anyway is to forget the past. Forget our troubles, not wallow in them. *Now let's go get a drink,*" he shrieked.

Ruck, unperturbed by his friend's outburst, picked up his cane and fumbled in his pocket for a smoke. "Dang, beau—I'da thunk you'd be a little more considerate of my condition. But yeah, I'd need a bracer to get my joint worked on by you. You crazy fucker."

Billy, a flash of lucidity and self-consciousness. "Of course you're right, Ruck—right as rain. Right as any of us."

"Wouldn't go that far."

"Listen to me, with all my drunken talk of dick-sucking." He tsk-tsked. "It's all an act. My little Andy Kaufman routine."

"I sure hope so."

"Let's go and collect these girls. I've been a sodden idiot tonight, and I apologize. Perhaps I'm going through a midlife crisis a little early." The two headed back around the corner.

"Everybody's been put through the ringer. Creed's divorce, all my bullshit. It don't never seem to end."

"I must say, that sister of yours?"

"Yeah?"

"She's a fine lady."

"I ain't been too good a brother to her. That much I know." Pausing. "Maybe I got a chance to make it up, now."

"Sounds like a beautiful thing."

"Man—you okay?"

"I was nervous about singing. Too much too fast."

"Been there; done that."

"Hey—forget all that talk back there."

"Already have. Booze fucks with your head, heart and soul, brother. You ain't got to apologize for nothing. Not anymore."

Billy and Melanie together on the sidewalk; he tried to put a good face on the fact that he yearned for Creedence, still. His throat closed in grief as they watched the siblings jaywalk over to the parking lot.

Ruck turned back and caught Billy's eye; the men, sharing a moment. The look they shared, portentous, like in a movie where the actor's faces represent emotions no amount of hoary scriptwriter dialogue could adequately convey.

He finally went to see the other passenger.

Dobbs and Libby Vandegrift, the happy couple, received Devin sitting on the floral-print couch in their tasteful, formal living room, a traditional family home: this corner-lot anchor situated on a quiet street in a subdivision not far from the new Tillman Falls interstate exit, why, it represented the American dream. Felt comforting in every way.

The couple had been married for fifteen years. Established, as folks say.

The cries of children at play, from another part of the house.

Devin, confused and nervous; told, beforehand, smoking not permitted.

Dobbs, no wheelchair.

Rising, effortless, to a standing position.

Presenting himself, a Christlike figure in pressed gray slacks, a sky-blue oxford stretched taut across a Southern man's belly. The famous curly hairline now in recession, feet shod with worn topsiders, a middle-aged gent who'd feel well at home anywhere in a place like Edgewater County.

Dobbs, whom they said would never walk again.

Dobbs.

Walking.

*His face is so young. Like ain't no time passed at all.*

Devin said this aloud, the words feeling glued onto a thickened tongue.

A shift in the refraction of brilliant light from an unknown source; Libby, her young self again, too, rose and greeted him.

Back to Dobbs, now become the man in the pool.

Hanging upside down in the corner.

Drifting, languid; his wheelchair sitting under him, empty.

Libby, glancing over to the apparition and smiling. Winking at Devin, a big thumb's up. Silent, her words nonetheless came to him:

*Life is just a bag of tricks!*

Waking up. Five in the *aye-yeem*. Cursing this latest shitty dream.

A thought, creeping in on cat's feet: the notion of a palliative to these terrible awakenings.

A shot.

A bracer.

An eye-opener.

Before going to see Dobbs.

Jamming his hands, freezing, under his armpits like in the days of the oldschool tremors, he shuffled to the bathroom he'd gone back to sharing with his sister. He took his toilet while singing:

*How dry I am, how wet I'll be.*

Back in bed, Devin switched on the light and read until the sun came up. He'd been going through old books from the bookshelf his mother kept as he'd left it—as she had every other part of his room. Like when he and Dobbs had hung out as teenagers, getting high and listening to records and playing Atari.

A museum exhibit.

A snake eating its tail.

*Like ain't no time passed at all.*

Yeah—it all fucked with him. Only day-by-day kept him going; kept him determined.

Seeing Steeple in such sad shape last week hadn't hurt. If that wasn't an advertisement for staying straight, nothing would be.

Only one niggling detail—Creedence told him how Melanie had all but blamed Devin's return on Billy's current status. Only his reading on recovery and its ideas about guilt being unproductive kept him from getting snippy over it. He had not asked anyone to come get him in Texas. He hadn't even been going to Texas before Billy called. Who was making whose reality, here?

Such a notion chapped his ass. Also made him want to drink it all away. But, what didn't?

Day. By. Day.

After dawn he dragged his ass out of bed, made breakfast for the house, and made sure his mother's pill-minder was stocked with her pain meds and other prescriptions.

And hoping she had a good day ahead. Mama had begun having more bad ones than good ones. It never rained but poured.

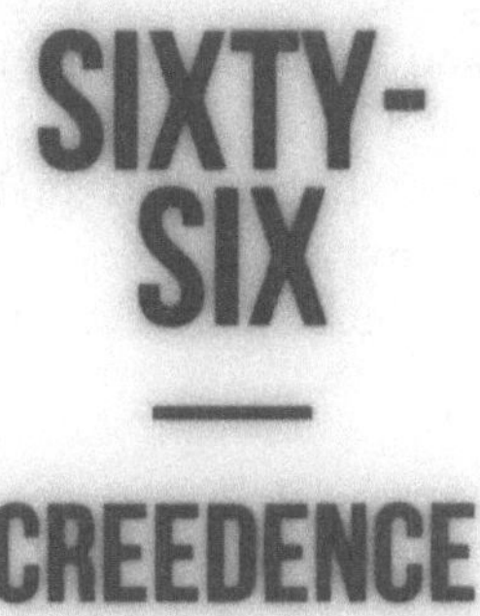


The phone number, long distance, unfamiliar. At first Chelsea thought the woman calling for Devin was a telemarketer.

Balancing the cordless on her shoulder, she stood chopping carrots; a salad underway. Healthy, her own food, that which was good for her, neither her ex-husband's diet nor her mother's rich indulgent cuisine, everything creamy and buttery and fatty to the point that half the time she awakened in the night with the shits. "You're who, now?"

"Millie. A friend of Ruck's. Millicent Haversford."

"You mean 'Devin'?'

She said she did.

"I'm his sister."

Silence, a low hum on the line.

"Hello?"

A voice halting, hesitant. "He—Ruck never mentioned you."

"And who may I say is calling, again? Millie, you say?"

"Yes."

Creedence, holding out the phone to Devin, standing with stiff body language in the living room.

Frantic, he waved her off as though directing an errant jetliner on the tarmac at Columbia Metro. *Forget it*, he mouthed. "Not ready."

"I'm sorry," hating to lie. "But he's not here."

Millie, all tumbling out in a rush. "He's not there. But, he's there—right?"

Chelsea, saying if she meant, did he live there? "Yeah. He's out buying groceries with Mama."

"I tried his mobile."

"I think he turned off his service. After he got out of the hospital—you don't know about that, do you?"

Millie, expressing shock and dismay.

"He fell down some stairs. They didn't know if he was going to wake up, but, then he did." Locking eyes with him across the room. "He woke up from a fifteen-year bender and a tumble down a flight of concrete steps onto his pointed little head like it wasn't nothing. Started smoking and cussing again without missing a note. It beats all anybody's ever seen," laughing despite the hot tears running down her face.

Devin, pinched and sour, cussed and went outside. He slammed the sliding glass door behind him.

"How bad is he?"

"Since he fell, he's sober. Near as anyone can tell."

"Thank god."

Millie, Chelsea thought, sounded like someone with an investment in hearing a sober Devin say 'howdy.' But she couldn't make him. No one could make Devin do anything. No one ever could. Except Libby. No help there.

"I'm thankful to hear this." Millie, searching. "We were both in the same boat, once. Together."

"So you knew him like he was before."

"Yes," definitive.

"I'm real sorry."

Millie, a laugh, a release of tension. "Me too—but you know what?"

"Say."

"After we got straight? He was okay, for the longest time."

"How do you mean?"

"Ruck seemed happy. Like he had managed to forget what had been troubling him. But, that could also be a function of my own disease and recovery. What they call 'euphoric recall'. He was dry for a time back then, to be honest."

"But he was never sober. He told me."

"He told you?"

"Yeah—but he never mentioned your name, either."

"I'm sorry."

"It's fine. I'm salty. I got a marriage gone messy."

"I went through a couple, girl. Ain't showed the best judgement at times."

A bonding moment.

Chelsea, relaxing.

"That butthole never told us back then he had gotten straight for a year or two. When he come home after Daddy and all—Daddy's funeral—we hadn't seen him in ten years. Longer."

Millie went on to describe her life with Devin. How much he loved watching movies on the couch with her at night, discussing them afterwards. He read books about movies and how they were made, always poring over the boxes of used paperbacks that came through the thrift store in which they had both worked together. Worked, and loved, and drank, but only at first, before getting straight. Drove up into the mountain passes west of Boulder. The winding roads.

"I remember trying to kiss him one time when we stopped at one of those scenic turn-outs. He got so sad, so sudden, on me. He started drinking again not long after. And yeah—after he came home for the funeral, he returned like a different guy."

"Bless you for putting up with him."

"He's got his sweet side. Even when he's drunk."

Chelsea, watching her brother outside smoking at the patio table and rubbing his temples, understood what she meant. She had seen that old self again, here and there. Mostly there.

Millie coughed and blew her nose. "Ruck kept talking about how he was waiting for his lucky day to come along. He'd never explain what he meant by that."

"Why did he go out there to Colorado away?"

"Said he'd started driving one day and that's where he ended up—said he stopped when he got to the mountains. Which didn't make any sense to me, not really. In road movies, they're supposed to end up at the sea, aren't they?"

"Yeah. The ocean."

Millie's voice now came small. "I want you to know I tried to help him. It didn't take—but I tried."

"Did he ever tell you what happened? About the car wreck? About Libby?"

"Car wreck? Not a word."

"That scar on his forehead. You can't hardly see it."

"He said it's from some bar fight."

"No, not a bar fight."

"Was it bad, the wreck?"

"Real bad. The only two who wa'n't hurt bad was him and his cat."

Chelsea could hear Millie crying. "Prudy."

"That's right."

Now they both had had mysteries solved.

"Anything you want me to tell him? A phone number?"

Millie, rattling off digits, sent Chelsea scrambling and fumbling for a pen. She chicken-scratched a smeary number on the back of a thermal receipt from the Piggly Wiggly.

"Please tell him I'm eager to talk. When he's ready."

"I'll do what I can."

Chelsea caught her brother's aggrieved gaze from on the deck outside.

He made a hard, slashing gesture across his throat. Mouthing the words *hang the fuck up now*.

Devin was stubborn. His old girlfriend would have to wait. If she counted the days like Devin, and it sounded like she did, at least she'd learned patience.

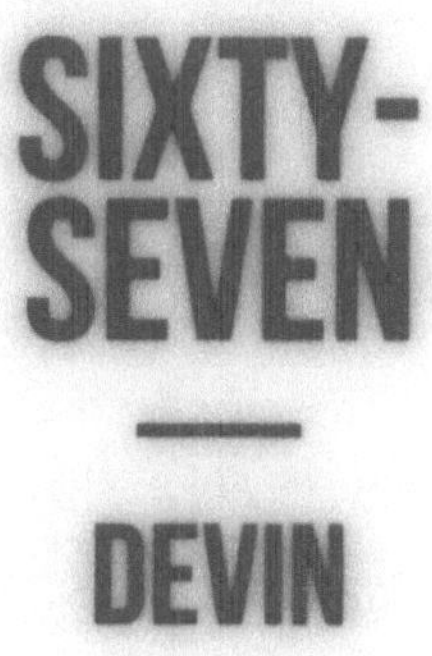



Devin, pitching his butt and cruising up the long ramp constructed along the front porch of the manufactured house, set back from the road on a weedy and sandy lot in a downmarket part of Edgewater County, had got up his nut. Had checkmarks to make on various lists of tasks, like making amends.

Dobbs and his mom lived outside the city limits of Tillman Falls, on the highway going to the airfield out past the high school. After all this time, the wood of the ramp had begun to look as weathered as the gray decking on the rear of the Rucker house. His daddy, if he were still around, would have long ago paid someone to pressure-wash it fresh again. Or done himself, more than likely. Devin would look into it.

Miriam Vandegrift opened the door with a sad smile. "There you are."

"Here I is."

"We were starting to wonder if you'd come calling. At all."

Two choices—shame, or in his case, self-deprecation. "Hey, I'm only fifteen years overdue."

The silence between them lengthy, her glare accusatory.

But she softened. "Get on in here, now. He's waiting."

Dobbs's mother, so stooped and old; he had only been able to picture the version he knew from childhood—dark-haired, slender. Musing how years of caring for a physically-challenged adult son had aged her, especially as she'd done it alone: Mr. Vandegrift, splitting the scene when Dobbs still young. Long before the tragedy. Their family, in his memory, always scraping by back when they were kids. Dobbs, eating over all the time. Always seeming so grateful. Their friendship had been an early window into class distinctions. Devin's daddy owned his own business, ran with the big wheels. Dobbs's daddy had fixed cars.

His heart fluttered and reflux fluxed. She led him inside by the elbow of the jean jacket, which his Mama had stain-treated and cleaned and stitched. He'd had Creedence sew one of those colorful dancing bears you see on bumper stickers, a Deadhead icon, over a gash in the side of the denim, one Devin claimed had come from another drunk's knife; over what issue, however, he couldn't, or wouldn't, say. His stories, no matter which ones told, were usually half made-up anyway.

Pausing, Dobbs's mother confided in a tight, hushed exhortation: "I've prayed and prayed, Devin; we prayed together over it, all these years. And tried to get him to see the truth. But he needs to hear it from you."

"Truth?" Yet knowing.

"He needs you to help him understand why."

"Why what? That a drunk passed on a double yellow line?"

Mrs. Vandegrift, hands wrinkled and gnarled by arthritis, working her fingers together in desperate supplication. "He thinks you've stayed away all this time because you've been mad at him. Because you blamed him."

Devin, writhing and hot all over. Cussing under his breath. Sweating. "I was ashamed. Not mad."

"I try to remind him about that drunk driver. How he run into y'all."

"Incontrovertibly so, ma'am."

"It is the truth, isn't it?"

Devin held out his meathooks. "I'm the jackleg who didn't see the truck in time. I been eat up with all that. Enough for both of us."

"No, son—we all know what happened. Those of us who choose to remember. Bless all your hearts."

Sober, unable to deny the truth, the facts unassailable in their fact-ness: No more fantasy, no more bullshit.

What happened, happened. The drunk ran into them.

So—what could have been done?

By Devin, Libby or Dobbs? Or Prudy, for that matter?

Everything.

Anything.

Another trip on another day, a traffic backup on I-26, a breakdown, a cop pulling over a big rig before the Tillman Falls/Chilton exit, a cop pulling them over, Prudy crawling into his lap, a flash of light, road construction, a dead dog, a rock hitting the windshield, a bug hitting the windshield, a stop for sodas or to pee out the beer they themselves had quaffed before getting behind the wheel—if not having a second one; it would have added another few minutes, no question—a sudden rain shower, another car accident, a leaf, a stone, a doorway in the sky opening up so the aliens could land at Jack Van Loan airfield over near campus in Columbia; how they had watched all through their time as students as small planes took off and landed, with Roy Earl commenting about one day purchasing his own aircraft.

Anything at all would have changed the timeline to place the tragic trio on a trajectory toward a different moment in a different space in a different universe from the one in which a drunk redneck going full-out down the two-lane blacktop, on the wrong side of the lines, obliterated the Mustang and everyone in it. Any little decision, it all goes another way. This mind-game had long driven Devin to have another forty drinks. Enough to stop saying what-if.

One bright interpretation? He'd read an article about some egghead's multiverse theory—all the timelines ran simultaneously in parallel. That meant lots of Libbys didn't die. They went their myriad ways. They were nearby now.

They lived.

But absent variables coming into play, the three friends and the cat were in this timeline placed where they were at that moment in the great unfolding of their personal history, fated, and nothing then or now to change the outcome... except in the imagination.

But real was real.

No movie magic to save the damsel.

No rewriting the screenplay now.

Change the title to Forever Facing College Street, maybe? That's the only revision they needed.

Hell—he'd sort it out, finally, by talking it through with the man in the wheelchair, endless in his patience, who waited for his old friend in the Southern sunshine pouring onto the screened-in porch.

Devin stood on a patch of worn outdoor Astroturf behind the wheelchair. "All right now, Dobbie—whatcha know good?"

Dobbs's body jerked, spasmodic, at the sound. He twisted around.

No words at first.

"Well."

"Yep."

Staring, speaking, saying simply:

"It's been a long time."

Devin, no courage to display, no sense of propriety needed; took two shambling steps forward and fell to his knees at Dobbs's feet. He mewled in quiet, aggrieved sibilance for absolution.

A string of gobbledygook, snot running out of his nose.

As though he'd been drinking.

Yet not.

Not this time.

Dobbs, stroking Devin's head, patted him on the back. Sniffling and drawing his own shaky breaths, he said, "Hush, son. Get up, now."

Devin, doing so far too quickly, became dizzy. He stabilized himself with the cane. He not only saw stars but suffered one of the awful flashes, too, of Dobbs's twisted body by the roadside. This symptom of PTSD, the disease Devin had been self-medicating for so many years, still flared up all the time. Banishing this phantom, seen here in the face of the real man, and most assuredly not in the form of an alcohol-induced hallucination, would push the one-day program to its limits.

His friend.

Real as the day was long.

Despite him being the one who'd squalled and collapsed like one of them old busted twin towers up in New York, Devin asked, "You all right?"

"The world outside endures—Eudora Welty wrote that."

"How about the inside world?"

Dobbs, shifting again in his chair, grimaced and lifting his arms, heavy, in a shrug.

He had other things on his mind: "I reckon you been resting all summer. Taking it easy around the house."

"Yeah. I been recovering from multiple mishaps, you could say."

"I was afraid you wouldn't be able to walk. Like me. When I heard how you fell."

Self-loathing filled him up the way a fried chicken supper did, with a dollop of guilt like fluffy mashed potatoes awaiting gravy—real potatoes, not flakes out of a packet. "Mama says I'm way too young for a cane."

"Took the words," he said, rolling his chair back and making room for Devin to sit on the white patio chair by a small glass coffee table on which lay stacks of books, magazines, the last few editions of the EDGEWATER ADVOCATE and the COLUMBIA RECORD. "Sit."

Devin had gotten around the county, all right, but not to see Dobbs. Had seen Libby's mother, in a nursing home up in Greenville; she had not recognized him, which made the visit short, merciful and pointless. Calling Libby's older brothers, both of whom he supposed, had turned into thick, graying middle-aged men rather than the thirty year-old lanky young bucks he remembered. Shelby Fordham, lots of phone calls and visits—she had the sweets for him, bless her heart. Yeah—since he'd been back, Devin had avoided no one, really, except Dobbs.

And the cemetery.

Devin? A goddamned selfish sonofabitch if he'd ever seen one.

"I been laying low, buddy-row. Sure enough."

A wan smile. "I heard you took a hard knock."

"One in a series." He had some weird vision issues, headaches and assorted shit, but what was new. "But I'm all right now."

Mrs. Vandegrift, fussing around, said, "Now that my boys are both here together—finally—what do we want to eat or drink?"

"Nothing, ma'am."

"Do y'all want some sandwiches and Cokes? Or Devin, do you drink coffee? I can make some real quick now—it's probably not as good as what you're used to: it's just Folger's, but we like it right good."

"Nothing, Mama."

"So—what can I get y'all?"

Dobbs, half-shouting. "We don't need nothing right now. If Devin wanted something, he'd say so." Turning to Devin. "You need anything?"

A reassuring head-shake. "I don't want for much, ma'am. All set."

Glaring. "See? *See?* Lord have mercy, but I wish you'd get out from under me today."

Chastened, hesitating, wanting to be included. "I'll just go look at my stories. Maybe I can fix y'all a snack later."

Dobbs and Devin sipped sweet tea that, despite their protestations, his doting mother served them anyway.

A fan with filthy blades turning and squeaking. The dog dishes, a poodle who skittered around inside on tiny claws and looked freshly groomed, and that had growled at him. Old junk out here, a rusty washer and dryer Devin remembered them buying at Sears back in 1983.

"Y'all ought to haul this old crap off to the dump. I'll help, if you want."

"What are supposed to use for a washer and dryer?"

Not-junk. "Oh."

Dobbs, at last posing a question, one loaded like no other—much of their time thus far had been spent with Devin spinning tales of ribald debauchery from his days lost in the funhouse, as he termed the period. Avoiding, for the longest time, any talk about that day on the road. Until, out of the blue:

"How much you remember?"

"More than I care to admit," Devin said. "You?"

Dobbs, squinting into the middle distance. "Not even the last couple of days before. All a big old blur, like a hole in there."

"Sounds familiar. Lost about a week leading up to me falling down them stairs like a dumb-ass. Last thing I remember is sitting in a bar called Chubby's out in Colorado, yapping on the phone with Billy about driving down to Texas." Chortling. "Billy says we had us a time there, and in N'awlins, too."

"It ended up saving you, in a way."

"What did?"

"Your fall."

"Least I got to sleep through detox."

Dobbs, *hm-hming* and *tsk-tsking*, occasionally swatted at gnats sneaking in through a rip in the screen. Devin thought he should fix it for them.

"May I tell you something?"

"Shoot, pard."

Dobbs—furtive, fidgety, hesitant—struggled to find the words.

Devin picked at his mustache, which unlike his still-stubby haircut he had let grow out to handlebar territory, asked, "What is it, hombre?"

"I hold onto this stupid fantasy." Dobbs, looking everywhere but Devin's eyes. "This ridiculous, dumb fantasy."

"It's me. You can tell old Ruck anything."

"I used to think about you coming back. And doing what we were talking about. Before the accident."

"What were we talking about? Before the accident?"

"What Libby suggested."

Feeling obtuse. "Spill it."

"About us all being roommates."

Devin's breath catching—of course. "You were going to move in with us in Arcadia." That fall, Dobbs, planning to live in the other bedroom where Billy'd ended up. A detail, not so much misremembered as lost in the maelstrom. "Weren't you."

His chin quivered. "If only."

Grabbing one of Dobbs's hands. "Might've-beens are for losers. And drunks."

Fighting off tears, haughty to the point of anger. "But it isn't mere nostalgia, Devin. I can't live with my Mama the rest of my life, now can I? Who's going to take care of me when—damn, son, she's old, now," lowering his voice. "I'm gonna die alone."

"*Beau*." Devin, panicked but concealing this through his usual sardonic sanguinity. "We'll get your ass squared away. I'm right around the freaking corner." Patting his knee. "Relax, chief. I'm not staying away like before."

Skeptical, Dobbs squinted against the blazing western sun now dipping toward the tops of the pine trees. "It'll be for the best. I'll die here alone, go home to Jesus and be done with it."

"Get out of here with that shit. You got a long time to live. Or, you don't. That's the game. That's the rub. So, yeah—you might die in this house. But not tonight. And not anytime soon. So give it a rest, drama queen."

Dobbs, deep in introspection, chin resting on his chest, rocked back and forth in the chair. "Thank god for my books, at least. Especially the Good one. That's one you ought to get more familiar with."

Devin, ignoring the bible reference. "Reading something good, are you? That's about all I do anymore. Like when I was a kid."

"Reading helps me forget."

"Word to that."

"But forgetting—that's been your biggest problem, hasn't it?"

"More to it than the forgetting. But, sure."

"You got to let me witness to you."

An ambush. Devin, waving him away. "Might as well save your breath."

"But I have to. You don't know how long I've waited." Desperate and beseeching, his bug-eyes reminded Devin of Eileen at her most shrill and demonstrative. "*I must.*"

Devin's instincts suggested flight, but the stark fact remained: he indeed owed his friend much, beginning with the courtesy of a listen.

And so, sitting with quiet patience, Devin nodded and *mm-hm*'d as Dobbs discoursed about Jesus and angels and light and a happiness beyond reason, an assurance beyond emotion, and how he knew in his heart that one day he'd walk again—upon streets of gold. How this answer, the answer of answers, lay hidden in all hearts, with only the search necessary to reveal the treasure. "'Ask and ye shall receive' is more than words."

Devin, nodding and counting the seconds until release. "Sounds good."

Noting with a degree of quizzical interest that his pious friend, once as irreligious as they'd come, seemed unable to look him in the eye. Dobbs, speaking with a stammering and quavering lack of a certain certitude one ought to expect from a person of such considerable and demonstrable faith. Devin, starting to wonder who between them needed convincing the most.

"Tell me: Can you feel what it's like to be alive anymore? Sitting here feeling sorry for yourself all this time? Can you?"

Dobbs, shocked by the impertinence, snapped his head around. "Edward Devin Rucker. Hush your mouth."

"Well?"

Dobbs, his ire deflating, gestured from the middle of his abdomen up to his face. "From about here up. You butthole."

"The part that works includes that big-old heart of yours, don't it?"

"I reckon."

"And what does your heart tell you about me? That I can be saved? That any of us can truly be saved in some fashion that makes all this crap add up to something? Saved like leftovers after Thanksgiving? Turkey sandwiches, for all eternity? Never running out, always tasting yummy and good and not all dried out?"

Ignoring the silly Thanksgiving metaphor. "You don't understand—my faith has made this bearable. After I took the Lord into my heart, it all made sense. You need to get you some of what I got going, son."

Devin, his skepticism a manifest, living organism all its own there on the crummy, cluttered back porch, dragged his gaze across the stand of longleaf pines, the fallen needles a carpet of rust, the trees autumnal brown and looking dry and thirsty. "I don't believe you. It's all an act."

"Oh, you little recalcitrant turd."

"I didn't come to listen to this. I came to see Dobbs."

Moist eyes unable to meet those of his friend. "'Dobbs died in the car that day. I'm nothing."

"That what being saved gets you? 'Nothing'?"

"Oh—p'shaw, Devin. Kiss my ass." He stuck out his tongue.

Now there, the old Dobbs. Devin smiled.

Yuck-yucking, the good old boy persona back in force: "Looky here, I'll tell you what's 'nothing'—this sky-pilot act you been putting on like it's some kinda durn Easter pageant. Them legs a your'n might not work, but up here?" He tapped his temple with the corner of his faithful Zippo. "You're so full of shit them blue eyes is a-turning brown. I swear to god-all-mighty if they ain't."

"Maybe you should go." Dobbs, verging on squirting a few. "You little pissant."

"God knows I probably should. But I just got here." Devin, slapping his knee with a sound that came sharp and sudden like a Snap'n Pop thrown in a quiet hollow school corridor during the middle of classes. "There, see? I got religion. Unbidden, I invoked the name of the Lord."

"Oh, *hell*." Dobbs, throwing hands into the air. "A body could go funny in the head thinking about all this mess. If only there was some kind of sign. To help explain."

"Wouldn't hold my breath."

"I believe, Ruck. But it's hard. It's a narrow way, as the book says."

Devin dropped his cornpone routine. "You want to know what I was up to for the last fifteen years? Looking for a sign, too. Or so I thought. An explanation I could buy—about Libby, about other stuff. But you know, funniest thing is that I thought I had it. I sure did. For the longest time, I thought I had been told secrets by someone, and damn if it didn't turn out... that it was true."

Rueful. Dobbs said, "Secrets. Now, that's something I know all about."

Devin, cursing himself, embittered with self-reproach, continued, "The only real secret I got told, though, was by Libby that day on the side of the road, with that lucky old sun beating down on us. I didn't realize it, but I had my answer. When the light went out of her eyes—? In her last breath came the big reveal. I couldn't see it then for what it was."

Anticipatory, Dobbs begged to know.

"That whatever we are right now—how much we love and live, sing and dance and drink and fuck and all that shit—in the end this body of ours ain't nothing but wormfood, and what we really are?"

"Yes?"

"I don't know that 'we' don't go somewhere different once 'this' is over. Someplace better. So maybe we're closer on metaphysics than farther apart."

Dobbs, sighing. "'This' can't be the end of everything."

"You don't want to live forever." A statement.

"Not live-*live*. But in a way, I mean."

"Like this?" Pointing to the wheel chair.

"No."

Devin, ruminative. "Maybe the answers and the questions are the same damn thing all going in a circle, with us stuck in the middle watching it all go around. Thinking we got a handle on what it is that's happening here. And so that's where I reckon I'll stay for now. Somewhere in the middle, watching it all spin around like my skivvies in Mama's dryer. I can live with that—I think."

"Maybe we could work on these questions. Together."

Devin, contemplative and melancholy with nostalgic awe. "We used to have this same damn conversation back when you and Roy Earl were getting all high-minded, so to speak. Didn't we."

"When you were Devin instead of Ruck. Yes. I miss those days. But, listen." Dobbs, hesitant and quiet: "Could you find me some?"

"Some what?"

"You know."

His gears ground. It took him a minute. "Wait—*weed?*"

Dobbs, hands up. "That used to be my happy place."

"I'll talk to Billy. If you think it might help."

"What do I have to lose?"

Afternoon into evening, sun gone down and the birds quieting, Devin arranged with Miriam to take Dobbs back over to the house for dinner. Calling home and hearing Eileen and Creedence both squealing and joyous.

Miriam, as well, delighted beyond measure. Now seeming not so much left out as gratified and thankful to Devin for his attention, his care of her son and his feelings.

And Devin, happy to drive Dobbs in his mom's customized van with its wheelchair lift. At Dobbs's behest Devin cranked up Led Zeppelin on the classic rock station; they cackled at the DJ, Doober Dougie, who'd been on Columbia radio for thirty years doing his rush hour drive-time routine. Devin, the Edgewater County wind on his face, felt the years melt away; they were the same best friends again, like back in the day when they would cruise around, sometimes with Roy Earl, listening to heavy rock and contemplating the geologic time of their lives that lay ahead in misty, inscrutable mystery.

Devin, pleased—if not yet enjoying complete and total closure, then at least approximating a feeling long foreign in his enduring march of emptiness and pain: now that they'd reconnected, he felt an unfamiliar sensation, something in the ballpark of relief. As with the eternal question of how to make love stay, would that the quiescence of his inner turmoil fraught with circular snake-eaten tails deign to persist.

Sketching and concentrating, Chelsea sat in the bright light at the front door with Bootsy, a petite, chubby tortie-girl who lolled in the sun and stretched out the black pads of her paws. A peaceful easy, feeling, like the soft classic rock on the radio.

She had been sitting in this spot with kitty-cats her whole life.

Here, she was safe—Bootsy, as well as her cat-mommy.

The thick drafting pencil felt good in her hand. Her expertise growing, Creedence, acquiring chops like she'd never had—as a girl she'd never worked hard enough, this she knew.

If she had? Maybe she wouldn't be sitting here trying to get said chops back.

But who'd encouraged her, other than her late father?

No one—and in the case of her mother, an active discouragement of anything resembling dreams, any course of action that would allow the child to go off and become an adult with its own sense of itself. Difficulty in understanding this condition, still, but as with an alcoholic, acknowledging the reality of a given problem the first and most crucial step to fixing it.

Mama, hanging in there. But so tired these days. She's handing off some of her bookkeeping work with the ELMS to a younger member, Rebecca LaFreniere—ugh. Yeah, pretty, tall, talented Becky LaFreniere, who had been one of the snooty rich bitches back in high school, way smart too, who went off to New York to be an actress for a while, which obviously didn't work out, but still. Who had never so much as looked at gawky Colette Rucker back then, and now only out of the corner of her eyes as she came to visit her mentor Eileen to have coffee and be trained in keeping the books.

What a doofus Chelsea had been, then as now. Who could blame Becky for ignoring her?

But Chelsea, time at last to catch up—the news had come that she'd been accepted into Southeastern, another milestone in her massive do-over that unfolded over the course of the tumultuous year. A year that'd been as full of change as any she could remember since Devin's car wreck. That had ended up causing the loss of both him and Libby, despite the fact that he had lived.

College. She prayed the young kids wouldn't make fun of her.

The idea hadn't sunk in, perhaps because when she thought of leaving—of moving only as far as Columbia, for heaven's sake—her stomach fell. Fear crawled all over her skin like the imaginary bugs Devin had described squiggling on his skin whenever he would try to detox himself from one of his epic benders, back when he'd been lost in what he kept calling 'the wasteland.' "*Just give us the gasoline,*" he'd always growl right afterwards, "*and we'll spare your lives.*"

Her brother, a grade-A nut job.

Chelsea, worrying and fretting about how to help him. His ability to stay sober. His plan for the future. At least he had gone earlier to see Dobbs. She wondered how it was going.

Toying with a suggestion—that after Christmas, they share an apartment together in Columbia. Not only to share expenses, but also for reasons of feeling maternal toward her long-lost, prodigal brother. Saying, he has returned as I'd desired, so I must keep and help him.

*I will protect him.*

In many ways, Creedence, in awe again of her brother—not exactly as two decades before when he'd been her teenage boy hero, hurtling toward manhood and freedom, no; instead, now incredulous at his having made his way back from the Purgatory of the wretched life carved out for himself after the accident. When, as he'd explained, his only goal had been a lonesome, drunken death, "On the side of the road somewhere—like Libby. But hard as I tried, it wouldn't never come. I always arrived alive. It beat all you ever seen."

Her blood had run cold. "I'm just glad you didn't hurt nobody else."

Devin, bitter, unrepentant. "Didn't I, though?"

He seemed most brokenhearted, in a way, whenever Prudy came up, the memory of whom haunted him like all the rest. She finally asked why.

"It's because I left her out west. Buried her in the woods, a real nice spot by a stream, and that's where she lays still." His face, a ghostly, pale shrunken skull. His hands, shaking. He licked his lips, wiped his mouth with the back of his hand. "But now I ain't got a place to go and remember her."

"You laid her to rest. She's with Libby again."

"The cat was the only thing what kept me going all that time. If you can believe it."

"My fur-babies? They're everything to me."

"Then you get it."

Two ideas, hitting her like near-simultaneous thunderclaps. Devin's Christmas presents would be covered by what the commercials called *unique holiday gift ideas*.

That only she could give him.

First, one designed to help him see through the tears and the pain, to remember the good times for once instead of the hurt, and this piece she could produce herself; a new test of her artistic and creative abilities.

The other, a final bit of closure for him and Prudy. That one she'd need help in procuring. She knew a place.

Christmas, important this year—with Devin the way he was, and Mama with her illness? Who knew when they would all be together again.

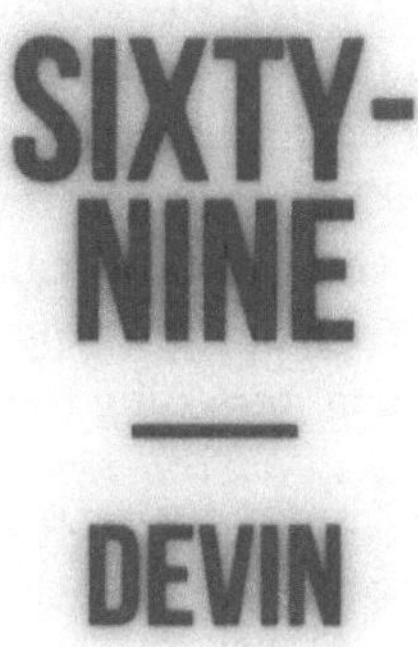




The scene deserved a title card, Devin later thought, like in a 1980s Woody Allen feature Libby had thought so profound, that they had seen early in their relationship; the one about the three sisters.

In any case, lousy timing for tensions to bubble—a day at the oncologist with his mom. No good news to be had.

But the biggest issue, bigger than her own death, was keeping her prognosis a secret from little 'Colette.'

What a crock.

Creedence wasn't oblivious.

Everyone was pretending.

He didn't make a fuss. Eileen's spirit and drive for control too strong. She projected an energy field like Sue Storm, the Invisible Girl. You could smell her will in the air, like ozone.

Eileen, thin as a stick and picking fussily at a pile of lima beans, told one of her fibs about how she and Devin had gone furniture shopping in Columbia that morning. Not to the doctor.

"I didn't like the prices I saw, though. Mercy, me. And driving in Columbia? Shut the door. I was terrified the whole time I was in that damn city. I tell you—I just don't know."

Creedence, her face as though carved out of stone, knew where it was headed. Loaded for bear. "You don't know what, mother?"

"About all your little—your little plans for the new year."

"My 'little' plans? Do tell."

"Oh, it's so much to think about—you moving out. This whole mess."

Devin, slurping up Mama-slop into his beak, reeled at the surreal nature of it all. Smacking and talking through his food like Brad Pitt, he knew not what to do except pretend right along with them:

"Mama, what's done is done." He gestured with a forkful of taters and gravy at his sister. "That's your daughter sitting there, ain't she?"

"*What's that supposed to mean?*" They almost said it unison.

"She's stubborn. There's nothing nobody can do."

Creed, whose eyes were red from drawing all day, said, "What mother wouldn't be happy about her daughter going to college?"

His fork against iced tea glass, *tink tink tink*. "Now, ladies." With their full attention: "Mama, this's your last chance to give her your blessing."

"*Last chance?* What on earth?"

Devin's face flushed hot. "Before she moves on with her life."

"'Moves on'. How melodramatic." Coughing.

"Mama, it ain't like I'm moving on from you. He means from Dusty and his mess."

"Say the words. Say the words to her, or I'll be damned if I won't stab you with this fork in that black heart of your'n."

It had turned into a prison yard brawl. Eileen barked with mocking laughter at her own son. "Devin, you ain't got the nerve to stick a fork in me."

Now he sounded like a TV newsreader: "*In other news, a drunken Edgewater County redneck drown-ded his Mama in a pot of chicken necks she had been boiling. Bystanders reported that the argument seemed to over the last packet of cigarettes in the house. As the facts emerge, we'll feature even more details on this horrific crime of passion.*" He busted out laughing. "What'll Rebecca LaFreniere and Ruth DeKalb and them think when they see us on TV, huh? Hoo-boy."

His jester act worked. They both sat waiting, neither looking at the other.

"What words, son. *Tell me what you want me to say.*"

"You know what, you goddamn hardheaded Edgewater County pack-mule."

"No, I don't."

"Tell her how proud you are of her taking charge of her life." Raising his iced tea to Creedence, a salutation that, coming from him, might have been taken for sarcasm. But not this time. "Finally."

"My own daughter knows how I feel about her."

"Do it, woman."

Eileen made a show of lighting up, grumbled about being addressed with such impertinence and high-minded, confusing drivel at her own damned supper table, at last coughed and began:

"If this university adventure is what you've got it in your bonnet to try, darling? Then you go on and move over to that damn city, and that damn university with all those people you don't know—blacks and Mexicans and Chinese, weirdos and perverts and drugheads and drunks? And, since I guess that's what your stubborn self has made up its hard-headed little mind to do, that's what you'll do."

Creedence, fake-grinning and bugeyed with irritation. "Which is the case. Yes."

"But here's the problem. I think it's so *late* now to be worrying with going to college."

"Late how?"

Hushed, humiliated. "You're over thirty years-old now, darling. Women with husbands don't go to college at thirty. They raise families."

Devin snorted. "Somewhere I hear the LEAVE IT TO BEAVER theme, Mama. Mercy."

"I tried that. Remember?" Creedence suffered a quivering chin. "I tried it. And fucked it up big-time."

"Colette—watch your mouth at this table."

"Yeah, you little motherfucker."

Devil-eyes at the son. He could but wink back.

Devin, noting the vibration in the room now cranked to eleven—ever since sobering up, extraordinary in his sensitivity to people's energies. Maybe he always had been. Hell, maybe that's why he liked to get stupid with drink, its soporific beneficence having proved numbing to his empathetic tendencies.

Mama lowered her voice. "Be that as it may, but divorcées in their thirties traipsing off to college to prove some point, why, it sounds positively ludicrous. Giving up a good home and husband to run off all willy-nilly with a pile of zit-faced teenagers almost half your age? As though you can do things over and make them all different, somehow?" She gazed to the ceiling, prayerful. "Lord have mercy on them, they know not what they do."

"Higher power," Devin mumbled, sipping tea. "Yep yep."

"Now, what you ought to be doing instead of all that mess is *trying to make another sweet little baby with your husband Dusty—*"

"—Mama, I swear, don't go there again—"

"—before it's too late."

"That train has left. Thank god."

"Lord help me. And I had taken to calling you and Dusty 'established' to the others downtown," a euphemism for her fellow ELMS. "I'm humiliated beyond measure. Humiliated," she wept.

"By my going to college."

*Boo-hoo-hoo*, Eileen said.

Devin produced the Zippo, *snap*, the first inhalation and humming to himself with commercial-worthy consumer satisfaction on his face; listening and gazing at his cigarette with affection, a loyal little pack of pals consistent in their friendship, carried close in a breast pocket nestled next to his flopping, thin-walled heart.

He thought it time to referee and bring everyone down to earth. No one may have wanted to discuss the fact this his mother had only months to live, so they may as well pretend, for an evening, to like one another.

"Mama here knows you deserve a second chance. Like I got one. She's just gonna miss you, angel face." He reached across to Eileen's bumpy, arthritic claw lying on the table by her ashtray. "We're both gonna miss you."

Eileen cussed and shoved his hand away. "I have plenty to occupy my time. I'm only being realistic about her chances of a return on the investment. Colette had no need to go to college, any more than you did, son. Look at what that wrought, in your case." Scoffing and bitter. "If I may say so. Your father's dream, like all entrepreneurs, was to apprentice you into the insurance trade like him. But you never even gave him the chance."

Devin, all pretense of amusement vanishing. All that talk skittered off him, but she needed to encourage the girl. If this pretense was to earn its worth and long stay at the Rucker mansion.

Not much time left.

Seriously.

His lips, working in soundless fury.

Damn if she didn't get him, though. Again. Like she always had.

His mother.

But Chelsea—Creedence—erupted on her own. Screaming like a crazy-woman, her plate of food went sailing across the room with a crash. Ginger-tom Arthur exploded from his perch on the empty, fourth chair—Dwight's chair—to bolt wild-eyed across the table straight through the platter of fried chicken, planting one hind foot with gray litter box grit between the pad smack-dab in the middle of a Pyrex dish full of creamed corn; the cat leapt off the table in a huge arc and scampered out of the room as though El Diablo Gato himself in furious pursuit. A further stampede, a symphony of sharp kitty-claws skittering against hardwood flooring; the mad scramble continued all the way up the stairs.

Devin, for his part, had come out of his chair, knocking both the lit cigarette into his lap. He did a shimmying Devin-dance, slapping burning tobacco from his jeans.

The energy settled. Creamed corn ran down the canvas of a Thomas Kinkade print which the cat had flung from its paws. Mama and Creedence both had visible auras, hot red light all around their heads. Devin tried not to bust a gut.

"For god sakes—look at this *mess*."

"I'm sorry." Creedence, her head in her hands. "I'll clean it up."

"Damn right you will." Coughing. "I don't know what's wrong with you. Either one of you."

"Devin wanted to give you a chance to tell me, for once, you thought I was doing the right thing."

*"The two of you wouldn't know the right thing if it come up out the commode and bit you both on them dimpled little pink butts I used to wipe."*

But for all her vitriol, Devin, noting that his mother's words came weak and weary. His Mama, barely able to get out of bed in the mornings. Time was short. She considered embarking on a course of radiation for a fresh spot of cancer on a nearby bone to the main tumor. He hoped she wouldn't, nor that any reasonable doctors would dare prescribe such a course of treatment. Not in her frail condition.

Devin, peering into her cloudy, tearstained eyes, the blue so pale against the red of her hair and thinking, *How my sister's matured into such a beauty.* Watching her take long walks and eating salads, her freedom from Dusty melting away a layer of ennui and dissatisfaction like snakeskin, molting off and revealing a fresh face. Devin, wanting her to succeed, to grow. His mother wouldn't be around to see in any case.

"At least Uncle Hill says it's time for me to get on with my life," Creedence said, clearing the table. "At least I got that going for me."

"That's because he loves you." Devin, a quiet, affectionate tone, regarding with newfound marvel his sister's cute, freckled features. "Like his own daughter."

Mama, pausing in the doorway, catching Devin's eye. "Of course he does."

Creedence, ignoring her mother to focus on Devin: "Him and Daddy were like brothers, he always says. He showed me a picture he carries in his wallet from when him and their other friends were in high school together. I thought he was gonna cry when he showed it to me."

"The bond between men is strong," Mama said.

Devin, a moment of grace—none of it mattered. Every bad feeling he'd ever experienced faded away, all problems and horrors mitigated, the feeling of connection with his sister, and his mother, like being washed in the blood.

He went to Creedence, held out his arms. She set Mr. Bubbie, who had jumped up on the table and started licking corn, down on Dwight's empty chair. A hug, held, the bussing of cheeks. "I missed my little sister."

"We're gonna make up for lost time."

"You betcha."

Creedence, yelling into the kitchen where their mother stood stooped over the sink, scrubbing dishes like always: "Mama, I'm gonna go find Arthur and Pickles. I done scared them half to death. Then I'll help in yonder."

"Just let me take care of it," Eileen called. "You'd just be in the way."

"See? That's why I never learned to cook worth a poot. She didn't never have no patience with me in the kitchen."

Devin, plopping back down in his chair, picked up Creedence's unfinished tea. He sipped and fished around in the cigarette pack with his free hand, finding one lone, crooked smoke waiting to be sparked.

At the last second, Devin, reconsidering. He put his brave soldier back into the reserves to wait for a later skirmish with his lungs.

He watched his mother dumping cat-adulterated food into the garbage disposal. He stood in silence until Eileen glanced, furtive, at him in the kitchen doorway.

"Oh—you scared the mess out of me."

"Let me ask you something, girlfriend."

Eileen's eyes shone like two opaque, hard stones set deep in the recesses of her brow. Her cheeks hung hollow. Displeasure with her firstborn oozed out of her like a fog. "Now what, son?"

"You did love Daddy. Didn't you, Mama?"

Those cold old eyes cut across the room and sliced into him. Her floral-print housecoat hung loose on her body as she dried her hands. "I had to, didn't I?"

He asked what she meant.

"He was your Daddy—wasn't he?"

"I never thought about it that way."

"Of course I loved him. Now you best watch your smart mouth in there," she admonished, "in front of your baby sister. Is that understood?"

"Yes, ma'am."

"It better be. And if you ever ask me such filth again, I'm going to whip your ass like I did when you were little. Like no time has passed at all."

"Mama—I believe you would."

Cursing, she went back to the dirty dishes, slamming the Pyrex almost hard enough to break it.

Only after closing the swinging door behind him did he let out his breath, bitter and hot. Swearing in the dim gloom of his past, a museum exhibit of his adolescent predilections, that neither tears nor rage would salve what ailed him. Struggling for over an hour with the compulsion to go.

Get.

Potted like a plant.

But holding fast. Shaking it off.

What'd occurred with Eileen, he said to himself, was good enough. Nothing left to say, not at least between him and his mother. A moment, this. What had he expected?

He enjoyed a realtime epiphany: 'this' surely had to represent growth. Was any of what went on with his folks and their friends his business?

Mulling it over in his old room he began to feel stuffy and stale, trapped inside a musty tomb in need of a good airing-out.

His sister had the right idea—to escape Edgewater County seemed like a plan, the first real one since his resurrection. Whatever enthusiasm he mustered, however, also came tempered by notions of a few chores remaining undone.

T'weren't anything earth-shattering.

Nothing he couldn't pull off.

Only paying tribute to Libby, finally.

*No sweat—I got this.*

# SEVENTY
—
## CREEDENCE

Her holiday drawing project, not only the most complex and challenging piece she'd ever attempted but also an important family Christmas gift, interrupted:

Again.

By Billy Steeple.

Calling now almost every day.

Hinting at first, now more direct about how the two of them 'getting together'—to catch up, as he kept suggesting—had become his 'primary action item.' Must be some university speak.

Together. To discuss Devin's progress. And whatever else arose.

*Arose.* His word.

Whatever his intentions, the idea, thrilling and naughty.

A stumbling block—Chelsea, wondering if Billy's little trophy-girl would be in attendance.

In a rush of hot resentment, with envy green like puke gushing from Linda Blair's mouth, she blotted out Melanie's face, her existence. Assumed she'd done wrong by Billy, treated him poorly in the sack and otherwise.

Yes—she hadn't been a good lover to him.

A hungry divorcée like Creedence? Mercy. She'd do him right. Billy was no fool.

Would let him do it over and again and over again.

*Now let's make up for lost time.* She planned this practiced catch phrase for the moment when, gently and patiently and in a state of high romance, he at last slipped inside her.

For now, however, it was only another hot bath night. Which helped for a few blissful moments of release. Afterwards, however, left empty and alone but for Devin, her sick Mama and all the cats.

A voice deep inside whispered how she might need more than a good lay; that this path with Billy could be wrong.

She ignored the advice. It wasn't the first time. Billy: an inevitability, now.

But the irritating good girl inside remembered again how her fantasy man already stood spoken for, and by a woman far more attractive and intelligent than Kookie Colette Rucker could ever hope to become.

And furthermore, wondering with a kind of self-consciously icky awe, what right did some dumb cracker from Chilton had to take Billy away from a rich, beautiful Pinckney girl from Charleston?

None.

Chelsea, nothing, a nobody. Jerking off in a bathtub in the middle of nowhere.

Pathetic.

And yet, Billy, calling again. Persistent in his need to make breathy, seemingly innocuous small talk.

Until murmuring: "Creedence—later on, if you could meet me soon, I want to eat out your asshole."

She couldn't speak. "*You want to do what?*"

"Don't you know how much courage that took?"

"Billy—I—there's no way I understood you right."

"God, I hate these fucking cell phones. I *said*, I hope you could meet me, 'if it's no hassle,' as I put it."

"Oh."

Her gut, like ice. How to play it.

Coy.

Coy was what men wanted. Wasn't it?

"My goodness. Meet to do *what*, exactly?"

Billy, at first making it sound like coffee, or lunch. To reminisce; to see if anything he could do for Devin or Ruck, as Billy always called him.

Then, as though she were dreaming, he said the words, she could hear them like a clear-chiming bell from on high:

"Fuck this. I'm through being cool, reserved and discrete, Creedence Rucker. Here it is. I'm—I've fallen in love with you."

"*You have?*"

"Yes. I'm calling you to arrange a rendezvous, in the parlance of olden times. I love you, and I must have you. And there's nothing for it but to come clean. If you'll agree to this, every dream you ever had will come true."

Creedence, telling this amazing man she didn't know what to say. That this couldn't be real. Like when she'd walked down the aisle with Dusty—unreal, but not a good unreal like this.

How she'd almost been a runaway bride.

How Mama had all but tied her up the night before.

How she harbored doubts. Said so.

"I know, I know—he asks on the phone? For real? What a dolt—"

"—oh, no, I didn't—

"—and of course you know I preferred saying all that in person."

She sat waiting. A single syllable escaped, a hushed whisper. "When."

"This afternoon?"

"Where?"

"A hotel downtown. It's a Marriott property, at Hampton and Main."

"All right. I can get there about—about—two."

"Perfect. Plenty of time to get my freak—rather, finish up some pressing work here."

She didn't know what else to say. "You—shall I bring a bottle of wine?"

He chuckled. Said all that would be more than arranged.

"Creedence?"

Her voice broke: "Y-yes?"

"I'm eager for us to make up for all the lost time."

She drew in her breath. Their minds as one, like with Mr. Spock on one of those old STAR TREK shows Devin sat around watching half the day on DVDs he checked out of the Edgewater County Public Library.

"I can't think of nothing to say, Billy. Anything to say, I mean. Except—well, I'm real eager, too."

"We've wasted so many years, haven't we?"

They had.

But today? Too soon. She needed to get fixed up right for him. The panic in her gut, not a good sign. She looked a fright today as it was.

"Wait, I can't. Mama's got—an appointment."

"Drat. Really?"

"Tomorrow? Please?"

"But angel—"

"Billy, is one more day too long to wait? Tell me it isn't. Please."

He cleared his throat. "Well. All right. A little delay will only make the end result all the better."

"Won't it? If we wait a little?"

"Indeed. The extra day will no-question provide for an extra-fizzy frisson of excitement. You cruel bitch—*I freaking love you for this.*"

To hear him calling her a cruel bitch in that ironic, Gen X way felt liberating and validating.

Yeah—screw Melanie Pinckney. Miss Priss had plenty of time to find another college boy for herself on campus.

"I think I might be in love with you, too." But the words—they didn't feel right in her mouth. "Thank you, Billy."

They rang off—same time, next day.

Breathless, with tension inside that felt like a stomachache, Chelsea next hurried herself making a variety of personal care appointments. These were important, yeah, but tomorrow was also the day Devin said he was taking Mama for her first bone cancer treatment, and how Creedence should keep pretending—for now—until he could see how well the old coot handled being irradiated. That way the house would be empty, and she wouldn't have to explain to anyone about her naughty errand all the way down in Columbia.

She knew the timing was bad on all this. She had to choose, though—Mama, or her future. Creedence chose.

# SEVENTY-ONE
## —
### DEVIN

Devin, reclining on the sofa in the living room of Roy Earl's duplex, hummed and waited for his buddy to finish an important, breathless businessman-type phone call.

The living room belied his pal's station—looked much the same as any other college-guy pad in the campus neighborhood: books on cinder block bookshelves, a Grateful Dead poster, a wall of books, CDs and DVDs like most kids all had.

But Roy Earl's junk held the smell of money about it. All the stereo gear was top-shelf, the kitchen of the old brick bungalow up in Herndon Hill above the Old Market tricked out in up-to-the-minute stainless steel and granite, cabinets full of exotic spices and interesting dry goods as though the good-old boy on his way to becoming some kind of hipster chef.

Roy. Who'd-a thunk it about that honkytonk man's grandson from Tillman Falls? Boy wasn't no redneck, not like Devin went around portraying. Roy used to talk about wanting to write poetry, books, that world. Not quite with the same passion Libby had shown for filmmaking, but he'd mentioned these dreams. Coffee and smoothies instead? Whatever worked.

He sounded as though negotiating a lease on a new endeavor, expanding the brand with another smoothie stand in the big new mixed-use retail and condo development to the northeast of the city; open by the late summer, he wanted the build-out done in time to catch the last of the summer lake season, the back-to-school rush. Also, he discussed training an entrepreneurial eye upon downtown Charleston, as well in the suburb Mount Pleasant across the Ravenel Bridge. Devin listened as he rattled off these plans, about scouting out-parcels for both smoothie stand, Roy explained, as well as another Carolina Beanery Café. The first of a franchise, maybe. "Who knows where it'll all lead."

America. Anything possible. Roy Earl, a businessman badass. Devin, proud.

Also thinking he ought to get on board the Pettus express. He could slop smoothies into cups all day, couldn't he? An honorable trade. Hell, in two years—two years—he could make manager.

Manager.

King.

God.

Or: Devin, launching into another form of hospitality trade, where the real money's to be made in a college neighborhood like this: *he could open a bar*. That's right. Roy and him, yee-haw, they could call it The Dixiana Too, have another franchise. License that iconically cool sign-logo facing a corner of the town green back home in Edgewater County to every town in America—what burg couldn't use a corporate shitkicker honkytonk to drive the fortunes of dying downtowns the nation over?

Kidding, thinks he.

Only kidding.

Hell, he'd take his inheritance from his daddy—his mother had finally gone through it all with him, shown him everything, in fact, about the stocks and the house and the land up by the river they owned where Dwight had planned to build a vacation cottage, a project he'd never gotten around to, unfortunately. Devin, bucks coming his way. He would have the wherewithal to get financing for whatever business he wanted to try. The wartime Bush economy was humming right along. America.

Roy Earl had called Devin about fifty times for him to come hang out, so Devin, at last succumbing and driving himself over for a visit.

All morning back home Creedence, however, a nervous, snippy little ass anyway, running from one end of the house to the other getting ready for an Important Appointment, she kept repeating, in Columbia on campus, she said, about her future. Hustling over to the Korean nail salon in downtown Tillman Falls where Mr. Halsey's Barber and Salon used to be, where Devin and Dobbs and Roy Earl and all of them had gotten their haircuts all those years ago, had been part of it.

Devin guessed she just wanted to put her best face on the rest of her life. Who could blame her? He worried that once Mama was gone, Creedence wouldn't know what to do with herself anymore.

Mama and Devin were supposed to have been over here today for a doctor's appointment, but Eileen, at the last minute, decided to cancel it. Devin had been glad. The time had come when doctors couldn't do anything without hurting her worse. That's what Devin had helped her decide.

Devin, on the way from his car parked down the street having gotten caught in a downpour—sunny as hell outside now, just his luck. While his clothes spun in the dryer he'd slipped on some of Roy Earl's duds, which swallowed him. His osteal frame looked like that of the last starving survivor to have staggered out of a death camp.

Still not eating much. His stomach hurt. All that boozing had done its damage. He should get some imaging on it. See how gaping the holes.

Eh. If you go to the doctor hoping to find something, they're sure to do it.

Devin, scowling and feeling revulsion at what he felt, which was: wanting a drink. Wanting to slam a few beers with Roy like in the days of old. Hit up some of the bar rails they used to shine with their expanding guts. Wanting fifty drinks, so bad he could already taste the hot-cold splash. The burning in his gut.

But holding fast, best he could. He had to—his people back home were counting on him.

Skating on the edge once or twice, but yet to fall.

Almost tumbling the day he'd called Shelby Fordham, thrilled to hear from him; one would have thought Elvis Presley himself had rung up from Costa Rica where he's been hiding out all these years:

"*I'd love to see you.* Even tonight, if you want."

"My calendar's clear."

"I could use it—things ain't been too good."

"How so?"

"I done split up with that butthole husband of mine again. This time for good, I reckon."

"That's too bad."

"Sounds more like you got good timing, sugar. Just sayin'."

"Understood." He felt chilled, not warm. "I don't want nobody chasing me with a gun, though."

"Shit. That turd's staying in a trailer in Mayfield Acres with this piece of white trash and—oh, wait. Ain't none of that worth telling."

"I don't even know who you got hitched up with."

She told him. He still didn't know.

"Let's forget about him. I know I'm trying to."

"Where you want to go? Run down to Columbia?"

"How about meeting me at The Dixiana? Would you be okay with that?"

The Dixiana.

Maybe it'd be fine.

Sure. "Sure."

"It won't be crowded on a weeknight—they ain't got no bands playing."

Devin, thinking Shelby Fordham either selfish, oblivious, or perhaps most accurately, not truly grasping the extent of his affliction, how far he'd gone around the bend—but how could she? Certain neither Mama nor Creedence had spread such sordid, embarrassing info around—what, after all, would people think?

Devin, fuck it; needing a test of his resolve anyway. They set a time.

Considering sprucing up the mustache, he searched his soul to make sure doing so wasn't vanity. If this were a date, however, he'd venture out without the old-man cane. Stronger every day. Better balance. He wasn't even forty years old, for god-sakes.

Arriving on the town green, he parked the Jetta in one of the angled spaces along the small park of monuments to various war dead, racist South Carolina forebears and generals. The honkytonk itself sat emblazoned with an old mural depicting the original Southeastern Redtails mascot 'General Reb' waving his Confederate banner, artwork over which folks sometimes protested regarding symbology and inclusiveness.

Devin, no dog in the fight. Confederate flag crap—to Gen X it always smacked of bad taste, lowbrow redneck shit. He never identified with such heritage—Devin, for all his phony redneck patois and yuck-yuck tone, had never felt Southern. Only suburban, adolescent, middle-class white, watching the same shimmering episodes of GILLIGAN'S ISLAND and THE PRICE IS RIGHT like everyone, awash in homogeneity. He had driven the roads of middle America. He had seen the sameness with his own eyes. He had lived it.

Inside the honkytonk, realizing in an instant how agreeing to meet her in a bar, of all places, represented the worst in a series of terrible ideas he'd pursued through the years relating to establishments like this.

The thirst, all over him.

Spots boiling.

Today was merely one-more-day.

A hug, her body thickened with age but no less shapely and appealing, Shelby still smelled the same as when they'd stolen a few adolescent kisses in the season before Libby.

Difficult to concentrate, the tables full of shitkickers eating burger baskets and barbecue all yakking and whooping and drinking, their conversations ebbing and flowing; Toby Keith blared from the jukebox in patriotic fervor; Roy Earl's granddad, Reynolds Pettus, a barrel-chested World War 2 vet nearing 80, hollered at the kitchen help, ragged on the curly-haired redneck girl working the bar; he still ran his own show.

Smoke, drifting from Devin's fingertips and nostrils; no antismoking bullcrud in Edgewater County, SC. No sir. Not yet.

Shelby, sipping a Corona Light, told Devin how unhappy she'd been; how she'd been treated; her travails; her bad luck streak. Her blue-eyed and blonde-haired cherubic cutie-pie face floating across the bar-gloom at him, the same as when they'd been teenagers.

Telling Devin how kind she'd always considered him.

Flirting, both implicit as well as otherwise.

"How we all prayed for you, after what happened." She reached across to touch Devin's trembling hand, damp from holding the glass of cold soda water he'd been nursing.

Squeezing back, he shook his head not only at how foolish her desire; here, another one like Millie, thinking Devin some kind of catch, a nice guy.

Also revolted by a small epiphany sneaking up on paw-pads. The wrong sort of what-if thinking.

"I always did like you, sugar."

"Back at ya. I remember some sweet smooches, back in the dewy dawn of adolescence."

"Oh, so poetic—but I was dating Sammy, and Greg. And you—well." Shelby, looking askance, tried to smile the way folks did who remembered it all. "You was going with Libby, all of a sudden. She moved here and scooped you right up, didn't she?"

"Along those lines."

"So it wasn't to be." A demure glance; holding his gaze. "Not then, anyway."

"Everything might have been different if we had."

"Ain't no way to know that."

Thinking through the alternative time line—Devin and Shelby married, him getting a degree and coming back home work at the Sugeree Nuclear Station, or maybe in sales, working for Uncle Hill. Kids. Football on Sundays; cookouts with Eileen and Creedence and Dusty and Daddy. An ordinary Edgewater County life.

Meanwhile, Libby, freed. Meeting someone else—hell, Billy, for that matter. In her class as peers; nothing to do with that Dead show or the drugs. The two of them, hitting it off. Living on to make their movies together.

Libby.

Alive.

It would all be worth it.

*Stop this foolishness.*

"It ain't never too late," Shelby said, husky. "I don't know about you, but —well I guess 'ladies' aren't supposed to talk this way."

She told him, in detail, what awaited him later. If he felt amenable toward getting his freak on with a gal whose radiator was running hot; a girl hadn't had nothing but pain for a long while.

"That sound familiar, sugar?"

Devin could but agree; but suggesting, in not so many words, that after what she'd already been through? To hook up with an irascible, shiftless ex-drunk such as him could hardly be the tonic her romantic life required for repair and redemption? And all?

"Honey, you ain't like the others. You never were."

"That's what I'm saying."

"Hush, silly man." Sudden, she leaned forward and kissed him, awkward, their lips mashing.

But then it clicked in. Soft, sweet.

"I'm-a get that check, I think," Devin said, high-voiced.

They ended up in a cheap motel room by the interstate, a grim reminder of many such places. Mind racing, surreal; the last intercourse had been with Millie, a couple of years ago now. Devin's sordid tales of scabby whores and drawn druggy lot lizards, all an exaggeration, all a hard-case act designed as nothing more than barroom tough talk. Boasting of evils committed, and yet without sin. Well—mostly. Here and there.

After less than a minute inside her supple and pulsing void, her hips meeting his with hungry enthusiasm, Devin, crying out and exploding.

Shelby sighed at first, but cooing reassurance she became a gentle, patient fellatrix until he'd again become erect. The second instance of coitus had been good for both of them.

Devin, at such intimacy, felt a spark of life inside.

Unsettled by the sensation.

Upon awakening in the morning they enjoyed a third time, slow and gentle and wonderful, until Shelby'd ruined the mood by peering up at him with eyes that'd shone with affection. He'd averted his own, rolling them both over so that she was on top, rocking and riding him until both came hard; Devin, worrying about being broken in half by her grinding.

No—more worried more about that loving look.

No way to allow actual serious involvement.

Not with somebody in his condition.

Whatever it was.

Since that morning he'd ignored her last few phone messages, the final of which had been left by a voice breaking with frustration and confusion.

"You don't have to be scared of me," she said. "I promise."

He'd square it with her, eventually. Or else keep hiding until it all went away. It wouldn't be right to starting anything serious right now. Not with Mama being so sick.

Devin would have shared all that with Roy Earl once he ended his phone call, except he knew his friend would be troubled by any mention of The Dixiana, of which he was not proud, nor Devin's presence inside.

But he did mention Shelby, and his friend, lonely and awkward back in high school and college, expressed delight and appreciation for one of his old crushes, another with whom he'd never made any inroads.

A real shame—Roy, always such a lovable guy. The right girl, presenting herself in due time. Eventually.

"Your stuff's probably dry, now." The dryer buzzed. "Ah, there's that Pettus intuition."

"You're a man in tune with his environment. Clearly."

"What's next? Thought we could grab a pizza. Watch some Thursday night football?"

He rattled off the names of the teams playing in the big game that week, the stakes, the star players and their relative strengths, breathless, information sifted and sorted that rang to Devin as inscrutable, like a coded language among initiates.

"Whatever you feel like. Just glad to hang out."

A couple of beats of awkward silence. "I know I keep saying this, but— boy, it sure is good to have ya back."

"It's good to be here." But in truth Devin not so sure. The future uncertain, the past threatening at every turn, the end always near. "Or anywhere."

"Word to that." Blooms of color in Pettus cheeks. "I've been looking forward to this. I've been wanting to talk to you so bad. About the old days, and stuff."

"Right on. Now's your chance."

What followed, a pent-up, rambling roundabout speech about the 1989 Dead show, about how things were never the same in their little group afterward, nor were they the same for Roy Earl inwardly. That they'd all done heavy drugs, and that, for all the good the experience had done him— he explained how he'd tripped a few more times, gone to a couple more Dead shows when they'd played in Charlotte or Atlanta, how the whole deal had been a net positive for him, and blaming drugs for shit people do is like blaming the bullets that come out of a gun somebody's used to consciously kill another person—he still wondered what happened, exactly. How Devin himself had seemed to change.

"Why'd Billy quit hanging out? Carmen told me her neighbor said they saw y'all fighting that night."

Why lie? "It was over Libby."

"I thought so."

"It all worked out, though." Devin, ironist, gave the bag-of-tricks wink and thumb's up. "Didn't it?"

"You and Libby were tight after that."

"There you go."

"Over the years I've thought about that night. And whether doing the acid—whether it'd messed you and Billy up. And Libby," he struggled with adding. "Whatever it was. Between y'all."

"Like I said, nothing happened. A misunderstanding. We were all fucked up."

Thinking of Libby, and the joyous months they'd had after Billy's foolishness. Libby, smiling and laughing, her innocent-yet-not expression, the Bradford pear blossoms floating in the air. Remembering—allowing himself to remember—the surprise at Libby having brought Prudy home.

Libby and Prudy, equalling life and love.

Devin, his face split by a smile and feeling as though his was the first smile on the first day by the first man to walk upon the fertile and verdant earth, the first human being to notice the pulse and joy and challenge of life —to be unconcerned with where it all led, good or bad—sighed and embraced the memories of his lost love. Of his dear kitty-cat. And of himself, innocent, before the fall.

And of only the moment at hand. Not the past. Nor the future.

"Beau, let tell you something." Devin, leaning forward and winking, hammered it up. "My life didn't *start* until that night. And yeah, afterward was the golden age, the best time I ever did have. So, no—the acid didn't fuck me up. Nor the Dead. They scared the hell out of me, but left something else there in hell's place. Something good and true and strong and real. But I lost it again."

"I know you did, Devin." Roy Earl broke out in a brief sob, hid his face in a chubby hand. "Damn, I swore I wasn't gonna do this in front of you."

"Don't you fret. We cried in front of each other plenty, when we was pups."

"True that." Embarrassed nonetheless, he wiped his eyes and blew some snot into a Spotted Banana napkin from a stack on the coffee table.

They sat in silence. Roy Earl went to pick up the TV remote, but a slight gesture of Devin's steady hand stopped him.

Roy Earl's face, reddening anew. "So I got one more issue. A question. Or, a favor. Something."

"Mysterious. Hit me, beau."

"It's about that long-legged sister of yours."

# SEVENTY-TWO

## —

## CREEDENCE

Chelsea, on the road, so excited and anticipatory she'd swallowed half of one of Eileen's generic Xanax taken by the matriarch every night for many years now.

Mama, gulping down pills left and right. Hiding in the pantry or the laundry room where she thought her daughter wouldn't see her. Sick as a dog after the first of her new treatments, trying to hide in the bedroom with 'a headache.' Continuing the charade.

Creedence, damned if she'd bring it all up now. She wasn't going to sit there dragging the truth out of the woman. Mama would have to decided to come down off her high horse and talk about her illness on her own. That she hadn't, well...

It probably meant the cancer wasn't nothing to worry about anyway.

Confused.

About Mama.

About Billy.

But going through with it.

Also wondering, incessant, how he could want dumb redneck Chelsea Wallis—Rucker—when he had Melanie, a hottie from a good Charleston family who lived in a big house on the battery or one of the marshes, as she imagined every person did who told her they were from Charleston.

A woman like Billy himself, from a family with money.

Who seemed to love and want him.

What was this foolishness?

And yet, Chelsea, pressing ahead: Preparations, an expenditure of money on what constituted an almost a total makeover—clothes, mani-pedi, hair trimmed and straightened, the wearing of teeth-whitening stripes that seemed to have accomplished nothing overnight but leave a funny taste in her mouth, new makeup, at last taking a hand mirror to trim her bush, nice, neat and all-but bare like the girls in the NSFW videos she'd discovered one day in the browser cache of her computer at work.

Buddy's doing, probably. His way of flirting. Since hearing about her leaving Dusty, Buddy, he'd been preening and prancing in front of her every chance he got. It was pathetic. DUSTY: THE SEQUEL was hardly the title she planned to rent from the Blockbuster Video of her future romantic life. She had put in her notice at the dealership anyway. With the holidays coming and school in the spring, it was time to cut that tie. Uncle Hill had been glad, but also cried.

Parking her Ford Focus in the hotel garage, she sat for a long time listening to Doober Dougie talk up the daily 'Floyd at Four' block of classic tunes. This time the tracks all came from the one with the man on fire.

She remembered Devin listening to Pink Floyd, how Mama had a fit. "That's drug music," she'd say, screwing up her face. "I don't know why y'all can't listen to the Beach Boys like we done. Good enough for us."

Getting out of the car and straightening the mid-calf length wrap skirt purchased at American Apparel, she eyed her shoes, also new, sexy slides; sheer shimmery control-top pantyhose, nude, the good smooth kind, in the egg. Makeup for the legs, girls!

Pantyhose. But, girls didn't wear hose anymore. She couldn't remember the last time she'd seen a woman wearing them. Maybe at the First Baptist Church in Edgewater County, when she and Dusty had taken a notion to try to start going, which hadn't lasted. Bunch of stuck up old biddies, looking down their noses. Eff that. She got it, though—hose felt like being stuffed into a sausage casing. But the pooch of her stomach and pale, freckled stems looked better. All that mattered. She would tease him by peeling them off slow.

The naughtiness, compounded:

Chelsea, lying to Hill Hampton about why she needed the afternoon off. Her cover story? That she'd be going to campus to fill out papers for the spring semester, and to look for an apartment, all of which she also told Devin and Eileen, who all fussed in their own way about her going by herself. As though she weren't a grown woman. Stupid and silly.

Guilty, though. Uncle Hill had beamed with pride. With love. So glad for her. That she was going to make love with some guy, a near stranger, to be honest.

Um; not.

Stomach flittering with butterflies, she hurried stiff-legged down a glass-enclosed walkway connecting the garage to the hotel. Caught a glimpse of herself in a reflection. The distortion made her look fat.

Inside, the hotel lobby loomed huge and open, with an atrium rising up several stories. Voices echoed. Connected to a large office building next door, everywhere she looked was busy, buzzing with activity—a Wednesday afternoon, people all scurrying around having important matters at hand. It felt like being in the city.

Would wearing hose make her look like a rube? Not a woman she'd passed had had on stockings.

Creedence, panicked, rushed into the public restroom in the hotel lobby, ducked into the first stall. She slipped out of her Candies—her come-fuck-me's—and slid off the hose, tried to stuff them down into her tiny clutch. Spastic and hurried and flustered and cussing up a storm, she ended up shoving them instead into the waste slot.

Her heart, pulsing inside her breastbone; breathing, difficult. For the first time in years feeling like she wanted to drink a wine cooler or a light beer, but on top of the zannie, probably a mistake. She could smell her feet, or so she thought. The whole bathroom stunk. Her stomach hurt.

Were they going to—what, exactly?

Sit and talk, first? Watch TV, maybe order a movie? Billy loved movies, didn't he? Wasn't that still his jam? She would have to learn to talk about movies the way she had NASCAR with Dusty. Going uh-huh, uh-huh, uh-huh.

And next?

Have room service?

Drink champagne?

Slow-dance to jazz on the radio?

A bouquet of flowers? A candy-red heart of chocolates, the finest money could buy?

Was this a movie?

No.

Condoms at the ready? One kept in his wallet like Dusty used to carry?

She should make sure Billy uses a condom, right?

Or is that bad? Like, unsexy?

And what would he be wearing, how would he smell, what would he do.

To her.

With her.

With that mysterious, thick peterpiper of his.

*I am going through with this.*

*Right?*

Sitting in the stall a long time, waiting for the right answer, she felt sleepy, queasy, dizzy. A vibration of uncertainty gripped her like an electric current. Tension flared in her stomach—what was the word for this? She felt it every time she lied, or thought about Mama being ill, or meeting Billy in the middle of the afternoon. In secret. She mulled.

# SEVENTY-THREE

—

## BILLY

Billy, stomping around the hotel suite.

Beside himself with frustration.

Pissed as fuck.

Beyond ready to go, for an hour now.

But Creedence, late.

And now? The ever-loving cell phone, *ringing ringing ringing* off the goddamn hook, so to speak, once again. Not Creedence—first it's *Dad*, then it's *Melanie*, then it's *Dad* again.

*No way I'm talking to them, or listening to messages or concerns or remarks, none of it. This is* my *fucking time here.*

His time to shine.

And Libby's, too, once she got her ass up here.

Or, Creedence. That's right.

Walking into the hotel room bathroom, lifting the lid on the toilet, he cursed with irritation: The phone in the pocket of his robe, ringing yet again.

*Melanie.*

Dropping the small metal bullet into the toilet with a wet *plunk*; pissing on the phone as his ringtone gurgled under the water—'Dark Star.' Flushing with a confident, satisfying flick of his wrist.

No time for calls or Dark Stars—Libby was late.

Shit. Not Libby. The lovely, lithe Creedence, still as engagingly youthful and coltish as when she'd been there ready and willing, but whom Billy'd spurned. Time to make up for this oversight, this slight. Past time.

A pastime.

*Remember—no accidents.*

In the bedroom of the suite, he had spent the first minutes she'd been overdue by obsessive checklisting: candles and incense; the bubbler already packed to the hilt with the blue-ribbon cultivated named-strain nugs, despite the fact that with each passing day he seemed to be losing interest in smoking pot; a fifth of Crown and a bottle of fine New Zealand Sauvignon Blanc in a chiller, in case Creedence didn't want whiskey guzzled hot right out of the bottle; a box of chargers and a cream canister, waiting to be filled with nitrous oxide but not cream, Billy convinced she'd be into some *wah-wah-wah*, how-high-can-we-try, pussy-pounding gas-fed excitement; should anyone find themselves feeling the slightest bit uptight, on the night table within easy reach lay available a tube of *Slick 69*-brand superlube; and finally, Melanie's silk kimonos, laid out side by side waiting and ready for when they'd need to take breaks, to peel grapes and feed one another, the two of them recovering from having ascended to a new level of passion and sexual satiety.

Or: Billy, needing bleach, a shop vac and a bag o'rags.

Nah. Control.

This? *This was love.*

Billy, using every inch at his considerable disposal to show her how much love he had to give; and that he knew where to put it.

"Fly high like a bird up in the sky." He sang shuffling around and waiting. And waiting. And waiting some more. "That's what she's gonna do. Soon as she arrives."

# SEVENTY-FOUR

—

## CREEDENCE

Chelsea had gone into the hotel elevator, headed up to the suite, but moving as though underwater: Bailing on the whole plan at first, changing her mind, fear of missing an opportunity. Worrying about her ability to discern the right decision. How all might be different if rich Billy Steeple had fallen in love with her when back he'd had the opportunity.

Her head, foggy.

Couldn't think straight.

Billy. If only he'd made love to her that night, gentle, patient, she would have shown him how special she truly was. And all would have been different.

*Melanie.*

*Poor Melanie.*

The doors, opening. Standing still, arms straight down, frozen, staring at the brass sign on the wall pointing out the room numbers. Seeing that to the left lay the room in which she was to go have unapologetic, mysterious sex with the man of her dreams.

Making no move.

Finally, a tone bonged and the doors slid shut, the lift awaiting instruction.

Chelsea, breathing a sigh of release—not sexual but spiritual, almost. Feeling as though changing her mind about the tryst the first correct choice she'd ever made.

So much out of her control—animal extinctions, warfare, religious hatred, the garbage, the plastic piling up in the ocean, people getting checks from the government who didn't deserve them, what really made the towers fall on 9/11, when they would find the WMDs in Iraq to justify us bombing the shit out of them. Here, though, a situation under her control—her own destiny. She could screw Billy Steeple. Or, she could look for an apartment, wander around campus, get used to the layout.

Billy, if he loved her—and she believed him, yes she did—would wait. Would do this right. He'd understand. She'd call him, soon as she was back home. So he couldn't talk her out of her decision.

Smiling and relieved, she chose L—in this case, not Lobby but Love, done right, taken and explored and nurtured in due time. Billy, worth the wait; Creedence Rucker, equally so. Would give her time to get to the next book in Oprah's monthly club: intimacy tips for partners new, as well as established.

The elevator, descending smooth and true and safe. Thinking through the eventual explanation to Billy of this decision and hoping for his understanding and friendship, and later, a long life together, married, loving, a new family. That's right, a baby born in love not deception, and cared for by him and all his money. As she would be.

And, to show her Mama, bless her soul, she could get get somewhere in life on her own. If there was still time. Once back on the road home to Edgewater County she called him to explain, but couldn't get an answer.

The little blue pills he now needed to perform kicked in. But still no Creedence.

Billy, striding heavy-footed around the hotel suite suffering a tree-trunk, pulsating and purple with hot insistent blood, jutting out of his robe frenzy, clusters of panic attacks. The sweats, a rubbery feeling in his knees. After, mind you, he'd already eaten two of the Viagra gel-tabs he kept at hand to deal with a steeplemeat maintenance problem plaguing him. Troublesome, but with all the stress of drunkenly agreeing to wed Melanie— he had no recollection of the conversation—certainly to be understood.

Damn this complicated nonsense.

To the Rucker wench's credit, she hadn't answered her phone because he hadn't called it, couldn't do so—his own unit, with her number stored in its memory, now flushed and useless; when the first drink of whiskey had loosened his bowels earlier, he'd gone and taken a power dump on top as well. No longer an option.

Time to go for a Blackberry anyway, one of those smart phones. Billy, needing all the help he could get. Hardy-har.

In the silk robe, forlorn and flopped in the lounging chair in front of the flickering television, tumescent to the point of pain, Billy knocked back the Crown, shot after shot. Cracking a creamer charger, another, another, each a rush into the canister; triggering and inhaling and holding the cold nitrous in his lungs like a hit of the finest cannabis.

Close to unconsciousness, he caught himself, barely, before pitching forward onto the coffee table. His senses returned. He cracked more chargers.

*Do it do it do it again.*

Convinced at last his girl wasn't coming because of cosmic intervention —Libby (Creedence) was surely dead, killed, arrested, or otherwise detained

—he relaxed. Billy, unable to ascertain a reason why she'd choose to miss out on a chance to be Steepled conclusively and with extreme prejudice, why Libby would abstain, demur, defer; clearly a car accident.

*Creedence, you mean.*

*And that's in poor taste, that car-wreck bit.*

"Understood."

Chugging the Crown, bubbling the liquor, once, twice, three times a drunk lady; crack, *whoosh*, an iced wind rushing through his throat, *wah-wah-wah* like approaching sirens, the hallmark $N_2O$ auditory hallucination.

Euphoria, sweeping through him; his vision, doubling.

Billy, faceplanted, awakened on the carpet of the hotel room smelling the sour, salty fungus-feet of those who'd trodden these floors before him.

Billy, resigned and angry but unable to leave—not with wood like this; folks in the lobby, they'd be impressed, no question, but they'd put him away for capital crime-level indecent exposure.

Switching on the television, he thumbed the remote and selected from the porn menu an adult premium choice twelve-hour package. Billy, throughout the long night, sat as the cold light of the pornography played; he pulled at himself, desirous of a release that despite several ejaculations not only never quite arrived, but neither ameliorated his painful erection.

After guzzling the rest of the Crown he bolted for the bathroom to puke up hot liquor, his everhard dick bumping against the cold porcelain of the hotel toilet. He passed out there, like in San Antonio. Woke up to a hard-on. Wept with frustration. A cold shower at last reduced the purple organ.

At home the next day, amidst calls from others he found one from Creedence on his voicemail. Saying, no no, now, this is too much, too fast. Let's hang out, instead.

Seriously?

*Maybe have you up here to Mama's for dinner one Sunday. Call me soon. I love you.*

Cowardly cunt.

But messages, oh my brothers, the others he had, these, a problem: To his annoyance, grief, amazement and mild chagrin, Billy, discovering the reason for all the calls: his grandfather had been rushed to the hospital, had been frantic. Asking for him, of all the man's relatives, to come to the bedside. Pleading for Billy, Billy, Billy, he kept saying—all this I leave to him. All this I leave to him. "I must see my grandson."

In any case, overnight the old man had died, with Billy now far too late.

This call with his father, furious, reporting to his irresponsible son, who could come up with no good excuse other than he had lost his phone, that it was beyond him how in this most important of moments, he'd been AWOL. "But it doesn't surprise me either, somehow."

Billy, listening and nodding. Yes yes, he said. So sorry. See you in a couple of days for the memorial.

Melanie, a wreck already at Billy's daylong disappearance; his father, apoplectic and bereaved, taking out his anger and grief on his wayward son; and Creedence giving him the high hat—what a farce.

But that was that re: the family largesse; the money at last his, the world at his feet, crouching, kneeling and slurping and wearing Steeple-logo kneepads, the universe wet and willing-ready to provide deep throat times infinity plus one.

The moment, at last at hand. A long slog, this.

*Libby, you, my dear, are an idiot. You and your myopic Sunday dinners at mother dear's table. You wait for another Billy to come along. Just you wait. Free advice? Go fuck yourself instead.*

As part of ongoing therapy, self-directed, Devin considered various methods of confronting the past which didn't involve standing over Libby's grave to play out some ridiculous scene like in one of her damnable cinema-plays.

Billy's wacky routine in Columbia, now that had left him dumbstruck. The boy needed to dry out.

What could Devin say. Fucking hypocrite.

Best to ignore Steeple. Let him work through his own crud.

Devin looked into the life of the asshole driving the truck that fateful day. Or intended to, but stopped by the idea that knowing more about a soul troubled enough to drink so much and drive was to wallow in familiar failings.

No answers there. He already had the answer.

Dude was drunk.

Dude was driving.

Devin, doing the same a million times. Before the accident. Since. What more did one need to understand?

And so another notion, different research, and yet not:

A man in a pool.

Asking Uncle Hill about that country club incident in the summer of Devin's fourteenth year. What he remembered—who the man had been.

"That must have scared the mess out of you, finding a dead retarded boy first thing in the morning."

"'Twas an eye-opener."

"In any case, that fella was Roosevelt Nixon's cousin, or nephew—the preacher on the radio. Built himself one of them mega-churches over yonder across the bridge."

Devin's skin, stippled with horripilation: The Reverend Nixon. Savior to

Prudy. The man of God who'd said grace over the steaming bleeding wreck of the car. This, the reason for at first believing the Reverend to be the Floating Man, come that day of the accident to collect the mortal rent. Their eyes, the same.

Coming back to him, now.

All of it.

He pushed it away.

Most of it.

Driving east until getting to the highway of Libby's death, now expanded to four lanes running from the interstate into Tillman Falls, he smoked and felt at ease. He crossed the long bridge over the coffee-colored Sugeree River and passed into the poor part of town, where the black folks were now being pushed out by mobile homes filled with Latino day laborers, families full of stair-step children and mothers-in-law; they called it Little Mexico across the bridge, now.

The Calvary Full Gospel Church of the Holy Redeemer remained in full flourish over in Easton township, the unincorporated area over the river. An old clapboard sanctuary sat next to a glimmering, modern glass and brick edifice reaching toward the sky; it reminded Devin of the county administration building downtown that had been constructed during his long absence. Here the work was so recent there remained a fenced-off quadrant of the parking lot with what construction equipment and supplies remained from the build. From the size of his congregation, the Reverend Nixon, a radio preacher, was doing all right, it seemed.

Devin, rolling onto fresh asphalt dark and smooth, the lines of the spaces crisp and defined, finished his butt and chewed some gum. Being a Friday, only a couple of cars sat parked outside. Devin, hoping a church secretary inside able to direct him to the Reverend.

Slicking his hair back and brushing off his jacket and pants, he thought: *No way is he going to remember me.*

"No way," Devin said to the empty parking spaces, loping to the sanctuary in his shuffling, post-fall gait. "Dime to a dollar says he won't."

A teenage boy appeared out of the double doors of the whitewashed, weathered older building. Startled by Devin's presence in the churchyard, he called out.

Raising a friendly claw, Devin hollered, "Y'all got a Reverend Nixon around here, pardner?"

A slight hesitation. "Yes."

"Wondered if I might have a word with him."

"May I ask what this is regarding?"

Devin, explaining best he could. "It's about a cat. And his cousin."

The boy took it in stride. "Parishioners—they come to my father with all manner of problems."

"Reckon it comes with the territory. But, this ain't no problem. I just need to thank him for something."

Tall, rangy and stoic, the teen, in workout sweats, gestured, poised and graceful, for Devin to follow him around the building. "He's around back."

Nixon, in shirtsleeves, wrestled a carton of what appeared to be holiday decorations out of a storage shed while two other, younger boys passed him smaller boxes from within, assembly-line method. He didn't hear them approaching at first.

Devin, shuddering at the sight of the strong, wide shoulders of the man, the rolls of flesh at the back of his neck, the dark skin and cropped dusting of now-graying hair, the sweat stains on his shirt; all familiar. More of him now to be sure, but without a doubt, this, the savior from the side of the road who'd taken Prudy. How Devin remembered Nixon best: while lying in the blazing sun, the shattered vehicle, the ticking hissing engine block, as the Reverend prayed over Libby and the other victims, voice quavering: *Bless and keep these children of God; mitigate their suffering to come.*

"Father?"

"Yes, my son?"

"A *visitor*." A manner Devin noted as code between father and son. "Right here."

Nixon, peering down his nose at the *visitor*, gave the skinny white man in the battered jean jacket and aviators the once-over. He handed off the cardboard box to one of his younger sons. Caution informed his deliberate movements.

He pursed his lips and tilted back his head. "Afternoon. You looking for work?"

Extending his hand and saying in a loud, nervous tone, Devin laughed, self-effacing. "Nah. Look here—a while back, you done me a solid. I came today to thank you for it."

"A favor?"

"It's long overdue. Name's Devin Rucker."

Nixon barked a short, mirthless laugh. "Devin Rucker. Now that's a name I haven't heard for a long, long time."

"Tell truth: You remember me?"

An enormous hand laid upon a bony shoulder. "I'm afraid so, son. Indeed I do."

"Sorry to hear that."

Nixon, a mountainous human being, seemed disturbed by Devin's skeletal frame. "Heavens, have you lost weight? You must let us feed you."

Nixon's son, at the adolescent stage when parental uttering often caused mortification, castigated his clueless father: "You make it sound as though he's a stray dog."

The Reverend, unmoved by his son's concern, motioned for the boys to totes boxes inside the new sanctuary. Unhesitant to abide his father's direction, he did so only with the pursed lips of teenage dissatisfaction.

"Had me a heckuva spread at lunch. But I appreciate the thought. I'll take a cuppa joe, if you got one."

"That much we can do." Nixon, looking upon the slender man with concern. "But, have you come here for help?"

The man knew a drunk or druggie when he saw one. "Like I told the young master there, reckon I'm getting around to saying thanks to a few folks. Or else, sorry for whatever I pulled on them."

"You're in recovery?"

Devin smiled. "You know the drill—people I come across who helped me out along the way. Or else who I might owe a kind word or two."

"Understood. We have meetings here three times a week. A bustling endeavor these days, I'm afraid."

"I been all over. Trust me—it's going around."

Roosevelt Nixon closed his eyes, nodded. "Yes."

"So—you remember the cat?"

"Of course." Putting his arm around Devin, he cautioned, "But your marker, if you had one, is more than clear with me. I begin each morning with a single request of this world, and it is for an opportunity to serve. But in any case, somewhere in my files I still have the lovely card your mother wrote thanking me."

Devin, fighting back a roll-tide of emotion. An enormous, sucking breath. "She sent you a card—good. More'n I ever did."

"Are you well, my son? Is your life a happy one?"

He shrugged. "Better than it was."

"Life is but our testing ground for how we'll be received for all eternity."

"Sometimes it does feel that long. Don't it?"

"Here's a lesson, a way to approach each new day: The past is complete, and the future is not ours to see, but right now? Right now is a gift, Devin. That's why they call it the present."

Devin grunted at what he considered a creaky cliché. "You ain't the first person to try to explain that to me."

Now for the other aspect of Devin's visit—to tell the Reverend of the day in the pool. Of finding the body, the floating man.

"Albert? Dear Albert? Another day I remember well. And, that was you?"

"Kinda blew my mind, finding him. But nothing like what was to come."

Shaking his head. "Another tragedy. He never got the chance to deal with his alcohol addiction. It cost him his life."

"It'd been so hot that day before—the hottest day of the year, or at least that's the way I remember it. I knew in my heart that, all that fella had wanted was to cool off. And he had to die for it? Don't nobody deserve to go over something so basic. Something so innocent. Do they?"

"Certainly not Albert. Despite his 'issues,' as afternoon TV talk show hosts would put it, he was a good soul, with a kind and innocent heart. Alcoholic, though."

"Another stupid accident. Him in the pool."

"It's fair to say so, yes."

"And as you say, he was a good man. Wasn't he?"

"Albert was relatively innocent of baser instincts."

"I tried to help him. That's why I jumped in. To save him, if I could. But too late."

"You shouldn't suffer guilt. His fate was sealed the moment he took a drink of that poison. The liquor, not the water in the pool, was his undoing. Something you know all about, don't you?"

He slapped his hands together. Ready, now, to skedaddle. "My Mama's waiting on me up the road a piece. Thank you again for helping me, and my cat. That's all I needed to say. That, and sorry it took me so long to say it."

"It was the least I could do."

"And yet not."

"You should know you're welcome anytime in our sanctuary here."

"I appreciate that."

Glancing over his shoulder at his new church, gleaming in the golden afternoon Carolina sun, he said, "There's someone inside you may wish to meet. If you have a moment."

Devin, perplexed. "Who?"

"Albert's mother."

"*His mother?*"

Nixon, a hand on the sleeve of Devin's jacket. "I don't think that she needs to know who you are, not in relation to her son and his death. It devastated her—his older brother had already passed away as well, as a serviceman overseas. But if it would help you to meet her, to say hello? This hour is the time."

"Can't think of a reason not to say 'howdy'."

The men ambled through a set of double doors at the rear of the sanctuary leading into the fellowship hall, with its folding chairs and tables and a small kitchen from which to prepare the bread of life broken amongst brothers and sisters there in the direct sight of God, a deity to whom the faithful were penitent, duly indebted, and, as Devin suspected, likely happy and satisfied at being in such condition.

A woman, stooped and elderly, nonetheless pulled an oversized tray of steaming blueberry muffins out of the oven as though it were no trouble. The whole joint smelled like a bakery. Devin had lied about lunch—his stomach lying empty grumbled at the heavenly scent.

Nixon called from the door. "Aunt Lechelle?"

Lechelle Nixon put her muffins down on the cooling rack. She regarded the hard-eyed white man standing next to her nephew. She took off her oven mitts and came over, a slow shuffle.

"Y'all like to made me come out of my skin."

"Come say hello to someone."

"Who this?"

"A friend of mine," Nixon said, smiling and beatific. "A dear, old friend."

Looking the visitor up and down, she wiped a hand on apron and held it out. "And how are you on this fine afternoon, young man?"

Devin, seeing her son's eyes in hers as well as the Reverend's, but not bulging and feral in horrific acknowledgment of death, instead twinkling with knowledge—with life—behind wire-rimmed glasses. Devin, guessing more than a few of the deep creases in her face attributable to the loss of her sons. "Right as rain, my dear."

Lechelle, folding her arms, inquisitive, acted like one of those intuitive types. "You got something to say, Mr. Man—don't you?"

"I do, ma'am."

"So I reckon you best be out with it."

Aching, empathetic, trying to find the words; Devin, holding out hands steady as rocks. "I'm not sure how to put it." At last he explained: "I knew your son."

Her face lit up. "You knew Albert? Or Dewayne?"

"Albert. He was a good fella."

They chatted for a moment; he didn't make up any lies. Only that he remembered him from them both working at the country club. Her love-light shined at getting to talk about the son she'd been missing for many years. Devin left wondering for whom, truly, this trip to the church today had been taken.

# SEVENTY-SEVEN

—

## CREEDENCE

Chelsea, grateful to pick up Devin's other Christmas gift, the one she couldn't make herself:

The small cube of a monument from the place over in Tillman Falls where Eileen ordered all the others for her beloved pets. Heavy for such a small stone, the engraving looked simple, perfect. Pleased, though not knowing what Devin might think about her gift. With any luck, a gesture to help him honor the life of his sweet kitty.

Chelsea, never again hearing back from Billy. That'd changed everything —he didn't love her. He had only wanted to fuck her, she felt. Typical man.

Or maybe he was playing hard to get.

But three weeks? Thanksgiving had come and gone.

Screw you, Billy. Enough of games. Her dignity and self-confidence, impugned. How could he not call to respond to the message she left? Her apology?

"I sure am sorry, Miss Rucker." The old woman working the counter at the monument company tsk-tsk'd as Chelsea scratched out a pink check with cartoon kitty-cat faces, number 103 on her new account. "I know how y'all Ruckers love your little ones so much. Your Mama and them ELMS has damn near paid for that whole new animal shelter they got set up over yonder."

"But this one, it's for somebody who's been gone for a while already. It's not so painful."

"Still, though. We grieve anew daily for our lost loves—don't we?"

"That's right. You don't ever stop missing the ones you lose."

# SEVENTY-EIGHT

## —

## DEVIN

The holiday season in the Rucker household, lurching from the highest highs to the lowest of lows.

The biggest ugliness occurred due to Eileen causing a stink on Christmas Eve, the traditional night upon which all the cousins and aunts and other scattered relatives gathered to feast and celebrate the birth of the Savior.

This year, like most others, finding the house overflowing with a rucksack of Ruckers and a bevy of Eileen-side Bevinses, all of whom were told Eileen had a thyroid issue resulting in her weight loss, general pallor and fatigue.

Devin, away for so long, had dreaded the holiday experience like few others. As did Creedence, both peppered with a thousand questions about what in God's name they were thinking by going to live in Columbia, as though the minuscule metropolis a Sodom teeming with sin, or else what Devin had been doing with himself for the last decade and a half.

Both siblings, for the most part, remained at their most diplomatic, working the room of aging folks who were taken with wonder at Devin's appearance back home. Thankful for sobriety, as he said again and again; a hand held in front of his mouth to shield his expulsions of coffee- and cig-breath.

But Eileen, bless her heart; she had to go and set one or more of her children off, and this despite a suspicious, prescient Devin having warned that, however much unbridled all-consuming emotion about family and the past and keeping everybody together might drive her every thought and movement, and despite her illness closing in from all sides—the latest scans, *no bueno*, heavy metastasization underway, darn it—if she pulled this one particular stunt? A no-brainer of a family crisis, if not outright old-school Devin-style trouble, likely to occur.

Picture this:

A Southern family, multigenerational, gathered around the long formal dining room table. A dozen grownups in total, a few youngsters to the side at a card table but not many, not since Devin and Creedence had failed to reproduce; as-yet, as Mama kept clarifying in a loud, quavering voice. Everyone laughing, talking, eating, most of them county natives, their speech with a musicality and a simplicity to the nature of their conversations: the condition of vehicles; children's and grandchildren's activities; the TV programs, daytime as well as primetime; how they understand neither computers nor the state of modern country music; NASCAR; their church pastor and his dramas; how the world was changing so fast; how the world was wicked; how the Lord had a plan.

Dobbs and his mother, also attending. Dobbs and Devin, together almost every day, now, hanging out if only to sit reading together like an old retired couple. Devin could now drive them, Dobbs and his mother, on outings; to movies, to the library, on errands. Good times.

Dobbs and Devin, reminiscing with cheer about Eileen cooking them breakfast before school, the scrambled eggs, how Dobbs liked ketchup on his; the albums they had played and cassette tapes too, riding around in Roy Earl's grandfather's pickup, listening to Blue Öyster Cult or The Who or any number of other classic rock bands.

Devin, weary and nostalgic, an uncommon condition—it must have meant Gen X was aging. "As wholesome and marvelous a childhood as anyone who'd ever lived. What we had."

Dobbs, a sad smile speaking poignant volumes. "It was a time of innocence and grace."

"I sure didn't know it then. But then, all that gets wrung out of you by life."

"Don't it?" Creedence, chiming in. "Don't it, though?"

An opportune moment for Eileen's guest of honor to appear out of the shadows of the foyer like a golem.

Dusty.

Devin, noting a new pink Izod polo shirt and charcoal slacks; betting dollars to doughnuts Eileen herself had bought the clothes for the erstwhile son-in-law, missed as he was so terribly. How ghastly this divorce business, she kept saying, which always made him chuckle. "Better to sweep things under the rug and soldier on."

Creedence, in shock, looked like Cool Hand Luke after eating the boiled eggs: bloated, eyes puffy, cheeks shot through with spidery thin veins. Otherwise, though, her face remained impassive. In control, other than the stainless steel pie server she clutched, a weapon at the ready; her hand, quivering.

"Well, Dusty—ain't this a surprise." Dobbs, dry and sarcastic. He picked at a piece of Eileen's hummingbird cake served on one of the Christmas dishes, of which Eileen had several generations' worth stored in the attic. "Didn't expect to see you here."

"No." Creedence, an icy winter queen. "We certainly didn't."

A palpable murmur of discomfort, a rash of throat-clearing, a hubbub of business-as-usual pleasantries. Dusty, doing well, he said in response to Hill Hampton, who occupied the far end of the table from Devin. Well as he could be, he said, under the circumstances.

Eileen, talking and talking, yappity-yap, to one of the aunts, Rosalee, Devin barely remember them all on his mother's side. Shaking her head, gazing up to the heavens with hands together.

Devin, reading her lips; his Mama, saying, *I'm hoping, I'm hoping for the best.* Literal fingers crossed.

Creedence, her head down, shoulders shaking; Dusty, coming over and trying to give her a buss on the cheek.

Cringing away from him.

A grimace.

A volcano.

A red veil, falling over his vision. Not the metallic boiling spots of old, but a different level of ire stoked by his mother's tendentiously disrespectful and flat-out wrongheaded behavior. When it came to Creedence's feelings, he didn't care how sick his mother might be.

A flash went through his spinal column like an electric shock. Some of the bar fights had been real. Devin had been trying to get killed, for a while, by goading biker and bangers into whipping his ass. Had learned to do some damage right back. Thought he was gonna have to do it that night on the street with Steeple, and all his drunken-ass, dick-sucking crazy-talk.

Devin, pissed about this stress. All day, he'd felt so centered and relaxed —an afternoon spent riding around alone in Columbia. Taking some boxes to the new apartment Creedence had leased over in Herndon Hill, walking distance to the Old Market and campus beyond. Holiday shopping at the sprawling Town Centre over in the sand hills of north Richland County. With all the stores, restaurants, and bars.

All afternoon.

By himself.

Dealing with what'd been ailing him.

Or rather, thinking about doing it. That's all he'd done. His memory on this came clear. Clear as it did on anything. He went into the bar, sat, didn't order a vodka.

Yep.

Going over and draping an arm around Dusty. He yelped, gaping at his soon-to-be former brother-in-law.

A hush descended. All eyes upon them.

"Looky here, son," Devin called out in the biggest and most expansive and generous of mellifluous South Carolina brogues, like the cultured and charming southern gentleman of means for whom his mother had hoped, "why don't we menfolk walk out on the deck so I can smoke one of these here coffin-nails?" The request, an absurdity. No fewer than five people including Eileen already sat puffing away, a wafting, blue pall blown around by the heating vents. "What say you, my boy?"

Dusty, hiking up the waistline of his Duckheads, looked doubtful. "I need to pee first."

"You can wee-wee on Mama's rosebushes. Make 'em all pretty and shit for next spring."

"But, Devin."

"*Move it, dicknut,*" he whispered with a smile, pointing to the sliding glass doors. "*Before somebody carries you out of here.*"

Outside, slamming the door shut, a thump. Background noise cut off clean, the two men on the deck. Dry, cold, bracing. Stars, twinkling in the clear winter night, wind whistling through a bad seam in the gutter by the garage. Devin, a withering glance back over his shoulder at his mother who watched them from inside, her hands still clasped together, nodding, a mad hollow grin splitting her withered and pancaked face.

The face of a dying woman, Devin allowed himself to realize. A pang of loss, welling in his thin-walled heart, made him want a snort.

Still mad at Dusty, Mama claimed. But understanding; how she kept talking about Creedence's lost baby; how, if only there could be another chance. How there wasn't much time left.

For Creedence, he thought she'd meant.

Now he understood. Not enough time for her daughter to meet somebody new. Get it on. Pop out the young'un. Before Eileen caught up with Daddy.

Dusty, pouting and hugging himself, paced around. "Coldest December I ever felt in my whole durn life."

Devin agreed, but this, a baldfaced lie: having slogged through Colorado winters, hoping against hope to be found one morning outside some watering hole beak-first in a snow bank, blue and stiff, Carolina Rucker, they called him out there, knew him some cold.

A Colorado public health department counselor, whom Devin visited for all of three sessions before declaring himself cured of alcoholism, had noted with interest how often he used words like cold or freezing or numb.

Devin, astute, remarked, "The cold, it's like the booze: another attempt not to feeling anything. I thought if I got cold enough I'd turn all the way to stone. It's the way I was already feeling inside. The rest of me hadn't caught up yet."

The therapist, an earnest young woman starting out on her career, seemed disturbed and concerned by some of his statements. Begged him to keep talking.

Nah, he'd told her. Ain't no thang. "I got this."

"I can't believe you getting around as good as you are. After all your shit, beau."

Devin, backlit by the deck floodlight, a paternal hand on a rounded shoulder. Tendrils of smoke, flowing out of nostrils. A dragon. "Let me axe you something—what the hell you doing here?"

Dusty's teeth, chattering. "It's Christmas."

A dark voice, scratchy, another Devin—a demon, Dirty Harry after gargling rusty bottle caps. "I don't give a damn if it's the end of days, the hour of the time, and Jesus comes riding up on a white magic unicorn, or, maybe a golden ark comes floating up the middle of the mighty Sugeree River running swift and hard and muddy over there down the ridge. No matter what, you ain't got no business here, son. Not anymore."

"That's what you say?"

"That's what your ex-wife says, son."

"She ain't my ex yet. And besides, Mama Eileen invited me. And don't call me 'son'. You ain't my Daddy. You ain't even been here in ten years."

Peering beyond Dusty's shoulder at the steps down which Devin's beloved sister had once tumbled, he imagined snapping Dusty's neck and running inside, screaming into his mother's face, *Oh, Mama—he was carrying a bag of groceries, and he tripped over his own two stupid feet and boo-hoo-hoo, now Dusty's dead...*

"Mama knew better than to invite you. But done it anyway."

"Mama Eileen said Creedence was the one who wanted me here. Since it was Christmas, and all."

"Dusty—?"

"What," petulant.

Devin, feeling silly. Relaxed. Thinking about sneaking away after dispatching Dusty. Some more private time. Christmas, after all. The warmth still in his belly from his earlier secret naughtiness that didn't really happen at the bar. Not if he'd convinced himself it didn't, that drink he'd coveted but spurned, especially as no one else knew.

No one must know.

*Not even you.*

A grim mantra. Devin, wishing for that therapist chick. Maybe finding another one.

And if he wanted to go whole hog and have some real fun? Which the voice in his head definitely said he should Go For with all due haste and speed? He'd kill this simpering little fuck—Creedence had confessed that she thought about asking him to do it—and run over to The Dixiana, call Shelby, get shitfaced and laid. Rock it out. Then go to prison. Die there in peace.

Bile, gurgling in his throat at this weak-ass sauce for reasoning. It sounded like the equivalent of pulling a FEAR—Fuck Everything And Run.

Devin, rubbing his eyes, pitched his butt into the yard. "My sister told me what happened."

"Ain't true. I don't hardly even know that girl."

"No—not the side-meat."

Dusty, dumbfounded. "—"

Devin jerked a theatrical thumb over toward the deck steps. "About her falling down that night."

"What you mean, son."

Working his eyebrows up and down like Groucho Marx. "How she dropped the groceries? Because they were so heavy?"

"Oh—right."

"C'ain't nobody figure out why she was toting a sack of Piggly Wiggly cornpone and chitlins up the back deck steps, but—well. That's the story. And we're sticking with it. Ain't we."

A literal gulp. "Yeah, sure was awful. And you's in the hospital too, which beat all I ever seen."

Savage, he whirled on Dusty, grabbing a handful of pink Izod. Dragon breath again, steam. "I'm saying that I know what happened for real."

"Quit it. I'll leave."

He released Dusty with a shove. "I ought to beat the ever-loving mud out of you. I've put people in the hospital, motherfucker."

Dusty, a stagger step back. "Don't feel like freezing to death out here no way."

Devin, offering a bromide about not letting the screen door whack him in the ass.

Thrusting a trembling finger. "Wanna know what I think? This is all *your* fault, somehow."

"*Da fuh?*"

"Everything was fine until last spring, when Colette said you were coming home. I knew there wa'n't gonna be no good come of it."

Devin, fighting for his New Balance not to find its way into Dusty's chubby ass rather than the screen door. A voice, exhorting—*HIT HIM HIT HIM HIT HIM*.

But another one, saying in more of a whisper:

*Don't.*

The first voice, not the real him; a phantom Devin, one banished but here resurrected; the voice he'd tried to drink into submission.

Devin, listening to the whisper, not the shout.

*Don't.*

"I didn't hardly do nothing in the first place. With that girl."

"Quit lying, dirtbag."

"Oh, hell." Dusty, spitting onto the weathered decking. "I didn't do nothing that nobody else don't do," the quadruple-negative of his declaration hanging in the air like fart-stink.

"Go on, bro. Before you have to pay rent you can't cover. If you know what I mean."

"Bunch of high-minded Ruckers, with your butts up on your shoulders. Maybe it's y'all's shit that don't stink. Ever consider that?"

Devin, calm, perhaps even warm and human inside, a sensation with which he'd found rare acquaintance over the course of his life, felt his heartsblood pulsing. Alive. "Buddy, it's all I think about."

Dusty, his hand on the sliding door handle. An accusation. "You're drinking again—ain't you."

Devin, mirth gone, stood ramrod straight. "Fuck no, bro."

"You sure?"

"I'm the one asking the questions here."

Dusty, face puckered with skepticism, weeble-wobbled his way back inside. "Tell me another one."

Lighting a new smoke, Devin took a stroll around the tombstones; a package of mouthwash strips appeared in his hand, furtive like a magician's concealed magic coin. He slipped one of the teal, jellied tabs onto his tongue like fiery communion. He noticed the burning of the alcohol, but only a little.

# SEVENTY-NINE

## —

## CREEDENCE

Chelsea, shaking inside at seeing Dusty waltzing into the dining room, knew the instant he appeared what had gone on; an obvious Eileen special.

*What does she think this is gonna do, make me change my mind?*

*Is that what this is? Trying to make me feel sorry for him at Christmas?*

*Lord love a duck.*

Watching Devin take Dusty outside. Making eye contact with her brother. Thinking, don't hurt him, just get rid of him.

Observing their body language: Dusty, cold and miserable, while Devin, leaning and bending and pointing, his cigarette cherry like a devil's eye, glowing and floating. Concerned her brother capable of rash action. Feeling guilty about when she'd fantasized for it to happen.

Thinking, not to worry: Devin, probably only producing a stream of filthy, smart-aleck remarks. Mean-sounding threats on which he was likely never to follow through. Not now he was sober.

Also watching Eileen, waiting. A bizarre, grinning visage, eyes dancing.

Moving over beside her daughter, she said, "I can't believe he came, Colette."

"You and me neither."

"Maybe it's a sign."

"A sign?" Menacing and deep, mimicking an angry Devin: "*Of what.*"

"A sign he still loves us all."

Chelsea, a fluttering in her gut like reflux. Noting that her mother had lipstick on her teeth, she said, "He don't know what love is."

"If y'all were to sit down and talk for a while—maybe y'all could make it like a date, a first date, all over again—who knows what you could figure out."

No longer any energy to cry. Only wanting Christmas, and the whole year, to end with a whimper. Or, for the sake of expediency, willing to accept an asteroid strike; a meltdown at the Sugeree River Station; a plague of locusts, or of virulent disease. Armageddon. The Rapture.

"You are such a fool. An old fool."

Furious. "Just like y'all to treat me this way. When I got so much going on."

Mocking. "P'shaw. You ain't got nothing going on."

Eileen, ignoring her daughter, pressing ahead, trancelike: "So when Dusty said he wanted to come over for Christmas, I told him, Dusty, I think that's grand. We all miss you so much, me and Daddy and Big Ma-maw and Papaw and the babies. And you know, I said to myself, I says, Eileen Rucker, you ought to go ahead and make plans. Just in case something special happens. What I'd like to think of as a Christmas miracle, Colette."

Chelsea burst out laughing. "Plans?"

"And so I says, Eileen Rucker, you better not get caught with your pants down, in case something *wonderful* happens. So, I went in your room and found your papers, and I called that man over there in Columbia who's leasing you that apartment? And I talked to him and tried to explain what all had gone on, and he was real sympathetic. He even said if we wanted to, we could take and go and just *tear up* that durn lease you and Devin signed."

Chelsea's stomach, dropping into the vicinity of her knees, like at the Myrtle Beach Pavilion riding the rocking pirate ship, which teenage Devin Rucker always referred to as the Vomit Comet. "Now I know you're kidding with me."

"It was a prudent action on my part, in case tonight you and Dusty got along again, and y'all decided to get back together. There wouldn't be no need for no apartment in Columbia. See?" She grinned, squeezing her grandmama eyes, a grandmama without any grandbabies to spoil, as she kept reminding her daughter. "I know y'all have done gone and put your house on the market, but—but I thought y'all could live here. Like when you first got married."

Chelsea, a hand drawn back. Lightning, slapping Eileen across the mouth. Hard.

Eileen, blinking and shaking her head. Beginning to speak.

Another slap, this time the daughter pulling her strength, but only somewhat.

Eileen, her cheek bright red, a look of horror. She sat down heavy in a chair at the children's dinner table, a metal folding chair the hard back of which seemed to hurt her Mama.

Coughing blood into her hanky: "Lord have mercy. Don't you realize how sick I am?"

"Oh, Mama—I'm so sorry."

"You didn't never have good sense. Sick as I am. You hitting me like that. God help me."

Shame, a warm bath. 'Sick'—she said the word. It was the biggest shock of Chelsea's life. The rocking pirate ship, a pendulum swing to the same awful gut-sickness, returned.

Before she could apologize further, the two of them, jumping—Dusty, charging in through the sliding glass doors.

"Lord, but it's cold out there. And Devin's got a bug up his butt sideways."

"Come on now, Dusty," Eileen, struggling to her feet. "Let's go and get the ham on the table."

Chelsea, staring daggers at the two of them—co-conspirators.

*Let me go*, she thought. Both of you.

"No, I got to get on, Mama Eileen."

"Oh, Dusty." Emotionless. "*Why*."

Thin, whining, defeated. "I reckon I got some last-minute shopping to do."

"Come back and see us when you can." Drifting into the kitchen, touching the side of her face. "I'm sorry, Dusty. I tried."

Dusty and Chelsea, left alone. Starting to speak, but Chelsea, turning her back, a wall of NO.

Hesitant, he shuffled through the dining room toward the front door, making a big show of sighing and sniffling, which only made her hate him more. Dusty had made Chelsea hit her own mother.

Her dying mother.

Panic. A panic attack.

But not saying a word to Devin. When he came back in, she wept, hard, and collapsed into loving arms that held her tight. She let him think it was all about Dusty. But it wasn't. It was Mama being sick.

It was herself.

All about herself.

Maybe that had been the problem all along.

How could she move to Columbia and leave her mother to die alone?

Devin, reading her thoughts, took her upstairs to his room for one of their oldschool chats. "I got to talk to you about something."

He closed the door. "I think maybe I'm gonna stick around here through the first part of the year. Help her do some crap. Maybe pressure-wash the deck. Repair that rotten threshold. Clean gutters. Grown-up stuff. Keep feeling like Daddy's list of home improvement type-deals must be a mile long by now."

"That ain't such a bad idea."

"You go on, though. Get going on school."

Relief, filling her like no lover ever had. "Are you sure?"

"Sister of mine, I got this. This one's on me. Besides—everything's fine. Mama's fine. She ain't going anywhere."

# EIGHTY

## — DEVIN

Christmas morning.

Devin, led upstairs by Creedence to receive his gifts, tokens kept secret from her mother, as well as him.

Eileen, cursing from downstairs, epithets coloring her accusations of rank ingratitude at such a display of secrecy and privilege. Gales of coughing and sputtering through her coffee and second of two morning cigarettes. For her sake, Devin had run himself ragged trying to make sure Christmas was 'normal'.

*But how normal could it be? You're back home, beau.*

Creedence, shutting the door to her room, smiled but seemed tense.

"What's all the suspense?"

Devin sat on the edge of her bed in lounging pants and a grungy old T-shirt, one Mama kept threatening to throw away. Rubbing swollen eyes, grunting as though suffering a headache and thirsty as all get out; since awakening he'd drunk what seemed a gallon of water, a quart of coffee. Dehydrated. For some reason.

Creedence, chewing her lower lip. "Promise me something."

"Yes, ma'am?"

"If you don't like these presents, my feelings won't be hurt. Not a bit."

"I'm sure it's great. Let's see what you got."

"Always impatient. Nothing changes."

Reaching behind the bed she pulled out a package, square and flat. "First, something I did myself."

Ripping into the bright holiday paper, snowflakes, silvery on an indigo background; Devin, seeing the back of a frame, a nice one.

"This better not be a picture of Dusty."

"Don't worry."

Pulling off the rest of the paper, turning over the frame, his crusty old

Devin-heart skipped a beat: Before him lay a beautiful, detailed charcoal drawing of Libby, standing in shafts of sunlight. Libby, holding kitten-Prudy.

He gasped, clutching the frame to his chest.

Devin, knowing the snapshot from which the image had been taken, a photo from the last time Libby and Devin had visited Chilton before the accident, only days after they'd adopted the kitten. The day they'd told their families about the move to Arcadia.

As in the photograph, the drawing of Libby depicted her happy, bright and alive. Libby, cradling the kitten like an infant.

A squiggle in the corner:

> *By Creedence,*
> *For Devin,*
> *Xmas 2004*

Devin, biting the inside of his cheek like Dubya and Poppy at the first inauguration, dignity and decorum demanding no tears must fall. "Bless you, my sister."

"I call it 'The Sunbeamers.'"

"You bet you do."

"I thought you might be ready to look at them both again."

Putting down the drawing, pulling his sister to him, he held her tight, possessive; he pressed his face into the shoulder of her ratty old terry cloth robe. "Thank god for my sister."

"There's something else, too. Ready?"

Pulling back, bussing her on the lips, he winked. "Gonna be hard to top the first one."

Leading Devin over to another box, a small cube on the floor beside her dresser, she held out her hands and waited.

"I thought that this might help, too. Even more permanent. Something to outlast all of us."

Devin, picking it up. "Dang. Heavy. This better not be a brick with a Wal-mart gift card taped onto it."

"Just open it on the floor."

Tearing into the paper. "Oh—god."

"I'm sorry."

"Don't be."

"Is it okay?"

Breathing hard, not looking at Creedence, he could only nod 'yes'."

Now a flood came, hot and silent, saltwater dripping onto the monument to his cat. Sucking wind. Coughing like his mother'd been doing all season long.

He settled down. "You got me with this. But in a good way."

"I thought we could put it in the backyard, if you wanted. With the others."

Devin, composing himself, put his hand on her freckled face. "I know a better place."

# EIGHTY-ONE

## — CREEDENCE

The new year, days away, found Eileen shuffling in a threadbare housedress, muttering and lashing out with sudden, vitriolic rages, many aimed at Devin. Such diatribes, Chelsea noted, ran off his back like warm duckwater.

He seemed to want to let her get it out.

Knew it was frustration over the cancer. Yeah.

Now that her brother had told her how bad, it all made sense. A hospice nurse was to come by starting next week. Creedence was still not supposed to know about that part.

Well. She still had to move out. If Mama wasn't gonna act like she was sick, to Chelsea she wouldn't be sick. She had to start thinking about classes, oldschool stuff like English and History. She'd have to sit through all that mess to get to the art stuff.

Like had bored her to tears in school.

She wanted to draw.

To look at things and draw them.

She'd get to that soon enough.

By the time she was thirty-five.

Or something along those lines.

*Double dang.* Mama's talk about her not needing to go to college had a ring of truth, suddenly.

Eileen, sparing only the cats her wrath: coddling and spoiling and babytalking the pets to a ridiculous degree, both hers as well as Chelsea's soon-to-be-transient brood; attached in particular to the aging, declining Mr. Bubbie, the once lion king of the house now able only to eat, sleep, purr, and shuffle around on unsteady paws that tingled from nerve damage—when she found him as a kitten, the tip of his tail had been broken in an accident.

The cat's time, nigh; the truth seen in his rheumy eyes, in the greasy coat he seemed no longer willing or able to clean.

She could see Devin getting the 'ick' in his gut over discussion of any such pet drama. Enough, already, was the look on his face. Which she understood.

Offhand, the night before, he had changed the subject of Mr. Bubbie's condition:

"I think old Roy Earl might still be sweet on you, girl. You believe that?"

"Too bad. He had his chance." She recalled Devin watching as her gears ground. "He isn't still single. Is he?"

"Hasn't found the right gal yet, he said Something about not enough freckles or pretty long red hair."

Oh, she had said. "Goodness. He didn't mean me."

Devin had snorted and shaken his head. He handed over a business card for Roy Earl's smoothie stand—little cartoon bananas.

"He said he drew them little banana-dudes himself. I thought y'all would have something in common."

She turned it over. A hand-scratched cell number. *Let's get caught up sometime!* with a smiley face.

How sweet, she had thought. How normal. Compared to Billy's refusal to respond to her apologies, which chapped her dimpled ass but-good, Roy Earl sounded like an actual gentleman.

Eileen, stooped over wiping down Mr. Bubbie with a special feline cleaning-cloth from a plastic packet beside her on the oriental rug, cooed a whispered mantra of love and assurance, when she wasn't coughing. Using an oxygen tank at night, now. She kept it in the closet during the day.

Helluva piece of theater, Devin kept saying, with genuine admiration, at Mama's attempts to keep Creedence pristine.

Hearing her old cat's motor revving into high gear, Creedence smiled. But also knew.

"He ain't too good, is he, Mama?"

Eileen, unfettered vehemence: "You ain't got the sense to take care of yourself, much less these damn cats." Coughing, heaving for breath. "I swear but you don't. Neither one of you. The thought of you taking him into yet another environment so soon—are you *trying* to kill this precious animal?"

Nothing had changed. Mama's words felt like being kicked in the stomach. "I wish you'd quit with these little scenes. I ain't gonna leave my pet behind. And look at you. Mama, you can barely take care of your own, much less my kitties. If you didn't have me and Devin to scoop your damn litter boxes, this place would smell like a zoo right now."

A long moment held, like on one of the TV shows right before a commercial break, the two characters having argued up to some dramatic peak to stand there, looking all bug-eyed at each other with music swelling. The mother, the daughter, the cat, purring and old and infirm.

The mother, infirm. But not old. *Mama and Daddy will both have died in their 60s*, Creedence thought. *Unless of course Mama pulls through. Nothing would surprise me.*

Mr. Bubbie, creaky, walked toward her on his shaky feet for a few steps. Before making it over to his cat-mom and with his breathing labored as though exhausted, he lowered back down onto the floor.

Chelsea allowed herself to acknowledge the truth: yes, it was Mr. Bubbie's time. Nothing told you like when their appetite went. And his was mostly gone.

"Maybe it is time to take him in. Do you think?"

"Oh, lord," Eileen wept. "I just don't know what to do."

"Mama, I don't know what to do either."

Creedence lurched forward—not to the cat, but to her mother. They fell into one another's arms and both howled with grief, their words coming in long strings of aggrieved gobbledygook like Devin's old drunk-speak.

At last the tears dried up. There wasn't anything to say. They hadn't been crying about the cat. Well—they had. And other things.

"He's fine for now, darling. Let's not do this to ourselves."

"I'll keep my eye on him another day or two. See how he eats tonight."

"That's right. Now help me go upstairs. I got to lay back down."

"You need to have your oxygen on."

Eileen gasped. "Hush your smart mouth. That's only to help me sleep."

Chelsea helped her to bed.

"Where's Devin been?"

"He said he was going to see Uncle Hill about borrowing a truck."

"For what?" Eileen remembered the moving plans. "Oh—p'shaw. Not that mess again."

"It's too much money, now, not to go through with it."

"Lord. Let me get in a nap before I have to fix supper later for you young'uns. I can't keep fighting these battles much longer."

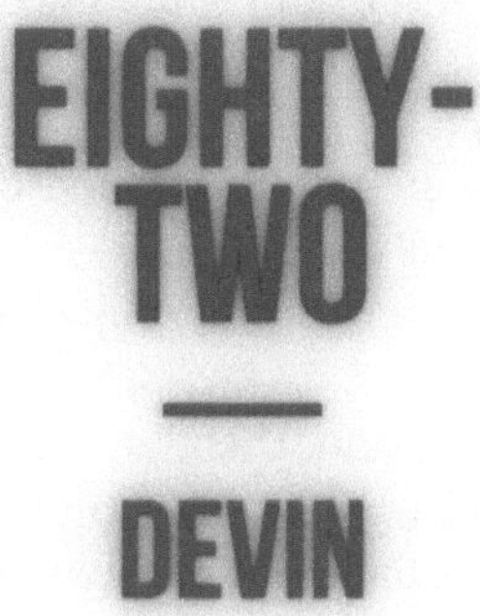

# EIGHTY-TWO — DEVIN

Devin, Uncle Hill, strolling the lot and shooting the shit—Edgewater County gossip, Redtails football, a big poker pot the car dealer won in the back rooms at Pike's Bait & Pawn, where redneck movers and shakers kept a private gentleman's club and speakeasy. The secret societies who ran the county, as Devin had learned from his dad, operated in the shadows. Had their own rules. The whole idea had made him sick.

Hampton told Devin of his plans to run for mayor of Tillman Falls; Devin, thinking it'd be an appropriate endeavor for a man of such prior accomplishment, wealth and connections. Wishing his quote-unquote uncle well in the effort.

"A member of the merchant class as well-known as you should ease right into office."

"Yeah—it's who you know. And I know everybody."

"I don't doubt it for a minute."

Devin, telling filthy jokes and crazy stories about his past on the road; Hampton, doubling over with laughter, almost choked on the juices from the plug stuck in his cheek.

A sample: "Why on Sunday afternoons do rednecks always do it doggy-style?"

Hampton, breathless from a previous ribald witticism, gasped *I dunno tell me*.

"So they can *both* look at NASCAR!"

"Lord have mercy." Hampton, wiping tears, his merriment in senescence. "Devin, son—you always was a handful."

"That's what y'all keep telling me."

"Means the world that you're here. You're home. And you seem whole. I speak for your daddy when I say that, you understand."

"Glad to be here. And—I understand. More than you know."

Putting his hands on Devin's bony shoulders, he squeezed the two hard bumps underneath the denim jacket hard enough to hurt. "You have been through hell, my boy."

"Hell, and back." Devin, an air of sanguine dismissal. "But I put myself through it, mostly. Don't forget that."

"You did the best could, son. Considering what happened. That's the way it seems to me."

"We better go with that version, then."

A hearty handshake. "And I got to say, Colette seems happier than I ever seen. At least since she was a little girl," his wistfulness here exponentiated. "Back in the day."

"Creed keeps talking second chances."

"Everybody needs one. But, I can't just go and replace somebody I trust on the switchboard, not somebody like my baby niece. It's one of the most important jobs we got here—if the customers can't get to the sales department, we don't move freight. Where to route the freaking calls is like the nervous system of the company."

"Putting it that way, I guess so."

Hampton and Devin went on to share their excitement over the Redtails' upcoming New Year's Day bowl appearance, but Devin, a big phony. Abhorring sports and most other entertainments, but faking his way through with reasonable alacrity.

Running out of small talk, they paused in front of the enormous American flag hanging from a fifty-foot pole. The big rigs downshifted on the freeway offramp a quarter mile away. The smell of charring meat wafted from the Hardee's. The grinding of a backhoe engine from another nearby parcel; the laying of another plain of asphalt for what Hampton said was going to be a nice-ass plaza with an upscale grocer as anchor.

Devin, rocking back on his heels, smoking. "Uncle Hill? A question."

Cursing his obliviousness, Hampton spat brown juice onto the asphalt of the iconic legacy car dealership he'd inherited. "You need a new car, don't you? That what this visit's all about. Shoot, say the word and you'll find a set of keys in your hand quicker than a New York minute."

Devin's gaze, flashing across the rows of sunstruck windshields, the stars and stripes hanging in heavy repose above their heads; the flag hung still as could be, awaiting a breeze substantial enough to lift such a grandiose shank of colorfully resonant cloth. "That right? Any car on the lot?"

Uncle Hill, ever the closer, slapped his hands together so hard a report like a gunshot slapped back from the huge glass windows of the showroom. "For you, son? Sign and drive."

"No more cars." Holding onto Hampton's meaty arm. "Just came to say how grateful I am for all the help you've given the Ruckers through the years."

Touched, tearful. "It's what you do for your loved ones."

"Only one other thing I need to know, Uncle Hill."

"Shoot."

Grinning like he'd won a contest against the odds. Against time itself. "You and Mama—y'all still sneak around?"

Hampton, the ruddy color draining from his face. "I ain't real certain I understand what it is you're trying to say."

"I'm sure Daddy didn't mind—since y'all were so close, and all."

Hampton, shamefaced. He examined the tips of his polished, snakeskin cowboy boots. "There's something you ought to understand."

"Do tell."

"Your Mama, son, she's a force of nature. When she makes her up mind she wants something—?" Grimacing as though physically pained. "Ain't much anyone can do about it. You appreciate what I'm telling you?"

Whatever ire previously felt now tempered by a twinge of empathy: "Beau—look who you're talking to."

Hampton, holding out his hands in a helpless gesture of *what can I tell you.*

Devin, playful, slapped at one of freckled bear-paws bearing rings: one from Carolina Military Academy down in Charleston, the other bearing the Masonic squared-circle. "I'm just funnin', you old devil."

"You like to give me a thrombo."

Devin, leveling a finger at the broad chest of his so-called uncle—the hard Devin, heart crusted over, mean enough to bite the head off a rattlesnake—returned for a bonus appearance. "Creedence loved her Daddy more than all the world. So, no matter what happens down the line, you'd best keep your secrets held close. Like I do. Deal?"

Hampton, subdued. "If only I had any decent secrets worth keeping, I'd probably be a happier man."

Devin, a slow nod. "You're one of the richest men in the county. You built this place and made it better than your daddy could've ever dreamed. You put dumbass Edgewater County field-hands of all creeds and races onto payment plans and with rims and wax and tape decks and the whole bleeding shebang. And I respect that. I really do. But there's only one more thing. One thing I got to ask you."

Hampton, blanching with anticipation, waited with a clenched jaw.

"Creedence said we could borrow a truck off you for a day or two. To move her stuff to Columbia."

"You got it," he said in a rushing cascade of relief. "Let's go inside and get the keys."

Hampton hollered for a supplicant to scare up an new F-150 to sign out for a few days to his nephew, who was in a hurry; to put Hill's personal DEALER tags on the vehicle.

Devin waited, smoking, a pervasive emptiness sweeping through his body—after all this time, the big confrontation. And, what? He had managed to make Hill Hampton self-conscious about shit that went down decades ago.

*Yippee—big deal.*

Devin, pitching his smoldering butt at the back bumper of a Ford Expedition, watched as the cigarette exploded in a tiny shower of ash. The resolution to one of the great emotional sagas of his life had come and gone like any other moment in the history of life on terra firma—there, and then not.

At least Hill had not asked about Eileen's condition. Hell, for all Devin knew, she'd kept it secret from him as well.

Other people's business—he wanted no part. Held no responsibility. He was Gen X. If they wanted him to help, they should have paid attention when they had they chance, when they could have been a good influence; instead they let the television sets raise their children—a cold medium. Oops.

Devin, driving back to Pine Haven in the blue F-150—new, only thirty-three miles on the odometer, shiny and chrome and with a specific Ford type of brand-new smell, like leathery men's aftershave—took the long way around. He did this often, to avoid the spot where Libby'd bled her death-water back into the earth, leaking out like the acrid vitals from the Mustang's pipes and valves.

Feeling lighter of spirit that at any time in memory, however, he made himself *not* go the long way.

Made himself say it didn't matter. Now was now and then was then, and what did then matter?

His ribcage vibrated and he got the creepy-crawlies. But he went and drove the old highway. Went and done it, dang it.

What he found: a new highway, expanded to four lanes all the way down thanks to the massive Wally-world distributor now located in the county, and in the nick of time since all the millwork was long gone. Trucks, coming and going—not drunk rednecks passing on a yellow line but big-old semis, the sort with which Devin had jockeyed on the hot, unforgiving slabs American of the highway system.

The ground were Libby died? All dug up and gone. Scooped out and turned into a concrete culvert. Like the literal space itself had been removed.

That felt good.

Devin, pulling into the emergency lane right whereabouts it'd happened, tucked a smoke into his mouth and turned on the flashers.

Devin, squinting and nosing his beak around, said, all different. The trees gone. Concrete where had been real grass, and fake grass where had been trees. In Devin's moment, it been grass and glass, trees and blood. Sunlight, yes, shining down.

But other than the current shimmering sun, more white than yellow, the landscape, transformed. What memories and ghosts floated here now so incorporeal as to be useless in provoking the old demonic memories—the anger, the black depression, the guilt.

The knowing.

The remembering.

Devin got out of the Jetta and ambled around. He stood smoking and looked down into the culvert as a couple of kids, Latino boys of ten and twelve, pedaled BMX bikes along the dry concrete culver. They passed below Devin going up and down its angled sides, back and forth, a double-helix dance among the four tires of the bicycles and the eight limbs of the boys; they rode away singing a melodic Spanish-language pop song.

No death here. Only right-now.

Devin, spitting and feeling all right, all right as he could, got back in the car. Enough with memory lane. But in a good way.

Satisfied, he went home to shove a load of crap into the pickup bed. He had gotten the hotfoot to go move stuff into the new apartment, but news of Creedence's date, with none other than Roy Earl, meant he'd need to stay.

Creedence, gorgeous and smelling like heaven, came downstairs. Devin, thinking Roy Earl likely to pass out at the sight of her. Checking on all the cats and Mama, she went outside to get in her fine little American-made Ford Focus.

But no need—outside sat Roy Earl Pettus, wearing a suit and holding a bouquet of flowers. He held the door open for her to his car, a Mercedes SL-350 convertible like Billy used to drive. There went some of that smoothie cash.

"I don't know what to say," Devin heard his sister say.

Roy helped her into the car. "I couldn't not come to get you a second time, angel." They drove off.

Eileen, haggard, shuffled outside in her housedress, dragging her oxygen tank.

"You need help getting out the door?"

"I'll be damned if I need anybody's help. Oh—so at least one of my children is still here?"

"Mama?" Devin stretched a strap taut across boxes in the bed of the midnight-blue pickup truck. "I need to axe you something."

"What, son." Breathless, annoyed and coughing blood-flecked spittle, she sat down on the front porch rocker.

"How long you got?"

"Till what?"

"You know."

The mother, the son, locking eyes. "I'm afraid don't have the slightest inkling of what you're talking about."

Nodding. Understanding. "A favor."

She waited.

"When you get there, let me know."

"Oh, p'shaw. You talk in riddles."

"Hey—know what I've been thinking?"

"What, darling."

Devin went to his mother. Leaning in and stealing a hug. Her body stiff at first, then molding itself to his. He felt her bones jutting out.

"I ain't got to move over there with her straight away. Creedence—she'll be fine. Roy Earl's right there. And so's Billy."

"Darling," she said. "Are you sure?"

"Sure as I am about anything."

"Well," she whispered, pushing back, straightening her hair. "I think that'd be lovely. Just wonderful, in fact. We can pay for your part of the rent ourselves, for now."

"That's right. We'll put checks in the mail."

"Yes, we will." Eileen, needing to say more. "Devin?"

"What, Mama."

"Let's you and me take Mr. Bubbie to the doctor tomorrow. So Colette don't have to mess with all that. Maybe it won't be as bad as we think."

"It's her cat, Mama."

"Devin—she wants us to do it. For her. To protect her. Don't you see?"

"Does she want that?"

"We both do."

Despite knowing the news wouldn't be good—it couldn't go any other way—he agreed. Least he could do for his little sister. And his mom. About that time the hospice nurse arrived, and they all went inside for her to take Eileen's vitals, check her meds, and answer any questions they had.

Billy, exhausted, greasy, shagged, spent; in other words, worn the fuck out, the prior evening having seen no small amount of energy expenditure, oh my brothers. It'd taken him until nearly dawn to dispose of the two accident-victims in the Green Hole, after he'd accidentally fucked them both to death during the wild threesome he'd engendered after picking up the middle-aged women at the Parlor.

Business types from out of town, they'd been attracted to Billy's free spirit and gentlemanly bearing. He'd gone out looking sharp, losing the tie-dye and flip-flops for a blue suit and loose tie like the lawyers drowning their perfidies in happy-hour oblivion. Showering, man-scaping, whole bit; he went out intending to get laid, have some fun. Blow off steam from the Creedence slight.

He'd yet to fully recover from it. That bitch.

Also, away from Melanie, with all her insidious planning.

Planning their life together.

Way way way ahead of herself.

Full of herself.

But he couldn't simply accident her out of the way. Not Melanie.

He halfway loved her, he finally realized.

Sickening.

How could he betray Libby? His love, full as a hothouse flower, remained only for her.

Yesterday he'd felt better, though, he had to admit, especially after picking up those skanks. Hell of a pop or two before things had gotten out of hand. He'd told himself it was going to be straight sex and how these women, drunk and amazed at themselves for agreeing to fuck this handsome stranger, would return home from their business trip gaping and sore, with only a headful of memories instead of grievous injuries.

But accidents, happening.
Quick.
Brutal.
He couldn't remember any of it with clarity. He'd been drunk. Lucky, again, his muscle-memory at dumping bodies continued to served him well.

But now, sitting in his old Mercedes, furtive, glancing at the quiet Old Market, lifting the whip cream dispenser to his mouth and inhaling, he didn't worry 'bout a thing. Holding in the gas, getting the sound of distant, hallucinatory sirens. No one would believe him capable of murder, nor of sucking nitrous oxide in broad daylight. Who would do this? Not I, said he.
*Wah-wah-wah.*
He'd bought a box of chargers and a fresh dispenser—his old one slipped out of his hand on the balcony and tumbled fifteen stories to the sidewalk below, shattering like a bomb going off. He'd ROLLED INTO the fancypants gourmet food shop across the way, buying his goods and hightailing it back to the car and setting to work.

Admittedly, he'd had a tough time calming down from the prior night's adventures in Eros and accidental murder. And for all he knew, Melanie—she'd gone home to Charleston to make wedding plans with her mother, was due back "before New Year's," meaning today, probably, the thirtieth—would return any second. Calling him every five minutes with her whole 'I love you' theatrical production.

No woman had loved Billy. That much he knew.

Billy, inhaling the gas. Wah-wah, like George Harrison said. Wah-wah-wah. It helped him forget the unloved thing.

Billy, scheming for a way to break into a hospital and steal a big honkin' blue tank of medical grade gas. Get it rigged with an octopus array of hoses. Recruit five or six bouncing betties together at once, get rocking and see if fucking that many at the same time helped quell the bothersomeness.

All could be arranged.

Billy, feeling nothing. Feeling relief at feeling nothing. But the moment, like all moments, coming and going, and soon the gas wears off. And he is Billy, again. Bothersome.

The purchase of the gas and dispenser a spontaneous addition to the plan at hand, to get a holiday gift he'd promised to his dad:

A shave and a haircut—neat, trim, Young Republican-approved and respectable, the slightest bit not-so-young—because, with Bush the Second reelected—who'd a thunk-it?—we would usher in what the pundits were calling a potential forty-year Republican majority in the government, one ready to expend political capital the way Billy, a firehose, shot thick ropes of Spiderman-webbing semen every which way.

With the election over, January 2005 begins a new cycle. And with conditions this favorable alongside his deep well of contacts on the hill—the folks with whom the family had long did business, and big business at that— the elder Steeple, it seemed, had decided to run in the 2006 midterms for a Virginia congressional seat he'd coveted. The district included any number of his military-industrial complex lobbying clients. Getting into the dome at last made sense.

Billy, having never gone back to work at Southeastern after getting Devin home back in April, felt more than onboard with a change of scenery. Already possessing the right clothes for his new position on the Steeple campaign—oxfords and khakis and penny-loafers, but with vibrant Garcia ties to set him apart from the rest of the politicos—he could transition as soon as his dad needed him.

The long hair, though? The hair, needing to go. It was fine. Jerry had been dead for ten years this year.

Billy, at peace with his decision. His Dad, running for congress like he'd always dreamt of doing, of serving his constituency and his country, he said? Righteous. More like doing the K Street Shuffle, as it was known, he held ideals he hoped Billy, with his writing skills, could help him convey to his media lapdog contacts who would promulgate the inevitability of a Steeple win.

A pip. A new scene, a new crowd.

Billy, ready to leave.

Leave his troubles behind.

Over Libby, at last.

Over it.

Darn it all.

Or at least that's what he kept telling himself.

In any case, Billy, starting work next month, hired onto the campaign full-time as a Paid Consultant, a title sounding loftier than the task itself: the elder Steeple wanting first to put Billy in the trenches. Answering phones, making coffee, intern-style grunt work.

Saying to his son: "The others will respect you more if we do it this way."

"What am I? Monty Clift in A PLACE IN THE SUN?'"

"Pardon?"

"Nothing, dad." Billy might have been over Libby, but he'd kill for a partner who knew movies.

Billy, not giving a shit about the campaign, the job, the dignity, so long remaining able to party-hearty, keep getting blazed and drunk and laid. He felt certain, as the son of the candidate, he could wander in late a few times a week, severely doubting anyone would have the temerity—the stones—to make hay out of his privileged behavior. It had been well-earned and would of course exist and unfold beyond any censure or reproach.

Complications, also necessitating Billy's current line of thinking: Crushed and angry to discover that the full inheritance not his yet after all.

Speaking of dignity? He had none.

At his father's Machiavellian insistence, prior to Granddad's death the two of them revised the terms of Billy's trust to add another ten blessed bloody years—fucking indentured servitude, this.

Difficult to take at first.

Humiliating.

Nearly fifty, now, by the time the real money at last rolled in.

But what to do? Run around screaming, blowing people's heads off, taking a shit on the floor, smearing it all over himself and flinging it at the audience like G.G. Allin? Holding his breath until turning blue? Raping and pillaging? Killing a string of women and concealing their bodies, instead of accidentally loving them to death to hide the fact of his lack of control?

Considerations.

As for Melanie, better not to have all that money at hand; all the harder to shake her loose, eventually, married or not.

Because of the campaign excuse, he had managed to put off a hard date for the wedding; continued fervent lovemaking, thanks to the miracle blue pills, with assurances that he wished not to (A) break it off, (2) break up, or (III) take a breather, all plans confirmed though postponed, life trajectories fixed and stable, had kept her quiet.

Melanie, balking, decried the long engagement proposed by him. At first. Not caring about finishing her degree. Ready to quit and be Mrs. Steeple.

Billy, disgusted. No career track? Housekeepers now did what women used to do. Late capitalism demanded careers, not caretaking. He wanted to puke.

Libby wouldn't have needed Billy. For anything. No wonder her strength had been so attractive.

Melanie, concerned about the drinking, though. Tiresome beyond measure. If it'd been good enough for Ruck, good enough for Billy. Hell, he couldn't say it that way, however, so he merely promised it all a passing affectation that DC life would cure.

Ruck. The dude had it all together. Had come through the fire. Was onto something. You want to see someone bounce back from the abyss? Call

Devin Rucker. A fucking superhero. Billy, not worthy of touching the hem of his jean jacket. Had let him almost fall to his death again.

Billy would die before he'd face his old friend again. Which almost felt worse than his shame, or anger over being thrown under the bus by Creedence. All of it toxic, he cracked another charger and tried to forget.

Killing the last of the nitrous out of the whip cream dispenser, Billy lurched out of the Mercedes with his head spinning. He staggered around, chuckling. Time for a drink.

Then, a vision—a girl, a grungy angel, a familiar face, a friend: his old intern Marleigh, peddling her bike the wrong way down Saluda Avenue toward the Beanery. At the sight of her, his mind and body, ramping into overdrive.

Here, another one that got away.

Throbbing. The way of the flesh, pink and wet and sticky and pulsating like some David Cronenberg-style makeup effects fever dream; one more chick, her mind blown at the sight and feel and staggering awesomeness of Billy. Providential; foretold, he speculated.

But he had felt the same about Libby.

And Creedence.

And them all.

*Maybe this time it'll be different.*

Billy, stagger-stepping after her, called out in good cheer.

Marleigh, stopping, putting her feet down, appeared cautious: "Dr. Steeple?"

Billy, trotting over heavy-footed, was glad she still thought him a terminal degree holder. "This unbelievably super-amazing, totally unbelievable incredibly good fortune is beyond all possibility of coincidence." He held out his arms to steady himself against a wave of vertigo. "Whoa. I think one of these cracks in the sidewalk just tried to crawl up my leg."

"What happened at the film archive?"

He ignored her. "What are you doing here? It's holiday break."

"My dumb parents went to Europe."

"This time of year?"

"My mom had to have Christmas in Paris. It's all she's talked about since HOME ALONE came out."

"No shit. Now that's movie fandom."

"I told her I thought the idea was idiotic. That they could count me out."

"Not HOME ALONE. God, I hate that shit."

"It's the worst."

"You get along with your mother otherwise?"

Marleigh frowned: *are you kidding?*

In secret, of course, Billy loved the movie. He watched it every Christmas, with it never failing to give him a serious lump in the throat. A boy untethered, making the most of the predicament, triumphing over directed and premeditated adversity, but getting the family back together as well; everything miraculously working out. Having cake, eating it too, a wonderful modern American fable. That thing fucking ROCKED, bro. He wanted to bash in her stupid girl-head for not appreciating HOME ALONE.

"So—may I ask? About the archive?"

Billy, trying to focus, smiled and said *shoot*.

Casting her eyes down, sheepish and concerned: "You walked out that day to go on your trip... And, like, never came back."

"Withdrawal in disgust's not the same as apathy, my dear."

"I was afraid you'd died, or something."

"Born again."

Cautious anew. "Oh-really, now."

"In a metaphorical manner of speaking. Not like you're thinking. I'm not one of these godly Southern crackers."

"So what happened?"

Billy, quick to answer. "No-no, it's not that something *happened-*happened. I chose to exercise the free will I had at my disposal. You realize, Marleigh, I was only doing that job for fun." Leaning in. "What you must understand is that I've got a veritable buttload of family money."

"Well, la-ti-da."

"It is what it is. But when the wind's blowing sour, I ankle the project. Sometimes I do it just to show people how easy it is for me to leave them hanging. How little I need them."

Marleigh, backing away from his hot breath, changed the subject. "I was disappointed I never got a chance to talk to you about that LEBOWSKI paper you were writing for the conference."

That stopped him in his tracks. Made his meatwhistle sing out of key.

Shame—he had finished his paper except for the citations, but he'd done nothing about preparing a presentation. He had bailed. Instead, he got drunk with Ruck. And come back to this life of lassitude and liquor.

He couldn't tell her any of it. "God—I didn't make you read that dreadful screed, did I?"

"I did get around to it."

"Well?"

"And I watched the movie again. And—well."

"Be honest, now."

"I dunno."

Billy, his heart thumping, seized the moment. Brash, gripping her forearm, leaning in, febrile and vibrating with goose-pimpled excitement and certitude, his charisma gushed like a tapped hydrant on a summer afternoon in a poor urban neighborhood. "We must go discuss this over scalding hot dark water. I still have time to revise the paper before publication. I need your help, Marleigh."

Hesitancy. "Um. I was gonna go in anyway. I guess."

Without waiting for a reply, Billy pulled her toward into the Carolina Beanery. He hoped to introduce her to Roy Earl, check in with the bossman, who had stopped returning Billy's late-night, drunken calls. Probably just busy.

The Beanery, with the university shut down for almost a month, sat all but deserted. Ceiling fans turned lazy in wintertime reversal mode. The black-and-white floor had been waxed. Businesses did repairs and chores while the students, their financial lifeblood and customer base, were on break.

With the Old Market in a state of relative slumber, the barista behind the counter, bored as hell and doing a crossword puzzle, leaned on a stool chewing her lip. An Asian guy sitting in the back corner on his Mac took advantage of Roy Earl's complimentary WIFI, tapping furiously, probably coding; a middle-aged guy in a rumpled suit came shuffling out of the bathroom, adjusting his belt; he picked up one of the alt weeklies and went outside with his espresso to smoke. Jazz played on the satellite radio—good, weird stuff; COLTRANE LIVE IN JAPAN, one of the tracks where his sax sounds like a honking donkey, perfect for a hipster coffee shop. The whole affair, redolent of baked goods and roasted coffee. Heaven on earth, a place of warmth and life. Of friendship.

Marleigh and Billy ordered coffee and repaired over to a rear corner table where Billy'd seduced many a grad student and fellow Southeastern staff member, erudition and the miraculous shank of veiny viscera nestled along his thigh friends in this regard—the corner table offered cover for placing a willing hand atop a khaki-colored polish sausage; to let them know it wasn't amateur hour.

Small talk, catching up, sipping coffee; Billy's future, a series of outrageous exaggerations regarding the DC gig. Saying that after he gets his dad elected to the U. S. Senate, the most exclusive club in the world, adding how he had an agent for a screenplay who thought a seven-figure deal lay in the future, with options for not one but three different other screenplays and options for sequels. Offers to set up first-look production deals at both Paramount and Universal. Leaving Columbia for good, heading west. Making all his dreams come true.

"That's Columbia, the city," he clarified, "and not the movie studio, which is Sony now anyway."

"No—I got it."

"So that's the real reason I quit. Sorry for the coldness of the gesture."

Marleigh, herself a budding filmmaker, lit up with amazement: "I'm so excited for you! I can hardly believe it."

"It truly is unreal. You have no idea how much."

Marleigh extolled the virtues of having become what she termed a "Netflix ho," renting so many films she'd not only missed out on, but screening many other interesting deep-catalogue titles. Running through a list of auteurs, some of whom were lacking in familiarity to Billy.

Alternately jazzed and envious of the young woman's knowledge. A little green.

A little titillated.

Or, a lot:

Thinking, Marleigh=Libby.

Trying not to consider such thoughts.

*But listen to her!* Yes, impossible to deny: A partner in cinema. Like Libby would have been. This, what he needed. All she needed was persuasion.

A universe of possibilities opened before his eyes, a swirling fractal maelstrom of infinite forgiveness and spiritual satori awaiting—*oh sweet mystery of life, I have found thee.*

"So anyway, Lebowski?"

"By all means."

"I get what you're saying, about how the movie is real symbolic, and the political stuff, the cowboy narrator character—?"

"The Stranger?" Billy's arm-hairs, stippling. "Omniscient, wise, all-seeing? I can dig it."

"Yeah, omniscient *and* all-seeing." Marleigh, teasing.

"Hardy-har."

"A narrator who knows. We can trust the Stranger. Can't we?"

"One presumes so."

"So there's narrator-as-God, all those White Russians, and the nihilists, as your paper says. And then 'Jesus,' a flashy pederast, a character of not only questionable fashion taste but also morality, serves as an extreme to which we may compare the political extremes, ironic in bearing but representative of deviancy in the populace. Walter, meanwhile, is the reactionary right-wing, the Dude a disaffected, failed hippie left-wing, would-be icon—that whole Port Huron Statement bit. And poor Donnie, he's caught in the middle between the extremes, another clueless everyman."

"Like most regular folks."

"Nobody in real life gives a shit about politics."

"Then there's the Big Lebowski, who epitomizes wealth and power."

"In the end we see him as not only a literally handicapped person, but a fraud to boot. A commentary on your own class, as it happens."

Billy, pleased, but trying not to show it too much. Trying not to seem eager-beaver, blow the whole plan. "Yes, yes. Go on."

"So I have to say: I don't think you followed through on your thesis."

"Wait—*what?*"

Drawing in a breath, her cheeks bloomed crimson before she pressed ahead. "Not that it's wrong, or anything. Just not quite—finished."

She had him there. "It was still in draft form. You've nailed me on that. I couldn't find the—didn't have the—too busy."

"You had the big preservation project. The one I was working on. You know they dropped it and canceled my internship," she said, downtrodden.

He didn't hear her. He wasn't listening. "That's it—I was too busy. You remember. The media archive. Meetings up the hill. Preserving the films. The movies. No way I could finish that paper. Too much else. Family stuff. All really boring. What's important in life? Some dumb movie? After all?"

"Well—I get it." Marleigh, puckish and innocent. "But the paper, it was ironic how you left out a discussion of the one thing that, like in the movie, could have *tied everything together*," eyebrows hinting.

Billy, slapping his forehead. "The Dude's rug—'it tied the room together'."

"So what do you think it means?"

Billy, musing, morose and moronic, felt his eyeballs pointing in two different directions. He needed another toot of nitrous; a headache creeping in. "Hell if I know how the gosh-darn rug ties it all together. Do you?"

"Maybe." She held up a finger, chipped turquoise nail polish, a mass of bracelets and other costume jewelry, light from the tiny halogen spots hanging from the ceiling glinting off her piercings. Patches, buttons—punk band logos, leftist political slogans, NO WHINING with the red negation slash on her right shoulder.

"So you're already talking about how these characters represent these different political factions, right? And what sets everything in motion is The Dude's rug, pissed upon by dumb hit-men who've mistaken him for a rich man who happens to have the same name. But anyway, again and again he hear The Dude invoking the rug's ability to 'tie everything together,' and as much as you want to say that, like in a mystery, it's some kind of red herring, I see it as the central symbol instead."

"Like Hitchcock's MacGuffin-dealie?"

"No, not at all. More like an objective-correlative. The MacGuffin is simple narrative misdirection. Sleight of hand."

"Oh, sure, sure." Billy. thinking her terminology sounded familiar from Max de Lisle's scriptwriting classes, concepts lost to time and inattention; thinking her like Libby reincarnated. "Right on all points."

"I was thinking about your thesis, and politics, democracy, governance, whole bit." Tapping the chipped nail against a coffee cup rim. "And like, what if the rug is the underlying idea behind our society—our Western style democracy, which is codified by a central document, a manifesto, a constitution. Commandments, of a kind. Sacred. Sacrosanct. In the case of this country, protection of the idea of every so-called man created equal, at liberty to be happy, to prosper, have redress of grievances, et cetera. But retaining the ability to create law. Maintaining order. Not forging happiness at the expense of anyone else, but in partnership. The golden rule. I mean— you yearn to be free, yes, but not free enough to, say, yell fire in a crowded theatre, or hurt somebody on purpose, or drive drunk, or, or—"

"*Drive drunk?*" Billy, his insect antennae twitching, leaned forward. "What the heck do you mean by that?"

Marleigh, taken aback by the brusque tone. "Just an example. Of—the violation of the social contract."

Suspicious. "Go on."

Getting back on track, she continued, "Think about it. The Dude's rights are trampled on left and right—pun intended—while he tries to regain the rug, with it providing him some ideal of security, an underpinning of order and reason. Linus's blanket, like. But more than that. A foundation that ties everything together, the disparate pieces of his life, into a manageable whole.

"And so maybe what they're saying is that by all of us choosing sides, or being forced or otherwise persuaded to choose sides, we're forgetting the reasons we're all in this relationship to begin with—if there are reasons. In any case: We're all human, after all. We all have to eat. We all have to pee and take poops," demure, giggling. "We all have to die, ultimately. Our country—our young country, compared to most—was supposed to be a new way of doing all that, or at least it was way back then. A new kind of social contract, building on the protections first established in, I guess, the Magna Carta? Not a history major, here. But, a new order. A new world order."

Billy, dumbstruck by her discourse. "So—?"

"*So*, maybe the rug literally does represent our constitution. Or the Declaration, or any codifying document. Like those dumb thugs enforcing a pornographer's sense of financial injustice, they're pissing on what the country's supposed to be—a democracy, where everyone, if they want, has an equal say, has rights, has a fair shot. The right to be left alone. The right to be right. The right to be left. To pursue happiness. To body art, or public demonstrations, or," lowering her voice, "to smoke dope. Or, like The Dude, to smoke dope and bowl."

"Retaining those rights'll be a challenge. Look at the war on 'some' drugs."

"Some people are selfish." Shrugging, a half-smile. "Like what they want is the only thing that matters. Well—fuck that, I say."

Billy, desperate to disagree, to say she was wrong, but he didn't have a blessed idea how the damned rug metaphor worked.

*Shut up and praise her—she's brilliant.*

And yet his words came haughty and dripping with condescension: "Well, that's one person's way of interpreting it all, one supposes. And now, the point's moot—no more academic papers for this moneyed and successful scriptwriter, not now that I'm jetting off to the big time. It's like hometown heroes Hootie and the Blowfish, on that night they took off in the lear jet from Columbia Metro to play the Letterman gig in New York—the moment of arrival."

Disappointed. "Just one person's opinion."

Billy, slapping his thigh. "I've got to see it again."

A smile, impish. "The rug?"

"No, silly—the movie. You game?"

"Oh—no. I can't."

"C'mon. You can't say no."

Marleigh, blinking, hesitant. A tiny head-shake. "I have work to do."

"Now, Marleigh." Billy, tilting his head, willing his eyes to twinkle. "Over the holiday break?"

"I'm starting to try to prepare for the spring. I've got scriptwriting."

A welling of emotion. "You do?"

"My first writing class. And to tell the truth—?"

"*Yes?*"

"I would love to pick your brain sometime. Talk scripts."

Blown away anew. "Could be arranged."

"I want to read the sci-fi epic."

"I have a copy up in the condo. You can take it. Give me notes."

"You—want notes from me?"

"Of course I do."

"Your news, it's just amazing. Congratulations, Dr. Steeple. But—I shouldn't come up to your condo."

Collecting himself at her resistance. Mercy. "Look, we can talk scripts all freaking night, girl. We can talk until the world dies. Since we're not colleagues anymore, it'd be okay to hang out. It's huge—my script, that is. Enormous."

Confused. "More than a hundred and twenty pages?"

"Oh, quite so, my dear."

"The pros say that's suicide."

Ignoring her concern—the lies, no agent, no finished script; who cared how long the damn script.

"Marleigh?"

"Uh-huh?"

"So, you get high?"

Her eyes, widening and uncomfortable. "Under certain conditions."

"Good enough, then, fair maiden. Shall we?" Billy rising, chivalrous, offered a hand she accepted, but only with great reluctance. "Conditions await."

# EIGHTY-FOUR

—

## CREEDENCE

Roy Earl and Creedence, strolling toward the Beanery together, smiled and chatted in soft tones. At the crosswalk his hand had rested on the small of her back for a brief instant while a motorcycle passed; the skin still tingled at his touch.

Inside the coffee shop, Creedence, breathing in aromas of fresh baked goods, thought she shouldn't eat another bite. They'd had dinner and a movie, a silly, loud action jam he'd chosen.

She felt so comfortable with him. Already. Like being at home.

"My word—that smell's heavenly."

"Scones are coming out for tomorrow morning. Want one?"

"Yummy," patting her stomach. "But since I moved back in with Mama, I've gotten big as the side of the house."

"You look fine to me."

"Quit it, now."

Bright-eyed, bashful, sincere. "I ain't just saying. You're beautiful. I always thought so."

Creedence, embarrassed but thrilled by the compliment. "Thank you."

The first-daters, at the movie: Roy Earl, reaching over and putting his arm around her, red hair spilling across his forearm. She scrunched over next to him. Creedence, warm all over, worried he could feel the pulse beating in her neck.

Roy Earl, chubby but handsome, was no-question successful. He told her he wanted to franchise his smoothie stands. Maybe the Carolina Beanery, too. "One in every foodcourt around the country would be a good start."

He would be a millionaire, soon.

Sitting across from one another in the deserted coffee shop, with closing time nigh, they made small talk; she discussed her mother's illness, and he looked heartbroken.

"Not Miss Eileen."

She held back a sob. "Yeah. I can't talk about it."

"I always did love her fried chicken, when me and Dobbs would be over."

"I remember those days."

With his manager busy breaking down, wiping, counting, straightening and running the dishwasher, Roy Earl enjoyed the last mocha of the day, a decaf; Creedence ordered a cappuccino. Grimacing at first, expecting the drink to be sweet. Roy Earl, explaining how if she wanted it that way, she'd better add sugar.

"Mama drinks Maxwell House. We ain't got a Carolina Beanery in Chilton."

"Not yet you don't."

Sweet, Creedence thinking, being the operative word for Roy Earl Pettus, along with thoughtful and attentive; feeling as though the first date the most meaningful on which she'd ever gone. Dinner at the upscale Italian restaurant also lovely. Roy Earl, asking her questions there, and in the theatre queue before the movie started, and on the drive back to the Old Market as well.

Wanting to know her.

To make up for lost time.

Creedence, feeling as though Roy Earl the first person to ever ask her what she thought about anything, other than perhaps her Daddy, god rest his soul.

But now Roy Earl appeared pensive. Chewing his lower lip. Tugging at an earlobe like Carol Burnett signing off.

Squeezing a smile at him. "Penny for your thoughts."

"There's something I been carrying inside me forever."

She sat waiting.

"Like I never truly and really said just how totally sorry I was? About not coming to get you like I was supposed to that night."

"Oh—that? I haven't given it a second thought in a million freaking years."

"Remember how I called you? To apologize?"

"A little."

"I ain't ever been sure it came through the right way."

"That's sweet. But, I accepted your apology back then."

"I didn't think you did. That's why I never tried again. But—there was Dusty, anyway."

"Don't remind me."

His rue, like a fog bank rolling in. Sweat broke out on his lip. "Damn it —I liked you so much, Creedence, but I was so shy. Growing up in some dumb place like Tillman Falls, in that stinking honkytonk, you don't learn how to talk to girls too good—or I didn't, at least. Had bad luck with them."

"Somebody broke your heart."

He stammered and hemmed and hawed and turned beet red as though busted. "Something like that."

"I waited in the rain for you."

Roy Earl, stricken. "You been mad at me all this time."

She patted his hand. "It wasn't no big deal."

"Devin said you cussed me up and down."

"I only wanted to see the Grateful Dead. And tell everyone back home how fun it all was. How cool I was, you know. For having gotten to go."

Roy Earl, epiphanic, all but shouting *eureka*. "You wanna go listen to it?"

"Listen to what?"

"The Dead show I made you miss."

"What, like, you got a CD of the concert?"

"Tapes, and CDs, yeah. Different versions. There's even a bootleg VHS —I need to get that transferred to a DVD. Billy, he made us all copies back then. The band, they let their fans record and trade the shows. A cool little sport, in a way, the taping. Blah blah."

Creedence, never hearing of such a thing. "Dang."

"So you wanna?"

"That'd be way cool."

Walking up the hill toward Roy Earl's house, their hands found each other, sudden and tentative at first, becoming more comfortable. Brisk outside, but not freezing. It barely ever froze in South Carolina. Maybe in the upstate. Never in Charleston. It's why the snowbirds come south.

The wailing of sirens, coming to them from the other side of the neighborhood closer to campus.

"Here they come."

"I called them on you, Roy."

"You did?"

"Yes—for stealing my heart."

As a spectral caterwauling came from the approaching emergency vehicles passing through the Old Market, she stopped her date under a streetlamp. Backyard dogs, howling. The glow of the streetlights. The city all around them. A first kiss before going inside; before making him hers.

Forgone: Creedence and Roy Earl never made it to the second CD of the three-disc set.

By the time the music twanged into silence, Roy Earl had already exploded inside her once, way too fast, gasping and swooning and gripping her like a life preserver, but the second time, oh yeah, thank goodness, she thought, and which had only taken about twenty minutes to get underway, now that one found Creedence smooching and stroking him back into full erection, clambering aboard, sliding down—slick!—and bumping and grinding atop him until catching herself a good one.

Coming hard.

Screaming, beating him against the chest, whipping her long red hair around and feeling like a woman, a real woman, hahahaha, alive and whole and awake.

Roy Earl, hollering and laughing, exploded for a second time.

Both of them, drenched. Nothing needed saying aloud.

Later, she woke up to him stroking and kissing her, half-asleep and murmuring and thankful; a trance of love.

"I must be dreaming," he whispered. "Please don't let me wake up. Please."

Creedence, snuggling over next to him, feeling adored. Well—wasn't that easy? He had been right there all along, waiting. Nobody knew.

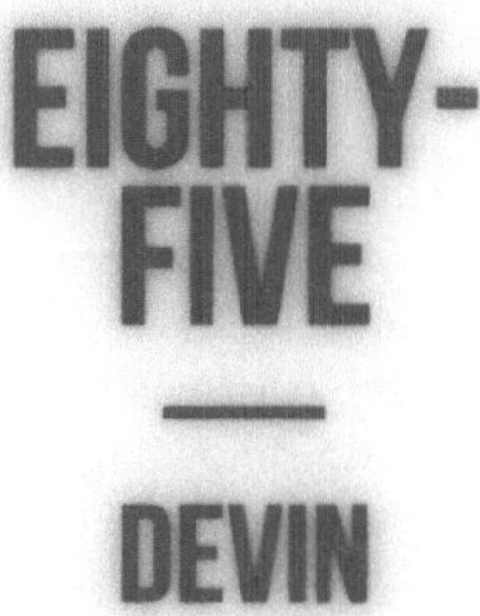


Devin sat alone in the empty apartment a few blocks off Blossom, in a 1940's-era house of four flats next to a huge orphanage on Millwood, with a tall oak tree and an open soccer field by the windows giving a sense of nature and green. Convenient, a five-minute drive to campus, or if by foot, an easy, level stroll mostly downhill in dappled Carolina light, with the chirping of the birds way up in hundred year-old trees back from when they first laid out this neighborhood, the first suburb of the city proper nearer the river. The American dream here; aging, but on display. Rah rah. Good class of people here. Creedence, if Devin weren't around that much after all, would be fine.

She could get another roomie, if need be.

Floating through the empty rooms, stashing the boxes here and there. Transoms over the doors, that's how old this creaky old place was. Its details bespoke its age like the lines around his Mama's mouth, the flesh that hung from her throat, the eyes that pierced him red and frustrated all the time, like an alkie forever waiting for the damn bars to open.

Devin, thinking, how many lived and loved here in this old house before?

A creaking sound came to him. The neighbors upstairs. Muffled voices. Spirits in the material world.

The hardwoods, refinished to a thick shine; footfalls echoing on the kitchen vinyl, peeling up underneath the lower cabinets; plaster-patched walls, a wrought iron fire escape leading from the back door down to a tiny, leaf-strewn backyard. Another resident's junker Fiat sat tucked into a leaf-strewn corner of the fence on blocks, its white finish covered in mildew, twigs, rotting flora. Old, ancient plaster, cracked, peeling paint around windowsills, burns and stains on the floor. This apartment a place where many had lived, in its modern era now serving college students. Beerdrunk students, hard on the furniture. Hard on the foundations of these old places. Hard on themselves.

But Devin, taking it easy.

One day at a time.

Devin, going outside, breathed in the cold air. Heavy traffic on the drive over, a long holiday weekend coming up, thousands making the pilgrimage down to the bowl game in Florida. Squatting on the dark stoop and smoking, eyes drawn by the red and green Christmas lights glowing in the windows of a house across the way, he heard dogs howling, and faraway sirens.

Feeling in his jacket. For the pint stashed therein. For a bracer, a toot.

"Good times." To nobody.

The bottle, not there.

Glad.

Feeling around in another pocket, pulling out a phone instead.

A female voice, answering on the first ring, though doing so nonverbally: Both silent, the age of caller ID allowing Millie Haversford foreknowledge of who'd deigned—at last—to call her back.

"Well, well."

"It is I, babygirl."

"A holiday miracle," a touch sarcastic. "How are you, Ruck?"

"Right as rain, honey. As right as a boy can be."

"This is wonderful. I've been waiting to hear that."

"Wellsir! There ya go."

A moment of grace.

Maybe. Millie would take some selling on his state of mind. "Are you really?"

Devin, yeah, into it, he said. Into the meetings. On the program. "I slipped for a week or two, but got right again."

"It's a slippery slope," sounding disappointed, cautious.

That he had gotten rid of his demons only after getting sober via the coma felt, at times, way too easy.

"You gotta be careful about getting arrogant. Thinking you've got it beat."

"How long you got now, girl?"

She told him—five years. "Long enough to stick. Or so I'm planning."

Devin, waiting to have more delusions like before, but nothing too out of the ordinary had come. Other than thinking Millie would want to hear from him. In general type-deal.

He could tell she didn't. All business from her end. Wary. Concealed.

She went on. "Recovery, it's a long road. And from what you've told me? You've got a good bit of work, yet."

"A work in progress."

"Healing takes a long time. And you—we—were sick."

"Still am. But I ain't, what-cha call it, complacent."

"Better not be."

"It wa'n't nothing but a put-on, girl. You got to know that. Not the alcoholism. But damn near everything else."

"Telling me something I don't know?"

Devin, wondering if she didn't think him some sort of weirdo. Again hearing sirens far off in the distance.

"Didn't know what to think."

"None of it had to do with you. Get it?"

His old gal-pal, asking, then, with whom?

"All me, little lady-friend. All for me. And the ghosts following me."

Dry. "How gratifying."

Hanging there in the foyer of the building like his cigarette smoke, her words cut to the bone. But she had a right.

"I think I'm done pretending, though."

"Baby steps. Know the ones I mean?"

He thought he did. Said so.

She told him to keep her posted; that she had to go.

"You're with somebody, aren't ya?"

She didn't seem to want to answer.

"I missed my chance—didn't I?"

"Let's talk another time. Bye, now."

"Okay."

Sounded good to him. So that was that with Millie. He guessed he would stop thinking about her. But, like Creedence and Roy on their date, who knew what was to come next in this crazy life of his?

Reaching down and pumping his bloody steeplemeat, Billy tried to maintain his tenuous erection; the moment upon him, but he hadn't time to pop a Viagra. Considering how much liquor he'd chugged while Libby had gone to the bathroom, a miracle he'd stayed hard as he had.

How she had shrieked with disgust. She came back into the room to find him nude. Erect. And huge, even at half-mast.

Also because he lunged for her.

How she'd recoiled from his fiery breath. Slipped from his damp grasp, hands greasy from lubing his meat.

He chased her around in the Media Hub, The Big Lebowski Five-Year Anniversary Edition Deluxe DVD Set playing loud from the speakers and the woofer. Marleigh. Billy. Multiple attempts and multiple ways and and means and feints and much shrieking and breaking of lamps and bongs and whatnot. SHATTER went not only the dope glassware, stinking up the joint with awful resinous weed-funk, but also a cacophonous crash from the heavy, bevelled, burdened tabletop full of liquor bottles and lubricant and his old Star Wars toys, pulled out of an archival storage bin where he kept the best of his old childhood mementos, the movie mementos and superhero dolls and one of those old twelve-inch, original GI Joe action figures.

But otherwise Billy, in control; no accidents happening this time. That was the old Billy. This would be straight sex, penetrative and fulfilling.

Cornering her, at last. "What do you say, Libby? Never too late?"

On the plasma screen, in eight billion colors and 9.1 surround sound, The Dude smoked the roach into his throat, spilled his beer, wrecked his beleaguered car. Billy, playing with himself and trying to stay halfway hard, loomed over her.

Marleigh, gasping and crying in disbelief, cringed into the corner. She grabbed a fistful of Criterion editions off the shelf nearest her. Threatened him with the arthouse classics. "You sick fuck. I'll kill you if you touch me."

"Oh, bother. Take a breather from all your blather. Now get those grungy cords off so I can give you what came for."

She whimpered, heaving a copy of Bergman's PERSONA at his face, which he batted away. The disc still had its shrink-wrap and price tag from B&N. She followed it with a weak heave of Antonioni's THE PASSENGER, which fell short.

Billy, dumbstruck by Marleigh's lack of enthusiasm, became vociferous and detailed in his criticism—he excoriated her every fashion, hair and cosmetics choice, her explication of his paper, her desire to write scripts.

"No wonder I can't get going. Not sexy. And put down my mother-freaking movies, if you please. We have all the time in the world, now, to watch them all."

Marleigh begged. "Please—*I don't do it with guys.*"

Billy let that sink in. "Not yet you don't," he finally said. "And besides, you owe me for that bong."

A challenge. Still, lesbian snatch better than Melanie. Where was the fun? Where was the thrill of the hunt? This, what he'd been waiting for. A game. A contest of wills.

His brief reverie, broken; Marleigh, a ghost, seemed to have swooped and slid between his legs like a base hit batter going for home. She bolted down the hallway.

"Say, now—where in the freaking heck do ya think you're going? We haven't fucked yet." Billy, his dick finally stretching and hardening, gave chase.

A huge crash. In the hallway he saw that Marleigh had tripped and fallen halfway into the living room.

Billy, skipping down the hall in a silly prancing gait, meatwhistle bobbing up and down, shouted, "Damn your execrable recalcitrance. I'm finally ripping a good one, here."

But Marleigh, sly; as he reached down for her, she rolled and put the hard heel of her hand up into Billy's strong jaw-line.

Billy, stunned, but barely. He yanked her up by her sweater, which ripped around the neckline.

Striking her backhanded across the face.

Hard.

Marleigh, limp, collapsed to the floor. Whimpering. Groggy.

Shocked with himself—he'd never hit a woman in his life. He loved them. This required reflection and introspection. "Wow. That happened."

As he vaguely watched Marleigh roll over and crawl away toward the kitchen, Billy, resigned to having done the action, yanked at his meat and said, "Crude, I know. But, if that's what it's going to take, I get it. Fine."

Libby, one for the ages, this battle. The naughtiest tail ever.

The naughtiest tale ever.

Ha-ha.

Panicking.

Why the hell all the drinking? Why couldn't he get high anymore? Panic, redoubling. Heart going like the triple crown winner.

Marleigh.

On her feet.

Disappearing into the kitchen.

"Libby? This is ridiculous. Let's do it in the bedroom. My bed, this time. Let's do this right... at last."

Marleigh, looking nothing like Libby Meade, met him in the kitchen doorway.

A war cry.

Lunging at him.

With a knife from the butcher block in her hand.

The cleaver.

Big enough to slice right through a piece of tough steak.

Like a razor—he rarely used it. Probably sharp as the day Billy bought the set.

Sharp as a whisper.

Slashing with it.

No chance for a big speech; a moment, not frozen and hanging there, but fast. A wet tugging, an arc of her arm motion stuttering and completing in a viscous torrent of what Billy thought at first was his own orgasm, Libby finishing him off with a hand-job about which they'd one day write epic poems and song-cycles.

Nope.

Seemed to be not-good, in fact.

Throwing the knife down, caroming off the doorframe and out the door, Marleigh became like a frightened deer, Billy thinking; a little scared whitetail doe like you'd see on one of Ruck's back roads over in Edgewater County, the ones on which he told Billy him and Dobbs and Roy Earl used to drive around, drunker than shit, because at their age—sixteen or seventeen—you couldn't go drinking at places like that honkytonk The Dixiana, not with Roy's grandpa running the joint. But you had to watch out for the wildlife, he advised.

Ruck.

Libby.

All this blood.

"Guys—this is bad." But his voice seemed to be gone. His breath, too.

Ruck had caught him and Libby. Had gone and cut his goddamn dick off.

How many dreams like this had he had? At least he'd wake up from this one, too.

But shit. What a dream, this. Covered in blood.

His balls, sitting there.

On the floor.

The heavy door, shutting behind her with a thud; Marleigh, the hell and gone. Must have gotten a second wind.

Billy, heartbroken. Epic fail. But why?

Pounding liquor. Resuming the movie, trying not to think about the next day. Hurting, but it'd pass. Bleeding everywhere.

The couch, wet.

*Fuck.*

Thinking about his new life. Matters working themselves out. He'd eat DC alive. He'd make contacts, some of them in show business.

Billy, on his way for real.

Fuck Marleigh, fuck the lies he'd told. He'd make his own reality, as his dad had always bidden him.

Searching for the phone, slipping around in his own creamy dream-blood, thinking about calling 9/11. Or 9-1-1, he meant. They got mixed up in the mind, now, that day of terror and the traditional emergency phone number. One of those crazy coincidences.

Billy, telling the nice person on the phone how he thought he might be bleeding to death. Saying, "Send 'em on over, pardner. Probably dying, yo." Sounding like good old drunk Devin. "Cut myself. Somehow."

Billy, staggering out on the balcony with his canister of nitrous oxide and the last of the brown liquor; Billy, bleeding and dickless, pondered how he was to keep on writing scripts if he had to work on all this campaign bullshit with his dad.

Thinking hard about a new idea he'd had: a real haunted-house movie, a corker, scary and action-packed as shit. The pitch was BLAIR WITCH meets THE EXORCIST meets ALIEN meets JURASSIC PARK meets THE SEVENTH SEAL, in which something ancient—That Which Was Forgotten—comes back to remind everyone of the real deal, in the process kicking major ass both onscreen and off; with CGI advances, to be made on an unlimited budget with a cast of superstars like one of those 70s disaster epics, the end result could be the biggest movie ever. Implausible, his dreams, but like in the movies, miracles sometimes happened—unexpected, wondrous dreams came true.

Like how he'd finally had the rare and different privilege of almost boinking Libby the second time in his life just now! And how shitty it'd turned out, and so this dream arrives as it had at the beginning, as a tarnished and sordid disappointment.

But still. Libby. Yo. Putting him in his place. Poetic, almost. Helluva day. He couldn't wait to tell Ruck, who would no doubt be pleased. They'd drink to it. Yes, they would.

Feeling lightheaded, like when he was really hard—it took so much blood to get that thing inflated it didn't leave much for thinking—he felt cold all over, a wave sweeping through him.

"Yo," he called out to no one. "I'm dizzy."

Taking the first toot of nitrous, expelling the gas in a satisfied, slow trickle, Billy saw images fluttering at the corners of his eyes; the anesthetic working into his blood. Feeling nothing.

Happy at this sense of nothing; acknowledging that happiness existed, hence, could not be nothing.

Confused. A weird feedback loop.

But his replacement cell phone, bonging with an annoying, generic ringtone and shattering the mood, irritated him.

He floated over to the balcony, by the railing. His legs were weak. A hot throbbing in his pelvis—his hard-on, he hoped, but he couldn't bring himself to look—felt bothersome.

Eyeballing the display: MEL, backlit in cool electronic blue.

"Like a fucking Swiss watch," in sniffling, sad disgust. "I was hoping it might have been the ambulance guys, wanting to be buzzed in—but, oh well. Hi, angel."

She said *sheesh, you sound terrible.* "You better not be drunk."

"Cool it, cool it—I'll get straight. Time you get up here. Yep."

"You're gonna sober up in five minutes? That I'd like to see."

"We got all the time in the world."

"Billy—are you more than drunk?"

"Nah, not at all."

"Okay, good," sounding cautious but relieved. "Cause we got a lot to decide, mister. And do."

"Righteous. I'll go buzz-buzz-buzz you in."

"No, I need you to come down here and help me carry in groceries. Nowhere to park."

"Ah—be right there."

He leaned over the balcony and squinted to see her down there amidst the distinctive shrubs cut into pyramids and the parking spaces and the red pavers of the walkway from the street: Melanie (Libby), waving up to him, pointed to her car in the fire lane with the hazards flashing.

Taking a huge draw on the cream canister and waving back, Billy, feeling, for once, glad to see her. She'd help clean up the mess.

Overcome by the gas—by the sillies—he heard sirens going *wah-wah*, saw color-splashes of red and blue on the street below from not one, but two arriving police cars, along with an ambulance. Giggled.

Leaning over, croaking, weeping, laughing, howling, stomping his feet, he went to call to Melanie, but felt instead only his center of gravity pitching forward and his mouth gaping open and fifteen-floor December night air rushing into it. As well an ebbing upward of PAIN from his groin, unbelievable pain. Passing a kidney stone, he speculated. Sucked on the gas.

"*Billy*," he heard Mel scream, faraway. He seemed to be going into nitrous-oxide warp drive. Cool.

Here now, the dream: Spinning around, breathing the nitrous out, the *wah-wah-wah* sounds starting again, different from what he'd heard before, less real, more real, he couldn't tell, the music sounding distorted, a clanging cymbal, *shoop shoop SHOOP*; and so dizzy, getting the spins like after those all-night draught beer-drinking parties in college, when you stagger back to your little bed and collapse and the bed, it starts spinning and spinning and spinning and you say *oh please don't let me puke* and you grasp clutching onto the sheets, grabbing at the fabric trying to get the whirl to stop, Billy reaching out but finding only the air rushing against his skin he thought *I'm passing out I'm passing out I'm passing out*, but the blood, rushing back into his head, and opening his eyes to hear a voice ringing out hollow and raw and there's Melanie (Libby), running, long arms flailing and policemen yelling toward him as though he were God, beneficent above the worshipful adherents gathering below, all of it happening in a rush of only seconds but stretched out to infinity and looping back around again, the ground rushing up toward him reaching out flailing and WAKING UP FOR REAL AND SCREAMING and finally grabbing hold of the bed sheet to stop the spinning, holding onto it, heavy, thick, red, white and blue; a loud *POP*, and the world flashing bright white, and all possible colors together as one, bubbling and melting into infinity.

The film, stopped in its tracks.

The print, ruined.

Billy's movie, unfinished.

No satisfactions, no permanence.
And then?
Endless.
Black.
Nothing.

# EIGHTY-SEVEN

## — DEVIN

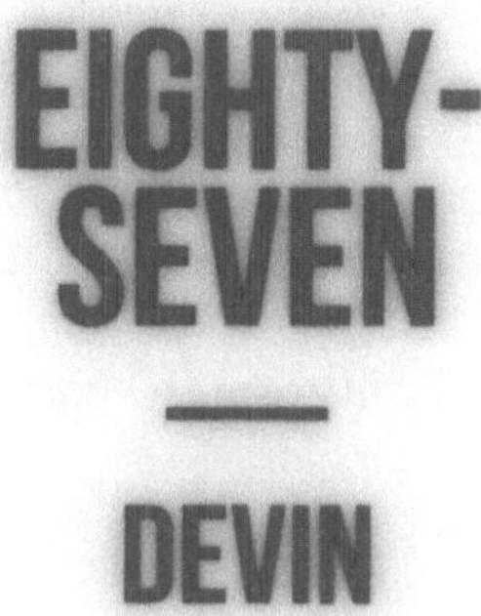

As if the mind-bending news about Billy Steeple planting it beak-first into the sidewalk hadn't been bad enough:

Devin, holding his mother's head as she vomited black sputum, a thick ropy strand which more dangled than erupted from her mouth into the pink plastic hospital tray the hospice care folks had provided. Oxygen pump, supplies, a subcutaneous pain pump had been installed. The nausea, they said, was coming from the fact the cancer had spread to her brain. Far as the rural county doctors at Edgewater Memorial could guess, anyway.

Once stable, time to return home to hospice care. As before, she pretended to not know what hospice portended.

The nausea, incessant. Still she smoked. Bedridden, delusional from the drug cocktail, howling with existential rage at dying before the light.

At least she had made it through Christmas. She had that going for her. And she was at home, and not among strangers. All Devin could tell anyone. Creedence mostly stayed to herself, letting her brother care for their mother.

He didn't mind. It was for her own good. Devin already had a head full of snakes. A few more wouldn't matter—like watching his mom suffer and die. No big whoop. It couldn't be as bad as what had happened with Libby.

No—but it could be bad all on its own.

Eileen had only made it through three of the radiation treatments Devin had dreaded, him driving her back and forth to the same oncology center in Columbia where she had driven herself so many times in secret, time and again, to take a mild enough form of chemo allowing her to keep Creedence in ignorance for the first months after her diagnosis.

Amazing, Devin thought, sitting in the sunlight lobby and waiting for her to come out from her doctor's office, upstairs from the radiation treatment wing. *Mama's always been real good at making her reality. You got to give it to her.*

She'd been retaining fluid, and wanted her regular oncologist to render an opinion. The radiologist had shrugged, said it seemed to him from her reports of constant nausea and diarrhea from the chemo how she'd been dehydrated, should have fluids.

His mother came shuffling out from the consult with a prescription for a diuretic. She had refused a wheelchair.

"Oh, darling—I'm so confused."

"Now what did those croakers say now?"

"Hush your mouth. They said I was dehydrated earlier, and gave me fluids. Then I complained about all this bloat, and Dr. Ackerman said, she said, to take these pills—more pills."

"Of course she did. It's what that damn mortician does for a living."

"Oh, lord. I can't take no more pills than I already do."

Devin, furious.

But later, he got the prescription filled at the pharmacy in the plaza next to the Piggly Wiggly. That's when she started going downhill, after that radiation treatment, the last she'd be able to take. Sick as a dog for the rest of the night.

For the rest of her life.

Maybe one day he'd return to the oncology center and burn it to the ground. A drunk like him, who had stories which ended with jail, with the hospital, and even a few with death, might be capable of anything.

After two days of Eileen Rucker doing her best not to vomit out her entire GI tract, followed by frenzied cleaning and laundry and Devin's own mortal exhaustion, circumstances had become dire enough he could tell his Mama he had to call in help. That's how they'd found out about the brain cancer.

One last weak, gurgling round of protestation from her, but undeterred he called the ambulance and his sister, in that order, who was already on her way back over to check on the kitties and Mama.

They sat looking at one another, waiting for the EMTs. Eileen moaned in pain and sickness. Creedence boo-hooed in silence.

The drivers had taken them to Edgewater County Memorial instead of one of the nicer hospitals in Columbia. Fury. Eileen said she was not going to die in that po-folks's hospital. And this, coming from a community leader, one of the mighty and powerful ELMS who secretly—or not so secretly— ran everything in Edgewater County, carried weight, she threatened.

Mama, no longer in her right mind.

The doctor in the ER, a smart guy from up north somewhere, had the sense to do the brain scan and find the lesions there. He delivered the news, shaking his head with a grim finality that made Devin want a good, stiff drink. His mother was dying for real, and soon.

Feeling as though the floor had dropped out from beneath the sneakers his mother had bought him for Christmas, the last shoes—the last anything —she'd ever get him, he had met with the folks from hospice. Had had to go tell her the news. He now had this, that, and the other thing to get handled.

Thank god he hadn't been drunk.

As for his mom's condition, now it reached the stage of all-but catatonia, morphine induced. Now all he had to do was walk back to her room to see if she was awake and lucid, which wasn't often.

Devin, trying to figure out how to tell her that the doctors had no plan for keeping her alive any longer; now nothing left to try.

Sorrowful, in one of her moments, she had said to him, "Maybe it's all a bad dream, and I'll wake up tomorrow. And none of this mess will have been real."

A gut punch. "I been thinking the same thing. For some time now."

"I'm sick to my stomach again."

"Okay."

"Get me the pan—where's my pan."

"Hold tight, Mama. Hold steady."

"Them damn doctors—they don't know their butts from holes in the ground."

"Ain't that the truth."

She moaned and begged for release from her agony. "Once I feel better from this bout," she said, gasping, "you must make me a promise."

"What, Mama?"

"You can't let me get like this again."

He promised her he wouldn't. Devin, realizing none of that old crap mattered now—it was over.

Her life was over.

And even before she passed, finally, a week later, he had begun missing her already. He had dealt with death before. Sure. But you only get one mother, now, don't you?

EPILOGUE

# LOVE IS ALIVE

WINTER
2005

Devin's Jetta, the good-old trusty fart-knocker of a road machine, retired. Cruising around Edgewater County instead in his mother's Oldsmobile.

The one she'd never need again.

The Olds, parked on a dusty track winding through the perpetual care cemetery, the rutted dirt road affording vehicles and their passengers ready access to the grave sites arrayed on the slight grade of the hillside: grassy, serene, color-dotted by blossoms real and otherwise. Dobbs, Creedence, Roy Earl, and Devin had come out here together, on a sunny late February Sunday to lay Eileen to rest beside Dwight, and now they all returned again.

Devin, dealing with Eileen's passing in a reasoned and calm manner, with no unfinished business left to haunt, had remained dry. Already coming to the conclusion that his mother, whatever her flaws, wasn't only a 'mother,' but first a human being no different from her baby boy, he did they thing they tell you about the past: he let it go.

Devin, moving on.

This is how he should've rolled ages ago, yo. But better late than never.

Except when it's too late.

Eileen, eulogized and lionized in an elegant obituary written by Bill Wimmel, the editor and publisher of the EDGEWATER ADVOCATE. Wimmil, a man Devin didn't know other than from the day of Albert Nixon's death in the pool, but one who'd obviously known his mother well. His piece described how much Eileen had done through the ELMS, and otherwise; projects and causes he'd never bothered to learn about. The good she'd done —for people and pets, especially, in her support of rescue organizations, shelters and spay & neuter programs. The kind of good a Gen-X wastrel like Devin could only imagine having accomplished. At least, that's what the mirror had said after he read the paper on the day of her funeral.

His father's obit had looked much the same. Back when Dwight had died, his tired old workingman's heart giving out on him five years shy of retirement, the paper had run as elaborate an obituary for him, too, but his son had only recently read it. During the funeral, Devin had been so far inside his own head he hadn't bothered to read his own dad's obituary. He hadn't had the courage to face up to what kind of man his father had been.

Or, who his mother was, either.

In any case, future generations would have a chance to remember, and judge the contributions of, Devin's late parents: one of the stately old oaks down on the town green, after a push by the ELMS and Hill Hampton, would be memorialized with a plaque as the Rucker Oak. Would remain there, he surmised, long after he and the remaining Ruckers were gone. Without a further lineage courtesy their children, however, the memory of Dwight and Eileen would have to be carried, if they cared, by nieces, nephews, cousins.

The day after Billy's death Devin had run himself down to the Old Market to find Officer McWhorter. He asked him what he knew about the incident. Upon hearing the circumstances—a young girl had been assaulted by a madman, the cop said—Devin offered to talk to the detectives working the case to inform them of Billy's past. That what had happened wasn't an aberration. That the boy had himself a history of aberrant sexual behavior. Only one incident he could vouch for, however; that Devin had witnessed. But still.

The plainclothes cops, who from the sound of them were ordinary South Carolina good-old-boys, thanked him for his information, albeit in the manner of men suspicious of stories from folks who looked like Devin; who never knew who might be stretching the truth.

"Might be useful for the victim to know that about Mr. Steeple, in the sense of healing and understanding the nature of victimhood. But the case is closed."

The other cop, also thoughtful, scratched at a thatch of black stubble on his chin. "But, of course, it's not your place to tell her of his history, Mr. Rucker."

"No—she's traumatized enough, I'm sure."

"The main thing I'm concerned about? How many more. Big-old longhaired boy like to killed her, he did. Like he was possessed, she said."

Damn, Devin heard himself whisper. "I can't explain it."

"Steeple kept calling her some other girl's name—what was it, Carl?"

"I don't need to know. It's okay."

"No, we got it in the report."

"Seriously, bro. I don't wanna know."

"No? Maybe it means something."

"Case closed, right?"

"You tell us."

What could he say to that? Billy, in the ground. "Reckon so."

"You say that like it's not a good thing."

"A complicated past with that old boy. He was a friend."

"Seems simple enough to me."

"Nothing ever is, beau."

"It is when you're a cop."

"Y'all often iron things out in such a straightforward fashion. I'll give you that much."

"It's a mindset."

"Understood." Devin, fishing for his smokes, beat it out of the cop station with the wind at his back.

No funeral for Billy in South Carolina; Devin, offering to accompany his body to Virginia, but Billy's father—or rather, an aide who called Devin back on behalf of Mr. Steeple—declining the offer. The father wanted desperately, Devin suspected, for it all to go away—Steeple Senior's run for the House would be undone by such an incident.

Devin hadn't known about Billy's father running for congress, or much of anything about his family other than the plastic-sack business.

Devin, he realized, hadn't known much about Billy.

Nothing, really.

Melanie Pinckney, understandably distressed at witnessing Billy's descent and impact on the sidewalk, now left a wan, quivering mess of her former energetic self, ran into Devin on the street outside Roy Earl's coffee shop one day. He went to hug her, but Melanie remained as stiff and unyielding as a mannequin.

Small talk. Her words, slurry and slow and stunned. She was in therapy; on medication. Moving back to Charleston. She'd see him around.

A woman destroyed by trauma; his mother, dead; Billy, dead; what destruction Devin had wrought by coming back. Everyone would have been better off if he'd stayed drunk and gone.

Sitting on the deck at home by himself, smoking and eating a sandwich, a pair of fighter jets from Shaw AFB screamed overhead on one of their training flight patterns. Or maybe they had been deployed on a mission—who knew, anymore. Time to roll another war out for the new TV season?

Cheney and Rumsfeld were pushing hard to expand the GWOT to Syria and Iran, if they didn't fall in line with the new world order. Good business was where you found it.

Devin, with nothing better to do but look at the accruing interest on his late father's investments, had become a news junkie. Had gotten cynical, already, about the leaders and their plans and their wars on other countries, on the civil rights of the people they were elected to serve.

A mess. Enough to drive a man to drink.

But no. None of that.

Close, a couple of times. The last week or two of Mama dying. But strong. Hanging tough.

A peal of birdsong, high and sweet. It rang out in emphatic, apparent happiness over Devin's sobriety.

Dobbs, following in Creedence's footsteps: his spirit reawakened by Devin's absolution, the former housebound, depressed homeboy applied to go back and finish the journalism degree he'd pursued before the car accident. That he could have finished afterwards, he said, if only he'd had the courage to stand up to his injuries. To stand up to the past, and to what fate had decreed would complicate his fortune, but not necessarily derail it.

"You don't have to lay down and take what life gives," Dobbs said.

"I thought I was standing up to it. Telling it to go fuck itself. Nope. In hiding from the truth."

"Same. I wish I'd have figured it out sooner."

"You and me both, spud."

And Creedence, beautiful Creedence, happy and excited and falling in love, if not falling far from the family tree once again; Creedence, living in the apartment only until, sudden and shocking to her, Eileen had died.

Afterwards, she started staying at Roy Earl's every night, using the groundwork her mother laid to get out of her lease after all.

Marrying him soon, she said; soon as the Dusty divorce was final, another month.

Creedence, Roy Earl, making a success out of their lives. Building his businesses. Making America great. How it all worked out for him; and now, for her.

Fine.

Which left Devin.

Sorting out his shit.

Or sifting, at this point.

Granular. That's right. The grains were now fine. And almost sifted.

Devin, cruising up the hill from his parents' graves, moved toward Libby's stone, a last sift here before taking a break from all this remembering. He'd been out here already by now, of course. The day of

Eileen's funeral and today, when they all came for Devin to place Prudy's mini-headstone in the ground next to Libby's.

Dobbs, Roy Earl, Creedence, all gathered behind him. Propping him up, literally, as he'd wept for his cat.

For Libby.

For his Mama.

At least he'd forgiven her. Before it was too late.

"Thank you for this." Creedence, holding Devin from behind, arms draped around his neck and pointy freckled chin jutting into his collar bone. "For giving me Prudy back."

"Least I could do for my big brother."

But now he was here alone, moving across the rows of gravestones, finding himself at last standing over Libby's simple, flat monument, only a yard or so away from where her own father Frank had been interred. He'd told the rest of them to go on back to the house, to stop and get fried chicken from the deli for supper. Told them he'd be right along.

Hanging for a spell at the marker:

### *Frances Elizabeth Meade*
### *December 30 1970 — May 10 1990*

But Libby, not there. Only a stone above a hole in the ground.

A box in the hole.

Nothing in the box but dust.

Devin, forced to bid a sudden and wretched farewell to her on the road in the hot sun, peering horrorstruck through the veil of blood and glass, had often felt no one could possibly have experienced grief in the manner in which God had forced him in those wrenching moments while waiting to be pulled out from the wreckage. Waiting alongside her. Forced to gaze into her dead eyes, hold her cold hand, and get used to the idea. And for all the years afterwards to come, Devin, kept alive by a nefarious, chuckling, scheming, sickly perverted wastrel, the God of Abraham, torturing humanity like ants under a magnifying glass.

And, oh, Devin? Devin 'Ruck' Rucker?

The center of grief's universe.

Epic.

Total.

Yeah.

No.

At last realizing such centrality wasn't and couldn't be so: Devin decided to begin cultivating a superb and perspicacious skepticism of all that lay outside of himself, of the greater world, huge and ancient, and of people, dying—and killing one another, and watching the killing, either reveling or else being driven mad, oftentimes both, by the relentless and pervasive and wholesale slaughter that's so far defined and shaped and driven human civilization—for as long as people had existed in these wretched and pernicious states of self-reflection. Which added up, all right. You bet it did. And yet didn't add up, not in the philosophical sense.

He had time to work on it all. Nothing but time.

The wind, shushing through the pines. A Sunday afternoon. Not much traffic on the highway. Quiet.

Devin. Examining the headstone for the ten-thousandth time—Prudy's.

Was it enough? Was he finished, now?

No. Something he left behind. In Colorado. To be retrieved.

Sure. They'd talked a few times since he'd finally called, her cold the whole time. Millie, wary. He'd need to go to her. To show her he was okay, now. To persuade her.

Hurrying and climbing into his mother's car, which purred into life, but needed an oil change, Devin, feeling filled with purpose. A puff of exhaust exploded from the muffler, hot, blue vapor set a-loose like a wraith drifting diaphanous and dissipating across the rolling slope dotted with gravestones and colorful silk flowers; Devin, cutting the midnight blue sedan, a dark shark of a cruiser, in a three-point turn on the dirt track.

Pausing, looking both ways before turning out onto SC State Highway 79, Devin, starting to fire up a smoke. Thinking better of doing so—he only had a few left, and a long night ahead.

Libby, sitting in the passenger seat; smiling, insouciant, her hair pulled back by a wide white ribbon. Libby, fresh and lovely as the day they'd moved into the Arcadia house together. Libby.

But it was no good.

"I'm not sure you should come on this trip."

"I've been on all the others."

He pressed his lips together. Shook his head. "Yeah."

"Aw—you want to be free of me. Don't you."

"Inarguably. But, never, angel."

"You never were any fun."

Libby Libby Libby; gone gone gone.

The empty seat, a signpost: the land-end into heaven. Responsible for no one's death, now, but his own.

Pulling out and cruising. A band of lavender horizon. The empty two-lane. Sweet highway air on his cheeks.

Devin Rucker's moment: Passing Pine Haven and the cavernous Rucker house therein, the family who awaited him. Eileen's cats, divided up between

Creedence and the surviving aunts. Most of the time no one living there, now, but Devin.

Which wasn't living.

Not alone.

He could kid himself all day long—he was heading to get Millie, who waited for him in Colorado. But she wasn't waiting. She didn't need 'getting.' It was only another story he told himself.

Passing the entrance to the subdivision where he'd had his latchkey childhood of beholding dead bodies, he chose.

Signaling and merging onto the freeway.

The big rigs and SUVs roaring past; Devin, up to speed, slipstreaming. Last of the sun, glinting off the aviators. His hands, steady.

In the glovebox, the tape of the Dead, but not playing it. Leaving it put away.

Driving.

Into the west.

Chasing the sunset.

But not drunk. This time, he had his wits about him. This time he would not only succeed at quelling what ailed him, he'd do it the right way—for keeps.

Hauling holy, ever-loving ass out of South Carolina. Again. Devin, ever after.

# CREEDENCE,
# DOBBS,
## AND
# ROY EARL PETTUS

WILL
RETURN
IN

# DIXIANA
# DOWN IN DIXIANA
# DIXIANA DARLING

**RETURN TO**
**James D. McCallister's**
**"EDGEWATER COUNTY, SC"**

in

*King's Highway*
*Fellow Traveler*
*Let the Glory Pass Away*
*The Year They Canceled Christmas*
*Dogs of Parsons Hollow*
*Dixiana*
*Down in Dixiana*
*Dixiana Darling*
*Reconstruction of the Fables (2022)*

# ABOUT THE AUTHOR

James D. McCallister is the author of novels, a short story collection and numerous other shorter pieces of fiction and creative nonfiction. A lifelong South Carolinian, he lives in West Columbia with his wife and beloved brood of cats, muses all.

*CONTACT JAMES D McCALLISTER:*
www.jamesdmccallister.com
editor@mindharvestpress.com